MARGARET THOMSON DAVIS

THE BREADMAKERS SAGA

The Breadmakers
A Baby Might Be Crying
A Sort of Peace

B&W PUBLISHING

Omnibus edition first published
by B&W Publishing 1993
This edition first published 2012
by B&W Publishing Ltd
29 Ocean Drive Edinburgh EH6 6JL

1 3 5 7 9 10 8 6 4 2   12 13 14 15

ISBN 978 1 84502 416 1

First published in Great Britain in 1972, 1973.
The Breadmakers © Margaret Thomson Davis 1972.
A Baby Might Be Crying, A Sort of Peace
© Margaret Thomson Davis 1973.

A CIP catalogue record for this book is available from the British Library.

Typeset by RefineCatch Limited, Bungay, Suffolk
Printed and Bound by Nørhaven, Viborg

THE BREADMAKERS

In loving memory of my brother
Audley S. Thomson.

Chapter 1

There was still unemployment and empty shops, but Duncan MacNair's bakery and general store had weathered the Depression and survived.

Women pushed in wearing aprons and slippers, or if they came from the maze of streets further along the riverside they arrived hugging heavy shawls around themselves, often with babies cocooned stiffly inside.

The traveller who shuffled through the open doorway of MacNair's, however, wore a long blue belted raincoat, underneath which his feet barely showed. The coat, shined smooth with age and years of carrying bulky samples, was topped by a milky-moon face devoid of any expression except resignation.

The shop bulged with people sweat-glistening with heat from the bakehouse at the back. Maisie the shop assistant was working at such a pace between the bakery counter at one side and the general store at the other, she was too breathless to talk.

But old Duncan MacNair, the master baker, ranted into his goatee beard as if all the customers were devils ganged up out of sheer badness to harass him.

The traveller manoeuvred his long raincoat among the hot flesh and, with a sigh, placed his case up on the bakery counter.

Feeling out his order book he began his usual monotone, 'Abdines, Askits, blades, bleach, Brasso . . .'

MacNair's bloodshot eye popped.

'I've no time for you today. Can you not see I'm busy?'

Well used to nobody having any time for him, the traveller went on with his list. 'Bandages, castor-oil and zinc, cough mixture, notepaper, french letters, pipeclay . . .'

'Beat it!' The womanish voice reached a top note that spurted saliva out.

'Sanitary towels, safety pins, Snowfire Cream . . .'

'It's the Old Govan Fair today,' Duncan howled. 'Did you not even see my horse out the front?'

'Christ, the Fair, I forgot!'

'Come on.' Two blotches of pride warmed old MacNair's cheeks. 'Have a look at the best dressed animal in the parade. He'll lift that prize again. By God, he will!'

Outside in Dessie Street, Sandy McNulty the vanman was chatting to Billy the horse. Sandy was so painfully thin it was as if a mischievous God in a cruel mood had caught him by the nose and feet and stretched him out of all proportion, leaving both nose and feet forever red and tender, and body without enough covering to keep it warm.

'You're a smart one, my Billy boy,' he was assuring the frisky, restless beast. 'There'll not be another horse in the whole procession to come near you.'

Old Duncan ignored him and addressed the traveller.

'Look at that!' He thumped a gnarled fist against the horse's rump, making it clatter its hooves on the cobbled street with indignation, and snort and toss its head.

'What did I tell you!' Sandy protested, grabbing the bridle.

A little crowd had gathered in Dessie Street to admire the horse. People going down the Main Road which cut across Dessie Street stopped to stare and others in the tramcars, trundling along the Main Road through Clydend to Govan Cross and further on into the centre of Glasgow, craned their necks round to keep staring.

Billy was a splendid sight and, judging by his proud prancing and the tossing of his head, he was well aware of his splendour.

Sandy had brushed and polished him with loving care until his red-tan hide gleamed. Even his hooves had been polished. A large scarlet and silver plume curled royally between his alert twitching ears; rosettes and flowers decorated his bridle; scarlet, silver and purple ribbons were plaited all over his reins and rippled from his tail; but the *pièce de résistance* was the magnificent saddle-cloth sparkling in the sun. Plush purple velvet was encrusted with silver and a many-jewelled design. The Dessie Street children were convinced that the fiery red and amber and emerald stones were real jewels and not coloured glass because rumour had it that, despite old MacNair's scraggy appearance and second-hand clothes, he was loaded.

Attempts had even been made to divest him of some of his wealth. The last try had been when a local gangster rushed into the shop brandishing a cut-throat razor and demanding all the money in the till. Old MacNair, outraged at the mere idea, had immediately screamed at him and chased him away down the street with a long butcher's knife lashing the air like a cutlass.

'I'll cut your bloody head off if I catch you, you cheeky big nyaff!'

Now he yelped at the traveller.

'Look at the float, too. Help me get the covers off, man. Don't just stand there like an accident looking for somewhere to happen!'

Between them, and to the mounting excitement of the onlookers hastily gathering in the narrow street between the high sooty tenements, they removed the covers from the four-wheeled vehicle standing behind Billy.

The crowd of neighbours - women in wrap-around overalls and slippers, some with masses of steel curlers in their hair, pale-faced men and little boys with skinny thighs in 'parish' trousers, girls bouncing up with heads straining - all jostled closer with loud ahs and ohs, inarticulate with admiration.

Bristly sheaves of corn hugged round the float. At the nearest end to Billy, a huge, flat wooden loaf stuck up displaying the words

MACNAIR AND SON

BREADMAKERS

'I'm going to sit up front with Sandy. Melvin will be in the back with the rest of them. They're going to be tossing pancakes as we go along and I've got hundreds of wee loaves packed in there to throw to the crowds. Christ!' The old man's excitement suddenly fizzled out and he nearly burst into tears. 'That bloody show-off of a son of mine'll be the ruination of me yet. You'd think I was made of money. This was all Melvin's idea. Hundreds of good wee loaves. Could you beat it?'

The traveller said nothing but looked vaguely impressed.

'He'll be wanting to pelt folk with my pancakes next. I'd better go and see him. He's through the back helping with the pancakes now.'

Knees lifting and cracking, he hustled back into the double-windowed corner-shop, punching customers roughly out of his way, and made for a piece of sacking that served as a curtain between the shop and the ill-lit lobby. The left-hand side of the lobby housed the lavatory and wash-hand basin. Next to the lavatory the side door led out to the close, and directly across from the curtain was the entrance into the white floury heat-haze of the bakehouse.

Melvin stood, tree-trunk legs well apart, one shovel-hand gripping white-aproned hip, bushy moustache bristling with concentration, neck muscles knotted, shoulder muscles bunched, arm bulging as he strained—ever-faithful to the rules of dynamic tension—to lift a Scotch pancake and imagine with all his might that it weighed half a ton.

All Melvin's fellow night workers, except Rab Munro who lived over in Farmbank, had been upstairs to their respective flats for a sleep and had returned to the bakehouse to help get everything ready for the Old Govan Fair.

A bald giant of a man, looking like an all-in wrestler with sweat splashing over his face, was bringing new batches of miniature loaves from the oven with the long handled pole or 'peel' and roaring in song.

The 'halfer', or apprentice, was over at the pie machine 'lifting' the pies.

Tam, another baker, his feathery white hair standing up on end, was swaggering along with more pancake batter for Jimmy the confectioner and Melvin, who, because of the special occasion, was helping him. Unlike Melvin and the other men, Jimmy always worked days along with his female assistant, Lexy.

Lexy nudged Melvin and laughed, making her own well-developed but softer flesh bounce and wobble.

'I bet you're dreaming about your new lady love. I've been hearing rumours!'

'She's got nothing on you, darlin.' Melvin's free hand suddenly shot up and twitched over Lexy's full melon breasts, making her squeal.

Suddenly old MacNair's high nasal tones snipped through the hilarity.

'Stop your messing about, you randy nyuck! And what the hell are you playing at with that pancake? Anybody would think it was as heavy as an elephant, or you'd glued the bloody thing down. If it wasn't for Jimmy here, where would we all be?'

Jimmy cast a long-suffering glance towards the ceiling as he continued rapidly flipping over the pancakes. Only the other day MacNair had insisted he was a 'good-for-nothing young Dago'.

Tam the white-haired baker smacked and rubbed his hands then gave Melvin's back a punch.

'You were awful concerned about Rab that last time he was off work, eh? How many times was it that you went over to Farmbank? We've heard about Rabs daughter. We've heard she's a beauty. Young, too. Sweet seventeen and never been kissed! Or is it sixteen? And a blonde as well. You'd better watch out for Baldy. He's a devil for blondes.'

Melvin scratched his moustache. 'She's a queer one but I'll soon knock her into shape.'

'You keep your hands off the girl or there'll be trouble. You're old enough to be her father. Where is Rab anyway?' grumbled old Duncan. 'He'd better be on that float tonight with the rest of us. I don't care if the big sod's dying.'

'One thing's for sure, I'm a damned sight fitter than her father,' Melvin said. Then, shoulder and arm muscles bulging, he went back to his tussle with the pancakes.

Chapter 2

The Old Govan Fair was always held on the first Friday in June and dated back to the fifteenth century, when Govan itself was barely a village and Clydend had no existence at all.

It had been originally granted by ecclesiastical rescript and at one time was the occasion of annual festival and holiday when the local deacon was elected.

The village band turned out to play for the retiring deacon at his residence, and it was also the custom for the band to halt at each public house en route in order to serenade the landlord. He, in return, was expected to come out into the street with a bottle of 'the cratur' with which he regaled all the bandsmen. The result was that although the music had been distinct and lively at the beginning of the march it deteriorated into a mere confusion of hiccoughing sounds long before the journey ended.

The main function, however, was not to pay court to the retiring deacon but to elect a new one. After the solemn business of the election was over, the proceedings quickly gave way to jovial rejoicings. A procession formed and marched to the boundaries of the village carrying the famous 'sheep's head' hoisted aloft on a pole and gaily decorated.

The sheep's head with its shaggy hair and big curling horns had always been the emblem of the Burgh. Legend had it that, long ago before ships were built in Govan, a pretty girl had come to serve in the manse and a young man had begun to court her and eventually asked for her hand. The cleric put his veto on the alliance and refused the youth permission to continue seeing the girl. The young man nevertheless succeeded in carrying her off and, in celebration, or revenge, he cut off the heads of the sheep in the glebe lands of the manse and left these grim relics lying on the ground.

The villagers, siding with the young couple, took the choicest specimen of the sheeps' heads and did it honour publicly by

14

carrying it on the Fair Day all along the village street to the ancient 'Ferrie Bot' hostel at Water Row, where they all got 'roarin' fou and unco' happy' drinking the health of the happy couple.

The traditional sheep's head was still carried but the procession had grown with the place. Govan had at one time been a village on the banks of the River Clyde, but over the years increasing industrialization exploded the once-peaceful water's edge with the endless clamour of the shipyards and the giant cranes crowding to reach the sky. Now, there were high honeycombs of tenement buildings behind the yards. Bustling shops with fruit and vegetables spilling out on to the pavements, draperies with dense doorways of hangers bulging with clothes. Dark brown, sawdust-floored pubs at every corner where money could be spent when men were working. When they were not, gloomy, dusty caverns of pawn shops with brass balls above where precious possessions might fetch a few shillings.

The roads of Govan formed the shape of a ladder, with the long, straight Govan Road nearest the Clyde and the more pliant Langlands Road further back. The rungs of the ladder joining these two main roads, from Clydend in the south to past Govan Cross at the City of Glasgow end, were - first - Burghead Drive, Holmfauldhead Road and Drive Road. At this point the ladder widened to encompass Elder Park with the public library at the corner. Then the rungs continued towards the Cross with Elderpark Street, Elder Street and Golspie Street. Next came Harmony Row with Burleigh Street angling off it into Govan Cross. Helen Street went into the Cross too, like Robert Street which arched from it.

Splintering back from the Cross, right on the river bank in the space between Fairfield's yard and Harland and Wolff's, there was a huddle of short, narrow, dark and very ancient streets, like Water Row, clustering around the Govan Ferry and the Govan Wharf.

Like Clydend they, with their rich tapestries of characters, were part of Govan and the Bacchanalian mother city of Glasgow, yet communities on their own with their own city-sized hearts, their own fierce loyalties.

15

The Old Govan Fair procession started at the marshalling point in Burghead Drive. All the floats gathered there prior to their triumphal progress from Langlands Road to Pirie Park, along Langlands Road and through the old Burgh.

Burghead Drive was electrified by noise and colour.

A huge crowd clamoured, laughed, chattered, squealed, heaved this way and that by desperate boiling-faced marshals fighting to make order out of chaos.

Spilling from both ends of the Drive were close on eighty decorated floats, motorvans and carts, unrecognizable in their gay dress. Horses were stampering, with whinnies and snorts, rearing at the excitement. Flags were fluttering; the noise of revving motor-bikes mixed with the ting-a-linging bells of flower-cycles. The Boys' Brigade, cheeky pill-box hats strapped tight under chins, were tippering drums. Heavy-jowled mustachioed police pipers were concentrating, tartan pipes wailing, screeching, squeezing under iron arms. Jarring jazz bands, with bearded wild-eyed maestros, thumped a bouncy New Orleans beat.

Further along in Elder Park another swarm of people waited impatiently, heads craning for the Govan Fair Queen.

A wooden platform had been erected and the Royal Naval Volunteer Reserve (Clyde Division) Band was playing with great energy and enthusiasm.

The first car to arrive carried the convener of the Fair, and he welcomed the guests and ushered them to the dais. The guests included Govan's member of Parliament and other local dignitaries. There were also representatives from the local hospitals to whom all the money collected at the Fair was to be given.

As each succeeding car approached, the crowd, agog to see whom it contained, leaned forward expectantly, on tiptoe to get a better view.

At last the clop of horses heralded the mounted policemen who were preceding the 'royal' landau. Thousands of lusty cheers welcomed the policemen and the car.

The sleek black landau drew up and out stepped the Govan girl who was to be crowned this year's Queen, resplendent in white organdie lace and purple robes trimmed with ermine. She was followed to the throne by her four maids.

The convener gave a little speech reminding everyone of the unlucky ones who could not be here to enjoy the festivities - the patients in the Farmbank Infirmary, the Elder Cottage, Southern General, David Elder, Shieldhall and Hawkhead Hospitals.

'We would like,' he shouted from the roof of his voice to make sure he could be heard in every corner of the park, 'to bring as much comfort as we possibly can to these unfortunates and we are looking to the big-hearted people of Govan to rally round and give every penny they can manage.'

Pockets, bulging with pennies ready to fling at the floats, eagerly jumped and jingled.

'And now it gives me great pleasure,' the convener continued in a voice already cracking and getting hoarse, 'to ask Mrs Struthers, wife of our Medical Officer for Govan, to crown Miss Flora Rattrey Queen of the Old Govan Fair.'

Mrs Struthers, flushed and pretty in a frothy confection of yellow hat, rose and the convener relaxed down in his seat, only to bounce straight up again, every nerve at the ready. His eyes bulged at the wolf-whistling multitude, and he gesticulated for silence with waving arms and thickly pursed lips.

Order was restored but the convener did not risk sitting down again. He hovered in the background strafing the crowd with sharp admonishing stares as Mrs Struthers lifted the crown.

'I now crown Miss Flora Rattrey Queen of the Old Govan Fair.'

With these words she laid the symbol of majesty on the Queen's head and cheering swooped upwards.

The Old Govan Fair procession was about to begin.

The streets were awash with colour. Red, white and blue Union Jacks of all sizes, and the gold and red lion rampant of Scotland, swayed and flicked and cracked. Streamers streamed rainbows, bunting puffed and flapped.

Melvin had instructed Catriona to secure a good vantage point on Langlands Road at the end of the park near the library.

'Make sure you come without your mother, mind,' he warned her. 'And as soon as the procession's over, I'll come back and

17

meet you.'

It hadn't been easy getting out without mother because all Catriona's life Hannah Munro had kept a conscientious eye on her and had insisted on accompanying her everywhere. It made the situation doubly distressing that she had been forced to give a reason for wanting to go off on her own. Unpractised in the art of telling lies, she could think of no alternative but the truth. Her mother immediately tried to restrain her and lock her in the front room, but to miss the Govan Fair as well as a meeting with Melvin proved too much for even a person of Catriona's timid temperament.

For the first time in her life she mutinied, actively rebelled, fought tooth and nail in fact, and rushed sobbing but triumphantly free from the house.

All the same, she was glad when she met Norma, a neighbour's daughter, and they crushed together on the pavement's edge outside the park and danced up an down giggling and squealing like children in eagerness for the procession to come.

Catriona's excitement at seeing Melvin was always sharpened by fear. He was an unknown (and now forbidden) quantity. She had not the slightest idea what was expected of her in speech or behaviour in any man's company and the extent of her newly-discovered ignorance appalled her. Melvin was her first male friend and she found herself, without warning, like the person in the experiment who is locked for days in the black-dark, silent, sound-proofed room, completely divorced from the normal stimuli of sight, touch and hearing, the measure, the criterion acquired through learning and experience with which to judge a situation and react with appropriate patterns of behaviour. Every time she was with Melvin, she was blind and deaf and alone.

'Here it's coming!' Half-laughing, half-crying, she clapped her hands.

'Here's the police!' A delighted yell broke out. At any other time such a cry in Glasgow would immediately disperse any crowd, clear the streets like magic, but on the day of the Old Govan Fair the City of Glasgow Police Pipe Band led the procession and a splendid sight and sound it was. Many a

Glasgow villain's heart warmed towards it and they felt proud, and boasted at having been 'nicked' by one of the big 'Kilties'.

The cheeky swaggering skirl of 'Cock O' The North' took command of the road. Pipers in the red tartan plaids and kilts of The Royal Stuart, giant men in bearskin headgear, short-stepping, kilts swinging, were in immaculate military order with each drone or bass pipe pointing up from exactly the same place on each man's shoulder.

Catriona felt so moved by the sight and sound of the pipe band she could have wept on Norma's shoulder. Emotion ranged free and, unused to the freedom, pride and happiness became distressing to the point of grief.

After the police pipe band came the sheep's head held aloft, then the Navy band, then the Queen's landau and the motorcade of guests. Then came another pipe band with a big mustachioed drum-major marching out front and tossing and twirling the mace with nonchalant panache, eyes glued straight ahead, not needing to watch the intricate manoeuvres of hand and arm, aggressively confident.

Then the decorated floats with motor-bikes weaving in and out of the procession, and in between the floats, too, bands and more bands until the whole of Govan rocked with sound.

And tenements towered above the procession and tenants were a crush of faces and arms and hands at every window and the sky became a chinkling, winking, sparkling copper-gold shimmer of pennies descending onto floats.

Catriona watched the big letters *MACNAIR AND SON - BREADMAKERS* come into view.

All the men on the float and the pretty bright-eyed girl were dressed in white trousers, white jackets, white aprons and jaunty white hats. Heads were tossing back, laughing, arms were jerking, throwing out, golden bread was pelting the crowd.

A tall young man, his curly hair blue-black against the white uniform, was tossing pancakes with intense concen- tration flipping high, higher, bumping, reaching, always catching. Catriona's gaze rested on him. Then she was startled by the unexpected pain of a crusty loaf flung by Melvin finding its target on the side of her face.

Chapter 3

'Leerie, leene, licht the lamps,
Long legs and crooked shanks . . .'

The summer's evening closed its eyes, shutting out light. Black velvet darkness softly muffled sound, hid the crumbling stone of the Dessie Street tenements, the ugly carving on the walls, the litter, the dust, the chalked pavements.

A bottom-flat window was open wide and a woman leaned out on folded arms. A cluster of other women lounged outside, some shoo-shooing infants at the same time as chatting about the Govan Fair and everything that had taken place during the eventful day.

A sheaf of youngsters propped itself up in the gutter to watch the lamplighter raise his long pole to the gas-lamps all along the street. The children chanted their song to him but with weary voices dragging fainter and fainter.

'Leerie, leerie, licht the lamps,
Long legs and crooked shanks . . .'

The street took on a cosy hue as the leerie's pole, like a magic wand, touched each lamp, springing it into brightness that faded into a circle of flimsy yellow on pavement and road.

Behind curtain-closed windows people slept, peaceful in the knowledge that life continued. There was always a baby exercising newborn lungs somewhere, its screeching muffled by high buildings and hole-in-the-wall beds. Someone was always having a 'hing' out some window and there were always a few men leaning or squatting at street corners. Across the Main Road in Wine Row, the street that ended at Clydend Ferry, the shebeens were supplying the winos with Red Biddy. The meths drinkers were down at the river's end, huddles of hairy spiders, not human, yet more pathetically human than anyone, hugging bottles deep in their rags, oblivious of everything except the individual world of fantasy to which they had retreated.

But in Dessie Street the bakehouse, the warm nucleus of life, was busy with breadmaking sounds as front closes puttered and hissed into flickering light and back closes became echoing tunnels.

Melvin had taken Catriona and Norma home. He had only succeeded in shaking Norma off for a few minutes in the park by dodging behind some bushes with Catriona firmly held in tow.

'If it's not your mother, it's your next-door neighbours!' he had hissed. 'I'm fed up with this. It's time we got married!'

'Married?'

'You heard what I said. It's time somebody cut your umbilical cord. Anybody would think you were an infant the way you're tied to your mother. Don't you know the law?'

'Law?'

'By Scottish law you can get married at sixteen without your parents' consent. Everybody knows that! I've got a palace of a house.'

'Have you?'

'I've got furniture, dishes, bedding, the lot. I'm a hundred percent fit and I've got a ready-made son - my son Fergus, a grand wee lad. What more could any lassie wish for?'

A silence dropped between them. Through the bushes he watched, with mounting exasperation, Norma coming nearer.

'Well?' His eyes bulged down at Catriona.

'Have we known each other long enough?' she queried, really anxious to find out.

'Och, we'll have plenty of time to get to know each other after we're married. I'll be good to you, if that's what you're worrying about. I don't drink and I only smoke the occasional pipe. Here's Norma! Come on, come on, make up your mind, woman!'

Catriona was prodded into giving a harassed 'Yes' and Melvin irrevocably sealed the bargain by announcing the news of his proposal and acceptance to Norma who could hardly wait to tell the whole of Farmbank.

Now he sauntered into Dessie Street and up the close,

21

shoulders back, big hands clinking coins in trouser pockets.

Already heat was blanketing out from the side door in puffs of white and beery fumes of yeast, and rolls were becoming golden, and bread steaming, doughy, sticking together, crusts floured on top.

Past the bakehouse door, he grabbed the iron banister and leapt up the stairs two at a time. Gulping in air, nostrils stretching, he paused at his own door on the first landing. Then as if unable to resist the challenge of the stairs he suddenly attacked the second spiral, pausing only for a minute between big Baldy Fowler's door and Jimmy Gordon's door before bounding up the last flight to the attics.

Lexy was a long time answering his knock and when she appeared her eyes were heavy with sleep and dark underneath where mascara had smudged against her pillow. She was absently rubbing the sides of her breasts making them quiver under her cheap cotton nightdress and the nipples tweak up.

'Ohi, in the name of the wee man!' she wailed, recognizing Melvin. 'Mr MacNair! I'd just went to my bed. Ohi!' Her hands flew to her face and hair. 'I was that tired, too, I didn't even bother washing my face.'

'You're all right.' Melvin strolled past her and into the house.

'Here, just a minute, Mr MacNair.' She followed him into the tiny camceiled kitchen, her bare feet slapping loudly on the linoleum.

'It's not time to start my shift yet. What's wrong? Has something happened?'

'No, not a damn thing. You're a fine figure of a girl, Lexy. Do you believe in physical jerks?'

Lexy gave an unexpected splutter of a laugh and Melvin glowered with annoyance.

'Nothing funny about that. I'm a great believer in exercise. That's why I'm so well-made.'

'I know, but could you not have told me that down the bakehouse? Are you not working tonight?'

'Baldy knows I'll be late.'

'Want a cup of tea? The kettle's sitting on the side of the fire.'

His good humour returned. 'No, thanks, darlin'. It wasn't

22

tea I come up for.'

She gaped at him, still glassy-eyed with sleep, but understanding splintered through with astonishment and another burst of laughter.

'Here, you're terrible, so you are!'

'Come on,' he grinned. 'I've seen Rab sneaking up here.'

'Rab's different. He's fond of me. And I'm sorry for him, so I am!'

Melvin put out his hands for her.

'All right, darlin', be sorry for me!'

'Away you go!' She ran light-footed across the room and clambered up into the high hole-in-the-wall bed, the exertion making her giggles become breathless.

Melvin followed at a more leisurely pace and, reaching the bed, stared at it with interest. He gave the mountain of mattress a punch, then heaved his solid bulk on top of it.

'Ohi! Get off, you daft gowk!' Lexy squealed. 'You'll burst my springs!'

'I've never been in a hole-in-the-wall bed before,' he admitted, settling down and loosening his tie, to the accompaniment of Lexy's piercing squeaks and her struggles to wriggle further up the bed and away from him. 'We've always had ordinary ones. It feels queer. Like being shut in a cupboard. But I suppose it's cosy in the winter tucked in here away from the cold draughts.'

'You're terrible! Away you go and try your tricks on with your own lassie!'

'Och, to hell! I'd need a tin opener for her!'

Lexy stifled a paroxysm of laughter with her fists but as soon as Melvin reached for her she punched him.

'You've a nerve! I told you - Rab's my man. He's real fond of me, so he is.'

'Rab's not your man and never will be. He's married and he's daft about his wife.'

Then, while her bleak smudgy eyes were still vulnerable with hurt, he gathered her to him.

Outside, the 'midden men', looking like coalminers with lights on their caps and string tied under the knees of their trousers, argued with one another about football. They filled their baskets with refuse from the overflowing middens in the back courts. Then, heaving the baskets over their shoulders, they returned, boots scraping and clanging, through the closes. The midden motor eased along at snail's pace while the men shook the refuse from their baskets on top of it.

A drunk with a bottle bulging from his jacket pocket lurched lopsidedly along the middle of the road singing, with terrible sadness and great enjoyment.

'The Bonny Wells o' Weary . . .'

A horse and cart rattled past him. Furniture and bedding and all the worldly possessions of an out of work family were roped on the cart. The family huddled on top, the children's heads lolling sleep-heavy, unconscious of the anxious world in which their parents could no longer pay the rent and had to 'do a moonlight'.

Over in Farmbank a lorry skimmed along, hugging the kerb, hissing water out, washing the streets.

Catriona lay curled in a ball in bed with 'Lovey', her pink hot-water bottle, clamped tightly between her legs. The violent scene of a few hours earlier when she had announced her engagement to Melvin was still flickering across her mind with the speed of an old-fashioned movie.

It had ended in a fight between her mother and father. Yet she knew that the question of her sudden decision to leave home and marry a man so much older than her and go and live 'in Clydend of all places', was far from finished. Her mother would nag on and on never-ending.

Catriona closed her eyes, tired beyond all measure of quarrelling and bitterness. She was thankful to be leaving.

Chapter 4

Usually, when Catriona thought of marriage, she thought of a house. She imagined herself going around it dressed in a frilly apron and holding a feather duster out before her like a fairy queen's wand.

And when she strolled up the imaginary drive she admired the size of her dream house, the solidarity of it, and the purple clematis swelling lushly round the door.

It had a carpeted hall; everywhere there were carpets, warm, luxurious and muted, shutting out the draughts of the outside world.

Inside was all comfort and safety and pleasure to the eye; luxuries everywhere - paintings, standard lamps, bedside-lamps, quilts and counterpanes on the beds.

She visited it as often as possible and never tired, never became bored. There was always another cupboard, another corner she'd never noticed before, or an alteration to make, some improvement to attend to, a piece of furniture to change to a more convenient place or something to add to her stock of requirements. 'Good gracious!' She'd mentally throw up her hands. 'I haven't any fish forks and knives!'

The house was far more real than the flat above the bakery at Number 1 Dessie Street.

She could still hardly credit the fact that she was going to get married and live in a place of her own. Often she had prayed for someone - anyone - to come and whisk her away from Fyffe Street and change her life from misery to happiness, from bondage to freedom, but she had never dared to believe that her prayers would be answered.

'Where's your daddy?' Hannah dispersed Catriona's pleasant haze of thought.

'I don't know.'

'You don't know!' Hannah eyed her with disgust. 'Well, I

know, all right. He's away hiding in some bar so that I can't get my tongue on him, that's where he is. But he's not going to evade responsibility this time. I'll see to it. He's going to speak to that man because it's all his fault.

'If he hadn't been off work with his filthy dermatitis, that man would never have needed to come here to give him his wages. And if he hadn't come here he would never have seen you and all this trouble wouldn't have started. I've told your daddy already - Clydend's one of the toughest districts in Glasgow. I wouldn't live there and neither will you. Sooner or later he's going to speak to that man. But we're going to speak to him right now!'

'Speak to him?'

'Get your coat on.'

'But, Mummy!'

She followed her mother along the lobby and watched her dive into a coat and jerk on a reddish-brown felt hat.

'Get your coat on!'

'What do you mean - speak to him?'

'You're coming with me to that bakery in Dessie Street and you're going to tell that Melvin MacNair you certainly are not going to marry him.' Her stare pierced through the shadows into the hall-stand mirror so that she could tug at her hat with both hands to make it sit squarely and aggressively.

'The very idea! He's old enough to be your father!'

'But, I want to get married.' Stubbornness gave emphasis to Catriona's voice. 'And I promised.'

'Nonsense! Here, don't just stand there, child, get this coat on. You don't know what you want.'

She hustled Catriona into a coat and buttoned it up with strong, deft fingers. Having fastened the top button, she tidied down the collar, whisked out some of the long fair hair that had become tucked inside and smoothed it neatly over her daughter's shoulders.

Suddenly she stiffened as if something terrible had just occurred to her.

'He didn't touch you, did he?'

'Touch me?'

26

'Like I told you Bad Men do?'

Catriona's mind wrestled to bring to the surface and sort out tales of Bad Men jostling against girls coming out of cinemas or theatres and injecting them with concealed hypodermic syringes, then carrying them off to sell them in the white slave market.

Or Bad Men in cafés putting powder in girls' tea then secreting them away to lock them in backstreet rooms.

Bad Men that lurked behind bushes in the park or under the water in the swimming-baths. Everywhere there were Bad Men trying to touch girls and 'dirty them' and have their own way.

'I don't think he touched me.'

She stared up at the purple threads on her mother' cheeks and the large black pupils of her eyes.

'God will punish you, you know. He has strange and mysterious ways of working. He'll send his messenger of death during the night to take you away into the eternal darkness. Or someone you love will be taken forever from you. Or an accident will happen when you least expect it. He's watching you, Catriona - you'll be punished. Oh, you'll be punished.'

Before she realized what had happened Catriona was pushed and pummelled from the house.

Rab Munro had escaped and he flew along Fyffe Street, eyes popping, the early morning air catching his lungs like champagne. He had just done a hard night's work but he was not so tired that he had to lie in bed at home and listen to more of Hannah's ranting and ravings about Catriona getting married to Melvin.

Too restless even to wait at bus stops, he determined to continue on foot as far as the Main Road and then take the tram along to Dessie Street.

Secretly revelling in the exhilaration of the air and the victory in managing to slip out while Hannah's back was turned, he covered Fyffe Street with long rapid strides, head lowered, hands dug deep into pockets. Only when he'd turned the corner into Farmbank Road did his pace even out a little.

He stared around. Farmbank Corporation Housing Scheme was certainly a better place than Clydend for the wife and family to live, he thought with satisfaction. He hadn't failed Hannah there. He'd readily agreed that the MacNair building in Dessie Street was no place for her. No one could deny she was a good-living respectable woman. His mind turned over some of her qualifications for goodness with the usual mixture of pride, admiration, envy and sarcastic derision: President of the Women's Guild, member of the Farmbank's Help The Helpless Club, and Grand Matron of The Band of Jesus.

He crossed to the James Street Public Park side of Farmbank Road and tramped along close to the railings, big hands bunched, head sunk forward, arms squeezed forward as if holding up his chest. He could hear the soft rustle of the bushes and feel them reaching out between the iron to tug at his sleeve. His nostrils widened with the smell of them and the new-cut grass.

Often he escaped into this place. A wooded part at the other end was dark and jerky with squirrels. Without relaxing, his fingers poked at the corners of his pocket. Finding no nuts, he was both glad and disappointed.

Pain settled on his head and down behind his eyes blurring them.

Without looking one way or the other he crossed James Street, continued down Farmbank Road past the grey buildings of the Farmbank Infirmary, across Meikle Street, then walked straight on until he reached the Main Road with its loud clanking and sizzling of tramcars.

He was thinking of bed, and Lexy. Sexy Lexy, they called her. Her bed, in one of the attic flats in the MacNair building, was wide and soft. He sunk into it in his imagination with a groan of relief. She'd be working now downstairs in the bakehouse, helping Jimmy Gordon cream and decorate the cakes, her spiky high-heeled shoes and bulgy calves almost completely hidden by the big white apron Jimmy insisted she tie round herself, but the apron and the long white coat did nothing to hide her hour-glass figure.

The rocking-cradle motion of the tram shuggled him off to sleep until the conductor's broad Glasgow bawl penetrated his snores and exploded in his ear.

'Hey, you! You get off at Dessie Street, don't you?'

He leapt spluttering to his feet, clueless about where he was and deathly cold.

'You doing an extra shift, eh?' The conductor grinned up from underneath a cap pulled down over his nose. 'Making your pile?'

'Sure . . . sure . . .'

He stretched an embarrassed smile at the conductor's ticket machine and poured himself off the tram as it trundled away.

The car stop was outside the high iron gates of the Benlin yards, and the equally high wall reared back along the Main Road as far as the eye could see, like a Scottish Bastille. Dirty newspapers flapped and skittered against it, and greasy fish and chip pokes moving more slowly and sporadically thumbed a nose at its bleakness, its harshness and its authority.

Past the stop, the wall turned into the part of Dessie Street that ended in the River Clyde and the Clydend Ferry, and had become known locally as Wine Row because of the shebeens up the closes between the warehouses.

Trams clanked back and forward along the Main Road as Rab stared across at the MacNair building. It was on the corner of the Main Road and the other end of Dessie Street that led to a jungle of side streets and grey-black tenement houses. The building itself wasn't bad: old but solid, a roomy, double-windowed, double-countered shop with office, lavatory, store-rooms and bakehouse at the back and, above, four good-sized flats and two smaller attic flats. Old MacNair had a gold-mine here - no competition, nothing but tenements except the Anchor pub at the opposite corner, and then about half a mile down the Main Road the 'Tally's', and he supplied both with pies, and rolls and bread for sandwiches, cakes, cookies and scones. There was nothing up the other end either except Granny's Café and MacNair supplied her, too, and of course the Ritzy Cinema, the local flea pit.

Sandy the vanman would be out delivering just now, his horse Billy clip-clopping, tail swishing, head up, ears cocked to listen for the Benlin one o'clock hooter that meant knocking-off time, a lively gallop to the stables, a big dinner and a long kip before brushing and grooming in readiness for the next morning.

Rab strode across the road, past the shop door and plunged

into the first close in Dessie Street. He suddenly felt sick.

This had been his secret place. Shadow-dark even during the day, it titillated the senses with hot smells of new bread and mutton pies and spicy ginger cake from the bakery's side door.

Up the spiral staircase, round and round.

Melvin MacNair's flat was directly above the bakery.

Catriona would live here. The fool of a girl - the very first man she'd ever known and she couldn't wait to sleep with him.

He fumbled blindly with the key of Lexy's flat, then made straight for her bed to lie head back, his face bitter and haggard. He didn't want Catriona to marry Melvin any more than Hannah did. Only he had more sense. He knew there wasn't a damn thing either of them could do to stop it.

He slept fitfully and wakened more ill-at-ease and guilty than if Lexy had been in bed, naked and pathetically vulnerable in sleep, beside him. It was as if some over-developed sixth sense warned him that Hannah was near.

Still cold and dazed with sleep and lack of sleep, he left the house in long reckless strides and clattered down the stairs, his boots sending hollow drum-beats up to the roof.

Until, unexpectedly, the ruddy-faced Hannah in war-like mood was blocking his path and he was clinging to the banister with the shock of seeing her there.

Catriona wept angrily beside her.

Chapter 5

The furnace heat of the bakehouse was immediately engulfing, and globules of sweat burst through every flour-dusted pore.

There were two entrances, one through the dough-hardened curtain of sacking from the shop end a few steps across the lobby that remained a slippery menace despite frequent moppings and scrubbings - and the other through the lobby side door that opened into the close.

The close and the stairs were washed regularly too but the flour had become part of the air, continuously moving and dancing a white haze in summer sunshine against the landing windows, in winter an irritant to the throat and chest, scraping up coughs as folk puffed round and round the stairs.

It kneaded underfoot with the grease making a glassy paste to twist muscles and break unsuspecting bones. It lent even more variety to the diet of the rats that rustled deep in overflowing middens in the back court.

It fed the army of cockroaches that burst up from the heat of the bakehouse to cover the floors of the houses above like a busy blanket, a crawling coverlet that magically disappeared with the click of a light switch.

The humphy-backed cleaner who lived in one of the attic flats cleaned slowly and wetly, smiling to herself. Like the men who attend to the huge Forth Bridge, by the time she'd worked her way down all the stairs through the close, the bakehouse, the lobby and the shops, the stairs were filthy and it was time to start at the beginning again.

Perhaps it was the frustration of this that made her the terrible torment, the practical joker of a woman she was. Old MacNair had warned her that if one more person was startled into screams by the sight of her kneeling in the shadows wearing a rubber mask, or if any more door-handles were found tied together or anything put through letter-boxes except letters, she would be finished for good, turfed out, lock, stock and barrel.

So the cleaner cleaned on and the flour thickened the air around her and her cloth slapped across the lumpy grease and her pipe clay squeaked as she decorated the grey stone with white intricate squiggles and patterns, and the heat crept up her back and the pungent smell of food made her mouth water.

The night shift had gone off. Big Baldy Fowler had stretched his muscles, rubbed his head in a cloud of flour dust, told the other bakers he was going for a kip, then gone upstairs as usual and made violent love to Sarah his wife.

Rab had buttoned his old raincoat over his sweaty shirt and flour-thick trousers and huddled into it, his face grey-gaunt over the turned-up collar, and, with only a tired nod, he'd slouched away to wait propped and heavy-eyed at a stop for a tramcar to Farmbank.

Melvin MacNair had carefully cleaned the two Scotch ovens with the scuffle, a long shaft or pole with a sack hanging on the end, a job he had always insisted on doing himself. Then he had hung his aprons in the lobby, washed himself in the lobby sink, changed his shoes, brushed himself down very carefully to remove even the slightest suspicion of flour, even brushed his hair and his moustache, donned a sports jacket and cap and gone smartly upstairs.

Only old Tam was left from the nightshift. He folded up the morning paper, flapped it on to the bench, scratched through his wispy white hair, then stretched luxuriously. The scraggy little body in the blue and white striped shirt with the tight rolled-up sleeves lifted for a second out of the big white apron then shrunk down inside it again with a sigh of satisfaction. This hour, after the night's work and before he went upstairs to face his wife and daughter, was to be savoured to the full. He had relished his breakfast: a big mug of strong sweet tea, a meat pie and a couple of hot rolls oozing with butter. He had enjoyed every item of the paper from the front-page headlines to the small printed sports results at the back.

Now his bright pearl-button eyes twinkled around. Jumping to his feet he rubbed and smacked his hands together, his gorilla arms developed out of all proportion to his undersized body by years of chaffing and kneading up the dough.

'Going to the match, son?' He grinned at Jimmy the confectioner who was leaning over and staring very seriously into the mixing machine.

'Sandy was asking,' Jimmy replied. 'He's got a couple of tickets.'

'Old MacNair gave me one.'

'Gave?' Deep-set eyes under jutting brows flashed round at him. 'Old MacNair never gave anything. Either he sells at a profit or there's strings attached.'

'Oh, I can't complain, son. He's supplied me with many a good feed without knowing it.'

'We work hard for all we get. And he gets most of it back for rent and food. Talk about daylight robbery!' Jimmy's words spattered out with machine-gun rapidity. 'Have you heard that song about the company store? It could be our signature tune.'

'Don't bother about me.' With a laugh he gave his hands another smack and rub. 'I've a lot more to worry me than old MacNair's baps. Anyway, son, you're awful young and you've a lot to learn about folk. There's a lot worse than old MacNair going around.'

'Your Lizzie, for instance. I know what she needs. A nice big fella!' Lexy flung her loud undisciplined voice at him as she passed with one of the cake tins she had been filling.

'Who needs a nice big fella?' Sandy the vanman, a giant bean-pole with red hair, a red nose and chronically sore feet, tiptoed gingerly into the bakehouse, his lips blowing and puttering, a habit he'd acquired while curry-combing his horse to keep the dandruff from flying into his mouth and up his nose.

'Tam's lassie.'

Lexy clattered the cake tray down beside Jimmy then returned to the other end of the bench, buttocks and bosom bouncing. 'How about you, Sandy?' Winking a heavily mascara'd eye at the vanman she patted the white cotton turban that covered the steel curlers in her hair. 'Or are you daft about me, eh?'

'I've enough to contend with, with my horse!'

Chortling to himself Tam went out into the lobby that separated the bakehouse from the front shop. The side door was

33

open and, as he was untying his apron, the halfer appeared, his freckled face creased in his usual grin, the scone or padded bonnet that protected his head against the weight of the boards pulled down over his eyes.

'Hi, Tam!'

'Hi, son!'

Hitching up his trousers the young halfer marched past him and into the bakehouse.

Tam looped the tape halter of his apron over a peg before leaving by the side door.

'I'm away!' he called. Into the close with a jaunty jog trot and up the spiral staircase.

Next to Melvin's, his door was the cleanest on the stair. Every inch of it was exquisitely polished and the brass name plate and letter-box and keyhole glittered bright yellow.

'Just let me catch any of them saying I don't keep a clean house,' Lizzie never tired of repeating. She had a bee in her bonnet about folk gossiping about her behind her back or trying to get at her in one way or another.

Carefully he rubbed his knuckles on his jacket before knocking exactly in the middle of the door. Then he waited, small on the doormat, faded and floury, praying that Lizzie wouldn't accuse him of spilling the white powder around on purpose.

Sarah Fowler was thirty-five years of age and despite her blonde hair and her slim figure she looked every minute of it. Easing herself downstairs she clutched at the iron banisters. Pain dragged at her lower back, belly, buttocks and thighs with exquisite precision. Her patchily made-up face had long ago set in a twisted pattern of suffering that could not untwist even when she smiled and she smiled more than most.

Reaching the first landing she rested thankfully between Melvin's and Tam's doors. Then, thinking she heard a sound from the latter, her nerves twitched into action and forced her feet down the rest of the stairs at twice her previous speed despite the pain. Anything was more bearable than a tirade from Lizzie - anything, she hastened to correct herself except the bagpipe moaning of Lender Lil, the mother-in-law to beat all mothers-in-law.

She stopped again in the close to get her breath back, shoved her message basket further up one arm and hugged her coat more tightly around herself.

She was beginning to dread the mornings. First thing Baldy did when he came off work from the bakery was get into bed beside her and have his loving. Not that she was complaining. She was grateful for and flattered by Baldy's attentions. It wasn't his fault that she'd had one miscarriage after another until her inside felt red raw.

That wasn't the only thing she felt. She had become so tired, so continuously and indescribably tired, even coming downstairs to the shop was like an expedition to the other ends of the earth. And the cold . . . oh, the cold! She closed her eyes, her scalp contracting, her icy fingers bending stiffly inside two pairs of gloves.

'Are you all right, hen?' Sandy McNulty came out of the side door as if on stilts, a bread-board squashing his ginger hair down.

Immediately Sarah's face crinkled into a grin.

'Och, aye. Just feeling the cauld as usual. It's ma watery blood. Got any guid stuff to spare?'

'We're two of a kind, hen. See this red conk? Everybody thinks it's a boozy yin. Booze be damned, I keep telling them. I'm just bloody frozen!'

'Ah think we'll have to emigrate, Sandy.'

He winked at her as they emerged together into Dessie Street, he with his stiff bouncy lope as if he were trying to avoid stepping on white-hot coals and she with her slippered feet and small tired shuffle.

'Just you say the word, hen, and ah'll be there.'

'Away with ye!' She poked him in the ribs before turning to go into the shop and although it was only a gentle shove it nearly over-balanced his bread-board.

Poor Sandy, she thought. She wouldn't have him in a gift. She felt keenly sorry for the vanman with his thin blood and red nose and the agony he suffered with his feet but she wouldn't exchange him for her Baldy, not in a thousand years.

35

There was nobody like Baldy. He was a real hefty hunk of a man who looked more like an all-in wrestler than a baker. He hadn't a hair on his head and he'd always been the same, with skin as smooth and shiny as a baby's, but muscle-hard as if crammed with rocks underneath. No one had ever dared to torment him about his hairlessness. At school he'd sorted things out to his liking right from the start by beating up his fellow pupils in the baby class as a warning of what *would* happen if they even though of tormenting him. But he allowed them to call him 'Baldy' because he'd never been called anything else.

Still smiling, Sarah pushed open the half-wood, half-glass door of MacNair's Bakery and General Grocers. Being the foreman baker's wife gave her a special status here.

Already the shop was busy and her tired eyes lit with pleasure at the sight and sound of so many familiar people. Carefully she shut the door. Gratefully she savoured the heat of the place as it wrapped lovingly, comfortingly around her.

Old Duncan MacNair, no longer spending his nights in the bakehouse but working from nine to five or six in the shop instead, was taking his time serving at the counter, his few grey hairs carefully parted and greased down over his head, his straggly moustache and goatee beard wet and drooping at the edges. He wasn't that old, of course, only about sixty-five, and he had vivid blue and red veined cheeks, and glittery if somewhat watery blue eyes to prove it. He could be quick when he wanted, rheumatic hands clenched, elbows bent, boots lifting and clomping like Sandy's horse; but this morning he did not want to and Maisie his assistant was being forced, much to her annoyance, to speed up her pace.

'Oh, come on, Duncan, man!' a customer tried to chivvy him on. 'We'll still be here when the hooter goes and nothing ready for our men's dinner.'

Duncan's words came from his nose, not his mouth.

'It'll not take you long to fry your sausage and open your can of beans.'

'You mind your cheek. I'm not Rab Munro's wife, remember.'

'Rab Munro's wife?' Sarah's small rusty voice echoed over her shoulder. 'What's she got to do with it?'

'She was in here arguing the toss with old Duncan. But *I'll* not argue with him. I'll be over that counter and chug the beard off his face.'

'Ah thought Rab's wife never came over here.'

'No, we're not good enough for her nor her blondie-haired daughter. She was trying to put a spanner in the works and stop the girl and Melvin getting married. Old Duncan chased her, didn't you, you auld rascal? I heard she went upstairs though.'

The first thought that leapt to Sarah's mind was that her husband had a weakness for blondes. Wasn't that why, no matter how tired she felt, she never failed to bleach her own hair? As soon as the brown roots began to appear she conscientiously attended to them.

A pulse twitched and leapt about her face and she hoped nobody could see it.

'Blonde, did you say?'

'Aye, long it was. I think thon hair must be natural.'

Lines of strain pinched Sarah's skin.

If only she had been able to give her man the wee laddie he wanted. It was right and proper that a man should want a son.

She felt ashamed - especially after all her man had done for her. Where would she have been, what sort of life would she have had without him? A bastard, brought up in a single-end - a dismal self-contained room - by a drunken granny, homeless when the old woman died and the factor put someone else in the house - where would she have gone but on to the streets?

That's what her mother-in-law always said.

The danger now lay in being ill and a nuisance to Baldy or being ill and having to leave him to go to the hospital.

A man needed to have his loving regular.

And then there was the worry about money, too. Baldy never complained but the expense of her being ill was terrible.

'Pretty, too, ah'll bet,' she quavered, her smile at its weakest.

'Not half!' The other woman unwittingly piled on the agony. 'No make-up or anything either, just a wee, long-haired bairn.'

Suddenly Duncan MacNair banged a gnarled fist impatiently on the counter.

'Come on, come on,' he ordered in his high-pitched nasal

tone. 'What do you want? Let's have it!'

'Cheeky old rascal!' The customer plumped her message basket on top of his hand making him yell with pain. 'I don't envy that girl coming here. If she doesn't watch out she'll have this one to contend with as well as the other.' She suddenly bounced with laughter, and straining round to Sarah she added, 'He's fit for anything. And you'd better watch your Baldy, hen. He's a great one for the blondes is Baldy.'

'Aye!' By some miracle Sarah found herself laughing instead of weeping. 'He's an awfi man!'

The house was cold with quietness when she returned upstairs. And the coldness and the quietness made the house grow and made Sarah shrink; her slippered feet quickened their shuffle across the hall, pulled as if by a magnet to her retreat beside the kitchen fire.

The fire was not long lit and smoke spiralled straight up, suddenly to bend and collapse, flutter and puff outwards. Huddled dull-eyed in her chair Sarah watched it. A mouse in the cupboard behind her nibbled tentatively, delicately, then, thinking the house must be empty because of its stillness, it began scraping and clawing and gnawing with reckless abandon.

Sarah had drifted away to her youth: perched on her granny's bottom-flat window-sill across the road, her skinny legs swinging, her short cotton dress covered by one of her granny's long cardigans instead of a coat, she breathlessly admired the boys playing football.

Old MacNair's shop door served as one goal area, her granny's close the other.

Dessie Street echoed to bursting point with male yells, oaths, criticisms of play and desperate instructions.

'Tackle him! Don't let him through . . .'

'Clear it! Clear it!'

'No goal . . . no goal . . . it wasn't off!'

If a goal was scored in old MacNair's doorway it had the added excitement of one of the boys, usually Baldy, having to swoop into the shop to retrieve the ball and shoot out again with old MacNair hot on his heels screaming for the police.

And when the police, in the form of Constable Lamont, materialized (usually from the bakehouse where he had been enjoying a jam doughnut and a big mug of tea), the boys scattered and disappeared like cockroaches and Sarah scrambled down off the window-sill and hared up the close to the cries of protest from women having a lean out their windows above.

'Och, they were no doing any harm, so they weren't! How do you expect the Rangers and the Celtic to get any players if you'll no let them practise in the street!'

Baldy had eventually got a job at MacNair's and flung himself into the flour of the bakehouse with every bit as much energy, noise and enthusiasm as he tackled everything else.

One night in the bakehouse, after a bear-hug behind the flour sacks in the storeroom and a kiss that tasted of hot cross buns and had the squelchy sound of the dough-mixer, she told him that the doctor said she was expecting and for the baby's sake they would have to get married.

Baldy hadn't batted an eyelid. 'Aye, as soon as you like, hen. There's plenty room round at Ma's.'

Ma meant Mrs Fowler or Lender Lil as she was more commonly known because she was Clydend's money-lender. She did not have an office. All her business was done at her flat in Starky Street and there was a stream of people lapping in and out of Lender Lil's all day.

She was continually complaining about them and when Sarah moved in as Baldy's wife her resentment increased.

'Oh, yes,' she said with heavy sarcasm. 'Everybody lives off me around here, so why shouldn't our Miss Sweeney?'

'Ah'm not Miss Sweeney. Ah'm Mrs Fowler,' Sarah stubbornly insisted. 'And you shouldn't be keepin' Baldy's wage packet now. Baldy's my man. He should be handing his pay over to me. Ah'm his wife.'

After her miscarriage she persuaded Baldy to leave his mother's and take the house in Dessie Street, and his mother's complaints instead of ceasing became worse.

'Fancy, after all the sacrifices I've made for him, after all I've done, after keeping him for years while he served his time in that baker's, he ups and leaves me before I've time to get a penny-piece back. My only son. Little did I think my Baldy would ever do a thing like this to his mother. Of course it's not him, the big fat fool! It's you and well I know it, Miss Sweeney! You've tricked my boy into marrying you, now you're making sure you gets your hands on all his money.'

Often her harangues ended in floods of tears, but Sarah felt sorry for her. She suspected the older woman must be very lonely. Lender Lil maybe had diamond rings and gold watches and quite a bank account with interest money but she had very few if any real friends.

Her sympathetic feelings towards Mrs Fowler however did nothing towards weakening her claims on her husband. Baldy was her man and the house in Dessie Street was their home, and she thanked God for them both, not Mrs Fowler.

But now, with the news that another woman was coming to live on the stair, she felt heavy with secret hopelessness.

She had been young and bonny once and full of life and loving. She had even once had long fair hair. She remembered brushing it and tying it back with pink satin ribbon the day that she and Baldy got married.

She was suddenly agonizingly aware of the change in herself, of energy and eagerness drained away, the dewy wonder, the vulnerability, the excitement of youth dried up and toughened.

The more she thought of the newcomer to Dessie Street, the more her mind shrank away from the idea.

Like a mirror to the child she could be no more and could never have, Sarah did not know how she could bring herself to look at Catriona, and dreaded the ordeal of seeing her as she had never dreaded anything else before.

Chapter 6

The staccato stutter of the Benlin riveters filled to bursting point the whole Main Road and Dessie Street and all the streets in Clydend with a fiendish metallic noise that echoed all over Glasgow, even drowning the rumble and clanging of the tramcars.

The people in Dessie Street had learned to live with it, to ignore it, to adapt their outside voices to broad, lusty bawls accentuated by elastic mouths that looked as if they were trying to make lip-reading as easy as possible for the deaf folk.

Women leaned out of windows and shouted pleasantries to each other and exchanged titbits of gossip. Little girls in the dusty street below squealed and giggled and teetered and tiptoed about in their mothers high-heeled shoes and too-long dresses and held on to huge-brimmed, feather-trimmed hats. Others were lost in rapt concentration, their eyes glued to a fast bouncing ball.

'One, two, three a-leary . . . four, five, six a-leary, seven, eight, nine a-leary, ten a-leary postman!'

One child was crawling along the pavement intent on chalking in as big letters as she could stretch to: 'Alice Campbell loves Murdo Paterson'.

Big boys and wee boys were racing and slipping and dribbling and kicking and shouting and fighting, playing football.

Upstairs in Number 1 Dessie Street Mrs Amy Gordon, widowed mother of Jimmy Gordon the confectioner, snoozed in her rocking-chair beside her kitchen fire.

Sometimes at moments like this she thought her husband was still alive. She would waken, startled into awareness by the sound of the front door, a rush of joy bringing his name to her lips. And then in the heart-rending minute as she remembered, the world emptied. She was alone. Seven long years he had been dead yet her subconscious mind, her unconscious heart still refused to accept it.

He had been a kind and loving husband, a conscientious if somewhat strict father, and a good hard-working baker for MacNair's although he'd never got much thanks for it; a big bully of a man like Baldy Fowler was thought much more of in that place. The bakery had killed him; the long night hours, the heat, the extreme change of temperature outside that the body never had time to adjust to, the heavy lifting and handling, the breathing in of flour dust through the mouth, the nose, the lungs and every open sweaty pore.

They'd vowed that Jimmy would never have to follow in his father's footsteps and encouraged the lad to stay on at school. They'd even dreamed of seeing him at university.

Jimmy had an intensely studious and searching mind. He was always experimenting with things and asking questions and he soaked up books, any kind of books, at a truly bewildering rate. He worked his way through the nearest library at Elder Park in no time and was soon spending hour after hour in the Mitchell Library in the city.

'It's the most marvellous place, Mum,' he kept assuring her. 'They've even got a music room there.'

It worried her how he lay reading in bed till all hours in the morning and then emerged, white-faced, to sit with his dark eyes still glued to a book all through breakfast, or at least until his father came in and snatched the book angrily from him.

'Can you not strike a happy medium? No good can come of going to such extremes.'

Her husband had been sorely tried with Jimmy's piano-playing as well. First the hours of laborious practising: the nerve-twanging scales, up, up, up, up, up, up, down, down, down, down, down, then the stumbling melodies, the suspense-filled pauses as Jimmy struggled to find the right chord.

'Is that you, son?' she called towards a sound in the hall, her rocking-chair squeaking forward.

Her answer was the strangely haunting notes of Sibelius's *Valse Triste* issuing faintly from the front room as if Jimmy were playing the piano miles and miles away.

She got up to make him a cup of tea, wishing he'd play more modern cheery stuff but nevertheless tum-tumming Sibelius and discreetly conducting with plump, ringed hands.

She sighed, but a smile deepened the creases round her mouth and eyes. He'd be sitting through in the front room now, covered in flour from the top of his curly head to the toes of his working shoes but not in this same world as her carpet and cushions.

The music gained in strength yet the gentleness of her son's fingers touched and stirred unknown levels of feeling. Her whole being was gathered up and carried along and swung into sadness with such poignancy that she stopped, tea-pot in hand, lips quivering.

Jimmy had had a rheumatic heart when he was a child and it still worried and distressed her. The doctor had said Jimmy was a fine big lad and he had youth on his side. His heart would heal and despite his excitable temperament he'd be all right, she would see.

Every night in her prayers she asked God that this should be so. 'Please, God, make my Jimmy all right.'

She made the tea, poured some into a cup, milked and sugared it and carried it carefully before her from the kitchen.

Outside the front-room door she waited automatically for the *Valse Triste* to stop, not daring to spoil the perfection of it. She made a strange and incongruous picture standing in the shadows of the hall, a little round barrel of a woman with grey-gold hair, a brown and green wrap-around apron and a cup of tea in her hand; while all around her swirled the music of the gods, quickening, dancing, saddening, pausing, swooping, gentling, gentling, until softly it faded away.

Jimmy's attention jerked as soon as his mother entered the room.

'You old rascal!' He grinned at her. 'Is this you spoiling me again?'

'Here you!' Laughing she handed him the tea. 'I'll have less of the "old"!'

He didn't want the tea. She always put far too much milk and sugar in it, but she was watching him, hands clasped over aproned waist, eyes eagerly waiting for him to enjoy it.

'Slàinte Mhath!' He swung the cup high as if it were filled with champagne then downed it in one go.

'Oh, my!' His mother radiated happy laughter and was a joy to see. 'You're an awful laddie!'

Affection for her surged through him and he just checked himself in time from flinging his arms around her and hugging and kissing her. It was unmanly to be emotional. At least it was unmanly in Scotland. Probably it was quite the reverse in countries like France or Italy. Which proved how ridiculous the whole thing was. Only a matter of social convention. It certainly wasn't a God-made rule. God, if there were a God, had given emotions to men as well as to women.

He wondered if other men felt as he did. Were they, too, isolating themselves on self-made islands of restraint?

'That was grand,' he lied, winking at her. 'You're the best tea-maker in Glasgow without a doubt, without a doubt.'

He preferred coffee every time. He enjoyed going up to town on Saturdays to buy a half-pound of the real stuff. The old polished oak shop in Renfield Street - with its overflowing sacks of beans and crystallized ginger in jars richly painted with Chinese dragons - had a grinding machine that produced the velvet smell of coffee as well as the smooth brown powder. A hundred delicate aromas floated in the shop, and together formed a warm drug cloud to anaesthetize and titillate the senses.

He lingered there, savouring the sight, the sound, the smell of the place for as long as possible, happy to pace around waiting while other people were being served, then happier still to burst into eager conversation with the old man of the shop. The old man always seemed genuinely pleased to see him and they spoke about new blends and methods of percolating, and little tricks like adding a pinch of salt or mustard; it was as if no one had been in the slightest interested in coffee all week until he had come in.

The old man gave him pamphlets to study and Jimmy in turn searched out books from the libraries and the book-barrows on the history of the coffee-bean and the use of coffee, and the coffee-drinking habits of people all over the world, and he loaned them to the old man.

It was a fascinating subject.

'Get changed now in case somebody comes in.' His mother's voice broke into his thoughts.

'Is the water hot enough for a bath, do you think?'

'Saints preserve us, you had a bath last night and the night before, if I'm not mistaken.'

'Don't tell me the boss is charging us for hot water now? Measuring it out, charging us so much the gallon?'

'Och, of course not, there's plenty hot water.'

'Well, well, then?' Black brows pushed up, dark eyes filled with fun.

'But Friday night's bath night. Everybody takes their bath on a Friday, son.'

'And Monday's washing day?'

'That's right.' Her round apple face shone with pleasure again. 'And Tuesday's the ironing.'

'And all the time you have a renegade son, a terrible deserter of tradition.'

'Och, you're an awful laddie. Away and have your bath if you want to. But I've never heard the likes of it in my life.'

'You're the best mum in Glasgow.' He stretched up from the piano stool, massaging and exercising his fingers.

She shook her head at him but her hazel eyes were soft.

'Away and take that floury apron off in the kitchen.'

'Your word is my command, my command, Mother!'

He gestured for her to go through the door first. As she passed him, small and plump and dear to him, her head nowhere reaching the height of his shoulders, he couldn't resist the temptation to touch her and the touch immediately sprang into a passionate bear-hug that triggered off laughter and squealing as he swung her round and round the hall, not putting her down or setting her free until they'd together crashed noisily into the kitchen.

'Saints preserve us! Behave yourself, you cheeky young rascal. What'll the neighbours think? What a terrible carry on. You're an awful wee laddie.'

'Wee, did you say?' His handsome young face twitched mischievously. 'Wee, did you say, Mother?'

Tidying back stray wisps of hair and brushing the flour off

herself Amy gazed ruefully up at him. 'No, you're no a wee laddie any more, are you, son? One of these days you'll be leaving your old mum to get married. Oh, here!' Her face suddenly alerted, remembering. 'You'll never guess who I had visiting me.'

Jimmy untied his apron, unbuttoned his white coat and stood naked to the waist, intent on stretching and massaging his shoulder muscles.

'Not Lizzie again. The old story, was it? What a good mother she'd make for Fergus? What a good wife she'd make for Melvin MacNair? She has as much chance of marrying him as I have of playing the piano in St Andrew's Hall.'

Amy screwed up her face. 'God forgive me, Jimmy. I'd like to be kind and civil and act as a Christian woman should but I'm sorely tried with her.'

'When have you been anything but kind to Lizzie, Mother?'

Amy shook her head, then, remembering again, she brightened.

'Och, stop putting me off what I was going to tell you. You're such an awful blether nobody else can get a word in edgeways. It wasn't Lizzie. It was Mrs Munro.'

'Mrs Munro?'

'You know, Rab's wife. She's the Grand Matron at the meeting - the Band of Jesus. She's president of the Women's Guild as well, and dear knows all what. Although she's quite a young woman. She can't be much more than forty. Well, maybe half-way between forty and fifty. A fine-looking woman. She does a lot of good work, that woman, and, oh, I was fair upset.'

'Hold it, hold it!' Jimmy held up his hand. 'Just a minute. Why were you upset? Who upset you?'

'Well, you see . . .'

'Sit down!' He hustled her over to the rocking-chair. 'You just tell me all about it.'

She smiled up at him, eyes twinkling.

'I will son, if you give me half a chance. It was nothing to do with me really, except that I was coming up the stairs with my messages and just as I reached the first landing and stopped to get my breath back, I heard raised angry voices from Melvin MacNair's house. Then suddenly the door burst open and out

46

stumbled a wee fair-haired lassie and Mrs Munro punching her between the shoulder-blades to help her on her way.'

'Grand Matron of the Band of Jesus!' Jimmy's lip curled with distaste.

'But it was so unlike Mrs Munro to be violent like that. Punching the bairn sore she was. But she explained it all to me later, poor soul. She was so overwrought and upset she just didn't know what she was doing. I had her up here for a cup of tea and she rested until she felt better.'

'What about the child? She was the one getting hurt and upset.'

'Well as it turned out, she isn't as young as I thought. I thought about thirteen or so. She just looks like a wee school-bairn. I can quite understand her mother getting all angry and upset about what Melvin's going to do.'

'What's Melvin going to do? What do you mean?'

'That wee lassie's the one he's going to wed.'

'My God!'

He could not help laughing.

Chapter 7

The Band of Jesus was having a special meeting in the front room. The proper meeting hall was in town in Dundas Street, a forbidding Victorian building of sooty black stone above the entrance of which a neon sign made a startling contrast, with bright busy letters telling the people of Glasgow that Christ died for their sins.

Special meetings of the Matrons, however, were held in the front room. The opening hymn wailed loud and long, some voices strong, others continually stumbling.

Catriona sat perched on the edge of the chair at one side of the living-room fire, her thoughts rapidly chasing each other. Her father filled the chair opposite, overflowed it, a gaunt silent mountain of despair staring helplessly at nothing, swamped, slumped, round-shouldered, long arms and square hands dangling.

Catriona felt as if there were a big placard hanging round her neck, shouting to the world in foot-high letters, IT IS ALL MY FAULT! She had not only been the cause of increasing her father's miseries but of her mother's obvious worry and distress as well.

There could be no getting away from the truth of what her mother said. If she had not agreed to marry Melvin MacNair, none of this would have happened.

First the embarrassing scene in the shop, then the anguish of seeing her mother, trembling and breathless, climbing the high stone stairs, hat slightly askew, hair-pins escaping unheeded from the bulky bun of hair at the back of her head.

'You wicked, wicked girl!' she kept repeating, puffing for breath and voice jerking near to tears. 'I don't know how you can do this to me, your own mother, After all I've done for you too. After all the sacrifices I've made for you.'

Melvin had taken a long time opening the door and when he

did appear he wasn't the dapper smiling man that they expected. His eyes had shrunk and become red-rimmed. He was needing a shave and his normally smooth, wax-tipped moustache stuck out like a bushy old brush. He stank of sweat, and, horror of horrors, he stood there for anyone to see in nothing but his pyjamas. The blue-striped trousers, by the look of things and the way he was holding them bunched forward in his hands, had no cord to hold them up and were an obvious, terrifying and hypnotic menace to both Catriona and her mother.

'I was in bed!' he accused. 'But come in.'

They remained rooted to the doormat, their eyes as one pulled along by his bare-footed, trouser-drooping stomp across the hall. Reaching his front room he had suddenly noticed they weren't beside him and twisted round, one hand clutching his pyjamas, the other pushing open the room door.

'Come in, if you're coming.'

Afterwards Catriona became convinced that her mother would never reach the end of her harangue about him.

'I've never seen such a disgustingly vulgar man. He's not modest, Catriona. He's a vulgar and immodest man. How can you have even thought of a man like that? You! A well-brought-up, well-protected, well-sheltered girl like you! How could you have thought of that man?'

Catriona no longer knew what to think of Melvin.

She hoped the meeting would be a short one. No chance of bed until the Matrons of the Band of Jesus left. They would be sitting stiffly-corseted and barrel-bottomed on the bed-settee.

Once, after a particularly long session, not of the Band of Jesus but the committee of the Help the Helpless, she'd burst out: 'Thank goodness they've gone! I've been dying to get to bed for hours.'

'How dare you, you impertinent child!' Ruddy cheeks had purpled with anger. 'This is *my* home and this is *my* room and this is *my* bed-settee. *Nothing* here or anywhere belongs to you and never you forget it. Every stitch of clothing you wear, I paid for, every crumb of food that goes in your wicked ungrateful mouth, *I* bought!'

Not that Hannah had many worldly goods herself. She

believed it her Christian duty to give everything away. Rab had two locked drawers in the bedroom to protect his treasures against his wife's generosity. Catriona's clothes and possessions were kept in a suitcase behind the settee but Hannah had long since wrenched the lock apart so Catriona had not Rab's enviable good fortune. Long ago she'd abandoned any idea of possessing real things. Her mother had got her hands on every single item from the dearly prized and jealously guarded bangle, a Christmas present from Uncle Alex, to her Sunday silk knickers.

As far back as Catriona could remember, Hannah had always loved to quote in a husky dramatic voice: "'Do not lay up for yourselves treasures on earth where moth and rust consume and where thieves break in and steal, but lay up for yourselves treasures in heaven, where neither moth nor rust consumes and where thieves do not break in and steal. For where your treasure is, there will your heart be also.'"

At other times she'd straighten her shoulders and raise her strong chin and look the fine figure of a woman that she was and make the impressive pronouncement: "'Therefore I tell you, do not be anxious about your life, what you shall eat or what you shall drink, nor about what you shall put on. Is not life more than food, and the body more than clothing?'"

But they'd all have to eat something and wear something at the wedding. That was one of the subjects under discussion at the Band of Jesus meeting now. Someone, it seemed, had offered the loan of a wedding dress.

'You *want* to marry me, don't you?' Melvin, the front of his trousers still puckered up in his hands, had asked.

She'd nodded wide-eyed.

'O.K.,' he said. 'As soon as possible, eh?'

She'd nodded again as if her mother later accused, he had hypnotized her or she was a puppet with him jerking the strings.

'And we'll make it a quiet affair, eh?'

Another movement of her head with her hair slithering forward and her eyes clinging to his unshaved, unwashed face.

'Nod, nod, nod,' her mother said. 'Like a gormless dumb donkey!'

50

The hymn singing stopped and now there was the drone of the Lord's Prayer. Automatically Catriona's hands clasped on her lap.

"'Our Father which art in heaven, hallowed be Thy name. Thy Kingdom come, Thy will be done . . .'"

'*Her* will, she means!' Rab sighed.

Catriona's eyes sprang open.

'What did you say, Daddy?'

He sighed again. 'Oh, never mind.'

The fire was dying in the hearth. Wind sang a melancholy tune in the chimney. Catriona's attention wandered round the room. An ancient railway-station waiting-place with limp cotton curtains, dark brown linoleum, a scratched wooden table, a few wooden chairs.

A memory of Melvin MacNair's house eased cautiously into her mind but guilt and fear flicked it away. Hastily she concentrated on Norma Dick next door. It would be nice if Norma could get married. What a lovely bride she would make walking down the aisle, a white veil frothy and spreading to vie in generous length with the long glistening train of her ivory silk brocade dress.

Norma would love to have a house of her own, full of things of her own, things like cushions and carpets and ornaments and . . .

'Catriona!' Her mother's voice exploded through the living-room door, and forced Catriona to her feet.

'Come through here at once and say thank you. Mrs Campbell's brought the wedding dress.'

Big women, fat women, double-chinned bewhiskered women, spread themselves in a circle round the room.

Smiling at everyone, like a performer acknowledging applause before doing a turn, Hannah prodded Catriona into the centre.

'Look at the nice dress Mrs Campbell is giving you a loan of. Say thank you like a good girl.'

'Thank you,' Catriona muttered, eyes down, not daring to look at anything.

'Mrs Campbell,' Hannah said at the same time, 'may the good Lord bless you, you're far too kind.' Then to Catriona,

51

'Don't just stand there, dear, hurry through to the bedroom and try it on.'

The dress had once been beautiful but it was now yellow-tinged with age and musty with mothballs. Catriona unrustled it from its wrapping paper and held it against herself without enthusiasm. There was a veil, too, limp and grey and sad-looking.

She put them on, then was hardly able to credit the humiliation of her reflection in the long wardrobe mirror. Little girls playing out in the street dressed up in their mothers' old clothes had looked better.

'It's no use,' she told Hannah, who appeared in the bedroom to circle her, muscular arms folded across her broad bosom. 'I'm too wee for it.'

'Beggars can't be choosers! It'll do very well. Come on through and let the ladies see you.'

'I can't do that!' Her voice raised incredulously. 'To be seen in your wedding dress before the wedding is bad luck. '

'Being seen in your wedding dress isn't what's going to bring you bad luck, my girl. Melvin MacNair's your bad luck.'

'No, please, Mummy. I read in a book. It's a bad omen.'

'Come on! Hold it up in case you tramp on it.' Hannah spoke at the same time as Catriona. Always, even after she'd asked her daughter a question, she never paid the slightest attention to the girl's voice.

Shame at her appearance, as well as fear, made Catriona dig her heels in, close her eyes, and stiffen her back when her mother pulled her.

Her mother let go. They both turned to speechless wax models. It was Hannah who recovered first.

'Honour thy father and mother,' she said and pointed dramatically towards the door. 'Go through there at once! No daughter of mine is going to break one of God's commandments. You've sinned enough as it is. He's watching you, Catriona. God misses nothing. Everything, every unkind, selfish thought, every cruel disobedient act, He takes note of and adds up for the terrible Day of Judgement when you'll stand before Him to await your final punishment. But make no mistake about this,

Catriona, you'll be punished here, too. For every sin you're guilty of, there's a punishment.'

Her brown eyes acquired a faraway glaze and her mouth drooped at the edges with the weight of her bitterness. 'Your disobedience, your ungratefulness, your wicked selfishness will be punished. After all I've done for you, this is what I get. I nursed you and protected you and wrapped you in cotton-wool as a child and wouldn't ever let a draught get near you. I wouldn't allow you to play with other children in case they hurt you or contaminated you with their germs. Nobody could have had a stricter Christian upbringing. I've gone out to work since you've grown so that you can stay in the house all the time and I still look after you and watch over you as conscientiously as I did when you were a baby. And this is all the thanks I get. This is all the thanks.' She heaved a big shuddering sigh. 'You leave me!'

Chapter 8

It was more like a funeral-day than a wedding-day, Rab thought as he hitched his trousers up, fastened his braces then buttoned his fly. He went through to the living-room struggling irritably with his back stud.

Hannah was still sitting over the fire, chair jammed against the fender, big flat feet splayed out inside the hearth, skirts pushed up, legs wide apart, palms nearly up the chimney. She hadn't done her hair yet and it flowed over her shoulders and down her back like a girl's, a river of rich burgundy, its fruity glimmer heightened by the flames of the fire.

There were times, and this was one of them, when Hannah exuded sensuality.

Forgetting his irritation and leaving his still-white collar dangling, he gently laid a hand on her shoulder and felt the gloss of her hair and the firm warm flesh. He longed to bend over her and slide his hand down over her bulbous breasts, and his breathing immediately became noisy, but with a quick disdainful jerk of her shoulder Hannah knocked him away.

'Have you no shame? Even on your daughter's wedding day, can you not think of anything else?'

She got up, bumping and crashing the chair aside, and began with brisk bitter movements to twist and pin up her hair. Peering at all angles of her reflection in the mirror above the mantelpiece she elbowed him out of the way.

'A lot you care about her, of course. The only person you care about is yourself.'

'What are you on about now?' He tugged furiously at his collar. 'You stupid fool of a woman.'

'May the good Lord forgive you for saying that, Robert, because I'm no fool and don't you forget it.' She faced him. 'I'll find out exactly why you were coming down those stairs at Dessie Street, and why when you saw me there you went as white

54

as a sheet with guilt and nearly fainted.'

'Guilt?' He raised his voice to a roar, fighting his collar now, avoiding his wife's eyes like the plague and hating himself for his lack of courage. 'Fainted! You're as mad as a hatter, woman. I never know what you're raving on about.'

'You were supposed to be home in bed, weren't you?'

'I told you, you fool! We've been over all this a hundred times before.' He sneered his hatred at her. 'I went back to see Francis MacMahon. He lives in one of the attic flats. So does his mother when she's not doing the scrubbing. So does his brother. So does his sister Maisie when she's not serving in the shop. Francis works in the yards. He promised to get me paint. I just wanted to remind him. That was all!'

'That was all?' Hannah faced him. 'Bad enough even if that was all! Don't you dare bring any stolen property into my house.'

'*My* house!'

'Oh, be quiet. I know who lives up there and it's an absolute disgrace, a young girl like that living in a house by herself. It's just asking for trouble and as long as there's wicked men like you going around, she'll get it!'

Unexpectedly Rab won the battle with his collar and sighing with relief he reached for his tie.

'If it's Lexy Brown you're referring to, she was downstairs working in the bakehouse all day.'

Depression swelled up like a pain in his chest and he sighed again. It would have been all the same if he had been at Francis's. She still wouldn't have believed him.

'I'll find out what's going on.' His wife's voice pushed close to him. 'I had enough to contend with that day with that girl and the MacNairs, but after this business is over with that girl today, I'll be down there at Dessie Street again and with the good Lord's help I'll find out exactly what's going on!'

His tie fixed, Rab wondered why he was all dressed up. Then suddenly he noticed Catriona sitting waiting and remembered what 'the business' was with 'that girl' today.

'Is that her ready?' he queried incredulously.

'So you've taken an interest at last, have you?' Hannah

plumped hands on hips and surveyed both husband and daughter. 'You're a bit late, are you not?'

'Whose granny dug that up? For pity's sake, Hannah, could you not have done better than that?'

'Could *I* not have done better? Oh, that's just like you, that's you all over. From the moment I found out about this awful business I've been trying in my own humble way to do my best for that girl. And I've been trying to get you to help, but would you, would you? Oh, no, not you! You were too tired. All you wanted to do was to shut me up and whenever my back was turned sneak out of this house and away to Dessie Street. And don't tell me you went trailing back there after doing ten hours' night-shift just to get a pot of paint from Francis MacMahon!'

'But look at her!' Rab said helplessly.

'If you'd taken the slightest interest in your own wife and family, if you'd given me extra money, I might with the good Lord's help have been able to buy her a new dress. But oh, no, not you. All you're interested in is that demon drink. And, of course, *you know what*!'

'I feel like a drink now,' he said, still staring at Catriona. 'By God, I do!'

'May the good Lord forgive you, Robert, for taking His name in vain. It's wicked, especially in front of a child.'

'A child?' Rab's voice gained in strength again until it worked up to a howl. 'If anyone's mad in this house it's you, you fool. She's not a child any more. She's getting married!'

'And whose fault is that? Who's to blame for that child getting married?'

'It's no use talking to you.' He lunged away in disgust. 'I'm away out.'

'What?' Hannah gasped in genuine astonishment. 'You're supposed to take her to the Hall.'

Already he was in the lobby and grabbing his jacket.

'I'll take her when I get back. She's not due to leave for another hour yet.'

Out before Hannah could run to stop him. Across the road like a bird. Along the street, swooping, swerving, crashing among people.

In at last, dry-mouthed, pop-eyed, to a pub called The Wee Doch and Doris.

It was the twelfth of July and all over Glasgow, from Govan to Springburn, from Gallowgate to Partick, from Cowcaddens to Gorbals, Orangemen and their families were gathering for the Orange Walk.

Sitting alone in the living-room at the back of the house, because her mother had left for the Hall and her father had not yet returned from the pub, Catriona thought she heard a band. Hitching up her dress she ran through to peer out the front-room window.

Farmbank Lodge was swinging noisily along Fyffe Street on the first lap of their march from Farmbank through Clydend on to the centre of Glasgow to mass together with all the other lodges from the various parts of the city and then onwards in a huge drum-beating, flute-tootling, accordion-twisting, bagpipe-screaming, high-stepping, swaggering parade to one of the public parks where they ate like horses, played boisterous games, cheered speeches and listened to the bands.

The fiery-haired, fiery-faced leader of the Farmbank Lodge was well out in front and thoroughly enjoying himself - elbows out - four prancing steps forward, four prancing steps back as if he were doing a barn-dance. Big white gauntlet gloves swallowed up the sleeves of his jacket, and the long pole of the standard he carried was secured in a white leather holster strapped round his waist. Other people were carrying flags and banners, one orange silk one stretching the whole width of the parade and held aloft by a man at either end.

The leader's standard was of royal blue velvet fringed with gold and he sported a fancy purple and orange sash over his Sunday suit. In the middle of the standard an orange-cheeked picture of King William curled and furled and flapped about in the breeze.

The flute band at his back was giving a high-pitched excited 'Marching Through Georgia', and the leader, like the followers of the band, was singing with great bravado and panache:

> 'Hullo! Hullo! We are the Billy Boys.
> Hullo! Hullo! We are the Billy Boys.
>   Up tae the knees in Fenian blood, surrender or ye'll die,
> For we are the Farmbank Billy Boys!'

Catriona had forgotten about the Orange Walk. Now she realized what a problem it would be for a car to reach Dundas Street until the Walk was over. She would never arrive at the Hall in time even if her father managed to come back in a fit state to take her.

It never occurred to her to feel angry, only guilty at keeping Melvin waiting. The noise, the movement, the excitement of the procession was infectious and, lifting her veil, she pressed her face close to the glass in case she might miss anything.

The men and the boys followed the band; then came the women, the girls and the smaller children, all wearing their best newly washed and ironed clothes, some with fancy blue sashes looped over their shoulders, some with sparkling white, others with vivid orange.

Quite a few of the men and some of the women too were fast becoming completely carried away, jigging about wildly, hands high in the air, heughing at the pitch of their voices, dancing their own riotous version of the Highland Fling.

The drummers, sweat glistening over their faces, used every ounce of strength and energy, especially as they passed the Chapel of Saint Teresa. The drums got big licks then, and teeth gritted with the effort, and muscles ached and sweat poured faster. Tum - tari - um - tari - um - tum- tum, louder and louder until heads reeled and swelled with the noise. Tum - tari - tum - tari - tuma - tuma tum!

At last, the end of the procession - the skipping, giggling, strutting children - turned the corner into Farmbank Road, leaving Fyffe Street comparatively silent and deserted. Only Rab Munro was left taking the whole width of the pavement. His big gaunt figure had not enough flesh on it to fill his suit, his shoulders were bunched forward, his hands delved down into his pockets, his eyes were earnestly struggling to see the pavement but he was stumbling then suddenly spurting and lurching forward at such a lick he hadn't a chance to focus on anything.

Catriona was waiting at the door.

'Daddy, come on quick! Splash your face with cold water. The car will be here in a minute.'

'Aye, all right, hen.' He leaned a heavy arm round her shoulders. 'You're Daddy's bonny wee lassie, eh?'

'Oh, come on, Daddy.' She had to turn her head away from the hot sickly blast of whisky and beer.

'Anthing I can do for you, hen, you've only to ask. You know that, eh?'

'I know. I know, but please hurry up.'

'It's an honorrarr . . . Marriage is an honrr . . honourable estate. Did you know that, eh? Did you know that, hen? I'm telling you marriage is an honourar . . . honour- rarr. Mummy's a bonny lassie. Always was. Always was.' He sighed. 'I'd never allow anyone to say a word against her. She's a wunnerful woman, wunnerful, wunnerful woman.'

'Daddy, please.' With a struggle, because she wasn't much more than half his size, she aimed him for the kitchenette and lurched along with him at an uneven rapid pace towards the sink.

Without a murmur of protest he allowed her to bend him over and wash and dry his face. The cold water did nothing to warm the grey lantern jaws and the blue-tinged eye sockets. It only dampened his enthusiasm down to a tearful moan.

'A wunnerful, wunnerful woman and it's true, perfectly true, what she says. I'm a heavy cross for her to bear, so I am. I have faults, so I have. Your daddy has faults, hen.'

'You're all right.' Suddenly Catriona felt weepy herself.

She thought she heard the screech of a car drawing up at the close. Sure enough there followed the clatter of a man's boots, then a loud rat-tat-tat-tat-tat on the front door.

'Daddy, that's the car. What'll I do?'

He straightened back his big bony shoulders.

'You'll take Daddy's arm and Daddy will lead you to Melvin.' Peering down at her, he swayed forward again.

'You're happy, aren't you, hen? Tell me everything's all right, eh?'

She nodded and looked away.

'Have you the pennies for the scramble?'

All the children who were left in the district had gathered round the big black Co-operative car. They raised a hearty good-natured cheer when Catriona and Rab appeared, and milled around, jumping up and down and shouting, 'Hard up! Hard up!' and, 'Mind the Scramble, mister!'

Somehow, they managed to get safely into the car, bang the door, wind down the windows and spray out clinking, sparkling pennies which were immediately pounced upon by the screaming children. And the children were left a writhing knot of arms and legs on the pavement as the car moved away.

By the time it joined the Orange Walk the Farmbank Lodge had met up with Makeever Lodge, the Clydend Lodge and the Govan Lodge and the procession was four bands and a good two thousand strong. Every other person was wielding, waving, swishing banners, the sky was crowded with jostling, jumping colour.

Govan boasted a pipe band with a tiger-skinned drum-major. Makeever had accordions, Clydend a mixture of raucous brass instruments being played with swollen cheeks and enormous gusto, and all the bands including Farmbank Flute were concentrating on different tunes and even the echoes of the tunes overlapped and clashed with each other. From somewhere in the far distance the joyous bouncy strains of 'Scotland The Brave' joined the cacophony of sound.

The car slowed almost to a standstill.

'Would you look at the crazy devils!' Rab raised his shaggy brows and flung a look out of the window without moving his head or the big bony body that had sunk wearily into his suit. 'It was the Irish that started all this. They came over here looking for food and jobs and brought with them their ignorant bigotry. The Irish Lodges come over now to keep it going, pouring off the boats at the Broomilaw like mad dogs rarin' for a fight. Listen to them!'

Catriona nervously eyed the scene outside.

'I'm a Loyal Ulster Orange Man just come across the sea
For dancing sure I know I will please thee.
I can sing and dance like any man
As I did in days of yore
And it's on the Twelfth I love to wear
The sash my father wore.
For it's old but it's beautiful
And its colours the are fine,
It was worn at Derry Okrim,
Enniskillen and the Boyne.
My father wore it as a youth
And the bygone days of yore
For it's on the Twelfth I love to wear
The sash my father wore!

'Why do we let them in?' Catriona asked, alarm heightening her voice.

Rab let out a roar of laughter.

'Why do we let them in!' He shook his head, making a lock of prematurely grey-streaked hair spread untidily across his brow. 'That's a good one!' His square hand thumped over her knee. 'Glasgow welcomes everybody, hen. Did you know that Glasgow was called the friendly city?'

Outside someone roared:

'King Billy slew the Fenian crew,
At the Battle o' Byne Watter,
A pail o' tripe came over the dyke
An' hut the Pope on the napper.'

'Will they be all right?'

'Who, hen?'

'The Catholics.'

'Of course!' her father scoffed, jerking his head towards the crowd outside. 'They're just out for a good time like at Hogmanay or a sail doon the watter.'

'But there's fighting in town, I've heard.'

'Och, there's fighting every Saturday night and oftener. Don't worry, nobody's going to go barging into houses and dragging

61

out Catholics, if that's what you're afraid of. Once they get a drink tonight they'll fight anyone who wants to fight. It won't matter a damn whether they're Catholics or Hottentots. Most of the time they'll be sparring with themselves.'

'The Twelfth of July,' someone bawled in broad Glasgow vowels, 'the Papes'll die!'

'Silly fool!' Rab mouthed dourly as he sank further back into the depths of the car seat. 'The Raffertys upstairs are Catholics.'

'Are they?'

'Sure! And the best of luck to them! Who cares!'

Chapter 9

A grey and white haze had settled over everything in the Fowler kitchen. Ashes were heaped in an old enamel basin on the rug in front of the fire, and the dust from the ashes hadn't been swept or washed from the tiled surround, and Baldy's floury footprints had hardened on the rug and all over the linoleum. The previous night's newspapers spilled off the chair where Baldy had left them and dog-ends crowded unemptied ashtrays. A greasy frying-pan, a kettle, dirty dishes, egg-yellowed cutlery balanced precariously on the draining-board beside the sink. The table in the centre of the floor was littered with the remains of breakfast: marmalade, rolls, a milk bottle, lumpy sugar in a bowl, a brown pot of tea gone cold.

Sarah's chair was pulled as close to the fire as she could get it and still she hadn't properly thawed out. The fire blazed. Sunshine poked yellow fingers into the dingy room. She wore a woolly vest, two pairs of knickers, two woollen sweaters, ankle socks over her stockings and a scarlet scarf that covered her ears and tied under her chin but was small enough to leave most of her platinum hair sticking out.

Her blood crawled cold in her veins.

Huddled back, she closed her eyes and listened to the ticking of the clock.

If only time would stop, as she had stopped, and wait until she felt better. If only she could stay sitting here in peace and quiet, absolutely motionless the heat of the fire mottling her legs, exhaustion suspended, senses lulled, awake, yet completely overcome as if under heavy sedation. She knew she was in her own kitchen by her own fireside and soon Baldy would come bursting through from the bedroom like a prize Aberdeen Angus bull and ravenous for his dinner. Yet she was separate, staring at the scene through black-closed lids from a place she'd floated to outside on the fringe of things. It suddenly occurred to her that this might be like dying. Immediately she opened her eyes and felt for a cigarette in her apron pocket.

She liked a smoke. Everything about the familiar habit brought comfort. The look and feel of the packet and the neat white lines of cigarettes, the promise of one rolling round between her fingers, then between her lips and sucking it before savouring the big soothing breath, then the smoke blanketing around her.

Soon she would have to heave herself up from the chair and drag herself about doing things. There was so much to be done, so many things she ought to be tackling. If she could just get organized. She strove to get sorted out in her mind, to plan her day bit by bit.

First she would set the table nice for dinner, really nice, with a nice clean table cloth. Only she hadn't got a clean cloth. All the cloths were in the lobby press with the rest of the dirty wash. The thought of mustering up enough energy to do the washing nearly swamped her.

She skipped the table.

If she washed the dishes first and put them away in the cupboard. No - put them back on the table for dinner. But there wasn't any dinner made.

If she emptied her shopping-basket first and put the things away in the cupboard, except the tin of corned beef. Baldy liked corned beef and cabbage.

The cabbage wasn't washed or chopped or cooked.

There was too much to do. She didn't know where to start. She didn't know *how* to start. She couldn't get things organized like other women - even the simplest things. She was no use. She was no use at anything.

Dragging at her cigarette, she fought to get the upper hand of her weakness.

'Aw, come on now, Sarah,' she said out loud to herself. 'Plenty folks have more tae worry them than you, hen.'

The words were barely out of her mouth when she heard the familiar thump-thump of Lender Lil at the outside door.

'But no much more!' she added wryly as she pulled herself out of the chair to go and answer it.

'About time!' her mother-in-law complained before pushing into the house.

Mrs Fowler was a big woman with a man's broad shoulders and a bosom rearing up over the top of her corsets like the Campsie Hills.

Sarah followed her back to the kitchen wondering if she would ever give up. Did Mrs Fowler really believe that she could break up their marriage and march Baldy back round to Starky Street to live forever under her thumb? Baldy wasn't daft; smiling at her mother-in-law, Sarah thought, And neither am I, you old bag!

'Like a cup of tea, hen?' she asked.

Mrs Fowler heaved her chest further up and sniffed.

'No, thanks, I'm fussy!'

Sarah shrugged. 'Suit yourself. I was just going to put the kettle on and yer welcome to a drink. Sit down and take the weight aff yer legs.'

'In a place like this? I couldn't sit in peace and I don't know how you can either. It's a disgrace. A young woman like you, too. I never kept a house like this in my life. My Baldy'll tell you. He's never been used to this.'

Sarah's face creased into a smile.

'*My* Baldy remembers how ah used to keep this place like a new pin. Ah had the floor that clean and shiny you could have ate your dinner off it.'

'I warned him. You're a fool, if you ask me, I said. You're leaving a good clean roof over your head and three square meals a day just to go and sleep with a bastard.'

'Look, hen,' Sarah struggled to retain some modicum of good humour knowing instinctively that this was the only defence she had that Mrs Fowler didn't understand or know how to fight, 'Ah've cabbage to boil for my man's dinner. Ah haven't time to stand here listening to you calling me names. Away you go and enjoy yourself somewhere else. Away home and count your money.'

'A bastard you were. You can't deny it. I remember your ma even if you don't. A proper tart, she was, a disgrace to the street. Your granny turfed her out. Back she came, though, and you in

65

the oven. Who your da was is anybody's guess. And your granny was nothing to boast about, either. Night and day that woman was at the bottle.' Her voice tuned up like the bagpipes. 'Night and day. If she wasn't in the pub she was in one of the shebeens. And to think my only son had to get mixed up with the likes of that.'

Distress skittered inside Sarah like panic. The kettle boiled. The lid hissed and danced. She switched off the gas, straining a cotton-wool mind to remember what else she had to do.

She lifted the heavy shopping-bag on to the table to search out the tin of corned beef and the cabbage but she had to lean her arms over the bag before looking into it, her belly pressed hard against the table's edge.

'A proper wife you cannot be to him, either,' Mrs Fowler lamented. 'How many "misses" is that you've had? I always said there was something wrong with you atween the legs. There's something wrong atween her legs, I always said.'

'There'll be something wrong between your eyes, hen, if you don't chuck it,' Sarah managed in quite a pleasant tone between grimaces.

'Strike me? Are you threatening to strike a poor old woman, Sarah Sweeney? Of fancy! Well, go on, then. It'll be worth it to put you behind bars where you belong. I'll have the police up here to cart you away in the Black Maria before you've time to draw another breath.'

'Ah'm Sarah Fowler, *Fowler*! Now chuck it, Lil.' Eyes shimmering with pain, she felt out the cabbage, shuffled over to the sink and doubling over it, standing on one leg with the other bending and twisting in time to the spasms of abdominal pain, she cut and cleaned the cabbage and stuffed it into the pot for Baldy's dinner.

She put the gas up high and it was boiling in no time and ready long before she'd finished wandering about washing and drying the dishes, opening the tin of corned beef, frying yesterday's spuds and setting the table all to the wailings of her mother-in-law.

Nearly every day without fail Lender Lil came round from Starky Street to Dessie Street, bought her messages at MacNair's then came up to nag and criticize her and either sympathize with Baldy, splash tears over him and tell him what a poor neglected lad he was, or rage at him and cuff his ear and accuse him of being all the big fat fools of the day.

'Hello, Ma!' The reek of cabbage now filling the house brought Baldy's big square box of a body crashing into the kitchen to crush, crowd and dwarf everything, even his mother, in size. 'Hey, Sarah, that's a rer smell, hen. Cabbage, eh?'

The boom of his voice and the bang of the door as he shut it and the screech of a chair as he pulled it out and thumped down on it made Sarah wince. It was strange how noise had an effect on pain, the dragging, the bearing down labour-type pains, they jumped and strengthened with noise and flared up to catch at the breath.

'Aye, and ah've mashed it with a big dod of butter.' She grinned. 'You and your big belly.'

'You and your big bum!' Baldy thumped a hand like an iron shovel across her buttocks, gave a coarse gravel roar of a laugh and turned to his mother again. 'How's tricks, Ma? Still coining it, eh?'

'You shut your cheeky gob!' Mrs Fowler's beady eye fought to extinguish her son's exuberance but filled with water and gave up.

Still reeling under Baldy's blow, Sarah couldn't get a grip of what was happening or where she was for a minute or two. She dished the dinner like a drunk woman.

'Could you eat some, hen?' She asked her mother-in- law automatically. 'You're welcome and there's plenty.'

'Fancy!' Mrs Fowler was genuinely exasperated. 'Dishing her man's dinner with an old pair of woolly gloves on. She's plain daft, if you ask me! A scarf round her head, too, as if the gloves weren't enough!'

'I'm awful cold rifed, amn't I, Baldy?'

'Never mind, hen, I know the way to heat you up.' With a bull-bellow he made to swipe her again but she plunked herself down at the other end of the table so quickly he missed.

She poured herself a cup of tea then wrapped her hands around it, hugged it, revelled in the heat of it. She watched Baldy enjoying his heaped high plate of food, stuffing it into his mouth with such rapidity she began to worry about his digestion.

The tea cleared her head and brought her back to grips with what was going on.

'You could have married her. You're a better man than Melvin.' Mrs Fowler sighed. 'A young thing like that, you could have trained her.'

Sarah's eyes wrinkled up with mischief.

'Hear that, Baldy. You've missed your chance, lad.'

He guffawed, squeezing a big eye shut in a muscle-hard face.

'Don't you be too sure, hen!'

Sarah sucked in another mouthful of tea.

'Today, isn't it, Lil?'

'The Band of Jesus Hall in Dundas Street. Nobody from Clydend's been invited. Just a quiet family affair Mrs Munro told Mrs Gordon. *Her* family she means, of course, but I can tell you this, everybody in this close and all old MacNair's customers are going to the Hall. Supposed to be to support Rab and Melvin but nosiness is more like it. Pity they hadn't more important things to do with their time. Anthing for an excuse to dodge work and enjoy themselves, it you ask me.'

Baldy opened his mouth in a roar of laughter that made some of his cabbage spill out.

'If I know Rab he'll need supporting. He'll be as drunk as a coot.'

'Maybe I'll go!' Sarah said in between sips of tea.

'Oh, yes! Oh, of course! You've nothing else to do. Not a thing!' Mrs Fowler wiped her eyes and it occurred to Sarah that Lender Lil needed to see a doctor about this continuous overflow which surely could have nothing to do with real heartfelt tears. 'I knew it,' the older woman went on, '"I know *one*," I thought to myself, "who'll be up at that hall in Dundas Street like a flash, if you ask me!"'

Sarah crinkled with good humour.

'Ah'm no asking you, hen. I'm just going.'

She couldn't explain why she wanted to drag her weary limbs away to town to the wedding. She knew instinctively that no good would come of it.

What was that word that Jimmy Gordon once used? A lovely fella, Jimmy. Up to the eyeballs in book-learning and it hadn't spoiled him one bit.

Massakists - that was the word!

She smiled wryly to herself.

'That's what you are, hen! You're a massakists!'

Chapter 10

Tam sat propped like a tailor's dummy between his wife Nellie and his daughter Lizzie on one of the hard wooden benches in the Band of Jesus Hall. At the other side of Lizzie perched Melvin's five-year-old son Fergus with his long blond curls like a girl and lantern jaws like an old man. Tam's whiter than white hair had been energetically brushed down and back but already the fuzzy wisps of it were springing up and spreading out in untidy excitement. His skin had been scrubbed clean and inspected by Lizzie, his shirt and collar had been starched with her usual fiendish efficiency so that he had no choice but to sit as straight and stiff as a poker with his head bulging up like a sugar-iced onion.

He felt sorry for Melvin. It looked as if Hannah Munro had won after all, because so far there wasn't a sign of the wee lassie.

He'd heard it said that Hannah was one of Christ's sergeant-majors. He chuckled to himself. He wouldn't mind being bullied by a Christian soldier like that.

Cautiously he stretched his head higher to get a better view of her sitting down front. Handsome was a better word to describe her than pretty. By God, she was a healthy looking specimen: fine ruddy cheeks, eyes full of fire, chin held high, hair thick and glossy.

Rab was a lucky man. Not content with having his fun and games with Hannah he had his bit of nonsense every now and again with Lexy as well.

Lexy would be holding the fort with Jimmy back in the bakehouse just now, bouncing and wobbling about wearing nothing but her white coat and apron. She couldn't wear anything underneath because of the heat, she always said. He could believe that. She was a hot piece of stuff was Lexy.

He wriggled restlessly in his seat, his trousers tight.

'I know what you're doing!' Lizzie hissed round at him, her

pink cheeks in shadow under a wide-brimmed straw hat. 'You're annoying me on purpose. Just because I'm upset today. Everyone's trying to take advantage. Don't think I don't know. I know!'

'You're wrong, hen. Nobody's trying to get at you, honest. We're all fed up sitting here waiting so long, that's all.'

Despite his high starched collar his head twisted round in a determined effort to see something, anything, to break the monotony.

'There's Sarah! Baldy's not here, though.'

Lizzie let a titter out. 'Maybe his mammy wouldn't let him!'

Tam choked short in mid-chuckle with a wince of pain and, mouth hanging open, he eased a gentle finger round inside his collar.

'Lassie, lassie, I wish you wouldn't make things so stiff. You're choking the living daylights out of me.'

His daughter's face tightened again.

'I know how folks talk. I know their rotten twisted minds. Their tongues are busy enough flaying me and making a fool of me behind my back. They're all gloating because they've done me out of my place there beside Melvin. I know the way they've been whispering and telling lies putting him against me. They're not going to say I don't keep you clean.' Unexpectedly her elbow pierced his side. 'Look what she's wearing!'

'Who?' He wheezed in pain.

'Sarah! I'm not surprised she's cowering away at the back by herself. She ought to think shame. Look at her. What a disgrace. In church with a scarf tied round her head - a *scarlet* scarf. I wouldn't be surprised if she's wearing her slippers. Have you seen these sloppy things she wears, red and fawn check with fuzzy red stuff all round them? Supposed to be fur, all matted and greasy. She's a filthy lazy slut. Look at her. She's even too lazy to sit up straight.'

'Aw, just a minute now, hen. She never did anybody any harm. Sarah's one of the kindest souls anybody could meet. All the wee bairns in the street go daft when they see her. She's always got sweeties on her somewhere.' Tam made a brave attempt at a laugh but was given such an immediate and violent indication to remember where he was and keep quiet that he dropped his voice to an apologetic whisper.

'Och, well, she's not had much of a life. I remember when she was a bairn herself - hail, rain or shine, there she was hanging about the streets or squatting in the close or on the window-sill waiting for her granny to come home. God knows what she had to put up with when that old harridan did arrive with the key. If it hadn't been for other folk in the street giving her a bite to eat, or a cup of tea, or a wee heat at the fire, I don't think that lassie would have survived.'

'I've had to survive, and nobody helped me. They've always been jealous of me, always gossiped and whispered behind my back.'

'Don't be daft, lassie!'

His attention retreated away from her, his head tugged round in the direction of the hall door. Still no sign of the bride and her father. Rab was a queer fish. A damned good baker but close, never much chat with him. And booze? Rab could drink anybody under the table, even Baldy. Rab could be rampaging drunk one minute and that sober, that depressed the next, it would take nothing less than a bomb to break up the terrible black cloud of him.

Nellie dug into his other side.

'Here they are at last, thank goodness. If I'd had to suffer another minute on this hard seat I would have fainted. My back's just about broke.'

Rab had had a few. He wasn't staggering but he was walking so straight and stiff with his head riveted so hard back it didn't look natural.

Brother Stevens, the nervous wee budgie of a man elected to perform the ceremony, obviously didn't know whether to relax with relief at the arrival of Rab and Catriona or to keep his already twittering nerves keyed up at the ready.

'"Dearly beloved,"' he began, too soon. '"We are gathered together here in the sight of God, and in the face of this congregation, to join together this man and this woman in Holy Matrimony which is an honourable estate . . ."'

From somewhere at the back of the hall, not at the front from

72

the bride's family where you'd expect it, came a sniffle and the scalp-tingling beginnings of a wail.

Brother Stevens secretly cursed whoever it was.

'". . .which holy estate Christ adorned and beautified with His presence . . ."'

The sniffle became a sob.

'". . . and is commended in Holy Writ to be honourable among all men and therefore is not by any to be taken in hand unadvisedly, lightly or wantonly; but reverently, discreetly soberly, and in the fear of God . . ."'

Sarah's sob burst into broken-hearted words.

'Mammy, Daddy, Mammy, Daddy!'

The words swelled up to a hair-raising wail of anguish.

'Mammy, Daddy, Mammy, Daddy!'

Brother Stevens damned the woman forever in hell, *and* her mammy and daddy!

Tam nudged Lizzie then Nellie.

'What's the wee lassie trembling for? Fear of God, Melvin, or the commotion at the back?'

Nellie sniffled a reply. 'That howling's upsetting me, Tam.'

'Not half as much as the preacher, lass. He looks as if he's going tae have a stroke.'

'Look at the disgrace of a dress!' Lizzie giggled again. 'Just look at it!'

'It was ordained for the procreation of children, for increase of mankind according to the will of God.' Brother Stevens was so unnerved he hardly knew what he was saying. 'And that children might be brought up in the fear and nurture of the Lord . . .'

All it needed now, he thought, was for someone to stand up and object. He gazed pleadingly at the congregation.

'"If any man can show just cause why they may not lawfully be joined together, let him now declare it or forever hold his peace."'

'Mammy, Daddy, Mammy, Daddy!' howled the tear-streaked woman in the scarlet scarf, huddled in the far corner at the back.

'"I require and charge you both."' He raised his voice determined not to be beaten. '"As ye will answer at the dreadful

73

day of judgement when the secrets of all hearts shall be disclosed, that if either of you know of any impediment, why ye may not be lawfully joined together in Matrimony, ye do confess it."'

The wailing and the sobbing reached such a pitch that everyone, including Melvin and Catriona, turned round.

Near to hysteria now, Brother Stevens shouted at Melvin's stocky back, '"Wilt thou have this Woman to thy wedded wife, to live together after God's ordinance in the holy estate of Matrimony? Wilt thou love her, comfort her, honour and keep her, in sickness and in health; and, forsaking all other, keep thee only unto her, so long as ye both shall live?"'

'Oh!' Sarah choked, exhausted at last. 'Poor, poor wee lassie!'

Chapter 11

Melvin said Lizzie would be willing to mind Fergus after the wedding for the few weeks until the Glasgow holiday fortnight started.

He didn't like leaving the business now that his father was on days instead of nights though. The days weren't so bad, especially with Jimmy on the job. It was the nights that worried Melvin. True, there was Rab and Tam and Sandy and wee Eck the halfer in the early hours, and Baldy was a good enough foreman, but they were all partial to a dram and if he wasn't there they'd be in the barm room drinking the stuff. They'd be stretched out helpless in all odd corners of the bakehouse in no time. God knows what kind of bread could be made and only Billy the horse sober enough to deliver it.

So there was no honeymoon until the Fair fortnight, and after the wedding tea they just went straight back to Dessie Street.

Melvin had decided to take the wedding night off but told Baldy that his father had instructed him to check on the bakehouse at least once during the night and they accepted this with sympathetic shaking of heads because they all knew old Duncan.

'Wipe your feet,' Melvin told Catriona as she stepped over the door holding up the long white dress she was still wearing.

She'd already wiped her feet on the prickly brown and orange mat on the landing. Now she silently repeated the process on the first little remnant of rug inside the hall. It slithered about awkwardly under her shoes on the highly polished linoleum.

'See that polish.' Melvin switched on the light and proudly surveyed the hall floor. 'Maybe you think that's a good shine. Lizzie MacGuffie thinks it's perfect and I've never bothered to contradict her but you should have seen that floor when my Betty was alive.'

'It's lovely.'

'Speak up,' Melvin rapped out. 'Nobody could hear a voice like that behind a car ticket.'

'This is my bedroom.' He flung open the door with a flourish. 'I decorated it all myself.'

'It's lovely.'

'I'll put your cases down here. You can go back to your mother's and collect the rest of your things in a day or two.'

Catriona lowered her eyes.

'I haven't got any more things.'

'Eh?' He laughed and hunkered down to chug loose the strap that held the cardboard case together. 'Is this all your worldly possessions, then?'

'Please!' Spurred into action by the acuteness of her shame and embarrassment, Catriona rushed forward to tug the case away from him. 'It's my things! They're private.'

Annoyance sharpened his laughing good humour.

'You've a lot to learn about marriage, haven't you? You're young, of course, and you've never been married before. I have, you see. Betty and I had a perfect marriage. There was never any secrets between us. There's nothing private between married people, didn't you know that?'

He flicked open her case.

'An old coat, an old skirt,' he cackled, holding them up then flinging them aside. 'A jersey. A pair of knickers. A pair of flannelette pyjamas. And a hot-water bottle?'

He fell back on his buttocks slapping his knees with merriment. 'Is that all?'

Catriona snatched up the hot-water bottle and hugged it and rocked it against herself.

'Come on. I'll show you the rest of the house.' He bounced to his feet like a rubber ball. 'I bet you can't do that and you're a good few years younger than me.'

'Do what?' She stared, mystified.

'Bounce up like that without any stiff joints or breathlessness.'

He repeated the process several times, up, down, up, down, hands spread over waist, knees expanding.

'You try it!'

Clutching Lovey tighter against her chest she shook her head vigorously over the top of it, making the veil flap about.

'I shouldn't do it in my good trousers,' he admitted, leading her into the next bedroom. 'That's where Fergus sleeps. The sitting-room has big corner windows, two looking on to Dessie Street and two onto the Main Road.'

Dazedly she followed him.

'Remember,' he said, 'you saw that before. Here's the kitchen. The bathroom's there beside the front room. A nice big square hall, isn't it?'

'It's lovely.'

In the kitchen he made straight for the mirror above the mantelpiece, smoothed back his thin brown hair, tweaked out his thick waxed moustache and dusted down his trousers.

'It droops in the bakehouse, you know. The heat and the ovens.'

'What does?'

'My moustache. The wax melts. Sometimes I think I ought to shave it off but everybody says it's so manly and it suits me.'

'It's lovely.'

'What are you hugging that thing for? You look ridiculous!'

She stared down at Lovey, hugging it all the tighter.

He laughed, puffing his chest like a prize pigeon.

'You won't need any hot-water bottles when I'm around. Away through and take that awful looking dress off and get your pyjamas on while I make a cup of tea and something to eat. I'm starving.'

Gratefully she concentrated on finding her way back to the bedroom, hurrying, glad to be away from him but shuffling and tripping, held back by the too-long dress.

She banged the bedroom door and leaned against it, eyes popping, heart battering. The thump of a man's feet shook the house, a clatter of a kettle vied with it, then the hiss of a tap turned on full.

What if he came through before she had her 'jamas' on? What if he saw her wearing nothing but her knickers?

She flung Lovey onto the bed and tore off the white dress, getting into a tangle with the thing bunched on top of her head and the sleeves too tight for her arms to escape and be rid of it.

She was gasping, choking, on the verge of hysteria by the time she did disentangle herself.

A piercing whistle now, and the chinkle of cups. Shivering with panic she hopped out of her knickers and into her pyjamas.

'Come and get it!' The sudden roar from the other end of the house nearly snatched the legs from under her.

She leaned a moist quivering hand on the dressing-table.

'Come on!' The voice bawled again. 'Never mind trying to pretty yourself up. You'll do! The tea's getting cold!'

Her mind ceased to function properly. She reached for her coat and buttoned it over her pyjamas wondering how she'd transport herself back home to Fyffe Street. She couldn't be away by herself. She'd never been anywhere by herself.

Even when she'd gone to school almost directly across from the house in Fyffe Street, her mother had been by her side, escorted her back, and even waited at the gate each play-time to make her stand under a watchful eye and sip a cup of boiling hot Oxo until the bell rang.

She had always been a delicate child, her mother insisted, and not fit to play. You never knew what you might pick up from other children, bad germs, bad habits, bad things they might talk about. Anything of the male species had been especially taboo.

Her mother had kicked up a dreadful fuss at school as soon as she heard the new gym teacher was a man, and thereafter had furnished Catriona with a note that excused her from going anywhere near the gym-hall. Instead she sat in the lavatory and dreamed dreams and waited until the gym period was over.

After school there had been homework or housework, visiting with her mother, attending the meeting hall with her mother, sitting at the front-room window, or acting shops by herself.

The cupboard in the living-room beside the fire was the shop and two wooden chairs placed side by side in front of it formed the counter.

There weren't any cupboards in the kitchenette, just a shelf along the wall for dishes, so all the food was kept in the living-room cupboard.

'Yes, madam?' she'd say smartly and politely. 'Can I help you? Jam? Certainly we have jam. Which kind would madam prefer, strawberry, blackcurrant or raspberry?'

'Strawberry?' Melvin was straddling the bedroom doorway hands on his hips, moustache jerking, throat caw-cawing with laughter. 'Blackcurrant? Raspberry? She doesn't just talk to herself. She talks shop to herself. Jumpin' Jesus, I've got a right one here!'

The bed was big. A long iron bar of a bolster stretched across it with two plumped-up pillows on top. It had grey army blankets hidden between pink flannelette sheets and a slippery rayon bedspread. The *pièce de résistance* was a thick golden cloud of satin quilt.

Catriona, blue pyjamas fastened neatly up to the neck, cringed back against the pillows, fingers digging into the pink flannelette, face closed, stiff, ashen.

'I always have my hot-water bottle!'

Unbuttoning his jacket and tossing it over a chair Melvin see-sawed between hilarity and anger.

'Well, you're not having it now. This is priceless! What do you want a hot-water bottle for? It's the middle of summer as well as being your wedding night!'

'I always have my hot-water bottle!'

Watching him flick down his braces, her voice cracked and her fingers retreated under the sheets. Deftly Melvin opened his fly, stepped out of his trousers and flung them over beside his jacket.

'You're a right one, you are. Never mind, I'll soon heat you up.'

He undid his shirt then stripped it off, taking care to avoid mussing up his moustache.

'How's that for a good figure?' He admired himself in the wardrobe mirror when he was down to nothing but his underpants. 'Not bad for a man of thirty-odds?' He suddenly gripped his wrists before Catriona's horrified eyes began contorting different parts of his anatomy, making them push forward, swell grotesquely, wrench up and round while all the time he kept talking and getting a little more breathless, a little more red in the face. 'I'm not the man I used to be, of course, but

79

I'm a miracle of fitness for a man who works nights in a bakery. Bakers are notoriously unfit. You'll never get them to admit it but they are. Stands to reason. Heart troubles, lung troubles, stomach ulcers, skin diseases, the lot. Bakers never last long. Either die or leave. We don't have them leaving so much. The houses, you see. Good houses these. My father's a crafty old devil. This building's the only one for miles around that has bathrooms. Did you know that?' He stopped talking for a minute to concentrate on doing unspeakable things to his stomach. 'See that abdominal definition?' A bulgy rolling eye demanded an answer.

Catriona slithered down in bed until only her head with a golden tangle of hair on top was showing. 'Yes,' she quavered feebly. 'It's lovely.'

'You're right,' Melvin agreed. 'Not even many champions can show an impressive "washboard" like that.'

Suddenly he began skipping with an invisible skipping rope. 'All the rest have lavies on the stairs,' he panted breathlessly. 'Most of them are just single-ends or room and kitchens and three or four families or more all share the one wee lavy. They never have lights, these lavies. You've always to take a candle or a torch.'

He stopped skipping, scratched energetically under one armpit and said:

'Ah, well! Bed!'

Immediately Catriona saw him bend, hairy hands ready to peel off his underpants, she shut her eyes.

It must be a nightmare. Her dreams had got mixed up. She twisted round on her side and curled up tight.

'"Our Father which art in heaven, hallowed be Thy name, Thy Kingdom come, Thy will be done on earth, as it is in Heaven, give us this day our daily bread and forgive us our trespasses as we forgive them that trespass against us . . ."'

Unexpectedly her whole body jarred and bounced a couple of inches up in the air as Melvin leapt into bed beside her. She kept her eyes stubbornly closed.

'"Lead us not into temptation, but deliver us from evil . . ."'

'Jumpin' Jesus,' Melvin groaned. 'Is that you talking to

yourself again?'

In the tiniest most inaudible sound, more a whimper than a whisper, Catriona finished.

'"For Thine is the Kingdom. the power and the Glory, for ever and ever, Amen!"'

'Turn round then!' The bed lurched about and the blankets untucked and let draughts flap in as Melvin made himself comfortable. Catriona, a small tense ball, refused to budge a muscle.

'Come on!' With one gorilla arm he scooped her up, rolled her round and held her, nose squashed against the hairy cushion of his chest. 'Let's have a cuddle and a wee talk first. It's not often I have a night off, so enjoy it while you've got the chance.'

They lay like that for a moment before Melvin broke the silence again.

'For pity's sake, take these thick things off. They're making me sweat.'

'What things?'

'These flannelette horrors.'

Before she could wriggle an arm free to protect herself he had unbuttoned her and was tossing her from side to side and up and down until he had agitated her out of both jacket and trousers.

'That's better!' he exclaimed, one hand pinning her body to his chest. 'Now, what'll we talk about?'

Shock set in. She lay wondering vaguely if she should make some polite remark about the weather while another area of her mind convulsed and shivered like a mad thing with malaria.

'You haven't much of a chest,' Melvin remarked, holding her back a bit. 'Just like a young lady. Of course, I suppose they've time to grow yet. See mine! What a difference! There's a chest for you! A hairy chest is a sign of virility. Didn't you know that? You're lucky, you know. Not many men of my age are as well put together as me.' He flapped the blankets down again. 'Betty knew how lucky she was. She was crazy about me. Used to call me her dream man. Once when she was in hospital she wrote me some letters. I've got them in a case in that cupboard. Did you see her photo on the room mantelpiece? What did you think of it?'

'It's lovely.'

'I'll let you read the letters tomorrow.' There was a pause. Then he absent-mindedly caressed her.

'How did your wife die?' His hand jerked clear of her.

'She was ill for a long time on and off.'

Silence.

'Fancy a cup of cocoa?' he queried eventually.

'No, thank you.'

His hand returned.

'Did your wife die having the baby?'

Again the shrinking.

'No, months after.'

It seemed he could not bring himself to touch her when he spoke of his Betty.

To Catriona this was, inexplicably, the worst, the most shameful, the most heart-rending humiliation of all.

Chapter 12

Jimmy had been too emotionally upset after reading the book even to think about playing the piano. It was a very vivid word picture of what had happened in the Highland Clearances.

A year after the defeat at the Battle of Culloden the chiefs began the terrible betrayal of their children. They decided they preferred sheep to people and drove the folk to the hills and glens from their homes with bayonets and truncheons and fire, to make way for the Lowland and English sheep-farmers.

The ill and the dying, the men, the women, the elderly folk, the young children, all with the same childish faith in the laird and all in their innocence refusing to believe the news of the burnings despite the black smoke rising high in the sky from elsewhere.

The burners came like an army - factor and fiscal, sheriff-officers, constables, shepherds, foxhunters and soldiers. They dragged out the terrified bewildered people. Families who escaped from the violence wandered aimlessly, not knowing where to find shelter or how to get their next meal.

One old man, sick with the fever, crawled into the ruins of a mill and his dog kept the rats at bay while he tried unsuccessfully to cling to life by licking flour dust from the floor. A man carried his two feverishly-ill daughters on his back for over twenty-five miles, staggering along with one, then putting her down, and going back for the other, and so on all the way.

Women watched their children die of exposure and starvation, and the tartan became a shroud.

After reading all this and more, Jimmy had locked himself in the bathroom and wept.

The trouble was, he thought, wiping his eyes with toilet paper, that people just didn't think. They didn't use their imaginations. They couldn't see events in vivid moving colour in their minds. Nobody, if they had really thought about it, really thought of what it meant in terms of human suffering, would have allowed such a monstrous thing to happen. The most important thing in the world, it seemed to him, was to try to encourage people to think, to increase their sensitivity, to develop a keen and painful edge to their imaginations.

At the height of his distress he'd tried to discuss the book with everyone but nobody wanted to listen.

His mother's normally kind, gentle voice had been impatient, almost petulant.

'It doesn't do to think so much on these things. You shouldn't read stuff like that and upset yourself and other folks. Why don't you get something nice and cheery out the library?'

Tam had still been in the bakehouse when he'd started his shift and he had actually laughed.

'Och, laddie, laddie, will you never learn to keep the head! And have a heart, son! Spare me the gory stories until I've had time to enjoy my breakfast!'

Lexy had wriggled and wobbled all over and made faces in front of him and behind his back and chanted in her sing-song Glasgow accent, 'Oh, in the name of the wee man! You're an awful big fella, so you are! Fancy getting all worked up like that about tewchters that have been pushing up the daisies for years.'

Nobody cared now as nobody cared then. All day his anguished eyes saw the suffering of the Highlanders, in the mixing-machine, in the fondant bin, in both Scotch ovens and in the proving press.

By the time he had finished a hard day's work he was more emotionally than physically exhausted. This lack of caring, this inability or refusal to tune into other people's distress - how many more tragedies of human suffering could it lead to in the future? It seemed to him to be a most dangerous state of mind.

His mother's practised stare took rapid stock of him when he returned upstairs: the tangled curls, the dark bleak eyes, the skin tight over his cheek-bones, a peculiar putty colour.

'No sitting in here reading or playing that piano all by yourself tonight,' she told him firmly. 'You're going to the pictures or away to one of these billiard halls the other lads go to and you're going to be like them and enjoy yourself.'

'Cheeky old rascal!' Laughing, he'd pretended to spar with her. 'Trying to bully me now, are you? Put up your dukes, up your dukes, come on now, come on now!'

'Och, stop your nonsense at once and do as you're told. Away with you. Get washed and changed and get out of here.'

He had gone, to please her. But he'd hung about in the closemouth for ages watching the children playing outside in the street and wondering what he should do and where he ought to go to pass the evening.

Lanky long-legged girls hopped spring heeled across chalked peaver beds. Others whipped draughty frames of skipping ropes round and round. Reedy voices chanted:

> 'Eachy-peachy, pear, plum
> Out goes my chum,
> My chum's not well,
> Out goes mysel'.'

Boys bellowed.

'Hey, Jock, Ma Cuddy, Ma Cuddy's ower the dyke, if ye catch Ma Cuddy, ma cuddy'll gie ye a bite.'

Balls thumped monotonously.

'House to let apply within, a lady goes out for drinking gin...'

Everyone walking by or just clustered around enjoying the evening together grinned cheery greetings and women hanging out of windows, arms folded and leaning with breasts comfy on sills, cried out:

'Hey, Jimmy! Have you sold your piano, son?'

Or, 'Hallo there, Jimmy boy, is it the jigging the night? You're a deep one, eh? Got a wee lassie and never let on, eh?'

He hunkered down to join in a noisy game of marbles with some laughing urchins in the gutter, and was soon excitedly shouting 'Sheevies' and 'High Pots!' and 'Knucklies' with the rest of them. But his heart wasn't really in the game and after a few minutes he returned to stand at the closemouth, long thin hands gripped behind back, tall lean figure dressed in shabby but good quality Harris tweed jacket with a scarf knotted at his throat. Other people in the district bought a whole new outfit every Easter and for every Glasgow Fair. Even folks on the dole managed to get some new togs at least for the Fair, helped by the Provident and various other clubs to which they paid their shillings religiously every week (except the Fair fortnight) all through the year.

Jimmy seldom bought clothes for the simple reason that those he bought were so expensive he couldn't afford to buy them more than once every few years. He liked good things. He enjoyed the look, the line, the feel of them.

'Are you going to be next then, son?' Josy McWhirter, the painter who lived across the street, poked his face out of the window over his wife's muscle-fat shoulder. 'First old Melvin and then you. What's that wee lassie and him doing up there?' His voice heightened into a squeal of delight. 'Hey, Melvin! Can you hear me? You're awful quiet up there!'

Jimmy smiled, shook his head, raised a good-natured fist at Josy, but felt the beginnings of a flush of embarrassment creep up from his neck. Best to make his escape before anyone noticed him actually blushing.

'Anything decent on the pictures?' he called out in what he hoped was a nonchalant manner as he strolled from the close.

Everyone immediately became intensely interested. Such a conflicting and enthusiastic bevy of film titles and criticisms assailed him and so many heated arguments arose as to whether he ought to go to the Ritzy, the local Clydend picture-house, or take the tram further afield to Govan, that he quit Dessie Street, chuckling and flapping his palms at them in mock disgust. Deciding not to bother with a tram, at least not for a few stops yet, because he felt so restless, he strode away along the Main Road towards Govan.

His pace had slowed a little by the time he was approaching Big Loui Lorretti's Ice-Cream Café, commonly known as the Tally's, which was situated at the corner of the Main Road and River Street.

He thought the crowd lounging at the corner looked familiar and, sure enough, as he got nearer he saw it was Slasher Dawson and some of the gang. Slasher was well known and feared in the district. Lil Fowler made good use of him as a muscle-man. Her extortionate rates of interest were seldom questioned when

Slasher was called in to collect. Slasher had more razor scars on his face and neck than any man in Glasgow. He couldn't be much older than Jimmy but his Frankenstein stitch-puckered face and his giant humped-up shoulders made it difficult to guess his age, and nobody wanted to. Nobody wanted to do anything to Slasher Dawson or say anything about Slasher Dawson, much to many a Glasgow policeman's chagrin.

His gang in comparison were unhealthy, undersized mice, nervous fleshless ferrets as much afraid of him as anyone else but under the continual strain of trying to keep up with his crime and violence in order to please him. They had no idea of any other way to survive, living as they did around the other corner in Dixon Street where Slasher also had his abode.

Jimmy was almost alongside them before he saw Lexy. They were all around her, sniggering and chatting her up and she was laughing delightedly, patting her hair, obviously flattered at so much attention being paid to her. But he could see the winks, the leering faces, the vulgar signs behind her back and he knew what they meant.

He strolled up to the group, his heart thumping.

'Hallo, Lexy. There's a good picture on at the Lyceum. Fancy coming? You're only wasting your time hanging around here.'

For a full minute there was silence. Even Lexy was shocked rigid and could not speak.

'Say that again!' Slasher dared, still incredulous at Jimmy's audacity.

Jimmy moved nearer until his black curly head was in between Lexy and Slasher, his face almost touching Slasher's grotesque twisted nose.

'How are you doing these days, Slasher? Haven't seen you for ages.'

One of the ferrets flicked out a razor. 'Let's do him, eh? Let's carve him up!'

'Saw your sister Sadie the other day, though, and your ma!' Jimmy went on talking straight at Slasher, completely ignoring the other young man in the thin frayed suit. 'I'm making Sadie's wedding cake. I suppose you know. They were in arguing about the icing and the way the cake should be decorated. You'll be going, won't you? Going to the wedding? By the way, tell your ma I want to see her again. Tell her to come tomorrow.'

The youth brandishing the razor giggled excitedly.

'Never mind tomorrow, eh, Slasher? Come on us cover him with red icing today!'

'Shut it!' Slasher growled without looking at his minion. Then, averting his eyes from Jimmy, he shrugged. 'Aye, O.K., Jimmy. I'll tell her. Ma'll be there, don't you worry. She's goin' mad about that bloody wedding. I'm fed up hearing about it.'

Only one person in the world Slasher Dawson feared and that person was, without a doubt, his mother.

'Good!' said Jimmy. 'Well, hurry up, Lexy! I told you. It's a good picture. We won't get in if we don't get a move on!'

All at once Lexy burst into a paroxysm of hysterical giggling.

'Ohi! Ohi,' she gasped and squealed. 'Oh, in the name, Jimmy Gordon. You're an awful big fella!'

Jimmy grinned and shook his head at Slasher with such obvious bonhomie that Slasher roared with laughter in return.

'Stuck with her all day and still not had enough, you big bastard.' He swung his bulk round to Lexy. 'You heard what the man said, you silly wee cow. Get movin'!'

'These heels of yours wouldn't last to the Cross,' Jimmy said. 'Come on! Here's a tram coming!'

Gripping her by the elbow he half-rushed, half-carried her along the street and swung her on to the tram just as it went clanging away.

She was gasping and giggling in his arms on the tram platform when an outraged conductor burst their bubble of frivolity.

'Come oan, get aff! Naebody's allowed to canoodle on my platform!'

Pushing Lexy, but hardly able to control his own breathless laughter, Jimmy manoeuvred her into a seat. The tram was mostly filled with women wrapped in tartan shawls lumpy with dummy-sucking babies. There were only a few men in shabby suits and caps pulled well down and mufflers knotted high at their necks. Jimmy settled down beside Lexy and had just managed to subdue both his own hilarity and hers when another young woman got on at the next stop and he immediately gave up his seat to her. Strap-hanging, he swayed, lost in thought, away in another world from Lexy and tramcars until the conductor bawled: 'Govan Cross! Any of yoos for Govan Cross?'

In strange silence Lexy allowed Jimmy to assist her from the tram. Her head held high, she bristled with ice-cold dignity. Jimmy didn't notice. He had wandered back to the Highlands.

'Here, you!' Lexy erupted eventually. 'What do you think you're playing at? Who do you think you are?'

He ruffled his fingers through his hair and stared perplexedly down at her. 'I don't understand what you mean. What do you mean? What are you talking about?'

'Well, I mean to say!' Lexy patted her curls. 'A fella asks a lassie to the pictures, the next minute he's cooled off that quick he doesn't even want to sit beside her. *And you never once opened your mouth either*!' she accused with a burst of renewed anger. 'What have I ever done to you? I mean to say. I'm not infectious, you know. I suppose you'd stand in the pictures too instead of sitting beside me if you got the chance. Well, I'm *not* infectious - *see*!'

'Lexy, Lexy, love!' Jimmy was appalled. 'I didn't get up because I didn't want to sit beside you!'

Soothed by the word 'love', and the unmistakable concern on Jimmy's face, Lexy's bristles settled down, indeed began to melt away with astonishing rapidity.

He hugged an impulsive arm round her shoulders. 'It's just ordinary manners, just manners, to give up your seat to a lady in a public conveyance.'

'Och, I'm sorry, Jimmy, so I am!' She melted so close to his jacket they had some difficulty in making smooth progress into the picture house. 'I hadn't realized, I mean, you're always doing such daft things. You're an awful big fella!'

'And I was quiet because I was thinking about that book again.'

'Och, never mind, Jimmy. I mean to say. It wasn't you that done it. Och, you wouldn't hurt a fly, so you wouldn't. You just hurt yourself, so you do. Where's it to be? Back stalls, eh?' Her

89

elbow jabbed his ribs and her squeal of laughter made him go red in the face.

He stared down, intent on finding his jacket pocket and the wallet he prayed it contained.

'Wherever you wish, of course.' He found the wallet, examined it as if he'd never set eyes on it before in his life, and selected a ten-shilling note with which to pay for the tickets.

A love film was showing inside but it paled in comparison with some of the performances taking place on the seats of the back stalls.

For Lexy's sake (after all, she was barely eighteen) Jimmy hoped she hadn't noticed as they settled in and he slithered comfortably down, long legs stretched out, elbows dug into the arms of his seat, chin resting heavily on clasped hands, ready to concentrate his full attention on the screen.

Unexpectedly, one elbow was knocked off balance, grabbed and hugged in a vice-like grip by Lexy.

'Fancy!' she hissed close to his ear. 'Just fancy! Here's me been working every day aside you and never realized you was such a lovely big fella. Ohi! Ohi! Jimmy!'

It was literally a most awkward position, terrifying, too! For a horrible minute Jimmy just sat there contorted to one side, not knowing what to do.

Then he sighed.

'Lexy. Here, sit round this way.' He put an arm around her and settled her comfortably against him.

It was her turn to sigh.

'Ohi, ohi, oh, in the name of the wee man!'

'Be quiet!' Jimmy commanded, his ears beginning to tingle with embarrassment. 'Be quiet and watch the picture. That's what we've come for, isn't it? The picture?'

'Ohi, ohi!' Lexy nearly choked. 'You're a scream, so you are. You're an awful big fella!'

Desperately he put a hand over her mouth.

'If you don't be quiet I'll make you. I'll keep my hand over your mouth like this all night!'

To his surprise she suddenly relaxed. She quietened her head pressed against his chest, her lips moving gently against his palm. Then the hot moist tip of her tongue tickled and disturbed him.

'Lexy!'

Why, oh, why, he kept asking himself, was life so full to overflowing with worrying situations, of anxieties, of responsibilities that had to be recognized and faced up to, decisions that had to be made and acted upon.

All through the film and all the way back home to Dessie Street, despite Lexy's chatter, he thought of his responsibilities towards her.

Was he going to be just the same as people like Slasher Dawson and his mob? Did the person, the place, the background make any difference to the moral question? Did a bed instead of a back-close make it all right? Did an invitation from Lexy make it right?

Lexy was eighteen and her mother was little better than a prostitute. Lexy had moved out of her mother's house in Pelt Street to come and work as his assistant and live in one of the attic flats.

He knew she was no innocent but she was no prostitute either, though what would it matter even if she were? Was he going to give her another push along the one-way street?

No man was an island. No woman, either. If man affected man, how much more man affected woman.

A few lines from one of his favourite poets came to his mind as he took Lexy up the spiral stairs to Number 1 Dessie Street.

> 'Then gently scan your brother Man.
> Still gentler sister Woman;
> Tho' they may gang a kennin wrang,
> To step aside is human
> One point must still be greatly dark
> The moving *why* they do it;
> And just as lamely can ye mark,
> How far perhaps they rue it.'

Robert Burns was a great man. An honest man and a man of wonderful love and compassion. Jimmy wondered what Burns would have thought of the Highland Clearances. He made it

91

obvious what he thought of a national thanksgiving service being held in church for a naval victory.

> 'Ye hypocrites! are these your pranks?
> To murder men, and gie God thanks!
> For shame! gie o'er - proceed no further -
> God won't accept your thanks for murder.'

Lexy rummaged in her handbag for the key to her flat. She opened the door. She smiled at him invitingly.

'Lexy!' He heaved a huge sigh. 'Oh, Lexy!'

Chapter 13

Everybody was talking about the Fair, the new clothes, the sail 'doon the watter' to Rothesay or Dunoon, the two weeks looked forward to the whole year and spent together, crowded into one comfortless room, or one room and a kitchen for which ridiculous prices were paid and paid gladly with typical Glasgow big-heartedness.

Dessie Street and surrounding district plumped for Rothesay, except Amy Gordon and Jimmy who had relations they went to visit in Dunoon. They sailed 'doon the watter' with the rest, of course. Dunoon was just not so far on. Neighbours and families crowded into the one flat, single-ends were packed, 'But and Bens', as one room and kitchens were called, were shared to overflowing, the flats next door, upstairs and downstairs were equally bursting at the seams with other neighbours for two glorious weeks.

Dessie Street, the Dessie Street side of the Main Road, Starky Street, Scotia Street, Pelt Street, Dixon Street, River Street, indeed most of Clydend, moved *en masse* to live for the Fair fortnight in even closer proximity with each other than they did for the rest of the year. And they loved every minute of it.

The only person who did not go away at the Fair was Duncan MacNair but he lived in a detached cottage in Meikle Street in the old part of Farmbank, the part that was, and he hoped always would be, unsullied by the Farmbank Corporation Housing Scheme, thanks to the huge tree-surrounded Farmbank Infirmary.

He hated the Fair (or so he said, but nobody believed him; such preposterousness was beyond any sane-minded body's understanding). All the Fair meant to him (he never tired of fighting to make them all see reason) was two weeks' loss of trade and money, a loss that would mean the ruination of him, a blow from which he would never recover.

'It'll be the death and ruination of me!' he whined through his nose to Maisie MacMahon who was filling the shelves with jars of apple jelly, and to the crowd of customers on the other side of the counter who were enjoying a blether and not paying the slightest attention to him. The death and ruination!'

At that point Lexy appeared from the back carrying a tray of iced German biscuits.

She was wearing her usual white coat, apron and turban but the steel curlers were noticeably missing; instead a thick sausage curl stretched across her powdered brow, and her face was flushed under her rouge and her eyes were shining bright like torches through lashes stiff with mascara.

'Anybody for Germans? They're lovely, so they are. Jimmy's just made them!'

A howl of laugher rocked the shop and even took old Duncan by surprise.

'What the bloody hell's so funny about my German biscuits?' he snorted indignantly.

'Och, it's not your biscuits, Mr MacNair.' Tiny, gnome-like Mrs MacMahon sidled up as close to the old man as the counter would allow. 'It's Lexy. She's started going with Jimmy Gordon. Did you not know?'

Automatically Maisie MacMahon cringed back against the shelves at the sound of her mother's voice. Mrs MacMahon, tiny, humphy-backed, smiling and innocent though she might look, was still Clydend's practical joker and her family had always suffered from her jokes more than anybody else.

'She's marrying him tomorrow! It's one of them hurried affairs.' Mrs MacMahon nodded sagely. 'You don't know what you've been missing back there. The things that go on behind that sack-cloth curtain. You wouldn't believe it.'

'No, I wouldn't, you old harridan,' Duncan MacNair replied. 'I know Jimmy. He's a cheeky bugger but he's not daft.'

'Aye, you're right, Mr MacNair,' Lexy agreed, completely unaware of the implied insult to herself.

'Och, but Lexy, hen!' Sarah squeezed to the front. 'You're no really goin' with Jimmy, are you? No harm to Jimmy. He's one of the best. A lovely fella. But ah don't think you'll get much fun out of him.' She leaned an elbow on the counter to give herself enough energy to laugh. 'Ah can't see him tickling your fancy!'

Lexy crashed the tray of German biscuits down on the counter, making old Duncan nearly weep for their fate.

'For Christ's sake!' His nasal whine loudened into a howl for help. 'Look what she's done to my Germans!'

Lexy ignored both him and his Germans and fixed a hoity-toity eye first on Sarah and then on the rest of the assembled onlookers.

'Hold your mouth, all of yoos! Jimmy Gordon's not that kind of a fella. He's cultural. And forby, he's got manners. You wouldn't get *him* sitting in front of a lady in a public convenience!'

For a minute or two everybody thought old Duncan was going to take, or had actually taken, a fit. He staggered about, bouncing first off the shelves and then off the counter, slavering at the mouth with hysterical laughter until his wispy beard was, as many a customer later described it, 'fair drookit'.

Without another word Lexy, her turbaned head held high, spun round and disappeared through the flour-sack curtain.

Gradually old Duncan was becalmed and the conversation returned to more normal channels - preparations for the Fair.

'I've heard of folk who've got some rare outfits, whole new outfits at the barras,' croaked Mrs Broderick, a comparative newcomer to the district, who had a mouth like a frog, was fat like a frog, and even had frog-like flat feet.

Suddenly the woman nearest to Mrs Broderick and to whom Mrs Broderick had so innocently spoken gave a ghastly shudder, took a menacing step that brought her even nearer to Mrs Broderick and yelled straight into Mrs Broderick's face.

'Don't you dare use that word to me. You big fat frog!' Then she stamped out the shop leaving poor Mrs Broderick blowing and puffing.

'Och, never mind, hen!' Sarah gave her a comforting pat. 'It was Mrs Tucker!' As if that explained everything.

'What did I say, but?'

'Och, nothing. It's just she can't bear the slightest thing to remind her. It all happened before your time.'

'Remind her of what, but?'

Sarah sighed. She had no inclination to use up what little store of energy she had on such ancient history but she felt sorry for Iris Broderick who after all hadn't meant any harm, and might all too easily do the same harm again.

'Well, y'see.' She shoved back her headscarf, leaned her whole self back against the counter until she could support herself by propping her elbows on top of it, and rubbed a slippered foot up and down one leg. 'Y'see, wee Andy Tucker - that's her man - he's a stevedore, though ye wouldn't think so, he's such a delicate lookin' wee soul. I'n't he?'

She glanced around for confirmation and got it. There could be no doubt about Andy Tucker's mysterious smallness, mysterious, that was, for a stevedore who worked like a Samson in the Benlin yards. Andy was four feet nothing. He looked as if he had been chopped off at the knees and he never could get clothes, especially trousers, small enough to fit him. His trouser seats always looked like hammocks and his trouser legs were far too wide all the way down. They flapped over the edges of his shoes and became tattered at the back where he kept treading on them. If Mrs Broderick looked like a frog, wee Andy Tucker was the spitting image of a seal, flapping along the road.

'Well, anyway,' Sarah pressed on. 'You know how there's always a lot of nickin' at the yards - if it's no whisky or something like that off the boats, it's cans o' paint that's just lying around. Anyway, for a while there was an awful lot of stuff goin' a-missing. The dock-police was nearly demented. Honest, everything but the ruddy ships were being lifted and wee Andy was their chief suspect. Oh, they hud their eye on wee Andy, them police at them Benlin gates.'

'Speak up, but!' urged Mrs Broderick. 'That's an awful habit your voice has of fading away, but.'

Sarah sighed again. Then she mustered up a smile before clearing her throat.

'He kept coming out wheelin' a barra piled high and covered that careful with sacks and things. The police stopped him every time and searched under them sacks until they were even usin' magnifying glasses, no kiddin'. There was always nothing but straw, just straw, but they knew, they said, that somewhere, somehow he was hidin' whisky or even drugs or diamonds, he was sneakin' something past them somehow and they wouldn't be beat.' Her voice was fading again but she managed to end with a crinkly face and a chuckle. 'Them police nearly did their nut when they did find oot what Andy was nickin'.'

'What, but?'

'The ruddy barras!'

Mrs Broderick opened an enormous mouth and let go such a yell of laughter she nearly burst her stays.

'Oh, what a scream, but!' She flapped, web-footed, towards the door, hitching herself together as best she could. 'Oh, here, I'd better away if I've tae be ready for the Fair tomorrow. I'll never reach the Broomilaw at this rate, but.'

Sarah's chest lifted with another big sigh. Sigh, sigh, sigh - it was all she could do these days. Still, a couple of weeks at Rothesay would soon put her right.

'Ah'm away as well.' She hoisted her basket over her arm. 'Ah haven't a thing done. No even a case packed.'

But she'd manage somehow, she knew. Anything to get away for a change, a paddle in the water, a breath of fresh air, anything to make her feel better.

She took a long time dragging herself up the stairs and felt most peculiar when she reached her own door on the second landing. A singing noise made light of her head and her tongue felt thick and tingly.

'Baldy!'

She felt her way into the silent house.

'Baldy!'

She shivered. 'Aw, come on, hen!' she begged herself. 'You've your man's tea to make and you've your case to pack. Just think of the morra. The morra, hen! That lovely sail doon the watter. And Rothesay! Aw, come on, hen. If you can just get yersel there, you're all right. You're a lucky lassie now. Come on. Come on. Count your blessings. At least your man's a foreman and he's got the money. All you need is the strength!'

The words were barely out of her mouth when the doorbell startled her. She wasn't expecting anybody except Baldy and of course it wouldn't be him because he had a key. She shuffled to the door using the wall to support her, trying all the time to gather enough energy to make herself smile and be ready to talk pleasantly.

It *was* Baldy, although he was barely recognizable. A taxi-driver was holding him up.

Sarah swallowed down her sickness.

'What happened?'

'Don't worry, hen!' Baldy swayed, bloody-faced, towards her, chunks of flesh sticking out and beginning to turn black. 'Ah'm perfi-per-per . . . Ah'm O.K. Ah just had a couple too many and tripped over masel'.' All at once he exploded into riotous song. 'I belong tae Glasgow! Dear old Glasgow town!'

The taxi-driver groaned.

'For pity's sake, man. Look at your nice wee wife. What makes you do a thing like this? Why do you live like this?'

Baldy pushed him aside and lurched into the house to tower over both Sarah and the cab-driver.

'Och, you silly wee ninny. If you haven't buried your face in the concrete you're not a man and you haven't lived!' Then his face squeezed into a smile and bled down at Sarah.

'Ah, there's my wee wifie waitin'. Pay the man, hen. I'm skint.' Suddenly he became very, very polite. 'I have not one halfpenny left in my possession.'

And with that he wended a zig-zag, hiccoughing, merry path towards the sink in the kitchen.

Chapter 14

The knock on the door was very quiet, so quiet that Catriona went on polishing the sitting-room surround, hearing it, yet not hearing anything at all.

Betty, Melvin's first wife, was a marvellous woman. Her death-bed had been the settee, under which Catriona was now sweating. It had been drawn close to the window so that Betty could be propped up to gaze down at life milling past in Dessie Street.

Melvin had done the housework during the day as well as work in the bakehouse at night and in the last few months of Betty's life he had looked after baby Fergus as well.

Betty adored him, he said, and couldn't bear that he should only be able to take a few hours' sleep and then have to get up to scrub and polish. Melvin liked the carpets scrubbed but everything else in the house protected by a hard gleaming polish. Many a time, he said, he found Betty creeping round the sitting-room floor in her nightie with a duster in her hand trying to save him the bother of doing the polishing.

Catriona wriggled from under the settee and squatted breathlessly back on her hunkers to gaze up at the huge golden-framed photograph of Betty that dominated the sitting-room mantelpiece. There was a medium-sized photo in the kitchen and one in the bedroom as well.

The knock at the door did not become louder but it quickened with irritation and insistence.

Catriona struggled to her feet and hurried out to the hall to open it.

A woman and a child of about five stood on the doormat. The woman had straight hair, a pink and white complexion and eyes like splinters of coal.

'I didn't knock loud,' she whispered, 'in case Melvin would be sleeping.'

'Won't you come in, please. You must be Lizzie.'

The child clung to Lizzie's hand. 'Want to stay with you.'

'I know you do, my wee son. You know who's good to you, don't you? Who gives you sweeties, eh?'

Catriona began to feel uneasy but she stifled her qualms and asked Lizzie to stay for a cup of tea.

'Sweetened with arsenic, I suppose,' Lizzie replied.

'What do you mean?'

'You can't fool me. I know you've had it in for me right from the start.

'I never even heard of you until the other day. Why should I want to do you any harm? I just want to be friends with everybody.'

Catriona shot the pale-faced little boy a worried glance. How did one talk to a child?

'Hallo.' Reaching the sitting-room she riveted her attention on him. 'You must be Fergus. I'm . . . I'm . . . You saw me at the Hall, didn't you? But your Aunty Lizzie took you home early so I didn't see you.'

'Don't you dare! I'm warning you. I'll see through every one of your tricks.'

'What tricks? What are you talking about now?'

'Trying to put my wee Fergie, my wee precious boy, against me. Me who's loved and cared for him like a mother!'

Catriona's heart thumped.

'I said you took him away from the Hall early. I was telling no lie or playing no trick. You *did* take him away early but no doubt you did the right thing. Little children have to go to bed early, haven't they?'

'I've been like a mother to that child and better. The fun we've had!' She smiled at him, bending over. 'Eh, Fergie?'

'I was hoping you'd help me.'

The child, who'd been like a wax dummy, suddenly exploded. 'I want my toys! I want my toys! I want my toys!' Leaping up and down, he zig-zagged in a mad dance around the room.

Catriona gaped at him.

'He's Aunty Lizzie's wee precious son.' Lizzie's voice dropped to a whisper. 'Aunty Lizzie will never be far away. Aunty Lizzie will always be waiting, across the landing, waiting behind her door.'

'Just a minute!' By the time Catriona recovered, Lizzie had limped heavily away.

'I wanted to talk to you,' she called after her.

The front door quietly shut.

'I want my toys! I want my toys! I want my toys!'

The mad dance erupted into the hall.

'Hush! Fergus! For pity's sake. You'll waken Daddy. Be quiet!' She chased after the tiny savage into his bedroom and immediately let out a cry of pain as a well-aimed metal toy hurtled through the air, and hit her in the chest.

Her mouth opened. Her face contorted. In agony she nursed her breast.

Other toys pelted about. Her nostrils widened as she fought for breath. Something sharp stung her leg.

'Stop it! Stop it at once!'

With arms outstretched she stumbled blindly towards him. Her hands found his dark-green jersey. She felt like strangling him but at the same time horror at herself changed her voice, pushed it back down her throat, gentled it.

'I'm your new mummy.'

He stopped. He stared warily up at her.

Her unexpected surge of passion evaporated as quickly as it had fumed into life and she gazed at the little boy with nothing but innocent curiosity.

He seemed to have calmed too; a wax dummy again, his eyes a bright still blue.

She smiled.

'We're going to be friends, aren't we?' Her mind roamed dreamily, searching for nice things to say. 'We're going to live together in this lovely house forever and ever and I'm going to love you and look after you like a real mummy and we're going to be happy and safe here together for always.'

How still he was! She'd never seen anyone or anything so motionless. Time stopped, life gone, only caution clung round his small bird-like figure, his long girlish curls. Then, with astounding rapidity, he lunged at her, his nails digging deep into

101

her legs.

'Fergus, what are you doing?' She endeavoured, gently at first, to pull him off. 'You're hurting me!'

He was hugging her legs with the strength of an iron-muscled maniac, his face hidden hard in her skirts.

'Fergus, don't be silly, dear.' Wrenching at him with increasing vigour but without the slightest success she fought to free herself. 'Fergus!' Her voice condensed in a flurry of alarm as her soft fingers, poking and prising at his fingers, found them statue hard, unbendable.

She didn't know what to do. She was a child herself, terrified. 'Melvin! Melvin! Melvin!'

The silky head moved. Fergus looked up at her, and in the moment before he released her, she saw the gleam of perverted delight in his eyes.

By the time Melvin had staggered through from the next bedroom in answer to her screams, unshaven, moustache mussed, face pouchy with sleep, hands fumbling with the cord of his dressing-gown, his son was quietly tidying away toys.

'Hello, Daddy!'

'Hallo, son.' A mumble before turning to Catriona and coarsening his voice. 'What were you making all that racket for? You wakened me out of a good sleep.'

Catriona stared at Fergus. She wondered if she'd imagined the whole thing.

'I'm sorry.' Her eyes flickered round to Melvin then lowered in embarrassment. 'It . . . it . . . it was nothing. I . . . mean . . . I . . . I . . . think.'

'Stop stuttering!' She caught the note of disgust and flinched under it. 'You sound like an idiot. And keep your eyes up when people talk to you. You look like a terrified mouse. We're not going to eat her, are we, Fergus?'

Unexpectedly he laughed, flung an arm round her shoulders, and kissed her wetly, searchingly and for too long on the mouth.

The child's eyes were burning a hole in her back.

In desperation she wriggled free. Melvin laughed again.

'Just kiss her.' He wiped his mouth with the back of his hand. 'Eh, Fergus?'

'Not in front of the child.'

'Why not?'

She didn't know why not.

'Why not?' Melvin repeated.

'I don't think he likes you kissing me.'

'Don't be daft. Why shouldn't he like anything I do? He's my boy. I brought him up myself. He's the best behaved child in Scotland. Lizzie likes to think she's helped and I let her think it to keep her happy but I looked after my son from the moment he was born. You like Daddy to kiss your new mummy, don't you, Fergus?'

Fergus nodded.

'See!' Melvin nudged Catriona. 'What did I tell you? You're daft! Come on through to the kitchen.' In the hall his tone turned conspiratorial. 'I'll show you how well-behaved and well-disciplined my boy is. Just wait till you see this. Fergus!' he called heartily as soon as he reached the kitchen. 'Come through here, son. Come and see what Daddy's got!'

By the time the child had arrived to stand before him, Melvin had produced two bags of sweets from the cabinet drawer.

'A bag of sweeties for Mummy.' He handed Catriona one of the paper bags. 'And a bag of sweeties for Daddy.'

A silence followed.

Catriona stood uncomprehendingly.

Melvin popped a toffee ball into his mouth and began sucking.

'Mm . . . good! Come on!' His eyes bulged impatiently first at her and then at the bag in her hand. 'You put one in your mouth, stupid! Hurry up!'

Well-trained to jump automatically to sharp command, she pushed a sweet into her mouth.

She felt sick.

'There now!' Melvin sighed with satisfaction. 'And what have you been doing today, son? Been having a good time, have you?'

'Yes, thank you, Daddy.'

'Right, away back and play with your toys, then.'

Fergus turned and walked obediently away.

103

'See that!' Melvin chewed the toffee ball over to the other side of his unshaven face. 'What did you think of that, eh?'

Catriona removed the sweet from her own mouth as delicately as possible. A twitch fluttered like a butterfly at her temple.

'I thought it was horrible.'

'Not the sweet, you fool,' Melvin laughed. 'Fergus! Anyway there's nothing wrong with the toffee balls. The old man sells them in the shop. There's very little he doesn't sell. Everything from a pan loaf to a sanitary towel. Well?'

She felt frightened. She didn't understand his lack of understanding.

'You tormented the child. It was horrible!'

'Don't be stupid. Fergus knows he can get sweets any day of the week. He can get anything he fancies out of the shop and I'm always buying him things up the town. See all these toys through there. I bought these for my son. There isn't another child in Glasgow who's got toys like some of those through there. Did you not see the size of that rocking-horse? And I always buy him a present for going away with at the Fair. Do you know what I've got for him this year? It's still down at the bakehouse. I was showing it to the men. What a laugh we had with it. It's a toy monkey. A big stuffed thing and real-life-size. I'll go down and get it later on.'

'Maybe you didn't mean to, but . . .'

'But what? My son's obedient and well-trained, that's what! Have you ever seen a child who could walk quietly away like that after everybody's got sweets but him? Have you ever seen a child like that before?'

'No, but . . .'

'Did he stamp his feet? Did he go into a temper? Did he shout and bawl: "I want sweeties. I want sweeties"?'

'No, but, Melvin . . .'

'Did my son cry?'

'He should have!' Catriona's voice teetered unexpectedly out of control. 'He should have cried and cried. A child should cry when he gets hurt.'

'Och, shut up. Don't talk daft. Obviously you've a lot to learn about me. Anybody in Clydend could tell you how devoted I've been to that boy. Hurt him? Me? You're a fool. More like you hurting him. What were you doing to him when I came through just now? Fighting with him, were you? Was that what all the screaming and fuss was about? I bet you cried when you were a child, always snivelling, I bet.'

Only now did it enter her head that she had never cried when she was a child.

'Where has his crying gone?' she insisted.

'Eh?' Melvin flung back his head and roared with laughter. 'That's priceless, that is! Where has his crying gone? Sounds like a line from a song.' Suddenly he blustered into the old Scottish tune 'Wha saw the Tattie Hawkers?' and went clopping round the kitchen like a Clydesdale carthorse. 'Where has his crying gone - where has his crying gone - where has his crying gone - it's gone up the Broomilaw!'

Catriona's mind retreated back to the bedroom to Fergus.

'Come on!' Melvin grabbed her, jigged her around a couple of times before stopping to fondle her. 'Remember we're off for our holidays tomorrow.'

Her eyes strained nervously towards the door.

'What's wrong?' Melvin pressed himself against her. 'What are you looking so frightened for?'

Catriona bunched her fists against his chest.

'The child might come in.'

'So what?' He pushed forward until he had made her stagger and fall into the cushions of the fireside chair. He lay heavy on top of her. 'My dressing-gown's tucked around you. He won't see anything.'

Shivering violently, pinned down by the weight of Melvin, her mind darted about seeking some solid ground of understanding, some yardstick by which she could properly measure the rightness or wrongness of events.

Betty's letters had been loving to the point of painful embarrassment. It had been an agony to read them. Never before in her life had she been so acutely distressed. 'My dream man' and 'my wonderful passionate lover' were favourite phrases of Betty's.

From the cheap notepaper and the weak spidery scrawl had

emerged the unmistakable and almost grovelling gratitude of a young girl already condemned to death but clinging desperately to the image of herself as a loving and vital woman - 'Any day now I'll be able to return to you and lie beside you and be a *real* wife to you, the kind of wife you want.' 'Please forgive me for being ill' was another phrase which kept recurring with harrowing insistency. 'Please be patient with me. Soon I'll be lying at your side and I'll be able to turn to you and love you and love you with all the energy that's in me. I'll be everything a good wife should. Everything and more, much more. Melvin, Melvin, I promise you, if you'll only love me still, and be patient.'

'If you're half as good a wife as Betty,' Melvin had informed her as he had pushed yet another letter under her nose, 'you'll do all right. You've a lot to learn though, but don't worry too much about it. I'll teach you just as I taught her.'

Now, over Melvin's shoulder she saw the kitchen door open and Fergus appear.

'The child!' she cried breathlessly. 'The child!'

'Aw, shut up!' Melvin breathed hoarsely in her ear.

Fergus had eyes like blue diamonds.

'Oh, Melvin . . . Oh, Melvin, please!'

The knocking at the outside door came straight from God, straight from the good Lord, to save her.

'Melvin, somebody's at the door.'

'Who the Hell can that be?' He heaved himself up, furious, hardly giving her time to twist round and hide herself from the diamond eyes and rearrange her clothing.

'Well, go on!' he fumed. 'Answer it.'

Hardly aware of what she was doing or where she was going, Catriona ran pell-mell into the hall and jerked open the door.

'Yes?'

For a minute Amy Gordon lost her voice. She stared at the pale sweating face, the expanding nostrils, the huge amber eyes filled to overflowing with what looked like terror.

'I'm Mrs Gordon from upstairs, remember?' Her freckled motherly face softened into a puzzled question-smile. 'Are you feeling all right, dear?'

Catriona longed to throw herself into the old woman's arms

and beg for help and protection but a lifetime of training in the virtues of self-discipline and an inborn Scottish embarrassment at melodramatic displays of emotion kept her firmly in check.

She lowered eyes and voice. 'Yes, thank you.'

'I brought you some of my home-baked scones and I wondered if you needed a hand with your packing. You'll hardly have had time to settle in Dessie Street, never mind get ready to go away to Rothesay.'

'Please come in!' Catriona led the way to the front room. 'It's awfully kind of you. The scones look delicious. Thank you very much. Can I make you a cup of tea or something?'

Mrs Gordon arranged her plump body comfortably on the settee by the window. 'Well, I really came to help you not to hinder you, dear,' she laughed. 'But I never say no to a nice cup of tea.'

'Oh, thank you. You're so kind. I won't be a minute.' Catriona backed stumbling towards the door, clutching the plate of scones against herself as if she were terrified they'd take wings and fly away. 'I'll just run through to the kitchen and put the kettle on. I won't be a minute. Please don't go away.'

She left Mrs Gordon more perplexed than ever, but, amused too, shaking her head and chuckling.

Melvin was tucking his shirt into his trousers in front of the kitchen fire. He always liked to get dressed in front of a fire.

'What the hell does she want?' His whisper rasped like sandpaper.

'To help me.' Flushed with excitement Catriona splashed water into the kettle and lit the gas cooker.

'Well, tell her you don't need any help! You've got me!'

She flung a curious glance at him as she clattered cups and saucers on to a tray. It seemed very odd to whisper when the whole width of the hall and more was between them and Mrs Gordon - and both the front room and the kitchen doors were shut.

'But the packing and everything. Women's kind of work.'

'I can do anything a woman can do and better. Cooking and baking's supposed to be a woman's job but I've yet to meet the woman who could cook a better meal or bake a better loaf than me!' He growled at her. 'You're not going to have females filling my house from morning till night. Tell her the packing's done and get rid of her.'

'But I've promised her a cup of tea. She's through in the front room waiting. And she brought scones - see, aren't they lovely? Wasn't that kind?'

'Stop your idiotic chattering! I've got a bakehouse of scones downstairs. Give her the tea and get rid of her as quick as you can. I want to talk to you. I can see I'll have to talk to you. There's a lot you don't know about marriage. And anyway,' his whisper strained as loud as his throat would allow, 'I've enough to suffer with Jimmy's piano. Sometimes I can't even hear the boxing. He drowns out my wireless. He's worse than the blasted riveters over at Benlin's.'

'What?' Her head was reeling as she rushed around making the tea and finding a milk jug and sugar bowl. 'Who's Jimmy?'

'Her son. Oh, you'll soon find out all about Jimmy. She never stops talking about him. A tall curly-haired bloke. You must hae seen him at the Govan Fair. He was tossing pancakes on the float. He works days. He's our confectioner. Look what you're doing! You've spilt milk on my good tray. That'll seep under the glass now.'

'I'm sorry.'

She hurried for a cloth but he beat her to it and reverently mopped up the milk. 'I made that tray.'

'It's lovely.'

'Carry it carefully and watch my good dishes, and remember I've done the packing and I want to talk to you.'

The tray sped across the hall, milk leaping, splashing, dishes, spoons clattering, chinkling, hysterical.

'Saints alive!' Mrs Gordon laughed out loud when Catriona exploded into the room. 'You're an awful wee lassie. But never mind, you'll soon settle down.' She accepted an eagerly proffered cup of tea with a sigh of pleasure. 'I understood your mother being upset, of course, with everything being so unexpected, and Melvin being a good bit older than you, but your mother doesn't really know Melvin or any of us very well, does she? No, thank you, I won't have a scone, dear, but you eat them up. You're such a skinny wee thing. I know who your mother was, of course. God forgive me, I don't manage to Meeting very often but I have heard her speak. A wonderful woman. You must be very proud of her. And I'm sure everything will work out all right and you'll be able to tell her not to worry. Are you listening to me, dear?'

'I'm sorry. What did you say?'

'Melvin MacNair is a good man.'

'Oh?' Amber eyes grew large, desperate to learn, yet astonished. 'Is he?'

Chapter 15

Sandy had been so upset when he'd heard about Baldy drinking and gambling away all his holiday money, he'd taken twice as long as normal to clear out his van.

His tall telegraph-pole figure, topped by his padded cap and the bread-boards, drooped in and out the Dessie Street close, tender feet pecking the ground like a hen on tiptoe.

He was thinking about Sarah, not Baldy. 'Poor wee thing.' He puffed and puttered into the bakehouse. 'And her looking as if she could be doing with a holiday, too!'

Jimmy shook his head, his young face a picture of misery, so keenly was he feeling Sarah's plight.

'How could Baldy do it? What harm has Sarah done anybody? What harm?'

Tam lifted his checked cloth cap to give his head a good scratch. He had escaped back down to the bakehouse as fast as he could. He was always escaping somewhere, the street corner, the pub, the bookie's, anywhere away from his own home and family. 'We'll have to all pitch in. We'll have to do something.'

Sandy's bloodhound mouth pulled down.

'Aye, but what?'

'Put round the hat, you mean?' Jimmy stopped piping cream into the sponges and looked up, eyes on fire. 'Start a collection?'

'Aye, son!' Tam smacked and rubbed his hands together. 'The very thing!'

Sandy's lip jerked out and in for a minute.

'There's not much time, Tam, and folks haven't much money to spare these days.'

'Och, don't fash yourself, Sandy. You know folks'll give as much as they can. I'll do the organizing. I'll go round everybody in the close for a start. Then the street. Even if everybody gives just a few coppers it'll be enough.'

'I could take you round the rest of the streets in the van.'

'Good man!'

'And we could trot over to Farmbank. Rab would want to give something. That's one thing about Rab. He's not mean. Nor's that wife of his. She'd give you the shirt off her back I've heard.'

'Christ, that's something I'd like to see - the shirt off her back!'

Sandy's teeth and gums came into view but Jimmy cut hilarity short.

'Tam, keep to the point. It's true what Sandy says. There isn't much time and everybody's busy getting ready for tomorrow.'

'Aye, you're right, Jimmy.' Sandy sobered down, then suddenly leapt into unexpected and unusual life. 'That bloody cuddy!' he yelled, and rushed away in an agony of speed as if he were propelling himself through a minefield.

He was too late! Billy the horse had heard the Benlin hooter and was off like Tam O'Shanter's mare, hell-bent for home.

Billy knew, the same as anybody else, and by the same token, that knocking off time was time to knock off.

'Ya bloody cuddy!' Sandy shook a furious fist at the horse and dangerously rocking, rollicking van as they disappeared into the distance, away along the Main Road. 'I'll get you for this. I'll teach you yet you stupid old ass!'

He drooped slowly back to the bakehouse where both Lexy and wee Eck were hugging each other, holding each other up, staggering about bumping into things, hysterical with laughter.

He puttered gloomily at them.

'I'll fillet that beast yet. I'll break every bone in his body.'

Not even Jimmy was shocked by this remark. It was common knowledge that Sandy McNulty loved Billy the horse, and often talked to the animal like a brother.

'Och, keep the head, Sanny. Take the tram along to the stables if your feet can't thole the walking.'

'One of them days, Tam, that bloody cuddy will do that once too often to me.'

'Well, then.' Tam hitched up his shoulders, smacked and rubbed his hands together. 'That's it settled, eh? We all put in as much as we can and get everybody else to do the same.'

'Great, Tam!' Jimmy radiated enthusiasm. 'Just great!'

'I'm away up, then.' Tam gave the vanman his usual punch as he passed, making Sandy's sad eyes roll and his red nose redden. 'You go and fetch King Billy while I pass the hat round the close.'

Melvin straddled the front of the fire, thumbs hooked in braces.

'Marriage,' he announced, 'is like two raindrops trickling down a window-pane, running into one another and becoming one.'

A giggle sprang unexpectedly to Catriona's lips, horrifying both Melvin and herself.

An outraged eye bulged down at her.

'I have always believed that marriage was a serious business. You obviously think it's just a joke.'

'Oh, no!' she hastened to assure him. 'Oh, no, I don't.'

'Well, what are you snickering for?'

She lowered her eyes.

'I'm sorry, Melvin. I don't know what made me do it. What were you saying?'

He fondled his moustache, hesitated, then once more took the plunge.

'Marriage is like two raindrops trickling down a window-pane, running into one another and becoming one.'

Sitting on the fireside chair, hands clasped demurely on lap, Catriona kept her head bent low.

'You're doing it again!' he accused.

'Maybe it's the idea of you being a raindrop. I mean . . . I mean . . . Oh, Melvin, please let me laugh!'

He didn't reply but a sound rumbled up from his chest like far-off thunder until it exploded in an open-mouthed roar of hilarity.

She smacked her hands over her mouth as if afraid she would go completely berserk.

Soon they were both mopping up tears of mirth that had all but exhausted them.

'OK! OK!' Melvin was first to recover. 'So I'm no raindrop. So shut up and listen to what I've got to tell you. Get up and let me sit there. Here, sit on my knee and sit quiet and serious and behave yourself.'

Not many occasions in her life had been happy ones. But she felt happy now. Sitting on Melvin's knee, her head held back against his shoulder, she remembered years ago being held like this by her father. The house had been very still and empty. They had clung together in silence and she had felt safe.

Melvin was restless.

'I mean this!' He cleared his throat. 'I'm not like most Scotsmen. The men round about here, for instance, make me sick. To them a wife's just part of their goods and chattels and their homes are just hotel rooms or lodging houses, places where they sleep and eat and get dressed to go out to football matches or pubs or bookies or out somewhere with the lads. Not me, I'm all for my home, and my wife and family. I've no interest at all outside this house unless it's to take my wife and family somewhere. And I neither gamble nor drink. I don't believe in wasting good money. That's why I always have a shilling or two in my pocket and a pound or two in the bank. Are you listening to me? It's time you gave yourself a shake and woke yourself up. There's always such a faraway dreamy look about you.'

'No, I'm listening, Melvin!'

'Well, anyway, as I said, I believe a happy marriage should be two people like one but living for each other, doing things for each other, trying to make each other happy all the time. To be a good wife you ought to study my every wish and comfort and your whole life from now on should be wrapped up in that. And I'll do everything humanly possible to see that you lack absolutely nothing to make you happy and keep you satisfied.' He suddenly gurgled. 'I keep you sexually satisfied, don't I? I know my sex, eh?'

This could not be denied so she kept silent. He turned serious too.

'There's something wrong with a marriage, I always say, if it needs to depend on anything from outsiders.'

Her eyes stretched with surprise. 'From outsiders?'

'Take Mrs Gordon, for instance. She was in here like a flash. She thinks it's going to be different because it's a different wife.

Well, it's not. It's a wonder Sarah hasn't been. She's usually first.'

Catriona shook her head.

'You jump about from one thing to another. I can't keep up with you.'

'Yes,' he agreed, giving her an affectionate pat. 'I've a quick mind and you're pathetically slow. Never mind, I'll soon get you trained.'

'But I get mixed up with them all. Who's Sarah?'

'Baldy Fowler's wife. The silly fool that spoiled our wedding day.'

'Oh, dear, wasn't it awful?'

'She's an idiot and a dirty slut into the bargain. You could stir that woman's house with a stick. But never mind her. The point is they would all be in and out here like yo-yos if you let them. That's the way they live. It would fit them better to mind their own business and keep themselves to themselves and busy themselves cleaning their houses.'   .

He tidied his moustache, smoothed, twirled it, pushed it up at the edges. 'But never mind any of them! The point is we don't need anybody if we're happily married. There's something wrong with a marriage, I always say, if the couple can't satisfy each other's every need.' His gaze acquired a hint of reprimand. 'Betty and I were perfectly happy together.'

Catriona sighed.

'What are you sighing for? What have you got to sigh about? You've a good husband, a ready-made child and lovely home. What more could a woman want?'

'I was just thinking that I'll never be able to be as good a wife as Betty. She seems to have had everything, even looks.'

'Oh, you'll do - if you do as you're told. I mean - if you just concentrate on your husband, your home and your family, that's all I'm saying. A good marriage doesn't need neighbours or friends or relations or anybody. Betty was an orphan.'

'Poor thing!'

'What's poor about that? You're better without parents half the time. All they do is interfere and try and cause trouble. Betty didn't need anybody. She had me! She dropped her girl friends,

114

even her best friend after we got married. Never saw them again, until the night before she died. I knew she couldn't last another night - down to skin and bone Betty was - a terrible sight. So I thought I'd give her a wee treat. She had been awful fond of that best friend - Jenny - Jenny something her name was. Funny how you forget. I've forgotten it now. Anyway I thought my Betty would like to see Jenny before she died so I sent for her and she came and I let her stay the night. Betty died the next morning. We were both with her - Jenny and I.'

A long silence followed in which Melvin played with his moustache and his eyes became glazed, remembering.

Catriona's mind darted about in distress. She looked round at the photo of Betty on the kitchen mantelpiece, stared perplexedly at the sad still eyes.

'Melvin, are you sure you're right? It says in the Bible to love thy neighbour.'

'Obviously Jesus Christ never knew Dessie Street or Starky Street or any of the streets around here or He'd never have said a daft thing like that.'

'But when Peter asked Jesus how often he was supposed to forgive people who'd sinned against him - "As many as seven times?" he asked, and Jesus said, "I do not say to you seven times, but seventy times seven."'

'Aw, shut up! You sound just like your mother!' He jerked her roughly off his knee and away from him. 'And I'm having neither your mother nor anybody like her in here. She knows her Bible, doesn't she? But a lot of good her knowing it did you! A squashed, dominated, stuttering little nonentity, that's what her and her holiness did to you. Folk like your mother are the biggest and worst kind of hypocrites in the world and they ought to be shot! They just use their religion to frighten folk and to get their own way. I bet your mother's frightened you silly all your life, eh? Hasn't she?'

Too many memories of too many fear-filled days and nights, of visions of retributions known and unknown clawed over Catriona's nerves. They could not be denied.

She stood before Melvin, head bent low, fingers twisting, a contrite child made all the more wretched by his withdrawal of affection.

'I'm sorry, Melvin.'

'I don't want your hypocrites in here.'

'I'm sorry.'

'You're young. You've a lot to learn about life and people.'

'I know.'

'That's what makes me laugh about you.' Unexpectedly he let out a guffaw. 'You always agree with everything anybody says about you. Good God!' His expression changed. 'That's that door again. Watch out of my way. This time *I'll* go!'

She remained facing his empty chair, her mind suspended with surprise. It had never occurred to her to disagree with anyone's criticism of herself. The mere idea was both astonishing and intriguing. And she had Melvin to thank for planting the idea in her head.

'Come away through, Tam.' Melvin returned, and gave his eyes a rapid roll towards the ceiling before turning to reveal the little white-haired swagger of a man behind him.

'Hallo, there!' Tam tossed his cap from his right hand to his left and came sauntering bouncily towards her, right hand outstretched.

'I'm Tam MacGuffie, your next-door neighbour, hen! Welcome to Dessie Street. You're a bonny wee lassie.' He grabbed her hand and pumped it up and down with such fervour she marvelled at the strength of him. 'We'll be seeing you at Rothesay, eh?'

'Not if we see you first!' said Melvin. 'Here's a quid and tell Baldy from me, he'd better watch it. I'll have his guts for garters one of these days!'

Catriona flushed a bright scarlet, tried to smile but failed and struggled to find enough voice to apologize for Melvin.

'Aye, he's a lad, is Baldy.' Tam laughed, apparently not in the least offended. 'Thanks, Melvin. You're a good sport, so you are.' He punched Catriona's arm and she staggered sideways against the chair and sat down with a thump. 'You're a lucky wee lassie to have a man like this. I hope you realize that.'

He squared up to Melvin as he passed him, ducked a couple of times then landed a good-natured punch on Melvin's chest

116

before trotting out of the kitchen. 'I've to meet Sanny. He's away along the Main Road chasing after his horse. Cheerio the now, hen,' he shouted from the hall. 'I hope you enjoy your sail doon the watter tomorrow! We'll all be there all together. Och, it's grand, so it is. You'll love it.'

Chapter 16

Rab had felt depressed before but never so hopelessly as he felt now. Looking back on his life he saw it as a complete waste of time and he blamed nobody but himself for his failures.

Low in his chair, head sunk forward, shaggy brows down, clothes hanging loose over big bones, he ignored Hannah's tirade, allowed it to pass him by, but in doing so each low-pitched, husky, nagging word sucked more of his vitality from him.

He did not need to argue with Hannah or answer her back or even listen to her to exhaust himself.

He recognized the fact, of course, that he never got enough sleep. Hannah's friends and neighbours were forever banging in and out of the house while he tossed and turned in the bedroom and punched his pillows and fervently wished eternal damnation on every member of the Band of Jesus.

Nevertheless the responsibility remained with him. It was his house and his wife and he ought to be able to keep both to his liking.

He had tried. Oh, he had tried, all right. He had accepted the challenge, fought the good fight - and been beaten. He'd tried to escape and been successful for a wee while but now even Lexy had grown sick of him.

She had asked for the return of her key. No explanation, no tender goodbyes, no regrets, no nothing. He didn't blame her. She was a healthy young girl. He was a middle-aged man, an unhealthy man.

Maybe she was afraid of catching the 'baker's dermatitis' that so often plagued his arms. Then there was his stomach ulcer. He'd confided in Lexy about that. Oh, how he must have bored the girl.

She had been more than patient with him.

No, he couldn't blame her. He was a fool! A bloody big fool!

118

Hannah was right. He was as mad as a hatter!

'You're mad!' she had bent over his chair and informed him quietly yet with dark triumph. 'I knew it. May the good Lord have mercy on your soul.'

She had been on at him for ages about his long silence, the moods of depression that alternated with wild bouts of temper. Then eventually, the day after Catriona's wedding in fact, she had, unknown to him, called in the doctor.

Lying in bed that morning, his mind roaming helplessly back over his life and all the things he regretted doing and all the things he wished he had done instead, he heard the knock on the outside door, the footsteps, and the whispering in the lobby.

Then, suddenly, into the bedroom marched Hannah followed by a young man, old Dr Grant's new assistant.

The shock, on top of the sleepless morning, after the long hard night's work, paralysed him to begin with.

He had never uttered a word while the doctor examined him, a confident young whipper-snapper with a whole lot of complicated new-fangled ideas; he had even started in a dazed faltering voice to answer some of the man's questions. It was only when Hannah began butting in and answering the questions for him that the realization of what was going on made his emotions burst alight and flame up until they almost consumed his body as well as his brain.

He'd leapt out of bed, sending the doctor sprawling and chased Hannah all through the house in his night-shirt bawling abuse at her at the pitch of his voice.

The young doctor quickly recovered and, like something out of a Charlie Chaplin film, had joined in the chase. Even when the eager beaver received a black eye for his troubles he had, it must be admitted, taken it very well.

There had been no malice in his voice when he had recommended a psychiatrist.

Rab squirmed inside. He'd heard it said that in America nobody thought a thing about going to these headshrinkers but in his part of the world it was unheard of. A psychiatrist was the luxury of the rich hypochondriac, and the necessity of the madman.

He sighed the past away and stared bleakly ahead at the future.

First a holiday up at Montrose with Hannah's Aunty Flora and Uncle Dougal who went to bed at eight o'clock and believed that the wireless was the voice of the devil.

Then after the holiday - if Hannah had her way - the headshrinker.

Slowly he raised his face. He glowered at Hannah.

'You'll have me in the asylum yet, woman!'

'That's where you belong!'

Just in time, the doorbell saved her.

Catriona was taken aback when she looked out the window and saw the straight-backed, ruddy-cheeked, familiar figure marching across the Main Road. Yet it was reasonable enough that her mother should wish to see her before they both left for their respective holidays.

Surely Melvin could not object to that? Still, she was glad he'd gone down to the bakehouse for Fergus's present and hoped he would be delayed there for some considerable time.

Her heart pattered with excitement at the prospect of showing off her very own home, although she still hadn't had enough time to convince herself of the reality of it.

She winged her way through the hall towards the kitchen and her soul caught its first sniff of freedom. Her mother could have no sway over her, could take nothing away from her here.

She was free, she was safe.

Round and round she danced, light-footed, long hair swirling far out then curling back close to her.

Fergus giggled when he saw her.

'Oh!' Her cheeks burned bright with embarrassment but she laughed. 'Granny's coming to visit us. You'll be a nice polite boy for Granny, sure you will?'

'Won't!'

'For goodness' sake, why not? I'll make tea and you can have some, or milk if you'd rather. And there's still some of Mrs Gordon's scones left.'

'Want to go to bed!'

'But, Fergus, I'd like you and Granny to be friends with each other.'

'Want to go to bed!' His toe poked the rug, then dug into it, then kicked it. 'Don't want a granny. Don't like a granny!'

Harassment quickened and sharpened her voice.

'Oh, all right. Go to bed, I don't care.'

Guilt flashed across her face but the problem of her mother's loud insistent ring at the doorbell was far more urgent.

Perspiring with excitement now, she flicked a glance of pride around the immaculate kitchen. The sink at the lace-curtained window was sparkling white and had a red-painted cupboard underneath it. The cooker shone, too, and the grey linoleum floor. A bright red fire burned in the hearth and its warm flickering reflected under and over the table on to the kitchen cabinet.

The hall was square, far bigger and more imposing than the narrow lobby in the house at Farmbank, and of course the bedrooms and the sitting-room were, by comparison, luxurious and beautiful.

She did another little jig of joy.

Freedom! Freedom!

As soon as the front door opened, the air became charged with anxiety.

'Are you all right?' Her mother came in, gripped her by the arm and, peering closely and worriedly at her, hustled her into the sitting-room. 'You don't look all right. What has that man been doing to you?'

In the front room she put her arm round her daughter's shoulders. 'What has he been doing to you, child?'

No one was more surprised than Catriona herself at the sudden waterfall of tears that came gushing up to overflow and spurt down her cheeks. Trembling violently, she hugged close to her mother.

'The wicked villain!' Hannah was trembling too. 'Men are all the same. All they ever want is to degrade a woman. They can do anything they like - if you don't fight to protect yourself - and a woman is at a terrible disadvantage, especially if a man gets her tied down with children. A woman has only one weapon to defend herself, and that weapon, Catriona, is her tongue. Oh, it's a man's world! You're beginning to find out what that means, no doubt. May the good Lord help and protect you!'

Hannah firmly disentangled herself, led the shivering girl over to the settee and pushed her down among the cushions.

'You wait there. I'll go through to the kitchen and make you a nice hot cup of tea.'

Visions of Melvin returning to find Hannah making herself at home in his kitchen came to sweat fear through every pore.

'No . . . I'm . . . I'm . . . I'm . . . all . . . right . . . m . . . m . . . Mummy!'

'Put your feet up!' Hannah grabbed Catriona's feet and heaved them up on to the settee for her.

'But . . . m . . . m . . . Mummy!'

'Just you relax and don't worry. I hope you're remembering to say your prayers. All this is a punishment for something you know. God has strange ways of working. Lie back. Don't move! I'll be back with a hot drink to revive you in a minute.'

The tears opened the flood-gate of emotion that had been held back by the shock of recent happenings.

She felt ill. She was glad to be lying down on the settee. She didn't think she could conjure up enough strength to stand up.

The horror of it all! She was actually, legally married, tied, in the power of a mustachioed monster of a man - for the rest of her life!

Her mother came striding back with the tea as confidently as if she owned the place.

Catriona envied her courage; especially when a few minutes later she heard the sound of Melvin's key turning and the front door opening.

'Oh . . . m . . . mu . . . mu . . . Mummy!'

'Just you keep lying there! Just you finish drinking your tea! That man won't dare say one word to you while I'm here!'

A nerve-stretching pause ensued. At long last the room door swung open, and Melvin came bumping in on his knees holding hands with a life-size monkey.

'Here we are!' he bawled. 'Ready for the Glesga Fair - wee Mickey and me!'

A stunned silence smacked over his face when his bulging eyes alighted on his horrified mother-in-law.

'Well!' Hannah was first to gather her wits together. She held her handsome head high and stared witheringly down at Melvin. 'There's more than one man in Glasgow needs to see a psychiatrist!'

Sarah just kept pushing herself on as if nothing had happened, as if she still had her holiday money and the noise from Lender Lil was not filling the house.

She fixed up the ironing board and stood, with what looked to Mrs Fowler like impertinent nonchalance, with her back to the sink, a cigarette dangling from her lips, smoke drifting up and making her eyes wrinkle as she ironed her husband's clean shirts.

Mrs Fowler howled and mopped at waterfalls of tears with a big white handkerchief.

'All that money! All that money! . . . But, of course, you'd drive anybody to drink. It's all your fault. My Baldy never did anything like this when he lived with me. Look at you - you're a disgrace. It's time somebody forced you to be decent. You're coming with me and you're going to stay at my place in Rothesay. You're going to do as you're told for a change and no more of your snash, Sarah Sweeney!'

'Sarah Fowler. Fowler! Ah'm sorry, hen, but if ah gave you an inch you'd take a mile. And if you think ah'm goin' to crush in with you you've another think comin'.'

'Fancy! Talking to me like that. You!'

Sarah removed her cigarette so that she could bend her mouth into a smile.

'Aye, just fancy the three of us in a wee single-end in Rothesay!'

'You and me in the double bed and Baldy on the couch, what's wrong with that?'

'You'll not separate me and my man, hen.' Sarah replaced the cigarette and continued slowly and heavily with the ironing.

'I'm going through to the bathroom to wash my face.' Mrs Fowler turned to an unusually silent Baldy who was hovering

123

huge and awkward in the middle of the floor. 'And you'd better put her in her place before I come back, do you hear? Stupid idiot!' Her fist shot out and punched him in the ear as she passed.

Baldy's ear turned scarlet but otherwise he didn't pay the slightest attention to the assault. He made straight for Sarah as soon as his mother swept away.

'Och, come on, hen, be a sport. We might as well do as she says. Why shouldn't she spend some of her money on us for a change? The old bag's loaded.'

Sarah sucked at her cigarette and said nothing.

Baldy put a muscle-hard arm round her shoulder and gave her a squeeze.

'Will I have a word with her, then? Butter up the old cow and see if I can't get her to loaned us the money for our own wee single-end?'

'Our own wee single-end.' For a terrible moment Sarah thought she was going to disgrace herself and embarrass Baldy by bursting into tears.

Instead she puffed violently at her cigarette then managed to choke and cough out, 'You haven't a chance in bloody hell!'

'Here. She's coming. I'll catch her before she starts on you again.'

In two or three big strides Baldy covered the kitchen, bashing into and crashing over a chair in the process.

Sarah shook her head, her mouth doing its best to contort into a smile.

Out in the hall, out of Sarah's hearing, and with the thunder of the lavatory cistern in the background, Baldy met his mother.

'Be a sport, Ma. Loaned us some money. I've enough to contend with with that dirty slut I married. Don't you let me down.'

Mrs Fowler punched him good and hard in the stomach.

'What are you blethering about? I'm offering to *give* you a holiday - pocket money and all. Don't you dare talk to me about letting folks down. What do you think you did to me when you got yourself mixed up with a useless article like that through there? You didn't need to marry her, you big fat fool! Our family's always been respectable. We've never had anything to

124

do with the likes of Sarah Sweeney.'

She pushed past him into the kitchen, but the sudden jangle of the doorbell stopped her.

'Ah'll go,' said Sarah with a hard-core of warning behind the weakness of voice. Nobody opened the door in *her* house but her.

Tam McGuffie and Sandy MacNulty were standing there like Mutt and Jeff. Tam was only about half Sandy's size but twice as lively. His checked 'bunnet' was pulled well down on his head but he was grinning from ear to ear underneath it, and smacking and rubbing his big hands and bouncing with gleeful impatience from one foot to the other.

Sandy was grinning too and showing as much teeth and gums as Billy the horse. He was holding out his cap and shaking it, making a chinkly noise.

Tam swaggered forward.

'There you are, hen. It's from the men and the neighbours. Take it, lassie. We know you'd do the very same for any of us. Take it. Sanny'll get his cap back after.'

The cap was pushed into her hands. She clutched it to herself, lips struggling, eyes squeezing.

Tam shoved her back so that he could jerk the door shut between them.

'See you tomorrow!' he flung at her in an unnecessarily loud voice.

Sandy leaned over Tam and cried a quick word of comfort.

'You're all right now, hen!'

Then the door banged shut.

Chapter 17

The paddle steamer *Caledonia* bulged fat and weighed low down with people. Yet more and more Glaswegians were queuing up at Bridge Wharf across from the Broomilaw and crushing merrily on to swell its sides fatter and fatter.

The hot sun sparkled the vivid kaleidoscope of coloured clothes and polished glass and dazzling paint.

Already the singing had started and men were chugging bottles of whisky from jacket pockets and women were chattering and laughing and children were dashing about getting lost.

A couple of middle-aged women, their fat bouncing and wobbly before them, were facing each other up for a dance, whacking their hands, galloping towards each other, pouncing on each other's arms and uttering hair-raising 'heughs' as they birled each other round, spinning faster and faster, with everybody watching, singing and shouting, clapping hands and stamping feet.

At last the gang-planks were lifted, ropes flung aboard. The steamer gave a warning hoot and with much creaking, groaning and splashing, the *Caledonia*'s paddles were set in motion, slowly at first, the water foaming and frothing; then gradually as it rocked away from Bridge Wharf, just by the George V Bridge, the paddles quickened and found their joyous rhythm and water-churning strength.

A band began to play in the centre of the middle deck. It consisted of four men in navy-blue suits and caps. One man strummed the banjo, another had a white hanky spread over his shoulder on which rested his fiddle and his head. Another energetically squeezed and pulled at a concertina and the fourth thumped with great concentration on an ancient piano.

Melvin, Catriona and Fergus sat forward on the top deck because they could get all the sunshine and fresh air that was going. They also got quite a breeze and Catriona's long hair swirled and twirled and flowed out behind her.

'Make sure you enjoy every minute of this,' Melvin warned. 'It's costing me a pretty penny!'

He had not yet recovered his good humour from the previous night's debacle with her mother.

Hannah had been either the stronger of the two personalities or the more practised in verbal warfare. Anyway, she snatched the last word before slamming away in triumph.

Long after she had gone Melvin had nagged his anger and bruised pride out on Catriona. In fact she had fallen into an exhausted sleep with his enraged voice pounding in her ears and awakened next morning to hear it, as if he had never left off, never paused for either breath or sleep.

'It's lovely.' She smiled round at him, flicking back glistening strands of hair that kept whipping across her face. 'And everybody sounds so happy. Listen to the singing!'

'Drunk, probably!' The corners of Melvin's mouth twisted, making his moustache droop low. 'They don't know how to enjoy themselves without a glass of whisky in their hands.'

The tubby *Caledonia*, brought specially up from its home-base in Gourock to help cope with the holiday crowds, waddled its cheery way past the docks, the ferries, the giant cranes jagging the sky, the ships all in different stages of growth balanced on stocks.

The yards were quiet because everything closed for the Fair. At other times when the steamers passed, the shipbuilders, swarms of men high up like ants on the sides of hulls, noisily banging and clanging, or leaning over, or up in the clouds working cranes, stopped and waved hands or caps and bawled friendly greetings.

'Haw, Bella! Why don't you buy a ship of your own?'

Today there was nothing to compete with the noisy paddle steamer except the hooting of other ships and the raucous screeching of gulls. The white-breasted birds swooped and dived alongside and followed the holiday cruises from Glasgow, knowing they were certain of generous and eagerly proffered handfuls of food right down the Clyde to Rothesay.

All the old Scots songs were getting big licks - 'Roamin' in the Gloamin', 'The Road to the Isles', 'Stop Your Ticklin' Jock', 'Ah'm The Saftest In The Family', 'I Belong Tae Glasgow'. Sometimes everybody sang together, sometimes one person went solo on the verses and everyone joined with them in lusty chorus.

'Fergus!' Catriona twisted round, then stood up to squint across and round the people in an effort to see where the little boy had run off to. 'Fergus!'

'Oh, leave him alone,' Melvin growled. 'He'll be all right. Sit down!'

'He's too wee to be away on his own. He might climb up high on something and fall overboard.'

She did not wait to hear any more objections from Melvin. The child made her nervous. He behaved very strangely at times. There was no telling what he might do.

Crushing her way along the deck, she caught a glimpse of his blonde head and blue and white shirt disappearing downstairs.

'Fergus!'

No doubt the music and singing were luring him on to the other deck.

Someone was shouting.

'Come on! Come on, Jimmy lad! It's your turn. Get away from that piano, Jock. Let a Clydend man show you how it should be played. A song as well, Jimmy. Come on now! Don't be shy. We're no going to take no for an answer!'

Suddenly a cheer went up then gradually tailed away as the piano rippled into tune.

Catriona stopped half-way down the stairs, arrested by the change in the music. The piano keys were being caressed more than played and the young voice was rich and tender.

He was very handsome. Her head bent to one side to study him.

Then, unexpectedly, dark eyes flicked up and found hers.

> 'They'll be pipes down the isle,
> Bonny Mary of Argyll,
> When the heather gleams like stardust in the glen.'

A hundred voices swelled into the chorus but she could still hear his gentle tone.

'I'll be sailing down the Clyde, in my arm you'll soon abide . . .'

Held by his strangely perceptive stare, life inside her, and outside, too, acquired a new intensity, an extra dimension; the sturdy Clydebank ship, the sunbright sky, the sparkling water, the people so happily singing, everything concentrated in time, and she saw, and she heard, and she was perfectly tuned in.

Moving away to continue her search for Fergus she felt so acutely disturbed by this new awareness, the strange heightening of sensitivity, she was not sure whether it made her happy or sad.

She found the little boy and returned with him, hand-in-hand, to where Melvin was lounging back scanning a newspaper.

'He wanted to spend some of his money in the shop. I let him get an apple. I thought an apple would be better than chocolate.'

Melvin grunted from behind the paper.

Sitting beside her husband, hands clasped on lap, Catriona closed her eyes but she could still see Jimmy Gordon staring at her.

It was a good thing she enjoyed the sail 'doon the watter', Sarah told herself afterwards, because the rest of the holiday was a nightmare.

It could have been grand, and no one realized more than she did that she was lucky to have any holiday at all. She was, in fact, hoarse from thanking everybody for their help, although the money gathered barely gave them enough to cover their expenses and Baldy's pocket-money. Her gratitude knew no bounds and, hoarse or not, she continued to thank everybody she met.

If only Lender Lil hadn't spoiled the holiday. Every day in Clydend, every afternoon, regular as clockwork she nag, nag, nagged. But in Rothesay her wail never stopped from early morning until late every night. Over and over again she assured Sarah that as long as she lived she would never forgive her for accepting the 'collection' money. Water had flooded down her coarse-skinned face.

'If everybody got up collections when somebody needed

money I'd be out of business. Money's my business, Miss Sweeney, in case you've forgotten! I'm a respectable business woman. I'm not in the habit of accepting charity and neither is any of my family. The Fowlers have always been respectable business folk and proud of it. You don't know the meaning of the word respectable - or pride - if you ask me!'

On and on and on, non-stop, except for the time when Baldy came in from one of his boozy dos with the lads. Usually the women, in between shopping and cooking under much more difficult circumstances than they were accustomed to at home, stuck close together on seats along the front and kept an eye on the children, and gossiped and had a laugh and did a bit of knitting and 'sooked' at ice cream.

The men very quickly found their favourite pubs and billiard halls and only emerged for food, a snore in the sun and some loving.

Baldy steered well clear of her during the day and she certainly didn't blame him, with his mother sticking to her side like a weepy crocodile. No man could be expected to spend his holidays listening to a nagging wet-eyed woman, so the only place she saw anything of Baldy was in bed where he energetically made up for lost opportunities.

The worst of it was, she had never managed to recover from the state of shock she had been whirled into before she left Glasgow. The change of surroundings and routine only made matters worse. Her mind and emotions felt as confused and bruised as her body. Never before had she been more vulnerable, never before had she been at such a disadvantage, in both preventing herself from drowning in Lender Lil's tears, and coping with Baldy's needs as a husband.

Defences down, she knocked about in a maze, stumbling miraculously from one day to the other, forgetting things, unable to concentrate, unable to hold things, continuously surprised at articles falling from her fumbling fingers. Little curtains came down over time and peering desperately back she could not see through them, could not prise open her mind to find out what she had done yesterday, or what had happened only a few hours before. Sometimes, to her secret shame, she could not even recall her own name.

All she could do was to keep automatically thanking everyone, and to smile her gratitude.

Free of the all-pervading flour that powdered his black hair and brows and long lashes, whitened his already pale skin, and dusted his clothes and shoes, Jimmy looked a new man. His hair had a gloss and seemed full of vitality. The fresh air had whipped colour to his cheeks and his eyes were brighter and shinier and more eager to find life and enjoy it than ever.

He explored Dunoon on his own and he enjoyed the aloneness as intensely and with as much appreciation as he did everything else.

His mother had soon settled down to her usual routine with her two unmarried sisters in their little house not far from the pier. She was perfectly happy to blether with them over endless cups of tea or go visiting Aunty Jeannie and Aunt Maggie's friends to have more blethers and more cups of tea.

'Och, away you go, son,' she told him in reply to his first polite offer to escort them around. 'It's no good for young laddies to be hanging about old women. Thanks, all the same, but never mind us. You get away on your own and enjoy yourself.'

Gratefully, he had escaped to walk for miles, shoulders back and - once he was away in lonely deserted places - breathing deeply in through his nose and out through his mouth in accordance with instructions in a book he had picked up at one of the book barrows in Renfield Street.

It had made fascinating study into the wonders that could be accomplished by proper breathing, exercises and self-discipline.

The self-discipline was the bit that worried him . . . the self-discipline. All his life there seemed to have been a tussle going on inside him for one reason or another. Take smoking. He reminded himself of the old joke, 'Of course I can stop smoking, I've done it hundreds of times!' The torments he put himself through trying to do without a cigarette - the torments, the depths he sunk to in defeat were just as bad, every bit as bad. After three or four days of wild pacing about and even wilder piano playing, he reduced himself to searching every pocket and ashtray in the house for dog-ends. It was always Sunday. The shops were always shut.

His mother would reprimand him. 'Saints preserve us, son, go and borrow some cigarettes from Sarah and don't stop smoking again. I can't relax when you're prowling about the place; you're like a caged tiger, laddie. You'll do more harm to yourself like this than by smoking, I'm thinking.'

Every time he persuaded himself that she was right; emotional strain was very bad for his heart. Gratefully, he rushed to have a glorious puff at one of Sarah's cigarettes. Immediately he took it he despised himself for his lack of will-power. Despised himself. He determined, if it was the last thing he ever did, the last thing, he'd master this smoking business. He just would not be beaten.

After the holidays, he would definitely give it up.

Scrambling up the Castle Hill after one of his walks he flung himself down for a rest and, propping himself up on his elbows, chewed a blade of grass as he gazed down at the pier and listened to the kilted piper playing one of the steamers away.

'Will ye no come back again?' the pipers lamented.

'Oh, we're no awa' tae bide awa',' the crowd on the ship lusitily sang, 'we're no awa' tae leave ye. We're no awa' tae bide awa' - we'll aye come back and see ye!'

Jimmy's gaze roamed across the shimmering water, back to the hills, then round to the rock on which stood the statue of Highland Mary, looking towards the coast of Ayrshire, where she met Robert Burns.

Highland Mary - Mary Campbell of Dunoon who went to work as a dairymaid or a nursemaid in Ayrshire, fell in love with the poet and, according to some people, married him 'Scotch style' by exchanging Bibles over running water.

He wondered if there were any connections between Highland Mary and the 'Bonny Mary of Argyll' of the song.

As he stared at the state of the woman so beloved by Burns, a sadness seemed to reach out to him.

He took a deep breath to chase the sadness away. Then he felt in his pocket for a cigarette.

132

As soon as he returned to Clydend, he automatically reminded himself, he was going to give up smoking.

Chapter 18

All the talk after the holidays was centred round Sadie Dawson's wedding. Slasher had long ago become sick to his back teeth of hearing about it but the women customers crowding into MacNair's for their daily supply of bread and groceries could not hear enough.

They knew, of course, that it was to be in the house, although how the house was supposed to hold the huge mob that was going was anybody's guess. MacNair's were supplying the food: steak pie, potatoes and peas, Scotch trifle, assorted cakes and biscuits and - the *pièce de résistance* - the three-tiered wedding cake with a tiny bride and a little model to represent Sadie's 'intended' perched on top under an intricate arch of icing-sugar. The cake was so big, old MacNair couldn't find a box to fit it.

The street outside the shop was deserted except for Billy the horse, Sandy McNulty's van, and a mucky-faced boy of about seven called Erchie who was always hopefully hanging about with the - to old MacNair - infuriatingly persistent cry of, 'Mister, mister, any broken biscuits, mister? Hey, mister, any broken biscuits? Any stale cookies, eh?'

The only other apparent life in Dessie Street was approaching with leisurely gait from the faraway end in the form of Arthur Begg's horse-drawn coal-cart. Arthur wore a greasy cap back-to-front on his head and a leather saddle-like cape to protect his shoulder-blades, but all that could be seen of Arthur himself was the bulging whites of his eyes.

Cupping his coal-black hand round his ear when he yelled his wares, he looked as if he were trying to catch what he was saying, which was not really surprising as everyone recognized his cry but no one understood a word of it.

'Co-o-ee any o-o-o-ee f-o-o-ee Co-o-ee!'

Arthur's mare plodded slowly along, the cart rattling and groaning behind her as she stopped automatically at each close, eyeballs rolling, white-showing, the same as Arthur's.

Inside MacNair's there was first an awesome silence when the wedding cake appeared, carried with great difficulty by old Duncan and Sandy, then the silence exploded into generous and noisy praise.

Old Duncan always insisted on carrying wedding cakes out through the shop into the van so that he could bask in the reflected glory of the exquisite confections. It was, after all, his bakery and his material and his employee who had made them.

Although he'd been chiding himself all morning for having anything to do with the wedding - 'God knows when I'll get paid for all this. Everybody in Clydend lives off me after the Fair. Nobody's got a halfpenny to their name. It's just tick, tick, tick, all the time.'

None of his grumbles dampened the excitement, however.

Jimmy and Lexy came through from the bakehouse to hover proudly in the background.

'Keep back! Keep back!' MacNair sounded as if he had a peg clipped over his nose. 'Out of my road, the crowd of you.' He staggered along at an awkward angle because he was trying to prevent his whiskers from touching the cake and also because Sandy, holding the other side of the huge pillared masterpiece, was so much taller.

The customers obediently made way, still singing praises.

'Oh, isn't it lovely! Sadie's a lucky girl, so she is!'

'It's a rer cake, but! I'n't it, but?'

With much grunting and sweating and agonizing warnings to take care and not bump into anything, they managed to ease their precious burden into the van.

Dixon Street where the cake was to be delivered was only five or ten minutes away, the other side of Dessie Street from Starky Street, but MacNair had no intentions of taking any chances.

'There's tissue paper in the shop. I'll pack some round it. And where's wee Eck? Tell him to sit in the back and hold on to it in case the Benlin hooter goes and that stupid nag bolts.'

'Billy's no stupid, anything but!' Sandy puttered indignantly. 'It's very clever of him to know what that hooter means.' With long stiff legs he stalked the old man back into the shop.

'Anyway the hooter's not due for hours yet.'

Seven-year-old Erchie, his small fists pushed deep into his ragged trousers, watched them emerge from, then return to, the shop. His pace changed to a brisk skip, ever-hopeful of success in persuading the old man to give him something to eat.

Near the doorway, however, his skip slowed to a gawky stop and his mouth fell open. A fascinating horrifying scene was being enacted before his eyes.

Begg the coalman's horse was trying to take a bite out of Mister MacNair's cake.

Erchie suddenly recovered his wits and flew into the shop.

'Hey, mister, mister!'

'Get away. You wee nyaff!' the old man whined. 'Can you not see I'm busy?'

'But, mister . . .'

'I'll mister you.' He made a swipe at the child's ear but Erchie, well-practised in the art of dodging blows, proved too quick for him.

'But, mister . . .'

'I haven't got any broken biscuits, or stale cookies, you dirty-faced wee devil.'

Erchie danced up and down with exasperation. 'The coalman's horse is eating your weddin' cake.'

'What?' Knees lifting, boots clattering, old Duncan beat everybody to the door.

The coal-horse, its wide, soft mouth placidly chomping, stared round at him in innocent surprise as he burst from the shop shaking fists and screaming.

'I'll murder you. You big fat thief!'

'Who's a big fat thief?' Arthur Begg emerged from the next close, took in the scene at a glance and dived in front of his horse, arms outstretched to protect it against all comers. 'Don't you dare lay a finger on my Nellie.'

'Lay a finger on her!' Duncan howled, wildly fighting to prise Arthur out of the way. 'I'll punch the big fool until she's unconscious.'

'Over my dead body!' Arthur rolled white eyeballs in a black face held high, chin shoved aggressively forward. 'Put up your dukes!'

'Right! Right!' Old Duncan's goatee beard bristled with fury as he rapidly arranged himself into suitable fighting pose. 'I dare you, you fat mucky-faced messin'!'

He was saved from the powerful force of the coalman's fist only by the timely intervention of Jimmy who pushed his way through the magically gathered crowd - one minute the street had been empty, the next it was packed - and grabbed both Duncan and Arthur by the scruffs of their necks and jerked them away from each other.

'What are you fighting for?' Jimmy's white coat and long white apron made a startling contrast to the coalman's black clothes and the khaki-coloured shop-coat old MacNair wore. 'Look, Nellie's only taken one wee bite off the top, one wee bite, and that's only icing. Come on, help me get it back into the bakehouse. I'll soon sort it!'

Puffing at a cigarette, smoke wafting up over her blonde, bescarfed head, Sarah had gone through to stare out of the front-room window in an effort to escape Lender Lil's tongue.

It was no use.

'You've nothing better to do, I suppose, but smoke my money away and stand around poking your nose into other folks' business.'

'I don't know anything about your money,' Sarah repeated automatically, 'I don't know what you're talking about, hen.'

She leaned her brow against the window, her tired eyes resting down on the street.

The wedding cake was beautiful. It reminded her of the cake Baldy had made for their wedding. Baldy had insisted on making the cake himself. And had he been proud of it!

She tried to smile but even thinking of weddings strained her, dangerously near to tears now. Emotion seemed to be building up inside her and losing its balance. Coupled with pain it was almost too much for her, nearly blotting out reason and swamping what little ability she had left to organize her resources.

More and more she longed for help and more and more she thought of the panel of doctors that sat in the converted shop they used as a surgery along the Main Road - the 'surgery yins' she called them to distinguish them from the 'hospital yins' because she already had so much to do with both. The cost of her previous visits was a shameful source of guilt that Lender Lil never allowed her to forget.

'You'll be the ruination of this family, Sarah Sweeney!' she kept saying, over and over again.

Mixed up with her need for the surgery yins was a secret sense of awe of all those in authority, people like doctors, schoolteachers, the clergy and the police.

The surgery yins and the hospital yins were important and busy men, and she shrank from bothering them and taking up any more of their valuable time in case they lost patience with her and accused her of being a nuisance.

Just as important was the fact that she had so much to do and organize before she could make a visit to the surgery.

She would have to have a bath and shampoo her hair and wash and iron all her underwear, indeed, attend to all her clothes in case she was suddenly despatched to hospital again. She'd have to go up town to buy a new nightie. She would have to see to all Baldy's clothes, too, and leave everything right for him. The house would have to be cleaned and extra shopping done; a thousand and one jobs would need to be seen to.

Even a visit to the surgery became immensely complicated, an impossible feat, once her thoughts attempted to grapple with it.

She longed to confess the terror that was emerging from the back of her mind like a monster to swim free with the upsurge of emotion.

She hardly dared turn her inward eye on the thought. Yet it was there, refusing to go away.

'Sarah, hen, you've got cancer!'

She had no clear idea of what cancer meant but it was what made Lender Lil and all the older women drop their voices to hoarse frightened whispers.

'They say it's - cancer! She's suffering agonies. She hasn't got a chance!'

The name 'cancer' was only mentioned by the more sturdy like Lender Lil. Most folk couldn't bring themselves to speak it out loud; instead it was darkly hinted at, as if they were afraid that the word itself had strange powers and was in some way infectious.

It was associated with vague but nonetheless horrible tales of women having their breasts cut off and their insides cut out so that they were left sexless, no longer real women that their men could love.

She felt ashamed; ashamed of the ever increasing untidy, and dirty condition of her house and of herself, ashamed of her lack of energy, ashamed of her inability to cope. Now her shame was spreading, mingling with terror, and entering into dark unmentionable places.

Clinging tenaciously to normal comforting little routines and habit patterns she eased herself away from the window, her emaciated body like a half-shut knife, and made a slow, shuffling, agonizingly painful progress towards the other end of the house; the kitchen, the warmth of the fire, her favourite chair with the soft velvet cushion, a cup of tea in her favourite cup with the roses round it.

'The kettle's on at low.' Her voice came out little more than a whisper so she cleared her throat and tried again once she and her mother-in-law arrived through in the kitchen. 'Fancy a cup of tea, hen? I'm making one.'

'It's about all you can do, you dirty slut. The whole day long you're making yourself cups of tea. Never you mind tea just now! When I came into this house I had five pounds in my bag. Five pounds for my messages. Now it's gone and I'm not leaving here until you hand it over. You'll not do me for money, Sarah Sweeney. By God, you'll not take my money from me. That's going too far!'

Ring-a-ring-a-roses. A game she used to play as a child came unexpectedly back to her. All the wee girls joined hands together and went skipping round in a circle.

> Ring-a-ring-a-roses,
> A pocketful of posies
> Atishoo! Atishoo!
> We all fall down!

139

'I don't know what you're talking about, hen.'

The cups were dirty, jammed in among a pile of pots and pans, of breakfast dishes and cutlery.

Sarah felt confused.

It wasn't nearly time for dinner yet. Lender Lil never came until dinner-time or afterwards, after she had done her shopping.

No, it wasn't nearly dinner-time yet.

They had barely finished breakfast.

She had given her man a good breakfast this morning.

There was the porridge pot, and the empty cream jug. There was the frying pan, the ham-grease hardened over crumbs of fried bread and shiny remnants of egg-whites.

'You know all right, you just haven't got the guts to look me straight in the eye and admit it.'

There was the empty marmalade jar and the small plates sticky with bread-crumbs.

The small plates had roses round them.

> Ring-a-ring-a-roses,
> A pocketful of posies,
> Atishoo! Atishoo!
> We all fall down!

Sarah smiled.

'Smirk at me, would you?' The voice suddenly gathered momentum like a train hurtling towards a tunnel. 'You impertinent article! You slut! Give me back my money or I'll strip the dirty rags off you and search them.' Her fist beat on Sarah's shoulder. 'You're a thief, Sarah Sweeney. A thief! A thief!'

Sound swelled up from inside and outside, and met, and made a mockery of the walls.

All the noise of a lifetime gathered and jabbled about.

The Benlin riveters, crowding inside high hulls, became frenzied. Trams rumbled and clanged and vied with the shipyards. Women called shrilly to each other. Men bawled and laughed and cursed and kicked balls. Children chanted. Somewhere a baby screamed. Suddenly Sarah screamed too.

140

Too rapid for thought, her hand darted out, grabbed a knife, whisked round and caught Mrs Fowler in the neck.

'Shut it! Shut it! Shut it!'

Mrs Fowler fell down.

Sarah stared at her.

Lender Lil was lying quietly on the floor.

> Atishoo! Atishoo!
> We all fall down!

An old woman lay on the floor in a heap.

'Poor soul!' Sarah murmured.

A noise at the door made her turn round. Baldy had come crashing into the kitchen in his shirt-tail.

'What the hell's going on?'

He froze at the sight of Sarah holding a blood-stained knife and his mother's body at her feet. Then he shrank, lost size as well as colour; everything about him squeezed smaller, until he was a pathetic creature trembling violently inside a too-big shirt. His legs began to buckle under him and he staggered, hands outstretched to grip the back of a chair for support.

Sarah rushed, arms ready to assist him, but like a wee boy he cried out in distress:

'Keep away from me. You've killed my mammy!'

Sarah looked down at the old woman again and in doing so noticed the knife. Opening her hands, she dropped it, waves of horror lapped away out, far out beyond her mind. She groped for something, anything she could do for Baldy before the tide came in.

'Go and get dressed, lad. Aye, that's what to do. We don't want folks seeing you like that, eh?'

'Then I'll have to go and get somebody. Oh, Jesus!' Baldy was muttering dazedly to himself. 'I'll go downstairs and tell Melvin. He'll know what to do. Oh, Jesus!'

'Go and get dressed, lad. Aye, that's what to do!'

Sarah wanted to remain where she was, thinking nothing, seeing nothing; only love of her man moved her on, and the instinctive knowledge, as yet unlinked with emotion, that maybe there wouldn't be much time left for loving him.

She followed Baldy out into the hall but when he floundered, still muttering instructions to himself, into the bedroom, she tiptoed to the front door.

She was the one who ought to tell Melvin. Baldy had done a hard night's work. He ought not to be upset. He mustn't be faced with the shameful ordeal of going downstairs to tell Melvin what she had done.

The waves were creeping closer as she clung to the iron banister, her feet hastening, stumbling down the spiral stairs. The waves rippled near, then receded with the assurance that nothing had happened. It was only a nightmare. Then they surged nearer to make her stomach heave and flutter, then disappeared again far into distance.

Melvin's wife opened the door and stared at her with huge eyes registering first a look of shy enquiry, then alarm.

'Your apron! There's blood! You've hurt yourself!'

Bewildered, Sarah stared down at herself, then up at Catriona.

'Ah've kil't Baldy's mammy!'

Different emotions scrambled over Catriona's face, changing and re-changing, jumbling senselessly together in panic. She jerked back, nursing her hands as if she'd been stung.

'Oh, no! Oh, no! Oh, what'll I do? Oh, how awful! Oh, but look at you! Oh, you poor thing. Come in just now. Come into the hall before anybody sees you.'

Sarah shuffled obediently in but her face creased and twisted 'I'm sorry, hen,' she apologized. 'Ah didn't mean to put ye to any trouble.'

'It's all right. I mean, don't worry about me. Wait there a minute. My mother's in. We were through in the front room having tea. My mother'll help you. You'll be all right. Don't worry. Just stand there a minute.'

She pushed the front door shut, her eyes still clinging with a mixture of horror and anguished pity to Sarah's bent, old-woman figure barely discernible now in the shadow of the hall except for the grey luminous face under the woolly headscarf and the fingers poking from thick woolly mittens.

Catriona flew into the front room and babbled out a rapid

stream of words to her mother.

'It's Sarah Fowler from upstairs. You remember, the poor soul that cried so much at my wedding. She's in a terrible state. She says she's killed somebody. I think she means her husand's mother. Oh, Mummy, talk to her, do something! Pour her a cup of tea while I waken Melvin. Yes, a hot sweet drink, that's good for shock. She's in a state of shock. She looks as if she doesn't know what's happened. She's waiting in the hall. I'll bring her through.'

'You'll do no such thing!' Hannah Munro managed to keep her voice down to a desperate hiss. 'Get that madwoman out of here! Get her out. Get her out before she murders the lot of us!'

For a moment Catriona's face froze in its expression of distress, then suddenly she burst into reckless speech again.

'You hypocrite! Hypocrite! Call yourself a Christian? Is this Christianity? What good's your Christianity if it's just a lot of talk?'

'Get rid of her, you fool! Get her out of the house before she murders us all.' Hannah was on her feet now, ruddy cheeks livid.

Catriona turned in a flurry of despair and darted back to the hall where Sarah was still helplessly waiting.

'I'll waken Melvin. No, my mother can tell Melvin. I'll help you upstairs. I'll make you a cup of tea.' She raised her voice. 'Mummy, tell Melvin! Tell him at once!'

She put an arm around Sarah, helped her out of the house and half-carried her back upstairs.

Sarah twisted round towards her, a pulse in her face pulling, throbbing, twitching, fluttering uncontrolled and uncontrollable.

'Ah'm terribly sorry, hen. Honest ah am. Ah'm that sorry for putting everybody to all this trouble!'

Chapter 19

Catriona sat at the kitchen table, hands balled on lap, head lowered. Opposite her, Fergus was kneeling up on his chair, his elbows resting on the table, his face cupped in his hands, watching her.

Melvin and Hannah sat on opposite sides of the kitchen fire.

'I'll never get over that as long as I live,' Hannah told Catriona for the umpteenth time. 'And the way you talked to me! I thought you'd gone off your head as well.' Her eyes rolled back to Melvin. 'And when I discovered she'd gone back upstairs with the murderess - may the good Lord forgive the poor woman - I nearly died!'

Melvin glowered.

'I told her to keep herself to herself. I told her not to have anything to do with the neighbours. I warned her especially about Sarah Fowler.'

'You needn't talk. If it hadn't been for you, she would never have been here, never got mixed up in any of this and I would never have come near the place either.'

'Nobody asked you to come.' Melvin stuck his face aggressively forward. 'But you've been here every day since we got married except for the holidays, and I suppose if you could have managed it you would have been with us then, too.'

'Yes, I would, I certainly would. I said from the beginning that no good would come of that girl coming here. I've good neighbours in Farmbank, kindly decent folk, but I told Robert - Clydend's one of the toughest districts in Glasgow, I said. I wouldn't live there and neither will that girl. But would he listen to me? Would he? Oh, no, not him! And now look what's happened. She's mixed up with a murder! A *murder*!'

'Well, it's all over now so for God's sake stop going on about it.'

'All over? All over? What about the trial? And have you

144

looked at that street down there? It's packed with sightseers.'

'It's nothing of the kind. There's a policeman moving everybody on.'

'Oh, yes, and we know where all the folk keep moving to. Into MacNair's shop, that's where they go. You're doing all right. You don't care.'

Melvin grabbed his pipe and tobacco pouch from the mantelpiece.

'You don't know what you're blethering about. I don't own the shop. I just manage the bakery for my father. I just get a wage like everybody else. Go and gripe to the old man if you've anything to say about how much money's coming in.'

'And that dreadful man - her husband - he's still there!'

'He didn't kill the old woman. Sarah did.'

'But he's insisting that it was him who took the money, borrowed it, he says, calm as you please. If I know anything about men, it's been all his fault!'

'Calm? Baldy? He's nearly demented. Do you not know anything about murders?'

'What a stupid question!' Hannah rolled her eyes. 'As if I'd want to know anything about such things.'

'Well, you ought to know that it's quite common to have people confessing to crimes when somebody's already been arrested. It happens all the time. In Baldy's case, he's obviously putting up a desperate fight to save his wife. No wonder the police won't believe him. It's pathetic.' He jerked his head towards Catriona who was still sitting in silence, eyes riveted on motionless hands, hypnotized. 'She told you what Sarah said to the police when they questioned her - "Ah stole Lil's money. Ah'm a thief." She kept repeating it over and over again so it's an open and shut case. It doesn't matter what Baldy does now. They'll hang her!'

For the first time Catriona looked up.

'Don't say that!'

'No,' Hannah agreed. 'You shouldn't talk about these things. You'll only upset her. Don't worry, child. The poor woman's mad. They'll lock her away in an asylum. Something has to be done to protect decent, law-abiding folk from people like that, but there's no need to talk about it.'

'What's the good of acting like ostriches? Murder with theft,' Melvin insisted. 'They'll hang her. And quite right too. Murderers are nothing but a menace. Whether we like it or not we've got to get rid of them. They're no use.'

'Sarah's no use?' Catriona echoed. 'Is that all there is to say about her?'

'Aw, shut up! There's been far too much emotional guff about the bloody murderer. Its always the same. What about the victim? Nobody ever bothers about the victim!'

'I saw her lying there. I'll never forget her as long as I live. But what good is killing Sarah going to do? It won't bring Lil Fowler back.'

'Well? Tell her!' Melvin cocked a head in Hannah's direction.

'Tell her what?' Hannah asked.

'An eye for an eye, and a tooth for a tooth! By rights she should get the same as she gave. Somebody should stab a knife into her throat!'

'Be quiet!' Catriona rose, shaking so much that the table rattled under her hands. 'Fergus, go through to the bedroom, please.'

'What are you picking on him for?' Melvin gaped with astonishment. 'What has he done?'

'He's a child. He shouldn't be listening to all this. He'll be having nightmares. Fergus, go through to the bedroom I said!'

'Stay where you are!' Melvin's voice coarsened. 'I give the orders in my house.'

Hannah gave a high-pitched sarcastic laugh. 'Would you listen to the conceit of the man. Well?' Her eyes prodded Catriona to speak again. 'Are you going to let him away with it, child?'

'Mummy, please!' She was sweating now, the tablecloth under her hands wet and sticky. She was shaking so much she was terrified that she was about to take a stroke. 'I don't need you to . . . to force words into my mouth, and I'm not a child.'

'You don't need me? That's what that evil man has been putting into your head, is it?'

'For God's sake,' Melvin groaned.

146

Hannah rose up. 'Look at him. Listen to him. If you don't realize what a coarse, selfish, vain brute he is, then you're a fool and I pity you!'

'But, Mummy!'

Melvin levelled his pipe at her. 'Will you stop that, you stupid, stuttering ninny! You're bumping my good table and making scrape marks on the linoleum.'

'Listen to him!' Hannah jerked on her gloves and snatched up her handbag in readiness to leave. 'Never in all the years we've been married has your daddy talked to me like that. I'm sorry for you, Catriona. You're not fit to cope with that man. The moment you married him you began making a stick to break your own back. He'll be the death of you yet that man. As God's my maker, I swear it. That man doesn't care about you or anybody else. All that man cares about is himself.'

Melvin aimed his pipe at Hannah. 'Get out of my house!'

'I'm going.' Hannah glanced haughtily round at him. 'But only because I'm good and ready to go.'

'And don't come back!'

'I'll come back as often as my daughter needs me. She'll need me, all right. The poor child obviously doesn't realize what she's got herself into.'

'I'll see you to the door, Mummy.'

'Stay where you are!' Melvin bellowed. 'You belong to me now, and you'll do as I tell you.'

Hannah let out another tinkle of sarcastic laughter.

'For goodness' sake! And here was me thinking your kind of Scotsman was dying out! You're needing to be taught a few lessons, my lad. You're needing to be brought up to date.'

Despite her mother's merry tone, it was obvious that underneath the haughty manner she was flustered. Her heart was visibly palpitating, and her ruddy cheeks looked hot. Catriona couldn't help admiring the older woman's courage and silently reviled herself for her own weakness, as she remained leaning on the table and allowed her to walk alone into the hall and away from the house.

She longed to run after her and beg forgiveness.

Melvin settled back to fill his pipe.

147

'Thank God that's got rid of her!'

Catriona's rage rushed up and out like boiling lava. 'Don't you dare speak about my mother like that. Especially in front of Fergus. And don't raise your voice to me and order me about. Don't you dare! Don't you dare!'

'You know,' calmly Melvin lit a match, held it to his pipe and puffed a few times, 'you look positively ugly.'

Her eyes immediately lowered. She sat down, her hands clasped in her lap.

'You're not much of a housewife, either, are you? My Betty used to have every floor in this house and every stick of furniture shining like a new pin. A good skin of polish protects things. Didn't you know that? Polish protects and takes care of things and makes them last. You've got to use some elbow grease of course. You've got to put on a good skin.'

'And, Daddy!' Fergus's high-pitched childish voice interrupted. 'My porridge was cold this morning.'

Melvin jerked forward in his chair, pipe forgotten.

'Do you hear that? His porridge was cold. What do you mean by it? What excuse have you got?'

Catriona looked up.

'An old woman has been murdered. A young woman, a neighbour of ours, is in danger of being hanged. And you ask me what excuse I have for letting Fergus's porridge get cold?'

'Aw, shut up! What happens to the Fowlers is their business. Your business is to attend to this house and me and my son.'

Catriona lowered her eyes and said no more, but she had learned something important.

She now knew how Sarah Fowler must have felt and how easy it would be for anyone to feel like committing murder.

Jimmy made his way slowly up the stairs. His face showed signs of strain. Thoughts of Mrs Fowler, of Sarah and of Baldy who was now practically living night and day in the bakehouse and talking desperately and incessantly about his wife and the trial - worrying thoughts were driving him to distraction. During the day while he worked, and tossing and turning and sweating in bed during the night, vivid three-dimensional pictures in realistic colour whirred and whirled through his mind, horrifying beyond all horror.

Fear for Sarah's fate jostled with anger and the intensity of his suffering for neighbour and friend. A thousand times in his imagination he was with her in Duke Street prison, a thousand times he made the imaginary walk with her to the scaffold.

He had known Sarah, Mrs Fowler and Baldy all his life.

He had not the slightest doubt that Sarah must have been strained beyond all human endurance. He had told the police so in no uncertain terms. The most terrible thing of all was that so many people did *not* know Sarah, or Baldy, or Mrs Fowler.

To strangers this appeared only as a brutal crime motivated by greed and theft, and perpetrated on a helpless old woman. A young blonde from a tough area of Glasgow had robbed a helpless old lady and when the old lady had pleaded for the return of her money the young peroxide blonde had calmly lifted a kitchen knife and stabbed her mother-in-law to death.

Letters in the papers, signed with pseudonyms like 'Off With Their Heads' and 'Vigilante' and 'Shocked', argued back and forward about capital punishment. The hate, the lust for revenge, the violence shown in some of the letters nauseated and depressed him beyond words. They talked of hanging being a deterrent. He couldn't understand why. There never had been any evidence to show that it deterred. It certainly had not deterred Sarah.

How many other Sarahs had there been, he wondered? How many Sarahs yet to come?

He stopped on the first landing, his chest tight, his breath catching in his throat.

'Are you feeling all right?' Melvin's wife was standing in her doorway, a polishing cloth and a tin of polish in her hand. She smiled a ghost of a smile at him, her eyes avoiding his. 'I'm Catriona. You're Jimmy Gordon, aren't you?'

'Yes.' He wiped his floury hands on his apron before offering her one. 'I only wish I was meeting you in happier circumstances. It's . . . It's . . .' He shook his head, words failing him.

'I know,' Catriona agreed. 'I can't sleep at night just thinking about it. That poor old woman. And poor Sarah . . .'

He was snatched back to the immediate present by the touch

149

of her hand. He found himself staring in silence at the gentle face, his fingers tightening round her fingers, surprised by the familiarity of the warm flesh.

'I listen to you playing the piano -' she broke the silence with a small tremulous voice. 'It's lovely.'

Their hands slid apart and Jimmy became aware of an aloneness he had never noticed before.

'Do you mean that?'

She nodded. 'Melvin has a piano in the front room. It used to belong to Betty. Nobody plays it now, though. I think it's badly out of tune.'

'I'll come down and try it sometime, if you like. See what I can do.'

'Thank you.' She blushed. 'You'll be welcome any time.'

'I love music,' he confided. 'At one time I had very grand ideas. Oh, very grand ideas. I was going to be a concert pianist. A concert pianist, no less.'

'Why didn't you?'

He hesitated, not wanting to talk of his illness in case it would decrease his manliness in her eyes, unable to explain about keeping a roof over his mother's head in case that sounded self-pitying or conceited.

'I wasn't good enough.'

'I don't believe it . . .' Quickly she looked up, her sincerity unmistakable. 'You're wonderfully talented!' Her blush deepened and she turned her attention to polishing her front door again.

'You're very kind.' He smiled, then continued his way upstairs, more intensely disturbed than ever.

Chapter 20

Duke Street Prison, official address 71 Duke Street, was a dark, long, antediluvian building with row upon row of high-up, heavily barred slits, and was bounded by a dismal wall. The jutting front gable of the building had a clock that the tram-traveller could see over the wall. The clock had never been known to go.

The prison used to be a house of correction for women 'where they may be whipped daily'. It had also seen many children punished in the past. In one year alone, there had been imprisoned in Duke Street five children under ten years of age, fifteen between the ages of ten and eleven, seventy-six from twelve years to thirteen years, and a hundred and fifty-nine prisoners in the fourteen to fifteen years-of-age class.

This was where Oscar Slater had frantically protested his innocence.

Along the west wall were tablets that marked the graves of hanged murderers. The initials of each murderer and the year of the hanging were inscribed on the tablets.

Unlike in America, the bodies of prisoners were not handed over to relatives. The reason stated in the Royal Commission report was: 'hanging leaves the body with the neck elongated'. The Home Office had stated that 'as now carried out, execution by hanging can be regarded as speedy and certain'. The Home Office was referring to a change in technique, a drop of variable length and a sliding ring which was supposed to hold the knot of the noose under the left jaw. This, they hoped, would prevent the difficulties of the past when the agony of suffocation without loss of consciousness could last up to twenty minutes, not to mention innumerable forms of mutilation: joints torn off by hitting the edge of the trap, heads partly or entirely torn off, and people having to be hanged twice and even three times in succession.

151

This innovation referred only to England.

When hangman Pierrepoint was questioned about the Scottish methods of hanging, he admitted: 'It is very very old, antediluvian. It is time it was altered in Scotland.'

These facts, gleaned from innumerable books, papers and authorities on the subject, milled round in Jimmy's mind as he accompanied Baldy on one of his visits to Sarah in Duke Street prison.

All the time that Baldy was talking loudly and aggressively about how Sarah was going to be all right and how he'd batter anybody to pulp with his bare hands if they even looked at her in the wrong way, Jimmy was silent, his thoughts completely swamping him.

Only the other day when he'd gone into town for his mother's prescription - she had become so worried and upset about Sarah, she couldn't sleep without taking tablets - he had overheard a snatch of conversation in the chemist's between a very respectable-looking man and woman. They had been voicing the opinion that they hoped the Fowler woman would not be hanged, although no doubt she deserved it - but, of course, they decided eventually, 'hanging is quick and clean - they don't feel anything - they never know anything about it!'

He had turned on them, eyes blazing, heart pounding like a sledgehammer in his chest, and told them exactly what hanging meant, described it to them in accurate detail, sparing them nothing.

They had been affronted and the man snorted indignantly. 'How dare you speak like that in front of a lady, you young horror! Don't you know you shouldn't talk about these things? It's not decent!'

'You made the statement,' Jimmy protested. 'You said that hanging was quick and clean and the prisoner doesn't feel anything or doesn't know anything about it. I've only told you the facts.'

'We don't want to stand here listening to horror stories from you,' the woman raised her voice, at the same time tugging her companion's sleeve, desperate for escape. 'I don't know what this country's coming to when respectable people can't come into a chemist's shop without being pestered.'

'I've only given you the facts,' Jimmy insisted.

But the couple had stamped away from the shop in a flurry of fury. No doubt they would soon calm down over a glass or two of brandy or a nice cup of tea.

The worst of it was that while people like that were tucked safely away in their own unthinking and unimaginative little worlds, others were being allowed to *act* and, as a result, people were suffering and had suffered and would continue to suffer in a million different ways; in poverty and in ignorance and in wars, and as a result of wars, on every side, all over the world.

As soon as they entered the prison, even Baldy fell quiet. The place was incredibly gloomy and oppressive. Inside this ancient building the Sarah they knew waited under sentence of death.

A petition for reprieve had been forwarded to the Secretary of State for Scotland. The petition asked that the death sentence be commuted to penal servitude and referred to evidence of mental aberration at the time she committed the crime. Reference was also made to the jury's unanimous recommendation to mercy.

Baldy left the silent white-faced Jimmy in the gatehouse and, barrel chest stuck out, big shoulders back, gorilla-hands clenched in pockets, he strode after the prison officer who led him across the prison yard and into the main building to where he could speak to his wife.

Sarah was looking prettier than she had done for years.

Her blonde hair was brushed back and shining and she was wearing a green dress and a pink woollen cardigan.

Baldy's muscle-hard face screwed into a wink.

'You're looking great, hen. You're going to be all right, eh?'

Her face crinkled.

'Ah'm all right as long as ah've got you, sure ah am, Baldy.'

'By God you are, hen. I won't let anybody lay a finger on you. You're my wife. Are they treatin' you all right, eh?'

'Och, aye. Everyone in here's nicer than the other. They're all that kind to me. Fancy, the polis and all the high-heed yins. They're all that kind. Ye've no idea! Even the holy yin comes to chat with me. And the food's just lovely too!'

'You're all right then, hen?'

'Och, aye, don't you be worryin' yourself so much about me. You're an awful man, so you are.'

There was a pause while she gazed at him and smiled at him. 'Know something?' He suddenly broke the silence.

'What?'

'You're just like what you were when we got married, remember?'

'Aye, fine.' Her voice saddened. 'Ah haven't been much of a wife to you, lad.'

'I told you not to talk like that so shut your mouth.'

The smile tried to flicker back but her eyes had gone wistful. She hesitated, the words on her tongue longing to come out but afraid of the embarrassment and the hurt they might cause.

'Ah've always loved you though, Baldy,' she managed at last. 'Have you been fond of me, eh? I mean before . . . Ah mean, ah don't expect . . . Ah don't deserve anything now . . . And ah'm that sorry, Baldy . . . ah'm that ashamed.'

'Don't talk like that, you dope!'

'Ah've caused you nothing but trouble, ah know.'

'You're my wife!' he insisted stubbornly as if that was enough, as if that settled everything.

Melvin had let Lizzie in and then gone down to the bakehouse to check with Jimmy about how much jam and fondant and fruit and other items needed to be ordered.

Catriona, nerves ragged with lack of sleep, was left feeling very ill-at-ease with her next-door neighbour. Already Lizzie had made several complaints and accusations against her.

Only the other day after she had put out crumbs in the back court for the birds, Lizzie had limped after her with a brush and shovel, swept up the crumbs and angrily complained to her: 'I know what you're doing, you sly little minx, but you won't get away with it.'

'I have no idea,' she protested when she recovered from her initial surprise, 'what on earth you're going on about!'

'Oh, you know, all right! Don't tell any of your lies! That baby-face of yours maybe fools the men but it doesn't fool me.'

'Know *what*, for goodness' sake?' Irritation at being bothered by trivialities at such a tragic time gave her voice unusual emphasis.

'You know that I've just hung up that washing, don't you?'

'Yes, but what's that got to do with me putting out crumbs for the birds?'

'You know those birds are going to fly over my washing to reach your crumbs. You know they're going to do their filthy business on their way over. All over my clean washing. You know, all right!'

'Oh! I've never heard anything so ridiculous!'

At any other time she might have giggled, but laughter, when Sarah was lying in the condemned cell at Duke Street prison, was something obscene. Everyone in the narrow cobbled street was talking in low-pitched whispers of voices, gathering in serious-faced crowds at corners and at close-mouths and in each other's houses.

She pushed impatiently past Lizzie and left her without uttering another word.

Now here she was again and at Melvin's invitation, to stop her thinking about Sarah no doubt.

'You're thinking and talking far too much about Sarah Fowler,' he'd exploded. 'And what you're wasting your time and mine on her for beats me. After all, whether you like it or not, the woman's a killer and she'll have to pay the penalty. She should have thought about the consequences before she carved up Mrs Fowler. She's nobody but herself to blame.' And eventually he had crushed the words of protest that came rushing to her mouth by his 'Aw shut up! Nothing you think or say or do is going to make one bit of difference. You're not the Secretary for Scotland!'

His contempt for her added flames of anger to her distress and she had tried to relieve her feelings by throwing herself into a frenzy of housework, working so feverishly at cleaning and polishing the place with such thoroughness that she felt certain he would never again be able to find any excuse to criticize her.

Yet he had been more furious with her than ever and had glowered at her and poked and peered about until, just before

155

stamping out of the house, he'd shoved the chip pan under her nose.

'Look at that. It's a disgrace. Do you not even know how to clean a chip pan? The outside's thick with filthy grease.'

Then she had heard him muttering to Lizzie on the landing and Lizzie had limped in with a gleam in her eyes, looking very pleased with herself.

'Hello, my precious wee son.' She leaned over Fergus who was on his way out to play in the back green. 'Here's a sixpence to buy yourself lots and lots of sweeties.'

'Lizzie, you simply must stop doing that,' Catriona gasped with annoyance. 'It just makes him sick and spoils him from eating a proper meal.'

'Huh!' Lizzie swung round and jerked up on her painful hip. You'll not tell me what to do, or what not to do with my own wee baby, you impertinent upstart. What do you know about my wee Fergie?'

'I know he's *not* your wee Fergie!'

Catriona immediately regretted her hasty words because she saw the wound they made before it was covered by hatred.

'How dare you talk to me like that,' Lizzie said harshly. 'You sly, wicked . . .'

'Oh, be quiet!' Irritation overcame her again. 'I'm sick of listening to your stupid talk. I'm not sly. I'm telling you straight to your face. I don't want you to keep interfering and spoiling Fergus.'

'Wait till Melvin hears about this! "Keep an eye on her, and Fergus," he says. "As soon as my back's turned she'll be wandering about there like the ghost of Lady Macbeth," he says. He'll hear about this, all right. You're not fit to look after a child. What children have you ever looked after before? What do you know about children?'

'There's the door, Lizzie!'

After it slammed shut with a violence that rocked the house, Catriona covered her face with her hands.

She waited. After the noise came the silence, and after the silence, her thoughts.

Suddenly she tore off her apron, grabbed the key from its

156

hook, flew from the empty house and pelted upstairs.

Amy Gordon, like a woman caught unawares by old age, shuffled across the hall in answer to her knock and peeked round the door, her motherly face bewildered.

'Oh, it's you, dear.' She sighed with relief. 'Come in, come in, I'm so pleased to see you. It's awful to be alone at a time like this, isn't it?'

She led Catriona through to her front room. 'I was just sitting here having a wee rest and looking out the window. Usually I've got Baldy in but he's next door just now with half the street in beside him and I'm glad. Poor man, he's trying so hard and with so much noise to make out he's not in the least bothered, but everybody knows he's nearly demented and he's awful hard to thole. I'm exhausted with him and glad some of the others are taking a turn. You'll drink a wee cup of tea, dear?'

'No, thank you.'

'Och, just a wee cup. It'll be no bother to make and you're welcome.'

'I couldn't drink it, honestly. I just wanted the company. I knew you'd understand.'

'Yes, of course, dear. Sit down and make yourself comfy.' Mrs Gordon sighed and shook her head. 'I'm worried about Jimmy, too. He gets so worked up about everything. He gets all excited about far less important things than this, so you can imagine what he's like just now.'

'I've been speaking to him. He looks awfully pale and dark under the eyes. Has he been keeping all right? He says it's lack of sleep but nobody's getting much sleep and I suppose we all appear a bit wan. It looks more than that with him somehow . . . he seems . . . I don't know . . .' Suddenly hot-cheeked she floundered in embarrassment but words - 'His face haunts me!' - escaped before she could stop them.

Jimmy's mother was too preoccupied with her own worries, however, to notice anything out of the ordinary about her guest's tone of voice.

'The lad was so ill.' Plump hands clasped and unclasped on aproned lap. 'Before your time, dear. A few years back. Rheumatic fever it was and it left its mark on his heart. The doctor said he'd be all right as long as he took good care of himself and kept himself calm, as if my Jimmy could ever do any such thing.'

'Oh, dear!' Catriona's heart pounded louder and louder stronger and stronger, like the beat of some fearful tribal drum, until it was shaking the very roots of her existence.

'He's got plenty of spirit,' Mrs Gordon went on. 'I agreed with the doctor about that. He said Jimmy had youth on his side too and he'd be all right but, oh, lassie, lassie, I'm awful worried about my boy. He's that fond of Sarah Fowler. She used to come in here every day and take a turn looking after him when he was ill and let me lie down for a wee sleep.

'She was that gentle with him, too, the way she used to sponge his hands and face, and he remembers, you see. She's always been such a kindly wee soul, Sarah, and aye ready with a smile or a joke. She used to have Jimmy grinning from ear to ear even while he was not able to move a muscle for the rheumatic pains.' Suddenly she stopped, her expression anxiously alerting. 'I think that's him now. Aye, he's coming through. He always makes straight for the piano every time he comes in.'

Her face acquired a forced brightness as soon as her son appeared in the room. 'Hello, son. This wee lassie's come upstairs to keep me company. Wasn't that kind? I'll go and make a cup of tea now.'

Rising she turned to smile at Catriona. 'He loves his cup of tea when he comes in.' Her smile returned to Jimmy who was standing very still, gazing across the room at Catriona. 'Don't you, son?'

He winked round at her.

'You're the best old tea-maker in Glasgow!'

'Less of the "old" I keep telling you, you rascal,' she scolded as she passed. 'Sit down at that piano and give the wee lassie a song and a tune. I won't be a minute and we'll all have a cup. It'll put some pith into us and make us feel better. There's nothing like a good strong cup of tea.'

The room was silent after she went out. Jimmy kept standing near the piano, massaging his fingers, his eyes never leaving Catriona until her cheeks flushed rose-pink.

'Please play something,' she said at last, wanting to keep the dark eyes holding hers, but terrified of the welter of emotion his penetrating stare was firing into life.

He sat down at the piano and allowed his fingers to flow over the keys before he began to speak to the music.

> 'I have heard the mavis singing
> His love song to the morn;
> I have seen the dew-drop clinging
> To the rose just newly born;
> But a sweeter song has cheered me
> At the evening's gentle close;
> And I've seen an eye still brighter
> Than the dew drop on the rose.
> 'Twas thy voice, my gentle Mary,
> And thine artless winning smile,
> That made this world an Eden,
> Bonnie Mary of Argyll . . .'

Chapter 21

'Sex and aggression,' Jimmy expostulated in between gulps of tea. 'Sex and aggression, beside tribal loyalty, are the most powerful biological drives.'

Hannah Munro tried not to look shocked. She had come upstairs in search of her daughter and also to wait while Rab next door took his daily (as well as nightly) turn with the rest at listening to Baldy and struggling to calm him down.

Hannah had never uttered the word 'sex' herself nor ever heard it spoken out loud - let alone in mixed company; and if Jimmy had not been such an obviously well-meaning young man she would have gathered all the dignity at her disposal and swept from the house. As it was, she remained straight-backed on the edge of her seat, sipping tea and bracing herself because she sensed, and rightly, that worse was still to come.

'And you see,' Jimmy's eyes flashed around, 'it's a question of keeping the savage inside all of us under control. Strictly controlled, you see. The sexual appetites usually find a reasonable amount of acceptable outlets but aggression has almost none. Here's where our danger lies. Lies waiting to rear up and destroy the civilized part of us. The murder trial appeals to the cruel savage hiding inside us; like a gladiator in an arena, a human being is fighting for his life and the thrill is the same as in the arena - will the thumbs go up, or down!'

'How true!' Hannah murmured, impressed despite herself. 'There's a beast in every man, right enough.'

'Now, now, son,' his mother pleaded. 'I wish you wouldn't get all worked up like that.'

'Oh, Mother, I wish everybody would get worked up.'

'Perhaps people are losing sight of the real meaning of charity.' Catriona gazed tentatively across at Jimmy, hoping she had said something that would please him, and seeing his nod of agreement, was encouraged to go on. 'Charity has come to

160

mean just putting a few pennies in a collection box, hasn't it? But the Bible says it's much, much more than that. It says . . .'

'Yes, indeed, child,' Hannah's strong voice interrupted. 'The Good Book says: "Though I have all faith so I could remove mountains, and have not charity, I am nothing. And though I speak with the tongues of men and of angels, and have not charity, I am become as sounding brass or a tinkling cymbal."'

'Yes,' Catriona whispered and lowered her eyes. But she could still feel Jimmy's gaze on her face, warm with understanding.

Her mother and Mrs Gordon continued the conversation but their voices were like meaningless droning far away in the background.

There was something far more powerful in the room, something silent, invisible, yet reaching out, touching, caressing the sensitive nerve ends of every secret corner of her soul.

'Bonnie wee thing,' Jimmy said very quietly. 'Cannie wee thing.'

His words, though almost a whisper, affected her like delicious electric shocks.

'Did you say something, son?' Mrs Gordon turned to him.

He smiled.

'I was asking Catriona if she knew any of the poems or songs of Robert Burns.'

'Oh, yes.' Catriona looked up, wide-eyed now, and breathless. 'I think he's wonderful.'

'Well, by jovie,' Mrs Gordon laughed. 'You and Jimmy should get on fine. He knows his Burns off by heart.' Then, as if suddenly remembering Sarah, and feeling ashamed at having laughed, she gave a big sigh. 'Aye, he was a great man. My husband was fond of him, too. Many a Burns supper he attended. Was that the door, Jimmy? Yes, go and open it, son.'

'It'll be my husband,' Hannah said, rising. 'It's time we were away, Mrs Gordon. We'll be over again, though. It's an awful business, isn't it?'

'You'll remember poor Sarah in your prayers, Mrs Munro?'

'Yes, I will indeed. May the good Lord help and protect her. Come on, Catriona. It's time you were going too, child.'

161

Jimmy was talking to Rab when they reached the hall.

'Is there still somebody with him?'

Rab nodded. 'Tam and Sandy are still there and two or three from down the street. They'll stay with him until it's time for work again.'

'You're dead beat,' Hannah accused him in a comparatively friendly, almost proud tone. 'Look at the colour of your face!'

Rab's shaggy brows pushed down. The matter of the headshrinker had been relegated, swamped by the more urgent and tragic turn of events, but he had not forgotten or forgiven Hannah. 'How can I look at the colour of my face, woman? I don't go around with a mirror hanging on the end of my nose!'

Hannah rolled her eyes towards Mrs Gordon.

'Men!'

Jimmy smiled down at Catriona when the others were making their goodbyes.

'I'll play for you,' he said. 'Will you listen?'

She smiled up at him, her glowing eyes giving him his answer.

Later, not long after she returned downstairs, the house began to echo, vibrate fill gloriously to the rafters with Beethoven, Tchaikovsky and Rachmaninov until Melvin flung down his newspaper and bawled through his moustache at the pitch of his voice, 'Jumpin' Jesus! If it's not one damned thing it's another! Has Jimmy Gordon gone berserk now? I can't hear myself think for that bloody racket!'

'Be quiet!' Catriona burst out before she realized what she was saying. 'How can you talk like that about such wonderful music, such perfect artistry?'

'I'll talk any way I like in my own house - and since when have you been a music-lover?'

Suddenly she felt frightened, not only for herself, but for Jimmy. Her eyes avoided the angry stare now bulging with suspicion. She shrugged.

'Anything to keep my mind off the murder and that poor woman lying in Duke Street prison.'

She said the words to protect Jimmy, yet she could not bear how disloyal to his talent they sounded. She sought and found for his sake a new well of courage.

162

'But why shouldn't I enjoy good music if I want to? That is good music, you know, and Jimmy Gordon is an unusually talented pianist.'

'What's going on here?' Melvin got up, his voice incredulous. 'Is there something between you two?'

'Don't be ridiculous!' Catriona stood her ground, her eyes refusing to be beaten down. 'Am I not even to be allowed to listen to music?'

'You're not going to be allowed to speak to me like that!' Suddenly he flung back his head and gave an ear splitting roar that reverberated painfully through her head.

'Jimmy, you bastard! If you don't give that bloody piano a rest, I'll come up there and kick it from here to Kingdom Come!'

The piano did not stop. It finished the piece it had been playing. Then it began another - the different, brighter, cockier rhythm of 'Gin a body meet a body coming through the rye'.

Melvin gritted his teeth.

'Hear that! He's a determined, impertinent young bastard! I don't know why my father puts up with him. If it was left to me he would have had his cards long ago!'

Catriona kept silent though she longed to flay him with bitterness.

What a fool she had been to marry him. She realized that now. She had been far too young and her world had been smaller, more confined, more naive than any nunnery. He had taken unfair advantage.

There were times when she tried not to blame him, when she fully accepted the responsibility herself, but this was not one of those occasions.

He had been older and far more experienced than she. He had rushed her into a loveless marriage of convenience. All he wanted was a housekeeper and someone to look after his son. He wanted sex too, of course - oh, plenty of sex and at the oddest, most inconvenient and nerve-racking times, as if he did it purposely to degrade and torment her.

There never had been any mention of love. They seldom kissed and when they did he had the peculiarly insulting habit of wiping his mouth and his moustache with the back of his hand

163

immediately afterwards as if to remove the slightest taste of her.

'Now he's got Lexy mooning after him, the old man tells me.' Melvin relaxed back in his chair again, forgetting his suspicions. 'Nuts about him she is, and making no secret of it. What's got into her all of a sudden I haven't a clue. She's been working down there since not long after she left school and never a bit of bother and now all of a sudden she goes all cow's eyes and weak-kneed over him. It's bound to affect her work. I told the old man - something'll have to be done about that guy. But all I get for my troubles is told to shut up. "I can manage Jimmy. You shut up and mind your own business," he squeaks at me. At *me*! The old sod's soft in the head. It's time he retired altogether.'

'Is that the girl that lives up in one of the attic flats?'

'That's her. Sexy Lexy they call her. She's a buxom piece.'

'She's pretty, isn't she?' Her voice struggled to sound casual and smother the misery underneath it. 'Is Jimmy in love with her?'

'Don't be a fool! She's as common as dirt. He's had her out though. I'll give you three guesses what for!'

She felt sick.

'Jimmy Gordon's not like you.'

'What?' Melvin suddenly guffawed with laughter. 'I wouldn't be too sure. He's only a boy compared with me, of course. I know what women like, eh?'

She froze, terrified to move or say anything that might incite him to demonstrate his sexual prowess right there and then.

'Well?' His voice loudened. 'Don't I?'

She managed to smile.

'Betty wrote some lovely letters, I remember. She must have been very fond of you. What age was Fergus when she died?'

Hearing herself, she felt amazed. It was like someone making polite conversation with a stranger. Then suddenly she realized he was a stranger and, to her, he would never be anything else.

Bitterness drowned in sadness. She didn't hate him. He didn't mean any harm. There wasn't necessarily a thing wrong with him as a husband - if he had the right wife, a wife like Betty for instance. On one point she was quite certain. She was not the right wife for him. Yet she had agreed to his proposal of

164

marriage of her own free will and had stood up in the Hall and agreed to love, honour and obey him until 'death us do part'.

Even now, she could hardly credit it.

I must have been mad, she thought.

'Oh, he was only a baby.'

'What?' Legs shaking, she groped for a chair.

'Fergus. He was only a baby when Betty died. I told you before.'

'Did you?'

'I don't think I told you about the christening, though.' He lounged back, a glaze of pride lifting his face. 'It was the best do folks round about here had been to in years. There wasn't a dry eye in this house.'

'What do you mean?'

'It was just the day before Betty died. I knew she couldn't last much longer and I wanted to do everything I could for her before the end. That was the day I sent for her girlfriend - Jenny something-or-other. I never could remember that girl's name. And I got a preacher to come and baptize Fergus and I propped Betty up on the settee in the front room and put Fergus in her arms. I invited all the neighbours to the christening. That room was packed and of course I had it looking lovely, all polished to perfection and clean curtains up and the carpet shampooed. I had given Betty a bath and bought her a new nightie and a bedjacket and brushed her hair - she had long hair the very same as you - but she was just skin and bone and she looked so pathetic and obviously not strong enough to hold the baby, so I knelt beside the settee and supported him for her while the minister conducted the service. I'm telling you there wasn't a dry eye in this house.'

Catriona sat transfixed on the chair opposite from him.

Eventually becoming aware of her silence, he eyed her curiously.

'What's wrong with you? You look as if you've seen a ghost!'

Her face crumpled.

'Come here, stupid!' He leaned forward, caught hold of her arm and dragged her across to him until she was sitting on his knee. 'There's no use crying for Betty now. I cried right enough and I'm not ashamed to admit it. I cried like a baby in front of everyone at her funeral and I've cried to myself many a time since. But crying doesn't bring anyone back. I had to face facts eventually.' He held her head down on his shoulder and stroked her hair. 'So don't cry, darlin',' he told her in the gentlest tone he'd ever used to her. 'You're my wife now. I've got you to look after now, eh?'

'Oh, Melvin!' She squeezed her fists against her mouth in an unsuccessful attempt to contain her sobbing. 'I'm frightened!'

Chapter 22

Early in the afternoon, telegrams from the Home Secretary, intimating that no reprieve had been granted, were received by the Lord Provost of Glasgow, Sir Andrew Finlay, and the town clerk, Sir Meikle Tate.

The telegram to the Lord Provost said: 'The Secretary for Scotland is unable to discover sufficient grounds to justify him in advising interference with the due course of law in the case of Sarah Fowler, now lying under sentence of death.'

No doubt Sarah's pleasant, well-balanced and co-operative behaviour before, during and after the trial had weighed heavily against her agent's plea of insanity.

Shortly after receiving the telegram, as was the custom, the Lord Provost and the town clerk proceeded to Duke Street Prison to inform the prisoner of her fate.

They were received by the governor, and Dr Stewart, and the Reverend McNeill who accompanied them in solemn, dignified procession to a room in the section reserved for women.

A female warder went to the condemned cell to fetch the prisoner.

Sarah welcomed her with a smile.

'Hallo, hen. Is it ma man come tae see me?'

'No, Mrs Fowler,' the woman said. 'It's the Lord Provost and the town clerk. Come on, I'll take you to them.'

'The Lord Provost and the town clerk?' Sarah was deeply impressed, deeply grateful. 'Would you believe it. Ah told ma man that all the high-heed yins were bein' that kind to me but ah never dreamt that anybody as high-up as the Lord Provost would come tae pay me a visit. And the town clerk, too!'

She tidied back her hair and tugged down her green prison dress and fumbled with the buttons of the pink cardigan as she accompanied the wardress along the corridor.

Entering the room she was more impressed and awestruck

167

than ever when she discovered not only the imposing figures of Sir Andrew Finlay and Sir Meikle Tate, but the governor, the doctor and the holy yin as well.

She cleared her throat.

'It's awfi kind o' ye all . . .'

'Sh . . . sh . . . !' the wardress reprimanded.

Sarah sucked in her lips in a gesture of embarrassed apology. Then, as if to make up for her lapse, she crinkled her face into an expression of rapt concentration on what the Lord Provost was obviously preparing to say.

'Mrs Fowler,' he began at last. 'It is with profound regret that I am obliged to be the bearer of a sad message. I am deeply sorry to inform you that the Secretary for Scotland has not seen his way to grant you a reprieve.'

Sarah's features relaxed. She looked bewildered.

She allowed the wardress to take her arm and lead her towards the door.

Then her legs buckled under her. The prison doctor rushed to the wardress's assistance and between them they supported and half-carried her from the room.

'Baldy!' The corridors began to echo with whimpers. 'Baldy!' The whimpers quavered louder. 'Baldy!'

And louder.

Until the pitiful cries for her husband were muffled by the clang of the cell door.

Jimmy paced back and forward.

'It's barbaric!' He stopped to twist out his cigarette in an ashtray. 'Barbaric!'

'Jimmy, son, please! Try to keep calm!' His mother pleated and unpleated her apron between her fingers, her anxious eyes never leaving his face.

Catriona was hovering near. Lexy was there, too.

'Calm? Calm?' He gesticulated wildly. 'How can I keep calm? They're going to strangle Sarah Fowler in the morning!'

'Ohi! Ohi! Jimmy!' Lexy's face twisted grotesquely as she burst into tears. 'Don't say that. She was always so nice to me!'

'But it's true, Lexy,' he said brokenly, and lit another cigarette.

168

Lexy began to wail and Mrs Gordon put an arm round her and persuaded her from the room.

'Jimmy, stop it!' Catriona blocked his way as he made to start pacing again. 'Nothing can be done now. You'll only make yourself ill.' She put a restraining hand on his arm. 'You've tried your best. You've written to the press. You've gathered petitions. You've organized pickets outside the prison. No human being could possibly have done more than you and Baldy and all Sarah's neighbours and friends.'

'Oh, Catriona, Catriona!'

'Sh . . . sh!'

Her hand tightened on him. She felt the warmth of his body and gazing up she longed to touch the thick unruly hair, the dear emotional face; to hold him close to her, caress him, soothe him with soft secret whispers, move closer and closer, melt into him, to be one with him, never to break apart.

'Catriona!'

'Sh . . . sh . . . Jimmy, love, please.'

She turned away as Mrs Gordon, accompanied this time by a red-nosed, red-eyed Sandy, came back into the room.

'Is Melvin still there?' she asked Sandy.

He nodded and his lips puttered in and out but he was, for a moment, incapable of speech.

'Sit down, Sandy.' Mrs Gordon took his arm and led him like a stiff-legged child over to a seat. 'There's tea in the pot. The wee lassie'll pour you a cup.'

'My father-in-law locked the bakery. The shop will be shut tomorrow, too.' Sandy nodded again and accepted the cup Catriona offered.

'He's still the same, is he?' Jimmy asked. 'Still the same?'

Sandy cleared his throat.

'Aye. Rab and the rest have been pumping whisky down his throat for hours and he's still stone-cold sober. Talk-talk-talking, though, as if he still doesn't believe what's going to happen. How he can keep talking at all, just keep on like that, has us all baffled. He's got us fair exhausted, that fella, and he's still going strong. He's never shut an eye once. I'm dreading the morning for more reasons than one. No fella can soak up all that whisky, not even Baldy, without repercussions. I'm telling you, that fella's going to go berserk.'

'Will I go back in again?'

'Oh, no!' Mrs Gordon and Catriona cried out in unison.

'Jimmy, son, you've done more than your share with Baldy.'

'Yes,' Catriona agreed. 'There's plenty of people in there and they're all staying until after . . . until - until morning.'

'Melvin says you've to go downstairs in case the wee fella wakes up,' said Sandy.

'I'll go doon with you, hen,' Lexy offered from the doorway where she was wiping her nose on one of Jimmy's big white hankies supplied by Mrs Gordon for the purpose. 'I'll stay the rest of the night with you till Melvin comes.'

'Thank you. You're very kind.'

Where was the dream and where the reality?

Surely she belonged with the man who was now walking with her in silence to the door? Surely she had known him all her life? He was the fulfilment of her need, he was the braver, better part of her.

Yet she was married to another man - a stranger.

At first, going down the dark stairs with Lexy sniffling at her side, she felt dazed. Then came the bitterness to kick and struggle angrily against fate.

She opened the door of her house and stepped into the hall - and hated it; hated the hard gleaming polish of the floor that both she and Fergus had been warned so often not to tread on. Little remnants of rugs lay like stepping stones between the front door and all the other doors.

She hated the bedrooms where the bed-ends, the top of the wardrobe and the skirting board had to be rubbed and rubbed and polished and polished. She hated the bathroom where Melvin was now insisting the high-painted walls ought to be waxed to preserve them against steam.

Most of all she hated the sitting-room, Melvin's pride and joy, with its pastel coloured Indian carpet that was an agony to keep clean and the pale gold standard-lamp on which she dared not allow dust to settle and the ornate brass front and fender on the fireplace over which, on Melvin's instructions, she had spent many back-breaking, sweating and wasteful hours.

Life was so short. Surely, there were better ways to spend it?

She led Lexy into the kitchen and flicked on the light. Every surface glittered and gleamed, not a speck of dust, not a crumb, could be seen. Not one hair on the fireside rug was out of place, not one cushion dented.

Lexy's sniffles stopped. Uneasily she sat down on the edge of a seat, uncomfortably she stared around.

She's longing to light up a cigarette, Catriona thought, but she's afraid to dirty the place or desecrate that brassoed ashtray.

Then it occurred to her that she was afraid, too; the realization made her hate herself with such intensity that she felt physically sick.

'Ohi, I hope Jimmy doesn't go in to Baldy again.' Lexy worriedly nibbled at her lip. 'He's terrible, isn't he? I mean he's a lovely fella.' She gave a big sigh. 'But, ohi, he's terrible too. I mean to say - isn't he?'

'Can I make you a cup of tea?' Catriona managed.

'Oh, in the name of the wee man! I've never stopped drinking tea all day and half the night. I couldn't drink another drop, even if you paid me. If I drink any more I'd be wetting my pants!'

'Well, come on through to the sitting-room. There isn't a fire lit there either but at least there's the electric fire. It'll heat us up.'

Through in the sitting-room she switched on all the lights and the fire and drew a couple of chairs in nearer. They sat for a long time, staring at the fire and at the slow relentlessly moving hand of the clock.

Catriona had begun to shiver, whether with cold or fear or with hatred or with all three she no longer knew nor cared.

'I've never been up this late before except at Hogmanay, have you, eh?' Lexy said eventually.

Catriona shook her head.

'Ohi - I'm gaspin' for a fag!'

'Go ahead then, have one.'

'Are you sure you don't mind, hen?'

'No, not me. Make yourself at home. You're welcome.'

'Oh, ta! You're a pal!' Lexy dived into one of her pockets and brought out cigarettes and matches. 'Here, try one yourself, hen.

171

It'll steady your nerves. I mean to say - what with one thing and another!' She rolled her eyes. 'I don't know about you but I'm nearly off my head, so I am!'

Catriona hesitated only a moment before taking a cigarette and accepting the light Lexy gave her.

She coughed and spluttered after the first couple of puffs but soon settled down to find the cigarette strangely comforting. She liked the feel of it between her fingers. It gave her something to cling on to. She enjoyed the sucking sensation, and the breathing in, and the breathing out, like huge shuddering sighs of relief.

They smoked in silence, and when one cigarette was finished they each lit another, and another. They tried not to listen to the clock ticking Sarah's life away.

'Here!' Lexy cried out, for the first time noticing the shivering and the white angry face. 'Are you feeling all right?'

Catriona was saved from answering by the sound of Melvin's key in the door.

They both got up and pushed back their chairs.

'Are you sure you won't have a cup of tea, Lexy?'

'No! Thanks all the same, hen, but I'd rather run back upstairs to my Jimmy!'

Catriona's heart wept hard stones.

'What the hell!' After Lexy had gone Melvin saw Catriona smoking. 'Put that thing in the bucket. You're not going to start that filthy habit in my house. You're not going to go around dropping ash on my good carpets or my good linoleum; and that's that!'

'No, that's not that! You smoke! Why shouldn't I smoke?'

'What? What did you say?'

'Oh, shut up!' Catriona shot the words at him then hurled the still-lighted cigarette into the spotless hearth with such force it bounced out again and landed on the Indian carpet.

With a howl of rage and fear for the damage it might cause, Melvin pounced on the cigarette and with garbled oaths and burning fingers he at last managed to extinguish it in the nearest receptacle which happened to be a fancy and much-prized fruit-bowl, one of the wedding presents he and Betty had received.

'Now look what you've done, you stupid fool!' he bawled.

'Look at my good fruit-bowl.'

'What *I've* done? I never touched your horrible fruit-bowl. You put it there, not me.'

You put it on my good carpet. What did you expect me to do? Leave it lying there to burn a hole - a hole in my good carpet?'

'Oh, shut up, shut up, shut up! Talk about jumping from the frying-pan into the fire. My mother's one extreme, you're the other, and the irony of it is - you're worse! I'm so sick of hearing about your furniture and your linoleum and your carpets. I don't care if this whole place burns to a cinder and all your precious possessions in it!'

Melvin surveyed her, his stocky legs wide, his broad hands digging into his waist. 'Now I know exactly what kind of horror I've the misfortune to marry.'

'That makes two of us,' she retorted bitterly. 'I certainly know what kind of horror you are now.'

'I've been a good husband to you,' he shouted indignantly. 'I've given you a good home.'

'This isn't my home. It isn't a home at all.'

'Look at all the things I've provided you with. I've even made you a present of Betty's clothes! What more could any man give you?'

She shook her head, the sickness and the shivering swamping her again.

'Nothing, nothing. I'm sorry for everything I said.'

'A fat lot you gave me! You'd neither a stitch to your back nor a penny to your name.'

'I said I was sorry.'

'You ought to be down on your knees to me in gratitude.'

Her eyes flashed fired and hatred at him again. 'You'd like that, wouldn't you?'

'What the hell are we standing here in the middle of the night arguing for?' He suddenly scratched his moustache as if a better idea had occurred to him. 'I'm away through to the kitchen and after I do my press-ups I'll show you the way to express your gratitude! Come on! Don't just stand there!' He chortled. 'There's been enough hot stuff on this carpet for one night. Let's see what you can do in the kitchen!'

Chapter 23

The room was heavy-clouded with smoke and thick with whisky fumes.

Sandy had dozed off in one of the chairs beside the fire. Tam sat nodding opposite, short legs splayed out, big muscly arms crossed over his chest.

Men were draped, in drunken stupors, over different chairs.

Francis and Eddie MacMahon and wee Andy Tucker were propping each other up on the settee. Josy McWhirter's cherubic face had flopped down and hung by his fat chin on the edge of the table.

Only Rab and Baldy were awake and still steadily drinking; Baldy with his sleeves rolled up and his unbuttoned shirt hanging open to the waist like a heavy-weight ju-jitsu expert or a huge all-in wrestler, and Rab leaning back, dark-jawed and big-boned, absently sliding his glass backwards and forwards across the table from one hand to the other.

Nobody noticed that Baldy had stopped speaking and was staring across at the window and at the clock on the mantelpiece, then at the window, then at the clock, then at the window.

Until suddenly a low snarl began to raise the hairs on the back of everyone's neck and by the time the snarl had increased in volume and menace to become first a growl as Baldy reeled from the table, then a terrifying gorilla-like roar, everyone was on their feet, restraining hands outstretched at the ready, mouths open in an agonized panic-stricken search to find the right words.

Baldy shot both arms up and sent the table, bottles, glasses, ashtrays, spluttering all over the room.

'The bloody cowards!' His big chest expanded. 'The bastards!' Lunging at the mantelpiece, despite the half-dozen or so men hanging on to him, he grabbed the clock and sent it hurtling through the window with an explosion, then a tinkling of

174

broken glass. A couple of white 'wally dugs' flew through the air next.

'Baldy!' Rab shouted as one of the china dogs hit the wall. He fought to twist Baldy's tree-trunk arm behind his back. 'You're wrecking your house, man!'

Baldy heaved round and sent Rab flying. 'What bloody good is a house to me now!'

Rab struggled to his feet again.

'Sarah wouldn't want you to be getting into a state like this.'

'Aye!' Tam cried. 'That lassie worshipped the ground you walked on. Think of her!'

'I am thinking of her, you stupid fool!' He yelled all the louder but tears were spurting, streaming down. 'I promised I wouldn't let any of them bastards touch her. She's my wife!'

After she had recovered from the shock of what the Lord Provost had told her, Sarah refused to believe it. Not that she had the temerity to suppose anyone as important as the Lord Provost would tell a deliberate lie, but because his words and the words of the learned judge - '. . . you will be hanged by the neck until you are dead . . .' - were beyond her realm of comprehension, had no place, did not belong in the world where the authorities and the powers-that-be had always commanded her secret awe, respect and admiration. She put the whole thing down to some sort of stupid mistake on her part. 'Sarah, hen,' she told herself, 'ye've picked them up wrong.'

Yet in the deeper lonelier layers of her mind she could not convince herself. She had done a terrible thing and she would be punished terribly. The thought came rushing in on a white horse of fear but was beaten back again.

It was the idea of respectable folk (the Baillies were going to be there) calmly walking her along and putting a rope round her neck that confused her. Even the holy yin seemed to think it was all right.

So it must be all right.

Yet she couldn't believe it.

But it was true.

The waves were surging in and in. And the cell was small.

Nowhere to escape, nobody to turn to. She was sorry.

Sometimes the shame of having disgraced Baldy and the MacNairs and the street was too much to bear.

She couldn't sleep.

There had been dirty washing in the lobby press, and the furniture and all the ornaments were dusty.

If folk were coming in and out looking after Baldy they would see it and Baldy would get a showing up. She should have left the house clean and tidy.

Her cheeks burned.

Had she *really* seen her house for the last time; her cosy fire, her chair with the velvet cushion, her bonny china with the roses all around?

No, in her heart she knew that was impossible. Soon, she would be going home again.

Baldy would come in. He was a lad, her Baldy, but they'd always rubbed along that well together.

He had been good to her. Never once had he complained. And what had she done in return? What kind of wife had she been to him?

'Och, Baldy, lad, ah feel that ashamed!'

In the morning she would go down to old MacNair's. It was a lovely shop that. The best shop in Glasgow. Warm as toast and smelling just as tasty and always somebody ready to have a laugh and nice wee blether. Many a laugh she'd enjoyed in there.

No more mornings.

She felt frightened. It was morning now.

The city magistrates and the governor and the town clerk's deputy and the chief constable of Glasgow and the doctor and the holy yin were there.

It seemed truly terrible to be putting all these important folk to all this trouble. She fumbled with her cardigan and with fast-beating heart endeavoured to answer their questions with fitting politeness. She crinkled her face up and smiled apologetically round and round at them all.

It was a very serious and dignified procession and she tried to keep decently in step.

No more steps.

The waves came pounding over her. Horror was the scaffold. Terror was the instinctive need to keep alive.

Impossible to escape.

No time to bridge the hopeless gulf between her and her executioners.

The pain that had continuously dragged low down at her back and her abdomen flared into unbearable anguish, and at the last moment, before a man put the cap over her head, she felt grateful for the custom of making condemned women prisoners wear rubber underwear.

Fear beyond all measure. Darkness - and death long-drawn-out.

There was only one thing left that Jimmy could do, and that was to go to Duke Street Prison.

He knew his being there, standing outside the big bleak wall in the early morning with the collar of his jacket turned up and his hands dug deep into his pockets, could do nothing to stop what was going to happen to Sarah. But he imagined she needed a friend close by and this was as close as he could get.

His eyes, black-shadowed in an unshaven face, stared up at the prison.

At one time, when an execution took place a man could be seen hoisting a square black flag on a flagstaff at the western end of the prison roof while the prison bell tolled a dismal announcement that the criminal had paid the penalty.

Now there was only the posting of a notice on the front wall.

No notice had been posted yet. He leaned against the wall and closed his eyes.

He wondered if there was a God. He had waded through the writings of Thomas Paine and other atheists and sceptics. He had come across some shocking atrocities in his reading about the history of the church.

All this weighed heavily against the existence of a deity, his mind tried to tell him. Still, in his heart he was not convinced. There was such bitterness, such derision in so many of the atheistic books and pamphlets. He wondered why they got so worked up about something they did not believe in.

As far as the church and some of the worst parts of its history were concerned, it seemed more reasonable to blame the *men* who had perpetrated the atrocities in God's name rather than God.

One had, he decided, to go back to the root of the matter. A Christian meant a follower of and a believer in Christ.

Did he believe in Jesus Christ?

He had no time for droning-voiced hypocrites who hid behind dog collars. Or all the pomp and jewelled crowns and expensive robes and impressive trumpeting of all the churches in the world put together.

But what had they got to do with Christ? The Christ who was a tradesman - a carpenter. The Christ who, when He went into the temple and found those who were selling oxen and sheep and pigeons, and the money changers at their business, made a whip of cords and drove them all, with their sheep and oxen, out of the temple, and poured out the coins of the money-changer and overturned their tables.

It needed only a little imagination to see that it took lot of nerve to do things like that, or a very strong character - or something more.

The miracle was that, despite the difficulties of translation, of words themselves as a means of communication and the human limitations of the men who recorded the books of the New Testament, in spite of the changing customs, despite men's varying interpretations of Him, the spirit and the reality of Christ had survived all down through the ages.

Yes, he believed in Him!

A creaking, scraping sound alerted his attention, made his eyes dart round, his chest tighten, his breathing become difficult.

A prison officer had opened the gate and stepped out, a piece of paper in his hand.

No, Jimmy thought. No! He stared helplessly, the words of the notice drumming in his mind and building up to pain in his chest, cramping his shoulder and making him feel breathless and more breathless.

No . . . No . . .

He wandered away, climbed on a tramcar and trundled back

178

to Clydend, his face a sickly putty colour, his whole attention now focused on the seemingly insurmountable difficulties of reaching the quietness of home, the relaxation of bed. Gasping, fighting to keep calm, he got off the car at the Main Road a few steps away from Dessie Street. The street was strewn with glass and broken pieces of pottery.

His feet crunched and clattered and stumbled over them into the close. Stop to lean against the coolness of the wall. On to the stairs, the banister hard and strong under his hand pulling him up.

Pain knifing him.

The first landing reached. Rest again, head rolling against wall. Pray for quietness to help keep calm. He wanted to live.

Noise swelled and reverberated around him like a riotous tenement symphony. Baldy shouting and sobbing. Rab and Tam and Sandy and a cacophony of other voices vying with each other in loudness.

Then from somewhere behind the door near which he had propped himself came another sound.

A girl was screaming.

Chapter 24

Catriona followed Melvin from the front room, across the hall and into the kitchen like an obedient child. Outwardly silent and subdued, she reeled inside, frantic for escape. She had been up all night imagining and dreading the hour of Sarah's execution. The hour was near. Now she longed for peace of mind to pray. She needed every last ounce of energy to plead with God to forgive Sarah in case more punishment awaited her after death. She wanted to beg Him for mercy. Somehow she had to gather the courage to say: '"Thy will be done", but if it is Your will that Sarah should die, please comfort her!'

She had to fight down revulsion and bitterness and hatred and ask His forgiveness for Sarah's executioners because it said in the Lord's prayer, 'Forgive us our trespasses as we forgive them that trespass against us.'

Before she dared open her mind to God it had to be very carefully prepared because He could see in every dark and secret corner. She had to be still and quiet, in awe and reverence.

Instead she was teetering on the verge of panic.

Melvin could not expect sex now. Not now! It was impossible. It could not be right. Surely it was obscenity to the point of madness to even think of sexual intercourse at a time like this?

Somehow her legs conveyed her into the kitchen where she had to hold on to the back of a chair for support.

Melvin was too busy to notice.

He stripped off his jacket, then his shirt and, naked to the waist, began limbering up. Muscles and veins bulged like balloons at bursting point as he jerked himself into different poses. Grunting, he grabbed his wrists and made his chest puff high like a woman's. He dropped his arms and made his shoulders swell up like the hunchback of Notre-Dame. He whipped round, arms held high, fists curled, and snorted over his shoulder at her.

'That back development's out of this world, you know. It has to be seen to be believed!'

He faced her again, hand clamped on waist, and began high-stepping up and down. He dropped low to squat on his heels and bounced to his toes again. He finished off by lying on his stomach and doing a few press-ups. Then he rolled around, gave his moustache a good scratch and grinned up at her.

'Come on then, darlin'! Let's see what you can do!'

She could hear Baldy upstairs, and the other men, and the thumping and the crashing. The world was noisily disintegrating. The child might waken at any minute and be frightened.

Was Sarah frightened now?

'Come on!' One of Melvin's broad hands groped up her skirt. 'Let's see you!'

She screamed - jerky, ceiling-pitched, staccato bursts, piercing. She clawed for the door, his hands imprisoning her.

The quick patter of feet in the hall and Fergus shouting.

The hands releasing. Escape. Into the hall, fight with the handle of the front door. The landing. Jimmy in the shadows. In exquisite gratitude she clung to the Harris tweed jacket, moved her face and lips in the warm hollow of his neck, prayed to melt safely inside him, be one with him, protected by his gentleness and understanding.

Suddenly love alerted her. All thoughts of herself forgotten she stared up at Jimmy's face.

'Jimmy, love . . . Lean on me . . . I'll take you home, I'll help you upstairs.'

He shook his head.

'Oh, Jimmy!'

With desperate, fumbling fingers, she loosened his tie and unbuttoned his shirt.

'What the hell . . .?' Melvin's iron grip wrenched her away. 'Right on my doorstep, too! I knew he was an impertinent bastard but this is bloody ridiculous!'

Jimmy twisted against the wall, his head to one side.

Panic swirled round Catriona again.

'He's ill! Can't you see? Are you always blind? Oh please, please, Melvin - help him!'

181

'I know him,' Melvin sneered. 'I've known him a lot longer than you. He's been to the prison. He's been working himself into a stupid tizzy over a useless dirty slut like Sarah Fowler. I'll deal with you at work tomorrow, Gordon. Right now I've a thing or two to say to my wife!'

The door crashed shut and they were in the hall and she was aching to kill him!

Only for Jimmy's sake did she pin down her voice and emotions.

'Go get a doctor. Please, please, oh, please, Melvin! I'll do anything. I'll promise. I'll never speak to Jimmy again. Only do something, anything to help him!'

'Watch where you're going. You'll dirty the linoleum!' Melvin raised his voice indignantly. 'Walk on the rugs. What do you think I put rugs on this floor for? I went to a lot of bother to get those rugs and place them just right to protect the good linoleum.'

'Dirty the linoleum? You're worrying about dirtying the linoleum?' She laughed with hysteria. 'You'd think there was nothing more to life.'

'But there isn't!' Melvin said, genuinely astonished at her ignorance. 'That's all life is - a fight against dirt.'

Darkness billowed around her. Wildly she struggled against the black cloth.

She fought with her fists, her feet, her teeth, her nails, all the strength that was in her, but Melvin's muscles bulged, proud of their superior strength, and the black cloth snaked around her, smothering her, whirling her down . . .

Consciousness returned and it seemed that she had never stopped struggling.

Only now she was in the bedroom, and she was trapped in a tunnel of blankets and her hair was flopping from one side to the other of a lumpy pillow.

'Take it easy,' Melvin was saying. 'Just take it easy, OK?' Reaching over he heaved her into a sitting position. 'The doctor's been and had a look at you. He's upstairs now but he'll pop in again later.'

'Jimmy!' She flung the blankets aside and would have been

182

out of bed but Melvin's iron arms restrained her like the bars of a prison.

His face acquired a solemn expression. 'It's too late.' He gave a long serious sigh. 'He wouldn't do as he was told, you see. We were always telling him - his mother, Sandy, Lexy, your father, Tam, and nobody more than me. Take it easy, we all kept warning him, don't get so worked up about everything - keep calm - don't bother - why worry? But we just couldn't do anything with him. He was always sticking his neck out; always ruffling himself up, and other folk, too.'

'Oh, no.' Catriona shook her head.

'Yes, he was. I knew him longer than you. He was always on about something or somebody. He even had the nerve to argue with the old man. They were always arguing the toss. This'll be a terrible shock for the old man. He liked him, you know. Och, to hell, I liked the fella too, even though he made a bloody nuisance of himself.'

'Jimmy's not dead. You said he was only upset.'

Melvin's face darkened with annoyance.

'I told you he'd been to the prison and got himself all worked up and I was right. How was I to know he'd gone too far and was going to die on my doorstep? I wouldn't have known yet, but Mata Hari across the landing was spying through her keyhole. She saw him drop and came hirpling straight in to tell me.'

'Jimmy's dead?'

'That'll be another night and day the place will be shut,' Melvin said. 'And he'll have a big funeral. Here, I bet the old man'll shut the shop on the day of the funeral as well. Jumpin' Jesus, that'll be three days.'

The veil of romantic fiction, the fairy-tales, all the comforting imaginings she had always hopefully clung to ripped away. Through death, she saw life.

'Oh, well!' Melvin scratched his moustache. 'As long as I get my wages!'

No fairy godmother. No Sir Galahad. No ship coming in. No last minute happy ending. Nothing round the corner.

'I'll need all the money I can lay my hands on now that you're pregnant.'

183

'Pregnant!'

Life went on. People went on, generation after generation, countless millions. Poseurs behind masks, duping themselves with self-importance, busy with minutiae.

'I don't suppose you even know what the word pregnant means. You don't know nothing, darlin'!' Melvin got up, stretching his muscles and laughing.

Life was the survival of the fittest.

Life was Glasgow, tough, harsh, complex, warm with humanity, with generous helping hands, with caring in abundance.

It was the caring that mattered.

'I'm learning,' she said.

A BABY MIGHT BE CRYING

To my sons Kenneth Baillie Davis and
Calvin Royce Davis with much love.

Chapter 1

Excitement crowded the Glasgow air like fast-bouncing footballs.
Flags rippled and crackled. Everywhere the Scottish lion cocked
up on its haunches, paws sparring. Headlines boasted:

EMPIRE EXHIBITION—1938

Alec Jackson felt on top of the world. Head and shoulders above
everyone else he swaggered along Springburn Road, whistling
through mobile lips well practised in exploring women as well
as sound.

He winked in passing at a huge fat wife with a wispy black
moustache and a head spiky with curlers.

'Hello there, gorgeous!'

The woman squealed with laughter then bawled after him:

'Wait till I get my hands on you!'

He twisted round without slowing his pace and bulged his
eyes in mock shock.

'Sex maniac!'

Then, still without bothering to look where he was going, he
swung into the dark close at the corner of Springburn Road and
Wellfield Street.

'Oops!' The pram he had bumped into creaked with the
weight of three children and was pushed by a grey ghost. 'You
don't need to use force, gorgeous. I'm all yours!'

'Alec!' The ghost changed with a smile, tightened, brightened,
became a self-conscious, coy young girl. 'What a fright you gave
me. You shot in the close like a bullet. Do you never take your
time?'

He pinched her bottom as he passed to go clattering up the
stone stairs.

'I would with you, love.'

He stopped on the first landing, his fist raised to rat-tat-tat at

189

the middle door, when he remembered that the Hunters had moved from their single-end to a room and kitchen on the top flat.

He took the other two flights three steps at a time and reaching the top attacked the door with a good loud thumping.

It opened in a couple of minutes and he followed Ruth Hunter to the left of the shoe-box hall and into the kitchen, his eyes never leaving the undulating flesh beneath her pink sweater and red skirt.

'Two shillings, is it?' she appealed, lifting her handbag from a chair and easing a softly rounded hand inside it.

'You can have it for nothing from me any day, gorgeous!'

One eyebrow arched up as she slid a look that cut him down with sarcastic disapproval, yet the sexual awareness still remained.

He snapped open his brief-case, tossed his book on to the table and thumbed through the pages.

Sammy Hunter was a lucky man. He could imagine Ruth pestering him for it, pleading with him every night.

With one hand Ruth slid a two-shilling piece across the table, with the other she guided her insurance book towards him. He marked up the book with a flourish.

'I like your new place.' Alec gazed around the kitchen as he tucked his pen into his pocket, and gave himself a pat. 'You and Sammy certainly have good taste.'

She forgot her sexy performance for a minute. Enthusiasm and childish eagerness rushed to take its place.

'You really think so?'

'Of course I do, love. Real high class, this place is. The pair of you have worked a miracle in here.'

'Sammy did all the electrical work. He studied a book on how to do it. We did the painting and decorating between us.'

'Good for you!'

'We had to get a plumber to shift the sink, though.'

He looked over to the kitchen window where all the houses had their sinks, with pot cupboards underneath. In place of a sink, a sewing-machine stood in front of the window. Gold curtains were drawn back on either side and, on top of the

190

machine, a vase of marigolds reflected the sun like glistening oranges.

'Shift the jaw-box?'

'Into the cupboard! Isn't it marvellous?'

Ruth knocked into a chair in her hurry to reach the cupboard door and two or three long strides took Alec over beside her to peer inside.

'What a bloody good idea!'

She flashed him a look and he apologised for the 'bloody', but she wasn't really annoyed. Sheer joyous pride swamped every other emotion.

'It's even got a light!'

The light clicked on, displaying Sammy's patient and conscientious workmanship of shelves and drawers fitted to the walls and under the sink. Alec could just see Sammy with a book in one hand and a screwdriver in the other. If he had managed a window that would have been something. Still, it was a bloody good idea.

'I like the colours.' He grinned and nudged Ruth, immediately electrifying himself with the heat and the bouncy resilience of her flesh. 'None of the old cream and green, eh?'

She shrank away but it was a graceful feminine movement. She had remembered sex again.

'I love pink and red. It's so nice and warm.'

'Yeah!' Alec's groan of enthusiasm aimed straight for the bulging sweater and skirt. Pressing back against the sewing-machine, wriggling quickly then slowly as if she were squashed up against him, she shrank further away.

'Do you like it here?' He gathered a kiss in his fingertips and flipped it to her. Ruth brushed past him, the invitation in her eyes hooking him and pulling him along.

'The room's the best,' she said and a pulse skittered through him.

The kitchen bed-recess had been made into a dining-area. That meant that the bed must be in the room. 'The room's the best all right,' thought Alec. Hallelujah! Unexpectedly Ruth stopped and indicated a cabinet made of the same polished oak as the sewing-machine.

191

'That's the bed. The mattress folds up inside during the day.'

Alec did not give up hope. He grinned cheekily down at her.

'I've heard of it happening in many a place but a cabinet's a new one on me, love.'

The sarcastic look returned, sarcastic, yet sexy.

'You want to see the room?'

'I'm fascinated.'

Across the small hallway she picked her way, high heels clicking on the linoleum, buttocks bunching and quivering. He could imagine her as a sultan's favourite concubine, or a king's mistress at a French court, or a hot-blooded temptress of a belly dancer. A belly dancer — couldn't he just imagine that!

In the front room, she swivelled towards him, her breasts jiggling like jellies.

'Of course, it's not nearly finished yet. Still the bare boards, but look at the paper! It's the latest thing. We got it in town. And see the hole-in-the-wall bed?'

He lit a cigarette to help keep his hands off her.

'Eh? Where?'

Delighted again, a child-woman, she giggled and wiggled, and pointed to the wall where the bed-recess ought to have been.

'Behind there. We're using it as a store place. Sammy made the wall, imagine! It's wood, papered over. Listen!'

She tripped over to press herself against the wall and knock on it.

She looked good enough to eat.

'Fascinating!'

'Are you laughing at me?'

'I was thinking you look good enough to eat.'

She struggled to cool her giggles, to flap superciliously at him with thick lashes on a tip-tilted face.

'It's really too early to show it to anybody yet.'

'Never mind.' He grinned. 'I'll be back.'

She ignored his innuendoes.

'Have you got tickets for the Exhibition, by the way?'

'Sure. I've got a season. I'll be there at the opening ceremony with the King and Queen in Ibrox Stadium tomorrow. Will you and Sammy be there?'

'No, we're going straight to Bellahouston Park. Sammy hasn't much time for royalty or the military or the powers that be. Sammy's very independent-minded.'

'Me too, but it's the wife.' He shook his head. 'Anything for a peaceful life.'

'There's going to be a march-past of all the services, isn't there? It's Sammy's father. You know what he's like, don't you?'

'Who doesn't?' He grinned. 'If it wasn't for his gammy leg I bet he'd be marching along beside them, bawling the odds.' He coarsened his voice to a snarl. 'Left, right, left, right, left, left.'

She shook her head and sighed as she opened the outside door but her eyes were smiling and her red mouth full and soft.

'Cheerio, Alec.'

'Cheerio, love.'

He savoured her all the way down the stairs and when he crossed the road outside he looked up at her front room window in the hope that she might be there to give him a wave. The double window in the old tenement building sparkled with cleanliness and was edged with royal blue curtains. It looked like a precious jewel in a crumbling stone setting.

Ruth had been on his book nearly three years now, almost from the time she married Sammy and moved into the single-end at Springburn Road. She had been sweet sixteen then but every bit as lush as she was now. He reckoned that she must always have been sexy. Even as a two-year-old those eyes of hers would have had a coquettish twinkle.

He had missed out on those years because, apart from being quite a bit younger than Alec, Ruth was a Springburn girl and he had been born and brought up at Townhead. He had always been secretly proud of his origins, although he would tell people that Glasgow could sink in the Clyde for all he cared; and that he would rather have been from wealthy blue-blooded stock, with the emphasis on wealthy. The truth was that he was proud to be a true Glaswegian, with his roots in the oldest part of town. Glasgow had not originated down at the Saltmarket on the edge of the River Clyde as a lot of people imagined.

Years ago, as a wee laddie sheltering from the rain in the public library, Alec had discovered that St Mungo, the patron

193

saint of Glasgow, had set up his monastery across the road, only a stone's throw from his own tenement building. St Mungo had chosen the very ground where Glasgow Cathedral now stood, grey and aloof yet not too far back from the crush and buzz of the Castle Street pavements, only separated by the small Cathedral Square, with its statue of King Billy on a horse with a broken tail that would wag in the wind.

From the Saltmarket at the river's edge to High Street and Castle Street then on to Springburn Road was practically a straight line on the map, right through Springburn to Bishopbriggs, once the bishop's riggs or fields.

Graduating from an infancy of tottering about his own back-court and close, Alec had first explored the area immediately surrounding it. Against the skyline of the Necropolis across the road, all crowding together, stood the cathedral, the towering Royal Infirmary, Duke Street Prison and the Drygait where, according to the book, such great lords as the Dukes of Montrose had their town houses long before the prison dominated the place, a giant black castle of doom.

He had chuckled at the thought of lords living there because he knew the Drygait only as a slum.

Then on his own side of the street was Provand's Lordship, the oldest house in Glasgow, now a museum. King James II and King James IV of Scotland and Mary Queen of Scots were all supposed to have slept there.

As he got older Alec had wandered further afield down High Street to the Gallowgate and along to the Barrows, or right down by the Saltmarket to Glasgow Green and the river.

He didn't very often travel up the other end towards Springburn because at that time there never seemed to be anything of much interest there. Springburn Park was the only exception. It meant a really wild game of football, plenty of swings, a pond with paddle boats, and if you took a jar you could catch minnows.

Alec had seen Sammy there long before Ruth had met him. The irony of it! Instead of bumping into Ruth, it had to be young Sammy. It would have been hard to miss him, of course, a red-haired, dour-faced unwilling conscript into his father's army.

Hodge Hunter, an ex-sergeant-major in the military police,

marched his brood round the park every Sunday and then forced them all through a variety of physical jerks. Kids came from miles around to jeer at them and risk a fractured skull from Hodge's silver-topped stick.

If only he had hung around Springburn Road instead of the park! Alec cursed himself as he legged along the road. If only he had lounged around the cafés, or the corners, he might have met Ruth before Sammy did.

But what was the use of worrying? The old shoulder-twitching bouncy swagger returned, and he was whistling cheerily by the time he turned right into Cowlairs Road past a few closes and right turn again into Cowlairs Road where he now lived.

His whistle bounced off the dark brick tunnel entrance of the Road and reverberated back from all sides like noisy drumming, with the clanging of two feet on the cobbles making a riotous accompaniment.

Emerging at the other end in the yard, with houses squashing in all round and the row of overflowing middens in the centre, he made a rush at a tin can and dribbled it across to the outside iron-railed staircase of Number Five. One last kick at the can before it was pounced on by a horde of howling footballers in short trousers and braces some sporting shirts, some jerseys, some vests, others bare-chested.

Up the stone steps two at a time, his brief-case banging against the railings. Then into the close, a wooden-floored one that thumped hollow, past the bottom-flat doors and up creaking wood stairs to his own right-hand door on the first landing.

The door stood open and Sheena the mongrel bitch lolloped out to meet him, tail a-wag.

'Down, girl! Get off!' He shied her away with his brief-case, rattling along the lobby littered with clothes pegs, pot lids and empty milk bottles.

Madge called from the kitchen:

'I'll murder Sadie and Agnes. They were supposed to pick them up.'

She was sitting wide-legged by the kitchen range feeding Maisie. Maisie was nearly a year old and Alec's mother said it was time she was off the breast but Madge just laughed.

'Och, what's the harm? If the bairn howls during the night, the breast's easier than getting up for drinks or to make bottles.'

They had produced four children in their four years of marriage, the four-year-old twins, Sadie and Agnes, Hector who was three, and Maisie the youngest.

'Sadie!' Madge yelled in the direction of the kitchen door and the room beyond. 'Agnes, come on, hen. Clear the place up for Daddy!'

Maisie sucked on regardless as Alec chucked her under her wet chin and fondled the heavy pendulous breast squashing against her busy pink cheeks.

'Get off,' Madge told him automatically, but she raised her face to be kissed, a square, shiny face with fine white skin smudged with freckles. His lips fastened warmly and wetly over hers and his tongue was just beginning to weave from side to side and push further in when she suddenly broke away, big-mouthed with laughter.

'Sheena! My God, her nose is cold.'

'Down, girl. Down!' Alec cuffed the dog's ears and its head bounced off Maisie who sucked on, ignoring it. 'I'll just put my case away, Madge, then I'll run down to give MacVene my line.'

'Hey, never mind giving the bookie your money. How about me? Remember you promised to take us to the Exhibition tomorrow. It's no use going without any money. Especially on the first day.'

'Don't worry, you'll get the winnings, you big-breasted beauty you!'

'Get off!'

She punched him and tucked her short straight hair behind her ears.

'Tea's ready. Don't you be long.'

Already he was whistling away to the room to put his case in his roll-top desk.

Sadie and Agnes were getting the bottles and the pegs from the lobby.

'Hello, sweethearts.'

He put his hand up Sadie's skirt and tickled her, and on the way back he stopped to fondle Agnes, slipping his fingers inside

196

her pants to feel the soft hot hairlessness of her, before whistling out of the house, across the yard and out of the Road.

MacVene was the bookie's runner who hung around one of the closes further down Cowlairs Road and collected 'lines' or bets for O'Hara the bookie, his ferret eyes all the time watching for the police.

Alec put sixpence each way on 'Starter's Orders' and went to join the crowd of men lounging and bantering at the corner of Springburn Road. At this junction Cowlairs Road joined Springburn Road at one side and Vulcan Street joined it at the other to make Springburn Cross. Springburn Road had existed for hundreds of years and there had always been some hamlet or village round about the Cross. There had once been an inn, so the story went, and a burn which started as a spring, hence the name Springburn. The mind boggled at the idea of country inns and green grass, burns and springs in this place.

Alec hung a cigarette on his lip, rasped a match up to light it and wondered who would want Springburn to be like that anyway.

Springburn Park was there for the kids if they wanted it. He had enjoyed his occasional safaris there but he had always found it alien land. It was more up the hill in Balornock than in Springburn, and could only have got its name because one of the gates was at the Springburn end, at the top of the Balgray Hill. Or perhaps the park had been there, with its marvellous view of Springburn and the whole of Glasgow, long before the existence of Balornock.

No, give him old Springburn just as it was, any time, any day, but especially right now with the hooters screaming and moaning and competing with each other for air space and the air stretching in the ears, alive, vibrating and painful with the racket. From all around Castle Street to the far end of Springburn men in dungarees and sweatshirts and dirty faces were surging on to the streets in enormous black waves. Men were mobbing from the chemical works, the locomotive works, the iron works, the younger ones whooping, shoving, tripping, punching and bawling in the exhilaration of suddenly being let loose.

Springburn was a man's place and men converged on the

197

Cross from all sides and clanging tram-cars lined up in Springburn Road rocking with the weight of men.

Cowlairs Road led down to Cowlairs works, the headquarters of the celebrated North British Railway Company's stud of bronze-green locomotives, now spewing out its men to mix at The Cross with the crush from the Hyde Park Works at the foot of Vulcan Street.

A tram-car ground and sizzled past from the town end and Alec caught sight of Sammy Hunter sitting at one of the windows, stockily built, in a navy suit and white-collared shirt, his thick hair spiking up from its brilliantine plastering, his bushy brows jutting aggressively forward.

Alec blew out a tight stream of smoke from a fluted tongue. His eyes were on Sammy but his thoughts had returned hot-footed to Ruth.

Chapter 2

In between serving customers at the general counter, Catriona kept glancing across the shop to the bakery side where her father-in-law was interviewing Mrs Jackson, a tall scraggy woman who had come about the cleaning job. Mr MacNair's brusqueness always embarrassed her.

In the first place he ought to have taken Mrs Jackson through to the cubbyhole office in the lobby at the back between the shop and the bakehouse, instead of keeping her standing there as he clomped about in his too-big boots serving customers with steaming bread and rolls, every now and again shooting a high-pitched whine of a question at her from a pink button mouth perched on top of a wispy goatee beard. The customers, crowding the shop, gossiped among themselves, stopping only to listen with unashamed interest to what was going on.

The last cleaner had moved to another district with her family, leaving one of the attic houses on the top flat empty. Now the spiral staircase of the three-flatted tenement above the shop that old Mr MacNair owned and let out to his employees was getting messier and messier. So was the shop itself.

The stairs and the bakehouse needed continuous scrubbing because of the rats, the cockroaches and the flour puffing up in hot grey clouds that dried the nostrils and parched the throat. The flour, not content with continuously swirling in the air, solidified into a slippery paste underfoot to make the bakehouse, the lobby, the shop, the close, the stairs and the landings a dangerous ice-rink.

The cleaner's removal had put the old master baker out of temper, especially since one of her sons had worked in the bakehouse and her daughter had served in the shop.

Catriona had been deployed from her flat above to help in the shop until the new counter assistant arrived.

'No longer than one week,' her husband Melvin had warned

his father. 'I don't want her wasting time gossiping to half the folk in Clydend. How's she going to have my dinner ready?'

Mrs Jackson was a widow and had been living alone in her house over in Townhead since her son Alec had married and moved to Springburn. Catriona had had the whole history before Mr MacNair had bothered to look at Mrs Jackson. The woman had rushed into conversation, a nerve twitching her eye like a wink. All about her son - what a good boy he was and how badly she missed him.

'His wife's a bit happy-go-lucky and extravagant. It worries me. Alec never complains but I know he worries too. It's the weans, you see.' She leaned closer to Catriona as if concentration on her stare and its nearness would help Catriona to understand. 'I'd like to help but I've only my widow's pension and what I get for a few hours' work in town. If only I could get this job at least I'd save on the rent.'

Old MacNair collected rent from all those employees who occupied his flats, as had the last cleaner, but this time he had made up his mind to pay no wages and instead allow the new cleaner the attic flat rent free.

'You'll do!' his nasal whine announced at last. 'Start on Monday and think yourself damned lucky.'

'Cheeky bugger!' One of the customers turned to Mrs Jackson. 'Don't pay any attention to him, hen.'

A bright red collar of fire suddenly appeared round Mrs Jackson's neck and quickly burned her face to the roots of the dry-fizz of her hair.

'Thanks, Mr MacNair. Thanks.'

The old man drowned her words by thumping a gnarled fist on the counter.

'Come on, come on! Who's next?'

Mrs Jackson squeezed between the customers to come back across to Catriona.

'Thank goodness that's over! Thank goodness!'

Catriona looked down with embarrassment.

'I'm glad you got the job.' Holding her hair back with one hand, she stole an anxious glance at the older woman. 'I hope you'll like it here.'

She was secretly wondering if Mrs Jackson knew about the murder. The MacNair building in Clydend at the corner of Dessie Street and the Main Road had made headline news not so very long before. The Street of Tragedy all the papers had called it.

Sarah Fowler, wife of Baldy, the foreman baker, had stabbed her mother-in-law in one of the flats upstairs. Never as long as she lived would Catriona forget the day when Sarah had appeared at the door, face apologetic, eyes bewildered.

I've kill't Baldy's mammy!

They had hanged Sarah in Duke Street prison and normal life as they had known it in the close at Number One Dessie Street had disappeared down the trap with her.

There had been other deaths, other changes. People had moved away, people had come to stare at the building.

Catriona herself had nearly died with a miscarriage.

'The trouble with you is you're too soft,' her husband Melvin kept telling her 'You don't do enough physical jerks.'

'Physical jerks!' Her mother saw red every time Melvin mentioned the words. 'You wicked man. May God in His infinite mercy forgive you. You and your physical jerks were nearly the death of that girl.'

Her mother had never forgiven her for marrying Melvin.

'Why? Why?' Even yet she kept asking, and she was always putting up prayers for her at the meetings of the Band of Jesus of which she was Grand Matron. 'Why, Catriona? That man's old enough to be your father. He's been married before and has a child. You were only a child yourself. You weren't seventeen when you married that man. And what you saw in him I'll never know. A vulgar immodest ignorant man like that, and you such a well-protected, well-sheltered girl. I even insisted on being over in Farmbank instead of in Dessie Street so that you would have the benefit of being brought up in a respectable district.'

She never tired of ranting on and on, digging mercilessly over and over again at old ground.

'It's your daddy's fault, of course. I've said it before and I'll say it again. If your daddy hadn't been off work with his filthy dermatitis that man would never have needed to come to the house to give your daddy his wages. And if he hadn't come to the house he would never have seen you and all this trouble would never have started.'

Why had she married Melvin? She had repeated that 'why' to herself far more often than her mother did. She had longed to leave her parents' house and have a place of her own. Perhaps that was the answer; yet Melvin's house had never felt and still did not feel a home of her own. It did not have the stamp of his dead first wife either, despite her photographs all over the house and the likeness in her little son, Fergus. It was Melvin's house. Everything belonged to him as he kept telling Catriona.

'Nothing's yours. You hadn't even a spare pair of knickers when you came here. By God, you were lucky when you got me, and don't you forget it.'

Think yourself lucky. Think yourself damned lucky. How many times had she heard those words? *Be grateful.* She was grateful for having escaped from her mother but living with Melvin had given rise to the hypnotic fascination and the morbid fear of sleeping under the same roof as a dangerous animal. Often she dreamed of a friend to help and protect her, and wistfully, yet without any real hope, she watched Mrs Jackson's golliwog head leave the shop.

'Here you!' her father-in-law yelped. 'Don't just stand there looking gormless. Get on with your work!'

Like a trapped bird beating its wings against the bars of its cage, Catriona flurried into action. Her hands delved into sacks to shovel up sugar and peas and beans and lentils and potatoes, her arm jerked backwards and forwards cutting sausages and black puddings, her fingers tinged over the till. Movement quickened her mind sending racing ahead to wrestle with all the work waiting to be done in the house upstairs.

She became conscious of the metallic stammer of the riveters in the Benlin Yards across the Main Road. The racket was always there as if the whole of Glasgow was filled to the skies with blacksmiths. Often she managed to ignore it, to accept it as part of the savage background that life had acquired since her marriage to Melvin. But now it filled her head, drowning out the buzz of customers' voices and the jangle of the shop-door and the rattle and clash of trays and tins in the bakehouse at the back, and the kettle-drum tattoo of metal-rimmed cart wheels on the cobbled street outside.

Until suddenly even the Benlin riveters were banished by the shock of seeing her mother, straight-backed, big-chested and angry, in the shop.

'What is the meaning of this?' Ruddy, purple-veined cheeks mottled with anger she swung round to face Mr MacNair. 'Are you trying to kill this child? Isn't one murder enough round here?'

'Mummy!' Catriona hissed, keeping her head well down in order to avoid everyone's eyes.

Her mother turned on her again.

'Get out from behind that counter and come upstairs at once!'

'But, Mummy!'

'Do as you're told!'

'Away you go, child,' old MacNair's voice sniggered. 'Do as your *mummy* tells you.'

Trembling with humiliation Catriona came round beside her mother who immediately punched and pummelled her out of the shop, leaving behind whoops of laughter.

'I'm not a child.'

'Oh, be quiet.'

Mrs Munro shoved her into the floury close, sickly with the beery smell of yeast, and up the spiral stairs to the first landing.

'I'm not a child,' Catriona repeated, but her trembling and the tears filming over her vision denied the words any authority. Her mother thumped on the door.

'I don't know what I have ever done to deserve all this worry. After all I've done for you, Catriona, after all the sacrifices I've made - and God knows I've made plenty, and I'm not taking the Lord's name in vain. After all these years . . .'

The door opened before she could say any more and Melvin, wearing striped pyjamas, the top lying open to reveal a hairy chest, stood glowering at her.

Catriona spoke breathlessly.

'I'm sorry, Melvin, Mummy knocked before I'd time to tell her I had the key.'

Melvin flicked his eyes upwards in disgust and stomped away, his bare feet slapping loudly on the linoleum.

He was not a tall man but Catriona was a fragile wisp of thistledown beside him. Melvin had an ape-like physique with a massive upper-arm measurement greater than Catriona's waist. Intensely proud of his muscle control, he exercised religiously every day, giving a cringing Catriona a nude display of muscles bunching, twitching, hunching, circling.

'For a man working nights in a bakehouse, especially a man of my age, I'm a marvellous specimen,' he never tired of telling her, despite his grey-white baker's face and the thinning hair that looked as if it had been parched with a lifetime's flour dust.

Now, not quite awake, he yawned and scratched his moustache as he returned to the bedroom, shouting out without looking round.

'I'm going to do my exercises. Put the kettle on.'

'Listen to that!' Mrs Munro marched into the kitchen and jerked out the hatpin securing the hat on top of her thick coil of hair. 'Lord Muck. He'll be the death of you yet, that man. You'll be the second he'll put under the clay, you mark my words.'

Catriona lifted the kettle.

'Do you want a cup of tea?'

'I'll do it.' Her mother snatched the kettle from her. 'You go and sit down.'

'I'm all right, Mummy. I wish you wouldn't worry.'

'If you weren't so wickedly selfish I wouldn't need to worry. You have been punished, Catriona, and you will be punished again. He's watching you, Catriona. God misses nothing. Everything, every unkind selfish thought, every cruel disobedient act He takes note of and adds up for the terrible Day of Judgement when you'll stand before Him to await your final punishment.'

She splashed water into the kettle, and clattered it on to the cooker. The gas lit with a plop.

'But make no mistake about this, Catriona, you'll be punished here too. For every sin you're guilty of, there's a punishment. Your disobedience, your ungratefulness, your wicked selfishness will be punished.'

The words were so familiar to Catriona, her mind was mimicking the speech all the time a split second before her mother got there.

Yet despite the familiarity of the words and her bitter if silent attempts to discredit them, they had long since become part of her. It did not matter how much her mind struggled to reason in her own defence. It did not matter how much hatred and bitterness she conjured up to help her hit back. In her secret innermost places, the darkest corners of her mind, she was convinced of guilt, of unworthiness, and of the awful punishment and retribution that forever hung over her head.

Her eyes shrank down. 'I'm sorry . . .'

'There's no use . . .'

'Mummy.'

' . . . being sorry. Do you want to die?'

'No, of course not.'

'Well? Why do you not have more respect for yourself? Stand up to the MacNairs, don't allow them to make a slave of you.' She strode about the kitchen finding cups and saucers, straight-backed, handsome, the sun from the window seeking out the burgundy richness in her hair.

'May God forgive the wicked villain! Fancy having you working down there in that shop after you've been so ill.'

'There's a girl starting tomorrow.'

'It's about tomorrow I've come. That man's dragging you off to the Exhibition, isn't he?'

'Yes, but . . .'

'I knew it!'

'But, Mummy.'

'And you've agreed?'

'Everybody will be there. There's going to be people from all over the world.'

'None of them will nurse you or care one jot when you're lying at death's door again. There's not a pick of flesh on you and he's going to make you crush through thousands of folk and walk for miles round and round, up hill and down dale in Bellahouston Park.'

'I'll take a cup of tea through to Melvin.'

'You'll do nothing of the kind. Put your feet up on that stool and drink your own.'

'But Melvin asked . . .'

'If he wants tea let him come and get it. He's a lot more able than you. Let *him* go to the Exhibition!'

'Melvin wouldn't go without me.'

'Let him stay at home, then.'

'But I want to go to the Exhibition.'

The door creaked open and Melvin, dressed only in loose-waisted trousers, came slowly into the room, concentrating on his exercises, his back, shoulder and upper arm muscles ballooning up.

'Where's my tea? See that tricep? There isn't another man in Clydend, probably the whole of Glasgow, with triceps like that.'

'You ought to be black-burning ashamed!'

Mrs Munro averted her face, her ruddy cheeks darkening to purple.

'Ashamed?' Melvin's eyes bulged with incredulity. 'What are you blethering about, woman?'

'Parading about half-naked. Displaying yourself.'

'Good God, anybody would think I was walking up the middle of Sauchiehall Street.'

'And don't blaspheme in front of me, either.'

'Where's my tea?'

Hastily Catriona poured him a cup.

'Here you are, Melvin.'

'Ta. My mouth feels like a sewer.'

Mrs Munro's nose twisted and her eyes shrunk away again.

'You're disgusting!'

Melvin downed the tea as if it were whisky and wiped his moustache with the back of his hand before turning away to continue his exercises

'Just you wait a minute,' his mother-in-law commanded. 'I've something to say to you.'

'Eh?'

His attention was not really with her.

'You are not to take that poor child to the Exhibition tomorrow. She's not fit for it.'

'Aw, shut up!'

He went away with his shoulders contorted into a grotesque hump that almost hid the back of his head. In a moment or two they could hear him cheerily whistling.

Chapter 3

From early morning, a rustle of excitement gathered momentum in the air. Purposeful crowds surged through the streets and squeezed together on buses, and tram-cars and trains rocking and rollicking them as they sped towards Ibrox and Bellahouston.

Limousines purred along, fat with distinguished passengers. Family cars honked and rattled, windows busy with expectant faces.

The sun grinned down at Glasgow competing for attention with an exuberant gusty wind.

Soldiers lined the packed pavements of Union Street to keep the boisterous crowds in check as King George VI and his Queen made the twenty-five-minute journey from Central Station to Ibrox in an open landau drawn by four of the famous Windsor Greys, with outriders and postilions.

All along the route, tenement buildings leapt to life with whirling, lurching, rippling flags. Open windows were crammed with spectators fluttering handkerchiefs.

Inside Ibrox Stadium sixty-thousand people jamming together in good-humoured breathlessness. Great masses of children energising the crowd, Scouts, Cubs, Boys' Brigade, white-bloused Girl Guides like banks of daisies. The whole arena animating suspense, rocketing every now and again into cheers of relief.

The children screaming at everybody and everything. The stand filling with notables, lawyers, bright stars from the Scottish Offices in their silk hats; Lord Elgin's party and the little girl who was to present the bouquet to the Queen; James Bridie, Will Fyffe, Sir Harry Lauder, all receiving resounding yells of welcome.

A groom busying himself about the lawn, paddock and pitch raising ear-splitting cheers. A policeman at the east end of the stand engaging in a nice bit of vaulting, falling on his face, and nearby Cubs roaring their hearts out.

Then twelve trumpeters appeared, scarlet and gold on the skyline like a row of toy soldiers, their fanfare blowing away in the wind and drowned by the great shout that welcomed the King and Queen as the Windsor Greys swept into sight.

Compared with the children the hearty cheering of the grown-ups was a performance without shape - self-conscious, ill-timed, hedged with Scottish shyness. Alec let out a slightly derisive hurrah, then laughed and glanced round at his family to see if they too were laughing. He had the girls up on his shoulders and Madge had Maisie struggling in one arm trying to pull herself up by Madge's hair and Hector stamping and jumping about on her hip in his efforts to see over the heads of the crowd.

'My God!' Hilarity escaped from Madge in jerks and spasms. 'I'm being murdered here.'

'Ma's meeting us at Bellahouston. She'll take them off our hands.'

'At Bellahouston? You're a scream! How are we going to find your ma at Bellahouston?'

'We'd better find her. We want to enjoy ourselves and not be lumbered with this lot.'

Alec heaved his shoulders up and down, making Sadie and Agnes squeal with delight. And the squeals mingled with the cheers like a great fan, vivid with gaiety, pageantry and colour. The ceremony became a confused flicker of impressions distorted by excitement.

The King's voice fighting determinedly to defeat its stutter:

'Scotland believes that the best means of avoiding trouble is to provide against it, and that new enterprise is the safest insurance against the return of depression. It is in this spirit that the Exhibition has been built, and I see in it the symbol of the vitality and initiative upon which the continued prosperity of Scotland must rest.'

The strong confident voices of the people joining together to deliver with gusto the Twenty-fourth Psalm:

'Ye gates, lift up your heads on high . . .'

The machine-like smartness of the services led by the Navy

and dressed by the right.

The fly-past seen from the start as sweeps of shadows at intervals across the grass.

Then the hurrying, pushing and heaving towards Bellahouston Park and the great Empire Exhibition of 1938.

Only one thing marred Tuesday the third of May for Sammy Hunter, and that was his promise to go to Balornock in the evening, when he and Ruth had been invited to have supper with his father, his stepmother and five of his eight brothers who had come up from England especially to be at the opening of the Exhibition. Then later in the week there was to be a return visit.

All his brothers had scuttled off to various parts of England as soon as they were old enough, getting as far away as possible from Balornock. Normally they only returned once a year, for Hogmanay, but the Exhibition was something that could not be missed.

The sixteen turnstiles at the Mosspark entrance clicked merrily, but as Sammy and Ruth crushed along in the queue, the thought of the two evenings with his father hovered over the back of his mind, black shadows threatening to engulf and reduce to insignificance the wonderful achievement of the Exhibition opening up in front of his eyes.

'We should have come earlier.'

Head tipped forward as he walked, he flashed a glance round at Ruth from under his brows, but Ruth's starry-eyed attention refused to waver from the impressive entrance with its sweeping curve, its slender pillars, its high fluttering flags.

'If your father's comin' to us on Saturday we haven't much time to get the house all ready,' she told him absently. 'We'll have to do the shopping on Saturday afternoon.'

Shadows lengthened and leaned forward. Yet he wanted his father and mother and brothers to come over on Saturday to see his new home. He was proud of his house, proud of the work that he and Ruth had done to it. They had transformed it from a rotting brown hovel, with rusted grate and flaking ceiling and wallpaper hanging from the walls, to a modern, tastefully decorated home.

Ruth, of course, was his greatest pride and joy. A great cook and housekeeper, a wonderful lover and wife, she had the same passionate enthusiasm for setting a table, whipping up an omelette or bewitching him to the shuddering point of ecstasy in bed.

Often he wondered what she saw in him and then the miracle of their relationship seemed like a fragile bubble liable at any moment to burst in his guts and leave nothing but himself.

'Don't remind me of my father. Why do you always have to bring him up?' he grumbled.

'He's here, isn't he?' She shrugged. 'We could bump into him, couldn't we?'

'In all this crowd there shouldn't be much chance of that.'

'Who cares?' Ruth clutched his arm and squeezed it tightly against her breast. 'Isn't this wonderful?'

They were inside now, staring at the Exhibition's greatest promenade and beyond it and above it in the distance the tree-encircled Bellahouston Hill with Tait's Tower on top - a giant of steel and glass that dominated the gleaming white city of palaces and pavilions below and the scores of smaller buildings spread gaily over the park from the foot of the hill, poetry in pastel shades of blue, red, yellow and french grey.

Who cared? He cared!

This was to be a day of days, a time of pride for Glasgow and the whole of Scotland. He wanted to bask in the glory and pleasure of it like everybody else. Nothing should be allowed to spoil it, especially for Ruth. Determination put length and purpose into his step, and Ruth began to giggle as she clipped along beside him.

They began pointing things out to one another, the lofty flagstaffs, the lake with its submarine floodlights and batteries of milky fountains, the pavilions competing with one another in splendour.

By the time they had worked their way round to the British Pavilion, even Ruth's effervescent spirits were beginning to go flat.

'Sammy, it looks wonderful, but couldn't we save it for another day? We could come some Saturday afternoon, couldn't we, love? Or any evening after this week.'

He squeezed her hand in acquiescence although he was keenly disappointed. He had been especially looking forward to seeing around the United Kingdom Government Pavilion with the great gilded lions at the doors of its entrance hall. This pavilion was said to be one of the most impressive in the Exhibition.

A pool or moat with a bridge across it from the main exit ran the entire length of the building. Scientific research was the theme of the exhibits inside and he had read in the papers how really sensational it was. The entrance hall was ninety-five feet in height and the exit had a gigantic steel and glass globe representing the world floating in space.

'My feet are killing me.'

Ruth hopped on one foot as she bent down to remove a flimsy high-heeled shoe, wiggle her toes and empty the shoe of grit and dust.

'We could take one of the auto-trucks,' Sammy suggested.

The thought of him with his self-conscious downcast glower perched back to back with another passenger on one of the little open auto-buses for everyone to see made Ruth's eyes brighten with mischievous laughter.

'I think I'll survive. But only if we don't trail round another pavilion. Can we just make our way round to Paisley Road now, love?'

'Wear sturdier shoes next time,' Sammy growled, but both of them knew he didn't mean it.

They both liked to look smart. Ruth always wore high-heeled shoes and Sammy changed his shirt and put on a fresh starched collar every day of his life. Ruth was very particular about his clothes and he about hers. They always went shopping for clothes together, although going into the ladies' departments of a shop even with Ruth hanging on one arm was always an agony to Sammy.

He sighed.

Dust was swirling up with the wind and the shuffling of a hundred and forty-five thousand feet, parching his throat, stinging his eyes, and dragging heavily at his spirits, but perhaps it was only the thought of the impending journey to Balornock that depressed him.

He tried to throw the mood off in a sudden bluster of bravado.

'Come on, then, step it out smartly or you won't get any supper. The rest of the horrible Hunters will have eaten it all.'

'Sammy!'

Squealing in protest, stumbling, choking with laughter, she clung to his arm and struggled to keep up with his rapid strides.

'Sammy, will you stop it? Do you want me to get angry with you?'

'I'll have no insubordination from you, woman! You'll go over my knee as soon as we get home. You'll get a good thrashing if you don't watch your tongue!'

He came to an abrupt halt outside one of the Scottish pavilions high on terraced walls, patterned after North Country dykes, and boasting a many-windowed tower, an immense statue of St Andrew in the entrance hall and a huge aggressive-looking lion rampant emblazoned in scarlet on the outside wall.

This Scottish lion standing on its hind legs, chest puffed, tail cocked, tongue curled, forepaws bunched up like fists sparring for a fight, was the emblem of the Exhibition.

There was something about Sammy, as he stared up at it, shoulders back, red hair spiking in the wind, that resembled the Scottish symbol. He had an aggressiveness, a prickling - 'I'm ready for any comers - try me if you dare!' - outer covering that completely hid the man underneath.

'Good old Scotland!'

'Oh, Sammy, we're not going in, are we?' Her eyes, her body and her voice softened towards him. 'Honestly, love, I'm exhausted. I'm not nearly as strong as you, don't forget.'

He turned away. 'Oh, there'll be plenty more chances before October.'

The lofty Paisley Road entrance was in sight now but he stopped again, telling Ruth and himself that they could not leave without spending some time admiring the cascades, yet knowing that he was only succumbing to delaying tactics.

He stared solidly at the two giant staircases and the multi-coloured cascades leaping down from the top of the hill between them.

'Imagine that at night. Imagine this whole place floodlit.'

'It looks marvellous right now. Everything does. I've never seen any place so marvellous.'

'Its a grand achievement, this Exhibition. It shows what Scotland can do.'

A pause grew in significance between them. Until at long last he broke the silence.

'All right. All right. Come on. We mustn't keep his bloody Majesty waiting!'

Chapter 4

'It's only fair that I should go home with Ma,' Alec told Madge. 'After all, Ma's the one who's been stuck with the weans all day.'

Madge readily agreed.

'Aye, it's a damned shame.' She tucked a lock of hair behind her ear and laughed. 'Come on, hen.'

'Not you, gorgeous. You go straight home and keep the kettle boiling for me.'

Their cheerfulness grafted across the weary wailing of the children. Even Maisie, normally a gooing, dribbling cottage-loaf of good nature, was brokenhearted.

'These weans need their bed,' Mrs Jackson accused her daughter-in-law. 'It's terrible!'

Madge's freckled nose creased up.

'Och, right enough. Poor wee buggers!'

Alec gave her an encouraging pat on the shoulder, rubbed Maisie's baby head lolling helplessly against it and fondled the bottoms of his other three children, clinging round his wife's coat-tails.

'On you go with your mammy and you'll be all right.'

'Da . . . dae!' Hector lamented and the twins took up the cry like a death-song.

Madge shifted Maisie on to her other hip so that she could give Hector a shaking.

'Shut up! Silly wee midden.' Her tone was good-natured despite her words. There was always a hint of a cheerful guffaw behind everything Madge said. 'You heard your daddy. He's to take Gran home. She's tired and fed up and I don't blame her.'

'Those weans need their bed.' Mrs Jackson spoke like a gramophone unable to get past one groove. 'It's terrible!'

'Och, I know,' Madge sympathised and struggled with her free hand to grab the clothes or whatever part she could of Agnes, Hector and Sadie. 'And they've still to go all that way in

215

the tram. I'd better get started.'

'Right. See you later on, hen.' With a quick convivial wave to his wife, Alec shepherded his mother off and both were soon carried away by the same crowd that was jostling Madge and the children, whose cries were fast reaching a crescendo.

'It's a disgrace,' Mrs Jackson told Alec afterwards. 'Fancy, poor tired wee bairns like that out on the streets when they should be in their beds. I always had you scrubbed spotless and asleep hours before this. These weans are always out till all hours. It's terrible.'

'Aye, there's not many like you, Ma,' Alec said, adding to himself, 'Thank God,' because half the time his mother talked a lot of nonsense. She had been out scrubbing here, there and everywhere and had never known when he was in bed and when he wasn't.

'Well, I'll leave you here, Ma.' He put an arm round her shoulders and gave her a squeeze, when they'd left the tram-car and reached her close in Castle Street. 'You'll be as right as rain now.'

Her parchment skin tightened bulging her eyes with panic.

'Aren't you coming up for a cup of tea, son?'

'Some other time, hen.'

She leaned closer to him and gave him a conspiratorial nudge with a bony elbow.

'I might manage a wee nip of whisky in it. Just seeing it's you.'

He spread out his palms and shrugged in a gesture of helplessness.

'It's the weans, hen. You heard them. They like me to be there.'

She struggled to nod her agreement, almost an imperceptible movement at first as if her scraggy neck had locked.

'Aye.' Her nod suddenly loosened, became briskly enthusiastic. 'You're a good lad.'

For no apparent reason a blotchy redness was creeping up from her neck to make her face look patchy.

'Cheerio then, Ma.'

'Cheerio, son. When will I be seeing you again?'

The words hung uselessly in the air and he was away- spring-legged, shoulders swinging; his piercing whistle vying with the clash and clang of the tram-cars.

He was wondering what to do next when he literally bumped into Rita Gibson, a girl he used to work with, in more ways than one.

'Whoops!' He grinned down at her. 'No need to rush me, gorgeous. Take it easy. I'm willing.'

'Oh, it's you, Alec. Still the same as well. An arse for a mind.'

'Aren't you lucky then, bumping into the only man in the world who's got two?'

'Aye, and my man'll kick you in both of them if he finds you with me.'

'I'll bet five bob that right now your man's either at the Exhibition or in the pub.'

She smirked an invitation up at him.

'Five bob? Is that all?'

He winked and jerked his head to indicate better things round the corner.

'Come on, hen!'

The house in Balornock was up near the park and Stobhill Hospital, a cottage facing Little Hill Golf Course in as near the country as one could get within the boundary of Glasgow.

It was a lonely place on a rough track that led to Auchinairn, and hidden from the Balornock Corporation housing scheme by the hospital buildings and the tree-thickened end of the park.

The nearest building to the cottage was the hospital morgue and many a nightmare the proximity of the place had given Sammy. He could vividly remember the terrors of coming home from school on dark winter nights, or returning from an errand and having to pass the place, a red brick coffin set well apart from the rest of the hospital. Worse still were the punishments imposed by his father. The 'sentry duty', the 'standing watch', the torment of being propped against the morgue and left there alone in the dark.

'Now, just ignore him,' Sammy urged Ruth, automatically lowering his head and his voice as he approached the house. 'Don't get upset.'

Ruth made no reply as the garden gate squeaked open. They walked in silence through the shadows of the thick bower that made a low-roofed tunnel towards the door. Heavy trees crushed around the cottage blocking the windows and darkening the interior.

Sammy turned the handle and went in.

'Come on. Come on,' he growled at Ruth. 'There's no one waiting to jump on you with a gun.'

But the mere sight of the place made anxiety descend on him like an invisible cloak of fleas.

They made their way in single file along the dark lobby and into the gloomy parlour.

Hodge Hunter stood huge and wide-legged, blocking the smouldering fire. Thumbs hooked in waistcoat, head sunk low in a coarse bull neck, he cocked a glittering eye at them.

'Well, well! Here's my youngest.'

'How are you keeping, Mother?'

Sammy went straight over to his stepmother, a delicate little English lady, Hodge's third wife, and kissed her on the cheek.

'Oh, she's fine, fine.' Hodge's sandpaper voice rubbed out Mrs Hunter's reply. Sammy flashed a look of disgust before turning to him.

'Ruth's going to help you with the tea.'

'Well?' Hodge cut in hoarsely. 'Where's my dram?' His voice surged up like sea roaring against rocks. 'Stop simpering over your mammy. Give your old father a dram.'

Hodge had made it a ritual on the few and far between occasions of family gatherings that everyone should toast the event and come well supplied with liquor for the purpose.

'Now, now, Father, don't be rude,' Mrs Hunter chirped smiling brightly round at Sammy's brothers, who could hardly be seen because the room was so shadowy and dark and they seemed to be shrinking back in their chairs as if desperately trying to make themselves invisible. 'We ought to offer our guests a refreshment. I have it all ready.'

'You mean thon filthy slops you made the other day, you daft gowk! Do you want to poison us all?'

'Tt. Tt.' Mrs Hunter ducked her tongue and flashed quick

218

apologetic smiles all round. 'He is a naughty man, isn't he? I've got whisky out as well, Father, but I thought perhaps Ruth might like to sample my raspberry.'

'Prrr-rr - !' Hodge made a loud rude noise. 'There's your raspberry!'

'For God's sake!' Sammy's face rivalled the dark red of his hair. 'Stop behaving like an animal. You make me sick.'

'I love your home-made wine,' Ruth interrupted, coming forward with a defiant tilt to her head and a swing to her hips. 'I can't stand whisky.' Hodge made a growling noise in his throat as if he were getting ready to spit.

'Ye've no taste in your mouth, woman.'

Ignoring him, Ruth accepted the glass of wine Mrs Hunter poured out for her.

'Now, Sammy, here's yours, son. The boys have all got . . .'

'Here's to Scotland's grand Exhibition!' roared Hodge, swinging his glass high.

His sons eased cautiously to their feet to mumble down their whisky, but their father's voice, bawling out again, made them wince into silence.

'Here's tae us, wha's like us!' He flung back his drink, clattered the empty glass on to the mantelpiece, then screwed a fat neck round to his wife. 'Where's my tea, woman?'

'I'm just away to the kitchen to dish it, Father. I've made a nice . . .'

'Come on, come on, jump to it.' His sarcastic black beads of eyes straffed his sons. 'Get round the table. Some have meat that cannot eat,' he suddenly roared piously heavenwards. 'Some no meat that want it. But we have meat and we can eat and so the Lord be thankit!'

'I'll come through and help you, Mrs Hunter,' Ruth murmured, fluttering a worried glance at Sammy who was sitting down with the rest, eyes lowered like his brothers but fists white-knuckled.

'Well.' Hodge marched stiff-legged over to take his chair at the head of the table. 'I hope you come up with something better. This time for your dinner was rotten!'

Sammy stood up and his stepmother immediately tinkled with laughter.

'Sh, Father, you rude silly man.' Then brightly to Sammy, 'Sit down, son.'

Sammy was leaning forward, heavy-jowled and ugly.

'Don't worry,' Mrs Hunter went on as if she were imparting exciting news to a crowd of favourite infants. 'We're all going to have a lovely tea, and a lovely time, and everybody's going to enjoy themselves!'

Chapter 5

Catriona was terrified to tell either Melvin or her mother that she was pregnant. She dreaded the look of revulsion in her mother's eyes that would greet the announcement, the shrinking, the twist of the mouth and nose as if it was a filthy stinking disease Catriona was harbouring instead of a baby. She was caught in claustrophobia, unable to escape. The horror, the uncleanness, the guilt, was at the centre of herself.

Often she puzzled over her mother's attitude, at the same time not wanting to see the answer, dodging it, being temporarily reassured by her mother's insistent concern and dogmatic protestations of affection, yet all the time knowing what the answer was. Her mother hated her.

Only a few years ago, before her marriage, her mother's hatred of her had been made only too obvious. She had been panic-stricken by stabbing pains between her legs and a sudden gushing of blood that soaked her knickers and made her woollen stockings cling to her legs.

Shocked, and certain that she must have developed some dreadful disease, she hobbled through to the living-room where her mother was down on her knees raking out the fire.

'What'll I do? There's something wrong. I'm bleeding!'

'Get away from me!'

She could still see the turning of the head, the loathing in her mother's eyes, the screw of the nose and mouth against something foul smelling.

After that, not daring to mention the shameful bleeding again, there had been many anguished months worrying about when she was going to die, months of secretly ferreting for odd bits of rags to mop up the blood, of trying to find efficient ways of securing the rags between her legs so that they would not fall out and shame her while she was at school.

She could not remember how or when she discovered that the

221

bleeding was something known as menstruation and common to every woman - only that the knowledge had come too late.

The intimation of her first pregnancy had brought the same grimace, the same disgust to her mother's face. Only this time the words had been different.

'You poor child! A lot that man cares if you survive this ordeal or not. His first wife didn't!'

Melvin had puffed up with pleasure when he heard the news and immediately delivered a long lecture about animals and their similarity to humans, the tits of cows and the maternal instincts of female monkeys.

She had appealed to him to stop these uncalled-for and revolting comparisons but her distress had only encouraged him to launch into further explanations and illustrations.

Nature was a wonderful thing, he kept assuring her, hitching his shoulders and bulging his muscles to prove it. He insisted that she show him her abdomen and her breasts every day. He made her stand naked while he examined her and then, still naked, do exercises while he sat close, eyes bulging; a smile making his bushy moustache spread up.

He told her she must be massaged with olive oil or her skin would be ruined and when she protested he further horrified her by declaring:

'You'll have a belly like a plate of tripe. That's what happens when you don't get oiled. After the baby's born your belly will shrivel up like a plate of tripe.'

So she had been oiled. Gleefully he massaged her while she stood in the middle of the room with head lowered trying to hide her growing deformity, her distortion, her unloveliness, by allowing her long fair hair to droop forward and her hands to act as tiny ineffectual screens.

Although Melvin and she were alone, she always felt her mother's eyes upon her, the stare growing and multiplying until every eye in the world despised her nakedness. The eyes never left her, could see beyond the outward sin to the greater sin inside, to the moment when despite self-loathing - she felt a quiver of pleasure.

The miscarriage had been her punishment, another scar in the mind, something to blank out and never speak of, yet a scar that would always be there.

The stabbing pain, the sudden gush of blood, the cry for help, this time to Melvin, and Melvin bawling out:

'For Christ's sake watch my good carpet! You'll ruin it. Wait till I get a pail or something.'

Kneeling on the carpet unable to wait, the horror of the spreading stain, far outweighing her physical agony.

'I'm s-sorry, Melvin. I'm s-sorry, I'm s-sorry,' she stuttered as he rushed about with pails and cloths before he even phoned for an ambulance.

Then the humiliations of the hospital examinations and the peculiar callousness of the abortion ward where doctors and nurses seemed to take it for granted that their patients, unmarried or married, had purposely caused their conditions. The whole staff were a vengeful God's representatives, whose duty it was to punish the miscarriers.

The thought of going through it all again appalled her. Even if she did not miscarry this time, the prospect was bleak. Her mother and her mother's friends had prepared her with plenty of gory tales about childbirth.

Most of all, she feared Melvin's reaction, and kept putting off the dreaded day of telling him until suddenly he said:

'For God's sake try and make a better job of it this time.'

'A better job of it?' she echoed, eyes anxious to understand.

'You've got another bun in the oven, haven't you?'

'A bun in the . . . ?'

His eyes bulged upwards with impatience.

'Pregnant! Pregnant!!'

'Oh.' She turned a deep pink, making the pale colour of her hair more noticeable in contrast. 'Yes, I am.' A delicate little sound as she cleared her throat. 'And please don't start comparing me with animals, Melvin. I don't like it.'

Melvin's moustache flurried out with a loud guffaw of laughter.

'I bet you don't like having a bun in the oven either but it's there, darlin'. You can't beat nature.'

She tried not to tremble. She struggled to smooth calmness

223

around her for protection because instinctively she knew that she must protect herself.

'It upsets me and I mustn't get upset while I'm pregnant.'

'Well, don't!'

'There was nothing physically wrong with me before. They told me. It must have been caused by nerves.'

'Well, don't have nerves. Physical jerks, that's the thing. And deep breathing.' He widened his nostrils and expanded his chest to enormous proportions. 'Nothing like physical jerks and deep breathing to keep you fit.'

An aura of stubbornness descended on her. She lowered her head, this time not submissively, but aggressively.

'Don't talk about animals.'

'"Don't talk about animals",' Melvin mimicked, then still with hilarity in his voice he added, 'Don't you tell me what to talk about. I'll talk about what I like.'

'Don't talk about animals and don't make me do exercises.'

'Aw, shut up.' He turned away.

'No, I won't. I won't.'

The trembling was beyond control now - a series of rapid convulsions growing in strength.

'You're the one who's like an animal. No, you're worse. You're coarse. You're ignorant. You're insensitive. I wish I'd never set eyes on you. I wish I was home! I wish I was home!'

'With your holy cow of a mammy?' he sneered, swinging round on her, broad-shouldered and long-armed.

'I wish I was home!'

'What home, you idiot? "Do not lay up for yourselves treasures on earth", your mammy's always quoting from her precious Bible, and she's carried it out to the letter, hasn't she? Your "home" is as bare as a railway waiting-room and you hadn't a stitch to your back when you married me. Your mammy's that holy and generous she's given everything away. What have you got to go back to? "Home", did you say?' He laughed again and suddenly pulled her into his arms. 'Forget it!'

She could never credit how different marriage was from the fairy-tale land of women's magazines and romantic novels. She had read so many of them after she had left school only a few years ago, and they had been so cosy and enjoyable that no matter what happened, part of her would always believe them.

In fiction-fairyland the husband never knew about pregnancies until he was told and then, after being speechless with joy for a few minutes, he suddenly rushed for a chair to ease his wife into as if she were made of the most delicate, the most precious china.

After that, during the whole pregnancy in fact, he watched her anxiously while she kept laughing and assuring him that she was perfectly all right. And she was perfectly all right, except perhaps for little fads and fancies like wanting a melon or a bowl of soup in the middle of the night, when the husband would walk miles searching for titbits.

In real life she had once taken a terrible craving for chips. She was usually in bed alone most of the nights because Melvin worked downstairs in the bakehouse but this had been his night off and she had timorously tugged at his arm until he had grunted awake.

'Whassa matter, eh?'

'Melvin, I'm sorry, but I fancy some chips.'

'You must be joking, darlin'.'

'No,' she assured him. 'I'd love some chips.' Her mouth watered at the thought. 'With plenty of salt and vinegar.'

'Chips be damned!' he chortled, pulling her towards the hot sweaty smell of his body. 'I know what you want!'

'No, Melvin, please!' She tried to flurry away his octopus hands but he jerked on top of her, his massive shoulders and hairy chest pinning her down gasping for breath.

Sometimes she hated the writers of romantic fiction for deceiving her so outrageously and yet all the time she longed for their rosy, gentle world and hoped that one day she might find it.

The only person in the family who took the news with acquiescence was Fergus, her stepson.

'You'll like having a little baby brother or sister, won't you, Fergie?' She knelt down in front of him and held his hands together.

'Yes, thank you,' he replied, his blue eyes empty.

'Oh, you will, you will!' she repeated more to reassure herself than the child standing so still in his scuffed shoes and drooping socks and school-cap slightly askew.

Her mind was speeding along two concurrent lines. She would have to tidy Fergus up before Melvin saw him or she would get a row. Melvin was almost as fussy about the care of Fergus's clothes and person as he was about the scrubbing and polishing of everything in the house.

'My house', he often expostulated, 'has always been the best furnished, best-looking place in Clydend and I want it kept that way. There isn't another floor in the whole of Glasgow that's ever had such a marvellous polish as that!'

Or about Fergus he would hitch back his shoulders and boast:

'That child is the best-behaved, best-mannered, most obedient child in Scotland.'

Indeed, for most of the time with adults, and especially with his father, Fergus was a model of quiet perfection.

Yet he was capable of unexpected extremes of emotion that frightened Catriona.

Sometimes she would walk past him when he was playing contentedly on the floor, or so it seemed, and suddenly he would lunge at her, clinging to her legs and hugging them with the strength of a maniac who would never let go. More than once after unsuccessful attempts to free herself, she had panicked and screamed for Melvin. But when Melvin arrived on the scene Fergus was always innocently playing with his toys again as if nothing had happened.

Now, since he had started school odd reports were reaching her of violent behaviour towards other children.

'You'll love a little brother or sister, and look after it, and be kind to it, won't you?'

'Yes, thank you,' Fergus replied.

She released his hands and allowed him to walk away. He was a strange child.

She struggled to her feet to stand absently nibbling at her nails. She felt far from happy.

Chapter 6

Sammy marched along Clyde Street from the office of the wholesale warehouse where he worked, hands in pockets, eyes down on shoes. Normally when he reached the Saltmarket he jumped on a tram car for home. This time he decided to stretch his legs and walk for a bit.

The Balornock ordeal was well in the past, with time deadening it, pushing it further and further away like a comforting growth of cotton wool. The return visit had become another milestone that he tried to leave far behind him too. Although visions still streaked across his mind's eye, and every now and again an echo startled him.

He hated his father's voice. It made him feel sick. His father sounded as if he were perpetually gathering phlegm in his throat in readiness to spit. His voice had the unnerving habit of changing in tone and volume, for no apparent reason. Even a normal remark about the weather was liable to swell into a lion-sized roar. It see-sawed between correct, carefully intonated English and a coarse Scots dialect that twisted into a sneer.

Sammy hated the sound of his father's voice but even more he hated his silences.

He had watched him enter the house in silence and silently march around poking at things with his heavy silver-topped stick as if he were conducting a kit inspection. He watched until he could bear it no longer. Ruth and he were painfully proud of their room and kitchen, proud but unsure. They had in their eagerness for originality and perfection experimented with colours and new ideas, and spent rather more than they could afford.

'There's still a lot we'd like to do,' he burst into his father's silence eventually. 'But we've had to call a halt. It's a question of money.'

Hodge poked underneath a cushion, caught a silk stocking on

227

the end of his stick and hitched it high in the air.

'You've had to call a halt!' his voice exploded before settling down to a hoarse rasp. 'About time, too!'

He had secretly cursed Ruth's untidiness, while knowing perfectly well that his father was to blame for purposely coming too early, before she had time to put everything away.

All the same he cursed her afterwards and a bitter quarrel had shattered the last remnants of pleasure in their grand new home. Until later, lying stiff and unhappy in the darkness, beside her in the cabinet bed he felt her toes and her fingers begin to edge caressingly towards him. Then her body wriggled gently nearer, melting his misery with its warmth and its voluptuous quivering flesh. She began kissing every part of him except his mouth although his mouth sought hers with increasing anxiety.

His temples, his eyes, his ears, her tongue tickling and exciting in exploration. The hollow of his neck, deep under his arm, his belly, his groin.

His pace lengthened and quickened after turning left into the Saltmarket. He banished Ruth from his mind and concentrated instead on his immediate surroundings.

Many famous names had been associated with the Saltmarket. Oliver Cromwell had lodged in the street when he occupied Glasgow. King James VII had visited a house here when he was Duke of York. Daniel Defoe had walked along this street. But it had been a different place in those days. Some hundred-odd years after Defoe's visit, the Saltmarket and the near-by streets, Goosedubs, Bridgegate, King Street, Trongate, High Street and Gallowgate had been described as 'a citadel of vice'. Within less than one sixteenth of a square mile there were a hundred and fifty shebeens and two hundred brothels.

Glasgow had been and still was a grim city. Yet it had a bouncy pulse of humanity and a humorous quirk that was the very essence of the place.

He liked the story about the crowds outside the Justiciary buildings in Jail Square on the left side of Saltmarket. Glasgow folk love a pageant, a procession, any kind of show, and crowds always gathered to watch the beginning of each High Court, with the trumpeters and the solemn-bewigged judges. A crowd gathered at the end of each big trial across the road at the entrance to Glasgow Green. The police, fearing trouble from the supporters of gangsters who had just been sentenced, and danger to witnesses leaving the court-house, decided it was imperative that something should be done. There was only one way to disperse a mob at this particular spot. The Parks Department of Glasgow Corporation planted a few flower-beds to break up the open space. No Glaswegian, not even a gangster, would trample over a flower-bed. Even a gangster being chased by a policeman would make a detour round a flower-bed and the policeman chasing him would do the same.

The South Prison used to be in Jail Square and prisoners were hanged in public outside it. The last thing a condemned person saw before he died was Nelson's monument in Glasgow Green - a fact which gave rise to the Glasgow insult, 'You'll die facing the Monument'.

The last person hanged there was an Englishman, a Doctor Pritchard who had poisoned his wife and mother-in-law in his house in Sauchiehall Street. Thirty thousand men, women and children had gathered to watch the hanging in eighteen sixty-five. Bakers and piemen did a roaring trade and as usual on these occasions, including the years when pickpocketing was a hanging offence - pick-pockets did their best business.

Sammy saw a white tram coming and raced for it.

A memory of his father had caught at his guts and the sudden burst of energy helped to excoriate it.

His father would have enjoyed public hangings. To watch someone suffer puffed him up with glee and to deliver the punishment himself was a luxury he indulged in as often as possible.

The Hunter family had always been organised along military lines. They mustered to attention by the sides of their beds at the crack of dawn for kit inspection. Then they route-marched to the park every morning before school and twice on Sundays and round and round inside the park before having to perform violent exercises to the sergeant-major roar of their father.

Some of the older brothers had been lucky. They could

229

remember a spell in their youngest days when Hodge had been away from home. Sammy being the last born had had no such luck.

Punishments ran along military lines, too - square bashing, at the double, and in full kit, and full kit could be anything heavy his father managed to find with which to weigh them down. Detention was being locked all night in the coal-cellar. Duty watch meant the mortuary. Hodge had also delved back in time and come up with punishments the army had long since abolished, like flogging and the old army custom of branding.

Only once had the latter punishment been meted out and Sammy had been the recipient.

His father had been asking the family, one by one, what regiment they would join if ever their country needed them. Each brother in turn mumbled the regiment of his choice but when it came to his turn, hatred suddenly rocketed up to distort his features and rush bile to his mouth with the word:

'None!'

'What regiment?' His father's face blocked sight, filled the whole world.

'None!'

'What regiment?'

'None!'

He could see the first wave of shock receding and the vision of punishment to come taking its place.

'Eh? Eh? . . . What's this? What's this? Would you not fight for your King and country?'

'No.'

'You're a disgrace to the name of Hunter. You're a bloody coward!'

His mother had been alive then, a pathetic shadow of a woman, and he always believed the ceremonial sadism of his branding had been the last straw that had killed her. His stepmother, not having been dragged down by constant child-bearing and the burden of his father, and having perhaps a spunkier nature, might have gone to the police for help, where his own mother struggled to protect him and failed.

The deep scar on his chest was still there.

230

He had told no one the truth of its origin, not even Ruth, brushing aside questions with irritable hints of road accident injuries.

He stared with grey marble eyes out of the tram-car window. It had left the Saltmarket, trundled beyond it up High Street, rocked round the bulge that was Castle Street before the long stretch of road from the Saltmarket straightened out again and became Springburn Road.

He allowed his body to rock and jerk with the motion of the tram and his mind open to the whirling grind of it as it struggled up the steep gradient towards the heart of Springburn.

First stop in Springburn Road - St Rollox works. Three stops past that - Springburn Cross. There at the hub of Springburn two streets diverged from the main road, Cowlairs Road on the left leading to Cowlairs Locomotive Works and Vulcan Street to the right leading to the main gate of Hyde Park Locomotive Works.

Over the railway bridge now at Springburn Station and the Atlas Works. Where else in all the world, it occurred to him, his spirits surfing on a wave of pride, could a passenger in a tram-car, in the course of a half-mile journey along a public highway, have found such a concentration of railway skills. Company works, private builders, major sheds, and a mainline cable-worked incline.

Away to the west, cranes of the Clyde shipyards spiked the sky. To the north stretched the magnificent sweep of open country across the Kelvin Valley to the Campsie Fells and the first West Highland mountains, including Ben Lomond and Ben More.

But down here where he lived was the next busiest part of Springburn to the Cross. The tenement houses, all with shops below, were old and often dilapidated but there was a homely buzz of life around them. Springburn was a beehive, always busy, busy with people, busy with movement, busy with talk. Traffic passed ceaselessly to and fro, courting couples swung along hand in hand, mothers heaved energetically at prams, and there were always railwaymen in dungarees and shiny caps

231

going on their shifts or coming off with black, soot-smeared faces.

He warmed to the place as he crossed the road to the corner where the usual crowd of men were standing arguing about football. Children were thumping a ball in his close and singing in light bouncy voices:

'One, two, three, a leary. Four, five, six, a leary, seven, eight, nine, a leary, ten a leary postman!'

He ran up the stairs, his young-old face brightening to find Ruth with the door open and arms wide waiting for him. He grabbed her waist and made her squeal with excitement as he heaved her up and whirled her round and round their freshly painted hall.

Then suddenly he stopped. He held her close, one hand pressing her dark head hard against his shoulder.

He shut his eyes. He prayed for the sadness to go away - and with it the premonition of something terrible, not in the nightmare past, but something still to come in the future.

Chapter 7

'Get your hands off my man!'

Madge battered through the swing doors of the insurance office just as Jean, one of the typists, was struggling with breathless laughter to forcibly remove Alec from her chair.

Draped nonchalantly back, his long legs propped on top of her typewriter, Alec had been enjoying the girl's hands tugging at him and her breasts bulging over the top of her blouse as she jerked back and forward under his nose.

The sudden arrival of his wife knocked both the typist and himself off balance.

'You rotten selfish little tart.'

Madge advanced, big-boned, high-hipped, feet and hands like spades.

'Playing around with a married man - and him with four weans!'

'No! No!' Jean protested. 'You've got it all wrong.'

'Oh, come on, gorgeous!' Alec slipped between them and pinched Madge's pale freckled cheek. 'As if anybody could lure me away from you.'

Madge knocked him aside.

'I was told about you,' she loudly accused the typist again.

'About me?'

'You heard.'

'What about me?'

'You've been seen going around with my man, hanging on to him like a leech. I'll leech you!'

'Alec!' the girl appealed.

'I'll Alec you!'

Madge's hand shot out and found bull's-eye on the girl's nose. Blood spurted in the silence for a horrified moment before Jean managed to wring out a long agonised scream.

Alec tugged at his wife's arm.

'Madge, for pity's sake, come on home before they get the police to us.'

The normally quiet sedate routine of the office had switched to uproar and typists were running, whinnying for Mr Torrance.

'Quick!' Alec urged, putting his arm round Madge and hauling her off. 'Before old Torrance arrives!'

As he told her later, on the angry march home:

'You'll be lucky if I'm not ruined and you're not in the nick by tomorrow. Then what would the weans do?'

'Women like that ought to be shot.' Madge tucked a straggle of short hair behind her ears then suddenly grinned. 'I did not bad, though, considering I hadn't a gun.'

They plunged into the gloom of the pend, their feet echoing like a stampede of wild horses.

'But look, Madge, I've enough trouble tangling with women at work without you making things worse.'

'I was there to help you.' Her voice became angry again. 'You ought to see Mr Torrance. You ought to tell him, Alec.'

'Tell him what?'

'That women won't leave you in peace.'

'What can he do, hen? Except to tell me to pack in the job. The married ones are the worst,' he confided. 'Some of the houses I go to - my God, I've to fight them off.'

'Which houses?' Madge stopped at the foot of the outside stairs, one red hand gripping the railing. 'Tell me which ones. I'll fight them off all right.'

'Sparrin' for a barney, eh?' One of their neighbours leaning on her window sill, plump arms folded to support her big chest, cosily joined in the conversation.

'It's a bloody wee midden in the office trying to get away with my man.'

'No!' Mrs White looked suitably shocked.

Alec shook his head.

'Honest to God, hen,' he appealed to the neighbour. 'It beats me where she got the idea.

'Mary down the road told me "A girl you worked with" she said,' Madge explained. 'Saw her hanging on to you like a leech and hauling you up a close in Castle Street.'

Gazing up at the older woman, her voice loudening, she added: 'And when I went in to the office today to find out which wee midden it was - I caught her - carrying on before my very eyes!'

'No!'

Alec chortled out loud. A case of mistaken identity. 'Mary down the road' must have got her beady eye on him on one of his visits to Rita Gibson.

'Madge gave her a straight right.'

Alec began jerkily sparring, head down, fists jabbing backwards and forwards, as he bounced up and down on the balls of his feet.

'And then a left hook and then a quick one, two, three to finish her off!'

With a howl of hilarity Madge punched and unbalanced him against the stairs.

'I gave her a bloody nose though!'

'No!'

A smell of kippers and ham and eggs titillated their nostrils. Windows were open, frying pans sizzling, getting-ready-for-high-tea-happy-sounds.

A little girl jumped up and down, legs twisting and knotting as if desperate to hold in water.

'Mammy, Mammy!'

'What is it?' (A bawl from inside one of the houses.)

'Mammy, fling me a jeely piece.'

'Yer tea's nearly ready.'

'Och, I'm starving.'

Then like manna from heaven a piece of bread, spread liberally with jam, sailed out one of the top windows.

'Come on.' Alec made a rush at the stairs. 'I'm starving as well.'

The children had been left in the house while Madge went round to the office and they spilled out with the dog the moment she opened the door. In a few months' time there might be another to add to the rush because Madge had 'missed' again. He hoped she was pregnant. Nothing like a baby to keep a woman out of mischief.

'Right, hen!' His hand slid between her buttocks and underneath to tickle her as the children milled around them. 'I'll go through to the room and have a look at the paper while you get the tea ready.'

His finger kept twitching the back of her dress as he walked close behind her, until she smacked at his hand.

'Get off!'

He went through to the room whistling and glad that his brood had followed their mother into the kitchen in the hope of something to eat.

The sight of the old roll-top desk reminded him of work and his mouth twitched. A case of mistaken identity - poor old Madge, always blundering into something or other. Just in case she blundered into Rita Gibson he had better be careful.

He had been making a habit of Rita since bumping into her the day the Exhibition opened. Her man was an engine-driver at Eastfield and worked shifts. Railwaymen worked damnable hours - never the same ones from one week to the next. His shifts went all round the clock, starting at a different time each week. He was older than Rita - past it probably - that would explain her insatiable appetite. Just could not get enough. He would have to cut her down. She was a right hairy.

Now take Ruth Hunter. She was different - a plum; ripe, succulent, juicy.

The door opened, interrupting an imagined energetic grapple with Ruth. 'I've given the weans theirs,' Madge announced, slapping her bottom down on a chair. 'So that we can have ours in peace after.' She slumped back. 'God, Alec, I'm tired.'

Now that he looked at her, he could see she was pregnant. Thick-waisted and high-bellied she sat with her knees splayed out and her hands hanging helplessly in the hollow of dress at her groin.

'Och, never mind, hen,' he comforted. 'I'll stay in tonight.'

Her freckled face brightened and she gave him a big grin.

'You mean it?'

''Course I do.'

'There's a good programme on the wireless.'

'Mm-mm!' He winked. 'Nothing as good as the programme

236

I've lined up for you!'

She laughed but her enthusiasm tailed off a little.

'No kidding, Alec. I'm beat.'

He came across to hunker down in front of her and slipped his hand gently up her skirt.

'You won't have to do a thing. You'll just lie back and relax and enjoy yourself.'

'Get off!' she protested, but remained in the same slumped back position as if she had not enough energy to move.

She sighed.

'You're a randy bugger.'

'Aren't you lucky!' he said.

'I'll kill you if you leave me for that wee midden in the office. And I'll kill her as well. Becky McKay's man went away and left her and she had to go to the poorhouse. Fancy! Becky McKay's in Barnhill and she gets chucked out every morning with all her weans. She's to walk the streets all day until they let her back in at night.'

With a jerk she awakened from her reverie.

'Alec!'

A stampede along the lobby made Alec sit back on the floor and Madge tug her skirt down just in time, as the door burst open and Sadie and Hector came yelling in the room.

'He stole my piece,' Sadie accused. 'I was helping Maisie eat her tea and he stole my piece.'

'Didn't! Didn't! Sneaky big clipe!'

Alec suddenly let out a bear growl and lunged at them on his hands and knees and they went hopping and skipping back along the lobby, with Alec after them, their fury changing to hysterical screams of excitement.

Madge followed, tucking her hair behind her ears and laughing.

The kitchen was small and hot because even in summer the fire had to be on to heat the oven at the side, and the hobs on top for cooking.

'It's sausages.' She tried to make Alec hear above the din. 'Do you want a couple of eggs with them?'

Alec got up and enjoyed a good stretch.

237

'I'll take anything you've got to offer me, gorgeous!'

'That's three slices of sausage and a couple of eggs.'

She grinned, adding good-humouredly to Sadie, 'Grab that bread knife from Maisie, hen, she's going to kill herself!'

Alec leaned over the iron sink to peer for a minute the window into the yard below.

He felt good. Life was good.

Turning back to his family and his tea he began to sing.

'Pack up your troubles in your old kit bag and smile, smile, smile . . .'

The children joined in, banging their spoons.

'What's the use of worrying? It never was worth while - so-o-o . . . !'

Chapter 8

Catriona's baby was due in November and now, seven, nearly eight months pregnant, it looked as if she was not going to miscarry. The baby heaved and kicked violently inside her. She could actually see it lumping up her smock as she sat resting her aching back against a pile of cushions on one of the sitting-room chairs.

It was obscene. She averted her gaze from herself but her eyes kept returning to stare at the jolting, mountainous abdomen.

'Is that the bell?'

Melvin flung down his newspaper as Catriona heaved herself up.

'I'll go.'

'Sit still! I'll see who it is.'

'I want to go.' She glared at him. 'I'm fed up sitting still.'

He bulged his eyes heavenwards and reached for his newspaper again.

A tall good-looking man stood at the door. Despite her misery and the hundred and one aches and pains that plagued her, dragged her down with the ponderous weight, she experienced a tiny thrill. The slim body, the dark hair, the twinkling eyes, reminded her of young Jimmy Gordon, the confectioner in the bakehouse who had died so suddenly.

Her eyes shrank down, her cheeks crimsoned with the shame of her appearance. Shutting the door a little she whispered round it.

'Yes?'

Alec grinned and winked at her.

'Hello, you gorgeous doll. I'm Alec Jackson and I've lost my mammy.'

Her hand flew to her mouth to stifle an unexpected giggle.

'I know I'm a big boy,' he said. 'But it's true.'

'Isn't Mrs Jackson upstairs?'

239

'Everybody in this stair must be dodging me, hen. I've knocked on every door and you're the first wee soul that's answered.'

'Maybe she's down in the shop.'

'You're a genius!'

Another almost imperceptible giggle was captured in her hands and timorous eyes peeped expectantly up at him.

He puckered his lips and bunched his fingertips against them to flick a kiss towards the gradually narrowing crack in the door.

'And a gorgeous wee blondie as well!'

The door clicked shut and she shuffled flat-footed back across the hall, rocking from side to side, a tiny boat a-bob bob bobbing.

'Well?'

Melvin's mustachioed face rose from the top of his paper.

Catriona slumped into the cushions.

'Well, what?'

'What do you mean, "Well, what"?' His eyes protruded with indignation. 'Who was that at my door?'

'Somebody looking for Mrs Jackson.' She shifted about irritably, restlessly. 'Anyway, it's not your door!'

'Not my door? Jumpin' Jesus, you're going off your nut like your mother.'

'If it's any kind of door, it's our door. Everything's always yours, yours, yours.'

'Well, everything is mine!'

Her fists bunched on her lap as if keeping a tight grip on tears.

'Nothing belongs to me and I don't belong anywhere.'

'What are you blethering about now?'

'Oh, shut up!'

'Don't you tell me to shut up!'

'Shut up! Shut up! Shut up!'

Melvin tossed his newspaper aside and stretched to his feet menacingly to hitch and bulge huge muscles over her.

'What are you going to do?' she queried, her personal discomforts niggling her far beyond fear. 'Challenge me to a wrestling match?'

He held his pose for a shocked second, then suddenly he flung back his head in a loud bellow of laughter.

She could not help laughing herself, although the hilarity that made her shiver in her nest of cushions was dangerously near the opposite extreme of heartbroken tears.

Melvin perched his heavy bulk on the side of her chair and put a gorilla arm round her shoulders.

'That's not a bad idea! Give us a kiss!'

Dodging his lips she pecked at his cheek.

'Melvin, I'm sorry but I'm absolutely exhausted. I'm fit for nothing until I get a cup of tea. Would you like to make it, dear? You do it so much better than me.'

She watched him hesitate and saw in his face the fear that he might be endangering his manhood. She pecked him again.

'I don't know what I'd do without your strength at a time like this. I feel absolutely useless!'

He guffawed with laughter.

'You are useless! Stay there. I'll go and make the tea. But you'd better enjoy it and be grateful, do you hear?'

'Yes, thank you, Melvin.'

He went through to the kitchen and she closed her eyes and sat with her arms hanging limply over the arms of the chair. She tried to relax. She tried to think pleasant thoughts to help her relax. It was no use. Her eyes opened; annoyance, vexation, harassment, elbowing for expression. Every few seconds she had to move, to hitch herself clumsily from one position to another, working herself through a hundred minute variations of body and limbs. And still she could not find a comfortable position.

Then she took an unbearable pubic itch. She looked furtively around to make sure that neither Melvin nor anyone else could see her, before having an exquisite scratch.

She felt sore, sore in the groin, sore in the back, sore in the breasts - her tiny boyish breasts now swollen, brown-stained, blue-veined.

In sudden pique she jerked her head from side to side at the same time bouncing her shoulders up and down, like a spoiled child stamping in a tantrum made worse by being so cruelly weighed down.

Her flurry of revolt against the injustice of it all gave her a throbbing headache and brought weak tears of defeat.

The only consolation she could find was that in a few weeks it would all be over. No more restlessness, no more having to trot to the lavatory every fifteen minutes and less at night. Her need to pass water had become so frequent she was like a sleepwalker staggering in and out of bed, in and out of the bathroom, the whole night long.

No more not being able to keep her stockings up, or fasten her shoes, no more indigestion and heartburn, no more gluttonous cravings that made her sick with shame.

For days now, unknown to Melvin, she had been consuming, one after the other, half-a-dozen rhubarb tarts. Fergus had caught her the other night and had stood, mouth drooling, dying for just one. But she had childishly clutched the box in her arms and told him to go away.

Porridge was another thing! She had greedily supped potfuls and potfuls of the stuff, often horrifying both Melvin and Fergus by wolfing into a tin of fruit salad immediately afterwards.

She would not be a bit surprised if, once the birth was over, she could never face porridge or fruit salad. She was perfectly certain that she would never, never look at that bottle-green bell-tent of a swagger-coat again.

Never! Never! Never!

Tears gushed faster. How did she know she would even be herself again. How did she know she would have the strength to survive the terrible unknown ordeal yet to come.

If only she could close her eyes and open them to find it had all been a nightmare. Hopefully, she tried it, though she knew there was no escape. The knowledge that she was trapped had been steadily closing in on her like unknown assailants in a pitch black room.

Terror that defied expression shuddered from her roots, clawed up years of black indoctrination, dogmatically instilled fear, ignorance, enforced severance from her contemporaries, imprisonment in her mother's iron womb.

'What's wrong now?' Melvin asked when he returned carrying

242

a tray of tea-things.

A minute or two passed as her sobs racketed wilder and she was unable to speak.

Unnerved by the unexpectedness of the outburst Melvin put down the tray and in his haste slopped tea into the saucers.

'Hell's bells!' he roared. 'Now look what you've done.'

'M . . . M . . . Melvin!' she managed to choke out eventually. 'I'm . . . I'm . . . frightened!'

'Frightened? Frightened of what?'

'M . . . M . . . Melvin! M . . . M . . . Melvin!'

He smacked a shovel of a hand against his brow.

'Jumpin' Jesus!'

'Please help me!'

He hesitated, his face screwed with an exasperation that quickly relaxed into a chuckle.

'Come here!' He stomped over and sat down in the chair opposite her. 'Come over and sit on my knee.'

She nodded, jerky and hiccoughing with sobs. Eagerly her hands clutched at the arms of her chair. She pulled, and heaved, grunted and wriggled, rocked and kicked out her legs but was unable to get up.

Melvin began to laugh. Tears of laughter dripped down and wet his moustache.

'Come on!'

She kept trying, breathless now, and skin shining with sweat, eyes big and soft and tragic like a seal's.

Until she stood in front of him, her strange heart rapidly pittering, and above it her own heart pounding with grief.

She knew at that moment what it was really like to be a woman, and she would never forget it as long as she lived.

'Come on!' Melvin chortled, loudly smacking his knees. 'Don't just stand there like an elephant!'

She waddled a few steps, pushing her abdomen in front of her and thankfully eased herself down on his lap. Then with a long shuddering sigh her head collapsed back against his shoulder.

'I know what you need,' Melvin said, his hand already searching out her breast.

'No.'

243

'I know what you need, better than you know yourself!'

'No!'

He pulled one tender milky breast from blouse and brassière, balanced it on his palm then flipped and smacked it up and down.

He was settled back in his chair, relaxed, taking his time, enjoying himself.

God who was a man, God who made all men, she thought, damn Him!

Chapter 9

The Exhibition flag on the tower was to be lowered at midnight on Saturday, 29 October, to signify the end of the Empire Exhibition to which Glasgow had been generous host.

Enormous crowds flocked to Bellahouston Park to enjoy the sights and smells and sounds of the Exhibition before the gates were locked for the last time.

Alec, Madge, his mother and the children went for an hour or two in the afternoon. Alec took the children on a screaming hilarious trip through the amusements park the giant wheel, the stratoship, the whirler, the crazy house with its walls and windows all out of perspective and its noisy mechanical cats. There they all wandered about eating new pink clouds of sugar called candy floss, and licking the latest thing from Canada - a whipped up whirl of ice-cream.

A special air of gay abandon stirred among the vast crowds a determination to toss all Scottish caution to the winds and whoop it up, enjoy themselves before everything packed up and went away.

Alec was no exception. He planned to take Madge and the family home and come back on his own to really have a time of it. After all, poor old Madge could not be expected to whoop it up. She was more likely to drop it down.

Anyway she had developed varicose veins, and something had gone wrong with her ankles, in fact she seemed to be puffing up like a balloon all over. He had never seen her look such a mess. Her hair, mousy at the best of times hung lifeless and greasy. One of the neighbours had cut it for her and made it too short at the back and too long at the sides. Patches of white skin showed at the nape of her neck but two lank tufts of hair kept straggling forward to cover her ears. Her freckles looked worse, too. Clusters of them seemed to have joined together to make brown smudgy patterns. The only decent things left about her were her eyes, wide-apart, bright candid blue, and that big-toothed grin she could always come up with.

'I think it's time I got you safely back home, hen.' He squeezed an arm as far as he could round the swollen waist. 'I don't want you collapsing here and being trampled underfoot by a mob like this.'

His mother's mouth worked with emotion.

'He's a good lad.'

'Aye,' Madge agreed, wiping away the remains of her ice-cream with the back of a red work-roughened hand. 'Alec is good to me, so he is!'

She had never been a daft sentimental type, but the love in her eyes as she smiled up at him was suddenly embarrassingly obvious.

He gave her bottom an affectionate pinch.

'Right home to bed with you!'

'God! Home to bed, he says!' She flung back her head with a shout of laughter. 'And him has to go out collecting and me all the weans to feed and put down.'

'Now, now,' Mrs Jackson reprimanded. 'Count your blessings. You've got a good man, he's out day and night struggling to make enough to feed you.'

'Och, I know,' Madge agreed.

'I'd come and see to the weans only I'm supposed to clean that . . . that what you call it?'

'Bakehouse,' Alec prompted.

Sometimes he thought she was going mad. In her bouts of forgetfulness his mother had been known to forget her own name.

'That's right. Clean that bakehouse before the late ones come in and you should see the place. You should just see what I've to do. I've to take a knife to that floor. Imagine! A knife to scrape it! It takes me hours and it's just as bad again the day after.'

'Och, it's a damn shame.' Madge scratched her belly. 'I'd be over giving you a hand if it wasn't for this.'

'Come on, you gorgeous hunk of woman, you!' Alec linked arms with her.

There was going to be open-air dancing after dark. He could

hardly wait.

Ruth and Sammy took their time going round. Right from the first day Ruth had admired the Women of Empire Pavilion with its orange sunblinds, its fluttering pennants, its girdle of scarlet geraniums and pale forget-me-nots, its handful of pink lilies in the lily pond. To please her, Sammy went round the building with her yet again.

Ruth also liked the Keep Fit Pavilion run by the National Fitness Council for Scotland.

There had been quite a *furor* over that particular pavilion at first. Three eight-feet-high photographs of nude female statues had been a feature of the place, on mirror panels at the back of an open-air stage.

Indignant complaints were made about showing female figures and quite a battle raged as a result. Eventually a compromise decision was reached. The promoters of the pavilion decided that nude female figures, even though they were merely photographs of statues, were not quite the thing for the general public. They could, however, be shown discreetly in a more inconspicuous corner. And until they could be moved they were screened off from public gaze.

Ruth and Sammy had a last look at the two Scottish pavilions, one telling of the old Scotland of history and romance, the other showing the questing new life of Highlands and Lowlands.

They took the lift to the top balcony of the great steel Tower of Empire on Bellahouston Hill and stared proudly down at the Empire spreading below in miniature but in miniature that was majestic in scale.

Good old Scotland! Sammy thought.

The clachan was their next stop. Ruth loved the little highland village. He preferred the Palace of Engineering although the clachan, tucked away on its own and separated from the rest of the park by trees, had an almost magical charm. Its rough shingled walks, its sedge grass, its crooked burn, its loch, and its kilted piper pacing its banks playing Scottish airs, was enough to catch at any Scottish heart, even one that preferred to live in a Scottish city.

In the thatched, whitewashed cottage with the plaque boasting 'Highland Home Industries', Ruth lifted one of the heavy walking-sticks topped by the traditional shepherd's crook. 'This would be a good gift for your father.'

'Put it down!' Sammy's voice crackled with anger at her for spoiling a pleasant hour. 'If he wants another stick, he can buy it for himself.'

'All right.'

Ruth pouted her lips a little as she put the stick back. To her, Hodge Hunter was only the man she saw for herself in the present. Sammy had never discussed his father with her. She must see, of course, that his father was a bully. She must despise him. She had quarrelled with him more than once, given up abominable cheek, yet the dislike she professed never seemed to run very deep.

Sometimes she even said things like: 'Your father must have been a fine figure of a man in his uniform, Sammy!'

Or: 'I can see how he managed to get three wives. A woman likes a forceful virile kind of man!'

'Forceful! Virile!' he'd spat in disgust. 'He's already killed two of them. The one he's got now is maybe trying her best to hang on but have you had a good look at her lately? He's going to succeed in murdering her as well.'

'Oh, now, Sammy.' She had actually laughed. 'Isn't that going a bit far, love? The first one died in childbirth, and you never knew her. Your own mother had a heart condition, hadn't she?'

'He killed them both. He killed them,' he insisted.

'All right, love. All right.'

She tried to soothe him but he could see she did not understand.

He wanted so much to explain, but where could he start? To justify his attitude to his father would mean the raking over of too many painful years.

His brows pulled down, his eyes glittered and his jaw set with stubbornness.

Did killing only mean a dagger in the back, a bullet in the brain or poison in the belly? No, there were far more agonising, far more long-drawn-out, more subtle ways to kill. The murderer who used the subtle methods never reached a court of so-called justice.

His father was a murderer all right. He would never forget his mother's last heart attack, and now he was watching the slow disintegration of another victim.

Yet his father was a much respected member of the community. He had had a splendid record in the army. He was an elder in the church. Oh, the irony to watch him, straight-backed and pious at church every Sunday. His friends included ministers, school teachers and upright ex-army men with medals and courageous forays to boast of.

How often he had listened to these stories, recounted over glasses of whisky, noisy laughter and hearty camaraderie, in the Balornock front parlour.

Listened and hated until he had been sick.

They left the clachan in strained unhappy silence. A horrible thought was growing in his mind.

Did Ruth like his father? Could it be that she admired him? Little incidents flicked across his consciousness, odd glances from Ruth's dark eyes, the way she laughed at his father's jokes or the coy way she had of reprimanding him if she thought his stories were vulgar, the heightened self-consciousness in the way she walked in his presence or sat or moved her hands or tilted her head.

The horror grew.

'I'm sorry, love,' Ruth said at last. 'I know how you feel!'

But she didn't.

Chapter 10

'May the good Lord forgive him!' Catriona's mother shook her head. 'The man's not only wicked, he's stark raving mad!'

Catriona had a feeling that for once her mother might be right. The birth was only a matter of a few weeks away and Melvin was insisting that she must accompany him to the last day of the Exhibition.

As he was always telling her, he believed in being a good family man and would never dream of going anywhere on his own. She tried to persuade him just to take Fergus along with him this time but without the slightest success.

'You know you want to go,' he kept assuring her. 'There's a massed pipe band parade and an anti-aircraft display. Planes are going to be coming across every ten minutes or so from Renfrew. It'll be marvellous. You'll love it!'

She could not imagine anything she would loathe more at this particular moment than the exhausting din of pipes and guns and planes.

Then there was the weather to contend with. Surely this had been the wettest summer for years!

'It's not a case of not wanting to go, Melvin.' She made yet another attempt to make him see reason. 'I'm just not able to trail around that Exhibition again.'

'Nonsense! There's nothing special about being pregnant. It's not an illness . . .'

'Oh, all right, all right!' she hastily capitulated, putting her hands up to her ears and squeezing her eyes tight shut. 'Don't tell me how and where any more animals drop their young, or I'll scream.'

He had been happy then, happy to be the good husband and father, taking his wife and son for a special treat.

She hated him as they set out for the Exhibition. Hatred battered inside her, hysterical for release, locked in and denied expression because of her need to lean on his arm for support, and to wheedle him for lifts on the autobuses, or reviving cups of tea, or to search for toilets.

'If you wouldn't drink so much, you fool,' he told her angrily, 'you wouldn't keep wanting to pee!'

'Sh-sh!' she miserably hushed him, her cheeks crimson with embarrassment. 'People will hear!'

'So what! Everybody's got to pee at some time or other. It's only you that goes to extremes!'

'You're awful!' she hissed. 'Awful!'

'Awful? What do you mean awful? I don't pee all the time!'

'Stop saying that word!'

'What word?'

Frantic with desperation, she struggled to quicken her pace, at the same time changing the subject.

'Listen, Fergus! Look! There's the pipers!'

A mass of swaggering swinging tartan, disdainfully ignoring the squelching mud underfoot, racketed along, sparking the air with patriotic energy. Young folk pranced in front of and behind it, delighted with the sight and sound.

The child's eyes grew large and round like baubles on a Christmas tree and he stamped up and down wildly clapping his hands.

Melvin laughed and cocked his head.

'He's having a grand time, eh?'

It was on the tip of her tongue to tell him that Fergus was over-excited but she bit the words down. The slightest criticism of the boy provoked his anger and indignation, and she had no wish and no energy for any more arguments.

They had waited in an enormous crush of people to get into the park, queued in fact for everything, and stood for what seemed a lifetime for a reviving high tea.

Buying a meal or even a cup of tea was an expense and a luxury that Melvin seldom indulged in and she had needed the rest and the food so much. Nothing in the future could ever compete with the utter joy of this.

By the time they had made their way to the anti-aircraft display the park was encased by a black night sky. The Exhibition sparkled in the darkness, a dancing fairyland of colour, the buildings caught in a flashing network of lights.

Despite the mud, people in raincoats and headscarfs and wellington boots were jostling and bumping together, singing at the pitch of their voices and dancing The Lambeth Walk.

'Any time you're Lambeth way,
Any evening, any day,
You'll find us all . . .
Doing the Lambeth Walk, oi!!'

Crowds were getting denser and the rain, now bucketing down, only served to increase their determination to have a riotous good time.

There was a wildness of spirit about the vast throng, a reckless abandon. It was as if the world were ending at midnight with the Exhibition and they would never be able to enjoy themselves again.

Catriona began to feel frightened.

'Can't we go home now, Melvin?'

'Don't be daft.'

'I'm tired.'

The understatement of the world, she thought. She felt so exhausted she could barely speak. Every bone, every muscle, every organ in her body throbbed. She longed to stop moving; she had wistful dreams of a barrow or something, anything, on wheels to run along underneath her heavy belly to support it. She shuffled along, flat-footed, wide-legged in a daze of fatigue, caught in the centre, pushed this way and that by a mass of over three hundred and sixty-four thousand people.

'We'd never get out of here before midnight,' Melvin said. 'Not through this mob, not even if we wanted to.'

The baby kicked and churned and protested inside her.

'Oh, Melvin!'

She tried to lean against him but he was lifting Fergus up into his arms.

'You're tired too, son, aren't you, eh? But you're not complaining. You want to see the guns and the planes, don't you? So does your mammy. She wants to see them, all right.'

'I don't like guns. Melvin, I hate guns!'

252

Her voice was flattened by the roar of the anti-aircraft guns of the army mobile section.

She stared through tears like a drowning man gazing through a deep undulating sea. She was beyond caring what anyone thought, or what she must look like.

Rain smacked down, making her headscarf a limp rag and her hair a dripping net across her face. Her voluminous coat clung stickily, outlining every bulging curve of breast, buttock and abdomen.

She wept loudly but nobody heard.

Automatics roared, spat flames and shook the trees and buildings. Searchlights, long and powerful, criss-crossed to and fro, blue across the black sky. A plane zoomed off into the night out of range and started the big guns booming again.

Behind the guns were anti-aircraft experts with height-finding, predicting, and sound-recording apparatus. An officer shouted brisk orders.

Then the searchlights picked out another plane flying high above the tower and simultaneously more guns blasted into action.

People had stopped trying to move and just stood making nearly two hundred acres of Bellahouston Park a solid block of humanity.

Catriona was too dazed to appreciate when the guns stopped, but gradually she became aware that a roar of voices had taken their place.

People grabbed hands, the park swayed.

'For auld lang syne, m'dear,
        For auld lang syne,
        We'll take a cup of kindness yet,
        For the sake of auld lang syne.'

The swaying heaved, quickened, jerked. Screams and laughter shot about like machine-gun bullets.

'So - here's- a- hand - my - trusty - freend,
        And - here's - a hand - o' - mine.
        We'll - meet - again - some - other - time,
        For - the - sake - of - Auld - Lang - Syne!'

Then, from every corner of the park 'God save the King'

thundered out.

It was nearly midnight. The lights in the Tower of Empire went out and the searchlights concentrated on the top of the tower where the Exhibition flag, the proud lion of Scotland, was being slowly lowered.

Then dramatically, unexpectedly a voice came echoing across the hundred microphones from every corner of the ground.

'The spirit of the Exhibition greets you,' boomed the voice. 'I am no individual. I am composed of all those who have contributed to its success.

'I express to all who have made me, to all who have entered me, gratitude for their parts in me.

'I die tonight. May memories of me abide in your hearts.'

In silence the crowd looked up while the strokes of Big Ben donged the hour and the flag slipped slowly down. It disappeared behind the wall of the top balcony of the tower and the Empire Exhibition was officially over.

It was the essence of Scotland that burst into one last song to the many thousands of visitors who had come from all over the world to visit their friendly city.

'Will ye no come back again?' Glasgow bawled heavenwards. 'Will ye no come ba-a-ck again?'

Then began the great exodus. It looked as if three international football matches were all coming out at once.

'What a night!' Melvin enthused, still with Fergus in his long, muscly arms. 'I bet you're glad you came. I knew you wouldn't want to miss it.'

Catriona kept silent. She had a tight grip of his coat-tail as they jostled towards one of the exits along with the rest of the crowd and her whole concentration was on keeping hold of him so that he could clear a path for her and get her safely home.

Pain screwed her. Delirium fizzing up like champagne. Clinging to the coat-tail, holding it up, praying. Pain throttling. Head to one side, nostrils panicking.

Going away. At ease. Easy now. Easy now. Easy.

No one else in the world. Alone in a lonely place. Fighting for existence. A wedding ring clamping round guts.

A broad gold band, strangling, tightening.

Relax, the magazines said. Take lovely deep breaths - and relax, you lucky, lucky mothers-to-be. One - two - three!

Who is the editor? Who is she? A man is the editor, he - he - he!

She did not recognise Dessie Street off the Main Road where cranes and ships towered up over the walls of the Benlin yards.

Leerie, leerie, licht the lamps,
Long legs and crooked shanks.

The shop at the corner had the blinds drawn down.

The blinds drawn down.

The blinds drawn down.

Gaslight wavered and flung deep shadows down the back close.

The spiral stairs wound round and round. Round and round. Round and round.

She sank to her knees at the foot of them.

Oh, my God! Her lips puttered out with pain as she nursed herself.

Oh, my Jesus!

'The thing that puzzles me,' she said, 'is how a big baby is going to come out such a wee hole!'

The spiral stairs went up and down.

Up and down.

Up and down.

Way up high.

She was floating, quickly, hurriedly.

In through the front door, across the hall, into the bedroom.

Bed.

Oh, how good God was to her.

Thank you God! Thank you, God!

The wedding ring was destroying her.

She fought it.

She tried to relax to please it.

She said she was sorry.

She cursed it.

She said she was sorry again.

And again. And again.

Yet it kept unbelievably contracting, crunching smaller and

255

smaller with herself inside it not knowing what to do, or what could possibly happen next.

Until she knew that she could not stand any more or no more pain could ever be any worse.

It was then that agony leapt to new heights.

'Jesus!' she screamed high. Higher and higher. 'Jesus!'

Then gradually she came back to the world again.

She felt the bed soft beneath her.

She saw the bedroom ceiling.

She knew she had experienced childbirth.

She told herself: Damn the women's magazines and all the romances in the world - don't you ever, ever forget this, girl. Don't you allow yourself to be conned into this ever again.

There was something soft, something making a strange crunchling sound against her. Utterly exhausted, she struggled to raise her head a little and peer down.

A red rubbery figure was sitting between her legs, tiny arms stuck out at each side and shiny matted head lolling helplessly.

Mrs Jackson was rubbing its back, then she suddenly grabbed it, held it upside down and gave it a resounding smack.

The cry echoed in Catriona's heart. With one last effort, she lifted, and held out her arms.

Chapter 11

The lights of Glasgow twinkling. Light beaming from shop windows and cinema doors. Neon sparkling high, winking busily. Trams and buses, bright yellow, swooping. Everywhere shimmery light

Alec never forgot the moment he and Madge came back out of the cinema and found that Glasgow had disappeared. There was only darkness.

Neither spoke for a minute, but stood staring at eerie blackness, skin contracting, hair rising.

Glasgow, second city of Britain, home of over a million souls, lay as dark and quiet as a wayside hamlet. Not a single light anywhere. Tram-cars and buses creeping through the black canyons of the streets without one spark of illumination. Shops, cinemas, theatres, restaurants, houses, invisible behind blinded windows.

Only little obscured crosses of traffic signals and the dimmed warnings of other traffic direction signs hung in the blackness like miniature moonbeams.

People waited quietly and patiently in crowds at the tram and bus stops to get home.

Arms linked, fingers entwined, Madge and Alec toed their way cautiously along until they found their car stop.

They could not see if it was their own tram that came forward like a shadow to the stopping place but out of the darkness they heard the conductor's voice.

'Springburn!'

'Is it war, then?' Madge asked when they had found seats.

'Naw,' he said. 'No yet.'

Alec chuckled and gave a match to his wife to hold while he searched for their fares.

'One thing's for sure. The courting couples will like this. Extra cuddles all round tonight!'

257

'Got yer call-up papers?'

Working in darkness seemed to have proved the last straw for the conductor, whose ghostly face was a bleak mask of depression.

'Go for the old medical tomorrow,' Alec told him.

'Well, I hope ye pass awright.'

'You must be joking,' Alec laughed, lighting up a cigarette. 'I'm praying I've got flat feet, ulcers, anaemia, and my intelligence is double-sub-normal.'

The conductor sighed.

'If yer warm, yer in!'

'He's applying for a postponement,' Madge said, pride lifting her voice. 'On the grounds of exceptional hardship - because of me.'

'You wouldn't be any hardship to me, hen!'

Madge enjoyed a hearty laugh.

'It's the weans. There's six now. Two sets of twins!'

'You'll never get off with that. Some folks have ten and more. Ah know a wumman down our street, so help ma boab, she's got twenty! There would be no Glasga fellas in the forces at all if you could get off with that!'

Alec blew out smoke and put an arm round Madge's shoulders.

'The wife's never been the same since the last two. Breech births, the twins were. Terrible, wasn't it, Madge?'

Madge gave another whoop of laughter.

'God, don't remind me! Talk about exceptional hardship!'

'Aw, well, anyways. The best o' luck to you, mate.'

Stumbling, groping and cursing, the conductor disappeared upstairs.

The tram crawled cautiously, and Alec impatiently kept count of the stops.

'This one's ours, hen,' he nudged Madge at last. 'Watch your big feet getting off!'

'They'll have to do something about this,' Madge giggled as she fingered her way along the shops and round the corner into Cowlairs Road.

'About this?'

'Get off!'

'Let's see your headlamps before you cross the road, hen.'

258

'Stop being daft and hold my hand.'

'I'll hold anything you want, gorgeous.'

'Alec, I nearly tripped and broke my neck there. Keep a hold of me, I said!'

The walls of the pend dripped to the touch and stank fustily.

A cat miaowed past.

Madge's laughter bounced around and kept echoing back to her.

'You couldn't mistake this place!'

'My little grey home in the west.'

'North!' Madge interrupted.

'Home, home on the range,' he loudly belted out in mock drunkenness. 'Where seldom is heard - a discouraging word, and the skies are not - cloudy all day!'

They staggered hilariously up the outside stairs, into the close, then up the hollow-beat wooden stairs to their door on the first landing.

Mrs Jackson's agitation clamped on to them and dragged them inside. A twitch was dancing around her eye.

'Thank God you're safe back.'

'How did the bonny wee wean-minder get on, eh?'

Alec chucked her under the chin before collapsing back in the horsehair sofa in the kitchen and draping himself across it.

'I'll never get back to Clydend tonight, Alec. What'll I do, son?'

'Stay here! She's welcome to stay here, isn't she, Madge?'

'Och, of course! Sit down here, hen. I'm going to make a cup of tea.'

'But my work. Oh, dear, dear.'

'Relax, Ma,' Alec advised. 'It'll still be there tomorrow.'

'But will *we*, son? Will we?'

Madge shouted with laughter.

'What's to stop us, for God's sake.'

Mrs Jackson came very close as if Madge had gone deaf.

'What's to stop us? What's to stop us? Any minute there's going to be a war. The last one was bad enough but this time there's going to be air-raids. You should do what your man tells you and evacuate yourself and the weans.'

'I don't want to leave Alec, and anyway, Ma, I don't feel able to go stravaiging away with thousands of weans. Puddling along with my own mob from day to day's bad enough.'

'She won't listen to me, Ma. I keep telling her it's for her own good.'

'You can shove two or three of them in the pram and there's always somebody would help. Somebody would help. Anyway, poor Alec is going to be called up.'

'He's trying for a postponement.'

'That poor lad will have to go. They won't listen to him. They never listened to his father.' Mrs Jackson's mouth went into a sudden grotesque paroxysm. She fought a battle with it and won. 'The least you can do is see that the weans are kept safe.'

'Ma's right, hen. I keep telling you. And you know what it said in the papers - Springburn's one of the bull's-eye areas.'

Mrs Jackson began wringing hands that plopped with sweat. 'You're smack in the middle of all these works.'

'You needn't talk.' Madge grinned round as she splashed water in the teapot. 'Dessie Street. At the docks?'

'Me being another bull's-eye doesn't help the weans. If you think anything of these weans, you'll evacuate them.'

'Och, poor wee buggers. I should, shouldn't I?'

'And the quicker the better if you don't want them blown to smithereens!'

'Och, all right, then.'

Alec lit up another cigarette and accepted a cup of tea.

'That's my girl! What's the latest from Dessie Street?'

'Up the close, you mean?'

'Uh - huh.'

His mother sat down beside him on the sofa and stirred vigorously at her cup. 'Wait a minute now. There's eh . . . there's eh . . .' Blotchy patches of red appeared on her face. 'Oh aye!' She gasped with the sudden relief of remembering. 'You know Tam McGuffie?'

'The wee white-haired baker?'

'Yes, he and his wife and daughter live next door to Catriona MacNair.' She leaned forward as if imparting a secret. 'His father's moving in with him.'

260

Alec chuckled.

'What's he called? Methuselah?'

'He's well over eighty and as deaf as a post. You know Catriona? Well, her father-in-law's coming to live with her too.'

Madge poked the fire into life before settling down with her cup.

'Is that that wee blondie one who was expecting at the same time as me?'

'That's the one. I delivered the wean. What a night that was. I'll never forget it. A nice big wean she had though. Did you no see him in his pram one day? Andrew, she calls him. A nice wee lassie she is, Catriona.'

Alec winked. 'A right wee beauty as well!'

'Here, you!' Madge warned. 'You keep away from her.'

Mrs Jackson's mouth quivered again.

'Keep away? The poor lad's not going to have any option. They'll take him away, I'm telling you, Madge. They won't listen about any postponement.'

'It's great when you think of it.' Alec shook his head. 'I've never even met a ruddy German in my life!'

'Och, I know,' Madge sympathised. 'It's a damn shame. All of them politicians should be put in a field and told to get on with it.'

'What a thought!' Alec grinned.

Laughter made Madge splutter her tea.

'You've got a mind like a sewer. Fight, I mean. If they want a fight they should bloody well fight it out between themselves.'

'They won't, though. Trust them,' Mrs Jackson said bitterly. 'They'll have that poor lad, that's for sure! They'll have him.'

'Shut up, Ma!' Alec's good-humoured voice had the beginnings of an edge to it. 'You're making me feel I've one foot in the grave already.'

Madge put down her cup and stared in inarticulate distress.

'Don't worry, hen.' Alec blew her a kiss. 'The Jerries will never be able to run fast enough to catch up with me.'

'Aye, son, you just take good care of yourself. You're a good lad. I couldn't stand you getting shot to pieces like your father.'

'Ma, I couldn't stand it either, so will you shut up! You're

261

scaring me rigid!'

'It's terrible to be a man, so it is!' Madge said.

'Pack it in, Ma. Let's get to bed. Where do you want to sleep, hen?'

'I'll just slip in beside the weans.'

Mrs Jackson nodded towards the high hole-in-the-bed behind the sofa where Agnes, Sadie and Hector sprawled in various poses of sleep. The three young children were divided between prams over in front of the coalbunker and the cot through in the room.

'Better you than me!' Madge sent a peal of laughter ceilingwards. 'Them wee middens kick like horses. Do you want to go through and use the throne, hen?'

The throne was an old pail kept in a curtained recess in the room and used on cold nights to save going outside to the icy lavatory in the yard.

Mrs Jackson shook her frizzy head, her eyes still twitching anxiously at her son.

'No, away you go.'

'I'll find you a nighty.'

'No, no. I'll be fine in my vest and knickers for one night. If only that was the only thing I'd to worry about!'

'Well, if we didn't know there was a war in the offing before,' Alec said, later in bed, 'we know it now!'

Madge cuddled close to him.

'Och, Alec.'

'What, hen?'

'What do they need you for? You're an insurance man.'

'Maybe they need a policy!'

He could not be sure whether Madge had started to laugh or cry against his chest. She was a big girl and she was making the bed rock and bounce. He laughed, just to be on the safe side.

Chapter 12

Melvin swelled with rage. His eyes bulged and blotches of colour stained his cheeks. Catriona had never seen him so angry.

'That settles it!' He hitched back his shoulders and flexed his muscles. 'I'm going to join up!'

She stared at him. Events were moving too fast for her comprehension.

The Prime Minister's broadcast still trumpeted solemnly in her mind like the heralding of doom:

'I am speaking to you from the Cabinet Room at 10 Downing Street.

'This morning the British Ambassador in Berlin handed the German Government an official note stating that unless we heard from them by eleven o'clock that they were prepared at once to withdraw their troops from Poland, a state of war would exist between us.

'I have to tell you that no such undertaking has been received and that consequently this country is at war with Germany . . .'

Then there was the terrible shock about Wee Eck the baker. Wee Eck had worked as an apprentice-baker at MacNair's for years until recently when he had taken his cheeky grin and freckly face off to sea as a steward on a ship called the *Athenia*.

Incredible that cheerful, hard-working Wee Eck was dead. She could not accept it. Her mind clung tenaciously to the belief that there must be some sort of justice, order and fairness in the world. God and the powers that be only punished the wicked. The wicked suffered varying degrees of hell on earth according to their sins. Then came the final judgement day when every deed, every thought had to be accounted for and the judgement was either acquittal to the safety of heavenly regions or damnation in the fires of eternal hell.

She could well imagine herself destined for the torments of the abyss, but to believe that Wee Eck had done anything to warrant the terrors of death by drowning was completely beyond her.

The Donaldson Atlantic liner *Athenia* had been torpedoed and sunk without warning two hundred and fifty miles west of Donegal. Bound from Glasgow to New York, she was carrying fourteen hundred passengers. Radio messages from the sinking ship brought British destroyers full speed to the spot and passengers had also been picked up by a Norwegian vessel and a Swedish yacht.

Most of the survivors were landed at Galway and Greenock, many of them wounded or suffering from shock, but Wee Eck had been one of the hundred and twenty-eight killed.

'Joining up?' Catriona echoed.

'That's what I said.'

'But what about your work and me and the children?'

'Don't be so selfish. You ought to be ashamed of yourself. At a time like this King and country comes first. Anyway there's Baldy - he's a good foreman and there's your father and Tam and Sandy McNulty. The army wouldn't give any of that lot a second look. Baldy's no use for anything except the bakery since they hanged his wife. Your father's got his ulcer and his dermatitis and every body knows about old Sandy's feet. No, it's men like me they need in the army.'

He stripped off his shirt to admire his bulging muscles in the sideboard mirror. Gripping his wrists, he grunted, wrenched himself this way and that and swelled himself up to grotesque proportions.

'Look at that neck! Look at those shoulders!' His moustache puffed. 'Have you ever seen triceps like that? Good job I asked the old man to come and stay.'

Jerking both arms up, elbows bent, fists clenched, as if he were about to punch himself in the ears, he forced his stomach muscles to do a circular rhythmic dance.

'The army won't have seen many men with muscle control like that.'

Catriona watched hypnotised, as each muscle in his body in turn performed its cocky, bouncing pirouette. She could never credit how he managed to do this amazing trick of sorting out all his muscles and making them work separately.

In the privacy of the bathroom, she had tried to make her own white body emulate his, but without the slightest success. The frustration of not being able to find any muscles at all nearly reduced her to tears. The only things she could jiggle were her small breasts and she managed that only when she jumped up and down.

'He'll keep an eye on things.'

'Who'll keep an eye on what?'

'My father. He's not that old. Only there was no sense in him wasting money on a woman to do his house over there and cook his food for him.'

'Who's going to keep an eye on him?'

'What do you mean, who's going to keep an eye on him?'

'You said he was drinking too much.'

'I said nothing of the kind.' Melvin stopped exercising and glared indignantly at her. 'He likes a wee glass after he stops work at night. It washes away the flour.'

'Your father may be the master baker but he's never baked for years.'

The unfairness of Melvin's having insisted the old man lived with them, without either discussion or consultation with her, was something for which she would never forgive him.

'Are you insinuating that my father doesn't work hard? Melvin's voice loudened as it climbed up the ladder of incredulity. 'He's downstairs working now while you're lazing there on your backside!'

'My father worked all night with flour filling in his nose and mouth and hair.'

'What do you mean - your father worked all night? *I* worked all night.'

'It's different when my father takes a drink, though!'

Her voice held a bitterness that encompassed far more than what she said.

He came over and pushed his face down close to hers, enveloping her in a suffocating smell of onions and sweat.

'Your father can drink himself to death for all I care!'

Daggers of defiance aimed from her eyes to his.

'Oh, I know you don't care. You don't care about anything!'

She would like to have added 'except yourself' but had not enough nerve.

Melvin straightened, bulged his eyes heavenwards and spread out his palms.

'Women! I've just said I'm going to join up and fight for my King and country!'

'Big man!' Catriona's mind twisted in sarcastic mimicry. 'Big, brave, strong, kind, thoughtful, unselfish husband!

'Oh, yes?' she said aloud.

'You don't believe me?'

Dutifully her gaze lowered, her voice smoothed out.

'Oh, yes, Melvin.'

He scratched his moustache, then grinned.

'The Argyll and Sutherland Highlanders. I bet you'd be as proud as Punch to see me in a kilt. I've got marvellous legs for it, haven't I?'

'Yes, Melvin.'

'Or the Black Watch. The lasses from Hell, the Huns called them in the first war. The Black Watch used to have a piper marching out in front, plying a stirring Scottish tune and behind him would come the men with fixed bayonets.'

He laughed and puffed his chest up. 'That would be a sight for the Huns. It must have scared them stiff. Can you imagine me in a kilt, eh?'

She could imagine him in the tartan all right, bulky shoulders, tree-trunk legs, kilts swishing smartly from side to side as he swaggered along.

'Well?'

'Yes, Melvin.'

'The Black Watch or the Argylls! Or how about the Cameronians?'

'I'd better make the tea.'

'You're a fine one to talk about not caring. What regiment do you think?'

'It doesn't matter what I think.' Catriona began setting the table. 'Your father will be through for his tea in a minute.'

The day he had told her that his father was coming to stay he had sat sucking his pipe, contented, at peace with himself and

266

the world, as he announced:

'Oh, by the way, I've asked my father to move in with us. He needs someone to look after him in his dotage and there's no use paying two women.'

Now, in the sharpness of her resentment, things that she had never noticed about the old man were becoming obvious. He was so mean, he never gave anyone any Christmas presents, not even his grandchildren.

'Just because I'm in business folk think I'm made of money,' he would complain in his high nasal voice. 'But I'm not. I've had to struggle all my life to keep body and soul together.'

He could never resist a bargain and often bought clothes and boots from customers whose menfolk had died. Or if there were no deceased's clothing forthcoming when he needed it, he would go and haggle for a cut-price garment at the local pawn-shop. Nothing ever fitted. Collars never matched his shirts and sagged forward over his straggle of beard. Suits of coarse, cheap material hung loose at his bottom and bulged at his knees. He always wore heavy boots and looked as if he were constantly on the point of walking out of them.

Every night at some time or other, he woke the baby with his clomp-clomp-clomping about.

But it was all Melvin's fault. The old man had not wanted to come.

'I see enough of Dessie Street when I work in the shop all day,' he protested, but Melvin kept persuading him until eventually he talked the old man round by pointing out how much money he would save.

When Melvin broke the news, Catriona visualised the years ahead, the lack of privacy, the extra nagging at the children, the anxieties, the responsibilities, the heavy nursing when the old man became bedridden.

'You want to be the envy of the other women. I know you. So be sure you pick the best.' Melvin scratched the surface of her attention. 'The Argylls have the glengarry. Cocky looking it is with a couple of black ribbons streaming down the back, a red and white diced band with one line of the red squares joined to remind folk of the battle of Balaclava. You've heard of Balaclava?'

267

'No.'

'You're a right one, you are! In Russia, you fool. The thin red line's famous.'

'I remember now. It was a painting.'

'A painting, be damned! It was a battle. The Argylls advanced in a great long line, all smart in their red tunics and kilts and white sporrans, bayonets at the ready.' He thrust his fists forward and struck an aggressive pose as if he were threatening her with a bayonet. 'There's nothing to beat the Jocks for tough fighting men. The salt of the earth, the Jocks are.'

She had wanted to say, 'You ought to have discussed this business about your father with me first. I don't know if I'm able to cope with him just now. I'm worried enough about the children.'

But it was because of the children that she said nothing. She must not put Melvin in a bad mood just when she was working hard to butter him up to a receptive frame of mind in an effort to get his help and advice.

Fergus needed constant watching since Andrew was born. She dared not leave him alone with the baby and had to keep alert and watchful every minute the child was in the house.

She thanked God for school and the few hours of comparative peace it afforded her. Or the few occasions like this one, when Fergus had been persuaded to go out and play.

The peace was suddenly shattered by a piercing scream that made even Melvin jump. They both flew, jostling and pushing at each other to get into the bedroom.

The side of Andrew's cot was down and he was lying blue in the face, and choking, his woolly jersey rumpled up, his nappy at his ankles.

She reached him first and snatched him into the safety of her arms to cradle the soft rubber-milk flesh, and nurse it close.

'Sh . . . sh! Sh, sh! Mummy's wee lamb. It's all right. It's all right. Mummy's here! Sh . . . sh! Sh . . . sh!'

Fergus was standing very quietly beside the cot, a golliwog in his hands.

'How did you get in?' Melvin asked in surprise.

'Granda left the door open again, Daddy!'

268

'Feggie!' Andrew sobbed and pointed an accusing finger. 'Feggie!'

Teethmarks were fast swelling into fiery lumps on the baby's thigh and spots of blood spurted.

Catriona felt sick.

'He had my golliwog,' Fergus said.

'Did you give him that golliwog, Catriona?' Melvin shouted.

'Yes, but, Melvin . . .'

'Aw, shut up! You fool! Why did you have to find him Fergus's toy? He's got plenty of his own.'

'I thought Fergus was too big for his golly now. I didn't know he still wanted it.'

'Never mind, son.' Melvin patted Fergus's head. 'Tea's ready. Away and wash your hands.'

'Melvin, I've been meaning to talk to you about Fergus,' she said, when the child had gone. 'I'm so worried. He does terrible things and I don't know how to handle him. The other day he was tormenting the baby and I just lost my temper and smacked and smacked him.'

'You what?'

Melvin pushed his face close to hers, moustache spiking out, eyes bulging.

The baby had stopped crying and was sleepily hiccoughing against her shoulder. She wondered if she should lay him down in his cot again and hasten from the room in case Melvin's anger frightened him.

Or would it be better and safer to keep him rocking in her arms?

'I don't know what to do about Fergus.'

'You want my advice, eh? Well, here's my advice. Don't you dare lift a finger to my son again or you're out on your ear.' He pushed his face closer. 'Is that understood? Has it penetrated that thick skull of yours? I'll throw you out of this house with only the clothes you have on your back. That's all you had when you came here and that's all you'll have when you leave.'

He would take Andrew?

Catriona's eyes twitched about.

She stood perfectly still.

269

'Well?' Melvin roared. 'Understood?'
'Yes, thank you,' she managed politely.

Chapter 13

'Sammy, you didn't!' Ruth's eyes guarded against panic.

'Why not? I do object!'

'You can't!'

His brows went down and his jaw set. 'Oh, can't I?'

'What will people think?'

'I don't care what people think.'

'You do. You know you do. We both care. And all your brothers have joined up.'

'They were always good soldiers,' he said bitterly. 'Theirs not to reason why, theirs but to do and die!'

'Sammy, your father!'

'What about my father?'

'Oh, now, please, love.'

'Forget about my father.'

'I can't forget about your father and neither can you.'

'Why not? What's so special about him?'

'He was a regimental sergeant-major!'

'Oh, yes?'

'Sammy!'

'Ruth. I've registered as a conscientious objector and I'm going up before a tribunal. That's all there is to it.'

'People will think you're a coward.'

'Let them!'

Anger widened Ruth's eyes. 'No, I will not let them. You're not a coward.'

He shrugged. 'What does it matter?'

'It matters a lot. I won't let them.' Her voice weakened and became petulant like a child's. 'It's not that I want you to go, Sammy. I hate the war. I don't even know what it's about. All I want is to have you with me in our nice wee house. We weren't doing anybody any harm. Just living our own nice quiet lives.'

A burst of humourless laughter escaped from Sammy.

'A nice quiet life! We've had that from now on.'

'But if you change your mind.'

'It won't change the war.'

'But, Sammy . . .'

'You can't have a nice quiet life during a war.'

'Oh, I don't know?' she flashed back at him. 'You seem to be making a jolly good try for one.'

'I was prepared for that from other people. But not from you.'

'I didn't mean it.' Ruth stamped her foot. 'I didn't mean it. I hate you for making me say that.'

'I'm sorry.'

'You can't be a conscientious objector.'

'I must.'

'Everybody will hate you.' She stamped again, her face twisting in tears. 'I can't bear it!'

He took her in his arms. 'As long as you don't hate me . . .'

'You always said you'd do anything for me.' Her body squeezed provocatively against his. 'Anything.'

'I know.'

'Well, don't be a conscientious objector. Please, Sammy. Please?'

'Ruth . . .'

'You could join a corps where you would just be doing office work the same as you're doing now.'

'Ruth, you don't understand.'

'Or the military police, like your father. Wouldn't he be pleased?'

He pushed her away.

'Oh, shut up!'

'Sammy!'

'The only connection I'll have with the military police is when they come to arrest me!'

'Don't talk like that.'

'After the tribunal they'll come for me.'

'And take you to the army?'

'Yes.'

She pressed wheedlingly close again.

'Well, if you're going to be made to go in the end, love, why cause all this fuss? Why bother with being a CO?'

A flush crept up from his neck and his voice began to tremble.

'I'll do nothing they say. I'll disobey every order. I'll refuse to put on the uniform. I'll have nothing to do with anything military. I hate them.'

She stared in bewildered silence for a minute.

'You feel as strongly as this?'

'I hate them.'

'Well,' she decided, 'if that's how you feel, that's how I feel. But your father will be furious!'

He nodded.

'Ruth, you'd better go out. Go to the pictures or something.'

'Go out? Now? Without you? Why? What do you mean?'

'He's coming.'

'Your father?'

'I went up today, to get it over with - to tell him, but he wasn't in. I waited for a while but I knew you'd be getting worried so I left a note. He's bound to have read it by now. He'll come.'

Ruth shrugged.

'Your conscience is your business. He has no right to interfere.'

'I don't want you getting upset. You don't know what he's like.'

'I'm not going anywhere without you.' Her full lips pouted. 'Imagine, me without you!'

She kissed him and he held her tightly and thought if nothing good ever happened to him again he would still consider himself a lucky man because of her.

'I think I'll go back,' he said suddenly. 'I don't want unpleasantness here.' With his arm still encircling her shoulders, he surveyed the immaculate kitchen. 'We've made a good job of this, haven't we?'

'It's just right.'

'In good taste yet homely and comfortable.'

'Everybody admires it.'

'Happy, too. There's a feeling of happiness about it. That's your doing, Ruth.'

'You're the one who's made me happy, love. Mum and Dad's place was never like this.' She groaned. 'All that crowd! Never any peace, any privacy, any security. I don't know how my mother stuck it.'

'She was a fine-looking woman.'

'I wished she'd lived just a little longer. Just to see me married and happy.'

Sammy shook his head.

'Sixteen children and your mother and father in that room and kitchen. My God!'

'She liked nice things, you know.' Ruth's eyes looked back and glimmered with amusement. 'She used to keep a half set of china and a sugar bowl and a milk jug locked away in the room cupboard and only brought them out at New Year or at other very special times when we had visitors. I used to think that china was marvellous. We just used tinnys, you know, tin mugs and the milk out of the bottles and the sugar out of the bag.' She leaned her head down on his shoulder. 'Now I use china all the time and I've a crystal sugar and cream.'

'If I had the money you would have better than this.'

'Nothing could be better than this. I've everything I want here.'

He kissed her on the brow and her gaze fluttered coyly up at him.

'Well, nearly everything.'

He sighed.

'A child, you mean? We're barely out of our teens. We've plenty of time.'

'We keep putting it off. Saving up for other things.'

'The other things you wanted,' he reminded her.

'I know, love, but I was thinking . . .'

'Don't worry, one day we'll get a wee house in Bishopbriggs with a patch of garden back and front.'

'For the baby's pram?'

Already the scene was melting in her eyes.

He nodded.

'I could save up the deposit in two or three years.'

'It would be a bit difficult here with a pram right enough. I'd never manage it up and down all these stairs.'

'I wouldn't let you.'

274

For a few minutes, surfing along on the tide of her enthusiasm, he had forgotten about the war and his father and been happy. Now, suddenly, there was a loud rapping at the door, and happiness scattered.

'Now, don't be upset, Ruth. Just keep calm. Blast! Blast! I ought to have gone back. I should never have given him the chance to come here.'

'Sammy, love . . .'

'It's all right. It's all right. Don't get upset. Don't worry!'

'One of us had better open the door before he breaks it in.'

'Now, don't you worry!'

'Sit down,' she said. 'I'll go.'

He was grateful to her for giving him the chance of a minute or two on his own to arrange himself in a casual, relaxed pose on the chair facing the kitchen door. He took a slow, deep breath.

He meant to say nonchalantly, 'Oh, it's you, Father! Did you get my note?'

But his father's eyes shrivelled him back to his childhood.

'You're a bloody coward!'

The silver-topped stick bayoneted out, cracked against Sammy's chest and doubled him up, rasping and red-eyed, clawing for breath.

'Leave him alone!'

Ruth rushed to his aid but was knocked aside.

Sammy rose from the chair still choking, but another blow reeled him back.

'You're a bloody coward!'

Hatred came pulsing to Sammy's rescue.

'Get out of my house.'

'Och, the big brave man, is he? But not big enough or brave enough to fight for his King and country.'

'Get out.'

'I could make mincemeat of you, son. I didn't spend half a lifetime in the army without learning how to make mincemeat out of the likes of you.'

Ruth clung to Sammy's arm, and he could feel her trembling.

'You heard what Sammy said.'

'He hasn't said what I came to hear and I'm not leaving until he says it.'

'If you're waiting to hear me tell you I'm going to join the army, you're wasting your time.'

'Och, I've plenty of time, son.'

'Mr Hunter,' Ruth tried again. 'If you don't leave us alone I'll go for the police.'

'You just keep your stupid mouth shut, woman. We've always settled our own affairs inside the family. We've never needed anybody else.'

'Oh, haven't we?' Bitterness weltered Sammy like a fire-hose shooting acid. 'That's where you're wrong. Somebody should have locked you up in an asylum years ago.'

Unexpectedly, the heavy-handled stick shot out again.

'Sammy!' Ruth's cry was panic-stricken.

From somewhere down a dark tunnel he managed to grab the stick and hang on, muscles straining as he heaved it towards the door, every now and again wrenching and twisting but still forcing his weight against his father with all the pent-up fury of years.

The door banged shut and he lay against it for a moment, his lungs hiccoughing for air. Blood was rapidly spreading over his best white shirt and he stripped it off as he returned to the kitchen.

Ruth's face was all ink-black eyes and a white blotting paper skin.

'Oh, Sammy!'

'Bastards!' he said. 'Bastards. All of them!'

Chapter 14

Alec read the notice again.

'"Parents should see that on the day of evacuation their children are equipped with the following: A gas mask. A change of underclothing. Night clothes. House shoes or rubber shoes. Spare stockings or socks. A toothbrush. A towel. A comb. Handkerchief. A warm coat or macintosh. A tin cup or mug." Well, hen,' he asked Madge, 'have you got six of everything?'

Madge tucked her hair behind her ears and grinned at him. She was ready at the front door with the babies crushed together in the pram and Hector, Agnes and Sadie and Maisie hanging on to her coat-tails.

'Combs and toothbrushes would be no use to them.' She indicated the babies, now christened William and Fiona. 'Poor wee buggers! Toothless and hairless!'

'Well, come on, gorgeous, don't dilly-dally.'

The grin still stuck on her freckled face but her eyes became worried.

'You're not just wanting to get rid of us, Alec?'

'Dope! If I wanted rid of you lot the best way would be to keep you here. The Jerries would soon blow you to kingdom come.'

'But what about you?' Her smile disappeared. 'You'll be here.'

'Not as much as you and the weans would, hen. I'm collecting, on the move all day, and often at night, remember, and now I've to do this fire duty. I've enough on my plate without worrying about you, so come on! I'll see you to the school.'

From early morning evacuees had been assembling at the schools in the evacuation areas where teachers and other harassed adults were endeavouring to make order out of chaos. Labels pinned to their lapels, gas masks slung over their shoulders and tin mugs tied to the gas masks; clutching coats, teddy bears and toys the children see-sawed between hysterical delight at the novelty of it all and the fearful dread of the unknown. They milled and crushed and pulled and pushed and giggled and waved good-bye and wept broken-heartedly.

Glasgow sprouted children as if an invisible Pied Piper was conjuring them up endlessly out of nowhere. They hustled down streets, packed buses and trams, and swelled stations and trains to bursting point.

Alec's mind boggled at the thought of so many unsuspecting country houses about to be forcibly invaded.

Billeting officers were empowered to serve house-holders with notice requiring them to provide accommodation for a certain number of evacuees and where actual rooms were commandeered, an offence was committed if they were not immediately vacated.

Failure to comply with the regulations could bring a fine of £50 or a three-months' prison sentence.

'My God, hen,' Alec laughed. 'And I thought I was the only one swelling the population.'

Although Madge laughed, she looked disconcerted. William and Fiona whimpered and Maisie sucked her thumb and looked tired.

'Where are they all coming from, Alec?'

'God knows! But just you keep with the teachers or whoever's in charge. Do what they tell you. They're organising everything.'

'Poor buggers! Better them than me.'

'Well, it's time I was back at work, hen. I won't pay the rent standing here.'

They had reached the gates of the school and small children and tall children, all lumpy with burdens and jaggy-cornered with gas mask containers, converged from every direction. Alec began to feel restless, hemmed in.

'I'll away then.'

Madge automatically wiggled the handle of the pram about in an effort to rock and quieten William and Fiona.

'Remember and send me some money, Alec.'

'The first weekend after you send me your address, hen, I'll be down to see you and bring you some.'

Alec leaned closer to her and pinched her bottom. 'I'll be

saving up more than money for you, I'm warning you - so be prepared!'

She flung up a big toothy laugh and then gave each of the children leaning against her a jab towards him.

'Say cheerio to Daddy.'

'I don't want to go away,' Sadie wailed, and Agnes, Maisie and Hector took up the words like a fugue ending in unison with,

'Dad . . . dae!'

Madge laughed again.

'Och, well, at least I don't need to worry about them making a noise. No one's going to hear them in the middle of everybody else's racket.'

Noise was attacking them from all sides and Alec's brains began to crash together like cymbals. He couldn't hear himself think.

Hastily he swung Sadie, Agnes, Hector and Maisie up into the air and kissed them. He dropped a kiss on William's and Fiona's cheeks, now hot and wet with the exertions of screaming. A quick kiss for Madge and he was backing away when, in an unexpected flurry of movement she let go of the pram, rushed forward and grabbed hold of his jacket.

'Now, Madge,' he laughed, inwardly groaning. 'It's not like you to make a fool of yourself, hen.'

She released him, tucked her hair behind her ears and began bouncing the pram again, laughing with embarrassment.

'You never said you'd miss us.'

'Gorgeous!' He blew her a kiss. 'I'll be miserable just living and waiting for that weekend.'

Never before in his life had he been so glad to escape.

He was up to the top of his head in sound and knee deep in children, wading, struggling through them. He thought he would never get clear, never reach the cool dark quiet of his favourite pub with its newly-opened, wet-floor, disinfectant smell more pungent than the beer.

Once the pub had been successfully achieved he celebrated his freedom and new-found bachelorhood with a double whisky and a big golden frothing pint.

'Cheers!' he said, raising the whisky to everybody and nobody. He felt on top of the world.

War, he decided, had its advantages.

For the first time in years he felt really free. No anxieties about keeping the peace at home, no worries about Madge marching in on him either at the office or at somebody's house.

She had nerve, Madge - he had to give her credit. Old Madge would barge in where angels feared to tread and there was a streak of violence in her that had to be seen (or felt) to be believed. She looked harmless enough with that freckly face and those laughing blue eyes but she packed a wallop like the back legs of a horse. Not that he had ever been at the receiving end. But he had winced in sympathy a few times when she had dished out a black eye or a bloody nose to some of his female acquaintances.

Madge was loyal to him no matter what happened; all the same he often got the feeling he was teetering along on a tightrope and one day he would slip and fall. Life seemed more and more a series of narrow escapes.

Now suddenly - freedom! Whistling cheerfully he returned to the street. He did not feel like working. The prospect of going home and making himself a meal did not appeal to him either, and he decided to take the rest of the day off to celebrate. First he would go over to his mother's in Clydend for a meal and while he was there try and get the chance to chat up the wee blondie who lived up the same close.

He had passed the time of day with her a few times already. The poor girl was sex-starved. She fluttered and flushed and became as excited as a child with Santa Claus if he even glanced in her direction. It was pathetic. Her man had always worked nights, of course, and now he had joined up.

A sex-starved wife and a crazy husband. It took all kinds to make a world.

Alec's mother was at home and welcomed him with unconcealed delight.

Blissfully unaware of the reason for his now more frequent visits she immediately began searching out the little titbits she saved up for such occasions.

280

'I've got a cake, son!' She came up close and gave him a conspiratorial nudge with a bony elbow. 'Tipsy! Your favourite! Tipsy cake.'

He winked.

'Great, Ma!'

'And a few potatoes. I'll make chips. It won't take a minute, a few chips.'

'Great, Ma!'

She would take ages. She was at the change of life he reckoned, and it affected her that way. She wandered aimlessly about, dropping whatever she touched, getting into mix-ups and forgetting where she had put everything from her corsets to her purse.

Restlessly, he strolled through to the room and stared down from the tiny attic window to the cobbled Dessie Street below.

Not every child had been moved to the safety of the countryside. Some still played with balls and skipping ropes, boys wrestled and punched, girls crawled along the pavement drawing peever beds with lumps of pipe-clay oblivious of their dangerous nearness to the docks across the main road and the high ships on stocks and other vessels crowding the river.

He returned to the kitchen lighting a cigarette. His mother was standing in the middle of the floor like a white-faced golliwog, her fingertips trembling against her mouth.

'This is my last fag, Ma,' said Alec. 'I think I'll run down for some.'

'I was just trying to remember where I put the cake, son. A tipsy cake. I know I have it somewhere.'

'Don't worry, Ma. I'm in no rush. Take your time, hen.'

Her lips were like elastic, stretching, pursing, moving about. Eventually she managed: 'You're a good lad!'

Alec shut the front door and stood for a minute or two on the landing.

Careful does it, he thought. The little blondie downstairs was maybe desperate for it but women were strange, touchy creatures and she was stranger and touchier than most.

For months now he had been doing a verbal minuet with her and it was proving the oddest experience of his life.

He still could not be perfectly sure what to make of her but he suspected that somewhere inside this delicate little butterfly there were emotions just as strong as those more obvious in Ruth Hunter.

Up till recently, of course, she had always been afraid of her husband suddenly appearing, and jumped and fluttered at the slightest sound, but now that he was out of the picture things should be different.

Not that her old man would have been justified in raising an eyebrow at anything that had happened so far: a chance meeting or two on the stairs, a few laughs and talks at her door. He had spoken to her downstairs in the shop, and a couple of times they had met for longer periods at his mother's place, the girl's gold hair and radiant face lighting up the dark attic room.

Puffing at his cigarette and blowing smoke out in front of him he went down the stairs until he came to the door marked Melvin MacNair.

He gave his usual rat-tat-tat-tat-tat. Tat-tat!

As always Catriona peeped timidly round a crack, then opened the door slowly, cautiously.

'Hello there, gorgeous. How do you do it, eh?'

Her eyes smiled, fluttered down, shoulders and hands squeezed up to stifle giggles.

'Do what?'

'Look more beautiful every time I see you. Look at that hair.'

Alec's hand went out to touch her hair and as usual she jerked back like a terrified doe. Only this time he was ready and his fingers reached and held, and wound round the soft silkiness.

'Anybody else in, hen?'

'No,' she whispered, cringing as if he were striking her.

He chuckled. She was just standing there letting him play with her.

'Aren't you going to ask me in?'

'I'm here by myself. The children are at my mother's and my father-in-law's down in the shop.'

'I've just come for six pennies for a sixpence for the gas. Ma was making me something to eat and her gas ring's gone out.'

'Oh! Oh yes, yes. Yes, of course.'

282

The girl wriggled her head from under his hand and flew across the hall towards the kitchen. He followed her into the house and quietly shut the door.

This was a lot different from his mother's poky place up under the rafters. There was a square room hall with various doors leading off it.

Polish was the keynote. The pungent waxy smell of it thickened the air. Everything was polished: even the walls, decorated with heavy embossed paper, shiny enough to see your face in. The doors, like the dark brown linoleum, gleamed and glittered, daring anyone to deface them.

Stepping stones of little rugs were dotted here and there. With great care he stepped on them until he reached the room into which Catriona had fled.

It was an immaculate, highly polished kitchen with sparkling sink and sideboard, table and chairs.

Funny, he thought, Ruth Hunter's place was as posh and well kept as this but so much more comfortable and homely.

'Find any, gorgeous?'

She gave a scream of terror at the unexpected sight of him that even he jumped.

'My God, hen!' He collapsed into one of the chairs by the fire, his hands on his chest. 'You just about frightened the life out of me!'

The girl's eyes remained enormous but laughter gurgled in her throat, escaping from her mouth in jerky little bursts. She put a hand up to try and control it, looking uncertain, apologetic, as if she were afraid he might be angry with her for making a rude noise.

Alec grinned at her and shook his head.

'You're an awful wee lassie.'

The fear went out of her eyes and she lowered her gaze and giggled childishly, and Alec immediately saw his cue. Here was a real Peter Pan, a girl who had never grown up.

'Come over here!'

He pointed to the rug at his feet.

Obediently she came.

'Am I a friend of yours?' he asked, trying to sound stern.

'W-w-well I . . . I suppose you are.'

'Didn't I carry your heavy message basket and your wean up the stairs for you the other day?'

'Yes, you're always very kind.'

'Didn't my mother deliver your wean?'

'Oh, yes. Oh, she's been terribly kind.'

'She's your friend?'

'Oh, yes, I don't know what I'd do without her.'

'And I'm your friend?'

She nodded and smiled tentatively.

'Well,' he said, his eyes beginning to twinkle. 'Don't you know how to treat your friends?'

Worry cast a shadow over her face and she did not answer.

He leaned forward and caught hold of her hands.

'It's easy, hen, just be friendly!'

Chapter 15

He pulled her on to his knees and into his arms before she had
time to realise what was happening and for a few minutes he
held her like a baby, rocking her, patting her. She stiffened at
first as though she were going to struggle but it was only for an
imperceptible moment, until she fell under tthe spell of the
gentle rocking.

Alec stroked and played with her hair and when he looked
down he saw that her eyes had closed.

His hand slid down over her blouse and found her small
breast. Immediately her arms flew up to hug herself protectively.

'What's wrong?' he queried in aggrieved surprise as if she had
offended him.

Her gaze shrank down.

'I'd better go and get the pennies for your mother.'

'There's no hurry.'

'I'd better go.'

He smiled.

'I'm stronger than you, hen.'

Before she could panic his mouth quietened her and he
burrowed down into a more comfortable position to enjoy a
long slow exploration, but she was trembling and shaking and
shivering with such violence that his plan to proceed in a
leisurely fashion had to be abandoned.

'No, please!' She struggled up for air. 'Oh, please. Somebody
might come in. What if somebody saw me?'

She wept broken-heartedly.

'Sh-sh!' He stroked her hair. 'I don't want to upset you - just
love you.'

'Love me?' Immediately her gaze beseeched him. 'You mean
that?'

'Of course.'

'You love me?'

'Adore you!'

'Is that the same as loving? Does that mean you care about me?'

'I love you. I really care about you. All right?'

'No . . . no!' She began to struggle again. 'Somebody might see me!'

'Gorgeous, you're in an upstairs flat. Are you frightened a passing pigeon will keek in?'

'I couldn't bear it.'

'Sh . . . sh . . . All right. All right.' He lifted her up in his arms. 'I'll take you anywhere you want to go.'

He carried her out into the dark hall.

'Where's the bedroom?'

'Oh, no, please, please put me down.'

'You know I love you, don't you?'

She shook her head, eyes wet and helpless.

'Well, gorgeous, I do!'

He let her slide down as he kissed her again.

'Come on,' he urged. 'What room?'

'No, somebody might see through the windows.'

'We could draw the blinds.'

'Everyone would know.'

The situation was becoming ridiculous but he managed to keep his voice low.

'Here then? It's dark and there's no windows.'

Furtively, fearfully she peered around.

'The doors are open.'

'Not the front door. It's locked.'

'The other doors.'

'Sweetheart, we can shut them if it'll make you feel happy.'

He kept his arm firmly around her as they went round the hall securing every door.

'All right now?'

Another fit of shivering took possession of her.

'Somebody could see through the letter-box.'

With an effort, he controlled himself.

'If we open this cupboard and stand behind it, nobody could see, not even through the letter-box.'

286

He manoeuvred her against the cupboard shelves.

'Anyway, it's pitch dark.'

'It's important.'

'What is, hen?'

'That I know for sure.'

'Nobody can see.'

'That you love me.'

'I told you.'

'Promise me you mean it.'

'I promise.'

'I want you to be perfectly honest. I need to feel sure.'

So anxious was she in testing his sincerity and anxiously searching his eyes that she was unaware of his fingers deftly unbuttoning and baring her. But the moment the heat of their bodies came together she gave a strangled cry of surprise and began struggling and fighting.

'Sh . . . sh,' he whispered. 'Somebody will hear you.'

At once she quietened and became motionless.

'Good girl,' he rewarded her. 'Good girl.'

He took as long as he dared. After all, the old man was liable to come up from the shop and for all he knew her battle-axe of a mother might be due to arrive on the scene.

'Your father-in-law or your mother might come,' he told her eventually. 'I'd better go.'

He allowed her to cling on to him and he kept his arm around her until they reached the outside door. He unlocked, then disentangled himself. 'Thanks, hen. I'll see you again soon.'

Her voice quavered out faint and high-pitched like an infant's.

'You won't tell anybody about me?'

'Don't be daft!'

He blew her a kiss before shutting the door and rapidly returning upstairs.

'I've got it all ready, son,' his mother greeted him, with a flushed, triumphant face.

'Just a minute, Ma. Give me a minute, hen, there's something I'm bursting to do.'

He staggered past her into the kitchen and collapsed full length on the sofa.

Laughter exploded up from his belly in jerks and swirls, madder and madder like a firework display. He writhed and clutched himself and flayed about shouting and howling.

'Are you feeling all right, son?'

Uncertainty tipped his mother's voice off balance.

He sat up, fished for a handkerchief and wiped tears of hilarity from his eyes.

'Great Ma! What's for tea, hen? I'm starving.'

She had committed adultery. She had committed adultery.

Catriona wandered back to the kitchen in a daze. Reaching a chair her legs tottered and gave way.

She had broken one of God's commandments.

All the sins that had harassed every year of her life faded into nothingness compared with this - this monstrous wickedness.

To think that only an hour ago she had been sitting here alone believing herself to be dangerously near a suicidal level of worry.

Since Melvin had gone she had somehow lost her grip on life. Old Mr MacNair and her mother between them had taken the reins.

Her father-in-law was becoming more and more of a whiner, harping on continuously about everything from the rotten weather and bad-paying customers to stupid nyucks in the government who'd got every one into another ruinous war.

If he was not complaining, he was depressing her with tales of disaster and death. He studied the evening paper's Deaths column with avid interest, often reading each announcement to her word for word, and had even indignantly complained on one occasion:

'There's only two deceased tonight!'

Apart from upsetting her, she felt sure the old man's conversation must have a bad effect on the children.

She confided in her mother and pleaded for advice, only to have the children promptly wrenched away from her.

'But, Mummy, you can't take them to stay at your place,' she had protested in panic. 'What will I do without them?'

'Oh, be quiet!' Her mother's face twisted in disgust. 'I'm sick of your selfish whining. You're as bad as that man.'

'It's not that Da means any harm. It's just he's getting old and . . .'

'Oh, be quiet.'

Her mother turned her attention back to Andrew, nursing him, smiling fondly at him, dandling him up and down.

'Granny's lovely wee pettilorums, wee lovey-dovey darling yes!'

'Give Andrew to me, Mummy.'

Feeling suddenly afraid, Catriona stuck out her hands.

'Please, I want him.'

'You're a wicked, selfish girl. What do you care if this poor infant's buried alive?'

'Buried alive?' Her eyes were enormous.

'This is the most dangerous place in Glasgow. May God in his infinite mercy help and protect you.'

'I want my baby.'

Catriona made a grab at Andrew and tried to pull him forcibly from the strong muscular arms, but was knocked back as Andrew let out a machine-gun panic of squeals.

'You wicked, wicked girl. Now look what you've done.'

Her mother began pacing the floor, bouncing Andrew against her buxom chest.

'Never mind that bad Mummy, lovey. Granny won't let that Mummy touch Granny's wee lovey again.'

Following her mother about the room, trembling with agitation, Catriona repeated over and over again:

'I want my baby. I want my baby.'

'Get out of the way,' her mother commanded. 'I'm taking these children to where they'll be safe and with the Good Lord's help properly looked after.'

'I can look after them and they'll be as safe here as in Farmbank.'

'Don't talk nonsense! There's only a council housing scheme in Farmbank. Why would the Germans want to bomb that? May God in His infinite mercy forgive you! You are putting your own selfish desires before the safety and well-being of these children. Come on, Fergus, you carry Granny's message bag.'

She swung round again. 'And you,' she said, 'had better pack

289

a case with their things and bring it over to me at Farmbank after you've seen to the old man's tea tonight. I'm warning you, Catriona, God has His own way of working. He'll punish you for your wicked selfishness. Something terrible is going to happen to you or to someone you love.'

She had determined to follow her mother and somehow snatch the children back again and this determination and the wicked selfishness of it had been churning around in her mind when she heard the unexpected rat-tat-tat at the door and Alec Jackson appeared.

Now she felt too afraid to face the children in case they might know what she had done and be ashamed of her. Her uncleanness was so abominable it was bound to be clearly visible to everyone's eyes.

Yet her ache for her baby tugged at her mercilessly. She loved and wanted Fergus too, but her feeling for him, try as she might, could never equal the acuteness, the exquisite pleasure-pain she experienced at the mere thought of Andrew.

She got up and began pacing the floor, desperate to run all the way to Farmbank and fight tooth and nail to get the children back, yet fearing that in her present shocked state she might do the wrong thing again, might go on heaping one dreadful sin upon another.

What if she did manage to bring Andrew back, and there was an air-raid and he was killed? She burst into tears and stood in the middle of the floor wiping messily at her face with the backs of her hands.

If loving meant really caring then she ought to care about the children, not herself, she ought to put them first.

She pressed her lips firmly together and breathed big jerky breaths.

Tea-time. Set the table. Clever girl.

For hours she wandered about the house trying to reassure herself. She longed for comfort. Not for Melvin's bullying voice, his harsh laugh, his heavy bull-body but for somebody who really cared about her.

Thoughts of Alec's gentleness relaxed her like an anaesthetic. Her hiccoughing breaths soothed and subsided. Alec would tell her what was best for the children.

It was late now and it was dark but she would go to him and he would make everything all right.

Her mind made up, she hurried to get her coat and find the tram-car that would carry her through the blacked-out city and to Alec's house in Springburn.

Chapter 16

The Society of Friends, the Quakers, held Fellowship Meetings and mock tribunals for conscientious objectors, to prepare them for what was to come, to help them clarify their position in their own minds and to give them practice in answering questions.

The Quakers were a revelation to Sammy, surprising him first of all with their obvious lack of prejudice. Everyone was welcomed at the Meeting House by the same warm shake of the hand and the same cheerful acceptance. It obviously made no difference if one was a Quaker, a Plymouth or any other kind of Brother, a Jehovah's Witness, an Independent Labour Party man, a Christadelphian, a Freethinker, a Christian Scientist, a Methodist, a Humanist, an atheist.

Sammy discovered that the Meeting House, a converted terrace house near Charing Cross, had its own library and before the mock tribunal started he had a browse through some of the books, and a few shy words with a Quaker called John Haddington, who came into the room to stand puffing at a pipe and heating his coat-tails at the fire.

The whole place was so unlike a normal church, both in appearance and in practice, that Sammy was quite intrigued. From what he had read and been told about them, he discovered Quakers believed that everyone, including women - who had enjoyed absolute equality with men right from the time of the founder George Fox - were part of the ministry. Therefore anyone could get up during meeting for worship and voice a prayer or anything he might feel moved to say.

Perhaps someone might recite a poem that had comforted or inspired him.

Another might stand up and give a few brief words on a special event.

After a silence another Friend might comment on what the original speaker had said, and so with respectful, thoughtful silences in between each speech, a little discussion might arise, a tentative spiritual probing.

Or the hour-long meeting might be held in unbroken quiet, a spiritual waiting in which the clamour of daily life was stilled. At the end of the hour notices would be read out, including the announcement that coffee was being served upstairs and all visitors would be most welcome.

'Coffee time's the best time!' John Haddington amused Sammy with his candour. 'We have a rare old talk then and thoroughly enjoy ourselves.'

As far back as Sammy could remember he had always had a church connection but it had never had much to do with enjoyment.

He had been marched to Sunday School and Bible Class. Eventually he had become a church member. The church was a background, part of the pattern of his life. Now he and Ruth attended church together.

But he had never given religion the same serious thought as he had other subjects. Ever since his childhood he had been an avid reader, and Ruth and he enjoyed going to the library twice or three times a week to change their books, but he had never bothered much with the shelves marked Religion.

His church membership was a prestige symbol, a sign of respectability more than anything else. It pleased Ruth if they dressed in their best and set out arm in arm for church on a Sunday. Their church connection gave them a place in the community and a set of decent standards to live by.

Here at Quaker Meeting House, he sensed with deep inward surprise that there might be something beyond and above this.

He sat self-consciously through the Fellowship Meeting and mock tribunal yet warming with gratitude for the practical help the Quakers, and John Haddington in particular, were giving him.

He had been completely in the dark about the coming tribunal; now, thanks to the Friends, he had some idea of what to expect, and could begin to prepare himself for the ordeal. He intensified his reading, taking pages and pages of notes to make his point on the day.

He had condensed the notes and rewritten them in a neat hand on a series of little cards that would fit in his wallet. He had muttered his arguments as he dressed, he had tried them out on Ruth until at last she asked worriedly, 'Do you think you should learn all this, love? You might never get the chance to say it.'

'But this is the basis of my objection,' he protested irritably. 'The point of these tribunals is to find out who really has a conscientious objection.'

'I know.'

She kissed him on the brow, then on the eyes, then on the mouth.

'Don't lose your temper. Especially at the tribunal. That's what you'll have to remember more than anything else.'

The day had come, and Ruth was helping as only she could. She took extra care in the washing and ironing of his shirt and insisted on pressing his Sunday suit, while Sammy brushed his shoes until they were like black mirrors. He had already been down the road to the public baths.

'One of these days,' he told Ruth for the hundredth time, 'we're going to have a house with a bathroom. It's terrible that people are expected to live in houses without bathrooms. What do they think we are - animals? They've a damned cheek, haven't they?'

She brushed him down as if she were caressing him.

'Yes, love.'

'They expect us to live in hovels and pay ridiculous rents for the privilege, work long hours for a mere pittance, never raise a voice in protest, and jump to their command when they want us to put on a uniform and fight for our country. *Our country*! What bit of country do *we* own?'

'All these dukes and lords,' she tutted.

'Yes, they're the ones who live off the fat of the land. Let them fight for it. You know what the Duke of Wellington called his men - the scum of the earth.'

She tutted again.

'A right military Charlie! They're all the same. My father used to yell, "Come on, you scum, pick-em up, left, right, left, right!" Well I'm not scum!'

'No, you're not.'

Ruth pouted her lips and teased his cheek with them.

'I told him. I was only so-high. "I'm not scum," I said. I was always stepping out of line. He could never knock me into shape.'

Her soft burring voice tried to soothe him.

'You mustn't let him worry you, Sammy.'

'Yours not to reason why!' Anger brought a tremor to his voice. 'Very convenient, isn't it? No questions asked. Just do as you're told. Well, I won't. Him and his patriotic jargon and heroic battle tales. If you look back on most battles they were a shambles of incompetence, stupidity and sheer lunacy at officer level.'

'You mustn't get angry.'

'I've a right to be angry.'

He tugged at his tie in silence for a minute or two. Then he said, 'Did you know they used to hold the tribunals in the Judiciary Buildings? Like criminal cases? The Quakers insisted the tribunals weren't criminal proceedings so they were moved to an ordinary hall.'

'Your tie's fine, love.'

'I'd better go. Now, don't you get worried or upset, Ruth.'

Her fingers caressed his mouth and she moved closer.

'I'm going to be fine,' she said. 'Don't you worry about me.'

At least Britain, unlike its present allies, made provisions for conscientious objectors and the treatment of them was, generally speaking, very good: a state of affairs which had had its roots in the revelation of the sufferings of the conscientious objectors in the 1914-18 war, when they had been subject to brutal treatment.

Even now a CO might fall foul of a tribunal or some individual on a tribunal who regarded it as his bounden duty to browbeat the applicants, but on the whole the tribunals were conducted conscientiously and fairly.

A vigilant eye was kept on the proceedings, wherever possible, by a small band of determined MPs, some of whom had themselves been COs in the First World War.

Sammy's tribunal was held in public and consisted of five

295

men - a university professor, a trade union official, a King's counsellor who was Chairman, a lecturer from the Education Department and an ex-sheriff. They made an imposing array up on the platform as if a higher floor-level was synonymous with lofty ideals.

The conscientious objectors were allowed into the hall one at a time from a back room and must answer questions sitting with necks craned upwards.

Sammy looked for Ruth as he walked in and was reassured to see her sitting beside John Haddington from the Quaker Meeting House.

Then, on the other side of the hall, he saw his father, crouched forward, palms resting on silver-topped stick, his eyes slicing him.

Sammy's chair made a loud creaking noise.

He prayed for a mind empty of past, divorced from present, a question machine. Question and answer.

'In your statement you say you hold as a principle that war is wrong.'

'Yes, sir.'

'You don't believe in fighting for freedom, for justice, and for a good and lasting peace?'

'No, sir. History shows that military means never resulted in a good and lasting peace. Victory has always sown the seeds of fresh war because victory breeds among the vanquished a desire for vindication and vengeance and because victory raises fresh rivals.'

He fingered his notes as if they were written in Braille and tried not to feel the mockery of his father's eyes upon him.

'In the seventeenth century we broke the power of Spain with the help of the Dutch. Then we fought three wars with the Dutch - we broke their power in alliance with the French. But within a generation we were fighting coalition wars against France. After six of these wars stretching over a century we succeeded in breaking France. But our chief allies, Russia and Prussia, became our dangers in the century that followed - together with France, the country that we had beaten.

'In the Crimean War we sought to cripple Russia's power in

alliance with the French. Five years later we were threatened with a French invasion of England.'

'What's all this tosh? The French are not the enemy now. You are being asked to fight the Germans.'

'If history teaches us anything it is this: after all the suffering and bloodshed, Germany will be our allies again. This is my point. Victory is only an illusion. A pause for changing sides. The germs of war lie with ourselves - not in economics, politics or religion as such.'

'Have you no loyalty to your King and country?'

'If you are thinking of the soldiers' dictum - "my country right or wrong" - the answer is no, sir. That kind of so-called loyalty is too often a polite word for what would be more accurately described as - a conspiracy for mutual inefficiency. I'd rather be loyal to the truth.'

'What if the Germans come over here? What would you do? Wouldn't you fight them?'

'War is futile. It has never gained anything. I would have nothing to do with military methods.'

'What would you do if a German came over here and assaulted your wife?'

'That is a hypothetical question.'

'It is not a hypothetical question. It has happened and can happen and will happen. What are you going to do about it?'

His hands were sweating and anger was burning up to his throat like bile.

'It *is* a hypothetical question. You might as well ask what I would do if a member of a Glasgow gang attacked my wife. I would have thought there was much more danger of that happening in the blackout at the moment. Or are all the gangsters already in the army?'

'Don't be impertinent, young man! A bit of army discipline is what you obviously need. Just answer the question!'

Fools! He glared hatred at them. Fools!

'I would do what I could,' he said. 'I would put myself between my wife and her assailant. I would use sufficient force to deter him but I hope I would not make myself a killer.'

'So you are not against force.'

297

'There is a difference between a hypothetical situation of either a German soldier or a Glasgow thug attacking my wife and Haig's blundering massacre of four hundred thousand men at Passchendaele.'

'Are you or are you not against force?'

'I am against military methods of trying to solve anything. History clearly shows . . .'

'Never mind about history! We don't want a history lecture from you. Answer the question. Are you or are you not against force?'

'I am against anything military.'

'Are you a church-going man?'

'Yes.'

'Do you know your Bible?'

'Yes.'

'Do you know that your Bible says: "An eye for an eye and a tooth for a tooth"?'

'Yes, and I know Christ made a point of contradicting that statement.' Even if you don't, he added to himself. Out loud he said:

'But I am not objecting on religious grounds.'

'You are just against the military.'

'I am.'

'You wouldn't care if Hitler and the whole German army came over here.'

'I am against any army.'

'But you don't want to fight?'

'I am fighting now.'

'Unsuccessfully. You need more training. The army is best equipped to give you that. Your name shall be removed without qualification from the register of conscientious objectors.'

His father caught up with him outside, stalking him stifffly. 'You'll be all right if you get to Maryhill Barracks, son. I've got friends there. I've already had a wee word with Sergeant-Major Spack. He'll soon knock you into shape. We'll make a good soldier of you yet.'

'Come on home, love.'

Ruth pulled Sammy away and nothing more was said.

He had expected his objection to be dismissed even before John Haddington had warned him. He was well aware that only the religious objectors stood much of a chance. Yet now that it had really happened he was shocked.

As a child standing still in the moving darkness outside the mortuary, his mind had shuddered not only with terror but with hatred and revenge.

One day . . . one day . . .

He had never cried as his brothers had cried when they were children. He had never run away like them when they had grown up.

One day . . . one day . . . he always thought.

Now his father was growing and multiplying like some evil fungus and spreading all over the world. His father and his war games and his map on the wall with all its coloured flags. His father gloating over how many men he had gutted with his bayonet. His father standing angelically to attention at 'God Save the King'.

His father shot up, a giant filling his mind in the waiting days that followed. Time blurred. The past caught up with the present and quick-marched it into the future.

Left-right, left-right, pick 'em up, pick 'em up. Come on! At the double - you scum of the earth!

The fungus had spread all over him and sucked him in.

'*What regiment?*' his father asked. '*What regiment?*'

And over and over again his mind ground out the same answer.

'None!'

Chapter 17

Alec was so fed up over the carry-on about Catriona MacNair, that in a reckless moment he volunteered for the Navy.

If he had thought that she could have caused half as much trouble he would have kept well clear of her.

He could still hardly credit that she had had the cheek to come over from Clydend to Springburn, actually seek him out at the pend.

Her arrival had been the second shock that night. The other was Madge's unexpected return from the evacuation.

He had been lolling back with a bottle of beer in his hand, his feet up on the mantelpiece, the wireless blaring, and had not heard the door open and Madge and the family come in.

He had never seen her look so tired and dispirited and the children were dirty-faced and dazed with fatigue. They all looked as if they would not be able to stand up for one more minute.

He turned off the wireless.

'Madge! What's wrong, hen? What are you doing back?'

'Let me get them to bed first. I'm going to fling them in the way they are. I'm not even going to take their coats off.'

She pushed the pram aside and lifted first Maisie, then Hector, Sadie and Agnes, heaved them into the hole-in-the-wall bed and covered them with blankets. The children immediately fell sound asleep.

'My God, Alec, what a day. I didn't even know where I was. They've hidden the names of every place. You can't tell what station you're at and there's all those posters up: BE LIKE DAD, KEEP MUM and IS YOUR JOURNEY REALLY NECESSARY? That was a laugh!'

She sprawled out on the sofa, her big thighs tightening her skirt and rucking it up.

Looking at her like that, pink suspenders showing and milky

skin bulging above the top of her stockings, he was glad she was back.

'Come on, hen, I'll undress you and put you to bed.'

'Do you know what my tongue's hanging out for?'

'I know what your tongue's always hanging out for.' He laughed. 'And you'll get it as soon as we're in bed.'

'Alec, for God's sake make us a cup of tea first.'

'Anything you say, gorgeous. The kettle's boiling on the hob.' He got up, whistling cheerily.

'It was bad enough here before we started.' Madge scratched her breast and made it swing about. 'All that noise and crush at the school, then the journey. God, it was awful. But it was worse at the other end. We were all crowded into a hall and this man started to separate us.'

'Separate you?' Alec widened his eyes in mock shock. 'So that's why you're tired?'

'Och, Alec, don't be filthy.'

'Separated you, you said.'

'Give us a cup of tea.'

'Promise you'll let me separate you and I'll give you one.' She sighed.

'He tried to take the weans away from me.'

He had never seen her nearer tears. Hastily he poured a cup of tea and handed it over.

'Who did, hen?'

'This billeting officer man. He said there was too many of us and we couldn't all go to the one place. He was going to separate us, send the weans all to different places. I was only to keep Willy and Fiona.'

'They would have been all right. He would have found them good houses.'

'They would have cried their eyes out without me and all separated from each other.' She took big noisy sups of tea. 'God, I'm enjoying this. No, I couldn't let him do it to the poor wee buggers.'

At that moment a knock at the door surprised them both.

'I'll go, hen.'

He went swaggering, whistling a tune through his teeth.

301

The landing was in complete darkness because of the blackout and he had not lit the gas in the lobby, but there could be no mistaking the small figure, the large eyes, the shimmering hair.

'The wife's back,' he hissed desperately. 'Hop it!' She just stood there looking stupid.

'Who is it, Alec?' Madge called from the kitchen.

'Beat it!' he whispered.

'Beat it?' Catriona echoed.

She was the stupidest creature alive. He fervently wished he had never set eyes on her.

He was about to shut the door in her face when Madge appeared at his elbow.

'There's a howling gale blowing in here with that door . . .'

She peered through the shadows.

'Is that Catriona MacNair?'

'She's come over to tell me that Ma's not well,' said Alec quickly.

'All this way, at this time of night in the blackout?' Madge gasped. 'Come away in, hen. There's a cup of tea made.'

'She's got to hurry right back, Madge. I'd better go with her.'

'Och, don't be daft. She looks frozen. Come in for a minute, hen.'

Back in the kitchen Madge poured out another cup and handed it to Catriona before slumping back down on the sofa.

'What's wrong with Ma?'

Catriona gently sipped her tea and stared round the kitchen as if it were about to burst into flames.

Alec wished he could snap his fingers and make her disappear. It was terrible that she should be here taking tea from his wife and only yards away from his children. It was downright indecent.

'There's no need to worry,' Catriona quavered, before he had the chance to answer Madge himself. 'There's nothing wrong with Mrs Jackson.'

'Nothing wrong with Ma?' Madge's tone changed. 'Then what have you come for?'

'What she means is . . . ' Alec began, but Catriona's wavering voice horrified him into silence again.

302

'I came to see Alec.'

'Oh, you did?'

Madge rose.

'No, Madge, hen, take it easy,' Alec pleaded. 'She's so much wee-er than you!'

'I'm sorry.' Catriona's cup rocked noisily in its saucer as she replaced it on the table. 'I feel so ashamed. I don't know how it happened.'

'How what happened?'

If only Madge would stop asking questions! Catriona was obviously a female George Washington. She was going to stand there in front of Madge like a wean who had pinched an apple and confess all. Alec groaned inwardly.

'Drink up your tea, hen,' he urged. 'It's time you were getting back.'

'You keep out of this!' Madge commanded.

'Maybe it was because Melvin's gone.' Catriona was wringing her hands now. 'Maybe it was because my mother took the children away. I don't know. I'm so sorry, Madge!'

'Sorry for what? What happened?'

'Well, you see, Alec came to the door for pennies for his mother's gas.'

Alec lit a cigarette.

'My God!' he said.

'You keep out of this!' Madge repeated, then to the girl, 'So?'

'I went in to get my purse and when I turned round he was at my back in the kitchen. And then . . . and then . . .'

'And then?' Madge prompted.

'Well . . . he said . . .' Catriona's voice faded. 'I should be friendly . . . I didn't know, I didn't think he meant . . .'

'Are you trying to tell me that my Alec laid you?'

'Oh, no,' Catriona hastily assured her. 'We were standing in the cupboard in the hall.'

Alec leaned against the mantelpiece to support his brow.

'My God!' he said again.

'I wouldn't have bothered him tonight only I didn't know who to turn to. My mother said the children wouldn't be safe with me at Dessie Street and she took them away.'

303

Catriona's voice suddenly changed to a horrible wail.

'I want my baby back and she won't give him to me.'

Alec could not stand it a minute longer. He had been as nice as ninepence to her, chatted her up, made her laugh and gave her a bit of loving when her man was away, and this was all the thanks he got.

'What a bloody cheek!' he gasped. 'I've a wife and six weans. I've enough worries without taking on yours.'

Unexpectedly Madge rounded on him.

'You're the only bloody worry in this house. My back wasn't turned five minutes and you were sniffing round somebody else.'

'No, hen, you've got it all wrong. You know what women are like with me.'

'She's only a wee lassie!' Madge suddenly let out a broken-hearted roar. 'And she's worried about her weans!'

Her big fist shot out, cracked his chin up, and bounced his head back against the mantelpiece.

He slithered bumpily down into sickly blackness and the next thing he remembered was coming to with a bit of rag rug stuck up his nose. He sneezed and howled with pain.

The light was out but the fire red-shivered the kitchen.

Maisie was making little puttering noises in the hole-in-wall bed and Hector, who needed his tonsils out, was snoring lustily.

Alec pulled himself up with the help of the chair, rubbing and working his chin about.

His bottle of beer still lay on the table and he took a swig, but it was warm and flat.

He undressed in front of the fire, not feeling in the mood to strip off in the freezing room. Once naked he heated his palms and rubbed them together, bracing himself for a quick sprint through and a jump into bed.

The blackout curtains hadn't been drawn and the front room was moon-filled with dancing grey dust.

He froze in mid-leap.

The bed was full, too.

Catriona was facing the wall, handless in one of Madge's long-sleeved nighties, her hair spread out like a silver shawl.

304

Madge was a protective mountain beside her, one freckled arm over the top of Catriona, cuddling her in sleep.

He had no alternative but to race back to the kitchen fire again. He put his clothes on, cursing fluently, then took one of the children's blankets, rolled himself in it and settled down on the jaggy sofa.

It was one of the worst nights of his life and he awoke to find life no better.

His big, cheery, always the same, happy-go-lucky Madge had changed.

She still marched about gaily making the breakfast and talking to the children and to Catriona but as soon as she turned her attention or her voice on him the good cheer hardened into cold steel.

Catriona was busily washing the children and brushing their hair.

He could have strangled her.

What right had she to come into his house and cause trouble between him and his wife?

Madge and she were as thick as thieves. Like long-lost sisters. Madge had even promised to go to Farmbank to rescue Catriona's weans. It wasn't fair. Why should Madge act like this?

He would have liked to remind her that he worked hard to keep a roof over her head and clothes on her back.

Instead he braved the icicles to give her a cuddle.

'How's my gorgeous hunk of woman this morning?'

'Get off!'

The words had been uttered many times before but never with the contempt they had now.

He felt genuinely worried but at the same time certain that Madge would eventually forgive and forget. He knew old Madge.

There were times later when he thought she had forgotten. Busy times alone together in bed. Or if they had friends in for a game of cards or if they were out visiting with the children she talked and laughed like her old self.

Yet she was not her old self. Quarrels kept flaring unexpectedly over silly, unimportant things and each time, before he knew what had happened, she had dragged Catriona up, then resurrected every other female he had ever known.

As if things weren't bad enough already, Catriona became pregnant.

He never could get over how such a harmless-looking creature was able to cause so much stir and trouble. He used to tell Madge he did not like using French letters because it spoiled making love: it was like eating toffee with the paper on.

Now every time he thought of Catriona he wished he had used half-a-dozen. The way Madge talked (and talked and talked) anyone would think he had planted a time bomb inside the girl.

The baby could be her husband's, for all they knew. He wasn't that long away.

Madge wouldn't hear of that, though.

'Oh, I know you. It'll be yours, all right.'

As if fathering a child had suddenly become a sin, and no other man would sink so low.

Alec began to feel restless, hemmed in, thoroughly fed-up with it all, and on a sudden impulse one day he joined the Navy.

So far he didn't regret it. He was a good mixer, cheerful, friendly and adaptable. In no time he was one of the lads, talking about 'the deck', 'the galley', 'skiving', and rolling cigarettes out of 'tickler' tobacco from an old tin. His cap tipped over his brow, his bell-bottoms flapping, he whistled along with his Glasgow swagger and his sailor's roll making him look jauntier and cheerier than ever.

In fact, there was only one thing spoiling a new and hopeful horizon: the war and where it might take him.

Chapter 18

'Put that light out!'

The shout resounded up the close and round the stairs together with the indignant clatter of feet, and the door battered and shook before Catriona had time to get to it.

She screwed up her face, fervently hoping that the children would not be wakened.

'There's a light from your house shining across on the Benlin Yards. You're endangering the whole of Clydend!'

The red-faced special constable could hardly speak, he was puffing so hard for breath.

'Oh, no, you must be making a mistake,' Catriona assured him. 'I'm very careful about the windows.'

This was true. She had big heavy curtains up on all the windows including the bathroom and she had followed the instructions in one of the government pamphlets which advised criss-crossing the glass with brown sticky paper to strengthen it against blast.

The special constable pushed roughly past her into the hall, hesitated for a minute to get his bearings then made a rush at old Duncan MacNair's room.

There were two bedrooms in the house and both faced on to the Main Road. Only the sitting-room had a window looking down on to Dessie Street. The smaller bedroom, which had once been the children's, was now the old man's room, and the children had been moved in with Catriona.

'Look at this!' the constable yelled.

The bedroom window stood bare and uncurtained.

Catriona sighed with exasperation.

'Da, how many times have I to tell you. You'll be the death of us yet.'

He was sitting on the edge of his bed in his vest and long-johns, his goatee beard quivering.

'What's the meaning of this?' His high-pitched nasal whine spluttering saliva through his ill-fitting false teeth. 'Bursting into my room with your fancy man when I'm getting my clothes off!'

'Da!'

The constable shut the curtains, satisfied himself that the window was thoroughly sealed, then approached with notebook and pen at the ready.

'Your name?'

'Away you go, you scunner. I want to get to my bed.'

'Name?'

'Da!' Catriona pleaded. 'Answer the man. You committed an offence. This is a policeman.'

'My name's Duncan MacNair,' he yelped. 'But you're not the police. You're too wee. The police are big fellas.'

The special constable, still heaving for breath, straightened in an effort to retrieve both authority and dignity.

'Address?'

'You've just come up the close. Do you not know where you are yourself?'

'I'm warning you, Mr MacNair.'

'Da!' Catriona pleaded, 'What about the shop if you go to jail? Things are hard enough as it is, without you making them worse.'

Old Duncan jerked on his pyjama jacket then began staggering about in a violent fight to get into his trousers.

'It's Number One Dessie Street.' Catriona wrung her hands in agitation. 'He's just had a wee nightcap of whisky.'

'I'm asking him the questions and he's perfectly capable of answering them himself. What's your nationality?'

Tangled in a trouser leg Duncan howled with rage.

'I'm a ruddy German, you silly wee nyuck. Get out my way!'

In desperation Catriona grabbed the constable's arm and pulled him into the hall, shutting the bedroom door behind her.

'I'm most terribly sorry! I promise it'll never happen again. I'll check the window myself every night. He's getting on in years and he feels the cold and takes a wee dram to heat himself up. He doesn't know what he's saying.'

'It had better not happen again.'

'No, it won't, I promise.'

'It's for your own good. You don't want the place bombed, do you?' He nodded at her swollen belly. 'Not when you're like that?'

Her head lowered miserably and she pleated and re-pleated a piece of her smock.

'All right?' he said sternly, his authority fully returned.

She nodded. Then, her head still lowered in shame, she showed him to the door.

After he had gone she tiptoed to her own room to take a peep at the children and make sure that they were still sound asleep.

She was always terrified that Fergus would waken, feel in a bad humour and take it out on Andrew. She had been tempted for the sake of peace of mind, and Andrew's safety, to leave Fergus with her mother, but conscience forced her to take Fergus home with Andrew in case he felt unwanted.

It was thanks to Madge that she succeeded in getting either of the children back.

Madge had gone with her to Farmbank and without wasting a minute in beating about the bush announced to Catriona's mother as they walked into the house:

'Hello there, hen, we've come for the weans.'

Then when her mother had rushed to prevent her touching the children Madge's firm big shovel of a hand had clamped over the woman's apron.

'Och, now, you're not going to stop the poor wee bugger getting her weans.' Suddenly her grin appeared. 'I don't want to knock your teeth down your throat, hen, but I will!'

The joy of getting the children back was indescribable. Hugging Andrew and kissing his petal-soft face and rubbing Fergus's head against her hip she had tried to stutter out thanks to Madge but had only succeeded in bursting into tears.

She was so glad to get the children home, it was worth suffering her mother's warnings of the retribution that would one day be heaped upon her head. As long as the children were all right, that was all that mattered. Yet the children's welfare was so bound up with and dependent on her own, she worried in case something might happen to take her away from them.

What if she died in childbirth? The thought haunted her and she tried desperately to look after herself and to be as brave as Madge, who insisted that she too was scared of childbirth but flung back her head and laughed when she said it as if it were a huge joke.

Try as she would, Catriona could not even raise a smile. The best she could do was to keep herself as busy as possible so that she would not have time to think about it all.

She rubbed and scrubbed energetically at the washing-board; she sweated down on her knees, her belly as well as the polishing cloth rubbing the floor. It was important to keep the place looking its best. Melvin had an obsession about polish and the fear kept nagging her that one day he might walk in unexpectedly and see something wrong with the house. She could not imagine her pregnant state angering him half as much or even being noticed before a neglected house.

Lying in bed at night unable to sleep she mulled over everything: the guilt and shame of her pregnancy, the coming agonies of childbirth, what Melvin would do to her when he returned home and found out.

Alec said neither Melvin nor anyone else need ever know.

'Except, of course,' Madge said, 'the poor wee bugger's sure to be Alec's double.'

When Catriona pointed out that Melvin had planned to have no more children Alec said:

'Who doesn't? He can make mistakes the same as anyone else.'

Alec and Madge, of course, did not know Melvin. Madge had never set eyes on him and Alec had only seen him once.

There was something different about Melvin. Catriona had never feared any man as she feared him; and terror went far beyond anything physical. Although, as Alec said, the mere sight of Melvin's physique was enough to scare anyone.

'For God's sake, hen, lie till you're blue in the face. That gorilla could murder me,' he said.

'Listen to him!' Madge hooted. 'And the bugger's at least six feet tall. It would serve him right if Melvin MacNair did murder him!'

310

She could not be persuaded that this was not really Alec's fault.

'If I had had a stronger character, Madge,' Catriona tried to explain. 'Or if I had been quicker-witted, or just had more common sense, this would never have happened. Anything that happens to me is my own fault.'

'You make me madder than ever at that rotten midden!' stormed Madge. 'You're that simple.'

'No. No,' Catriona protested. 'All I'm doing is accepting the responsibility for my own actions.'

'You're daft, hen.' Madge shook her head. 'You shouldn't be walking around loose!' Then turning to Alec. 'See you! You rotten sneaky dirty midden! I'll never forgive you!'

A day or two later Alec took off and joined the Navy.

It was awful how people affected each other's lives.

Because Wee Eck had been killed, Melvin had rushed off to fight in the war, and now because of the trouble she had caused in Alec's life, he had suddenly shot off to the Navy.

Catriona hoped that neither Melvin nor Alec would be hurt, and would have prayed for their safety, but she was too afraid to open any communicating link with God, in case by doing so she might somehow be made more easily available to Him and He would bring further sufferings to her or through her to the children.

Often, as her pregnancy dragged wearily on, she longed to pray for herself. She longed to say,

'God, please give me strength. I'm frightened.'

But her mind dodged the words behind the rapidly pulled blind of other thoughts.

It was strange how Melvin had had no leave. As far as she could gather he had been sent to France. He had never been much of a letter writer and what letters she had received, hinting that something big was on, had had bits of them cut out by the censor.

Rumour had it that his regiment was in the fighting somewhere in France. It did not seem possible, somehow.

The war had not much reality for her. Certainly there was rationing. Some foods were very scarce. Others had disappeared

311

altogether and become only mouth-watering dreams of the past.

Still, Catriona was lucky because of the shop, and sometimes she managed to scrape up a little extra for herself and Madge.

The shop was short-handed, since the young women were being conscripted and the older ones were making better money in munitions, but they found a solution to that problem.

Mrs Jackson and Madge between them had been carrying on Alec's insurance book and one of the customers was Ruth Hunter. Her husband, a conscientious objector, had been taken to Maryhill Barracks.

The wife was living alone and needing work, but in loyalty to her husband she did not want to take any kind of war job.

Mrs Jackson had told her about the shop assistants leaving MacNair's to go into munitions and Ruth had come over to see about a job.

The only drawback was the travelling distance in the blackout. Even using the Clydend Ferry did not help much. She would still need to use a bus or tram-car as well.

Tentatively Catriona had suggested to Ruth that they might be good company for each other and said that Ruth was welcome to come and stay with her at Dessie Street for as long as she liked. They were about the same age and both their men were away: it seemed silly for both of them to be lonely.

She had not had much hope that Ruth would consider moving in with a pregnant woman, an old man, and two children, but to her surprise and delight the girl had jumped at the chance.

It turned out that she adored children and she was to move in at the end of the week.

The only worry again was what Melvin would do if she was still living in the house when he came back.

The house was beginning to get - it would seem from Melvin's point of view - cluttered and disorganised.

What had once been a tidy bedroom for them alone had now an extra bed squeezed in for Fergus and also Andrew's cot.

The other bedroom had never been the same since old Duncan moved in with his empty beer bottles and sticky glasses under the bed. Then there were his ashtrays full of pipes and

312

crumbs of dark brown tobacco, spilling into every corner. The tobacco was not only from his own pipe but from the pipe of Angus MacGuffy, the old man next door who was a regular visitor and who, although almost stone deaf, carried on loud and determined conversations with Duncan in between glasses of whisky.

Now Ruth Hunter would be sleeping on the sitting-room bed-settee.

These were some of the changes the war had brought and it was strange to see the close all shored up and the brick baffle walls outside the entrance. Some said the baffle walls were supposed to protect the tenement buildings from the blast of bombs, others insisted they were to stop shrapnel and splinters flying up the closes. The only thing they had done so far was to cause innumerable black eyes, bloody noses and broken bones in the black-out.

The black-out, as far as Glasgow was concerned, had caused the only violence, injuries and deaths. Every night more and more people were being killed. Yet at the same time the darkness of the city seemed to heighten the senses. The apprehensive ear caught sounds ringing louder, tuned into more hollow echoes, as if each street were a tunnel. The eye saw nothing, only blackness, yet the ear became acutely aware of a wireless talking in the tunnel, or the clang of a dustbin lid, or a measured footfall.

There had been a few alerts - the jerky panicking whoo-whoo-whoo of the sirens echoing in her stomach and making Catriona run for the children and take them down to the windowless lobby in the bakehouse where everybody in the building gathered believing it was the safest and certainly the warmest place to be.

But nothing ever happened. The long wail of the All Clear had gone and everyone had thankfully climbed the stairs and disappeared into their own houses.

Catriona could not conceive that anything ever would happen. The war was a nightmare unreality.

The only real things in life, the only things that meant anything to her were the times she had Andrew on her knee sucking his thumb against her breast and Fergus kneeling at her feet his elbows on her lap, cupping his chin, his eyes wide, intent on listening to her telling a bedtime story.

Or when she was down on her knees with them on the floor playing 'mummy bears' and seeing their eyes sparkling and their heads flung back with the joy-bells of laughter.

War seemed very far away. Like Melvin.

Chapter 19

While Alec's ship was in dry dock for repairs he managed to get a couple of day's leave.

The first thing he noticed when he reached Springburn was the number of women wearing dungarees, dirty faces and turbans.

On the tram-cars, tough, loud-voiced cursing knots of them leaned forward, calloused hands gripping knees, screeching with laughter at dirty jokes. Lines of them strolled along Springburn Road, dungarees straining and bursting with bouncing footballs. There were no longer any men lounging at the corners, but women again, clusters of them, thumbs hooked in belts, chewing gum or smoking. One woman wolf-whistled him as he passed to turn into Cowlairs Road and another bawled:

'Hey handsome, you can sail me up the river any day!'

Alec made juicy kissing noises with pursed lips before swaggering jauntily across the road, and the women exploded in great yells of pleasure and hilarity.

The pend stank. It had always been a bit smelly, but he never remembered such a sour stench as this.

Face twisting, he screwed his eyes around. The cobbled pend with its brick arch was always dark even in daytime and it took him a minute to discern the two bins at the yard end. Then he remembered that Madge had told him in one of her letters that all the vegetable peelings and waste scraps of food had now to be put in these pig bins. Nothing must be wasted. The corporation collected the bins and sold the contents to farmers for pig food.

Government films were shown in the cinemas urging everyone to be careful not to put in safety pins or anything that might prove too indigestible or dangerous to the pigs.

'To hell with the bloody pigs,' Madge had written. 'We *eat* all the scraps here. I even grudge the buggers my peelings. The

315

rations are so tight we'll be eating peelings and all soon!'

Alec had managed to cadge some butter from the galley. He had some NAAFI chocolate for the kids and a pair of stockings for Madge and that ought to keep everyone happy.

The yard was cluttered. No room for a dribble at a tin can now.

Back to back with the line of middens stood an ugly brick erection which was supposed to protect all the occupants of the surrounding tenements from blast.

Alec sprinted up the stairs, calling a cheery greeting to Mrs White from next door.

'Hello there, Alec,' she called back. 'Hey, Madge and the weans are not in.'

'Out with her fancy man, eh?' He grinned. 'Och, well, that leaves you and me to have a wee bit slap and tickle on our own!'

Folding her arms across her chest she enjoyed a good bouncy laugh.

'My man'll slap and tickle you if you're not careful. I would have watched the weans but I had to go out myself and everyone else is away at their work.'

'Any idea where she is, hen?'

'Aye, in the queue round at the coal yard in Atlas Street. It's not so cold now but we need something for the cooking. It's all right for the well-off yins that have cookers.'

'Thanks, gorgeous!'

Alec gave her a salute before clattering back down the stairs, across the yard, out through the pend and round the corner on to Springburn Road again. He crossed over and went whistling, rollicking up towards Atlas Street, his round sailor's cap perched well back on his head.

Springburn had changed quite a bit. It did not look so busy. Instead of the usual rush and squash at tram-stops pople queued quietly. There were long queues at various shops too, although it was hard to see what they were waiting for. The shop windows were empty. Alec had never seen so many empty windows.

Signs were up at the licensed grocer's saying in big letters: NO WHISKY. He refused to believe them. There was bound to be a wee nip somewhere.

He cut off to the right at Atlas Street and in a matter of minutes was at the coal yard. A long straggly queue of women and children and a few old men had come with prams and boxes on wheels and suitcases and shopping bags and baskets for any kind of fuel they could get.

He saw Madge and the children before they saw him and he felt a pang of disappointment. Madge had been letting herself go. That was the worst thing about marriage and put many a bachelor off taking the plunge. Once a woman captured her man she just let herself go and got steadily worse and worse looking. When they were married Madge had been a fine, big, healthy specimen of a girl with laughing blue eyes and a ready grin. Maybe she had never been a raving beauty; she had too many freckles for that. But she had a fine skin all the same, pearly and soft, and her hair used to have a glossy bounce to it. Her figure had always been buxom but her legs were long and shapely.

What a difference now! Her legs were streaky and dirty-looking with the orange-brown paint the women used now, instead of stockings, and she was wearing the most unglamorous shoes he had ever seen. They had thick wooden soles and as the queue moved up she clumped along like a cart-horse; but the shoes were nothing to the monstrosity she had on her back. Hanging loose and shapeless it completely hid her figure and looked like an old army blanket.

'Hello there, gorgeous.'

Reaching her he put an arm round her and gave her a hug before lifting and kissing each of the children in turn.

She had the youngest two in the pram and Maisie was sitting in a wooden box on old pramwheels.

Madge's face lit up.

'Alec! Thank God! You can pull the coal home. I didn't know how I was going to manage.'

He laughed.

'What a welcome! Here, I like your new coat, hen. A Paris model, is it?'

To his astonishment she took him seriously.

'You really like it, Alec? Is it all right? I made it myself.'

'Made it yourself?'

317

'Yes, out of an old army blanket. It didn't need any clothing coupons.'

'Great, hen!' he assured her. 'Just great!'

Unzipping his hold-all he produced bars of chocolate and handed them round to a hysterical chorus of delight.

Their turn came, the box was filled with fuel and he towed it towards home, Maisie, Hector, Agnes and Sadie perched on top with black bottoms and chocolate mouths and the old wheels buckling and squeaking. At his side Madge pushed and heaved at the big pram, jostling and bouncing Willie and Fiona so that they kept missing their eager open mouths and spread chocolate all over their faces.

As they hurried towards home, Alec indicated a long line of people.

'What are they queuing for?'

'God knows. You daren't stand for a couple of minutes anywhere now or a queue's likely to form at your back. And see half of these shopkeepers? Talk about Adolf Hitler! I'm telling you we've sprouted a few wee dictators round here.'

The pram bumped through the pend and the box on wheels jangled the air with sound, and Alec helped Madge up with the pram, then went back for the box of fuel and children, then he pulled Madge into his arms, and kissed her and fumbled to unbutton the grey blanket-coat. In no time she pushed him away.

'The cheek they give you!' she said.

'Who?'

He couldn't think what she was going on about.

'The shopkeepers, and they don't give you a bag or even a scrap of paper to wrap anything in. I was buying a bit of fish the other day and he slapped it straight into my hand. I thought he was joking but when I asked for paper the cheeky midden shouted, "Do you not know there's a war on?" That's what they're always saying, "Don't you lot know there's a war on?" As if we didn't. Another thing they do now is draw you aside as if they're doing you a big favour and whisper out one corner of their mouths that they've had a delivery of something. The last time it happened to me it turned out to be bottles of some horrible smelling cough mixture.' She laughed, remembering. 'When he said "bottles" I thought he meant whisky.'

He grinned at her.

'What did you say? I bet you soon told him what he could do with it.'

'Oh, no!' She was surprised into seriousness. 'I bought a couple of bottles. You can't afford to turn anything down nowadays, Alec.'

He lit a cigarette, settled down on the sofa and watched her strip off her coat, tuck her hair behind her ears, then kneel down on the rug to set and light the fire.

'How are you and Ma managing the book?' he asked.

'Oh, not bad.' She laughed. 'But, my God, up and down so many stairs is murder on my veins. I do most mornings, as often as Mrs White can look after the weans, and Ma does most afternoons.'

'I thought they had nurseries now for the young ones, and what about the others? Aren't they at school?'

'Och, they say it's too dangerous all the weans together at that school so we all take turn about to have a few of them. A teacher comes here with half a dozen or more once or twice a week.'

'The classes are held in houses?'

Madge grinned up at him.

'You know "Mary down the road"?'

He blew out smoke. 'Don't tell me they have a class in her wee single-end and Dougal on constant nightshift?'

'He snores like a pig as well. They shut curtains across the bed but it was no use. They could still hear him snorting and wheezing away. The teacher complained. She said he was putting everybody off. The teachers get awful harassed, poor buggers. But there's times you've just got to laugh.'

Chuckling, she rested back on her heels.

He could see she was about to splurge into a series of domestic reminiscences and restlessness needled him.

'Hurry up with the fire, hen,' he urged. 'This place is as bleak as a dungeon without it.'

'Och, I know. I won't be a minute. Then I'll make the tea.'

'What have you got, gorgeous? I'm starving!'

She struck a match and watched with pleasure as it crackled the fire into life that warmed and softened the room.

'I've dried egg,' she told him, struggling to her feet.

'Dried egg?' he echoed, with visions of himself chewing away like a martyr at yellow cotton wool.

Immediately she bristled like an angry porcupine.

'Oh, maybe your fancy women can do better but we're lucky if we manage to get dried egg here!'

Hastily he spread out his hands.

'Great, hen! Great!'

The more he saw of civvy life, the more he was glad to be in the Navy. At least the food was good and there was plenty of it.

'Where are they sending you?'

Madge's voice was still a bit needly, and she pushed it over her shoulder at him as she washed her hands.

Trust old Madge to put her big foot in it and remind him.

'There's a rumour we're off to France soon. The BEF's in dead trouble.'

'The BEF? What's that?'

'The British Expeditionary Force. The Jerry Panzer divisions are beating the hell out of them.'

She gave a whoop of derisive laughter.

'God, I hope the poor buggers aren't depending on you to save their bacon.'

He laughed along with her and hoped the same thing.

Chapter 20

Sammy's father had often gleefully related stories about tough English soldiers who had served all over the world yet who dreaded being posted to Maryhill Barracks. Its prison-like reputation was legend.

Now, bumping along in the army landrover between two soldiers and with the corporal in charge sitting beside the driver, Sammy viewed the approach to the place from the bottom of a deep well of anxiety.

The barracks were enclosed within a high wall constructed in bastion form with a series of projecting angles, and the main gateway had impressive stone piers.

The landrover screeched to a halt inside. A soldier appeared and spoke to the corporal. The gates closed behind them. The landrover jerked into movement again and Sammy's world vanished.

This other world smelled different. The air was a heady mixture of cordite, oil, carbolic, brasso and paint.

Gone was the leisurely rocking of the trams, the pleasant untidiness of people strolling this way and that, stopping to enjoy a talk in straggly groups whenever or wherever the fancy took them. Gone was the interesting undulating broth pot of humanity.

Here life was all mechanised. Men drilled on the parade ground like robots with stiff jerking necks and limbs.

The rhythmic clump of boots grew louder and louder. Someone screamed through a crocodile mouth wide open and high.

'Iya- eft - ick- ar! 'Eft 'ight 'eft 'ight 'eft 'ight 'eft 'ight 'eft 'ight . . .'

A flag crackled in the wind.

The landrover stopped. The car horn gave two rapid blasts.

'Out!' They scrambled from the vehicle.

321

'At the double!'

They were outside another gateway now. This one had a huge iron door with a small wooden window. A soldier peered from the window before the iron door creaked and squeaked and clanged open.

They were entering the detention part of the barracks, high-walled off, separate. Into an office at one side of a small yard. The corporal gives Sergeant-Major Spack their papers. The corporals and soldiers go away.

Sergeant-Major Spack bristles short grey hair on head and lip and has a bouncy enthusiasm.

'Hallo! Hallo! Hallo!' He struts smartly around Sammy examining him from head to toe. 'What have we here? The black sheep of the Hunter family? Well, lad, no nonsense here, remember. You're with my bunch now. The army, lad. Nothing to beat it. We'll soon make a soldier of you, eh? Eh, Hunter? The guards here will help keep you right. Good men. From Blackrigs. You know Blackrigs, Hunter? Eh? Blackrigs?'

He knows Blackrigs.

Other districts like Springburn or Clydend or the Gorbals were cosy old places compared with Blackrigs housing scheme. There, new council houses had windows broken and boarded, doors chopped up for firewood, streets continuously swirling and flapping with old newspapers, broken beer bottles and other litter, and everywhere buildings, walls, pavements and roads chalked with gang slogans and obscenities.

There also, insurance men and others who dared go about their business in the scheme were beaten up and robbed, and taxi, van and lorry drivers passed rapidly through with their heads down, huddled low over steering wheels to avoid being hit by flying stones or bottles.

'Reeight, Hunter. Reeight, jump to it. Strip off! At the double!'

Sammy glowers defiance.

'You don't know the routine yet. The routine, Hunter. First everybody strips off. Reeight. Reeight! At the double!'

'Why?'

'Why?' Spack looked genuinely astonished. 'Why? Nobody

322

asks "why" in the army!'

'I do.'

Spack nods to the soldiers.

'Ree . . . ight!'

He struggles, getting redder and redder in the face with the violence of his exertion. Close-cropped hair bristling close to his eyes. Khaki sandpapering him. The soldiers have numerical advantage and they are older and heavier men. In a matter of minutes he is naked.

'Ree-ight, Hunter!' Spack's voice bellows louder. 'You've got three minutes to get across that yard, have a bath and be back here. Get going. At the double!'

Sammy stares impertinence through grey-green marble stones of eyes until one of the corporals digs him in the ribs with the truncheon he carries.

The air blasts against his skin, darting it with sharp needles of rain. The bath is in an open-sided hut which also houses four wash-hand basins. The water turns his blood to ice. Back across the yard again still naked.

A heap of clothes lie waiting for him on the floor of Spack's office. Prison clothing of khaki denims and plimsolls. Under the conscientious eyes of the sergeant-major he dresses in silent hatred.

Across the yard. This time into the prison building, ancient black stone with small barred windows like vacant eye-sockets. The iron door of each cell has a spy hole so that the guard can watch every move.

Into a cell where the barber is waiting. The corporal knocks him down on to a chair. The other soldier cuts his hair off. Crops it scalp-close.

He is prodded and pushed along to another cell. Inside there is a locker and a bed. The mattress is rolled up tightly with the blankets folded neatly on top. He puts the small kit he has been issued with on top of the locker and hangs the khaki battle-dress inside. He sinks into the silence.

He sat motionless on the edge of the bed and thought of Ruth.

His main worry was that Spack might not allow him to write to her or receive any of her letters. It was up to him to decide what mail a prisoner should be allowed to receive or send out, and all mail incoming or outgoing was read by him.

The sergeant-major also decided if a prisoner was to be allowed any visitors.

He did not expect that Ruth or anybody else would be allowed to visit him but he did hope for some contact with her, even if it were only an occasional letter.

All that sleepless night he longed for her, imagined her in his arms in the cabinet bed in the kitchen. And how was she going to manage. She had assured him that she would be perfectly all right. She would find a job, she said.

It was terrible to think of her having to go out to work. At home she could suit herself and be her own mistress. She was so proud of her home.

To Ruth, it was probably the same as to most women, home meant many things and was terribly important. Home was the roots of civilised life, home was security, home was the reflection of achievement.

He remembered the fuss Ruth and all the other Springburn women made at Hogmanay. Soon after tea-time on December 31, Springburn quickened with household activity. Women energetically cleaned windows so that the first light of the New Year should not shine through dirty glass. Flushed faces and flyaway hair told of much scrubbing and polishing and conscientious cleaning of every corner so that they and their homes could start the New Year right.

In the last minutes of the Old Year there would be much scurrying of feet on the tenement staircases as the women carrying their kitchen ashpans, ran to the dustbins to get rid of the last ashes of the dying year.

Then everything would be ready, the house sparkling, the fire crackling, the bottles and glasses mirrors for dancing light, the plates of sultana cake and cherry cake and black bun and shortbread piled generously high. Everyone waiting, newly washed and brushed and wearing clean clothes.

Springburn hanging breathlessly in unnatural stillness.

From somewhere down by the Clyde, a solitary tentative blast from a ship's siren heralded midnight. From the Springburn

Parish Church came the glorious clamour of bells. Springburn exploded in welcome. Countless railway whistles shrieked. Over the hill from the direction of St Rollox came the deep Caley roar. Above it all was the steady crack of the detonators spaced along the rail and being happily exploded by one of the engine crews.

Everyone happy and wishing everyone happiness. Happy camaraderie spilling out of every door.

He awoke to bleak reality.

'At the double! At the double!'

For years he had been sick of the words. 'At the double! At the double!' A favourite army phrase and one his father never tired of using.

It was five a.m. and the first duty of every day was to scrub out the cells and then work down the central hall and from there through the various rooms, corridors and offices.

At seven o'clock there was breakfast at a long table in the central hall with the other prisoners, a guard sitting at each end of the table. Other guards strolled around the hall, ever watchful. Talking or smiling were punishable offences so that the meal was a dour and silent one.

Back to the cells again to fold the blankets and roll the mattress, and brasso and blanco all the kit and set them out for inspection. The stupid waste of time, the sheer useless idiocy of polishing the studs on the soles of the boots irked him beyond words.

He knew the army 'bull' so well, had been nurtured on it for as far back as he could remember. He had been polishing the soles of boots and washing and whitewashing coal while his contemporaries were out playing football.

Yours not to reason why
Yours but to do and die . . .

He had long ago come to believe that the army, far from being an institution for the defence or preservation of mankind, was in fact the most dangerous, the most destructive force, not only to the body but to the mind of man.

The professional soldier's profession was to kill and he believed that - especially at officer level - they wanted war because peace bored them. They wanted to play their army games, not with little flags but with real people.

He believed the militarist ideal was to drill and regiment, the process of regimentation beginning at school where every independent, individualistic urge could be crushed and disciplined.

Instead of aiming at the development of every faculty to its highest capacity the militant ideal was the creation of efficient machines; not fostering a sense of individual responsibility and a questioning inquisitive intelligence but making a virtue of unreasoning obedience.

The military used harmless-sounding words to mask manoeuvres that meant death, suffering and destruction. They pinned on medals and played brass bands. Statues went up and poppy wreaths were laid. Impressive ceremonies covered multitudes of sins.

He hated the militarist ideal more than anything else in the world.

The kit was perfect, ready and waiting when the adjutant with his entourage of sergeant-major, corporals and guards came in to inspect it.

Without looking at Sammy, the adjutant jerked out his stick and knocked the kit on to the floor.

'Get that kit cleaned properly.'

'What's wrong with it?'

The adjutant's eyes flashed round and for a minute he gaped.

They all gaped. Before their faces disappeared behind their military masks again.

All his enemies.

Chapter 21

The sirens started so scream, breathlessly, jerkily, just as Catriona and Ruth were about to get ready for bed.

'What do you think we should do?'

Ruth came from the sitting-room leisurely brushing her hair, arms reaching up and back, brushing, smoothing, breasts lifting, pushing.

Each siren followed hastily the one before, until it sounded as if the whole of Glasgow was exploding with sirens, each one competing in feverish excitement with the other and every one out of time and tune.

Catriona put a hand to her brow.

'They'll waken the children!'

'It seems a shame to lift them, doesn't it? Nothing's happened so far, has it?'

'I know. They're liable to get their death of cold being lifted from their warm beds and taken down that draughty stair. Still . . .'

Catriona nibbled at her nails, eyes straining with worry. 'What if anything did happen? Oh, dear, and there's Da as well.'

'You can't make him go downstairs, can you? His safety is his own responsibility, isn't it?'

'Oh, no!' She was shocked. 'Melvin would blame me if anything happened. Oh, dear!'

'Something might happen to you if you're not careful, mightn't it?'

'It doesn't matter about me.'

She avoided Ruth's eyes, thinking what a good thing it would be if she had a premature birth. Only things never happened the way you wanted them to. It would be just typical if this baby was late.

Ruth raised an eyebrow.

'Doesn't it? What about the baby? And what about Fergus

and Andrew if anything happens to you?'

Catriona could have wept.

'Oh, well, I suppose we'd better get started. At least this time the alert went before we were undressed.'

The sirens wailed gradually away fainter and fainter until the silence was only broken by people stirring in the building and beginning to make their way down the stairs. Old Angus MacGuffie from next door who thought everyone was as deaf as himself was protesting loudly to his son Tam, who had run up from the bakehouse to help his father down because neither his wife Nellie, nor his daughter Lizzie could do anything with the old man.

'You're always doing this!' Angus was roaring. 'Hauling me out of my bed for no rhyme nor reason!'

'There's a raid on, Paw!' Tam roared back.

'A raincoat on? No I will not put a raincoat on. It's too cold!'

Ruth laughed and tossed back her hair.

'He's started already. Isn't he a scream?'

Catriona rolled her eyes. 'Mr MacGuffie and Da are as good as any turn at the Empire. Mr MacGuffie with his bums for bombs, and Da calling them booms. I'd better get the children.'

'How about just lifting the pram down? And Fergus's mattress?'

'What a good idea! I could get one of the men to help.' Catriona's small face lit up with gratitude. 'I'm so glad you're here, Ruth. I don't know what I'd do without you.'

She ran and opened the front door.

'Tam!'

'Aye, lass?'

Tam strained a red face upwards, puffing for breath as he struggled to get his father safely down the spiral stairs.

'Could you send Baldy to help us bring the children down? I'll just keep Andy in the pram and maybe he won't even waken.'

'Right, lass, just as soon as I get this thrawn old buffer down to the lobby.'

Nellie and Lizzie appeared loaded with all their usual accoutrements, cushions, knitting, peppermints, shawls, earplugs, thermos flask, gas masks.

'Hello,' Catriona greeted them. 'Isn't this a nuisance?'

'I read in the paper they had a terrible time in England last night,' Nellie confided. 'There was this woman who just went back upstairs for a hanky when the bomb dropped and she was killed and the rest of her family escaped unhurt.'

'Poor thing!' Catriona tutted. 'Fancy!'

They always discussed the details of other lads and made sympathetic noises in the same way as they enjoyed little gossips about local scandals. The happenings themselves held no deep reality. Reality was the friendly exchanges, the neighbourliness, the warmth of shared conversation.

Lizzie limped across the landing and peered close through thick glasses.

'*I'll* take Fergus down. *I'll* see to my wee baby.'

Immediately Catriona retreated back into the house, her face stiffening.

'I'm seeing to Fergus, thank you.'

She shut the door. Lizzie had taken charge of Fergus when the child's mother died and had never forgiven Catriona for appearing on the scene as Melvin's wife and taking over.

Lizzie had queer ways and Catriona felt sure she had done Fergus nothing but harm.

'Lizzie again?' Ruth queried.

Catriona nodded.

'She gives me the creeps that woman. If I've to go to the lavatory or anywhere else will you watch Fergus for me, Ruth? Don't let that woman near him during the night if I'm not there. She'd waken him up and frighten him. She enjoys frightening the children. It's terrible.'

'Don't worry!' Ruth went through to the sitting-room to put her hairbrush away. 'I can't stand her either.'

'Poor Mrs MacGuffie and Tam.' Catriona heaved her heavy belly across the hall towards the bedroom and the children. 'They can't have much of a life.'

She kept a hold-all packed ready and she checked it as usual to make absolutely sure that everything was all right. Extra clothes for the children, their favourite picture books and toys, a mug and plate and spoon each, ear-plugs, gas masks.

329

The door-bell went and before she had time to shuffle, flat-footed, wide-legged into the hall, Ruth had answered it and ushered big Baldy Fowler the foreman baker into the house.

Since his wife had been hanged Baldy shared his upstairs flat with Sandy the vanman. Baldy had the build of a huge all-in wrestler and although heavy drinking had taken its toll, nevertheless to bump the pram downstairs with Andrew still sleeping peacefully inside was no bother to him. In a few minutes he was charging like a bull back up the stairs for Fergus.

Catriona noticed how he kept looking at Ruth and how Ruth's dark eyes fluttered coyly up at him.

Ruth worried and perplexed her. Often in the evenings they talked and talked and Ruth told about her husband Sammy and what a good man he was and how much she loved him.

There had been times when she had gone through to the room for something after Ruth had gone to bed and found her weeping for Sammy. Yet there seemed to be something dangerous that switched on inside her every time a man appeared. It was as if men turned a spotlight on her and she immediately began a sensuous performance, each movement a studied provocation.

Fergus had woken up and was getting a 'coal-carry' on Baldy's shoulders. The mattress and blankets were under Baldy's arm.

'Come on, hen.' He bull-bellowed laughter towards Ruth. 'I'll carry you down under the other arm.'

They were all out on the landing and Catriona was locking the door. Ruth wriggled and giggled back against her as if for protection.

'You wouldn't dare?' she said in her husky burr that always lilted up to pose provocatively.

Baldy's shovel of a hand shot out, whirled her round and smacked her soundly on the buttocks before grabbing her round the waist and clattering noisily down the stairs with her.

Fergus bounced up and down and laughed and screamed with excitement. Ruth was laughing and squealing and kicking her legs wildly out behind.

'Let me down! Let me down! You're tickling me! Baldy, please! Please?'

'Aye, you've a rare soft belly. Oh -' He suddenly burst into riotous song. 'Stop yer ticklin', Jock, stop yer ticklin', Jock, stop yer ticklin', tickalickalickalin', stop yer ticklin', Jock!'

They did not seem to care who heard them.

Feeling strangely depressed, Catriona held on to the banisters and slowly and carefully negotiated her clumsy body down the stairs.

The narrow windowless lobby that separated the bakehouse at the back from the shop at the front was packed, but a space was somehow made for her and with much difficulty she managed to ease herself on to the floor. People sat on cushions, backs propped against the walls. The pram and the mattress were in the middle of the floor. Only the two old men, Duncan and Angus, had chairs. They were talking very loudly on topical subjects like black-outs, rationing and bombs.

None of these things were acceptable to old Angus and he was always saying so in no uncertain terms. Again and again he tottered into shops and bawled for his sweeties and baccy and whatever else he fancied. He was completely deaf to any explanations about rationing.

As for the black-out, his utter disdain of the whole procedure was only matched by that of Duncan who also believed it to be a lot of nonsense.

'I was reading about them insenary bums!' Angus roared at the pitch of his voice.

'Aye.' Duncan's high pitched nasal voice fought to rival his friend in loudness. 'You put them kind of booms out with sand!'

'With your hands?' Angus shouted incredulously.

'No, no!' old MacNair yelled, nearly spluttering his false teeth into Angus's ear. 'Sand, SAND!' Then a lot quieter. 'You're a deaf wee nyaff.'

Eventually they both dozed off, gnarled hands clasped on bony laps, mouths loose and drooping, puttering to life only with snorts and snores of long high-pitched whistles.

'Where's Ruth?' Catriona asked Nellie, but before Nellie could answer, Lizzie said:

'Where do you think? Through in some dark filthy corner of the bakehouse with Baldy. It's disgusting!'

331

'What's disgusting?' Catriona's cheeks burned. 'Ruth will be making us a cup of tea, that's all.'

'Her man's a conchie, isn't he?' Nellie said.

Catriona nodded.

'He had to go to Maryhill Barracks.'

'Och, well, the best of luck to him. How about a song to cheer us all up?'

Immediately someone burst into 'Pack up your troubles in your old kit bag' and everyone joined in. Then they had 'Roll out the barrel, - we'll have a barrel of fun - '

Fergus lay watching and listening, propping himself up on his elbows, saucer-eyed at first, then gradually as the night wore on he slithered down with fatigue, while Andrew slept peacefully through all the noise.

'Sit down, Ruth,' Catriona pleaded, when Ruth had brought in the tea. 'Don't go through there again. There's too many windows. It's too dangerous, and Mrs MacGuffie was telling me about a woman who just ran upstairs for a hanky and was killed.'

Ruth curled gracefully down on to a tiny space on the lobby floor like a beautiful sleepy-eyed cat, while Catriona tried to lift her belly over to give her a bit more room.

Someone handed round banana sandwiches made with mashed parsnips and banana essence and everyone began to munch.

Sandy the vanman's mouth undulated like a big rubber band. Then he swallowed and said:

'The raids are more often now. Have you noticed?'

'Aye!' Nellie agreed. 'All over the place. Did you read about that woman buried alive for nearly three days?'

They all nodded, settling down to eat their sandwiches and drink their tea and enjoy a good chatter about all the strange things that were happening outside their own safe, cosy little world.

Until the all-clear wailed loud and long and folk suddenly realised how stiff and tired they were. Terrible tangles of legs and arms, buttocks bumping in the air, and yelps of pain as everyone struggled to their feet, and jostled about, and gathered up blankets, cushions and cups.

'Mummy,' Fergus began to wail. 'Do I need to go to school today? I'm tired.'

Duncan MacNair woke up with a splutter, fumbled for his big red hanky and loudly blew his nose.

'Christ!' His high-pitched whine sounded as if he were about to burst into tears. 'I might as well just go through and open the bloody shop now. It's not worthwhile going up the stairs to my bed.'

Tam came through from the bakehouse, grabbed his father by the lapels and jiggled him about in his jacket.

'Paw!' he bawled in Angus's ear. 'Paw!'

'Eh?' Bloodshot old eyes screwed open indignantly. 'What do you think you're doing? Take your hands off my good jacket!'

'Come on, Paw. I'll help you up the stair and you can go right to bed and rest yourself till dinner time.'

Tam hauled his father up by his bony elbow.

'Ah could have been in my warm bed all night if you hadn't dragged me down here.' He turned, tottering, to old MacNair. 'Ah can't see the sense in it, can you, Duncan?'

'No, I can't, Angus,' MacNair whined. 'They must think we're awful frisky.'

'Eh?' roared Angus. 'Who had a hauf o' whisky?'

'Awful frisky!' Duncan yelled furiously. Then, clumping away in his too big boots, 'Christ, you'd need a bloody horn for that wee nyuck!'

Catriona stood at the door waiting for everyone to leave so that the pram and mattress could be lifted out. It had become quite a habit to stand there, hands clasped over swollen waist, smiling shyly at everyone as they left. As if she had just had a party, and was saying goodbye and hoping that everyone had enjoyed themselves.

And because the bakehouse lobby was a MacNair lobby, and she the hostess, everyone smiled in return, and thanked her, almost as if they had.

Up the stairs with the pram and mattress and the children now. And Baldy laughing and Ruth giggling.

Up the stairs slowly, pulling on the banisters, one foot, one stair at a time. Not sure if the baby is starting or if it is only

333

fatigue that is causing the pain.

She is so tired she does not care if the baby is starting.

Only she wonders - what kind of place is it coming into? And for a terrible minute she stops on the stairs feeling frightened of the world outside over which she has no control. Then she hears Andrew wake up and sob and cry out.

'Mummy, Mummy!'

And she goes on up the stairs, hurrying now, getting breathless but managing to shout.

'It's all right, love. Everything's all right. Mummy's here!'

Chapter 22

Before he joined the Navy, Alec used to pretend to Madge that he had a hard job fighting women off. In Dover it was literally true. The place was swarming with prostitutes. Some rumour had brought them from all over the country and the faster the police cleared them out, the faster they appeared.

He had seen two real hairies clawing, kicking, twisting and screaming at each other in the middle of the road, completely oblivious of a lorry that had nearly knocked both of them down.

The place was seething with rumours. It was said that labourers were already digging vast communal graves enough for several hundred people. A sailor was supposed to have brought a revolver and two rounds of ammunition home for his wife. Some women, it was said, were carrying knives and poison capsules. Somebody was already rumoured to have committed suicide.

The British troops in France were getting beaten and this meant that hordes of Germans would be coming over.

Yet nobody, including Alec, really believed a word of it.

They had lived for eight months in the belief that Lord Gort's BEF was invincible. It was not easy to re-adjust.

Even after Alec was half-way across to France in HMS *Donaldson* he still had no clear idea of the true position.

'Dunkirk?' He deftly rolled tobacco in a cigarette paper. 'Never heard of it.'

He was lounging over the side talking to one of his mates as the ship churned busily across the Channel.

Suddenly Alec jabbed his cigarette skywards.

'Hey, Jack! Are they . . .? They are!'

German dive-bombers snarled unexpectedly from a peaceful sky.

Alec beat the other sailor for cover by a full five seconds. Crouched below one of the guns, he felt the ship swerve violently from port to starboard as it tried to dodge the hail of bombs.

The old destroyer creaked and shuddered and jarred but bustled towards its destination, visible now on the horizon in its pall of doom.

Oil refineries, warehouses, quays were a holocaust of fire, and smoke belched upwards and sideways, giant beanstalks spreading into black clouds that extinguished the sun.

Dive-bombers whirled and wheeled and swooped and screamed and fire exploded and water shot high white mountain peaks into the air.

An officer came half crawling along the deck.

'You . . . you and you . . .'

Alec groaned to himself, following as best he could.

He had a sinking feeling he was going to be forced into the thick of things and soon found from a hasty briefing that he and a dozen or so other 'volunteers' were to go ashore and reconnoitre the place.

Already they were caught in the middle of the inferno, only one of many ships, large and small, a motley armada jostling for space in a fiery sea.

Above them the sky darkened and became heavy with Stukas. The planes screamed with eerie piercing whistles that Von Richthofen had specially invented to splinter nerves and scatter panic. The Stukas fell from the air, swooping, diving so low to drop their bombs that pilots' faces could be clearly seen before the planes rapidly swerved, dipped and shot upwards again.

Ships cracked in two like nuts and sank within seconds.

Noise engulfed the world. The pounding howl of the destroyers' guns, the metallic banging of the Bofors guns, the shriek of bombs, the hysterical stutter of the Vickers guns firing two thousand bullets a minute.

Alec could no longer hear what the officer was nattering on about but he set off in the motor launch with the others, towing one of the empty whalers, and prayed as he had never prayed before in his life that he would get back all in one piece.

Dead men and live men were bobbing about cheek to jowl in the water. Hands were outstretched and mouths open in screams for help that Alec could not hear; but he could see that soldiers were being weighed down and drowned by heavy clothing and equipment. The launch nosed nearer the shore and suddenly troops rushed out at them from all directions.

Now he could hear the screams. The boat rocked with frantic clawing hands while the officer bawled himself hoarse and nobody paid a blind bit of notice.

Like shoals of piranhas, troops swamped the whale. A major's gun cracked out from the beach and shot a floundering young officer through the head.

Christ! Alec thought. Whose side's he on?

He struggled ashore and stood soaked to the skin beside his mates. They surveyed the scene on the beaches, under aeroplanes endlessly diving like vultures. A vast multitude of battle-fatigued men, shell-shocked men, demoralised men were milling and wandering about. Others had dug themselves into the sand for safety, only to be buried alive by bomb-made avalanches. Some were just stumbling around like bewildered children.

Alec could not help remembering the times he had stood at the corner in Springburn watching men stampeding from the works lusty with good spirits and pride in themselves, confident in their skills and what they could produce and create.

Here, he thought, could be the same men. What a waste!

Different parties of ratings each with an officer in charge were to take over agreed sectors of the beaches and organise the troops in groups of fifty. Later they were to be led to the water's edge and checked for arms. The last order from the Admiralty, according to Alec's officer, had been 'Mind you bring the guns back.' But first they had to reconnoitre Dunkirk.

The town of Dunkirk had once been much the same as many another seaside town with its promenade and its three and four-storey terrace boarding-houses, its hotels, its souvenir shops. Now, as they walked along with broken glass grinding under their feet, Alec saw a toy shop with its front blown away and crowds of wax dolls with pink cheeks and glassy eyes staring out. He saw dead civilians, men, women and children, littered around like pathetic heaps of rags. Soldiers too weighed down and bulky with equipment and long coats and rifles and tin helmets, as if they had sunk exhausted into death.

The place stank of death and smoke and stale beer and putrid horse flesh and rank tobacco, cordite, garlic and rancid oil.

Noise battered continuously at the ear drums. An abandoned ambulance's jammed klaxon vied with the terrified screaming of French cavalry horses wheeling and panicking as the guns thundered; and all the time there was a steady chopping and crunching as millions of pounds worth of equipment was destroyed.

Soldiers, some alone, some in menacing-looking bunches, staggered about the street blind drunk.

From underground cellars of hotels came rabid sounds of intoxication.

Yet, despite the madness of those sounds and the racket of the guns, Alec heard sobbing from one of the buildings.

He went in and looted about like a blood-hound until he found the child, a girl of about three, cowering behind a chair on which slumped a dead woman.

'Hello there, hen,' he greeted her cheerily. But as he picked her up he inwardly cursed his rotten bad luck. Weans! Even in foreign parts he had to get lumbered with them!

He emerged from the house with the baby hanging from him like a too-tight tie.

The officer, already harassed beyond endurance, glared venomously at him.

'You effing big fool! We've enough on our plates trying to organise the army. We can't cope with civilians as well. Put that kid back where you found her!'

Alec hesitated. He could feel the child's puny arms clinging with desperate defiance round his neck. At the same time he saw in his mind's eye the vast chaotic army surging about the beaches between fountains of sand sucked high in the air by bombs; men who were scrambling into the whalers so fast that the crew could not handle the oars.

The officer repeated himself, adding:

'That's an order, Jackson!'

Alec turned back into the building. 'You'll be safer in here, hen,' he said.

It was dark and smelled of gas. A rat skittered over some old

338

newspapers. Alec bent down and untangled himself from the child's grasp. Small fingers scraped futilely at his neck in a frantic effort to hang on. Baby round eyes bulged with ageless terror in a face, dirt-streaked and snotty-nosed.

He was suddenly reminded of his own children.

Often they had clung to him snotty-nosed, their dirty faces streaked with tears. Their familiar wail had a startling immediacy.

'Daddae! Daddae!'

His stomach screwed up. He pushed the French child away from him. Incredulity and panic mixed with the horror in her face.

'You'll be all right, hen,' he said straightening up 'Your daddy'll come back and get you.'

As he walked away she ran after him but fell and cut her knees on some broken glass.

That last glimpse of a baby crying helplessly on the floor of a derelict house in Dunkirk would, he knew, remain with him for the rest of his life.

Christ, he thought, what's happening to the world?

Chapter 23

Melvin arrived unexpectedly just as she had always feared. Catriona went to answer the door, thinking it was Mrs Jackson from upstairs and there he was.

'Where's your key?' she asked in surprise.

He had always been so particular about the keys to his door.

'Key?' A strange high-flying laugh careered into song. 'Beside the seaside! Beside the sea!'

He pushed past her and she hurried after him with short agitated steps like a little Chinese girl. She was thinking of the newborn baby sleeping in one of the bedrooms. Robert, she had called him, after her father.

'The place looks as if it's never had a lick of polish since I went away,' Melvin accused, striding into the kitchen. 'My God!'

He came to an abrupt stop and stared around.

'You could stir this place with a stick. And this floor's filthy. Look at my good linoleum. You've been neglecting my house while I've been away. Look at it!'

'Please, Melvin, there's no need to get angry. You always get everything out of all proportion.'

'All my life I've worked hard to build a good life and a good home, and be decent and respectable. You're not going to drag me down and make my place like some of the miserable slums around here or in Farmbank.'

'You're exaggerating. You always do.'

Despite her words, her voice had gone a bit vague. Now that she got a good look at him in the light she felt frightened for him as well as of him.

His brown hair had darkened to grey. His wiry bush of a moustache now drooped like uneven strands of wool. His eyes were ringed with black and his cheek bones looked higher and more pronounced than before. His shoulders were still enormous yet weight had slipped away from him, shrunk him inside big

340

bones and a hairy skin.

'I'll clean it and polish it myself rather than have it look like this,' he vowed. 'I used to be able to see my face in that floor. Everybody used to remark on it. This house was like a show place. A place to be proud of.'

'I know, Melvin. I'll do it tomorrow. Don't worry. I just haven't had time today. I'm sorry. You should have let me know you were coming. Fancy walking in like that!'

'Well! Now that I've arrived, don't just stand there!'

'Oh, yes, you'll be needing a cup of tea and something to eat.'

'Sure. Sure. After!'

'After?'

'Come on. Come on. Get your knickers down!'

'Melvin! Don't be horrible!'

'What do you mean, "don't be horrible"? You're my wife, aren't you?'

'There's things to talk about.'

'After. After.'

He moved towards her and she backed hastily away, stumbled and thumped down on to one of the chairs. Immediately his hand shot up her skirt to rub at her with iron fingers.

He looked an ugly stranger and she cringed underneath him and strained to lever his arm away.

His voice lowered with concentration.

'Come on, darlin'. Down on the floor.'

'There's other people in the house.'

'What do you mean?' He stopped in surprise. 'There's people in my house?'

'Your father's in one of the bedrooms playing dominoes with old Angus from next door.'

'Old Angus? Who the hell's he?'

Taking advantage of his surprise, she tugged her skirts down and twisted them round her legs like a tourniquet.

'Tam's father. And then there's Ruth.'

'Ruth?' He jerked to his feet. 'Ruth?'

'She sleeps on the bed settee in the sitting-room. But, oh, Melvin, please try to understand.' Her voice gained speed. 'She's been such a comfort to me while you've been away and you've

341

been away such a long time. She works downstairs, you see. We needed her in the shop. Everyone else went to munitions, you see.'

'No, I don't see.'

'Well, she couldn't go into munitions.'

'Why couldn't she? Has she got a crowd of weans through there messing up my good sitting-room?'

'No, no. She hasn't any family. It's not that. She couldn't go into munitions because her husband's a conscientious objector.'

A broken roar exploded from him. 'Jumpin' Jesus! I've been fighting all this time in bloody France, and you've been keeping conchies in my house.'

'No, no. Not her husband. He's in Maryhill Barracks. Ruth's the only one that's here.'

Her heart changed its beat from a rapid pitter-pat to a big slow, regular drumming.

'And, of course, your new wee son, Robert. I called him Robert after Daddy. Is that all right?'

'Is . . .? Is . . .?'

Melvin opened and shut his mouth like a walrus.

'Maybe you'd rather I'd called him Melvin. But Daddy always . . .'

'Shut up! You weren't pregnant when I went away.'

'I was! I was!'

She lied so vehemently, so convincingly that she almost believed herself.

'How can you say such a thing? Remember before you went away I wasn't feeling well? Remember that first day you told me you were going to join up. That was the day Fergus bit Andrew and we got such a fright. I was sick that day, remember?'

Melvin's rage was extinguished, leaving his eyes bleak and a nerve flickering around his face as if it were lost.

'Why didn't you write and tell me?'

'I thought you'd enough to worry you. You went straight into the thick of things you said. Anyway, you never wrote much to me after you went overseas.'

He gave a bitter laugh.

'No, I didn't get much of a chance for letter writing.'

'He's such a good wee boy, Melvin. He never cries and he's no bother at all. He's so like you and he's really terribly clever.'

He laughed again but this time he managed to sound pleased.

'Well? Let's see him, then!'

'Oh, yes.'

Delight irradiated her features and she went flying to the bedroom, calling excitedly back over her shoulder.

'You'll love him, Melvin. You'll just love him!'

She returned slowly, nursing the baby with great tenderness in her arms.

'Isn't he wonderful?'

Melvin restlessly jingled coins in his pocket and stared at the doll-like infant in the long white gown as if it were about to blow up.

'Everybody says he's like me, do they?'

'Yes, everybody! Can't you see the resemblance yourself?'

He edged a little nearer.

'Three sons now, eh? Some men try their damnedest all their lives and never manage to produce one.'

'I know.' Gently she kissed the sleeping child's brow. 'I feel so lucky.'

'Well!' Suddenly he exploded with impatience. 'Don't just stand there drooling over him. *I'm* here!'

Still nursing and cuddling the child close to her she went to replace him in his cot. All the time at the back of her mind, terror simmered. Melvin must never, never find out the truth. He had often threatened to take the children away from her and throw her out in the street for far less heinous crimes than adultery. She had no idea of the law but had never needed to look any further than her immediate surroundings in Clydend for examples to illustrate the Scottish tradition that the man was the boss, the proverbial 'lord and master', the privileged one, and a woman was merely part of his goods and chattels with which he was perfectly entitled to do whatever he liked.

Back to the kitchen she flew to try to keep Melvin in a good humour and in her rush she crashed the door open, sending it banging noisily against a chair.

Melvin's reaction was unexpected and frightening. He spun

round, crying out in rapid staccato bursts, eyes bulging, mouth jerking spasmodically under the grey wool.

'I'm sorry, Melvin. I'm sorry!' She stared at him in distress. 'I didn't mean to startle you.'

'You fool! You've always been the same. You've always hared about like a hysterical idiot. You've never had any sense.'

'What's wrong? You look ill. What have they been doing to you?'

'What do you mean, what have they been doing to me? Nobody does anything to me.'

He straightened and squared his shoulders and bulged his arms and tried to perform with all his old panache. And failed.

'I showed them. I showed them what a Jock could do!' His voice deflated. 'You didn't sleep with anybody else, did you?'

Impulsively she rushed to him and threw her arms around his neck.

'No, dear, don't be silly. You're just overtired. Fancy thinking a thing like that.'

'I was looking forward to coming home. It was meant to be a surprise. I thought you'd be pleased.'

'So I am. I am! You know I am.'

'It was a right rammy,' he murmured, absently fondling her breasts. 'The dirty Huns outnumbered us. We haven't finished with them yet, though. Britain always loses every battle but the last. You like me doing that, don't you?' He chuckled. 'You enjoy it. Open your dress and let's see you.'

Clutching at the neck of her dress she looked miserably away. 'Oh, Melvin.'

'What do you mean "Oh, Melvin"?'

'We'll be going to bed soon. I'll be getting undressed when I go through to the bedroom.'

'I want you to get undressed now.'

'Not here!'

'Here!'

'I was going to make you a cup of tea.'

'A good idea.' He laughed excitedly. 'Parade around. Make the tea in the buff. Come on. Come on!'

Getting a grip of her dress he jerked it down to her waist. He twisted and tugged and wrenched at her clothes until she was naked.

'Right. On you go!'

Her voice reached scream-height without getting any louder.

'Somebody might see me! Ruth! Your father! Old Angus! The children! If somebody sees me, I'll die!'

'Serves you right for having so many folk in my house.' In sudden irritation Melvin scratched violently at his moustache. 'What's that racket out there now?'

'It's old Angus going away.' She grabbed her clothes and clutched them up in front of her. 'What if your father decides to come through here?' She began to sob and moan and weep without tears. 'Oh, please, Melvin, hold the door, hold the door. Don't let anyone see me. Don't let anyone see me!'

'Da's bawling his head off.'

'Old Angus is deaf.'

Shaking as if she had malaria Catriona struggled into her torn dress and with clumsy fumbling fingers buttoned it over her nakedness.

'I don't care what he is. That's bloody terrible, shouting and stomping about like that. All it needs now is the conchies to come out and join in the chorus. And I thought I was going to have a bit of peace and quiet in my own house.'

'I'm sorry. I'm sorry. Oh, for goodness' sake, let's just go to bed.'

'All right,' he growled. 'But it's a disgrace. I might have known everything would be reduced to pigs and whistles when it was left to you. God knows what else you've been doing behind my back.'

'Nothing, nothing. Let's go through.'

It was only when she reached the bedroom that she remembered Andrew, who slept in the bed with her now since baby Robert had the cot. Andrew was still a baby himself. His hot pink cheek dented the pillow and his thumb, newly escaped from a moist mouth, lay ready to give comfort.

'I'll lift him out,' she whispered shakily. I'll put him with Robert. He'll be all right at the bottom of the cot.'

'He's the conchies' as well I suppose?'

'What?'

Catriona's voice squeaked incredulously and she twisted round with Andrew lolling soft and heavy in her arms.

'His wife's here. Don't tell me he hasn't been here.'

'You mean Sammy? I've never set eyes on the man in my life. Melvin, I wish you wouldn't talk like that. It doesn't make sense. You're frightening me.'

She arranged Andrew in the cot, making sure that his limp bandy legs did not spread over and brush Robert's feet.

'You know his name.'

'Of course I know his name. I've heard Ruth say it dozens of times.'

'Does she know that you know him?'

'I don't know him.'

'Has he never been in my house?'

'I've never seen the man I told you. Why are you nagging at me like this?'

'She's in my house.'

'Because I know her doesn't mean to say that I know him.'

'He's never been in my house?'

'Of course not. But even if he had . . .'

'Has there or has there not been a conchie in my house?'

'Melvin!'

'Has he, or hasn't he?'

Harassment needled her.

'I'm not going to listen to any more of your mad talk.'

At that moment, as if to add to her miseries, the sirens sounded and Melvin flung himself on to the floor halfway under the bed.

'What on earth are you doing now?'

He got up slowly, fumblingly, keeping his back towards her.

'I fell, you fool. I tripped and fell. This house is a bloody disgrace. Toys and rubbish lying everywhere.'

'For pity's sake, Melvin, I wish you'd just get into bed and try not to worry. Oh, dear, if it's not one thing it's another.' She hesitated. 'We always go down to the bakehouse lobby during an air-raid but I don't think we'll bother tonight. I'm tired as well. Anyway, nothing ever happens here. Although this is supposed to be a bull's-eye area and they're so fussy about the black-out. There's always wardens or police or somebody shouting "Put that light out!" You can't even shine a torch around here. It's impossible to see where you're going. It's really dangerous.'

'Dangerous.' He laughed bitterly. 'Dangerous! You don't know what danger is, you fool.'

'Oh, don't I? You don't know about the baffle wall in front of the close.'

'What do you mean, I don't know about the baffle wall? I nearly broke my nose finding out about it on the way in.'

'You see! You see! The children are always banging against it and hurting themselves. It's an absolute menace, that thing. I'd better go and tell Ruth that I've decided not to go down. I don't suppose she'll bother going either.'

'I'll see about this tomorrow, do you hear me? I'll see about this.'

She turned at the door, her face creasing with exasperation.

'See about what?'

'Strangers and conchies in my house.'

His eyes bulged red-veined at her in the shadowy light from the bedside lamp.

'You tell that woman I'll be talking to her tomorrow.'

She escaped from the room to find Ruth in the hall wearing nothing but a clinging low-cut night-dress. She was stretching slowly, lazily.

'This is getting monotonous, Catriona, isn't it? And exhausting. I feel as if I haven't had a decent sleep for years, don't you?'

'Let's just go back to bed,' Catriona suggested. 'My husband Melvin's home.'

'Is he?'

Ruth woke with interest.

'Good night, Ruth.'

Catriona edged back into the bedroom and closed the door. The bedside lamp had been put out and for a moment she felt alone in the darkness with the thrum-thrum of the planes passing overhead.

347

She did not usually pay much attention to them. They came with the darkness every night and filled the sky like a pregnancy, a menace she knew was there but just had to live with and accept.

She slipped out of her clothes and groped for her nightdress.

'Maybe they're ours,' she said, just to make conversation. 'Probably it's the RAF.'

'Don't ever mention the bloody RAF to me!' Melvin burst out with unexpected loudness and venom.

Catriona hastily hushed him and scrambled into bed.

'For goodness' sake, what are you shouting like that for? You'll waken the children.' Then her own voice rose with surprise. 'You've still got your clothes on. Have you a chill or 'flu or something? You're shivering!'

'There's nothing wrong with me. If I want to sleep with my clothes on, I'll sleep with my clothes on.'

'Oh, dear, maybe I should get the doctor!'

'Jumpin' Jesus, I'll take them off if it'll please you.'

Melvin tugged at his battledress under the blankets, writhing and bumping about.

'There's nothing wrong with me now, I keep telling you.'

'Now?' She caught anxiously at the word. 'What was wrong with you before?'

'Nothing, you fool! Everybody went to transit camps and rest centres. I was rested and fêted and treated like a lord for God knows how long. I'll soon show you if there's anything wrong with me or not.'

He bunched up her night-dress with his big fists and jerked her against him.

She wanted to plead with him to be gentle, because she was still tender from Robert's birth, but she was afraid to remind him of the baby.

She squeezed her hands down to act as a buffer and shut her eyes and tightened her muscles for the terrible invasion of pain.

Instead something small and soft kept bumping futilely against her. Then after a long time, Melvin said:

'I've gone right off you. You're no use. I've gone right off you, do you hear?'

348

She did not answer and they both lay very still in the darkness and listened to the planes.

Chapter 24

To learn that Melvin despised her came as no surprise to Catriona. What puzzled her was that he had ever wanted her in the first place.

But her husband's rejection of her brought a shame more acute than she had ever experienced before, and her inability to cope with the changes in his behaviour made her feel insecure and confused.

He nagged at her in unexpected bursts and spasms. At other times he shot out sudden crazy accusations.

He could hardly bear to stay under the same roof as her any more, and for the whole of his leave he padded about, high-shouldered and long-armed like a gorilla behind bars.

The continuous movement of him nearly drove Catriona to distraction. Round and round the house from one room to another he prowled, with a cigarette in one hand and the other hand busy jingling coins in his pocket. He sucked in smoke as if it were nectar and blew it out fast. He tried his pipe now and again but mostly it was a continuous chain of cigarettes.

'There won't be any cigarettes left for the customers if you go on smoking like that,' she told him eventually. 'They have to take some Pasha in their ration as it is.'

'Pasha. My God!' He tossed away a half-smoked cigarette and lit another. 'Somebody lit up one of them in the shop the other day. It stank the place to high heavens. What are they made of - camel's shit?'

A couple of times he helped her down to the close with the pram and then he brightened when Tam and Baldy and Sandy praised 'the new edition to the family'.

Tam had punched him enthusiastically.

'You're a lucky man, eh? Three braw sons. Are you aiming to build up your own football team, eh?'

Melvin had laughed with pride and pleasure then.

'Aye, my Robert's the best behaved infant in Glasgow. I've three sons to be proud of. They're all grand lads.'

But mostly he just laughed with Ruth.

When Catriona introduced him to Ruth, he was obviously impressed, and now in his restlessness to escape from the house he often went down to the bakehouse or the shop and did not come back up again until closing time. Then he and Ruth would return together, their laughter spinning round and round the spiral stairs.

'You said you hated conchies,' Catriona reminded him.

'Don't you ever mention that name in my house!'

'Ruth's a conchie.'

He guffawed and smacked his knees.

'You're jealous!'

She flushed.

'I'm stating a fact.'

'She's a fine-looking woman. That's a fact.'

She could not deny this. Ruth oozed beauty. Her black hair and her dark eyes gave her a kind of gypsy magic, and speaking to Melvin about Ruth only seemed to make him worse.

He seemed to take a pride in developing a noisy bantering relationship with the girl and sticking it out in front of Catriona like an impudently cocked thumb.

It cut her out as completely as if Melvin and Ruth were members of a secret society that she was not qualified to join. She kept telling herself that neither of them meant to do this to her and it was only her own distress that isolated her, but it was no use.

In between, attending to the children and doing the housework and cooking the meals, she snatched time to brush her hair and tie it up with a ribbon, and powder her face, and dab herself with perfume. It made not the slightest difference, but every time Melvin's eyes lit on Ruth they bulged with delight and back came his old peacock swagger. He puffed out his chest when he spoke to her and every now and again he roared with pleasure at some flattering remark of Ruth's. Ruth was good at the flattery, Catriona noticed.

Indignation mounted with the pain of her wounds until one

351

day when she was alone with Ruth she blurted out:

'Why don't you ever go and visit your husband?'

Ruth's smile vanished as if the words had smacked it from her face. She pouted.

'Do you think I haven't tried? They won't let me, will they?'

'Something must be wrong, Ruth. He's been shut away for such a long time. I heard the other day about a conscientious objector who got out after six months.'

'I know. I went to see the Quaker man, John Haddington. Remember I told you about him? He explained to me. He says they must be giving Sammy a whole lot of short sentences one after the other so that he's always under detention. That means jail, doesn't it? I didn't understand all he said. Something about a court martial, I think. He's going to try and see Sammy and he's going to try and make them give Sammy a court martial.'

'That doesn't sound very good.'

'It doesn't, does it?' Ruth played with a curl of her hair, winding it round and round her finger. 'But Mr Haddington seems to think it'll help. Anyway, he's going to see what he can do.'

Melvin had gone to the bedroom to put on his slippers and when he returned, sucking energetically at his pipe, the conversation about Sammy was abandoned.

'To hell with this pipe!' he exploded at last. 'I've gone off it as well. I'd rather have a Pasha.' He ruffled Ruth's hair as he passed. 'Did you bring me up more fags?'

Ruth arranged her long legs, relaxing back and smiling up at him. 'Did you think I'd forget? They're on the table.' Now for the first time, Catriona wondered if Melvin had told Ruth about 'going off' her. Her cheeks burned with shame at the thought and she slipped miserably from the room, longing for a breath of air.

Lizzie opened the door across the landing as Catriona closed hers.

'It's a disgrace. I don't know what the street's coming to!'

'What are you talking about?' Catriona queried sharply.

She had never had much patience for her neighbour's daughter and had long ago discarded any pretence of liking her.

352

'That conchie's wife. She's got no shame. I knew she was a dirty slut when I saw her carrying on with Baldy. I sized her up right away. And to think a woman like that is under the same roof as my wee Fergie.'

'He's not your Fergie now.'

'No, and he's not your Melvin either!'

'I didn't come out here to listen to your silly talk, Lizzie.'

'Oh, it's not my talk. It's everybody's talk. She can't take her eyes off Melvin. Down in the shop, for everyone to see, they're ogling at each other. It's shameful. And the other night I caught them in the office when I was down looking for Da. Disgusting, it was!'

Catriona whirled round to her own door again. She knew her legs would never carry her downstairs.

'The trouble with you, Lizzie,' she said, fumbling with her key, 'is that you've a dirty twisted mind.'

Once inside she leaned against the door for support. She could hear Melvin and Ruth laughing in the kitchen.

Suddenly she hated Ruth. If only Melvin had carried out his threat and flung her out. But soon his leave would be over and he would be gone.

'I'll show them yet,' he had vowed. 'I'll show them!'

Melvin was sitting on the arm of Ruth's chair, turning the pages of a photograph album on her knee; and Ruth was giggling as each page turned as if Melvin were touching her instead of the album.

'You've seen all these photographs before, Ruth,' said Catriona.

'Have I?'

'You know you have. I showed them to you weeks ago.'

Melvin glowered across the room.

'So what? Why are you talking so nasty all of a sudden? It's my album. She can look at it again if she likes.'

She ignored him.

'It's a while since you've taken a look at your nice wee house in Springburn, Ruth,' she said.

'It reminds me of Sammy when I go over there.'

'But you should keep your husband in mind, surely? I always

353

keep my husband in mind all the time he's away,' she said with more emphasis than truth.

Ruth flushed a deep scarlet but her chin tilted up.

'I meant that it made me sad because Sammy's in prison. Anyway, the house is sublet now, isn't it? Have I offended you in any way, Catriona?'

'Oh, no!' Catriona replied, furiously offended.

How dare this stranger, this conchie's wife, how dare she come here and make herself so much at home and behave so disgracefully.

Ruth got up.

'I think I'll go through and write to Mr Haddington again,' she said.

'A very good idea,' said Catriona, too angry to look at her.

Melvin laughed incredulously as Ruth left the kitchen.

'What was all that about?'

For a minute or two she stared at him uncertainly. Then she went over and sat in Ruth's place.

'I've an awful sore head, Melvin,' she murmured, like a child, leaning her head down on his knee. 'I've a sore back, too. I don't feel at all well. I'm so glad you're here.'

Melvin laughed again but this time he sounded pleased.

'You want me to make you better, eh?'

'You've always been stronger than me.'

'That's true.'

'You've always been an unusually strong man.'

'I know.'

'You still are.'

'Of course I am! Why shouldn't I be?'

She waited for his usual display of physical jerks, the wrenching and hunching and twisting and swelling up of every muscle in his body. Instead he placed his fingertips on either side of her temples and lifted her head up.

'Do you feel that?' he said, his stare bulging with excitement. 'Do you feel that, eh?'

She eyed him cautiously.

'Yes, dear?'

'That strength, that power sizzling from me through my

354

fingertips into you?'

'Yes, dear.'

'Your headache's going away, isn't it? You feel electric shocks sizzling from my fingers into your head, burning the pain away?'

Impulsively, she grabbed him round the waist and hugged him as tightly as she could.

She would order Ruth from the house if necessary. She could not stand her any more. How could she lie under the same roof as someone she no longer trusted, someone who had tried to steal her husband away. The wickedness of the woman, after all she had done for her! She had been nothing but generous and kind to Ruth Hunter from the time she had taken her in. Hunter! She was well named. A huntress, that's what she was, a horrible plundering female.

'I could hypnotise you as well.'

Melvin's eyes bulged and he waggled his fingers in front of her.

'Pain, pain, go away!'

She was suddenly reminded of a jingle from her childhood.

'Rain, rain, go away!' she sang out merrily. 'Please come back another day!'

'Bend over my knee and I'll massage your back. Where is it sore?'

Her heart began to palpitate but she did as he suggested.

After a long silence, he said:

'You're enjoying this, aren't you?'

'Let's go to bed, Melvin. Ruth or Da or somebody might come in.'

'It's early yet,' Melvin laughed. 'Don't rush me.'

'No, it's not, Melvin. Come on, dear. Let's go to bed.'

'You go through just now then. I'll do some exercises first. I've been neglecting my physical jerks. It's a mistake to get lazy like that. Physical jerks is what keeps a man fit.'

Worried, she got up.

'You won't stay long, will you?'

'Don't rush me, I said.'

Out in the hall she hovered anxiously, her eyes creased, trying to discern Ruth's door in the darkness, then made her way reluctantly to bed, her eyes still straining towards the sitting-room, her feet hesitating as if the floor could no longer be depended on.

She lay stiffly on her back clutching the bed-clothes up under her chin, eyes wide, ears alert. Time seemed to stretch on like a never-ending road and when Melvin did at last appear, she started nervously.

The yellow saucer of light from the bedside lamp left the rest of the room in darkness but she could hear his big noisy gasps for breath. The bed tossed her from side to side with the weight of him clambering in beside her. Then she saw his scarlet face and his moustache puffing and flurrying out in agitation.

'I'll maybe spare you a few minutes.' The words shuddered out from heaving lungs fighting to grab in air. 'We'll see!'

Chapter 25

Cell 14, the punishment cell, was upstairs. Sammy had come to know it very well. He hung against the wall, his arms stiff above his head, his wrists handcuffed to the bars of the small window.

To be manacled like this was not a punishment created solely for his benefit. Countless soldiers had been handcuffed to these same bars over the years. He wondered what it had done for them. Had it made them into good soldiers?

He would be damned if anything he had experienced so far in Maryhill Barracks would change his mind about being any kind of soldier. He would see the whole army and all their barracks burn in hell first. Everything that had happened had only heaped fuel on his hatred and redoubled his resolve to be as uncooperative as possible.

The punishment had been more commonplace at first, going round the parade ground at the double with full kit, or being on half or quarter rations. Eventually his diet shrank to bread and water alone.

The corporal's truncheon had been used. Long periods of solitary confinement had been tried, too. Now it was the manacles.

He shifted restlessly, changing his position as best as he could. The handcuffs sliced scarlet rings round his wrists. He shifted again, his face contorting with the agony of pulled shoulder muscles and bones hot and dry.

The cell door opened and one of the guards unlocked the handcuffs. Sammy viewed him with a dislike shared by most of the prisoners.

At first, he remembered, before all his 'privileges' were taken away, he and the other prisoners had been allowed an hour from seven to eight o'clock each evening in a special room where they could talk and smoke one cigarette. During that hour there had always been murmurings against certain of the guards.

'A couple of right gets,' somebody said. 'One dark night, after I'm out of this lot, I'm going to enjoy putting the boot in them!'

'At the double! At the double!'

A truncheon jabbed Sammy back to the present and kept on jabbing until he reached the parade ground.

Time for PT now, and he knew what would happen.

He would refuse, as usual, to obey orders. Nothing, but nothing, was going to make him jump to their tune. The guard would report him to the sergeant-major and he would be summoned to Spack's office.

'You again, Hunter?' the sergeant greeted him. 'You're a right one, you are! We can't have any more of this, lad. No more messing about. You're in the army now. It's time the army taught you a lesson.'

This cheerful speech bounced off Sammy's stony silence and the sergeant gave a brisk nod to the corporal who hustled Sammy away.

What, he wondered, without much interest, was going to happen next.

He did not care. All he worried about was Ruth. No physical suffering could compare with the mental anguish he felt by being out of touch and not knowing what was happening to his wife.

Perhaps she was ill. Maybe people were victimising her because of him.

His mind was still trying to tune in to distress signals from Ruth when all the cell doors were opened and everyone ordered out into the main hall for tea.

He ate automatically, not knowing or caring what went into his mouth, and when the meal ended he rose with the others to return to his cell.

'Not you, Hunter!'

Still obsessed by thoughts of Ruth he looks round at the corporal.

He keeps on looking.

All the other men disappear. Iron doors clang shut. Keys turn in locks.

Silence.

One of the corporals has black cropped hair and skin of

358

coarse grained leather and is called Morton. The other man's head is khaki and his name is Dalgliesh.

Morton stands legs apart, shoulders hitching, neck stretching forward, hands jerkily beckoning.

'Come on! Come on!'

Sammy stared at him in disgust.

'Away and play soldiers with somebody else. You make me want to puke.'

'Frightened, are you, eh? A right cowardly bastard, aren't you?'

Sammy eyes Dalgliesh who is already clomping towards him.

'It takes two of you, doesn't it?'

'We're going to teach you how to fight.' Dalgliesh laughs, enjoying himself. 'F— conchie bastard!'

Dalgliesh's hands shoot out, smack-grab down on Sammy's shoulders. Before he can burst free Dalgliesh's head cracks like a rock against his nose.

Blood messes across his face and fills his mouth.

He heaves up his arms and breaks the shoulder grip. He aims through flashing coloured lights until a jarring of his wrist gives pleasure. But only for a moment before he doubles up with a scream as a boot digs kidney-deep.

'Give the bastard to me, mate!' Morton rumbles. 'Let me have the f— yellow-belly!'

Morton's fist catches him under the chin, lifts him straight, reels him back. The floor thumps up.

Dalgliesh gouges a boot full-force into Sammy's groin.

Sammy's scream heightens with rage and he punches with both fists. He feels the rhythmic crunch-crunch of his fists as they keep slamming away at their target until the skin bursts from his knuckles.

Noise from everyone and everywhere and everything, joins in. All the prisoners kicking and battering and clanging and banging at cell doors.

The leather face bounces off the table. The table does a noisy somersault and Morton disappears. Fountains of chairs spurt through the air. Dalgliesh grabs one and axes it across Sammy's chest before swinging at him with first one fist then the other, weaving him backwards to the left side, then the right, then to the left again.

'F— conchie bastard.'

Sammy hits the wall and bounces back to Dalgliesh and hangs on to him, blood hosing from his mouth over Dalgliesh's shoulder as they struggle.

Morton heaves the table away, staggers up and gets the boot in again. Sammy wrenches Dalgliesh round and the next boot-blow mistakenly finds Dalgliesh's face.

They both come at him now. Morton's fist hits him like an iron hammer and explodes teeth in his face.

He hangs on to Morton until he manages to wrench out his truncheon. The success in getting the truncheon acts like a slug of whisky. He swings about like a madman. The truncheon cracks through the air. Crack - crack - crack.

He cannot stop. He staggers about still wielding the truncheon, slower and slower and slower.

He can no longer see the hall. His spine bumps blindly against cell doors, moves along an iron wall until the wall opens and he is sucked in. He falls backwards like a parachutist tumbling into nothing.

In slow motion he heels over, knees floating up, arm floating too, gently surging in a patient effort to catch the bed.

The bed is no use. The mattress is doubled up with all the blankets folded neatly on top. Orders are that they should not be touched before eight o'clock.

To hell with army orders. The floating arm claws at the mattress until it is flat and he is stretched over the top of it, blood wetting it, and warming it.

Until a whiplash of icy water hits him and from somewhere he hears the sergeant's voice.

'You vicious bastard! You've nearly killed my men. Good men, Hunter. Worth a score of your kind. We won't forget this. Don't think you'll get away with it. You won't. You've nearly smashed their skulls in, Hunter. Some bloody pacifist!'

The cell door clanged and he was left with pain closing in on him. He struggled to ignore the pain, to concentrate on his mind instead of his body.

'Some bloody pacifist!' The sergeant had accused. What was a pacifist! He knew his dictionary definition off by heart. A pacifist was an adherent to and believer in pacifism. Pacifism was the doctrine, theory, teaching of the necessity for universal or international peace, and the abolition of war as a means of settling disputes; pacifism was systematic opposition to war and militarism.

Yes, he was a pacifist and he would continue to be a pacifist until the day he died.

Being a pacifist did not necessitate having a placid, saintly or unemotional temperament. On the contrary, he believed that in terms of the causes of war, placid unemotional people could be most dangerous.

You had to be emotionally involved. You had to have strong feelings. You had to care and you had to care *enough* and caring enough meant caring *all the time*. It was no use caring too late.

That was the difference in the pacifist. He had to be emotionally violent in peace-time. Peace was the pacifist's battleground. A pacifist was a peace-tired fighter. The victory he fought for was the prevention of war. His was the unglamorous, the unpopular, the never-ending chore of keeping well informed about what was going on in the world and passing on that information to people who did not want to know; reading newspapers and other organs of information with a questioning suspicious mind. To be particularly sceptical of the leaders of men and every sentence they uttered no matter how cleverly phrased and charmingly delivered. To be courageous enough to swim against the tide, to contradict in public places among strangers, or in private gatherings with friends.

Being a pacifist involved fighting after the First World War was over. It meant arguing about treaties. It meant shouting from the house-tops that a Second World War would grow from the victories of the first and the way in which these victories were used. It meant insisting that the end of the First World War was a *prevention-point* when precautions should have been taken against German grievances, not against German aggression.

It meant protesting about Britain's stand on behalf of dictators in the Spanish Civil War. It meant insisting that here was another *prevention-point*. Here was where Hitler and Franco and Mussolini tested themselves, put the first boot forward, stretched the first muscles and found nothing but encouragement.

Why had the powers of Freedom and Democracy not lined themselves up firmly and politically against the dictators?

Theirs not to reason why? No, theirs to reason why, *all the time*!

Pain intensified, swelled to enormous proportions, became like an iron giant stamping mercilessly all over him.

He vomited teeth and blood over the edge of the bed to the floor.

He would teach his unborn children to question. He would teach them that in each individual lay the seeds of both love and hatred, peace and war and in every individual conscience lay the responsibility for which of the seeds should flourish.

He tried to move but the iron giant kicked him all over and began to grind him underfoot. He tried to suck in air but a gush of blood choked him.

He thought of Ruth. His mind struggled towards her.

Ruth . . . Don't worry . . . One day . . . One day . . . !

Chapter 26

'Have I done anything to offend you?'

It was the second time Ruth had asked that and Catriona hated her for putting her in the position of having to deny it. She had no proof that Ruth had any particular designs on Melvin any more than on Baldy or any other man. Ruth offended her just by being Ruth, but she could not tell the girl that. It was not fair. She hated Ruth for making her feel guilty and unfair.

Ruth had no right to like men so much. It was just not decent. Ruth enjoyed men. She viewed them as if they were a box of Turkish Delight that she was aching to get her teeth into.

Did her relationships go further than a giggling, wriggling, teasing manner? Catriona had no idea but she felt she had enough to worry about without somebody like Ruth adding to her difficulties and anxieties. She wished the girl would go. She wished she could tell her to go, but that would mean being left without a shop assistant and she could not cope with the shop herself, with Fergus and the two babies to look after.

She flushed, avoiding Ruth's eyes.

'No, not really,' she protested.

But, she added bitterly to herself, you might at least have had the decency to let me say goodbye to my husband by myself.

Melvin's leave had come to an end and he had caught an evening train for the South of England. He would not allow her to see him off at the station.

'You'd be sure to lose yourself or do something stupid trying to get back to Clydend in the black-out,' he insisted. 'I know you. You'd better stay here.'

So they said goodbye at the front door and Ruth stood there saying goodbye too. Right up to the last minute, Ruth and Melvin laughed and joked together. Then Melvin said, 'Cheerio, darlin'!'

His words were accompanied by a guffaw of laughter and the

delivery of a resounding smack on Ruth's bottom.

Catriona's anxious eyes detected the brief second the hand lingered on the flesh, and the eager movement of the flesh quickly pressing itself into the hand.

'Melvin.' She pulled his arm away from Ruth. 'Promise you'll write and let me know how you are.'

'Sure, sure.' His lips under his hairy bristle of moustache met hers in a noisy enthusiastic kiss. Then he said in a sudden change of tone. 'You behave yourself, do you hear? And remember, keep my house clean!'

They both stood watching his big khaki shoulders swoop down the stairs. They listened to his army boots clanging and echoing into silence. Then they went back into the house and shut the door.

Ruth said she would make a cup of tea.

'That would be nice,' Catriona replied stiffly.

While Ruth was putting the kettle on, she escaped into the bedroom. The children were all sleeping but Fergus was kicking restlessly and making moaning sounds. She straightened his blankets and hushed him and smoothed back his tangled hair.

Andrew was back in her bed tonight and she looked forward to cuddling into his warm pliant body and going to sleep with his small hand clinging to her nighty. The cot containing baby Robert had been put over in the corner at the far end of the room, away from the bed, while Melvin had been at home.

Melvin's moods had seemed so mercurial and unreliable that sometimes she feared for the baby's safety.

She had tried to have as little as possible to do with Robert or Andrew while Melvin was around so as not to draw attention to either of them, although to ignore them for any length of time was an agony.

If Andrew was up and about the house of course, he refused to be ignored. He kept slipping his hand into hers and leaning his head against her skirts while he sucked energetically at the thumb of his other hand. Or, still thumb-sucking, he would clamber up on to her knee to settle his cheek against her breast.

Robert could only lie alone in his pram in the close or in his cot in the room but every time Melvin's back was turned she hurried anxiously to the pram or cot to whisper loving reassurances to him. He always rewarded her with the most beautiful smile in the world.

No one would believe that a baby as young as Robert could smile. They laughed and pooh-poohed and insisted it must only be wind. But she just needed to look a the adoration and trust that made calm pools of Robert's eyes, and she knew, and felt a thrill, and was grateful.

Now Melvin was away the cot could come back beside the bed, and she tugged and pushed at it until she had it tight against the side. It was her idea of perfect bliss to lie in bed with Andrew cuddled into one side of her and the cot close to the other so that she could slip her hand through the bars and gently trace Robert's features with her fingers; the downy head, the nose that was the tiny centre of the rounded rose-petal cheeks.

Sometimes, unexpectedly, his eyes would open and such love and trust would shine out through the darkness at her, she had to hug up her knees and press her arms against her breasts to contain the ecstasy. And she would lie staring into his eyes, drinking in the love and loving back with desperate gratitude.

The bumping and scraping of the cot wakened him now but he did not cry.

'It's all right, love,' she whispered, smiling down at him. 'Everything's all right. Mummy's here.' Then her whisper gently rocked into song.

'I left my baby lying there,
Oh, lying there, oh, lying there,
I left my baby lying there.
When I returned my baby was gone . . .'

The door-bell rang. She tiptoed from the room and went to answer it.

Madge stood on the doormat looking larger than ever with one of her brood clinging to her hand and hiding her face in her skirt.

'You'll never guess,' said Madge. 'That big midden of mine is back from France!'

Before she could control it, Catriona's face lit up.

'Alec is back?'

'What are you looking so pleased about?'

'For you! For you!' Catriona hastened to assure her. 'I'm pleased that you got your man back as well. I had Melvin. He's not long away. Aren't you coming in, Madge? Ruth's making a cup of tea.'

'Well, just for a couple of minutes.'

Madge followed Catriona into the kitchen with her little girl still attached to her skirts and bumping along beside her and behind her like an awkward tail.

'Hello, Ruth,' Madge greeted. 'How are you doing, hen?'

'Oh, not bad, Madge, except that I'm missing my man, aren't you?'

'Am I hell! The dirty big midden's upstairs just now with the rest of the weans, seein' his Ma.'

'Alec is back?' Ruth's face lit up, but Madge did not notice. She was struggling to peel her child off her leg.

'Come on, hen, don't be shy. Say hello to your Aunty Catriona and your Aunty Ruth. He'd lumber me with another wean if I'd let him. I told him to watch it but he just laughed.'

'Aren't men awful?' Catriona sympathised. 'As if you hadn't enough with six.'

'Seven's a lucky number, he says! Not for you, I says, and bounced his head off the wall and knocked him unconscious!'

Ruth started to giggle and Catriona squeezed her hands over her mouth in an effort to suppress her mirth.

Suddenly Madge exploded in big-mouthed big-toothed hilarity.

'Served him right, the dirty midden, eh?' She accepted the cup of tea that Ruth offered. 'Ta, hen. No word from your man yet?'

'Mr Haddington's written to our Member of Parliament about him.'

Madge sucked in a noisy mouthful of tea.

'Fancy!'

The outside door burst into life with an energetic rat-tat-tat-tat-tat. Tat-tat!

'That'll be that stupid bugger,' Madge said after another drink of tea. 'Ruth, tell him I'm just coming, hen. Don't let him in.'

366

Catriona had half-risen from her chair. She sank down again, eyes following Ruth's back as it disappeared with eager haste from the room.

'Help yourself to something to eat, Madge,' she said absently.

'My God, you've got biscuits!'

Even the child cautiously emerged to gaze in awe at the plate.

'Put them in your bag and take them home.' Catriona strained her ears to listen to the laughter and the tantalising rise and fall of conversation in the hall. 'I've got a few more in the tin.'

'Oh, ta.' Madge's big, square hand grabbed the biscuits and stuffed them into her bag. Then she took one out again and pushed it towards the child. 'Here, hen, get your molars stuck into that.' Then she rose. 'Well, I'd better be getting back to Springburn. It's time the weans were in bed. Poor Ma! She's always going on about that. Right enough, it's a shame. The poor wee buggers get dog-tired.'

'It makes them girny, doesn't it?'

'Mine don't just girn.' Madge laughed. 'They howl blue murder. That's them started. Would you listen to the racket. My God! All I need now is for this one to join in.'

Catriona followed Madge's buxom figure into the hall.

'She's a good wee girl aren't you, pet?'

She patted the child's head. The little girl was still hiding into Madge's skirts but her cheeks now bulged with biscuit.

'Och, aye!' Madge agreed. 'Right enough!'

Bedlam reigned on the doorstep. Alec had a sobbing child in each arm and others leaning or hanging on to him in various degrees of heartbroken fatigue.

'Hello there, hen!' he called cheerily over the noise to Catriona. 'How are you doing?'

Madge pushed out in front of him.

'Never you mind how she's doing. It's none of your business how she's doing. Come on!'

'I'm coming, gorgeous. I'm all yours!' said Alec, giving Catriona a quick wink before turning away.

She hoped Ruth would not notice her flushed cheeks or hear the pounding of her heart when she returned to the kitchen.

Dreamily stirring her tea, Ruth murmured half to herself:

'He's awful, isn't he? But you can't help liking him, can you?'

'He's all right, I suppose,' Catriona replied casually.

'He's got something, hasn't he?' Ruth's husky voice melted all her words together. 'It's not just that he's handsome, is it? There's something likeable about him even though he's awful at the same time, don't you think?'

'Madge can be very violent. She wasn't joking.'

'I know. Poor Alec.'

'Not just with Alec. She can be violent with women as well.'

'Oh?' Ruth fluttered starry lashes and sipped daintily at her tea.

Catriona pressed the point home.

'Yes, I believe Madge is terribly jealous.'

'Well, you ought to know!'

Like guns, Catriona's eyes shot up.

'What do you mean?'

'You and Madge are such good friends.' Ruth smiled. 'Aren't you?'

There was no doubt about it, Catriona decided; Ruth would have to go.

Chapter 27

Madge knew he had gone up to the insurance office to see old Torrance earlier in the day so later all he needed to say was:

'Old Torrance was too busy to talk. The place was going like a fair. He's asked me up to his house in Balornock for a drink tonight, though. He's not a bad old stick. You know what he's like, of course. A drink to him means quite a few. Better not wait up for me, gorgeous.'

So here he was, with an alibi for tonight, with everything arranged, and actually on his way to Ruth. He had never felt so excited in years. He could hardly credit his good fortune.

He had tried to talk to her at the door of Catriona's place that other night but didn't get a chance for the weans and eventually he had burst out more as a joke than anything else.

'My God, what a life! It's not worth living any more. I wish I could get you on my own the way I used to.'

To his astonishment Ruth replied with a sigh, 'You're right, Alec, but my house is sublet just now, didn't you know? There was no use it lying empty, was there? This way I can make a few shillings extra, can't I? Then, of course, it's being kept filled, and it's being taken care of, isn't it? But we could meet somewhere else, couldn't we?'

'How about the Ritzy?' He snatched at the first thing that came into his head. He had noticed the local cinema's advert only a few minutes earlier in his mother's place upstairs.

She nodded, brightening.

'We can talk about old times.'

'Yeah!' he agreed enthusiastically.

The Ritzy had been a good idea. Any place in Springburn or even in the city might have meant bumping into some friend or neighbour who would pass the word on to Madge. Over here at the other end of town in Clydend, Madge knew no one but his mother and Catriona and neither of them would be out after dark. Catriona had to stay in with her weans and his mother took so many tablets now that she was asleep half the time.

The tram stopped quite near the Ritzy and his eager stride had him outside the cinema and up the front steps in a matter of seconds.

She was waiting for him in the foyer, looking more desirable than any woman he had ever seen in his life. He gave her an appreciative wink.

'Hello there, love, you look good enough to eat!'

She smiled.

'Hello, Alec.'

He could hardly take his eyes off her as he bought the tickets and gestured to her to proceed him up the stairs to the best seats in the house. He did not touch her but made the gesture like a caress and knew by the purr in her eyes that she understood.

The film had already started when they reached the dark darkness of the gallery. They found two seats in the back row, and took their time settling down. Slouching back, Alec arranged his long legs as comfortably as he could in the small space available. Ruth relaxed and crossed her shapely legs, resting her elbows on the arms of her seat while she slowly eased off her gloves, one finger at a time like a strip-tease artist.

It was better entertainment than what was going on on the screen, but Alec forced his gaze if not his attention away from her. He was still making love to her. By stretching out the suspense, by not watching her, he was intensifying her eagerness to be watched. Making love was an art, and one he believed he had a particular talent for.

This time he had everything carefully thought out. They were going to enjoy each other, Ruth and he. This was going to be a night to remember.

In a few minutes he would change his position slightly so that he could drape his arm along the back of her seat. She would melt into him, her soft flesh pressing close. His arm would tighten round her shoulder. Her head would move back, face tilting, moist mouth opening with invitation.

But first he would kiss her hair and brow and ears and eyes. And all the time his hands would gently stroke and fondle.

He would make sure, though, that he did not go too far. Even if she begged him, and she probably would, he must not go too far. The back row of the Ritzy's gallery was not for them. Not when there was a perfectly comfortable spare bed in his mothers place in Dessie Street.

He had a key to the house and by the time the show finished and they got back to Dessie Street his mother would have taken her sleeping tablet and be dead to the world in the kitchen bed. Ruth and he would slip quietly into the house, make straight for the bedroom and bolt the door.

He was just about to move towards her when something unexpected caught his attention.

A notice had flashed on the screen:

'An air raid is now in progress. Any patrons wishing to leave should do so now in a quiet and orderly manner.'

'Oh, hell!' he protested indignantly.

'Sh . . . sh!' Ruth's eyes glimmered mischievously at him through the darkness. 'They often do that, didn't you know?

Just looking at her made his indignation melt away. He grinned and winked. 'Yeah! Who doesn't!'

She giggled.

'Everything you say sounds awful! You've always been the same, haven't you?'

'You too, hen. You sex maniac you!'

Suddenly the building jerked at its roots with a dull thud. Everyone stood up.

'That was close,' Alec said. 'Close enough to be the docks!'

The screen went dead.

'Oh, Alec!'

'Come on, hen. I'll take you back home.'

People had begun to crush into the passage-ways, but there was no panic. It just looked like the normal nightly crush to get home after the show had finished.

Alec shouldered a path for Ruth and reaching the emergency exit a few yards from where they had been sitting, turned to allow her to go through the door before him. At the same time his eyes seemed to explode. Everything around him disintegrated in an angry roar. His hands, clutching out for support, caught

371

at the lintel of the exit door and hung on.

Sound crumpled down under a huge puff of dust. Then there was silence.

He heaved himself out through the door and allowed his feet to slowly, carefully descend the stairs.

The emergency exit led to a narrow lane at the side of the cinema. Alec stood staring dazedly towards the Main Road.

There were sounds of running feet in the black-out and weak little fingers of light from torches frantically criss-crossed. People were shouting and an air-raid warden wearing a steel helmet came clattering over the cobblestones of the lane towards him.

'Are you all right? Did anybody else get out this side?'

Alec stared at him.

The warden rushed in through the emergency door, aiming his torch upwards. In a few minutes he came out again.

'We'd better go round to the front.' He got a grip of Alec's arm. 'This wall doesn't look too safe. You've been lucky, Jack!'

Alec allowed himself to be led on to the Main Road. A pale moon showed the Ritzy lying open at the front like an old doll's house and full to overflowing with a mountain of rubbish. It spilled out on to the street, with lavatory pans and fancy tiles, broken bricks and slabs at grotesque angles like tombstones in an old graveyard and gold-painted plaster, and great beams of wood, and red plush seats gone grey.

Already people were moving over the mountain, a black swarm of burrowing ants. Others were standing dazedly at the foot as he was standing. Some wept.

One woman was moaning and sobbing and talking to herself.

'We had a fight and he took the wean and went without me. Him and the wean liked them cowboy pictures. I wanted him to mend the pulley. He'd been promising to mend it for ages. Tommy, I says, if you go out tonight again, that's us finished. But him and the wean liked them cowboy pictures, and they went without me.'

The air-raid warden asked Alec his name and address, and if he had been with others, and if so, did he see any of them here, and if not, what were their names and addresses?

'Don't worry, Jack. It'll come back to you. You're still shocked. Here, have a cigarette and just stay there until I've time to see to you.'

Alec inhaled, his nostrils pinching in with the smoke.

The warden had joined the other ants scrabbling and pulling at the debris.

No one would notice, Alec thought, if he walked away now. He could walk and walk until he felt better. Then he could jump on a tram-car and go home. He could go to Madge as if nothing had happened. No one need ever know.

Somebody was repeating angrily, brokenly beside him:

'Bloody war! Bloody stupid war!'

He seconded that. War was the stupidest thing that men had ever thought up. Life was short and there were so many better things to do with it. War was a bloody stupid waste!

He saw the warden crushing towards him and tossed away his cigarette. Now was the time to go, the time to say a silent goodbye to Ruth. He cursed himself bitterly because he could not do it.

'Feeling better, Jack?'

'It's Alec. Alec Jackson. Cowlairs Pend, Springburn.'

He flung himself down on his knees with the others to claw desperately at the bricks and the wood and the stone . . .

'Someone belonging to you in there?' the warden sympathised.

'A woman.' Dust stung Alec's eyes and cracked his voice. 'Ruth Hunter.'

Catriona would have fainted when she learned about Ruth but she discovered that fainting was a luxury she could not indulge in. To escape into unconsciousness when two children were clinging to one's skirts and a baby was gurgling trustfully in one's arms, had to be out of the question. She must force herself to go on dandling baby Robert and telling the other children to behave themselves. She must light the fire and dress Robert and cook breakfast and pick up toys in case the old man tripped over them. There were nappies to be washed and beds to be made and she had to decide what to cook for dinner.

Life went on. Mercilessly. There was no escape. The young

girl inside her panicked, flapped futilely against the reality of an ordinary housewife shackled with weans, one wife among millions, having to go on and on struggling with endless responsibilities, disappointments and problems, having to accept the pitiless erosion of age and the irrevocable finality of death.

Having to face guilt, having to look herself in the face.

Poor Ruth, she kept thinking. Oh, my God, poor Ruth!

The funeral had been a nightmare and the Quaker meeting for worship afterwards, in which there had been endless painful time to think, was no better.

This was the first time she had seen Sammy since they took him away and what she saw brought more horror.

His head was shaved to a dark red stubble that laid bare bright scarlet weals. His eyes were inflamed and badly cut. Stitches puckered his shin. His nose was smashed and his face twisted with discoloured swellings.

He sat opposite her in the small room of the Quaker Meeting House, his stocky body rigid, his grey pebble eyes hard.

Long wooden forms were arranged in a square with a small table in the centre. On the table a vase of daffodils made the rays of a wintry sun look faded. The clock on the wall ticked interminably like tiny droplets from a vast sea of silence.

Catriona's gaze wandered over some of the others in the room then she tried to concentrate on the daffodils to keep her mind safely empty. But she kept thinking: Poor Ruth! Oh, my God! Poor Ruth.

She remembered how she had confided in Ruth one night not long before Robert's birth. She burst into tears and confessed to Ruth that she felt frightened to go to bed on her own in case the baby started during the night and she was not able to help herself.

Ruth had immediately flung her arms round her neck, hugged and kissed her and assured her that she would love to look after her and she must never feel lonely or frightened ever again as long as she was with her.

From that night until Robert's birth Ruth had slept with her, cuddled into her back with her arm protectively round her swollen waist. And before saying good night every night she

374

would ask in that lilting voice of hers:

'You're all right now, aren't you? You'll tell me if you need anything else, won't you?'

She remembered the luxury of cups of tea in bed in the morning brought by Ruth before she went down to her day's work in the shop. She remembered a thousand little kindnesses eagerly, lovingly, generously given.

In an agony of remorse she recalled her jealousy of Ruth, her coldness to the girl and her eventual wish to get rid of her.

If only . . . If only . . . The words prefaced a dozen thoughts as she sat in the Quaker silence opposite Sammy.

John Haddington, who had finally managed to get Sammy out of Maryhill Barracks, had wanted to take him home with him but Sammy had come to Dessie Street because Ruth's belongings were there.

'You can sleep on the bed-settee in the sitting-room,' she told him. 'You can stay here as long as you like.'

She dreaded to think what would happen when Melvin came home again but she would have to face that problem when he arrived. She had no alternative. Life went on. You kept doing what you could in your own way. You made mistakes. You struggled to understand. You failed. You tried again. You took one small step after another. Only kings, politicians and madmen took big steps like war.

You just took one small stumbling step after another because you believed that life was a pattern of small things, a chain in which every tiny link mattered.

She wanted to talk to Sammy on the way back to Dessie Street, to try to explain. She sought to bring words of comfort to her inarticulate tongue but no words came.

And perhaps she had no need to say anything.

In the kitchen, while she was making a cup of tea, Sammy chatted quite naturally to the children and when Fergus, in an embarrassing burst of honesty said: 'What an awful looking face you've got!' Sammy laughed and replied, 'I know. Think yourself lucky you haven't got one like it. You're a handsome wee lad!'

He took it in his stride, too, when the old man spoke about Ruth.

'A fine figure of a woman!' Duncan chewed nostalgically on his pipe as he kept repeating in high-pitched aggrieved tones. 'A fine figure of a woman. It's terrible. What am I going to do down in that shop without her?'

'Da!'

Catriona tried to silence him with a hiss in her voice and a cup of tea in her hand. But Sammy's gruff voice had assured her.

'There's no need to get upset. It's all right.'

Afterwards he had dandled Robert on his knee while she prepared the child's evening bottle.

My God! she thought. Alec's child!

But she smiled and said what a good baby he was and Sammy too admired him.

Madge had agreed that Sammy must never know that Ruth had been with Alec that night, but that was as far as she would go.

'I'll make Alec pay for this,' she vowed. 'I'll make the dirty rotten midden regret this for the rest of his f— life.'

'Madge!'

Catriona had been shocked and distressed, not only by Madge's language but by the ugly bitterness twisting the normally placid, good-natured face.

'Madge, please. What's the good of being like that. You'll only make yourself ill. I'm sure Alec will regret that night without you making his life a misery.'

'What do you know about misery!' Madge shouted. 'What do you know about anything! Coddled and spoiled and doted on all your life by your "mummy".'

'Madge, don't.'

'Your own man wasn't good enough for you. You had to have a taste of mine as well.'

'You're upset. I know how you must feel. But hating me won't change Alec.'

'You mind your own f— business. You've had more than enough to do with my man. God knows how many other wee cows have had their fun and games with him as well. To think there was a time when I actually trusted him. But never again! He's made a fool of me once too often. Don't tell me how I should or shouldn't be with him!'

She agreed, however, that no good purpose would be served by allowing Sammy to know.

It was comfort Sammy needed, and that first night in Dessie Street, Catriona's tongue still desperately searched for words. Eventually, before saying good night to him, she managed:

'Ruth used to talk about you all the time, Sammy. She loved you very much and she was always so proud of you.'

Was that small step a failure, she wondered, lying in bed across the hall from Sammy, sharing the same darkness and the terrible sound of his sobbing.

She clutched at the bars of the baby's cot, longing to go through and hold the man, and hush and soothe him as she would the baby.

But she remained clutching the bars, imprisoned.

Chapter 28

'You're like a hen on a hot girdle,' Duncan complained. 'You're more of a hindrance than a help in this shop. Ruth took her time but she got things done no bother.'

'All right! All right! So I'm not Ruth!' Catriona hissed, turning to the next customer.

Her father-in-law was still muttering and salivating into his goatee beard after all the customers had gone.

'I'll leave you to lock up, Da,' she told him. 'I'll have to hurry upstairs.'

'Some employee you make!'

'I'm not an employee.'

'Ruth always stayed behind and saw to everything. I never needed to worry.'

'Well, *I* need to worry. I've a baby lying in a pram in that draughty close and I've another baby upstairs in Mrs Jackson's and Fergus has been home from school for ages and I dread to think where he is and what he's doing. And I've everybody's tea to see to.'

'That conchie nyuck up there should be doing something for his keep. What's he doing, eh?'

'He's paying good money for his keep and he's away seeing about a job today.'

'Aye, he'll be getting himself fixed up in one of them boom factories. He'll make his pile here while the likes of Melvin's away earning coppers. I told that stupid ass that I could have got him deferred. He's no right to go away and leave me to look after this business by myself at my age. If the likes of that conchie can stay here and make his pile . . .'

'Oh, for goodness' sake, Da!' she interrupted impatiently. 'Sammy would rather die than go into munitions. He's a pacifist. He's gone to see his Quaker friends. They have an ambulance service. They do jobs like that.'

'Bloody pacifists! They ought to put them up against a wall and shoot them!'

'Da, you know you don't mean that. You're just tired and needing your tea. I'll away upstairs and get it started.'

Unexpectedly the door-bell pinged and a traveller shuffled in with no legs, only feet showing on the end of his long blue belted raincoat The coat, shined smooth with age and years of carrying bulky samples, was topped by a milky-moon face devoid of any expression except resignation. His black homburg looked as if somebody had stamped on it and twisted the brim in a fit of rage, a misfortune he had no doubt suffered with the same stoic lack of emotion with which he put up with everything else.

'What have you got?' MacNair eagerly pounced on the traveller before he'd even had time to heave his case up on the counter.

'Bana . . .'

'Bananas?'

Excitement exploded Catriona and the old man into one voice.

'Banana essence. You can make a spread for sandwiches with it. I've got a recipe in my case somewhere. Parsnips or swedes or something like that you use. If you can get them. You cook them and mash them up with the essence.'

Catriona sighed.

'Everybody knows that.' She took off her apron. 'Fancy my Andrew has never seen a banana in his life. It's hard to imagine that I actually used to eat them and never give them a thought.'

'Bananas!' the traveller sighed, remembering. 'Marvellous things!'

'Them were the days!' the old man reminisced along with him. 'Before all these ration books and coupons. Christ, you need to be a Philadelphia lawyer to sort everything out now. It's terrible.'

The traveller looked around the empty, dusty shelves.

'This place used to be packed. You always carried a good stock.'

The old man chewed his loose dentures for a minute before saying dreamily:

'Everything from currant buns to sanitary towels I had in here.'

'Now we spend most of our time cutting out bits of paper from ration books.' Catriona rolled her eyes heavenwards. 'Forms, and ration books and coupons. I know how Da feels.'

'Aye, my shop used to be the best stocked shop for miles around, but now look at all I have! A silly wee lump of butter and a wee bag of tea and sugar. That would have been just enough to feed one family in them days. Now I've to share it among everybody. Remember my mutton pies and my nice white bread and rolls?'

'My God!' the traveller said.

'Thick and juicy with meat them pies were. And the bread snowy white with a crisp crust on the top.'

'Da, don't be cruel. Tormenting folk doesn't help. I'm away upstairs.'

Catriona pushed through the piece of sack-cloth that served as a curtain between the shop and the lobby at the back, and went out through the side door into the close.

Despite the hood of the pram being up, and several blankets and covers, a woolly bonnet, coat, leggings and mittens, Robert's face was pale with cold and his nose looked like a maraschino cherry.

'Och, mummy's poor wee love.'

Hurriedly Catriona lowered the hood and began to unfasten the waterproof cover.

'I would have had you inside in the lobby but you've go to get some fresh air some time.'

His eyes beamed love up at her and his mouth opened the whole width of his face, and her heart melted towards him as he showed her every part of his toothless pink gums.

'I'll carry the pram up.'

Sammy's voice made her swing round. It had a jerky gruffness that always startled her when she was not expecting it. She could never quite get used to his appearance, either. His spiky hair, his broken nose and aggressive stare made him look more like a prize-fighter than anything else.

'Oh, it's you. I didn't expect you back so early.'

She lifted the baby and followed Sammy up the stairs.

'I came across in the ferry,' he told her. 'It saves a bit of time and it's handy being at the end of the street.'

'I never use it. I don't like walking down Wine Row.'

'Wine Row?'

'The other end of Dessie Street. Everybody calls it Wine Row because of the sheebeens and the meths drinkers.'

'I don't suppose they'd do you any harm. They seem to be away in a world of their own.'

'Oh, it's not that I'm frightened. It just makes me feel sad to look at them.'

They went into the house and Catriona hurried through to the kitchen to see if the fire was still lit.

Any kind of fuel was desperately difficult to come by and coalmen no longer bothered to deliver what little they had.

You had to go to the coalyards and queue up in the hopes of getting a ration of coke or wood, or now and then some briquettes made from nobody knew what.

Catriona had built the fire up very carefully with wet newspapers, a few briquettes and plenty of dross.

'Oh, good!' she said, seeing the faint red glimmer underneath all the smoky black. 'It's still in. Now wee Robert's nose will get a chance to thaw out.'

Tenderly she kissed the nose before sitting down, balancing the baby on her knees and stripping off the bonnet, mitts and coat.

Fergus was lying back on the opposite chair reading a book.

'Hello, son,' she greeted him. 'Are you hungry for your tea?'

'I've been hungry for ages.'

'Well, it won't be long now. You start setting the table and maybe Uncle Sammy will run up to Mrs Jackson's for Andrew.'

'Right,' Sammy agreed. 'I'll go and fetch him now.'

Fergus carefully put a marker in his book before laying it down and it was a minute or two before a question registered in Catriona's mind.

'What was that you put in your book, Fergus?'

'It's to mark my place.'

'I know. But what is it? Let me see.'

It was a letter from Melvin.

'When did this arrive? How did you get it? You're a very bad boy, Fergus. You must never touch other people's letters.'

'It was Andrew,' Fergus said. 'Andrew gave it to me.'

Catriona sighed.

'Oh, Fergus, for goodness' sake go and set the table.'

She propped the happy, gurgling baby against the cushion behind her and hastily ripped open the letter.

One minute later she had torn the envelope and its contents into shreds and was about to poke them into the fire when she realised that one jab at the carefully balanced dross might collapse the whole thing in a belch of black smoke and completely extinguish the tiny red promise of heat.

She put the poker down and stuffed the paper into the pocket of her dress instead.

Lizzie must have written to Melvin and told him about Sammy staying in the house.

'By the time you get this letter', he wrote, 'I'll be overseas again and what have I got to think of when I'm away? I'll think up ways of doing that conchie. I'll practise my physical jerks night and day, especially my hand grips. Even under my blankets at night I'll do my hand grips. Because the first thing I'm going to do when I meet that conchie is to take him unawares and shake him by the hand. "Hello there," I'll say in a big friendly voice while I'm crushing his hand to pulp and splinters.'

Sometimes she suspected that Melvin was a little mad and now she feared that the madness of war might combine with his own madness and swell it to dangerous proportions.

She looked ahead to the time when Melvin would return, and a wave of apprehension threatened to swamp her. Then Andrew's plump little figure appeared at her elbow and she had to hold back the wave. She had to smile lovingly down at him.

'Are you a hungry wee boy too, eh?'

It was a blessing, she told herself, that she had plenty to do to keep herself occupied. She was almost glad now that she had to help in the shop. To keep busy with a host of little tasks and duties was essential. This was the lifeline to which she must cling. The little things were the most important. The tin of beans she was busily opening at this moment to feed her children with. The pot on the cooker to heat them. The spoons the children were clutching in eager anticipation.

All the little necessities of normal life. The washing up cloth. The plug for the sink. The baby's bottle, bouncy brown teats. His bath in front of the fire. The cracked yellow duck that swam lopsided.

The chipped cup that she kept for herself. The extra cup of tea in the teapot to be drunk after all the children were attended to. Teddy bears and golliwogs and comforters. All the bits and pieces that were needed in life and were part of the pattern.

'You look tired.'

Sammy flashed her a look from under jutting brows.

The kitchen was cleared, the children asleep, and the old man was listening to his wireless and enjoying a pipe through in his own room.

Catriona nodded. She was thinking that it was time for the air-raid warning to go, and her eyes strayed up to the clock as the sirens began to wail.

She felt so tired, she would have liked to close her eyes and drop off to sleep right there and then on the chair.

No hope of that, though. There was not much chance of a sleep anywhere now. She might as well get ready for the trek downstairs.

The nightly racket had become earsplitting, the painful din of giant fireworks exploding and vibrating all the time in the echo chamber of the head.

'Nothing to worry about,' people assured each other. 'It's only our own guns.'

The big guns on the ships and the guns on the docks. And all the ack-ack guns firing from the street.

As Sammy carried Fergus and the mattress downstairs to the bakehouse lobby and then Robert in his pram and then Andrew, Catriona struggled to concentrate on gathering together all the bits and pieces and odds and ends, trying not to be engulfed or confused by the appalling din, the hysterical wailing of sirens, the low thrum of planes sounding too heavy for the roof to hold, the sharp crack-crack so near that it violently rattled the windows, the (so-far) distant crump-crump of bombs.

They greeted each other cheerily in the bakehouse lobby, shouting at the pitch of their voices to make themselves heard above the pandemonium outside.

'Hello, Nellie! Is your stomach still bad, hen? I've brought a wee pinch of baking soda just in case.'

'Oh, ta! You could have had a spoonful of my sugar if it hadn't been for Paw. I was saving it in a jar,' Nellie wailed. 'Paw thought it was washing soda and emptied it into a basin of hot water and steeped his feet in it.'

'Oh, my God!'

There was a howl of sympathy.

Angus's son Tam, the wee white-haired baker with the big muscly arms, came barging through with two chairs above his head.

'Here's your seat, Paw, and yours, Mr MacNair.'

The old men's chairs were always placed as near as possible to the lavatory door. Robert's pram and the mattress with Fergus and Andrew were set in the middle. Then with much squeezing and pushing and grunting everyone settled down, their backs supported by pillows, cushions and lobby walls, arms and legs tangled together.

'Watch my feet, for pity's sake,' Sandy the vanman pleaded. 'See, if anybody tramps on my bunions . . . !'

His floppy bloodhound face screwed up at the thought.

'Look at that wee pet.' Catriona nodded towards the baby. 'Wide awake and not a whimper.'

She was sitting on the floor at the side of the pram with her knees hugged up under her chin. Leaning her head to one side she began to sing to the baby, who stared at her wide-eyed with delight.

'Wee Willie Winkie,
Runs through the town,
Up stairs and down stairs
In his night-gown,
Tirling at the window,
Crying at the lock—
Are all the weans in their beds,

For it's now ten o'clock?'

Baldy Fowler appeared, huge and merry and slightly drunk, staggered over everybody and made a place for himself.

'Come on! Come on!' he hollered. 'The crowd of you aren't cheery enough tonight, where's all the Glasgow spirit gone?'

'Down your throat!' somebody replied and sent up a roar of laughter.

'Let's have a song.' Baldy waved a fist about as if he had a flag in it. 'Let's have a good old Glasgow song!'

'Right!' Tam smacked his palms together and gave them an energetic rub. 'Here we go, then. Everybody together:

'I belong to Glasgow!
Dear old Glasgow Town—
But—there's somethin' the matter with Glasgow for—
It's going round and round!
I'm only a common old working chap, as anyone here can see
But—when I get a couple of drinks on a Saturday—
Glasgow belongs to me!'

After several repeats, delivered with great gusto, it was decided that it was time for Catriona to make tea.

She smiled to herself as she set the cups out on a tray.

They were belting out another one now, their road voices energetically bouncing and swaggering with typical Glasgow panache.

'Just a wee doch and doris,
Just a wee yin that's a',
Just a wee doch and doris,
Before ye gang awa',
There's a wee wifie waitin'
In a wee but and ben,
And if you say "it's a braw bricht moonlicht nicht",
Yer aw richt, ye ken!'

The song screeched to an end in a howling bedlam of laughter, above and outside of which Catriona distinguished a fast, piercing whistle.

Then the building collapsed.

For a few minutes the protesting roar of the tenement took possession of Catriona's brain. She was deafened, blinded, knocked off balance. She found herself on her hands and knees wandering around in circles like a bewildered animal. The air parched and thickened with plaster dust. Her eyes stung. She began to cough.

Then other sounds filtered through the blackness. Moans, and muffled bursts of screaming punctuated by brief disbelieving silences. There was sifting, sighing sounds, and creaking, splintering sounds. The old building groaned as it disintegrated, with as much anguish as the people who were part of it.

A high, reedy voice squealed:

'Mummy! Mummy! Mummy!'

It stabbed Catriona to life, made her claw like a maniac towards it, ignoring the jagged stones and twisted metal tearing at her body.

'It's all right, wee lovey. It's all right, Mummy's here!'

She reached Andy's legs and wrenched up the piece of wood that covered the rest of him.

'You're all right, Andy. You're all right, son. You're all right.'

Blindly she fought to pull him into her arms.

'Mummy's going to make everything all right. Mummy won't let anything hurt you.'

Mummy won't let anything hurt you. Who took this right away from me? she thought.

She waited for endless time, hushing and holding the child in her arms, waited and listened to the moans and the screams and the sounds of people far off. Until at last hands came towards her and lifted her with the child out of the tomb into a dark winter's morning.

An army of black ghosts was wandering across the Main Road towards the ferry.

Dazedly, with Andrew cradled in her arms, Catriona joined them.

There was nowhere else to go. All round her Clydend was burning.

Chapter 29

Across at the other side of the river people were gathering to watch helplessly as Clydend went up in flames, a red ball in a black sky.

When it was realised that their side of the river might soon be an inferno it was decided to get survivors shuttled as far away as possible from the docks and the built-up working-class area, away to the wealthy country districts of Bearsden and Milngavie.

Already, as if the thought had flown around the inhabitants by telepathy, motor cars were rolling in to block the streets by the riverside, queuing nose to tail. Hands gripping steering-wheels, eyes straining to peer through windscreens, their drivers waited impatiently as the Clydend ferry slid towards them, emerging slowly and smoothly from the flames over the black mirror of water. The Clyde was a riot with leaping, glowing reflection as if a red-hot sunrise had exploded across it.

As the ferry drew in and the heavy chains clanked, the drivers contracted stomach muscles, clutched steering-wheels tighter and braced themselves for the hysterical invasion of the hurt and the distraught.

Instead, the ferry brought only a strange immobility and utter silence. The whole thing was uncanny. The people of Clydend stood packed together yet completely alone, every soul suspended in silence behind a vacant mask.

For a minute or two, the watchers fell into the same immobility. Then suddenly movement scattered everything in a flurry and rush.

People squeezed on to the ferry, took the Clydend folk by the arms and led them off in a buzz of activity and strange posh accents.

Somebody put Catriona into the back seat of a car and she sat automatically nursing Andrew in her arms and staring straight ahead. She had never been in a private motor car in her life. She just could not be in one now. It was a fragment of a dream. A dream that she was a part of, though as in all dreams she was watching it from somewhere outside. All she needed to do was to be patient. Sooner or later dreams, even nightmares, came to an end.

The car sped on and by the time hands helped her out darkness was beginning to fade into misty grey light.

Somebody said:

'You're all right now. Don't worry, nothing ever happens here. This is Bearsden!'

The air reeked with burnt porridge.

Another voice:

'The ladies are making breakfast for all of you in the church hall.'

'I want my baby,' Catriona said.

'You've got your baby in your arms, dear. George, I suppose I ought to take the child from her. Under all that dirt he might be injured. Oh, my God!'

A woman's face came nearer. The face was delicately painted and topped by a glossy fur hat. The hat was knocked sideways in the woman's struggle to wrench Andrew away.

Andrew was gone.

People milled about. The porridge smell grew stronger. Faces blurred in a confusion of movement and an excited babble. Expensively dressed women fluttered about near to tears and waving spoons. Voices swooped into a circle of echoes and spun around.

'My baby! My baby!'

'Yes, yes,' somebody gasped with harassment. 'Lots of families have become separated. There's children all over the place. We're trying our best to get everybody organised.'

Over at the other end of the hall she saw Fergus, listening intently to a man who was hunkered down in front of him holding his hands.

She thought she saw Sammy.

'I want my baby!'

'There's lots of places he could be,' a kindlier tone assured her. 'They've taken children to Milngavie as well. Try not to worry. You'll find him.'

She wandered away from the hall and discovered the road outside busy with movement. A stream of cars was shuttling to and from the river. In comparison the pavement was quiet and cool. It glimmered with early morning dew like a carpet of stars. The stars winked at her, here, there, everywhere, minute yet diamond-clear, flashing up in vivid sparkle, disappearing, darting, dazzling.

She had been walking for a minute or two before she became aware of a car slowing alongside her. The driver, a young man with an eager to please face, was asking her if she wanted a lift. She got into the car without saying anything and the young man eyed her uncertainly and asked:

'Are you all right? Are you sure you know what you're doing?'

She knew what she was doing, all right. She was going back for Robert.

It was daylight now and the fires of Clydend had been extinguished. Most of the tenement buildings or parts of buildings were left standing. Some people had returned to, or perhaps had never left, those houses that had escaped serious damage.

Ambulances were trying to manoeuvre through blocked streets. Air-raid wardens and police in steel helmets and men in shirt sleeves and women with dirt-streaked faces were digging in the grey mountains of rubble.

Catriona went to the heap of stones and debris that once had been Number One Dessie Street. Her feet stumbled over it until she was picking her way cautiously on all fours. She stopped at what she thought might be the right part. Maybe under here was some remnant that would prove to her that she was home.

She began lifting stones and chunks of rubble and setting them neatly aside.

She found a red velvet cushion and a pudding spoon, a rubber hot-water bottle and a knitted woollen rabbit.

Important things.

She concentrated on her digging with great care and attention.

But from somewhere a wireless was harassing the air with unnecessary sound.

'. . . we shall not flag nor fail. We shall go on to the end. We shall fight in France, we shall fight on the seas and oceans . . . We shall defend our island whatever the cost may be. We shall fight on the beaches, we shall fight on the landing-grounds, we shall fight in the fields and in the streets, we shall fight in the hills . . . we shall never surrender . . . and even if, which I do not for a moment believe, this island or a large part of it were subjugated or starving, then our Empire beyond the seas . . . would carry on the struggle . . . until in God's good time, the New World, with all its power and might, steps forth to the rescue of the Old . . .

'Let us therefore brace ourselves . . . that if the British Empire and its Commonwealth last for a thousand years, men will say, "This was their finest hour"!

'You ask, what is our aim? I can answer in one word: Victory - victory at all costs, victory in spite of all terror, victory however long and hard the road may be; for without victory, there is no survival . . .'

'Oh, shut up! Shut up!' Catriona said, and went on with her digging. 'A baby might be crying!'

A SORT OF PEACE

The Moving Finger writes; and, having writ,
Moves on: nor all thy Piety nor Wit
Shall lure it back to cancel half a Line,
Nor all thy Tears wash out a Word of it.

The Rubáiyát of Omar Khayyám

Chapter 1

Old Duncan MacNair kept more and more to the tiny bedroom allocated to him. There he crouched inside his second-hand, loose-fitting clothes, his boots toeing the fender, his gnarled hands palming close to the heat of the gas fire. There he chewed his dentures and scratched uncomprehendingly at his beard and filled sticky glasses from bottles he kept hidden in the wardrobe.

He had never recovered from the shock of losing his property. He had owned a general grocery and bakery shop with a bakehouse at the back and above three stories of flats and a couple of attics.

He never tired of rambling on about War Damage Premiums and how he was going to rebuild his shop and bakehouse and carry on business as usual. He was over seventy now and Catriona could not see much hope of it happening.

On her way to work each day she passed the place that had once been her home. Her husband Melvin MacNair, old Duncan's son, had been so proud of that flat above the bakery. She remembered how he strutted like a peacock as he showed her round and told her how his first wife had polished the floors, and the doors and even some of the walls until they shone like glass.

'There's not another house in Clydend or even in the whole of Glasgow that could hold a candle to this,' he often boasted.

She had been sixteen then, much younger than Melvin and as innocent and unsuspecting as an infant. Only the romantic fairy tales she avidly read and her desperation to escape from her mother's house had made her blurt out a rash 'yes' to his sudden proposal of marriage.

Now Melvin was in a prisoner-of-war camp in Germany, and Catriona had capitulated to her mother and moved to her parents' house in Farmbank taking the children and old Duncan with her.

In Farmbank the pale grey uniformity of the houses created their own desolation. It was not very far from Clydend but there the MacNair building had been mellow with age and its tenants and customers spiced with a richness of character that the Farmbank housing scheme lacked.

Travelling to the centre of the city every day she felt magnetised to the right-hand side of the tramcar where she could sit rocking gently to the motion of the tram and gaze out the window, her eyes searching for Dessie Street. The hope never left her that maybe that night three years ago in 1941 had just been a dream. Only in nightmares could things like that happen. Over and over again her mind groped to sort out the facts, like a schoolteacher determined to make a stupid child comprehend . . .

The sirens go. Everyone in the building troops downstairs to the bakehouse lobby. The bakehouse lobby is warm and safe.

They gossip:

'Did you know Slasher Dawson's home on leave?' somebody says. 'A friend of mine in Govan was telling me she saw Slasher sauntering along with a pal when one of these incendiary bombs dropped in front of him. "Sandbags," he bawled, and quick as lightning his pal, a wee bachly fella about half the size of Slasher, streaked into the nearest close and came staggering out with sandbags on his back. With a flourish Slasher flicked a razor from his waistcoat pocket, slashed at the sandbags and emptied sand on top of the bomb. It frized out, no bother, and he strolled away.'

Everybody laughs.

They are sitting arms and legs atangle on the lobby floor. Fergus's mattress and Robert's pram are crushed in the middle.

She says, 'Look at that wee pet. Wide awake and not a whimper.'

She is crouched on the floor lose to the pram with her knees hugged under her chin. Her head is leaning to one side as she gazes at her baby. She begins to sing to him. He stares back at her, wide-eyed with love and delight.

> Wee Willie Winkie
> Runs through the town,

> Upstairs and downstairs
> In his nightgown,
> Tirling at the window,
> Crying at the lock,
> "Are all the weans in their beds,
> For it's now ten o'clock?"'

There is more singing. Broad Glasgow voices. Somebody leads with the shout, 'Everybody together . . .'

'I belong to Glasgow,' they sing.

She goes through to the bakehouse to make tea. It is her turn.

They are belting out another song now. Voices are bouncing and swaggering.

> Just a wee doch and doris,
> Just a wee yin that's a',
> Just a wee doch and doris
> Before ye gang awa' . . .'

She smiles to herself as she sets cups on a tray.

'. . . And if you can say, "It's a braw bricht moonlicht nicht", Yer aw richt, ye ken!'

The song screeches to an end in a hurricane of hilarity.

Despite the noise of the laughter she hears a fast, piercing whistle . . .

Catriona's mind kept stalling with horror at that point. She remembered what happened but the pain of it was to much to bear. Yet she had borne it. She had wept. She had not wept. For long hours she ignored all thought of it. At other times she moaned and nursed herself, and saw Robert's face, eyes beaming adoration up at her, mouth opening in toothless trusting smile.

'I told you so,' her mother kept saying. 'I told you you ought to have let me keep those children safe with me in Farmbank. God works in strange and mysterious ways, Catriona. I told you you'd be punished and someone you loved taken from you. If you had done what I told you, that poor wee lamb would have been alive today!'

Grief sank into secret places. Guilt carved terrible wounds. Now the blue tramcar clanged along the side of the Benlin shipyards, and Catriona's heart raced with hope. Opposite, at the corner of Main Road and Dessie Street, was the MacNair building. Above the shop were her windows with the shiny gold curtains. Inside the glistening promise of the windows had been home, privacy, a place to rest, comfortable chairs, familiar beds, a nice square hall, a kitchen with children's toys strewn about.

Smells from the bakehouse had wafted up the stairs with the warmth, hot spicy gingerbread, juicy meat pie, crispy rolls, crusty new bread smells. They had blended with other aromas from the houses: porridge, chips, bacon, rich Scotch broth, toast burning, milk boiling.

Sounds too: a wireless medley - the jaunty strains of 'Peg o' my heart, I love you'; echoes of Alvar Liddell's polite new announcements, his voice like a tranquil river that nothing can disturb.

The bickering of a husband and wife eddying to and fro in the distance then hastening louder into whirlpools of anger. Little girls playing with happy concentration:

> 'I wouldn't have a lassie-o,
> A lassie-o,
> A lassie-o,
> I wouldn't have a lassie-o,
> I'd rather have a wee laddie,
> Laddie, laddie, laddie . . .'

The shock of seeing the now desolate piece of waste ground instead of the familiar tenement building never lost its impact for Catriona.

Every day the tram jangled to a stop opposite. Every day she stared and stared. Then the tram carried her away. As usual she alighted further on at Govan Cross and took the subway from there because it was quicker; she could get out at St Enoch's station and just cross over to Buchanan Street and Morton's, the shop where she worked.

Buchanan Street was one of the greatest business and shopping thoroughfares in the city and a most popular rendezvous of the wealthy. There were some very old established and expensive shops in Buchanan Street and Morton's was one of the oldest. The war and higher-paid jobs in munitions had led to a shortage of staff but there were still a manageress, two elderly 'alteration hands' and another saleslady called Julie Gemmell.

Julie was nineteen and up in the clouds about going to marry an Air Force officer. There were so many of these rushed wartime affairs now and they reminded Catriona of her own over-hasty although pre-war marriage. The mere thought of Julie's unsuspecting eagerness distressed Catriona. She had agreed to be Julie's matron-of-honour, as married bridesmaids were called, and she looked ahead to the ceremony with nothing but dread.

Only four years separated them in age, yet Catriona felt so much older and sadder. In outward appearance she could have been taken for younger than Julie: despite childbearing she still had a small, boyish underdeveloped body, and her fair hair and timid hazel eyes were on a level with Julie's shoulder.

Julie came from the Gorbals and had a habit of repeating, in a slightly aggressive tone as if she thought you had not heard her the first time, that she was not in the slightest ashamed of the fact. She would toss her glossy hair and make her pageboy roll spring and bob about, and her eyes would acquire a dangerous green sparkle.

'There's nothing wrong with the Gorbals, you know. Plenty of decent, hardworking folk live there.'

Catriona agreed wholeheartedly every time she said it.

Julie's excitement about her romance with Reggie Vincent was embarrassing to watch. Her skin took on a fiery hue as if she ran a temperature when she spoke of him.

'An officer!' In an ecstasy of joy she clapped her hands. 'Fancy me going with an RAF officer, Catriona. And he's so well educated and all that. Did I tell you he's been to the university?'

She had innumerable times before.

'And imagine, just imagine - he comes from Kelvinside!' Julie always laughed then and repeated with a comic roll of the eyes and an exaggerated accent: 'Kailvinsaide! Cain yew jast aimaigine me raisaiding in Kailvinsaide, Caitriona?'

Memory splintered Catriona's eyes with pain.

Kelvinside was away at the north-west end of the city along Great Western Road, its elegant crescents and terraces curving up on either side and giving the road an even wider and more splendid appearance. Great Western Road led to Bearsden, with its sprawl of large villas and gardens and trees and high walls.

399

Catriona had been taken there after the Clydend blitz and been fed burned porridge and soup in the Bearsden town hall. Afterwards, but before her mother came to collect her and hustle her off to Farmbank, she had been given sanctuary in what seemed to be the house of her dreams. Too shocked and dazed, she had not paid much attention at the time. Often since, though, she had remembered the place and been amazed at how it matched her pre-war childish imaginings of the home she would have when she married. Many a time as a young girl curled up in the lumpy bed-settee in Farmbank she had seen that house, felt the comfort of it, the luxurious carpets, the fluffy satin quilts.

She thought of it now. One day she would have another home, she vowed. She would have a home of her own for herself and her children, and it would be like that.

Her husband, Melvin, never came into the picture. She dared not allow his big gorilla body and his bulbous-eyed mustachioed face to harass her mind. Fear had always been the strongest emotion Melvin aroused in her and she had not yet gathered enough courage to confess to him in her letters that the house and business and everything that meant so much to him had gone.

She persuaded herself that it was kinder in his circumstances that he should not know. Surely it must be torment enough for Melvin to be locked up behind barbed wire. He had always been such an active man and so proud of his physical fitness; he never used to miss a day of conscientious practice at his physical jerks, as he called them. That was how she most vividly remembered him, hairy hands gripping wrists, shoulders hunching, muscles rippling and ballooning.

Yet every now and again other memories disturbed her like rumbles of thunder that warned of a coming storm.

The last time he had been home he had come straight from Dunkirk and he had been a strange Melvin, thinner and hollow-eyed and prey to mercurial moods that twisted her fear into panic.

Her thoughts dodged him and other harassments. A protective barricade grew inside her head but its walls were never quite

400

high enough or strong enough and always seemed on the verge of crashing down.

Everyday strain, mostly caused by her mother, heaved at her defences.

Her mother had literally snatched the children away from her and insisted on doing everything for them. At the slightest sign of protest or attempt to have anything to do with the children, her mother would remind Catriona of her sin in causing baby Robert's death. If her father, Robert's namesake, tried to come to her rescue, his wife's tongue would immediately lash him, her face twisted with contempt and bitterness.

'Why are you alive and my baby dead and buried?'

Catriona's angry reply snapped out like a reflex action:

'He wasn't your baby! He was mine!'

'May God in His infinite mercy forgive you!' The retort never varied. 'You ought to be ashamed to admit you're a mother. You're not fit to lay claim to the word. What kind of mother were you? What did you do to a poor, helpless, trusting wee infant?'

And so it went on, leaving Catriona drowning in a secret whirlpool of agony.

The shop gave her some respite and sometimes, chattering and laughing with Julie, she forgot to be unhappy. Then something Julie would say about love or marriage would unexpectedly tug the strings of her hidden pain and she could barely keep up the pretence of girlish normality. She just wanted to cry and turn away.

On the Saturday before Julie's wedding, Julie explained all the arrangements. The ceremony was to be on Monday at 3 o'clock in Blythswood Registrar's Office. They were both being allowed the afternoon off work. It was a quiet time and the manageress assured them that she would be able to manage and the alteration hands could always come forward and serve if necessary. Julie was to have the next day off as well so that she could spend some time with her new husband before he went back.

'We'll both go straight to the Gorbals from the shop,' Julie instructed. 'You remember and bring all you need. We'll have a cup of tea and a sandwich or something, and change and then take a taxi to the Registrar's Office.' Then she did a little dance and gave a strangled, 'Yippee, Reggie, here I come!'

A couple of late shoppers appeared and forced her to stop talking of her plans. They both went to attend to the customers, Catriona shyly, with a timid smile of enquiry, Julie, head tossed high, swooping forward in style, arching pencilled eyebrows.

'Yes, modom?'

Afterwards they said a giggling goodbye at the corner of Argyle Street and St Enoch's Square.

'Reggie's telling his mother tonight and I'm visiting there tomorrow for afternoon tea. Afternoon tea ait Kailvinsaide, no less!'

'I hope everything goes all right. I hope his mother will like you. You know what mothers can be like.'

'Och, I've seen a photo of her. She looks quite a nice wee soul. And don't you worry!' Julie patted her hair and arched her brows and gave a little bouncy wiggle of her hips. 'After I get through with myself tonight she'll think I'm the cat's pyjamas. I'm going to clean and polish myself from top to toe. I've got beer in to give myself a special shampoo and all the old curlers are lined up at the ready. And I've bought a new nail buff. I'm even going to polish my toes.'

She gave a nonchalant demonstration of buffing her fingernails. 'Buffety-buff-buff! I'm telling you, pal, once my future mother-in-law sees me, she won't want to change me for the Queen of England! Don't forget to bring your glad rags to the shop on Monday.'

Julie waved gaily as she swung off and disappeared among the jostling Argyle Street crowds.

Catriona's laughter faded. The hand raised to return Julie's wave drifted down. Uneasiness itched her mind. Talk of Julie and Reggie's wedding made her think of her own marriage again. Somehow it had brought Melvin closer.

She trembled as she turned into St Enoch's Square, as if her husband might be waiting for her.

She must tell him about the air-raid. She did not dare pretend any more.

Chapter 2

'For God's sake, Madge! Have a heart!' Alec Jackson appealed to his wife. 'I could go back off this leave and never be seen again.'

Madge wrestled with the nightdress over her head while he lay in bed boggling at her nakedness. At last her freckled face popped into view and she wriggled the nightdress down over milky body and brown nipples and curly pubic hair.

'I couldn't be that lucky. Not me! Oh, no, you'll come f—ing back all right.'

'Madge!'

He could not get accustomed to Madge using the swear word. On the ship it was used all the time and he never gave it a thought, but to hear it coarsen his wife's mouth shocked him deeply.

Not that Madge had ever been an angel. She could bloody and bugger occasionally and she was never above a bit of violence either. Many a female acquaintance of his had been chased off by a battling Madge, dishing out squashed noses and black eyes. He had been at the receiving end of Madge's fist himself and although his mates back on the ship thought it a howl of a yarn when he told it to them, in actual fact it was no joke. Madge had nearly knocked his teeth out.

Still, she had always remained attractive with it. Big, high-hipped, melon-breasted Madge with her long, lean legs, her toothy grin and candid stare.

Only now was he beginning to notice the change in her. She had lost the naivety that he had once found so attractive. Sometimes there was a hard twist to her mouth and her eyes could change to ice chips. Perhaps the change was more noticeable because he had not seen her very often these past few years, what with Dunkirk and one or two other places. Join the Navy and see the world, they said. After this lot was over they could keep

403

the world. Give him Glasgow any day and his wee house in Springburn and Madge and the weans.

There could be no escaping the fact, though, she was definitely not the same easy-going big-hearted girl she used to be.

Take sex, for instance. She had never denied him before and certainly never quarrelled as she was doing now about him not having a French Letter.

'The queue was about a mile long, hen,' he tried to explain. 'I would have missed my train if I'd waited.'

'You're not bothered about what I might miss. You've never bothered. I've had six weans and I would have had more by now if the bloody Royal Navy hadn't hauled you off.'

'Och, you wouldn't be without one of the weans.'

He made the mistake of sounding too sure of himself, even quite jocular. Her bonfire of anger immediately flared up again.

'No!' she bawled. 'But I'll make f—ing sure I'll be without any more!'

'I wish you wouldn't use that cuss word, hen.' He felt genuinely harrowed. He had always been pretty good-natured himself and he certainly had never laid down the law to Madge before. Anything for a peaceful life and a bit of loving, that was his motto.

This was so unlike her. Granted, she had never been quite the same since she found out about his wee bit of nonsense a few years back with her friend Catriona MacNair. Later on too she went a bit wild when she discovered he had made a date to go to the pictures with an old customer of his, Ruth Hunter, who was lodging with Catriona at the time.

It had only happened once with Catriona and it had meant nothing. Surely Madge had forgiven and forgotten that long ago? She was still friendly with Catriona, as far as he knew.

As for Ruth Hunter, he had never as much as touched the girl, worse luck. If he had told Madge once, he had told her a thousand times. Ruth and he had barely seated themselves that night when the cinema was bombed. The whole place had caved in and he had never set eyes on the poor cow again. Alec had been lucky to get out alive. He was about the only one who did.

'Shocks you, does it?' Madge flung back her head and roared

with laughter, hands on hips, legs apart, the clinging blue of her nightdress straining.

'I don't like to hear it from you, hen.'

She climbed into bed over the top of him like a St Bernard dog with backside high up and knees digging down. He let out a howl as one knee almost ground into his crotch.

'For God's sake, Madge! You nearly denied yourself a lifetime of pleasure.'

'You'll have been getting your pleasure, all right.' She flapped the blankets energetically and the hot sweet smell of her talcum powder puffed up his nostrils. 'Sailors are supposed to have a girl in every port but, if I know you, it'll have been every girl in every port.'

So that was it! Poor old Madge was terrified he had not enough to go round, and of course before this leave she had been deprived of it for a long, long time.

He struggled to encircle her with his arm.

'Anyone would think, to hear you, that I had been away on a pleasure tour. Listen, hen, I've been concentrating on one thing and one thing alone - keeping alive. That's the God's truth. I'm telling you, Madge, half the time I'm scared rigid. I keep wishing I was a wee fella, about four feet nothing.'

She giggled, and taking advantage of her good humour he slipped his hand between her legs, hitching her nightdress up with stealthy fingers.

'Why four feet?' she wanted to know.

'I'm a hell of a target at six feet, that's why, and not only for Jerry planes and guns. It's our own mob as well.'

'Eh? Our own guys try and shoot you?'

Surprise slackened her, and he is in there with his hand right away, caressing the moistness of her, making her quiver and arch and make little absent-minded moans of protest.

'It's officers,' he murmured in answer to her question, at the same time wriggling his other arm free to manoeuvre her nightdress up above her breasts. They hung to one side, tender-looking with delicate blue veins and coffee-coloured nipples beginning to harden. He tickled them with his tongue in between each word and felt them twitch as if his tongue were electrified.

'When they look for volunteers everybody tries to merge into the background and disappear. I can't. I try, but I stick out like your lovely wee titties!'

'Get off!'

Her words held no conviction. Already she was enjoying herself too much and it made his pleasure twice as keen. His mouth searched with increasing urgency, moving down from her breasts to her abdomen until he was burrowing between her legs, his tongue sword-sharp with passion.

She began to moan and squeal with such abandon he was afraid she might waken the weans and they would come through from the next room.

He did not stop what he was doing but he whispered hoarsely, 'Shush, hen, shush!'

But it only made her cry out all the louder:

'Oh, God, Alec, I love you!'

Afterwards, when they were lying quiet and exhausted, she gave a big shuddering sigh and announced:

'I hate you, you rotten big midden!'

He laughed as he reached for a cigarette.

'You hate me to stop, you mean!'

'You don't care a damn about me.'

'Madge, you're my wife. There's nobody to beat you in the whole world, hen.'

'And you've tried them all.'

'Och, now, Madge . . .'

'It was bad enough trying to keep track of you when you were an insurance man and just going around Springburn. Now you're gallivanting all over the globe. God knows where you've been and who you've been with.'

'Madge, I keep telling you . . .'

'I know what you keep telling me. You were telling me the same thing when you were sniffing around Catriona MacNair and Ruth Hunter.'

'I'll swear on the Bible if you like - I never touched Ruth Hunter. As for Catriona, you know what she's like. She asked for it.'

'Asked for it? Don't give me that. She was just a wee lassie.

You laid her before she knew what was happening. And her man away in the Army as well. You're lower than a worm, Alec.'

'Look, hen, it meant nothing to me, absolutely nothing.'

'It meant a lot to her though.'

'What? You must be kidding. She's a nut-case. She couldn't love a man if she tried.'

'She can have a bloody wean without trying.'

'All right! All right! So she had a wean. So I said I was sorry. I've been apologising about that for years. Are you never going to forgive and forget?'

'The wean was killed. In the same raid that killed our mother.'

He puffed at his cigarette in silence for a minute.

'I know. Poor wee bastard. She'll have got over it by now, though.'

'That shows how much you understand.' Her voice cracked with bitterness. 'You think you know all about women, Alec, but the truth is you're such a randy bugger you never see past their arses.

He shook his head uncomprehendingly.

'Anybody would think she was your wee sister, the way you go on.'

'It's not her. It's you. And me. You've probably given me a wean.' Her voice turned into itself, became incredulous, as if she could not believe what she was saying. 'Another wean would make seven. Seven! You come here, have your way with me, then you buzz off to enjoy yourself somewhere else. You don t care about how I'm going to manage or how I feel.'

He began to get rattled.

'Look, hen, will you get this daft idea out of your head once and for all? This bloody war isn't a picnic organised specially for my benefit that I can get around and keep supplied with girls. If I thought I'd get away with it, I wouldn't go back. There's nothing I'd like better than to stay right here with you, believe me. You should see the build-up of men and hardware down south. My God, hen, there's going to be a hell of a fight any day now. And I've a horrible sinking feeling they're going to shove me in first!'

She started to laugh, quietly, gently, then louder and louder until she was seesawing between hysterical hilarity and moaning tears.

'Women!' he groaned to himself, but he pulled her into his arms and nursed her like one of his children.

'Shush, hen, shush. It'll be all over one of these days and we'll be able to get back to normal.'

'I used to trust you, Alec. I really trusted you. You always said it wasn't your fault, it was just that the women wouldn't leave you alone. And I believed you.'

'Well, it was true.'

'You were always fighting them off, you said. You didn't want anybody else except me, you said.'

'Neither I do. Madge!' He cuddled her closer. 'I'm just counting the days to when I can come back here to you for good. That's the God's truth, so help me!'

She snuffled and wiped her nose on her nightie.

'I miss Ma as well. She was a good soul, your Ma, and a great help with the weans and the book. God, I get tired at times, Alec. I just had to give up the book. Climbing up and down all them stairs collecting every day fair beat me. I don't know how you used to do it and keep so cheery all the time.'

'Don't worry about the book, hen. It couldn't be helped. I'll get fixed up with something when I get out, either with the Co-op or the Prudential.'

'I put most of the money straight into the Post Office. I had to dip into a few pounds. The weans were needing so many things and it's not easy with me not working and sometimes I've to pay extra for things on the black market.'

'We'll manage all right.'

'As long as I've got you, Alec. I'll murder you if you leave me with all them weans.'

'Don't worry.'

'I wouldn't need to worry if you didn't give me anything to worry about. How would you like it if I got off with one of them Yanks?'

He laughed, secure in the knowledge that Madge would never look at another man.

'Which kind? A gum-chewing skinny one with steel-rimmed

glasses and cropped hair or a gum-chewing hefty fella with tight trousers and a big bum.'

She tried not to laugh.

'They get the girls all right. You should see the gum-chewing girls hanging on to their arms and all the kids running after them shouting, "Any gum, chum?"'

He had seen the girls. Tarts mostly, with pencilled eyebrows and maroon mouths and hair curling on square-shouldered coats or tucked into ropey hair-nets called snoods. Gripping shoulder-bags, they bounced along on streaky orange-painted legs and dumpy shoes.

He was reminded of an experience with a right hairy he had met up with in Pompey. They had been getting along all right until she disappeared into another room, reappeared carrying a whip that looked like something out of *Mutiny on the Bounty*, and invited him to have a go.

'Our boys hate them,' Madge went on.

'The girls?'

She dug an elbow into him with such force he yelped in protest.

'The Yanks, stupid! Because they get all the girls.'

'And the Poles, and God knows who else I bet! When I was crushing through the crowds at Central Station I could hardly hear a Glasgow tongue. I'm not surprised our lads are peeved. Outnumbered in their own backyard. Wait until after the war, though. Our turn's coming.'

'Not your turn.' Madge's voice hardened. 'You've had your turn.'

'For God's sake! When I said that, I didn't mean . . .'

'You never mean anything you say. I found that out years ago.'

'You're not going to start that all over again.'

'I never started anything. I never let you down. I never told you lies. I never slept with your friends.'

He groaned and turned over and tried to escape in sleep. Madge twisted away too, leaving a cold tunnel of air between them.

Depression suddenly knocked the props from under him. For

the first time in their married life Alec felt Madge had failed him, somehow let him down. All she seemed to think about was herself. All he had heard since he had arrived home was one petty grievance after another. He hadn't been kidding either when he said this might be his last leave. The whole of the Allied armies, navies and air forces seemed to be massing down south. He was beginning to think the only thing that prevented the British Isles from sinking under the weight of it all was the barrage balloons, important and aloof in the sea like fat cigars.

He felt sick at the thought of repeating the experience of his last visit to the French coast. His number had nearly come up then, not to mention a few times elsewhere. It seemed really tempting providence to have another go.

At the same time, like everybody else, he felt sure that it would be the other chaps that would cop it, not him.

His good spirits surged up as quickly as they had sagged. He rolled over and cuddled into his wife's back. She remained stiff and cold and unresponsive. He slipped his hand between her legs and tickled her. Then, straining his head up, he whispered close against her ear in broad Glasgow accent:

'Hullo, therr!!'

Chapter 3

At last Catriona wrote the letter:

'My dear Melvin,

I've been so worried about whether or not I should tell you all that has happened. I know you must have suffered terribly in all the fighting and then to be captured and held prisoner.

It was only because I couldn't bear to think of you suffering any more that I put off telling you until now. But the war won't last for ever and I'm beginning to worry about the shock you would get if you arrived back in Glasgow not knowing.

Melvin, my dear, there have been air-raids here and our place was hit. I told you that wee Robert had died. What I didn't tell you was that he was killed. He and most of the others in the building were killed when Dessie Street was destroyed by bombs.

Your lovely flat has gone, Melvin. And the shop. But I've managed to salvage a few bits and pieces and some of the machinery from the bakehouse is still all right and in storage.

Please try not to get too upset, dear. Da is very keen to buy another business and as soon as this terrible war is over and you are home again we'll be able to start afresh.

We'll get another house too, don't worry. Pass the time just now planning how nice you'll make it and all the nice new things you'll have.

You'll understand now why I'm staying with my mother and father at present. Da is here too, and of course Fergus and Andrew.

Fergus and Andrew are doing well at Farmbank School. Andrew is still in the "baby class" but Fergus has only about another year to go before he sits his qualifying exam and moves to secondary school.

They send you their love. I'm sure you'd be very proud of

411

them if you saw them setting off to school together each morning. They look so smart in their blazers and caps and white shirts and school ties and both with their school bags on their backs. Andrew is still quite plump and small but Fergus is fairly shooting up. I think he's going to be very tall. He's as thin as ever but very energetic. Andrew has plenty of energy as well and they both love football. I'm afraid when they arrive home each day they don't look smart. Their caps and ties are askew. Their socks are hanging over their shoes. Their shoe-laces are trailing loose behind them. And you should see the filthy state of their faces, their shirts and their knees. Sometimes I get awful angry and rage at them. But then my mother rages at me. I'm afraid she tends to spoil them.

I don't mind telling you, Melvin, I'll be glad when we get another house. Things haven't been too easy for me either. But I mustn't complain. You're worse off than me - away in a strange land and a prisoner. At least I'm getting on fine at my job and saving my wages as hard as I can so we'll be all right for money. I didn't even buy anything new for Julie's wedding.

Julie is the girl I work with. She lives in the Gorbals and is getting married on Monday to an RAF officer from Kelvinside. I'm to be matron-of-honour.

I'd better sign off now, Melvin, as I promised mummy I'd scrub the bathroom and kitchenette floors. It's about the only thing she'll allow me to do. I mean, she insists on doing everything for the children, even washes and irons their clothes in case I don't do it right.

I get so annoyed with her at times, but it doesn't matter what I say, she talks me down and goes on doing exactly what she wants to. Honestly, Melvin, I do try. The other night she decided to take the boys with her to visit a friend. She'd had them out with her the night before as well and I had visions of them becoming so tired they'd be falling asleep at school the next day.

I said they weren't to go, but of course they wanted to go. They love their gran because she lets them stay up late and spends all her sweets coupons on them. My father's about as bad. He gives them bags of chips in bed and tells them ghost stories and then they're up half the night - Fergus with nightmares

412

and Andrew with indigestion.

But as I was telling you, the other night Mummy was taking them out again and when she refused to listen to me I tried to physically restrain her from taking them out of the house. I mean I actually got a hold of the boys and started pulling them back into the sitting-room, but what with them struggling and my mother punching at me I had to let go before I was half-way along the lobby.

I really don't know what can be done with somebody like my mother. I've never known of anyone with such a strong personality. And yet sometimes I wonder about her strength. She seems to need people so much, it's almost as if she's afraid to be on her own. Maybe all that iron determination hides a very lonely and unhappy person underneath. Anyway she's happy just now with the children here. But I was wondering, Melvin, if I shouldn't be looking around for a wee temporary place. I'd have enough for a deposit and of course I'd keep working and what Da would pay me for his food and board would help.

I don't want to hurt my mother and I feel guilty about leaving her but at the same time I don't know if I can stand it much longer here.

For one thing, there really isn't room. As you know there's just one small bedroom and your da has that. Remember the sitting-room and the bed-settee where I used to sleep before I was married - well, Mummy and Daddy have that now and the boys have a mattress on the floor beside it. I'm on the sofa in the living-room, jammed up against that big old-fashioned table and wooden chairs. I used to think sleeping on that lumpy settee in the sitting-room was bad enough but at least it made down into a bed. This horsehair sofa is too short even for me and so narrow I'm afraid to turn in case I fall off during the night. Mummy rams the chairs and the table up against it to stop me falling out.

Talk about being in a prison. Every night I'm jammed in there and peering out through the bars of the chairs watching Mummy striding about as happy as a lark, getting the boys' clothes and everything organised for the morning.

Sometimes she sets the table for breakfast and one night the

413

breadknife was lying on the table within my reach and, Melvin, I know this is wicked, and I pray that God will forgive me, but a terrible feeling came over me.

I was lying there very quiet and still, just watching Mummy striding about and singing to herself and folding the boys' clothes, and suddenly this terrible feeling came over me. I wanted to grab that breadknife and plunge it into my mother again and again. Just for a minute the temptation was almost overwhelming. I was frightened at myself, Melvin.

It made me remember poor Sarah that time in Dessie Street when she stabbed her mother-in-law to death. Maybe that was what she felt. I'm frightened in case that feeling comes over me again. I think I'd better look around and try to find some wee place. We can get a bigger, better house after you come home.

I said ages ago that I'd better sign off and here I am pages later, still writing. I seem to have got quite carried away. It's just that it's so frustrating living at Farmbank like this and there's no one I feel can talk to about it

Poor Madge has troubles enough of her own with all that crowd of children in a wee room and kitchen in Springburn. They haven't even an inside toilet.

My friend, Julie - that's the girl I told you about, the one I work with who's getting married on Monday - she's so happy at the prospect of her marriage to her marvellous Reggie she's blissfully unaware of anything or anybody else.

I hope everything goes well for her. I wouldn't like to see her get hurt. I don't know why, but I worry about Julie a lot. I try to feel happy for her but instead I just feel sad. I can't help it. I wish I wasn't going to the wedding.

Honestly, I'm dreading Monday. I know it sounds stupid but even the thought of it depresses me.

Now I feel guilty as well at writing all this to you and making it such a morbid letter.

But of course it couldn't be a cheerful one when its purpose was to tell you about the air-raid.

I know how you'll feel, Melvin, and I'm so very sorry about the house and everything but it wasn't my fault. There was nothing I could do.

Just try to think about the lovely new house you'll have and all the nice things you'll put in it and I'll keep everything all beautifully clean and polished just the way you like it, I promise.

You've always been a strong man, Melvin, and I know you'll be able to weather this bad news and get over it and start planning for the future like I've said.

If your Da can do it - you can do it.

Please try not to worry. Everything will work out all right.'

She signed the letter, folded it, put it in an envelope and carefully printed the address.

The house was quiet and empty. Her father was out at the pub. Her mother had taken the boys to the pictures.

Catriona gazed bleakly around at the outsize furniture, dark relics of the Victorian age which had once belonged to her grandparents.

Melvin had often said that it was a disgrace, the way it had been ruined. The table was scratched and burned and ring-marks overlapped in a maze of patterns.

A handle was missing from one of the sideboard doors and it kept squeaking open to reveal a higgledy-piggledy assortment of cups and saucers and plates, a sticky jar of jam, a piece of margarine on a saucer, a jug of milk and a bowl of sugar.

A bulge of damp dross in the grate occasionally spat out bluish flames or puffed black smoke.

The house in Dessie Street had been warm because of the bakehouse underneath.

Catriona crossed her arms on top of the letter and made a nest for her head. There had been times when she had hated the house in Dessie Street because of the way Melvin made a god of it and bullied her into endless scrubbing and polishing.

Yet she wished she could go there now. She longed to go home, to shut the door behind her, to wheel Robert's pram into the warm kitchen.

'Where's my wee boy?' she always used to say before she lifted him out and dandled him on her knee and took off his blue knitted bonnet and coat. He always smiled hugely, his eyes melting up at her with adoration. She saw him now in the crook

415

of her arm and nursed herself with tense-faced, monotonous anguish.

Chapter 4

Gorbals! The name exploded in his mother's face like one of the ten thousand pounders Reggie's bomb-aimer dropped from his Lancaster over Berlin.

'Oh, no!' Muriel Vincent allowed her husband Norman to coax her into a chair. 'I don't believe it.'

'I'm sure if we discuss the matter in a . . .'

'Oh, be quiet.' She snipped Norman off, then softened round to her son who seemed far too young to be sporting a thick handlebar moustache: 'Reggie, tell me it's not true.' Her voice changed again. 'It's one of those silly university pranks, isn't it?'

Reggie retreated behind a bravado of laughter.

'Good Lord, the "Varsity"? I was just a kid then.'

'You're only twenty now.'

'Twenty-one actually, mother.'

'Only a boy.'

She remembered him as a skinny child, trotting jerkily beside her towards his first day at Kelvinside Academy. She remembered his hand twisting in her loving grip. He always had a tantalisingly elusive quality. Something of him kept evading her no matter how she kissed or cuddled. Not that she had been a possessive mother. She was sure she had not. He had led a normal happy life with lots of friends of both sexes. No one could accuse her of trying to keep Reggie to herself, of being selfish, or of not wanting him to get married. Her whole life had been devoted to seeing that he got the best of everything. She had always sacrificed herself for Reggie and she had been delighted when he had shown obvious interest in Sandra Brodie, whose father was one of the partners in the well-known firm of Glasgow solicitors, Ford, Brodie and MacAllister.

The Brodies had a detached villa in Bearsden.

Only a few weeks ago she had been enjoying afternoon tea in

417

Mrs Brodie's elegant lounge and weaving with Mrs Brodie delightful plans for Reggie and Sandra's wedding. Over teacups and sighs they pictured Reggie, tall and dashing in his RAF officer's uniform, and Sandra, beautiful and superior-looking in Brussels lace and sweeping train.

Definitely a superior type of girl, Sandra, and so perfect for Reggie. Such a good background. Bearsden, of course, was *the* district, and Sandra had gone to the private school in Bearsden and graduated from there to another fee-paying school off Great Western Road, then on to teachers' training college.

Mr Vincent edged his pipe to one side of his mouth to allow his words to escape from the other.

'I must admit this has come as rather a shock to me too, son. The Brodies. Solid people.'

'I know, Father. It's just one of these things!'

'Just one of these things?' Muriel cried out. 'How can you sound so casual about ruining your whole life?'

'Oh, come now, Mother. How do you know my life is going to be ruined? You don't know anything about Julie. You haven't even met her yet.'

Muriel thought of the book which she had innocently acquired at the local lending library not so long ago. The picture it vividly painted of the Gorbals had left an imprint of horror in her mind.

In sordid, stinking rabbit-warrens of tenements, people who were worse than animals urinated in kitchen sinks, got raging drunk on 'Red Biddy' and sprawled in their own vomit. Gorbals women had been depicted as completely immoral and the men apparently roamed the streets in gangs and fought each other with razors. No doubt the inhabitants would not all be like that, but still . . .

'The Gorbals!' She shuddered. 'Of all places!'

Reggie flushed.

'I thought . . . I was hoping . . . Oh, come on, Mother, be a sport, let her come and stay here.'

'Here? In Botanic Crescent?' She refused to believe he could be serious. She patted her finger-waved hair that curled in a spaghetti roll against her pearl earrings. 'And her unemployed father as well, I suppose. I can just imagine him popping into

418

your father's bank and asking for a loan!'

'Holding it up, more like,' her husband guffawed between comforting sucks of smoke.

'What do you think you're laughing at?' She turned on him, her eyes shocked. 'How dare you make a joke of this. How dare you! If you had any backbone you'd do something!'

'Muriel, my dear, what can I do? Under Scottish law Reggie has been free to marry without parental consent since he was sixteen.'

'Trust you to talk about the law and remind me of Ford, Brodie and MacAllister's. Reggie might have had a partnership. The Brodie money could have been his too, one day. And the villa in Bearsden.'

She began to cry, her sobs rushing away with her while she struggled to catch them and subdue them in her lace-edged handkerchief so that the neighbours would not hear.

She could visualise the peaceful crescent outside, with its elegant sweep of terrace houses, in one of which her mother and her father, the Reverend John Reid, still lived. At this end stood the mellow red-sandstone tenement which Norman and she had occupied since their marriage. Norman could not afford one of the terrace-type houses. They were very large, of course. The flats, although spacious, meant much less work and no one could criticise a close like theirs with its tiled walls and Sunday hush every day of the week and each landing church-like with its stained-glass window, ruby red and royal blue.

They were just in the crescent and no more. Botanic Crescent looped up off a green houseless part of Kelvin Drive.

Not that there was anything wrong with Kelvin Drive or any of the other Drives or Roads or Gardens in the district. Few districts could compare with Kelvinside for sheer beauty and convenience. After all, they were only ten minutes away from the centre of the city.

But here in this quiet little crescent, so near to the busy Great Western Road, yet separated from it by the Royal Botanical Gardens, the River Kelvin and - immediately across the road - the loop of green grass and trees of the crescent, they were in a secret little backwater, a private place of their own. Here Muriel

Vincent had been born and brought up. Here she had taken her doll for its daily outing, crossed the road, swept through the gate, bumped the pram down the steep steps to the Kelvin, paraded with dignity along the banks, stopped occasionally to tidy the pram covers, then returned via the other steps that emerged at the tenement end of the crescent where she now lived.

She belonged here, cushioned with beauty and the sighs of trees and the serenading of birds and the sleepy humming of insects.

The idea of coarse, loud-mouthed people - because she was sure the girl's father would not be her only relation - invading this peace appalled her.

What would the neighbours think?

Her weeping loudened brokenheartedly.

'Mother!'

'Muriel, my dear!'

She clutched at Reggie's hands and clung to them, squeezing them tightly against her cheeks and mouth, cupping the smell of her perfume in his palms.

'I can't sleep at nights.' Her eyes widened up at him as she strained to discern his face through her tears.

'All the time you're away, Reggie, I'm sick with fear. Nobody knows but your father. I keep a brave face for outside. I tell them I'm glad you're doing your bit for your country. I tell them I'm proud and I am proud, Reggie. Even though I'm ill with fear at the thought of you flying that bomber. Every night I've gone with you to Germany. Every night I've lain awake watching those German searchlights trying to find you in the sky so that their guns can shoot you down.'

'Mother!'

'I have. Oh, yes, I have, Reggie. And I've prayed and prayed and you've always come back safe and I've been grateful. I've always thought one day it's going to be all over and everything's going to be all right and you'll be settled with a nice girl and have a happy life. It's the only thing that's kept me sane.'

'You mean the whole world to Mother, Reggie, and she's never let you down. She's worked hard to do her bit for chaps

420

like you when they happen to be in Glasgow. She slaves in that church canteen every spare minute she can.'

'I know, Father.'

'And I've always kept a brave face for you, Reggie. Have I ever made a fuss like this before when you've come home on leave?'

'No, of course not, Mother.'

She struggled to find courage now. She released her hold of his hands.

'All I've ever wanted was for you to be happy and to get the best out of life.'

'I know.' His voice was weakening with misery until his father suddenly announced:

'I'll go and make a cup of tea.'

Immediately Reggie brightened with gratitude.

'Righteo, Father.'

'Oh, yes, you do that!' Muriel called bitterly after Norman's retreating figure.

Then in the trap of silence that sprang between them, she wondered how she could reach her son.

Impossible to fathom the Reggie she knew in the setting of the Gorbals. Impossible that Reggie should have anything to do with a product of such a place.

Kelvinside and the Gorbals, although both districts of Glasgow and their inhabitants all Glaswegians, were surely poles apart. She was reminded of the quotation, 'East is east and west is west and never the twain shall meet.'

'Wait until you see her, Mother. She's A1. Absolutely splendid.'

'You used to say Sandra was splendid, a really nice girl.'

'So she is.'

'You've known Sandra for years and she adores you.'

'Mother, I'm going to marry Julie before I go back on "Opps". I was hoping you'd understand.'

'Don't talk about going back,' she wailed. 'You've only just arrived.'

'There's something big building up, Mother. I think it's the invasion. We're been giving Jerry hell these past few months. I think it's to soften him up before our troops move across the Channel.'

Dabbing at her tears, she shook her head.

'Poor Mr Churchill, he has so much to worry him. I'm beginning to feel that I've more than enough to cope with myself.'

'It's because of this, you see. I mean because of me having to go back not knowing when I'll get leave again that . . .'

'I still maintain it's not like you at all,' she interrupted. 'Mrs Brodie said that you told Sandra you didn't think rushed wartime marriages in registry offices were fair to a girl.'

'I still don't, actually. Anything could happen to a chap and that's a pretty bad show for the girl he leaves behind.'

'Oh.' She gave a mirthless laugh. 'I suppose the RAF pay good allowances.'

'Yes, that's what Julie says.'

'Oh, Reggie, Reggie!'

'No, no! She didn't mean it like that! We want to start saving for a house of our own, you see.'

'Why isn't she here tonight? Why isn't she telling me it's not like that?'

'Steady on! This was my idea.'

'You don't want to rush into marriage, Reggie.'

'The way things are, I believe it might have been better to wait. But I'm crazy about Julie and . . .' He flashed her an unexpected grin. 'You know how determined women can be. You're quite a strong-minded gal yourself.'

'Are you going along to see Nanna and Pappa?'

'Yes, of course.'

Just then Norman rattled the tea-trolley into the sunlit high-ceilinged room. He brought it to a halt in front of the chair near the window where she was sitting. The peach china edged with gold took on an extra lustre and became pearlised in the sun.

She noticed with a ripple of irritation that he had cut the home-made fruit loaf too thick. Anyone would think he had never heard of rationing. Not that she grudged Reggie anything. If the loaf had been cut in small pieces he could have taken two. It was just not the done thing to serve large thick slices.

In Bearsden, Mrs Brodie offered her guests the tiniest of sandwiches and pinky-fingers of cake, exactly one of each for each person.

Tucking her handkerchief into the pocket of her dress she proceeded to pour tea from the silver tea-pot. Next to Reggie, the tea-pot was her pride and joy. She would match her silver tea-service with any in Bearsden. The shapely tea-pot and sugar bowl and cream jug were family heirlooms handed down from generation to generation.

'The napkins, Norman.' She spoke in the quiet, gentle monotone of the long-suffering. 'And the hot water.'

Reggie half rose from his seat.

'I don't want anything to eat, Mother.'

She passed him a cup of tea and a plate with a look of reproach and he sunk back down with the weight of it.

'I wouldn't say anything to Nanna and Pappa about all this, Reggie. Not tonight at least. Let them enjoy your visit for a few hours, all right?'

'I'm not ashamed of Julie. She's a wonderful girl. I'll be proud to have her for my wife.'

His father patted his pockets as if to make sure his tobacco was still there.

'It may very well be that she is a nice girl, in her own way. The point is you were already committed, my lad.'

'No, I wasn't, Father. The truth is . . .'

'Norman!' Muriel interrupted. 'The hot water.'

Her eyes jabbed daggers into his before smoothing back to Reggie again.

'Nanna and Pappa will be so glad to see you. They barely caught a glimpse of you the last time you were here. I knew no good would come of you going to that dance-hall in town. I suppose that's where you met her. I know you wanted to show that English RAF friend you had with you around and give him a good time while he was here, but what was wrong with the Bearsden Town Hall? Or your own church, or local tennis club dances? You always enjoyed them before.'

'Everything's different now, Mother. The war has mixed us all up.'

'Well, it's high time everybody was unmixed and back to normal.'

423

'I doubt if anybody will ever be the same again.'

He finished his tea and dabbed at his mouth with his napkin, taking care not to spoil the silky twirl of his moustache.

She watched him, marvelling at his debonair good looks and at the same time cringing inside with a sore heart.

Despite Reggie's tall sinewy body, he would always be to her the same evasive, vulnerable little boy.

She still remembered the time years ago before the war when she had been whipped away to hospital to have her appendix removed. A tiny startled Reggie had not even kissed her goodbye. Yet he had rapidly developed a dangerously high temperature and such alarming symptoms that he had very soon to be taken to the hospital himself.

It eventually occurred to one of the hospital doctors what the cause of the child's unidentifiable illness might be. By this time her operation was over and she was enjoying the luxury of her private flower-filled room and the chocolates and fruit everyone had brought her.

Norman had decided it was better not to tell her about Reggie. She had never forgiven him for that. Afterwards, she raged at him with quiet persistence to make certain he never made such a stupid mistake again. Her little boy might have died while she was lying there idly flipping through magazines and eating chocolates. Her son had needed her, but it took a young doctor, a man with more perception than Norman, to realise this. He brought Reggie into the private room so that he could be reassured that his mother was all right.

Then he was all right. It was the first time she realised what a passionate child he was and she looked ahead with fear to the time when he might be at another woman's mercy. A cruel, ignorant or insensitive girl could use Reggie's vulnerability to suit her own purpose and make his life a misery.

In two days he would be marrying Julie Gemmell from Gorbals Cross. Tomorrow afternoon he was bringing her to meet them for the first time. At best the girl would probably sit dumb and allow Reggie to do all the talking. The atmosphere would be polite and restrained and in no time at all they would make excuses and leave. Panic began to grow and swish inside

424

her like brooms.

Reggie was on the verge of ruining his life. He did not know anything about Julie Gemmell. How could he? There was not enough time for any of them to find out anything.

If only she could talk to the girl on her own, plead with her, if necessary. Then it suddenly occurred to her that she could. All she needed to do was to take a subway train from Byres Road to Bridge Street. She had sat many times in the subway on her way to the centre of the city, staring idly at the map above the windows opposite, so she was familiar with the route. Across the map snaked the blue River Clyde and the underground railway formed a circle that crossed, or, rather, went underneath the river at two places.

She eyed Reggie and Norman, calculating what their reaction would be to her plan of 'bearding the lion in its den' - so to speak.

Their immediate horror, she felt sure, would swamp her intentions and prevent her from moving an inch from her chair. Both her husband and son tended to be over-protective. They had always underestimated her, she felt sure.

She decided that it would, at this stage, be simpler and safer not to discuss the matter with them.

Rising, she gathered the dirty teacups on to the trolley. Norman rose too.

'I'll see to that, my dear.'

'No. You go along with Reggie, Norman. I'll follow later.'

'I insist you go and powder that pretty little nose of yours.'

'Norman,' she said evenly. 'I have other things to do. I want to follow on later.'

'Oh. Oh, very well, my dear. Ready then, son?'

She wheeled the trolley out without daring to look at either of them. Already she was protesting to herself with apprehension.

She heard the front door close and hurried back to peer out of the sitting-room window.

Anyone could see they were father and son. They were both tall, and lean, and fair, and they both had the same crooked smile, but Norman stooped as if his head kept tugging his shoulders forward. His step had slowed and he had lost most of his hair.

Her anxious eyes strained to follow the two men all along the crescent until they disappeared inside one of the terrace houses at the other end. Then she retreated into the bedroom to change into her dusty pink suit and hat and to arrange her fur tippet, a present from her parents, high around her throat. Then she tucked her handbag under her arm and smoothed up the fingers of her gloves.

She decided to cut through the Botanic Gardens. That way was most pleasant and she would not be seen from her mother's house.

The iron gate creaked open and she carefully descended the steep steps to the river bank and the bridge. On the bridge she stopped for a minute to gaze at brown water bulging slowly and the green mountains of trees on either side, gently swinging and bouncing and dipping down.

She would have liked to stay there enjoying the peace for a few minutes more and then go to join Reggie and Norman at her mother's house. She would have been welcomed into her mother's spacious hall by Jessie, her mother's servant, who would have taken her fur. Jessie had worked for her mother for as far back as she could remember. Over the years she had become silver-haired, rather deaf, and a bit of a hypochondriac, but she could still do a decent day's cleaning and fortunately her age saved her from being called away to the forces or munitions. She just continued serving the family and cleaning the house and trying to ignore the war as if it had never happened.

If only it had never happened. Still, it was really too bad of Reggie. One could not blame everything on the war. He should have had more sense.

She turned away in exasperation and distress, her heels clipping on the bridge, then up the steps at the other side and through the main part of the Botanic Gardens. She emerged from the Queen Margaret Drive entrance, at the corner of Great Western Road.

Great Western Road was busy with traffic. This part especially tended to be difficult to cross because of the intersection of Queen Margaret Drive and Byres Road opposite.

Her fingers tightened round her handbag as she waited until

the traffic cleared and she could walk across and make her way down Byres Road. She moved purposefully enough, yet she had a fragile quality that stirred men to help her on to buses and immediately to rise and offer her their seats. Even the colour of her and the texture of her clothes had a delicate perfection.

'Bridge Street, please,' she asked at the subway ticket counter. 'Thank you.'

A wind sucked up from the subway with an earthy smell. It flurried the fur round her throat and her soft rose-coloured suit as she descended and it brought with it a wave of fear.

Yet she knew she could not allow her only son to ruin his life without trying to do something about it.

She drew on the thought for courage as the subway train thundered her away into darkness.

Chapter 5

History was in the very air of the place. At night it whispered up from the river and drifted through the narrow streets in Scotch mist. During the day it swirled with the dust in the tenement closes. All the time it clung to the old grey walls.

Gorbals was famous for the manufacture of firearms, drums, spinning-wheels, cuckoo-clocks and swords. During the fifteenth and sixteenth centuries it was so celebrated for its sword-manufacturing that Gorbals swords were judged to be as good in temper and edge as those made by the famous Andrew Ferrars. Its harquebuses or handguns were equal to those of Ghent, Milan and Paris and by the first quarter of the nineteenth century the only individuals in the west of Scotland who manufactured guns were found in the Gorbals. Gorbals was a busy place, especially during the wars between England and Scotland.

The beginning of the nineteenth century also saw cotton-spinning as one of its principal industries. Since then numerous iron-founding and engineering works had been erected within the old Barony, including the famous Dixon's Blazes that lit the sky over Glasgow like a giant ball of fire.

Julie's father, Dode Gemmell, had been a moulder in one of the foundries. He had sweated his strength away at the furnaces and outside in the cold Scottish winds he had caught chill after chill. The chills became pneumonia and the pneumonia, tuberculosis of the lungs. He had been forced to give up work and for a long time now he had been on the dole.

He wore a checked cloth cap, or 'bunnet', and a white muffler instead of a collar and tie, except when Julie had visitors. Then Julie shoved a clean collar at him and said:

'Right, you bachly auld tramp, make yourself respectable or I'll be disowning you.'

'You canni dae that, hen,' he'd chortle. 'Anybody can see

428

you've got the Gemmell beak!'

He was a good-natured, cheery man despite his sucked-in face and eyes set in dark brown parchment; his gummy grin made no secret of the fact that he had not one tooth in his head. He hawked and coughed a lot and hung about the close or one of the street corners at Gorbals Cross, rubbing his hands and shuffling from one foot to the other. Always eager to plunge into energetic conversation on football or any subject at all, he would jerk his head and give a cheery 'Aye!' of greeting to anyone who passed, friend or stranger, it made no difference.

He was proud to belong to the 'Red Clyde', a staunch supporter of the Gorbals Labour MP George Buchanan, and an enthusiastic admirer of Jimmy Maxton, the long-haired fiery-eyed member for Bridgeton.

He identified warmly and experienced keen fellow feelings with workers in other districts, towns or countries and his admiration for Soviet Russia knew no bounds.

Ordinary working men in Russia had successfully risen up in revolt against the injustices and indignities that all working men suffered. This knowledge gave Dode's life real hope. He followed the Russians' progress in the war as if they were his much cherished brothers.

At some Red Army victory he would proudly shout to passers-by, 'What do you think of Old Joe now, eh?'

He had never been much of a drinker of the 'hard stuff' but the moulding had been thirsty work and made a man need a few pints.

No longer fit for work, he still enjoyed his beer and Saturday night in one of the Gorbals Cross pubs had become a ritual. He eagerly looked forward to the arguments about football and politics, among the noisy, sweaty crush of men. He shouted and cursed and laughed with them in the coffin-shaped bar with the sawdust floor and enjoyed the complete lack of restraint that the absence of women afforded.

Sometimes, if his horse came in or if one of his mates won a few bob, there would be whisky as well as beer and he would get a 'wee bit fu'. He was even cheerier and friendlier in his cups and Julie could never bring herself to be angry with him for long.

Although she would punch him on the arm and scold:

'Do you want to disgrace me? You drunken auld rascal. Away through to your bed!'

She never invited any friends to the house on Saturdays. Sunday she considered to be her best day because she had time to prepare everything and also to do a bit of shopping. The whole of Scotland might be as quiet as a grave on Sundays with shops, pubs and all places of entertainment closed and everybody observing the Scottish Sabbath. But in Gorbals it was always different.

Most of Glasgow's large population of Jews at some time or other had lived here. Many still did and most of the small shops and businesses in the area were owned by Jewish families who kept Saturday as their 'Shabbos'. As a result the Christian Sunday to them meant business as usual, and all the shops did a roaring trade and the Gorbals streets were crowded.

Mrs Goldberg who lived downstairs from Julie was a very orthodox old Jewish lady and her beliefs prevented her from doing anything on her Sabbath, even cooking, or lighting a fire. So every Saturday morning before leaving for work, Julie ran in to Mrs Goldberg's house and lit her fire and made her a cup of tea. On the way home she looked in again to see to things and each time the old lady gave her the same greeting.

'A goot voch to you, Julie.'

And Julie would laugh and give the Jewish greeting back.

'And a bessern to you, Mrs Goldberg!'

The last visitor to the Gemmells' had been Catriona and she had come on a Sunday. Julie remembered with pride how clean and tidy the house had looked. The tiny room and kitchen flat with the cavity or hole-in-the-wall beds had been so spotless it was practically antiseptic. She had been especially proud of using napkins at tea-time. She had made them from an old tablecloth and they looked really classy. Her only worry had been that her dad would forget what they were for and do something terrible with his, like using it for a hanky.

She knew that the MacNairs were business people and quite well-off but no one, not even a MacNair, was going to be allowed to say that just because the Gemmells came from an old

Gorbals tenement they were dirty or ignorant.

She was as good as anybody anywhere and so was her dad and so were their neighbours. It was not their fault that there was not any hot water in their tenement and the lavatories had to be shared and were outside on the landings. In fact, in a cupboard-size room and kitchen with a smoking iron grate, and a lightless lavatory as cold as the North Pole, and only a shoe-box of a sink served by one cold water tap, it was difficult to live decently. It took guts. Those who did keep clean and respectable - and that meant the majority of Gorbals folk - were better, not worse, than people from the so-called better-class districts. Julie believed the people of Gorbals deserved a Victoria Cross.

That Saturday, after leaving Catriona at St Enoch's Square, she swung along, skilfully weaving in and out and round about the waves of people that surged along Argyle Street. There was a bounce to her walk and a jiggle of buttocks and breasts and a bounce of hair. It was good to be young and in love and buoyantly alive in dear old Glasgow.

She loved the place almost as much as she loved Reggie. Sometimes she felt so happy she almost bounced right up in the air and floated along high above the crowds in heady communion with the city.

Dear old, dirty old, friendly old, beautiful old Glasgow!

She could see the Tolbooth at Glasgow Cross now but she turned off to the right before the Cross and went down Stockwell Street towards the river.

Stockwell Street used to have a well called the Ratten Well that was notorious for its impure water, and the Ratten Well featured in the story of how Stockwell Street came by its name. There had been a skirmish there between a small party of Scots led by Wallace and the English, and afterwards the victorious Scots flung the dead English into the Ratten Well to Wallace's cry - 'Stock it well, lads, stock it well!'

It had been in Stockwell Street that the wealthy Robert Dreghorn, or Bob Dragon as he was nicknamed, had his bachelor town-house. He was the ugliest man in Glasgow. Tall and gaunt he had an inward bend to his back and an enormous head with one blind eye, one squint eye and a Roman nose that twisted to one side until it nearly lay flat on his cheek. Bob Dragon had an appreciation of beauty and used to follow admiringly any pretty girl he saw in Argyle Street, only being diverted if he noticed another prettier girl coming the opposite way. Then he would about turn and follow her until an even more beautiful one caught his eye and changed his direction and so on, backwards and forwards, criss-cross, round and round.

If Bob Dragon had still been alive he would certainly have followed Julie as she crossed the Victoria Bridge swinging her handbag, admiring the view of the river and the other bridges coming across it. Bouncily she sang to herself a tune that was always being played on the wireless:

'Praise the Lord, and pass the ammunition.
Praise the Lord, and pass the ammunition . . .'

Now at the other side, her feet were on Gorbals ground.

The Victoria Bridge led straight into Gorbals Street, the Main Street, and five minutes along it brought her to Gorbals Cross.

Her heart warmed to the old grey tenements. Their age, their cosy familiarity made her feel wonderfully safe. They crowded round her winking their tiny glass eyes in the sun, their close mouths dark caves of shelter.

Children in multi-coloured clothes swirled and bobbed around all the streets like vegetables in a broth pot.

Street songs and games frothed into the air.

'The big ship sails through the eeley ally o'
The eeley ally o'
The eeley ally o'
The big ship sails through the eeley ally o'.

Little girls were playing peaver and Julie hopped into their midst and took a kick at the peaver.

'Hey you!' somebody shrilled. 'Whit do you think yer daein?'

Further along others were intent on another game.

'In and out the dusty blue-bells,
In and out the dusty blue-bells . . .'

Reaching the Cross, Julie waved to her father who was at the corner rubbing his hands and shuffling from one foot to the other, and showing all his gums like a delighted infant as he laughed with a neighbour. Immediately he spied her, he returned her wave and scuttled up their close to go and put on the kettle.

Gorbals Cross was really a circle with an iron-railinged Gents' underground lavatory and a clock standard in the middle. Four streets led off the centre like spokes of a wheel. Their close was on the corner of Gorbals Street and she crossed the road towards it and entered its dark tunnel-way swinging her handbag and jauntily whistling.

As usual Julie went in to attend to Mrs Goldberg before going upstairs to her own house and by that time her father had the tea-pot ready on the table and was taking the fish suppers from the oven where they had been keeping warm since he brought them from the local fish-and-chip shop.

Before starting to eat she filled a big kettle and also a pot full of water and put one on the gas ring and the other on the fire to heat. As well as hot water to wash the greasy dishes after the meal, she needed water to wash her hair and also her underwear and the blouse she planned to wear to Kelvinside the next day.

Immediately the meal was over she chased her father out of the way with a few extra shillings in his pocket and reckless orders to enjoy himself.

'Be like me, Dad, get happy!'

She decided to leave the dishes and see to her hair and the washing first. Then while her hair and the washing were drying she could clear the table. Tomorrow morning would be time enough to tidy the room.

On Saturdays, with helping Mrs Goldberg, she never had time to do anything in her own place and although her dad always bought the Saturday fish suppers, infused the tea and emptied the suppers from their newspaper wrappings on to the plates, that, and seeing that the fire did not go out during the day, was his sole contribution to the domestic scene.

The newspaper wrappings were still crushed in a heap on the table where he had discarded them and as usual he had put the milk bottle out instead of using a jug and the sugar bag instead of emptying the sugar into a bowl and he had cut the bread in thick ragged hunks.

As she rolled her hair up in curlers she sighed at the mess. He was an awful man. He had not even emptied the ashpan and it overflowed on to the tin sheet with the painted artificial tiles on the floor in front of the fire until the ashes reached the fender. Not that she blamed him. There was something terribly humiliating in the predicament of a man who had done a man's job for so many years, having to stay at home and do women's work while the woman of the house went out to earn the money.

It was pathetic how pleased he was when he won a few shillings on a horse. No matter how much she protested, he insisted on going halfers with her.

'Here you are, hen!' He would present the money with a nonchalant flourish. 'You deserve it. Go and treat yersel tae something. Have a treat on your auld dad.'

He and Reggie had got on like a house on fire. Her father had been such an eager enthusiastic listener that Reggie had become quite flattered and carried away with himself. He had recounted all his exploits in the air with gesticulations and noisy sound effects like a little boy swooping about the room with a toy aeroplane.

'By God!' Her father could not contain his delight and admiration. 'You're a rerr lad, Reggie. Ah'll be damnt proud tae huv you fur a son!'

She was determined that she would be as big a hit with Reggie's folk. Why not, after all? She knew how to behave and how to dress. She had good taste. She was neither ignorant nor common. To talk with a posh accent was easy too. She talked posh in the shop every day. She would not overdo anything, of course. A lady never went to extremes.

Tomorrow when she went to Kelvinside she would be well groomed but discreet in her black suit, and white gloves and blouse and her mother's fine gold locket, and her manners would be impeccable.

She lit a cigarette, lay back on the chair by the fire and put her feet up on the side of the old black range.

Through the cloud of tobacco smoke she dreamed her dreams.

434

She heard the knock on the door and automatically bawled, 'Come on in, it's no' locked.'

Her mind was still in Kelvinside watching herself being a hit with Reggie's mother. Then, suddenly, Reggie's mother was standing in front of her.

There could be no mistaking the dainty woman in the pink suit that made her own best black costume look like something out of Woolworth's.

Julie stared at the confection of pink hat and the exquisite pink and white face underneath it. She was too stunned to drop her feet down or stub out her cigarette.

At last she forced herself to rise. Apologies lumped in her throat. Apologies for her sweaty feet, swollen with standing in the shop all day, apologies for her head, an ugly mass of steel curlers, apologies for the bottle of beer that she had been using for a hair rinse, apologies for the shameful state of the house. She swallowed down the lump and it left a bitter taste.

Her stare hardened, became impudent. She plumped her hands on her hips and arched her brows.

'Well?'

The other woman glanced around with only a suspicion of distaste before enquiring in reasonable moderate, ladylike tones.

'May I sit down?'

Chapter 6

Muriel prayed for calmness as she lowered herself gracefully into a chair and eased off her gloves. Never in her whole life had she been in such a sordid place. Never in her worst nightmares had she imagined such a monstrous partner for Reggie. The girl was as common as dirt. There was a brazen impudent look about her. Hard emerald eyes glittered with venom and made Muriel feel afraid. With fast-fluttering heart she managed to speak:

'I take it you are Julie Gemmell.'

'So?'

'I'm Mrs Vincent, Reggie's mother.'

'Oh?'

'I thought we could have a little talk.'

'Today.'

'Yes.'

'Not tomorrow.'

'I thought it would be better to have a chat on our own.'

'Why?'

Muriel longed for help and protection. Daggers of hurt tormented her. How could Reggie do this to her? she wondered.

'I'm worried about Reggie. He hasn't been himself recently. Oh, I know it's this awful war. It's upsetting everyone's lives. But I can't allow it to ruin Reggie's future as well as his present.'

Julie lit a cigarette.

'I'm not with you, pal.'

'What I'm trying to say is . . .' The older woman's desperate gaze retreated for a moment. With trembling fingers she opened her handbag and plucked out a lace-edged hanky. 'Poor Reggie is risking his life every day just now so that a decent future can be secured not only for himself but for everyone.'

'So?'

'Reggie deserves a decent future.'

'Sure!'

'But with the strain and pressures of the war, with everything mixed up, people are making hasty and foolish decisions in their private lives, decisions they will later regret most bitterly.'

Julie guffawed with laughter and flopped into a chair. Even the way she sprawled out had a defiant impudence.

'Look, Mrs Vincent, if you've come here to tell me I'm not good enough for you, why don't you just spit it out?'

'Not for me.' Muriel's heart made a tight drum of her chest. 'For Reggie.'

'Reggie thinks I'm fine.'

'At the moment he does.'

'We're getting married on Monday. Haven't you heard?'

'That's why I'm here. I wouldn't have bothered if he had just had an affair and left it at that. It's perfectly understandable that men under such terrible tensions and dangers should want to indulge themselves when they can.'

'You mean, sex?'

'But under normal circumstances they would never dream of marrying the person.'

'You're a dirty-minded wee bitch.'

Muriel felt ill. She prayed for Reggie or even Norman to come and carry her safely away from this claustrophobic, filthy beer-smelling slum. She longed to flee from the place. Only her love and concern for her son gave her enough courage to remain sitting.

'Reggie was going to marry a girl from Bearsden and I was very happy for him. It's not that I object to Reggie getting married.'

'So long as it's a girl from la-de-da Bearsden and not from common old Gorbals.'

Julie's mimicry of her Kelvinside accent made Muriel flush.

'You are a most impertinent girl. I cannot imagine what my son sees in you.'

'Too bad.'

Muriel made to rise. Then forced herself down again. Her delicate pink face had gone an unhealthy white. She looked like a wax doll.

'I love Reggie. He's my only son. I cannot allow you to ruin his whole life.'

'Look, pal, you can do what you like. You can talk yourself red, white and blue in the face. But nothing's going to change my mind about marrying Reggie on Monday.'

'Why are you doing this to him? Is it for money? Is that it? I'll give you every penny I have if only you'll leave Reggie alone.'

Julie sprang to her feet like a cat, green eyes sparkling.

'How dare you come here and insult me! First of all you insinuate that I'm little better than a prostitute.'

Clutching her handbag and gloves, Muriel rose too.

'You're putting words into my mouth.'

'Then you try to buy me off with money.'

'I'd sacrifice anything for my son's happiness.'

'I don't want your lousy money. I don't want anything from you.'

'What do you want?'

'Want! Want! That's the only way you can think. I know your type. I'm serving women like you every bloody day in Morton's. Spoiled, selfish little Modoms just like you! You don't care about Reggie or Reggie's happiness. All you're worried about is yourself. Your ideas, your wants, your plans.'

'That's not true. You don't understand.'

'I'm not daft. I understand all right. You've been spoiled rotten all your life. You've had it soft. You've had it all your own way. Well, not with me, pal. Not with me!'

Muriel closed her eyes and crushed her handkerchief against her mouth. At last she managed:

'Maybe I've said all the wrong things. If I have I'm sorry. I didn't mean to hurt you.'

'You haven't hurt me, pal. You haven't bothered me one bit.'

'Or insult you. I swear to you I'm not thinking about myself. The only one I care about is Reggie.'

She held up a restraining hand to Julie who looked ready to flare into speech again.

'Oh, I admit I would have liked Reggie to marry Sandra Brodie and I had dreams of Reggie eventually having a partnership with Sandra's father. But I don't care about that any more. All

I ask is that Reggie should not be rushed into a wartime marriage that he would later regret. That you might regret, too. My dear, I know it seems very exciting for things to happen suddenly. There's a certain glamour about all this impulsive, reckless behaviour, but what about afterwards? Do you really think you could fit in and be happy as a professional man's wife in middle-class suburbia?'

'I'm as good as you any day, anywhere, pal - and I'll make Reggie a good wife. One thing's obviously never occurred to you. *I* love him!'

'If you loved him you wouldn't marry him. You couldn't.'

'That's the daftest thing I've ever heard.'

'You know what I mean. You'll have to face up to the truth sometime. All I'm asking you, begging you, to do is face facts now before it's too late. You and Reggie have nothing in common, absolutely nothing. What basis is that for a marriage? You come from such different backgrounds and levels of education it just couldn't last. He'd end up hating you.'

'You don't know what you're talking about.'

'Oh, yes, my dear, I do - I know my son. He'd feel worried, then embarrassed, then trapped, then he'd hate you.'

'He'll have no reason to feel any of these things. You're the only one who's likely to worry or embarrass Reggie. He's not going to thank you for coming over here badgering me for a start. Now do you want a cup of tea before you leave?'

'You know that I'm telling the truth.'

'Mrs Vincent, Reggie and I are going to get on fine, just fine. Everything in the garden's going to be lovely, believe me.'

'How can I believe you? Look at you! Look at this place!'

'I'm not in the habit of letting folk see me in my curlers.' Julie's voice iced up with anger. 'I never asked you to come here. And I haven't had all day to potter about the house like you. And I've been working hard in a shop from morning till night. Too bloody bad if I can't have a breather for five minutes after I come home without a la-de-da like you floating in and peering down your toffee-nose at me as if I were dirt. I'm as good as you, pal, and I've nothing to be ashamed of.'

Just then the door opened to reveal a skeleton of a man with

439

hollow toothless cheeks and shabby clothes that flapped loosely over his bones.

'Hey, whassup, eh? Is this toff upsettin' you, hen?' He staggered into the room belching beer and whisky fumes in Muriel's direction.

She looked away in disgust.

'I think I'd better leave.'

'Hey, jussa minute, missus.'

'Shut up, Dad.'

Muriel heard the crack in the girl's voice and was moved to pity.

Going down the draughty stairs and out through the dark tunnel to the street she felt harrowed by the whole encounter.

She had never before seen people living in such conditions. A whole new, distressing world opened up and she felt in danger of being swallowed by it.

She felt sick, claustrophobic, frightened. Her feet quickened towards home. If only she had never left Kelvinside. No good would come of her visit to the Gorbals. She knew that now.

What could she say to Reggie? That she had nothing against the girl personally? That she wasn't being snobbish or class-conscious?

But she *had* something against the girl. She was as common as dirt. She was ignorant and impudent. She belonged to filthy, sordid surroundings and had a dreadful unemployed drunk for a father. How *could* such a person be suitable for Reggie? The very idea was preposterous.

Reggie might think she was interfering or causing trouble for him just now, but later he would understand and he would thank her.

She would do everything in her power to dissuade him from making a fool of himself. She would plead, weep, have hysterics, if necessary. She would become ill. She would tell him that she would rather die than see him go through with this ridiculous farce of a wedding.

Yet all the time she knew the worst was going to happen. She thought of the little boy who had trotted beside her on his way to school and all the hopes she had always cherished for him.

Bewildered and completely brokenhearted, she kept asking herself, 'Reggie, how could you?'

Chapter 7

The taxi crawled across the River Clyde like a black beetle through a yellow flame. Then suddenly darkness sucked it under the Stockwell railway bridge. A fusty smell filled the cab and people's feet echoed.

Julie shivered.

'Are you all right?' Catriona asked.

'Of course! Why shouldn't I be?'

Sunshine again as they curved into Argyle Street, then up Hope Street to West George Street.

'Maybe they'll be there after all.'

'His people? Not a chance. Not after Saturday.'

'Fancy her turning up like that. What rotten bad luck.'

Julie whirled round, her face softly shaded by her wide brimmed hat, her green eyes luminous.

'She did it on purpose! That woman meant to humiliate me. I'll never forgive her. I'll never forgive that woman as long as I live.'

Catriona mentally wrung her hands.

'Maybe she just thought . . .'

'She thought she could stop me marrying Reggie, but she's had to think again, hasn't she!'

'It's a pity though. I mean, with you not having a mother of your own . . .'

'I'm a big girl now. I don't need the likes of her.' Julie rustled the skirt of her taffeta dress and tugged at its matching bolero jacket. 'Are you sure I'm all right?'

'You look lovely.'

'Well, don't say it as if I'm about to be executed. Let's get one thing straight before we get out of this car. I don't want you letting me down by howling and blubbering.'

Catriona's head nodded in silent abject agreement.

'Come on, then!' Rustling and flouncing, and keeping a good

grip of her hat, Julie alighted from the taxi.

A noisy navy-blue and white wedding group of WRNS and matelots were being bullied into position for a photograph on the pavement. Another party spilled from the building, the bride and bridesmaid in square-shouldered utility costumes on which the roses on their lapels looked as incongruous as the pink carnations pinned to the coarse khaki uniforms of their partners.

Reggie and another man in air-force blue were waiting inside. At the sight of Reggie, Julie flushed and her chin tilted in the air, but her attempt at nonchalance failed and she looked more in love and vulnerable than ever. Reggie linked arms with her and their eyes exchanged caresses as if they had already made some sort of holy communion.

Catriona felt so distressed, so desperate for escape, it was as much as she could do not to turn tail and run.

'You look wizard, Julie,' Reggie said. 'Doesn't she, Jeff? Didn't I tell you?'

Jeff's moustache vied in luxuriance with Reggie's handlebar of blond hair, and his hearty guffaw made Catriona cringe.

Yet another bride and groom and bridesmaid and best man exploded past them as they tried to squeeze into the room in which the marriage ceremony was to take place.

It was bare, like a waiting-room only smaller, containing just a desk at which sat a dull-eyed, middle-aged man. He stared pityingly at Julie and Reggie. Then he rose with a sigh.

'Will all of you please stand in front of the desk. Has the best man got the ring?'

The ceremony consisted of identification, a brief explanation and finally an oral declaration by both parties.

Reggie spoke in a clear polite voice.

'I know of no legal impediment to my marrying this woman, Julie Gemmell, and I now accept her as my lawful wedded wife.'

Gazing up at him Julie repeated:

'I know of no legal impediment to my marrying this man, Reginald Vincent, and I now accept him as my lawful wedded husband.'

Catriona began to weep.

They were back out in the corridor in less than ten minutes.

That's all it takes to ruin your life, Catriona thought. In a few minutes, a mere snowflake of time, you can step over, change paths, start on a narrow road of suffering too private, too complex, too terrible for a free person to understand.

The years of her marriage to Melvin weighed down, pressed in, choked her like the MacNair building on the night of the air-raid.

'For pity's sake, Catriona!' Julie laughed. 'This is the happiest day of my life, and look at you! I've heard about people crying at weddings, but this is ridiculous!'

Water gushed down Catriona's cheeks and she stuffed a handkerchief tightly against her mouth. It was a still silent kind of weeping. She just stood there, eyes open wide and tears overflowing.

They were all laughing. People laughed as they surged past defying the rule not to litter the place with confetti. The air shimmered with colour.

Wiping her face, Catriona began to laugh too.

She allowed herself to be thrust outside to the waiting cab. Soon they were honking towards The Rogano licensed restaurant and from there to Green's Playhouse to dance to Joe Loss and his band. The dance-hall was on the top floor. Underneath it, Green's Playhouse Cinema boasted the biggest seating accommodation in Europe.

The lift spilled them out and Julie grabbed Catriona's hand and almost skipped into the ladies' cloakroom.

'Gosh, that wine's gone to my head!' She rolled her eyes and pretended to stagger. 'Casheeona, aye shink aym a lirrle tiddly!'

'Stop it!' Catriona hissed with embarrassment and nudged her and darted a look around. Then feeling reassured that no one was paying them any attention, she captured an explosion of giggles in her hands. 'I feel quite light-headed myself!'

Julie clenched her fists, screwed up her face and closed her eyes.

'I'm so happy, happy, happy, and I want you to be happy too.'

Catriona had an affectionate impulse to hug her friend, but instead she laughed and said:

'Tonight I'll forget all my troubles and really enjoy myself,

444

just to please you!'

They squeezed their way through the crowd of girls in front of the wall mirror and pushed their faces close to the glass to concentrate on smearing lips, and curling eyelashes and tidying eyebrows with stiff wet pinkies.

A high-pitched crescendo of chatter beat against the walls and filled the cloakroom with heady excitement. Outside men laughed and smoked and mooched and chewed gum while Joe Loss pounded the building with the bouncy 'In The Mood'.

After fluffing powder over their faces and lightly teasing their curls, and screwing round to check the backs of their dresses and the seams of their stockings, Julie and Catriona pushed through the swing doors and rejoined Reggie and Jeff.

The foyer was just a raised part at the back of the hall and in a couple of minutes they had descended the steps into the ballroom. It was a huge hall with pillars holding up a balcony where people sat at small tables littered with ash and empty cigarette and chewing gum packets and sipped lemonade and coffee. At one end of the floor, raised on a stage, Joe Loss in white tie and tails jumped and twisted and flashed his teeth and flayed the air with his baton. His men earnestly pulsated and blared out and pulsated and blared out above the bobbing heads of the dancers.

Julie and Reggie melted into one another's arms and floated away, cheek to cheek. Jeff gripped Catriona tightly against him and swooped her off with long fast strides that kept speeding unexpectedly into dainty spring-toed steps. She was never quite quick enough for the change of pace and kept stumbling and trampling on his feet.

Other dancers jostled them as people vigorously contorted themselves about. Men threw women high in the air and twisted them round their bodies like snakes and swooped them down to side between their legs. Women bounced and twitched and twirled, skirts spun and opened like umbrellas to show wide-legged French knickers. Plum lips and rosy cheeks glistened and thin pencilled brows arched high with effort and excitement.

Catriona giggled. 'I'm trampling all over you. I'm sorry. I'm afraid I'm not used to drinking so much wine. I feel quite dizzy.'

She pushed without success at his shoulders to try to lever him off.

The drink, the music, the heat, the frenzied people, all intensified her reckless need to be happy, but to be happy she needed to escape from Jeff. The mere fact that he had a moustache was enough to remind her of Melvin.

'Please, Jeff, let me go. I want to stand at the side for a breath of fresh air from the window.'

Her voice wheedled and softened with promise and Jeff gave one of his excited whinnies and led her from the floor. Once out of his grip she felt delirious with freedom, pleaded with him to go and fetch her a glass of lemonade, then as soon as his back was turned she slipped away to hide by herself.

She could have swirled around and danced by herself and shouted to everyone that tonight she did not care about anything. Instead she edged through he crowds whispering, 'Excuse me, please, excuse me,' and avoided people's eyes and kept her gaze lowered shyly.

She had never been to a dance before. She had barely finished school when Melvin wrenched her from her mother's apron strings and installed her in his house in Dessie Street. Now, for the first time, she caught a glimpse of a dimension to life she had been missing. Not that she wanted to participate; she felt much safer being a spectator and observer of the scene. It was more than enough to listen to the music, to watch the dancers, to quickly brush against the men as she passed, and feel the heat of them and smell the tobacco and the sweat, and the cloying perfume of the women.

But a hand gripped her elbow and stopped her in her tracks like a startled doe and before she knew what was happening she was in a sailor's arms and shuffling with him cheek to cheek.

Up on the platform someone mouthed close to the microphone:

'All of me . . .
Why not take
All of me . . .?'

The lights had gone out and a spinning ball of mirrors sprinkled a confetti of colour through the darkness.

The sailor did not speak but held her with comfortable familiarity and after the dance he kept a grip of her hand and smiled and winked at her before drawing her to him for the next dance.

She noticed the Canada flash on his shoulder and wondered what Canada could be like. Before the war she had only heard Canada and America mentioned at school. They were just statistics to be learnt parrot-fashion for exams. They never had seemed real places where real people lived, reality had always been bounded by Glasgow.

'What's Canada like?' she asked curiously.

His voice in reply was a slow, gentle drawl that enchanted her.

'It's God's own country, honey! God's own country!'

'What a wonderful voice!'

He eased her back for a moment to give her a lopsided grin and an amused stare.

'I guess you're the sweetest little thing this side of the pond!' he drawled.

Wide-eyed against his chest she watched the speckle dancers drift around. It seemed as if she were in fairyland.

The sailor was called Johnny and was French Canadian, she discovered later over a glass of lemonade. He talked nostalgically of a lovely old city called Montreal, Quebec, and how his father had been a peace-time skipper on one of the boats that worked the great lakes.

Catriona listened entranced, elbows propped on the small table, hands clasped under chin, as she gazed admiringly at the sapphire blue eyes, the tanned face crinkling kindly.

They danced again and again. The band played the haunting 'Lili Marlene' and everybody sang.

They were still clinging together and moving around the floor in a kind of dream when the band played the last dance.

> 'You must remember this . . .
> A kiss is just a kiss . . .
> A sigh is just a sigh . . .'

'You're wearing a wedding ring, honey,' he murmured. 'Does

that mean there's a husband somewhere you're crazy about?'

Suddenly the impact of her personal tragedy drained her happiness away. She had not only lost a child, she had lost her own life too. In the middle of a song called 'As Time Goes By' she remembered about Melvin.

'I'm afraid I'll have to go now,' she told the sailor abruptly.

'Can't I see you home?'

'No, I'm sorry.'

In a panic of distress she fled before he could speak to her again. A whirlpool of dancers sucked her away and by the time she reached the outer side of the hall she had lost sight of him. She caught a glimpse of Jeff laughing and talking and obviously making a hit with a warm-eyed brunette. Julie and Reggie were nowhere to be seen.

The colourful, crowded scene disturbed her all the way back to Farmbank. The feel of it, the sight of it, the sound of it, each facet of the experience stayed alive and became more vivid in contrast to the house in Fyffe Road.

Everyone was in bed and, after checking that the boys were safely asleep, Catriona retreated to the living-room and to her horse-hair sofa prison where she crouched in an almost unendurable fever of restlessness.

Chapter 8

'I won't let you down, Reggie. You'll never need to feel ashamed because I come from a working-class family.'

'Of course not, darling.' He folded his uniform neatly over a chair beside the bed. 'You talk such rot at times. Who worries about class nowadays?'

'Your mother!'

'Oh, I know how you must feel about Mother, but honestly, she isn't as bad as you think. I admit she's old-fashioned, a minister's daughter and all that, but give her time. You'll find her pretty decent once you get to know her.'

'Do you think I ever will?'

'For my sake you will.'

'Oh? You're very sure of yourself.'

'I'm sure of you.'

'That doesn't sound very complimentary.'

'You do love me, don't you, Julie?'

His eyes became suddenly very young and anxious. In a face that confidently sported a handlebar moustache and sideboards his youthful uncertainty seemed incongruous but it was an incongruity matched by the vest and pants and woollen socks he was wearing.

Julie giggled.

'I'm glad you don't wear Long Johns!'

She lay in bed happily watching him. She did not care in the slightest if he looked ridiculous. For better or for worse, he was her man, and a background of the crowded tenements had long ago taught her the true facts of life. She had romance, she was bubbling over with the excitement of her whirlwind romance with an RAF officer, but she had no romantic illusions. Reggie was her man and that was that. In the Gorbals no woman thought or spoke of her 'husband', it was always her 'man', and

Julie felt there was something basic, fundamental and right about the expression. It got back to the root of things, to the time of the cavemen when a woman depended on a man's physical strength to protect her or to kill something so that they could eat and survive. Yet woman's physical weakness had caused her to become much more wily and tougher in spirit, and there was something marvellously right about that too. One strength complemented the other. Sometimes the one strength helped to endure the other and that was as it should be.

She had watched marriage in close-up in the overcrowded tenements, seen husbands who worked hard and always handed over their wages and never raised their hand in anger. Their wives spoke proudly of 'my man'. She had seen other husbands who gambled and drank and beat their partners and their wives spoke of 'my man' with the same possessive lilt to their voices.

Julie savoured the words as she watched Reggie strip.

She had a wonderful feeling of completeness, of something accomplished that would never change. She did not like change. She had lived in the same house in the same district all her life. She had attended only one school. Her loyalties had clung tenaciously from childhood to a single friend until that friend married and moved to England. Since leaving school she had worked for only one firm.

Reggie was the first man she had ever loved and she was happy in the certainty that he would be her only love.

She felt unashamedly proud of him. She felt like a cavewoman who not only fulfils the basic necessity of finding a mate but who succeeds in ensnaring the very best mate in the cave.

'I'll always love you,' she told him.

He looked away, stubbed out his cigarette in the ashtray on the bedside locker.

'Damn this bloody war!'

As he said the words, Julie's quick eye saw his mind drift far away from her.

'Come to bed.' She pushed the covers down to reveal white breasts bulging over a black nightdress. 'Forget about the war.'

He came in beside her and she sighed with satisfaction. 'We're all that matter. We love each other and we belong to each other

450

and we're here in this hotel in each other's arms. Nothing in the whole world could be more important.'

She could feel him trembling against her and she was glad of her soft woman's skin and breasts and belly and full hips arching under his exploring hands. She was his and it was right and proper that he should be pleased with her.

Here was her strength and her love and generosity guided her in an infinite variety of ways to increase his pleasure until she was exhausted but triumphant and he was gasping for breath and half-weeping in her arms.

Gradually his jerky breathing soothed and after a long peaceful silence, she remarked:

'I think there's blood or something on the sheet.'

'It's all right, darling,' he murmured sleepily. 'That happens when it's the first time.'

'But it's on the sheet.'

'Don't worry!'

'I can't stay the night in a hotel and leave dirty sheets on the bed next morning.'

'Darling, the sheets are stripped off every morning.'

'I'm not having people say that I left stained sheets.'

'They'll know what it is. They probably gossip and laugh about these things all the time in hotels.'

Immediately the bedclothes flurried back. She struggled up.

'Well, they won't get the chance to gossip or laugh about me!'

'What the devil are you doing?'

'Get up! Come on, I want that sheet! It won't take a minute.'

'You're joking!'

She tugged the sheet from under him.

'It's only a small stain. I'll get rid of it in a couple of minutes at the washhand basin and then hang it over the chair at the window to dry.'

'Good Lord!'

'I've got my pride, Reggie. I don't sleep in other folks' beds and leave stained sheets.'

Her breasts jiggled about and she became pink in the face and breathless as she attacked the offending part of the sheet with a soapy nailbrush.

Reggie relaxed among the disorder of blankets with his arms folded behind his head and roared laughter up to the ceiling.

'Be quiet!' she scolded him. 'Somebody might hear you. How would it look if we were chucked out the hotel for noisy behaviour in the middle of the night? I'd never live it down.'

She held the crumpled linen under a gush of cold water and then wrung the water out, her face contorting with the exertion. 'There, that's better. I told you, Reggie, I'll never let you down. I've got pride and I'm not afraid of hard work. I've always kept a spotless clean house and my mother before me.'

Reggie grinned over at her. 'You're only nineteen. What do you know about keeping house?'

'I've kept one for seven years. My mother died when I was twelve. Move over till I tidy the bed, you big oaf.' Her voice softened reminiscently. 'I remember Mammy, and my wee brother. He died just before her. There was first one funeral and then another, and do you know what sticks out most vividly in my mind?'

'What?'

'The worry about money - about not having any, I mean! Mammy used to worry about that all the time when she was alive. As long as we can manage to keep a roof over our heads and a brave face to the world - she always used to say. And she always managed. But at the funeral it was terrible. You know how there has to be a funeral tea for everybody. Well, talk about feeding the multitude with a loaf and a few fishes!'

She rolled her eyes. 'I knew Mammy wouldn't have wanted me to borrow from anybody. But I thought it would be all right to take the stuff Mrs Goldberg offered. We always lit her fire and did odd jobs for her on Saturdays and I reckoned she owed us something.' She cuddled into bed beside him. 'Dad kept wailing - "I'm no use without my better half." But I told him, "We'll have to show everybody we can manage right from the start or they'll have me away in a home and you'll end up in 'the Model' and what would Mammy think about the disgrace of that?"'

Reggie's arms tightened around her. 'I want to look after you for the rest of your life. I don't want you to have to worry about money or anything else again.'

She sighed with happiness.

'Oh, Reggie, just think - we've our whole long lives before us. We've so much to plan and talk about. What kind of house do you reckon we'll have one day?'

'A small one, to start with anyway, modern and easy to run. Life's for living, old girl. I don't believe in women being chained to the kitchen sink and all that rot. No, were going to enjoy life and we're going to live it together!'

'A bathroom's a must!'

'Definitely!

'And a kitchenette. It's terrible this idea of sinks and cookers and beds all in the one room. I'd like to have met the man who designed Glasgow tenements. I'd have given him a piece of my mind.'

'Tenements aren't all like that though, darling. You must see our flat. You'd love it.'

'Your mother and father's, you mean?'

'Yes. I was hoping you could have stayed there while I was away.'

'Reggie, your mother hates the sight of me! She made it perfectly plain she didn't even want to see me at her place on Sunday.'

'She didn't mean it, darling. It was just the shock of everything. You must admit it was a bit sudden. In her day there were long courtships and everything was so different.'

'Everybody knew their "place", you mean? People from the Gorbals stayed in the Gorbals and never sullied the fair banks of the Kelvin?'

'Julie! She just didn't expect me to get married so suddenly, that's all!'

'That's what you think, pal! But anyway, what about my dad?'

'Oh, he has plenty of good friends and neighbours and plenty of time. He could manage. It's you I'm worried about. You work all day and then have to go back there. Its a bad show. I'd feel much better if you were in Botanic Crescent. Mother could have a good meal ready for you every night and you could relax and take things easy in civilised surroundings!'

She jerked up.

'There you are! You're as bad! I come from uncivilised surroundings, do I? Well, let me tell you I'm as civilised as your mother any day!'

'Darling!' He soothed and pulled her back down into his arms. 'Idiot! I was talking about the lack of hot water in the houses, and cavity beds, and lavatories outside on the stairs and the cold draughty tunnels of closes. I know these things aren't your fault.'

Her ruffled feathers gradually settled.

'Well . . . all right then.'

'How about calling there tomorrow afternoon?'

She screwed up her face.

'Oh, Reggie . . .'

'I promise you, Mother won't slam the door on you if that's what you're worried about.'

Julie sighed.

'You're fond of her, aren't you?'

'She's my mother.'

There was a little pause before she said, 'I remember how I felt about Mammy right enough.'

'Does that mean you'll come?'

'If it's what you want, Reggie.'

'Oh, I love you, Julie!' His young voice trembled with gratitude and excitement. 'And I know Mother will love you too. It's simply a matter of getting to know each other.'

She suddenly became perky.

'I'll come on one condition. You come with me to the shop first.'

'The shop?'

'Morton's, where I work. I want to show you off.'

He laughed.

'Darling, you've got the day off. They'll think you're mad if you turn up.'

'No, they won't. They'd love to meet you. Go on, Reggie, be a sport. There's just the manageress and the two alteration hands. You've met Catriona already.'

'But why?'

454

'I told you. I'm proud of you and I want to show you off. I think you're the most handsome, the most wonderful, the cleverest man in the whole world!'

'Hold on, old girl. Handsome, maybe, but clever never!'

'You fly these big planes. I've seen pictures of the instrument panels on some of them. I can't imagine how anybody could begin to understand them. You're an absolute genius as far as I'm concerned.' She hugged him and showered him with kisses. 'And I'll love you for ever and ever. Will we call into the shop tomorrow? Just for a couple of minutes on the way to your mother's.'

'Righteo.'

She immediately detected the note of false cheerfulness.

'What's wrong?'

'Oh, mentioning planes reminded me of the war and of having to go back to it tomorrow night.'

'Reggie, I'm sorry. I shouldn't have said that.'

'It's not your fault, darling.'

'Can we come back here for a little while tomorrow night before you leave?'

'Yes, we'll just call on Mother for half an hour or so in the afternoon.'

She snuggled closer to him and opened her mouth in eager invitation against his, and they made love again, and again, and again, until Reggie rolled over on to his back, his arms flopping helplessly at his sides.

Her mouth still slid over his body, warm and full and eager.

'Reggie,' she urged.

'I don't think I could again, darling.'

She kept forcing her face against him like a cat rubbing itself.

'Reggie,' she whispered. 'Reggie!'

Chapter 9

'Snap - snap - snap - snap! Grandpa, I said it first. I said it before you did. I did! I did!'

Rab Munro roared with laughter as his broad baker's hands fought to snatch the cards from Fergus's eager grasp.

'No, you didn't. I won. Snap!'

'Grandpa! Give them to me! They're mine. I said it before you! Grandpa!'

Catriona could not stand it any longer. There was nothing wrong with a game of snap but this one had been going on too long. It was nearly eleven o'clock and Fergus was getting far too excited. He would never be able to sleep.

'Daddy, that's enough. It's time Fergus was in bed.'

'Och, Grandpa, don't listen to her. Come on!'

'Now, now!' Rab's lantern-jawed face lengthened in sternness. 'None of your cheek, young Mr Skinamalink.'

Fergus erupted into high-pitched giggles.

'You're an old Mr Skinamalink.'

Catriona rose.

'Fergus, put the cards away now and no more nonsense. You've school in the morning.'

'An old Skinamalinky long-legs with four eyes and frizzy hair.'

Rab grimaced in mock rage and gave a giant-sized roar.

'What? Let me get my hands on that rascal. Fee-fi-fo-fum! I smell the blood of an Englishman!'

Fergus began to squeal with excitement and brought Andrew skipping into the room in striped pyjamas. His grandmother had been bathing him and his curly hair was matted and showed patches of white scalp. Freckles peppered the bridge of his nose and his cheeks were scarlet beacons. Gleefully he joined in the shouting.

'Fee—fo—fi—fum!'

456

'Now don't you start. This is ridiculous, Mummy. He should have been in bed hours ago. I'm getting worried about their health.'

'Oh, be quiet!' Hannah Munro pushed her daughter aside in disgust. 'You're a bit late with your worrying. If you had worried when you'd reason to worry, my wee Robert would have been alive today. That lovely wee pet who did nothing but smile at everyone.'

Rab tugged off his reading glasses and tossed them aside.

'Now can you see what I've had to suffer all these years, Catriona? She never gives up. She goes on and on.'

'Oh, yes, you'd like me to keep quiet, wouldn't you? It would be much easier for you if you were just allowed to drink all your wages away every week and play around with any woman you fancied.'

'Too bad if a man can't have an odd pint of beer to wash the flour dust away.'

'Grandpa, play with me!' Fergus yelled. 'Play with me! Play with me!'

Catriona determinedly began scooping up the cards.

'Fergus, you're giving me a headache. It's eleven o'clock at night and time you boys were in bed. Now off you go. I won't tell you again.'

Andrew glowered and for the first time Catriona saw a look of Melvin about him.

'Granny said I could stay up until I got a cup of cocoa and a piece on jam.'

Hannah patted his head.

'That's right, Andy. You tell her.'

Rab groaned.

'There's no need to encourage the child to be cheeky. She is his mother, you know. Or have you conveniently forgotten that important fact?'

'There's a few things you've conveniently forgotten, Robert.'

'Oh, no, no, you'd never allow me to do that.' His big boned frame sunk back into his clothes and he added bitterly more to himself than to her: 'On my deathbed you'll be standing over me casting up every fault I've ever had.'

'Grandpa! Grandpa! I've got the cards!'

'Fergus, give those to me at once!' Catriona's voice sharpened with irritation.

She had been on her feet all day at the shop and since she had arrived home there had not been one minute's peace and quiet.

'There you are!' With gales of laughter Fergus tossed the pack of cards high in the air scattering them around every corner of the room. Almost at the same time Catriona's hand shot out and smacked him across the face.

His laughter collapsed into an offended whine then jerked into broken-hearted sobbing.

Immediately Andrew burst into tears of sympathy and apprehension.

Catriona put her hands to her ears.

'Oh, shut up! Shut up! Get to bed, both of you!'

Miserably they trailed off, wiping their wet cheeks with their sleeves.

Hannah at last found her voice.

'That's terrible! I'll talk to you in a minute, my girl. Come on, boys, Granny'll give you a nice cup of cocoa and piece'n'jam in bed.'

After they'd left the room Catriona said to her father:

'Jam in bed! They'll get into a sticky mess and their teeth will be ruined!'

'You shouldn't have hit the boy.'

'I didn't mean to. It happened before I could stop myself.' Abruptly she changed the subject. 'Daddy, I've been looking for a place of my own.'

His dark eyes filled with alarm and she got a glimpse of how fond he really was of the children and how much their company meant to him. He did not say anything and she lowered her gaze to her hands and went on.

'I've got this room and kitchen in Byres Road - I just heard this morning. I didn't want to say anything until it was safely settled.'

His balloon of tension puttered down with a sigh.

'Oh, well, it's your life, hen.'

'You'll still be able to see the boys, Daddy. You know you'll be welcome to come over any time.'

He nodded as if not trusting himself to speak. Then after a minute's silence he got up and at the living-room door he muttered without turning round:

'Time I was in bed, too.'

Catriona ran towards him, and hugged him before he left the room. If only her mother would take the news with equally quiet resignation.

The temptation to postpone telling Hannah was strong. Catriona would have liked to whisk the boys and old Duncan away to Byres Road and avoid the ordeal of breaking the news to her mother. But, for one thing, the old man was fuddled with drink most of the day and it was difficult enough to prise him out of the bedroom at mealtimes. It was going to be a sizeable operation to transfer him from Farmbank to Byres Road. He would complain loudly and long about leaving his chair in front of the gas fire and having his radio-listening and his routine shuffle to the local off-licence interrupted.

The boys would not take kindly to leaving their grandparents' house either, but desperation kept pushing Catriona on.

As soon as her mother came through she burst out:

'Mummy, I've something to tell you.'

'I've something to tell you, you wicked girl. Don't you dare raise your hand to an innocent child. The Bible gives a warning about what can happen to anyone who does such a thing.'

Her voice raised and filled out with the strong dignified tones she used when addressing the Band of Jesus. '"It would be better for him if a great millstone were hung round his neck and he were thrown into the sea. And if your hand causes you to sin, cut it off; it is better for you to enter life maimed than with two hands to go to hell, to the unquenchable fire."'

'I've found another place to live. There isn't enough room for us here. It's not right that Da has your bedroom and . . .'

'Don't talk nonsense,' her mother interrupted. 'Mr MacNair is no bother at all. He's perfectly happy and comfortable in the bedroom.'

'But you and Daddy . . .'

'Daddy and I are fine.'

'The boys . . .'

'I know what's best for the boys. I'm older than you, Catriona. I've lived longer and learned more. I'll worry about the boys. Just you get to your bed. You're always complaining about being tired in the morning. Well, I'm not keeping you up.' She made a grand sweeping gesture and it occurred to Catriona what a fine-looking woman she was with her thick burgundy-hair and strong tipped-up chin and rigid back. 'There's the sofa and don't forget to say your prayers and remember to ask God's forgiveness for all your sins, especially for causing so much hurt to people.'

'I mean it, Mummy. I'm grateful to you for having taken us all in after the air-raid. I don't know what we would have done without your help.'

'That's something you've still to learn. Families are supposed to help one another. Now get to bed.'

In a gesture of dismissal, Hannah began making preparations for the morning, striding backwards and forwards, crashing dishes and cutlery about in the sideboard and clattering them on to the table.

'Mummy, I'm sorry, but whether you listen to me or not - whether you face it or not - I'm moving to Byres Road with Da and the children. It's all settled. I've paid the deposit and everything.'

Her mother stopped.

'But you can't go.'

'I must.'

'You selfish, wicked girl. What about the children? What about their schooling? You're always whining on about that. This just shows the lies and the hyprocisy that's been coming out of your mouth. A lot you care about those poor boys.'

'It's because I care . . .'

'May the good Lord forgive you, Catriona. You're talking about uprooting these children just when they've begun to get over the dreadful shock of what you done to them before.'

Like a time bomb, Catriona exploded in hysteria.

'You keep blaming me for the air-raid! The quicker I'm out of here the better before you start blaming me for the whole

460

bloody war!'

Hannah was shocked speechless for a minute. Her ruddy cheeks faded to reveal fragile threads of purple capillaries criss-crossing. But she remained bolt upright. She lost none of her dignity.

'How dare you!' The words were savoured slowly and with a very correct accent. 'How dare you use bad language to your own mother. Little did I think I'd ever live to see the day my own daughter would sink so low. Get to your bed at once. I don't want to hear another word from you. You're not fit to be in charge of young children.'

Catriona wept with frustration and distress.

'It's all settled,' she repeated helplessly.

'Well, you can just unsettle it.'

'I can't stay here for ever. There's Melvin.'

'What about Melvin?'

'There isn't enough room for us. What happens when Melvin comes home? Where could he sleep?'

'There's no question of that man coming back here for years and years yet.'

'No, you're wrong! The war could finish quite soon. They say there's going to be a big invasion any day now. The Allies are ready to pour across the Channel and sweep the Germans off the map.'

'Who says?'

'Everyone says.'

'Everyone's been saying things like that for the past two years.'

'Maybe they don't know when or where or how, but something's bound to happen soon. We keep getting customers in the shop who've travelled around, especially down south, or have had word from there because you can't get into some of the places now - they're so packed with soldiers and sailors and equipment.'

'Glasgow's been packed for years.'

'Yes, but nothing like what they say. They say every inch of sea for miles around Britain and every river and every port is chock-a-block with warships and all sorts of queer landing-craft

461

and artificial harbours and things. And there's so many more ships being built they're even putting them together in streets and children can stand on their own doorsteps and watch the welders and riveters.'

'What nonsense!' Hannah scoffed. 'And don't try and evade the issue, my girl. These children through in that room are perfectly happy and content where they are and you have absolutely no excuse for uprooting and upsetting them just now.'

'It isn't nonsense, Mummy. The streets are full of army trucks and tanks and guns as well, lines and lines of them, half up on pavements in front of houses and folks having to squeeze past or walk out on the road to get round them.'

'Well, if it's God's plan to have an invasion - there will be an invasion. So stop whining on about it and get to your bed.'

'I was just explaining how Melvin might get home sooner than we expect and I've got to be ready. I've got to have a place for him to come to.'

'You don't care about that man. Why you married that man I'll never know.'

'So that's why I've got this wee room and kitchen in Byres Road.'

'You've not even any idea about how to manage with rations. You were lucky before. You got extras from the old man's shop. Now the only way to manage is to pool all our books and coupons the way we've been doing. And I'm well known and respected at the shops along the road and if there's anything special comes in they let me know or keep a share aside for me. You don't know a soul in Byres Road. Now I'm tired, if you're not, and I'm going to my bed. I don't want to hear another word from you. I've had enough of your stupid selfish talk for one night.'

'But, Mummy . . .' Catriona began again and stopped in mid-air.

There was no use talking.

Chapter 10

Restrained by roll upon roll of barbed wire, Britain was shrinking fast. Overcrowding had become claustrophobic. There was no longer any escape from the uniformed multitude jostling shoulder to shoulder with the civilian population.

Noisy activity whirled to a climax. Ports seethed with an astonishing variety of shipping. More and more vessels kept crowding in. Ships sprang up everywhere, not only in shipyards. In narrow streets and alleyways, in workshops round every corner, steel skeletons clanged and reverberated.

Into the small island crushed more and more assembly points, ammunition dumps, vehicle parks, camps, training-grounds, embarkation 'hards', barbed wire, airfields, anti-aircraft and searchlight sights. Day and night fast convoys roared at breakneck speeds in endless streams along narrow streets making houses shudder and echo to the thundering of wheels.

On 6th April 1944 all military leave was stopped. Troops and armoured vehicles crammed the coast ten miles deep. Plans for each day and enormous feeding and other necessary arrangements had to be made. In trucks lining seaside streets, typewriters clicked busily. Orders were triplicated in mobile offices complete down to waste-paper baskets.

A vast armada of ships swelled the waters of every port and harbour and buffeted for space with thousands of 'things' that floated like the huge artificial harbours called Mulberries.

Restless confined men played cards and thought of women and beer and home and argued about invasion dates.

In great concentrations of armoured equipment the sound of bagpipes could be heard as Highland units, destined to be the spearhead in France, practised for the final piping of troops into battle.

On 2nd June the ships had begun loading and by the early

hours of 5th June every craft was crammed and some had already set off, the tin-hatted men down below jampacked tightly, lumpy with equipment and guns clashing against each other. By four a.m. the recall went out by broadcasts from the shore for their return because the weather had worsened. Fog closed in but the civilian population could hear the continuous thunder high above them in the darkness as thousands of RAF and American Air Force night bombers set out to bombard the coastal batteries commanding the landing beaches to be assaulted.

In the landing craft the packed troops tried to get some sleep while a ferocious gale made the vessels roll and heave and plunge and smack waves against thin plates. Men vomited and had to remain in their vomit, and the stench mixed with silent fear and tobacco and khaki sweat.

On 6th June, General Eisenhower's order of the day was read by commanders to all troops:

'Soldiers, sailors and airmen of the Allied Expeditionary Force, you are about to embark on the great crusade towards which we have striven these many months. The eyes of the world are upon you. The hopes and prayers of liberty-loving people everywhere march with you.

'In company with our brave allies and brothers-in-arms on other fronts you will bring about the destruction of the German war machine, the elimination of Nazi tyranny over the oppressed peoples of Europe and security for ourselves in a free world.

'Your task will not be an easy one. Your enemy is well-trained, well equipped and battle-hardened. He will fight savagely but this is the year 1944. Much has happened since the Nazi triumph of 1940-1. The United Nations have inflicted upon the Germans great defeats in open battle man to man. Our air offensive has seriously reduced their strength in the air and their capacity to wage war on the ground.

'Our home fronts have given us an overwhelming superiority in weapons and munitions of war and placed at our disposal great reserves of trained fighting men.

'The tide has turned. The free men of the world are marching together to victory.

'Good luck, and let us all beseech the blessing of Almighty

464

God upon this great and noble undertaking.'

In a creaky old destroyer in a channel choked with ships, Alec Jackson said:

'To hell with the whole thing! Just let me get back to Glasgow, mate!'

It was around seven in the morning and smudgy battleships and cruisers were steaming up and down drenching the shores of France with thunderous broadsides that killed French women and children as well as German men. Holiday houses and hotels gushed with fire.

Nearer the sea's edge spurts of flame shot up from the beaches in high snake-like ripples. Guns flashed and yellow cordite smoke curled into the air.

Invasion craft crawled down the ships' davits like beetles, and headed towards the shore in long untidy lines. Inside them the backs of men heaved as they vomited while bursts of spray broke over the sides and the craft smacked and lurched about. They tried to draw strength from the fact that everything had been meticulously planned; they had been trained for months for what was to come and there were officers to tell them where to go and what to do. They did not realise then how plans could go wrong, how orders could become impossible to fulfil and how quickly officers could get shot.

Sometimes when orders were given and blindly obeyed in true military fashion the men fared no better than in the American Sector of the beach code-named Omaha. There, tank-landing craft dropped their ramps in unexpectedly deep and stormy water and, at exactly the correct time ordered, the first tank moved forward to drop like a stone and never be seen again. Commanders in the second, third and fourth tanks in each craft watched the first tanks and crews disappear and drown. They had orders to launch, however, and they launched. One by one they vanished beneath the waves without trace.

Within two or three minutes twenty-seven of the thirty-two tanks were at the bottom of the Channel and nearly one hundred and fifty men were drowned.

Only one commander away at the western end of the beach decided conditions were not favourable and waited until he could go right in and land his tanks on the shore.

In the crush of naval craft of all types incidents like those at Omaha went unnoticed.

Men were waiting silently in landing-crafts, ears alert for the thudding of shells, hands clutching rifles. The wallowing of the craft eased as they approached shallower water and gently nosed through a mass of debris until an explosive jar lurched everyone forward.

Now they had arrived. Ex-office clerks and bricklayers, and shopkeepers and toolfitters and students were sharing the same apprehension. Now ramps crashed down, leaving them naked to machine-gun bullets that twisted them into grotesque ballet dancers and spattered the sea with scarlet. Now mothers' sons became butcher-meat caught up on barbed wire, became flotsam, became beach litter with faces buried in sand, became mere objects robbed of human dignity, rumps poking in the air.

Wave upon wave of men were spewed out to trample over the dead and dying to get a foothold in France.

Beyond the beaches glider-planes crashed and glider-planes landed and paratroopers speckled the earth with white and desperately shouted the rallying cries they had been taught.

'Able—Able!'

'Baker—Baker!'

'Charlie—Charlie!'

They were not surprised at being lost or confused. They had been told before setting out:

'Do not be daunted if chaos reigns. It undoubtedly will.'

On HMS *Donaldson* Alec felt he had been plunged into the centre of a maelstrom of hell. Noise was incredible and continuous. German shore batteries duelled with the ships. The whole shoreline flashed with white from the big guns, plumes of smoke curled high in the air and blood-red flames rampaged out then shrank under billowing clouds of dirty smoke.

Above, a constant umbrella of bombers and fighters darkened the sky. The air groaned and throbbed with the engines of the heavy bombers, and fighters streaked noisily underneath them.

Alec shaded his eyes with his hands and peered back towards home. He had never seen so many aircraft in his life. He wondered where they were all coming from. Britain was a small island and there were limits to what it could hold. Surely there could never have been enough ground space for all these planes to take off. Yet they kept being tossed skywards. They were still zooming over.

His tired eyes, gritty and bloodshot, trailed after one massive formation as it roared above him and away across France. He saw some of the planes explode in the high distance like red cherries and others dive down, charcoaling the sky with black lines.

'Poor bastards!' he muttered.

Never before in his life had he felt so disgusted, so sick to his guts.

'What am I doing here?' he asked himself.

Suddenly the whole thing seemed like a horrible charade.

The padre had led them in prayer before it began and asked for God's blessing. The German padres would no doubt have asked the same God the same thing. It was ludicrous.

He remembered Madge telling him about some Quaker set Catriona had got to know. Apparently that lot believed there was a bit of God in every man. He remembered how Madge had joked about it.

'A bit of the devil in you, more like!'

Now his normally good-natured mind twisted with sarcasm.

'Well, if there's a bit of God in every man, mate, this day man's being bloody disrespectful to his Maker.'

Thinking of Madge brought memories of his children crowding in.

Since he had been in the Navy they had grown away from him. They were like strangers. More and more his thoughts turned to them as they had been before when they were all at home and carefree and happy together. As ships turned broadside on and belched destruction towards the shore he saw his children through the sheet of flame. They had polished faces, white bibs, and sat at the kitchen table. They were singing and banging time with their spoons. Above the bedlam of war he heard their reedy voices:

467

'It's a long way to Tipperary,
It's a long way to go.
It's a long way to Tipperary,
To the sweetest girl I know.
Goodbye Piccadilly,
Farewell Leicester Square -
It's a long, long way to Tipperary,
But my heart's right there.'

Chapter 11

'How can I ever repay you, Julie?' Catriona longed to cling to her friend and weep tears of thankfulness on her shoulder but she kept emotion in check.

She was always uncertain of Julie's reactions. Julie had a perky brusqueness that seemed to repel displays of affection as if they were a weakness or an embarrassment she had no patience for. Yet at times she gave the impression of being a bouncing time bomb of emotions herself.

No use embracing or kissing Madge in an attempt to show gratitude either. She had already tried that and Madge had knocked her roughly aside with one of her big hearty laughs.

'For God's sake, hen, grow up. Stop acting so stupid!'

Julie shrugged and lit a cigarette. 'What have I done except give you a few old cups and plates and a couple of chairs?'

'And all the other things. Both of you have been absolutely marvellous. Gosh, I can hardly believe it. A place of my very own.' She closed her eyes with the relief of it. 'I can do what I like, come and go as I like, please myself about everything.'

'What an imagination!' Madge laughed. 'You're a scream, hen. You've spent all your savings on the deposit for a wee room and kitchen that's really your man's and you're having to share it with two weans and an old man. Still, you're lucky to get the place. Houses aren't so easy to come by nowadays. And you're not so crowded as me, eh?'

'Yes, no harm to your new house, Catriona.' Julie strolled over to the window puffing smoke as she went. 'But better you than me living here.'

Catriona's small face tightened with anxiety.

'Why? What's wrong with the place? Byres Road's supposed to be a good district, isn't it? I know this isn't the best building in the road, but there's a lovely view. You can see the Botanic

Gardens.'

'It's too near my mother-in-law, that's why.' Julie's green eyes suddenly twinkled with mischief. 'Just think, she'll probably pass here every day going for her messages. Maybe one day a bus'll get her crossing Great Western Road.'

'Julie! Don't tempt Providence by saying things like that!'

Madge tucked a straggle of hair behind one ear, shifted her pregnant belly to a more comfortable position and gave a toothy grin.

'Is she an old cow, hen?'

'Tairaibly Kailvainsaide, yew know!' Julie rolled her eyes. 'Tairaibly refained and all that. She nearly died when she found out about me. She thinks I'm dirt because I come from the Gorbals. I told her straight. I'm as good as you and better, pal. Reggie told her as well. You ought to have heard him. Reggie's loyal and all that. He's fond of his mother but, as he says, now that we're married his wife comes first. He'd do anything for me.' She gave a long sigh. 'He's so handsome too. Isn't he, Catriona?'

'Tall and broad-shouldered with marvellous blue eyes and blond hair,' Catriona enthused, happy to have found a way to be of service to Julie.

Madge stretched her big frame out on one of the chairs.

'Aye, they're all great lads at first. I remember when I used to think my man was marvellous.'

Julie coloured with the sudden intensity of her feelings.

'But Reggie *is* marvellous! He really is! He's the nicest, most wonderful person I've ever met. He's such a gentleman and so well educated. He's been to the university, hasn't he, Catriona? Yet there's no side about him at all. My dad and him got on like a house on fire. One time he took my dad out and bought him a drink. I'm not kidding you, everybody in the Gorbals met Reggie that day. Dad was so proud he was stopping strangers in the street and showing Reggie off.'

Madge grinned and scratched the side of her breast, making it swing and wobble about.

'Och, well, the best of luck to you, hen. You're only a' wee lassie yet! I just hope you'll never be trauchled with a squad of

470

weans in your wee place in the Gorbals the way I am in Springburn. I hope to God my crowd aren't ruining the Botanic Gardens across there just now. I'll murder them wee middens one of these days. They never pay a blind bit of notice to a thing I say.'

'Oh, no!' Julie sent a confident stream of smoke darting from full pursed lips. 'Reggie and I are only going to have two children, one of each sex. We've got everything planned.'

Madge spluttered out a howl of derisive laughter. Catriona giggled before she could stop herself and immediately felt guilty and hastened to make amends.

'We know what you mean, Julie.'

'Well, what are you laughing at? What's so funny?'

'We're a lot of bloody mugs, aren't we?' Madge remarked quite pleasantly. 'We're that easy conned.'

Julie's eyes lit with anger.

'What do you mean, conned? Nobody cons me.'

'What Madge means is . . .' Catriona began, but Madge interrupted.

'Things don't turn out the way we bloody well plan, that's what I mean. If you don't keep your eye on that good-looking fella of yours, hen, the chances are some other lassie'll be having a squad of weans to him as well as you.'

Julie's brows and her voice pushed high.

'My Reggie? You don't know him. He's so sincere and sensitive. A perfect gentleman. Isn't he, Catriona?'

'Oh, gosh, yes!'

'I knew all I needed to know about my man the first time I looked at him.'

'Well, hen, I'm sorry to be such a wet blanket but I still say you're just a wee lassie and you've a lot to learn. If you ask me, men are all the same - selfish, randy buggers. That's all they care about. All they want is to enjoy themselves. If you ask me, hen, you'll be trauchled with a dozen weans before you're done.'

'I'm not asking you. I know my man!' The hand that stubbed at her cigarette trembled. 'He's not selfish. But if he ever does decide that he wants more children, that's OK with me, pal. If my man wants a dozen kids, that's OK with me. Whatever my

471

man wants is OK with me!'

Madge's freckled face spread into a smile and she hauled herself up.

'Well, the best of British luck to you, hen. I'd better go and round up my dirty wee middens while there's still some of the Botanic Gardens left. God, my varicose veins are killing me.' She laughed. 'I've piles now as well! They're some other things you're liable to get that you didn't plan for. Och, there I go again. It's a shame, isn't it! Don't pay any attention to me. The trouble with me is I've got such a rotten bugger for a man. Honest to God I hate that dirty midden.'

An awkward silence followed as she struggled into the grey swagger coat she had made herself out of an old army blanket to save clothing coupons.

Catriona felt guilty and ashamed at the mere mention of Alec and she miserably lowered her head.

'And he'd better not say a word to me about his book money when he comes back or he'll get this down his throat.' Madge brandished a red fist. 'I had to keep dibbling into it to pay the doctor for the weans and all the things he said they were needing. That house of ours is that damp it gives them coughs and God knows all what, poor wee sods, and what with this new one . . . See, if Alec says anything about me not managing right with the money . . .'

'Madge, what are you getting all upset about?' Surprised, Catriona looked up. 'Alec's not the type to get on to you about money, is he? You've never said anything about him being like that before.'

'Maybe it's my conscience bothering me.' She sent a great gust of hilarity to the ceiling. 'I've spent all the bugger's money. Serves him bloody well right! Well, I'll away, Catriona. I'll see you next week, hen. Cheerio, Julie. Come over to Springburn with Catriona any time and visit me. Talk about the Gorbals being slummy. My God, you've seen nothing until you've seen Cowlairs Pend!'

'The Gorbals isn't slummy,' Julie snapped back 'There's plenty of clean, hardworking folk in the Gorbals.'

'You'll get a clean, hardworking fist in your eye if you're not

472

careful, hen.'

'Send my two across when you're in the Gardens, Madge,' Catriona hastily intervened. 'It's long past Andrew's bedtime. He'll probably take ages getting used to sleeping in the kitchen with me talking and moving about.'

'Och, well, my crowd have survived sleeping in the kitchen so I suppose yours will as well.'

The word 'survived' brought the night of the air-raid rushing back and she wanted to cry out with the agony of losing baby Robert. Instead she smiled at Madge as she saw her to the door and said:

'As long as they've got a bed, that's the main thing.'

'Aye,' Madge agreed. 'And a roof over their heads. Poor wee buggers, they're entitled to that. I'm glad you managed to get a place, hen. In a real posh part as well! My God, you're fairly coming up in the world, eh? I'd give my right arm to live here but I'm having a hard enough job paying the rent for the dump I'm in.' Her freckled face split wide open with laughter and she gave Catriona a nudge before leaving. 'You'll have to tell me who owns some of the buildings around here so's I can try giving him the wink!'

Back in the kitchen, Julie rolled her eyes.

'What a character!'

'She's terribly kind. Too kind, in fact; that's half Madge's trouble. Look at the stuff she's given me - sheets and pots and pans and dear knows what all. Not to mention the bag of messages she brought today to give me a good start, as she says. She can't afford any of it, you know. It's terrible! You saw me fighting with her, trying to make her take at least some of the stuff back, but she just laughed and wouldn't listen.

'How about a wee cup of tea before the boys come in? You're in no hurry to get away, are you, Julie?'

'No, I told Dad not to wait up for me or anything. He tends to do things like that - worry and fuss a bit since Mammy died.'

Catriona put the kettle on and found two cups and saucers in the cupboard beside the fire.

Grief tortured her. She longed for comfort, for Julie to stay the night and not leave her alone. Longing groped desperately this way and that but could not escape the agony in which she nursed her baby in her arms.

'Will I make a bit of toast?' she asked. 'It's ages since we've had our tea.'

'I know what you're trying to do.' Julie smoothed down her skirt and patted her hips. 'Sabotage my figure. Jealousy'll get you nowhere, pal.'

Catriona laughed.

'Yes, you'd better be careful. Remember what Madge said.'

With a roll of her eyes Julie took a couple of slices of bread from the bread tin and put them under the grill.

'Obviously she's not been able to keep her man, and I'm not surprised. Look how she's let herself go. There's no excuse for a woman looking like that. Did you see her streaky leg make-up? And her ankles were filthy. Her hair could have done with a wash, too, and why doesn't she let it grow a bit and put curlers in?'

'Och, she's pregnant, poor soul, and she's already got six children to look after. She's never been too strong either since that last set of twins was born. She had an awful bad time.'

Julie deftly turned the toast.

'She looks as strong as a horse. I thought she was going to land one on me. Believe me, pal, I was scared rigid!'

Suddenly they both began to giggle. 'If she had socked me, I would have howled,' Julie raised her voice in mock distress, '"I'll get my Reggie to you. He's more your size, you dirty big bully!"'

'You and your Reggie!' Catriona shook her head. 'You're an awful girl. Watch the toast. You're going to burn it. That'll be the boys at the door! I'll go.'

As she went into the small hallway she could hear Julie scraping butter on the bread and singing:

> 'There'll be blue-birds over
> The white cliffs of Dover,
> Tomorrow, just you wait and see . . .'

Catriona opened the outside door ready to give the boys a row for being late but was taken aback to see Julie's father in the shadows of the landing.

'Mr Gemmell! Come away in. Julie's in the kitchen.'

He seemed reluctant to move and hovered uncertainly on the doormat, his eyes evasive in their brown hollows. He looked ill.

'Is something wrong?' Catriona asked.

Dode shuffled down the hall, peeling off his cap.

'Aye. Ah've got bad news.'

'Not Reggie!'

'Aye, lass, a telegram!'

'Oh, no!' Catriona wrung her hands. 'Oh, no, Mr Gemmell!'

'What am ah going tae say to her, hen?'

They both listened in anguish to the sound of Julie's happy singing.

Miserably Dode twisted his cap.

'Ah'm nae damnt use.'

'You'll just have to give her the telegram. Oh, dear, you'd better go in.'

'Dad!' Julie gasped as soon as she saw him. 'What are you doing here, you auld rascal?'

She had been eating a bit of toast and she tongued her teeth and flicked crumbs from the corner of her mouth. 'I'm big enough and ugly enough to see myself home. All I need to do is get the subway down the road, for goodness' sake!'

Abruptly Dode produced the telegram and stuffed it into her hand.

'This came. I opened it, lass. Reggie's missing. Failed to return, it says. But don't you worry, hen. He'll have been taken prisoner like Catriona's man.'

Julie stared down at the telegram. Her firm cheeks sagged and went grey like an old woman's.

Catriona thought she was going to faint and hurried to put her arms round her and help her into a chair.

'Yes, look how I heard from Melvin. That's what happens, Julie. They get picked up and taken to a camp and eventually the Red Cross or somebody traces them. It's happened lots and lots of times.'

'I want to go home, Dad,' Julie said.

Dode nodded. He was still twisting his cap and tears shimmered his eyes.

'A damnt shame!'

'Come on.'

'Isn't there anything I can do?' Catriona queried, still clinging round the girl's shoulders. 'Stay and have a cup of tea. Stay the night if you want to. Both of you. We'll manage.'

'No, thanks all the same.' Julie became suddenly brisk and rose, tidying down her skirt. 'I just want to go home with my dad.' Catriona followed them to the door with short steps.

'Julie, something's just occurred to me. What about Reggie's parents? Shouldn't you go and tell them?'

Julie's face twisted into a travesty of a smile and she ignored Catriona's question.

'Best of luck in your new house, pal. Be seeing you!'

The door banged shut.

Catriona was left helplessly wringing her hands in the empty hall.

Chapter 12

The gate creaked open. Open, then shut again, lazily, like the motion of the trees. The Gardens and the crescent were a green shimmer. Tall trees allowed heavy branches to lean, to undulate, to whisper and ripple.

From where she sat Muriel Vincent could see nothing but gently dancing green framed in the big windows of her sitting-room.

'Pretty as a picture,' she had often said. 'Such a nice outlook.'

The room was quiet, so quiet she was sure she could hear her tiny gold wrist-watch ticking.

The stiff-faced girl in the chair opposite said, 'I got these.'

She handed over some letters.

The first one had Reggie's squadron and air station address at the top.

Muriel read:

'Dear Mrs Vincent,

Prior to receiving this letter you will have received a telegram informing you that your husband Flight Lieutenant R. Vincent had been reported missing from an operational flight which took place on the night of 6th June 1944.

It is with very deep regret I am writing this letter to convey to you the feelings of the entire squadron following the news that your husband has been reported missing.

On Tuesday evening last an aircraft and crew of which your husband was pilot and captain took off to carry out a bombing attack on the French coast. This flight was vital and one of the many fighting and courageous efforts called for by the Royal Air Force. The flight should not have taken very long but although other aircraft completed their mission your husband's aircraft failed to return.

The most searching enquiries through all possible channels and organisations have so far revealed nothing but of course it will take some time for possible information to come through from enemy sources and I can only hope your husband and crew are prisoners of war. Meanwhile further information may come available; if so, this will of course be passed to you immediately.

A committee of officers known as a Committee of Adjustment has gathered your husband's personal possessions together and will communicate with you in the near future.

May I again express my personal sympathy in your great anxiety.'

The letter was signed by a Wing-Commander.

Another communication headed 'Casualty Branch, Oxford Street, London', began:

'Madam,

I am commanded by the Air Council to express to you their great regret on learning that your husband, Flight Lieutenant Reginald Vincent, Royal Air Force . . .'

The letter from the chaplain was written in a spidery longhand:

'Dear Mrs Vincent,

I am writing to express my profound sorrow that your husband F/Lieut. R. Vincent is missing after operations on the night of 6th June. I understand the uncertainty and anxiety which you must feel. I was up waiting for the crews and it was a great grief to us when your husband's plane failed to return.

I can only hope that your husband and his crew may have escaped disaster by baling out and have become prisoners of war. But of course there is no certainty of this, and it is not until official information comes through via the Red Cross that your terrible suspense will be ended.

You may rest assured that whatever this news, it will be communicated to you at once.

I know that whatever has happened to him he would not have you overcome with sorrow, and you can be sure that his chief thought was less for his own safety than for loyalty and devotion to duty.

Like so many other brave men, he has willingly hazarded his life for a great cause, and we may be proud and thankful for his example.

During these times, we can but commit ourselves and our anxieties into the hand of God, who cares and suffers in the griefs of His people.

I pray that you may find in God your comfort and be made strong to bear your heavy load of suffering.'

The last letter was neatly typed and signed by a Fight Lieutenant for the Group Captain commanding Reggie's base station:

'Dear Mrs Vincent,

As the officer disposing of the effects of your husband F/ Lieut. R. Vincent, may I be permitted to offer you my most sincere sympathy.

In accordance with Air Ministry regulations your husband's personal effects are being forwarded to the RAF Central Depository, Colnbrook, in order that certain formalities may be completed under the provisions of the Regimental Debt Act. All enquiries regarding these effects should be addressed to the Officer Commanding, RAF Central Depository, Colnbrook, Near Slough, Buckinghamshire.

A bicycle, BSA with dynamo and lamp, was found in the effects and is being retained on this station pending disposal instructions from the Central Depository.'

Muriel passed each letter in turn to her husband Norman whose face contorted in ugly sobs and had to be hidden and mopped with a handkerchief he fumbled from his trouser pocket. He was shaking all over like an old man.

Muriel viewed him with cold unloving eyes He had never been an use in a crisis. Oh, he fussed and made cups of tea and insisted on calling in the doctor if she was ill. He could hold on to money, too, and she could depend on the fact that he would never squander all he had and leave them penniless. He did not drink or gamble or go with other women. But he was a weak man.

Long ago she had discovered he was a weak man and she secretly despised him.

She remembered overhearing two women confiding in each other over cups of coffee in a restaurant near Norman's bank. One of them had obviously been having trouble with an overdraft and Norman had taken advantage of her predicament. She was furiously recounting to her friend:

'My dear, he'd always been such a gentleman before. I could hardly believe my ears. You wouldn't speak to me like that, I said, if my Nigel were here! No, my dear, he's no gentleman. He's just a horrid ferret-faced coward!'

Muriel's stare raked over his lanky body, his faded eyes now red with tears, his thin features. Quite a good description she had thought at the time and she still thought so.

The bitterness inside her hardened into a spearhead that aimed straight for Norman's heart. Somehow whatever had happened to Reggie must have been Norman's fault. Norman was a cheat and a failure. He had failed her right from the start. His pathetic ineptitude in bed had sickened her so much she had long since abandoned having anything to do with that side of their marriage.

Often she marvelled at Norman's managing to father one child. She thanked God he had managed, of course. Having Reggie, loving him, watching him grow, planning for him, dreaming about the wonderful future he was going to have, had been the only justification for her marriage, for her whole life, in fact.

Nothing Norman could possibly feel would ever match the torture she was in now. Yet he was reduced to blubbering and making a fool of himself in front of the girl. Reggie's wife had more backbone than his father.

In disgust she averted her gaze from Norman. Her eyes wandered over to the window again then came back to the girl sitting opposite.

She stared at the erect figure, immaculate in the black suit and crisp white blouse, hair like polished mahogany, curling neatly inwards and contrasting with creamy skin and hard green eyes.

Reggie loved this girl. Over and over again he had told her, 'I love her, Mother. I thought you'd understand. I really love her.'

Understanding began to grow in the silent room that had been so familiar to Reggie. How often had he sat in that same chair in which his wife was now sitting.

Muriel cleared her throat.

'I had a letter too. From Reggie. "In case anything happens to me, Mother", it began. He must have written it at the same time as the one you told us he wrote to you.'

Julie raised a brow.

'Oh?'

'He asked us to look after you.'

'That won't be necessary. I'm perfectly all right, thank you. Well, if you'll excuse me.' She rose, tucking the letters neatly into her handbag and closing it with a snap. 'I'd better be going.'

Muriel rose too, smiling politely, calmly, yet plummeting down a ski slope of panic as if she would be alone in the world if the girl went away.

'Must you? I . . . I thought perhaps you could stay for dinner. We have plenty, I can assure you.'

'No, thank you all the same, but my father's expecting me.' Julie turned, hand outstretched to Norman.

'Goodbye, Mr Vincent. Chin up and all that! Reggie wouldn't want you to be upset.'

The contrast between the man and the girl was striking. For the first time Muriel saw the proud tilt to Julie's head and thought that there was no danger of her breaking down and acting the fool.

Yet she was only nineteen.

'Mother, will you please take care of her for me,' Reggie had written.

She could see him writing the letter just before he went on that last flight, his blond head bent in concentration over the paper. He always wrote in spurts and flourishes with long pauses in between when he thoughtfully chewed his pen.

In the taut silence as Muriel followed her daughter-in-law

481

across the parquet-floored hall, her son felt very near.

At the outside door Julie said jauntily:

'Well, goodbye, Mrs Vincent. Thanks for the afternoon tea.'

Just for a second Muriel thought she saw her own anguish mirrored in the green eyes.

She touched the girl's arm.

'You must come again.'

'Aye, aw right.'

The brittle voice lapsing unexpectedly into broad Glasgow accent gave it a pathetic droop that Muriel found unbearable.

She suddenly ached to take the poor child in her arms and comfort her, but already Julie was away down the stairs, the clumping of her wooden heels filling the stained-glass sanctuary with unaccustomed noise.

Muriel returned hurriedly to the sitting-room and went straight across to peer out of the window.

It seemed as if Reggie were at her elbow, all the time anxious. *'I love her, Mother . . .'*

Recklessly she did something that she would never have dreamed of doing before. She rattled her fist against the window.

Julie jerked round in the crescent below. She gazed up. Muriel waved.

A stunned look dulled the young features for a moment, then they tightened and brightened. She smiled and waved back.

Muriel watched the girl clip briskly away in the Queen Margaret Drive direction, then turned back into the quiet sitting-room where Norman was still fumbling a handkerchief over his face.

'You ought to be ashamed of yourself.' She passed his chair, smoothing the skirt of her dress close to her legs as if it might be contaminated by any contact with him.

Norman shook his head.

'Our only son!'

'Oh, be quiet, Norman. Reggie's all right. Where's your faith? We'll be hearing from him one of these days. It's just a matter of waiting. For his sake, if for nobody else's, try to wait with some dignity.'

Norman just kept shaking his head.

482

'You've always been the same.' She picked up the white polo-necked sweater she was knitting for Reggie and tucking the needles under her arms she started them clicking busily.

'Muriel, for pity's sake put that away. I can't bear to see it.'

The needles continued as if they were taking pleasure in their jabbing movement.

'Reggie's sweater?'

'Muriel, please!'

'He gets cold. You've heard him say how cold it can get in that bomber.'

'He's been shot down.'

'And taken prisoner.'

'Muriel.'

'He'll be glad of this in a horrid prisoner-of-war camp. And I'll see that he gets it. I'll contact the Red Cross.'

'Our only son!'

'Oh, be quiet. Control yourself. Try to remember you're a man. That girl has more backbone than you! You're always the same, Norman.'

'My dear, I'm only facing facts and accepting them. His wife doesn't believe he's alive any more than I do.'

'That's a lie. How do you know what she believes? You were so wrapped up in yourself and your own feelings all afternoon you hardly gave the poor girl a glance.'

'I couldn't bear to look at her. She reminds me all the time of Reggie. He spoke so much about her that last time he was here. I hope she doesn't come back, Muriel! What's the use, after all?'

'That's so typical of you. It doesn't matter, of course, that Reggie asked us to look after her.'

'We'll give her money, see that she never lacks for anything.'

'Money! That's all you know about. I've said it before, Norman, and I'll say it again. Thank God Reggie has me. You've never understood him.'

Her knitting needles quickened and every now and again she gave a sharp little tug at the ball of white wool.

Norman stood up, crumpling his handkerchief between his hands.

'I understand he's dead.'

483

'Don't say that! You don't know what you're talking about. I keep telling you, Norman, Reggie is alive and well. You're like a poisonous weed. Spreading gloom and depression. Julie must have felt it. You upset her. I could tell. I'm going to see her again as soon as possible and do my very best to reassure her. This dreadful war isn't going to last for ever, I'll tell her. Soon it will be all over and Reggie will be home.'

Chapter 13

D-day, Alec reckoned, had been the beginning of the end. He thanked God for the end but the whole business still sickened him. He could not forget the cost.

Wave upon wave of men, countless British, Canadian, American and all the rest, had been killed and mutilated in the process. Unarmed thousands of civilians had been caught in the centre of the fighting, had clung desperately to their homes and when their houses had been hit by bomb or shell they had run out to crowd together in search of shelter, only to be hit again and again and left to die in the smoking ruins of once serene little cities.

A soldier survivor of a typical battle for a French town had said:

'We won the battle but, considering the high price in American lives, we lost.'

It reminded Alec of what he had read of the First World War. From his level, that of the ordinary man being sent in to fight, all wars were the same, just a reckless slaughter. It seemed to him as if some determined top brass had his hand on a tap of human life and turned it on and kept turning it on.

Life gushed out, as easy to come by and as cheap as water, and was swilled just as easily down the drain.

He was so sickened, he felt ashamed to be part of the human race. The top brass, and the politicians, the folk that were supposed to be so much cleverer than the likes of him - with all their brains, their civilisation, their so-called Christianity - was this the only kind of solution they could come up with? Was this the best they could do?

Now the European war was over and he was fortunate enough to be among the first to be released. Some poor mugs had been kept in because they were still needed in the Far East, but

485

he was out, on his own, changed from a number in the Navy to a number in the Labour Exchange, or Buroo as it was known locally.

He had wasted no time in signing on at the Buroo and agitating for work. With a wife and seven weans to keep he could not afford to waste a minute.

As well as taking the precaution of signing on for Buroo money he hurried back to his old office, burst cheerily in, expecting the same old camaraderie; but most of the men he had known were no longer there and he did not even get a decent welcome from the girls. Afterwards, trying to piece together his shattered ego, he decided that they must all have acquired American boyfriends with fancy uniforms and plenty of money or men of some other nationality equally glamorous. Compared with a money-flashing Yank or a heel-clicking Polish officer he could see that he would seem dull stuff.

He shrugged them off and wished them luck. As for the men in the office, they were polite and amiable but at the same time surprisingly distant. He felt like a stranger, an uninvited guest who was putting a strain on the party.

The same applied to other men in other offices. He tried to storm quite a few. They were all ticking over very nicely without him. They all had their established routines. They were all fully staffed.

Despite the cheerful bantering bluster that gave energy to his long legs and sent them racing up stairway after stairway, three or four steps at a time, and his fist rat-tat-tat-tat-tatting on prospective employers' doors, he began to feel embarrassed as well as bitter.

'Damn them!' he thought. But his thoughts did not help. Then he told himself: 'Early days yet!'

He was barely demobbed and the war in Japan was not even over.

Yet he knew that more and more men would be coming home and it would get harder, not easier, to find work.

He kept trying, never letting up because he had always been an active energetic man. Now as well as his natural exuberance he had acquired a new restlessness. It seemed to have been born in the Navy and was tuned to the continuous movement of the ship. It was a kind of impatience that made the tiny overcrowded room and kitchen in Cowlairs Pend close in on him like the bars of a prison.

Worry about money tormented him, too. The overcrowding and the bad condition of the house had affected the children's health. One or the other kept needing the doctor. Fiona coughed all the time and Madge was always dosing her with something.

Day after day he struggled to simulate normality, to ignore his worries. He tried to fit in with the children, be the same overgrown playmate he had once been to them, the loved and respected boss of the Jackson gang. But he found the same strange rejection here as in all the places he visited to ask about work. The gang had closed its ranks. His family resented him. His children had grown into an impertinent, unruly, rebellious mob and his wife had given way to being a slut.

He missed the way it had been before the war when he had been able to take Madge out for treats to cheer her up, when he had been able to burst into the house with an armful of presents for her and the weans. But it went deeper than nostalgia. His inability diminished him.

He tried to talk to Madge, to make half-joking yet desperately serious attempts to explain his feelings, not to mention his money worries, to her.

She swatted away his embarrassed gropings as if he were a fly on something she was going to eat.

'Never mind feeling sorry for yourself. Think yourself damned lucky. What about me? I've been stuck in this dump with them wee middens of yours for years. You lumbered me with this lot and even that wasn't enough. You had to have your fun with other women as well. I can't even trust you with my best friends. You're no use. Now you can't even get a job. You that's such a bloody charmer. You that's so clever. You'll be expecting me to go out to work to keep us next and how can I with me still feeding this wee midden.'

She indicated their latest, a plump infant of nearly three months, called Charlie, who was energetically sucking at her breast.

'I don't know what we're going to do. I used to trust you. You were my man and I trusted you and somehow that made everything all right.' She scratched her lank hair and shoved it behind her ear out of the way. 'Now everything's all wrong and I don't know what's going to happen.'

He got so fed up, he escaped to the pub and drank himself stupid a couple of times. He took the whole width of the Pend, bouncing off one side, staggering across the cobbles and bouncing off the other on his way home, and on his arrival he immediately tried to force himself on everyone in a desperate effort to ingratiate himself in their affections. Nothing but bedlam resulted. The older weans had shaken free of him, loudly sneering in disgust, 'Get off!' and the younger ones had screamed and sobbed and yelled:

'Mammy, Mammy!'

Afterwards he felt guilty and ashamed, not only of worsening relations with his children but because he knew he could not afford to drink.

He was also angry at himself for giving Madge something else to nag about.

Fortunately, his inborn Glasgow humour kept coming to his rescue and sometimes Madge had to laugh in spite of herself.

'Have a heart, hen,' he'd say. 'I admit I'm an unemployed rapist but don't tell me I'm a hopeless wino as well!'

Sometimes they would chat together almost like normal and Madge would tell him all the gossip.

'Catriona MacNair's man's coming back. She heard the other day and she's in a right flap. He's been a prisoner of war, poor bugger. Still, he's lucky compared with some. You haven't met Catriona's pal, the one she used to work with, have you? Julie Vincent, a bit of a haughty piece but quite a nice wee lassie all the same, comes from the Gorbals. Catriona and her used to work in Morton's in Buchanan Street. Well, her man was shot down on D-day. It's the queerest thing that, Alec.'

'Queer? Being shot down? My God, hen, if you'd seen as many shot down as I've seen . . .'

'No, no,' she interrupted impatiently. 'Julie's mother-in-law.'

He laughed and shook his head.

'Women! I don't know what you're talking about, hen.'

'Catriona says Mrs Vincent wouldn't have anything to do with Julie at first. Then Reggie - that's Julie's man - got shot down and from that moment, Julie's never been able to get Mrs Vincent off her back!'

'You're sure it wasn't Mr Vincent Catriona said?'

'Don't be filthy. Trust you to make a joke of the poor lassie's trouble. You don't care a damn about anybody.'

'I'm sorry, hen. I'm sorry!' He hastened to veer her back into the path of good humour. 'You mean Julie's man was killed?'

'They weren't sure at first but word came through that he was dead not long after he was posted missing. Och, that was a while ago now. Must be a year or more. Aye, he went missing on D-day. But that's queer about her mother-in-law, isn't it? Catriona says it's fair tormenting Julie.'

'She's probably at the change of life. Remember Ma went a bit queer?'

'Aye, poor soul. My God, if it's not one thing it's another. Women just get free of bringing up weans and then they've "the change" to suffer.'

'Well, I never invented it, hen.' He laughed, then realised too late that in laughing he had blundered.

'Aye, laugh, laugh!' Madge shouted in his face. 'It's a great joke for the likes of you. As long as you're getting your f—ing way, you've nothing to worry about!'

'Madge, the weans!' he pleaded. 'They'll be talking like that next.'

She laughed bitter, ugly laughter.

'Oh, listen to Saint Alec. I was just stating a plain fact in plain words.' She shook her head. 'I wouldn't have cared, Alec. I would have struggled along being pregnant all the time, being trauchled and tired and mixed up and not being able to manage and I still would have been quite content and happy if I'd thought you cared.'

He groaned.

'But, hen. I do care. My God, you go on like a gramophone record. You've got an absolute obsession, Madge. It's really getting terrible.'

'I've got an obsession? I've never lied to you. I've never . . .'
'Oh, shut up!'

He couldn't help it. It was just impossible to sit quietly listening to another long spiel about his heinous infidelities and in his rush to get up and escape he stumbled over Charlie who was sitting on the floor with a dummy teat stuck in his mouth. The dummy teat spurted out to dangle on its yellow cord and Charlie let out a scream of protest.

Madge hauled herself up.

'You kicked that wee wean, you dirty big coward!'

'I did not!'

Madge's red shovels of hands punched out wildly and in desperation he gripped her by the wrists.

'You're mad!'

'If I'm mad it's you that's made me.'

Her freckles were ugly brown blotches on an unhealthy grey skin and her eyes strained huge and wild with anger.

'See him! See him!' she shouted round at the now screaming children. 'See what a rotten midden you've got for a daddy!'

To Alec, this was the last straw. He flung her wrists aside.

'You're a great help,' he said bitterly. 'A great help. Well, you might as well know it all and really get to work on me. The rent's so much in arrears now we'll never be able to make up the money. You said you didn't know what we're going to do. Well, I don't know what we're going to do either.' His voice broke. 'The way things look I'm going to be in the jail and you and the weans in Barnhill.'

The screaming and sobbing of all the children lifted to a crescendo at the mention of the word Barnhill. They all knew it was the poorhouse.

'Shut up!' Madge bawled above them. 'And get away through to the room, the whole crowd of you. Charlie and all. Haul him out along with you.'

Alec lit a cigarette and thought bitterly of how any time now everybody would be celebrating VJ-day. The end of the war. What they had all been fighting for. Freedom. Victory. A decent way of life. What a joke!

As soon as the kitchen was empty and quiet, Madge

faced him.

'What are you talking about us all getting separated for? You're my man and we're your family.'

'I know, hen. But with these doctor's bills and the medicines and one thing and another . . . You must have seen it coming yourself. We've been robbing Peter to pay Paul.'

'They'll try and sell all our furniture, all our things, everything we've got, Alec.' She gripped the back of a chair for support. 'They'll try and separate us.'

He grabbed her angrily into his arms.

'If I could just get a bloody job. I'm going back down to that Buroo again. I'll plead with them. To hell with collar-and-tie jobs and offices, hen. I'll empty bins. I'll sweep the streets. I'll do anything.'

'What if they don't have anything? The rotten middens haven't had anything so far.'

'We'll just have to do a moonlight.' His handsome face, already fatigued and embittered by war, now creased with worry. 'But where we'll go I've no idea. Who'd take us in, with all our mob! How will we even get a lorry or something to move all our things?'

Madge thought for a minute.

'I know!'

'What, hen?'

'The McNairs still have their bread van somewhere. That'll do fine. And see over the West End where she lives, Alec, there's big houses lying empty. It's wicked! Why should there be houses lying empty and weans needing a roof over their heads? Some squatters have moved into one already. We could go there, too.'

'Oh, just a minute, hen. I don't know if I agree with squatters. Everybody can't just go about taking everything they want!'

She pushed him roughly away.

'You're a fine one to talk! It's all right when it's taking a woman you want, is it? But it's different when it's taking a place for your wife and weans?'

'All right, all right.' He groaned. 'But don't you see, Madge, it's illegal. They'll have me in the end.'

'No, they won't. They won't.' She brandished her big fists but

491

he could see that she was trembling. 'Nobody's going to take you away from me again. I won't let them. Do you hear, you dirty big midden? I won't let them!'

'Och, Madge!' He took her in his arms again. 'If it's what you want, hen, we'll go right away.'

He shut his eyes and tried to blot out the terrible picture of chairs and rolls of linoleum and cots and brushes and mattresses and all the pathetic paraphernalia that they had collected over the years, not to mention the weans, all being crammed into an old bread van in the middle of the night and setting off rootless and defenceless yet still dependent on him, to he knew not where.

'I'll go and see Catriona,' he said.

'*I'll* go and see Catriona,' Madge corrected. 'You stay here and look after the weans.'

'But this house out her way . . . I'll have to know exactly where, won't I?'

'We'll all go then.' She swung round towards the door and blasted it with an enormous yell. 'Sadie! Agnes! Hector! William! Fiona! Maisie! Come back through here at once, and bring Charlie!'

Chapter 14

'I can't eat it!' Melvin's red-rimmed eyes glared down at the large chocolate cake. Brown crumbs speckled his moustache proving that he had tried. His mouth warped with bitterness.

'But, Melvin, I thought you said you'd been dreaming about a chocolate cake for years. Don't worry about rations or anything. I'll manage. Eat it, Melvin. It's all yours. I made it specially.'

'I can't eat it, you fool. My belly's shrunk!'

'Oh, dear!'

This was yet another problem Melvin had brought home. During the day he could not eat and at night he could not sleep. The cavity bed had been out of the question.

'I'm not going to sleep in that hole in the wall.' He had swung away in an effort to hide the apprehension in his face but she had seen it and been moved to put her arms round him and comfort him like a child.

'It's all right, dear.'

He pushed her aside with a bluster of bravado.

'I could if I wanted to. I don't choose to, that's all. It's space I want now. Space to breathe and stretch myself.'

'Yes, all right, Melvin, but what can we do? There's no place else. Except the floor.'

'Well, what's wrong with that? It's only a temporary measure. I've got plans, big plans.'

So she had pushed back the table and chairs and made up a bed as best she could on the kitchen floor. She crept in first and watched with a mixture of fear and compassion as he undressed to reveal the skeleton of the man he had once been. Yet he still had plenty of swagger.

'I've got about five years' pay lying. Think of that!'

'That's lovely!'

'And I had a few pounds stacked away before that.'

'Fancy!'

'I'm going to speak to Da, get things moving about a new business.' He hitched big bony shoulders inside his pyjamas. 'You can't keep a good man down!'

'No, dear.'

She strained up to peer at his grey hair, his sallow face deeply carved with lines, before crumpling back with her feelings in disorder. He was an old man. An old man scratching himself and stomping over to come and lie beside her. She wished she could pluck herself out of the room and throw herself to the winds. She had crazy visions, rapid jerky pictures of herself escaping, being free, starting life again.

But there were the children. Her stomach contracted with immediate fear at the thought, no matter how fleeting, of leaving them.

Melvin's lovemaking touched a need inside her, let at the same time it flared up a disgust of herself. She turned away afterwards and tried to blot herself out in sleep but Melvin kept his hand between her legs and refused to stop fondling her. For hours she lay unable to sleep, fatigue and the invasion of her privacy irking her beyond measure. The thought that even if she did sleep, he would still be 'using' her seemed to take away any last vestige of pretence that she had ever been or would ever be a free human being with dignity or rights of her own.

Resentment and anger simmered in a cauldron of repressed emotion. But he had suffered years in a prison camp, she kept reminding herself, and because of this she kept forcing herself to be patient and to please him.

She had baked the chocolate cake to please him and he had taken one half-hearted nibble at it and then put it down.

Fergus and Andrew were at the table, too, waiting eagerly, eyes on the cake, mouths drooling. Then Fergus kicked Andrew under the table and Andrew reacted obediently to cue.

'Can I have a bit then?'

Melvin's reaction was so violent it startled all of them, including old Duncan who had been chomping noisily at a crust of bread with his too-loose dentures.

'Leave that cake alone, you ugly fat little bastard!' His voice was not loud yet it shook the air with venom. 'You've enough fat on you to keep you going for years. Mummy's spoiled brat, aren't you? Mummy's plump wee cuddles?'

Andrew's eyes stretched enormous in a face gone white. His lips trembled but he did not utter a sound.

Catriona was outraged.

'What are you picking on him for? Fergus wants a bit too. He's too fly to ask, that's all.'

'Yes, Fatso's always been your favourite. I wonder why?'

'Have you gone mad or something?' Catriona got up from the table, ready to bodily protect Andrew if necessary. 'What does it matter about the stupid chocolate cake. You said you didn't want it.'

'I didn't say I didn't want it but, oh, let him have it. Let him have it. All of you have a bit. Eat it all. Don't worry about me!'

Catriona sat down again. Lack of sleep plus the new irritations of the day had started pain pressing in at her temples. 'You mean you might eat it afterwards? Well, that's all right then. I'm sorry, boys, but I made the cake for Daddy and he might . . .'

'No . . . no!' Melvin interrupted, pushing the cake into the centre of the table with a grand gesture. 'Eat it! Eat it! Don't worry about me!'

'But, Melvin . . .'

'Eat it!'

In miserable silence the children pushed pieces of chocolate cake into their mouths.

Eventually Melvin said:

'We're getting out of this place for a start.'

'It's nice here,' Catriona muttered resentfully. 'In a nice close, in a nice district. The children play across in the Botanic Gardens.'

She wished he had never come back. She had been content pottering about on her own as if she were a little girl again playing at houses. There was a cosiness about the new place and it gave her a sense of achievement to look at it and realise that she had found it, paid the deposit and negotiated everything herself.

495

It was a bit cramped with her father-in-law in the room and Fergus kept harassing her with objections about having to sleep with the old man. Still, at night once they were settled and Andrew tucked in the kitchen bed and the fire was flickering, a glow of security and real pleasure warmed her. There was a kind of happiness in busying herself doing odd jobs, or gazing out the window at life ebbing back and forth in Byres Road.

Sometimes she curled up beside the fire and read a book. Sometimes she crept in beside Andrew and enjoyed a read in bed. Every now and again she stole a thrill by gently touching the little boy as he slept, caressing his hair with her fingertips, or the childish contours of his face. Or she would lie for a long time holding his hand.

'This kitchen's not much bigger than the bedspace I had to live in in the prison camp and not nearly so tidy or well organised. I never could stand poky disorganised places. I always had a house to be proud of and that's what I'm going to have again.'

'I suppose that means I'm going to be a slave to the polishing cloth like I was before. I don't understand you.'

'You wouldn't know a good polish if you saw it. You should have seen the shine on my floors when my Betty was alive.'

Catriona rose and began to gather up the dirty dishes.

'Oh, for pity's sake, we're not going to go over all that again. I had enough of your marvellous Betty years ago.'

'Don't you dare talk to me like that.' His voice never rose but the menace in it was unmistakable. Duncan shuffled to his feet.

'I'm away to the room, son. Maybe there's something good on the wireless.'

'I'll come through and talk to you later. We'll have to get another business.'

Old MacNair scratched his beard.

'Aye, I know, but it's easier said than done. There's businesses to be bought, oh, aye. There's old Russell. I meet him often across in the Gardens and we have a blether and a smoke on one of the seats. He was telling me he's thinking of retiring. He's got a place just down the road. Been here for years. But there's all the bother about allocations. You've got to have allocations in the district. Our allocations were for Clydend.'

'We could soon swing the allocations. What's to stop us paying a few hundred extra for "goodwill"?'

'Not having a few extra hundred,' Duncan replied tartly. 'That's what could stop us. I'm away through to the room.'

'He's got it all right and plenty to spare,' Melvin growled after the old man had left. 'He's made thousands. I've done his books and I know. For years I worked for that old skinflint for no more than pocket money. He took me out of school and paid me a few bob for working like a slave. It was like drawing blood out of a stone to eventually get a decent wage off him and for that I ran his business. He's been no bloody use for years. This time I'm going to see that I get a partnership.'

'Do you think you'll get him to agree? It is his money.'

Melvin's eyes bulged.

'Are you deaf as well as stupid? I've just been telling you how I earned that money. I slaved for it for him and I took him into my home so that he didn't need to pay for his house and all his expenses. He's going to be fed and looked after for the rest of his life, thanks to what I've done.'

'Yes, and you never as much as mentioned it to me.'

'What do you mean, mentioned it to you?'

'You never said a word to me until after it was all settled and I'm the one who's got all the work and worry.'

'You!' he sneered. 'What work have you ever done? What worry have you ever had?'

She turned away and put the dishes in the sink. She could not bear the pain of saying - my baby is dead.

'Nothing! Nothing! My life's been just dandy since I met you!'

'Yes, well remember that,' he warned, taking her seriously. 'What's the top-notch houses round about here? The really best ones you've set eyes on?'

'Houses?'

'That's what I said.'

'Why?'

'Just answer my question.'

The children began to argue in the background and she

recognised the pattern of sound. Fergus was tormenting Andrew about something and at any minute Andrew was either going to erupt into violence and pitch himself bodily at Fergus or burst into noisy tears of frustration.

'Away out and play, boys. Fergus, here's money for sweets.' She smiled, hoping to bribe him into a better humour. 'And there's some coupons in this book. Share them with Andrew and take his hand crossing the road. He's only a wee boy and I'm depending on you to look after him.'

Immediately the words were out she worried about whether she ought to have mentioned about taking Andrew's hand and looking after him in case it revealed any preference for Andrew and incurred any further jealousy or displeasure.

She tried to console herself by thinking that surely it was natural for every mother to feel a special kind of love for her youngest, her baby. Then pain so terrible that nothing in the world could ever soothe it away took possession of her. She could feel the milky-smelling softness of Robert in her arms, see his round eyes drugged with sleep and adoration as she nursed him and sang to him.

> I left my baby lying there,
> Oh, lying there, oh, lying there,
> I left my baby lying there,
> When I returned my baby was gone . . .

She pressed her hand against her mouth.

'The houses! The houses!' Melvin insisted.

'What houses?'

'Jumpin' Jesus, wake up!'

'Och, there's lots of nice places round about here. The West End's full of nice places. Where Julie's in-laws lie is nice. Julie's a girl I used to work with. She took me round there one day.'

'Round where?'

'Her mother-in-law lives in a big red sandstone flat facing the river at the other side of the Botanic Gardens.'

'Show me!'

'Now?'

'Now!'

'I'm doing the dishes.'

'Now, I said.'

'Oh, for goodness' sake!'

'For goodness' sake,' he mimicked. 'What do you know about goodness? I don't believe that last brat was mine.'

The unexpectedness of his words rocked her. She clutched on the sink for support.

'Melvin, please, you don't know how I feel.'

'I'm not so sure about Fatso, either!'

'You don't know what you're saying.'

'I could get rid of you, you know. You think yourself damned lucky. I'm doing you a big favour keeping you on. But just watch it. Watch it! What are you standing there for, then? You look as if you're going to puke in the sink. Hurry up!'

'Is this how it's going to be?'

'What do you mean, "Is this how it's going to be?"'

'Are you going to torment me all the time and make my life a misery?'

He guffawed with laughter and shot big hands out to fondle her breasts and make her immediately shrink away from the window.

'Somebody might see!'

'You love it, don't you!'

Shrivelled miserably into a corner, her hands and arms twisting in an effort to protect herself, she said:

'I thought you wanted to go out.'

'Sure! Sure! Get your coat.'

He tugged at his tie and buttoned the jacket of his demob suit, a crumpled navy-blue pin-stripe that nipped in at the waist.

Outside, striding along Byres Road and across into Queen Margaret Drive the breeze flapped the trousers of the suit against his bones and sunlight made shadows hollow his face. Darting a look up at him she wondered what he was thinking as he marched along, his moustache puffing up and his thin hair feathering.

Was he dreaming grand dreams of a house without cavity beds? Did he expect one in Mrs Vincent's building to be empty, ready and waiting for him to command?

She sighed and took his arm.

'Was it terrible for you in the prison camp, Melvin?'

'Och, I was hardly ever in a camp,' he scoffed. 'I was escaping all the time. Nobody could get the better of me. They couldn't pin me down, not even the Gestapo. It's a fine place here, right enough.' He took big breaths as they went over the Queen Margaret bridge. 'A lot different from Dessie Street. Remember all the dust and noise? The yards across the main road and the street all lumpy with cobbles?'

She made no reply.

'This is the place, all right.' He gazed around, puffing out his chest. 'For - for a king!'

'Round to the left,' she said, then after a minute or two: 'This is Botanic Crescent.'

He stopped and stared at the big three-storied terrace houses until she became embarrassed and tugged at his arm.

'People will see us. Come on, Melvin. The tenements are at the other end but don't hang about there either. Julie's mother-in-law might notice.'

He began marching along at such a cracking pace she was harassed into taking little running steps to keep up with him.

On an impulse she nearly blurted out the news of how quite a few of the houses in the West End had been invaded by squatters and only the other day Madge and Alec had installed themselves in a place already occupied by a crowd of other families. She had since heard they had barricaded themselves in and the police and other officials were trying to evict them. However, fear of mentioning Alec's name in case it might arouse Melvin's suspicions held the words in check just in time.

'Oh, yes!' Melvin eyed the tenement building with satisfaction when they reached the other end of the crescent. 'Very nice! Very nice indeed! Come on, which close is hers?'

'Why?'

'If there's any houses going around here, she's the one to know, stupid. She's on the spot, isn't she?'

'I've only met the woman once. Oh, I don't like it. Come on home, Melvin please!'

'Don't be stupid. My God, if I left everything to you, where would we be?'

'I found a nice wee place.'

'Look, it's obvious from here that those are lovely big flats. There's no comparison with the likes of this and that poky wee hole you call a house. Which close is hers?'

She led him up Mrs Vincent's close, her flaxen head lowered.

'This is ridiculous!'

'What do you mean - "This is ridiculous"?'

Over-awed by the dignified silence of the tiled close and church-like windows of the landing, both their voices lowered to hissing whispers.

'I've only met the woman once. What'll she think?'

'What do you mean - "What'll she think?"'

'For goodness' sake!'

When they reached Mrs Vincent's door which was half stained glass and half polished oak, Melvin immediately pulled the bell but he nudged Catriona and said:

'You do the talking.'

She glanced up at him, her irritation mixed with surprise. She thought she detected a tremble in his voice.

The door opened to reveal a petite well-preserved woman with black hair, a flawless skin and a beautiful fragrance around her.

'Yes?' Her eyes were expressionless but the slight raising of her brow and tilting of her head indicated a polite interest, a willingness to listen.

'I'm a friend of Julie's,' Catriona began and, once started, desperation forced her to race along in a performance of smiling confidence. 'Catriona MacNair. We have met once but you probably won't remember. This is my husband, Melvin. I hope you don't mind us coming to your door like this but we wondered if you might be able to help us.'

'Perhaps you had better come in.' Mrs Vincent stood aside and allowed them to enter the hall. Then she led them to the sitting-room.

'We have a very small room and kitchen flat in Byres Road.' Catriona kept the smile stuck to her face. 'And we're looking for larger accommodation. Now that my husband's home we're rather overcrowded. Melvin's been in a prisoner-of-war camp in

Germany.'

She saw the pain flit across the other woman's eyes and she hated Melvin for bringing her here and making her hurt Mrs Vincent. She wished she could break through the invisible barriers that separated one human being from another. She longed to say, 'I lost a son too. I know how you feel.' Instead her soft voice kept lightly, breathlessly chattering.

'This area is very nice and we were wondering if you might know of any flats here that are likely to become vacant in the near future. My husband was just saying - someone on the spot is the best person to know about these things.'

'Do sit down!'

They accepted her invitation and perched themselves side by side on the edge of the settee and waited tensely in the silence that followed.

'I'm so sorry to bother you, Mrs Vincent.' Catriona's words tickled the perfumed air again. 'It's not fair of us to be putting you to any trouble.'

'Not at all. I'd like to help. But I'm afraid . . .' Mrs Vincent lapsed into silence for another few minutes. 'I simply cannot think of any flats around here that are liable to be for sale. I'm sorry. The only thing I can suggest is that you keep watching the *Glasgow Herald*. You might see something suitable advertised and I'll certainly pass on anything I hear from any of the neighbours.'

'That's terribly kind of you. I'll give you our address.'

'No,' Mrs Vincent said hastily. 'Please don't bother. I can always see Julie and tell her.' She turned to Melvin. 'Were you in the RAF, Mr MacNair?'

'No,' Melvin said. 'The Army.'

'My son was killed over France.' She blinked across at the mantelpiece. 'That's his photograph.'

'A fine-looking lad.' Melvin bounced up to go over and take a closer look.

'Yes, he was always very good-looking even as a child. I have some other photographs here.' She reached for her handbag and lowered her head as she fingered through its contents.

'That's him when he was seen and here's another taken when

502

we were on holiday at Dunoon.' She passed around one photograph after another and both Melvin and Catriona admired each in turn.

All the time Catriona was telling herself she had no pictures of Robert, no clothes, no trace. One day the memory of his face she cherished in her mind might fade away and she would have nothing.

At last they rose to go, politely refusing the cup of tea they were offered.

'I'm sorry I haven't been of much help,' Mrs Vincent murmured as she showed them out. 'The only place I know of that's going to be on the market soon is the big terrace house next to my mother's at the other end of the crescent. The old lady who lived there fell and broke her hip. She's been in hospital for a long time now. She'll never be able to come back and look after herself again. They've moved her to a home and her solicitor is attending to the sale of the house. But I don't suppose that would be of any interest to you. I must see Julie and tell her you called.'

The door was barely closed when Melvin whispered excitedly:

'Fate, that's what it is! I was admiring these terrace houses on the way here. "*That's* what I call a spacious house," I said to myself. "That's the kind of place anybody would be proud of." Come on, we'll have another look.'

She could hardly believe her ears.

'You can't be serious.'

'It's fate, I tell you.'

'Melvin, they're huge. Don't be ridiculous. They've got three storeys not counting the attics and cellars. We couldn't possibly keep a house like that. Julie says Reggie's grandmother has money of her own. They've got a living-in servant and a daily char.'

Melvin hitched back his shoulders. 'Maybe one day I'll be able to employ servants too. I'm not going to be content with a small bakery business this time. I'm going to build up something really big. MacNair is going to be a household word before I'm through. And I'm going to have that house. And it's going to be like a palace.'

'You're away in a world of dreams,' Catriona said.

Chapter 15

Julie's greatest fear was that the letter would disintegrate or in some way vanish. She opened it tenderly and read it. She had already consumed every word a hundred times or more.

'My own dearest wife,
    You'll probably never receive this. I certainly hope you don't.
    I just thought I'd dash off a few words in case I "failed to return" - as they say.
    Well, I've always returned so far, and I've more reason than ever to come back now that you're waiting for me.
    I keep thinking what a lucky chap I am. Wasn't it a stroke of luck you liked Felix Mendleson's Hawaiian Band and went to hear him that night at Green's Playhouse? I thank my lucky stars over and over again that I decided to go there that night too.
    It was the merest chance, darling. I sweat every time I think of it but I nearly went to the Locarno.
    I might never have seen you standing there in front of one of the pillars with your head in the air and that perky look that seemed a kind of challenge. I might never have felt the smoothness of your skin, sweet talcum-smelling like a baby's. I might never have shared those precious private moments when you gave yourself to me with such loving generosity.
    I couldn't bring myself to say this to you in person, darling, and probably I'll always be too embarrassed to say the words to your face, but - thank you for loving me.
    I love you, Julie.
    But, my own dear, proud little brand-new wife, if anything should happen to me tonight, don't spend the rest of your life thinking about me and what might have been. You're too young for that.
    I want you to be cherished and looked after. I want you to be happy. I want you to have a lifetime of love and happiness.

From your adoring husband,
Reggie.'

She folded the letter away in her handbag. She did not know what to do. She lit a cigarette and watched her father briskly splash water on his face then attack it with a towel. He was getting ready to go out again.

'Everybody's acting like they want me fur their best pal the day, hen.' He rubbed his hands and did a little joyous shuffle. 'I've had that many laughs and blethers wi' folk ma head's spinning.'

'I know what's making your head spin. You don't fool me, you auld rascal. When you come in tonight - it's straight through to the room with you, do you hear? Don't you dare come staggering into this kitchen wakening me with any of your drunken chatter.'

'You're no' staying in, are ye, hen?'

'I don't know what I'm going to do. I'll probably go over to Catriona's. Away you go and don't worry about me.'

She turned away stretching lazily, as if she had not a care in the world.

'Cheerio then, hen. Try and enjoy yersel'.'

'Aye, aw right. Cheerio, Dad.'

She took a deep drag at her cigarette then tossed it into the fire.

She stared at herself in the mantelpiece mirror. There she was. Dark glossy hair. Milky skin. Emerald eyes. Not bad-looking. Good figure. Twenty years of age. Widow. Widow about to celebrate Victory day.

What victory?

She lit another cigarette and went out still smoking it. Her mother-in-law would not approve of that. Smoking in the street. Tut tut. Not that she would criticise. She was too much of a lady for that but she might gently advise or exude that aura of ladylike suffering that made it only too obvious you were offending her sensibilities.

She wished Mrs Vincent would leave her alone, get off her back, forget she had ever existed. It was a strain never knowing when she would pop into the shop and invite her in that casual but determined way to lunch in MacDonald's or Wylie & Lochead's. Or phone the shop with an invitation to Kelvinside to see about something or other. Letters often arrived asking the same questions or, worse, just anxiously enquiring about her health.

Shaking Mrs Vincent off had proved impossible for more reasons than one. Julie had tried. Over and over again she had made promises to call at Kelvinside and then never turned up. It only made the situation worse. Her mother-in-law rushed to contact her again to make sure that everything was all right. She refused to take offence and never stopped pressing invitations and presents on her.

Julie knew how she felt. It was not that Mrs Vincent cared about her. Her son was all that had ever mattered and in his wife she somehow saw her last link with him.

Often Julie felt the same way. Occasionally loneliness overcame her and she went to visit the Vincents of her own free will. Always she regretted it. If Mr Vincent was there she felt out on a limb, lonelier than ever, isolated in that special kind of severance peculiar to widows. The pain of this could flare into agonising proportions by just being in the company of a married couple, even though the married couple's relationship was far from perfect. They still had a relationship. They were a pair. They could fight together, gossip together, eat together, sleep together.

She was neither one thing nor the other. She was no longer the single, carefree, uninitiated girl she had once been. Oceans of sadness cut her off from single girls. Yet she was not married like married women either. Night after night in bed she fevered to have her husband by her side and this physical agony was only a small part of a world of grief at losing him.

If Mrs Vincent was alone the visit was no happier. There would be the torment of seeing Reggie's photos and hearing all about his exploits as a child. They spoke about him nearly all the time. It was terrible.

There seemed so much of Reggie's life she had never shared. She wanted to see the photographs, to touch his cricket bat and his old school bag, and his favourite books, to sit on the chairs he had sat on, to hold close to her the clothes he had worn.

Yet it was terrible. She avoided going to Kelvinside as much as she could.

Tonight she felt compelled to go somewhere and her conscience nagged at her that it might be a kindness to visit Mrs Vincent. Walking smartly round to Bridge Street to catch the subway, she tried to be sensible, to fight the strange horror rising inside her. Maybe she would drop in for a few minutes after visiting Catriona.

Visits to Catriona were different now. Her husband had returned and Catriona was obsessed by all the apparent worries this entailed. They were in the throes of buying some ridiculously big house and Catriona did not know how she would ever be able to clean and polish it all.

She had shrugged and told Catriona:

'Well, don't.'

But she envied Catriona her trouble with her house and her husband, her planning, her worrying, all her homely harassments.

It was obvious when she arrived at Byres Road and Catriona opened the door that she had been weeping. Her hazel eyes were inflamed and her face looked hot and blotchy.

'Oh, come in, Julie. It's nice to see you.' Her voice shrivelled to a whisper. 'He's got this business and he's wanting me to manage the shop as well. Did you ever hear anything so ridiculous? The house has ten rooms counting the attics. I don't know how I'm going to manage that.'

Before Julie reached the kitchen and entered the family circle she already felt out of it, an intruder. Before she was inside, she itched to escape. To be a non-participator, an observer, meant spending the rest of the evening smiling hypocritically on an icy fringe. It was unendurable.

'I've only dropped in for a minute. I thought I might say hello to the old ma-in-law and then scamper off to join the celebrations in George Square. Aren't you lot going?'

Catriona darted an uncertain look at Melvin.

'Actually, I wanted to take some things to Madge.'

'Of course we're going. This is VJ night.' Melvin allowed his

507

words to puff out in between sucking at the pipe he kept gripped firmly between his teeth. 'The police pipe band's going to be playing in George Square and the City Chambers is going to be floodlit and they've got fairy-lights in all the trees. I knew we'd win in the end.'

'I've these things to take to Madge first, Melvin. I won't be long.'

'What do you mean, you won't be long? She lives in Springburn!'

'No, they're squatters now. They're in a house over in Huntley Gardens.'

'Squatters?' Melvin aimed his pipe at her as if it were a gun. 'You wash your hands of them. No wife of mine is going to get mixed up with that mob. A crowd of right no-users.'

The red blotches on Catriona's face merged into a scarlet flush.

'Nobody's ever any use as far as you're concerned. You always seem to see the worst in people. Well, Madge helped me when I needed it and I'm going to help her now.

'OK. OK.' Julie laughed. 'Call it a draw, pals. I'll deliver the goods. Where are they?'

Catriona hesitated, taken aback by the offer as if she had forgotten Julie existed.

'That's very kind of you, Julie, but I shouldn't ask you.'

'You're not asking me.' Shrugging, she lit a cigarette. 'I'm at a loose end. It'll give me something to do.'

'It's just some food and odds and ends in this basket. Well, all right but stay and have a cup of tea first.'

'No, thanks all the same but I'd rather be off.' She lifted the basket. 'Take it easy, pals. The war's over, remember.'

Catriona followed her apologetically out to the hall.

'I'm sorry you're having to rush away, Julie. Come again soon and stay for a meal.' Her voice contracted into a hiss. 'Isn't he terrible? You know where it is, don't you? Cross the road and . . .'

'Stop worrying!' Julie laughed, but returning back down the stairs she kept swallowing at the lump in her throat. It would have been different if Catriona had been on her own. They could

508

have spent the evening giggling and gossiping together. It would have been company and something to do.

She flicked her cigarette into the gutter when she reached the street and crossed the road with quick capable steps. At the other side she glanced round to see if Catriona had come to the window as usual to give her a wave. The window was empty. Catriona would have completely forgotten her and returned to the absorbing world of conflict that she and her husband shared.

At the sedate little backwater called Huntley Gardens, in a terraced house thundering with the noise of children's feet on bare floorboards and vibrating at fever pitch with the racket of voices, Julie had the same experience of being alone, on the outside of a world shared by absorbed, together people, a world in which she belonged, yet had no longer any place.

Madge's husband invited her in and introduced himself as Alec. He was tall and broad-shouldered and had a tanned face with dark, sexy eyes that immediately awakened with appreciation when he saw her. He held out his hands.

'If you're a policewoman come to arrest me, I'll come quietly, hen, but you'd be safer if you put the handcuffs on!'

She chuckled.

'Do I look like a policewoman?'

'You look gorgeous!'

Madge came striding into the hall then with a baby hanging on her hip, its mouth plugged with a dummy teat and its legs wide like a frog's.

'What do you want?' she asked, tucking her straggly hair behind her ears and at the same time hoisting up the slithering baby.

Julie held out the basket.

'Not a thing, pal. Not a thing. These are from Catriona.'

'Och, she's a good wee soul, isn't she?' Madge was slightly abashed. 'I'm sorry I can't ask you to stay for a cup of tea, hen. There's God knows how many other families here and only one cooker.' She erupted in a bluster of laughter that jerked the baby off his perch on her hip again. She hauled him back up. 'It's hellish, sure it is, Alec.'

'You're not kidding!' Alec groaned. 'And it'll get worse, not

509

better. They say they're going to turn off the water and electricity.'

'Och, we'll manage somehow.'

'But, Madge, hen, I keep telling you . . .'

'I know what you keep telling me . . .'

'But we've got to face facts sooner or later.'

'We're facing facts now but we're facing them together and that's how it should be!'

'Excuse me, pals, I'll have to go. I'm off to George Square to join in the wild celebrations and all that,' Julie interrupted. 'I hope you manage all right, Madge. I'll be hearing from Catriona how you get on.'

Back outside again, she walked smartly yet without paying any attention to direction. She was away down Byres Road before she could see through her mist of wretchedness. It had been her intention to pay Mrs Vincent a visit and then take the blue tram into town. Her heels went off beat, slowed a little, made to turn, then stopped. She knew she would not be able to bear the Vincents tonight. Yet she longed to make some contact, some sort of communion with Reggie.

University Avenue led off Byres Road and on impulse she started walking quickly along it until she reached the grey spired and turreted university building, then she went straight in unchallenged with her shoulders back and her head in the air.

Some young men wearing long university scarves came down the steps of one of the buildings. She wondered if they realised how lucky they were. The war was over. They would have a chance to live. She turned away from the building and gazed at the magnificent view of Glasgow stretched out underneath as far as the eye could see, from the hill she was standing on to the far hills in the distance.

Down to the right beyond fat green banks of trees was Kelvin Park and the art galleries. To the left high on the horizon rose the elegant ring of terraced houses called Park Circus. Hidden by more trees but on a map looking like the tiers of a wedding cake, were the other beautiful terraces, some of the many examples of Glasgow's fine architecture.

Reggie had loved Glasgow, too. He had been much more knowledgeable about it than her, of course. She remembered one day he had taken her out on a tour of the city. Buildings she had passed every day, places she had known all her life had taken on new meaning and interest. Hand in hand they stopped and stared and gazed up as he told her little anecdotes about the history of different places.

She had never been in Glasgow Cathedral until that day when Reggie had taken her and she remembered how she had enjoyed him quoting Zachary Boyd who had once been bishop in the cathedral and who had fancied himself as a poet. Apparently Zachary Boyd had left his money to the university on condition that they published his poetry. The university had taken the money but could never bring themselves to fulfil the condition.

'That wasn't fair!' she protested, but Reggie laughed and said: 'You haven't heard any of his poetry. Listen to this:

> And Jacob made for his wee Josie,
> A tartan coat to keep him cosie,
> And what for no?
> There was nae harm,
> Tae kep the lad baith safe and warm.'

She laughed then too.

'Well, he had a good Scots tongue in his head. There's nothing wrong with that.'

They were going to have such a wonderful time together. He had been going to teach her so much. They were going to love each other so passionately and for so long.

She ached for him now. She tried to suck his spirit from the air around her. But it was flesh and blood and reality she needed. She hurried away from the university again and caught a tramcar into town.

It was beginning to get dark. The city was ringed with bonfires and a ceiling of sparks glistened all the time in the air. Around the bonfires children and adults danced. In every street there were rings of dancers. People had been celebrating all day. Public houses had been so busy that they had run dry and closed two hours earlier than the normal time. Revellers spilled out on to the streets. Thousands converged from the suburbs to the centre of Glasgow. People buzzed from buildings as if the place was a city of hives.

Every vehicle that passed was a throng of riotously happy figures clinging to running-boards and luggage-racks. Crowds of uniformed men roamed the streets drinking out of bottles. The air cracked and quivered with flags. Bugles blew. Trumpets tooted. Men in shirtsleeves pranced about the streets playing wildly on accordions to dancing crowds. Kilted pipers swaggered along followed by strutting, laughing children.

Young people marched in battalions through the centre of the city and were joined by thousands of others to besiege George Square.

By the time Julie crushed and jostled her way towards the square it was a solid mass of completely abardoned, riotously happy people, many of whom were climbing up the statues and trying to bring cheer to stone faces by the offer of whisky.

Coloured lights were strung over all the trees surrounding the square and the City Chambers were floodlit.

The most outstanding feature of the square, however, was the noise. Julie's ears had never been subjected to such a continuous racket. It had reached such a peak of loudness it was impossible to distinguish separate sounds. Impossible to hear the sounds of singing and cheering, the sounds of bagpipes, whistles, kettledrums, mouth organs, rattles, squibs and rockets. At a range of no more than thirty yards it was even impossible to hear the rumbustious music of the Glasgow Police Pipe Band. The air stretched with just one high-pitched yell like a locomotive's whistle that never died away.

The square dragged Julie in. Noise engulfed her, confused her. Someone whirled her into a dance but there was no room to dance and she stumbled and bumped about and laughed until she was breathless. Someone else gave her a swig out of a whisky bottle and tipped the bottle high so that she gulped too much and choked and spluttered. She danced arm in arm with a long line of service-men and women. Then she found herself in another dance, arms hugging the waist of a man in front while someone behind clutched at her.

The dancing swung drunkenly backwards and forwards, round and round. Again and again bottles of whisky and beer were passed about and shared.

There were civilians and there were servicemen of all kinds but Julie could only see air-force blue uniforms. She clung to one eventually, refused to let go, closed her eyes, rubbed and pressed her face against the muscly arm.

Lips close to her ear sent words wandering through her alcoholic haze.

'I'd better take you home, beautiful. Tell me where you live?'

'Gorbals Cross,' she slurred without opening her eyes. 'And don't you dare say anything about the Gorbals, do you hear? There's plenty of good, honest, kindly, clean-living, decent . . .'

'Sure . . . Sure!'

She felt as if he were using her as a battering ram to force a way through the crowds but she clung on tightly and every now and again she opened her eyes and saw the blue material close to her face and was comforted.

She moaned with pleasure. Soon they would be out of the square, over the bridge across the Clyde, into dear old Gorbals, home, and bed.

Chapter 16

Catriona was in town spending some of her clothing coupons on much needed socks for the children when she felt tired and went into a café in Argyle Street for a reviving cup of tea. It was while she was sipping tea at the back of the cafe that she saw Sammy Hunter come in and sit down at a table near the door.

The sight of his fiery hair and his pugnacious broken-nosed face, with its jutting brows and cleft chin, catapulted her back to the night of the air-raid more vividly and immediately than anything else could. Sammy had come to Dessie Street to sort out his wife's things after she had been killed in a previous raid. His wife Ruth had left their home in Springburn to work in the bakery and stay with Catriona while Sammy was imprisoned in Maryhill Barracks for being a conscientious objector. One night, unknown to anyone, Ruth had gone to the Ritzy cinema with Alec Jackson and the place had got a direct hit. Ruth had been buried under the debris.

Sammy had been released from detention shortly afterwards. Then while he was at Dessie Street there had been the other raid.

Sammy had dandled wee Robert on his knee. Sammy had carried the baby downstairs to the bakehouse lobby, the crowded, floury, heat-hazy place of mouth-watering smells where everybody thought they were safe.

She could see them now, she could hear their voices shouting to make themselves heard above the other sounds; the hysterical wailing of sirens, the low menacing thrum of planes, the crack-crack of guns so near that they made windows rattle, the distant crump-crump of bombs.

'Hallo, Nellie . . . Aye, Tam . . . Come on, Lexy . . . Isn't this damnable, Angus . . . There you are, Sandy . . . Hallo, Baldy, lad . . . Here we are again, Catriona . . . How are you, Sammy . . .'

All her good friends and neighbours.

They had been singing, she remembered, when Dessie Street

collapsed. She and Sammy had been two of the very few survivors.

She kept seeing him with her baby in his arms. Then suddenly Sammy's eyes flashed up as if he had sensed her anguished stare. The sight of her brought him immediately striding towards her.

'Catriona! I never noticed you come in.'

'I was here a while before you. I've finished my tea. I was just about to leave when I noticed you.'

'Have another cup. Stay and tell me how you're getting on.'

She smiled and nodded and he settled opposite her.

'Is your husband back yet?'

'Yes. We're in a room and kitchen in Byres Road but we're about to move into a bigger place in Botanic Crescent.'

'He's managed to get another business then?'

'Yes, on a very good site. Do you know Byres Road at all?'

'I know it's a busy shopping centre. He should do well there.'

'Yes, I believe he will. And of course it's a much bigger shop and bakehouse than the one in Dessie Street.'

'So life is treating you well.'

Her lips tried to stretch into a smile of agreement but trembled and failed. She shrugged instead.

'And you? Have you married again, Sammy?'

'No, still a widower and still in the house in Springburn. I think you knew I was with The Friends' Ambulance Service?'

'Yes. The Society of Friends - they were the ones who helped you,-weren't they?'

'I've been around a bit with them, I can tell you. You know, it's amazing what they do. They're a hardy crowd. Even the old ladies I've met seem spunky. There's one I know, well over seventy and believe it or not she still goes hill-climbing with her husband. They're great ones for enjoying nature. People have the wrong idea about them, Catriona. So did I at one time. Like everyone else I thought they were some narrow, strait-laced sect who wore white collars and high black hats. Not a bit of it. They believe in living their religion, not preaching it. They really care about people without wanting any recognition or glory for what they do. But just you read some books about the history of the Society and about some of the Quakers of the past. For such a

515

small number of people it's amazing the amount of reform they've achieved and influence they've had.'

He suddenly grinned. 'Of course don't get me wrong. They're not all angels. I'm a pretty lousy one for a start.'

'You're a Quaker?'

'Is it such an incredible idea?'

'I can't imagine you joining anything.'

Sammy's muscular face tightened when he laughed.

'It's a lot different from the Army, you know. The exact opposite in fact. There's a wonderful sense of individual freedom and equality. Of course, this can lead to difficulties and disorganisation at times. And, as I say, they're not all angels. There's good and bad among them just the same as anywhere else, and sometimes individuality can stretch into eccentricity. Sometimes some of them nearly drive me mad. Yet I love their eccentricities and their mix-ups. It doesn't matter to me what they do. It's what they're trying to do, what they're struggling to achieve that's important. I don't know why but I feel I belong with them and feel at home. But you're quite right, I haven't joined. That's another thing I like about them. Nobody tries to convert you or put the slightest pressure on you to become a member.'

'Are you still doing ambulance work for them?'

'Now that the war's over I'm having to think of going back to my old job. Although, to be honest, I don't feel the same about working in an office any more.'

'Isn't it marvellous that it's all over?'

'Yes, of course. But at the same time, I can't help feeling depressed, Catriona.'

After a minute or two, in which he ordered more tea for both of them, she said:

'Because of all the people killed and injured, you mean?'

'Haven't you read anything about Hiroshima and Nagasaki?'

Her face twisted in distress.

'Poor things! I was just saying that to Melvin the other day, but he maintains they had to drop the atomic bombs to stop the war.'

'And create a better world. A world fit for heroes to live in.

That's what they always say. Now they're trying to justify the dropping of atomic bombs.'

'Melvin was reading a report the pilot made and it sounded so business-like and ordinary. It said things like, "The trip out to the target was uneventful." Apparently he was awarded the Distinguished Fliying Medal immediately he got back.'

'Oh yes,' Sammy said bitterly. 'He would! And they needn't kid us the raid was a last-minute emergency they were forced into. One of their precious brigadier-generals has let it out that the exact date for the dropping of the first atomic bomb was set well over a year ago. Anyway Japan was beaten before the bombs. Her navy was finished. Her air force wasn't able to defend the country. The new US bases had made invasion possible and the Japanese armies on the mainland couldn't stand up against Slim's men.'

Catriona said, 'I keep thinking of the children.'

He shook his head.

'I saw some of the pictures. Children with the patterns of their clothes burned into their skins. Imagine - the bomb was dropped at 9.15 a.m. Japanese time. Typists were taking the covers off their typewriters ready to start work. Shops assistants were behind their counters and customers were wandering in. Housewives were drinking cups of tea and children in school were just beginning to chant their lessons. Then suddenly there was this blinding flash and the whole city and everything and everyone in it, including emergency facilities, were crushed and burned by the terrific pressure and heat. And for miles outside there was and still is horror and suffering. And not only that, future generations are going to suffer.'

'I don't want to imagine it. I get too upset.'

He sighed.

'I don't enjoy thinking about these things either. But surely someone's got to. If we don't end war now - and I mean for good this time - war's going to end us.'

'I don't see what we can do. We're just two individuals.'

'The world's made up of individuals. Although I must admit I haven't a great deal of faith in our generation. There hasn't been much protest about the bomb or anything else, has there?

517

But maybe the next generation, maybe your children will be different. Maybe they'll think for themselves and have more of a social conscience.'

Catriona could not help laughing.

'All they're doing at the moment is playing football, getting dirty, tearing their good clothes, and, I'm afraid . . .' she eyed him mischievously, '. . . fighting!'

Sammy smiled and looked down at his cup in the shy, awkward way he had sometimes.

'Oh, I did plenty of that kind of fighting when I was young. What age are the boys now?'

'Fergus is nearly thirteen and Andrew will be eight in October.'

'I probably wouldn't recognise them.'

They drank their tea in silence for a while, both thinking of the changes that passing time had wrought in their lives. Then Sammy said:

'Do you ever see Alec Jackson these days?' Catriona's gaze betrayed momentary panic. She wondered if he knew about Alec and herself and the one shameful lapse that had resulted in baby Robert. Not that she was ashamed of Robert. Her thoughts scurried to blot out the word shame - as if somehow Robert might be hurt by it. In case somehow, somewhere he still existed and might feel that she did not want him or love him. She had always wanted him and loved him. And she always would.

'Catriona?' Sammy's deep-set eyes were studying her curiously.

'Oh, sorry. I was dreaming. What were you saying, Sammy?'

'Remember that insurance man we used to have in Springburn?'

'Oh yes - Alec.'

'His mother lived in one of the MacNair houses, didn't she? Ruth used to speak about him in her letters.'

'Oh!' She felt even more uncertain of her ground.

'I never see him in Springburn now,' Sammy went on. 'I used to bump into him quite often.'

'Look, Sammy. I'm awful sorry but I really will have to rush. The children are still on holiday from school and they get into so much mischief when I'm away like this. It's time I was getting home and making their tea.'

518

He rose too, his craggy face wistful.

'It was nice seeing you again, Catriona.'

Smiling and edging away from him towards the door she said:

'You must come and visit us after we're properly settled in the new house.'

'I would like to very much.'

'I'll drop you a note.'

'Don't forget.'

She waved goodbye and escaped from the café. It had been good to see him again but she felt confused and disturbed.

So many things had been happening recently one on top of the other that she did not know how to cope any more: the negotiations about the house in Botanic Crescent and the cleaning of it in preparation for moving in and the new business. The form-filling for that had been incredible, not to mention problems about staffing.

Melvin had persuaded her father to give up the good day-shift job he had in Farmbank and come over to Byres Road to help out. But, as she kept telling Melvin:

'Daddy doesn't keep well. You can't expect him to travel back and forward from Farmbank indefinitely.'

'He can do a day shift here,' Melvin said. 'I'll do nights.'

Melvin had never been afraid of hard work and Catriona had always regarded him as a practical down-to-earth person. Now, she was having to rethink even these basic attitudes. Melvin was very full of grand ideas but seemed so often to lack the initiative to organise them or put them into practice.

He needed her to help make his dreams of grandeur come true. Although he would rather have died than admit it. He had to have all the glory and the more she did the more credit he took.

He was the one who raved on to everyone about how his shop was going to be the poshest, best-looking business in Glasgow. She was the one who planned the colour scheme, went to search for paint and carried it back to Byres Road. She was the one who struggled up and down ladders, painting the place every spare minute she had.

He boasted that one day everyone in Glasgow would seek out

MacNair's Bakery to buy their specialities. But it was she who thought up new ideas for recipes. The whisky liqueur cake had been her idea. At first Melvin had scoffed and sneered and said it would never work out. But together they had experimented with ingredients until a delicious sweet moist whisky-tasting confection had been produced. Already people were coming from all over Glasgow to buy it. The only drawback was that the ingredients were scarce. Even Melvin's friend who owned the pub nearby could not supply him with enough to meet the demand.

'But wait! Just wait!' Melvin said excitedly. 'Rationing and shortages won't last for ever and then this will go like a bomb!'

The word bomb reminded her of what Sammy had been talking about.

She was reminded too of the family album old Mr MacNair kept in his room. Faded brown prints of mothers and fathers, and grandmothers and grandfathers, in their babyhood, their youth, their prime, then old age.

The pages flicked them past as hastily as life itself. And in that flicker of time it seemed so senseless for people to inflict suffering on each other.

'Oh, God, for the sake of the children,' she thought. 'Please don't let there be any more wars.'

Chapter 17

'Now behave yourself,' Catriona hissed at the children. 'Remember there's a minister living in the next house!' She eased open the back door as if there might be crocodiles outside waiting to snap at her.

'So what?' Fergus said.

'So you behave yourself, that's what.'

Irritably she punched his shoulder and immediately became more tense and anxious at the sight of the cold fury in his eyes. He did not say anything else and both boys left the house quietly. She knew however that there would be reprisals. Fergus would torment Andrew, perhaps by some constantly repeated act like knocking down Andrew's carefully set-up soldiers or perhaps just by following Andrew around peering closely at him all the time like a hypnotist.

Andrew would lose his temper and erupt in violence. Then Fergus would either hold the freckly-faced, wildly punching, struggling child at arm's length and taunt him with laughter, or he would twist his arms or hurt him in some other way.

She wondered if tormenting or bullying by older children happened in other families.

She realised that Fergus's tragic early years - losing his real mother and then being looked after by Lizzie next door in Dessie Street - must have something to do with his character. Lizzie had been a quiet, twisted person who had tormented Fergus.

'I used to tell him I'd wait behind the door and pour petrol over his daddy and set fire to him and burn him all up. I loved to see the expression on wee Fergie's face! What laughs I used to have!' Lizzie had told her.

It was not surprising that Fergus seemed twisted inside at times. Yet Catriona blamed Melvin too. He had constantly repressed the child's emotions in the mistaken belief that he was training him to be 'the best-behaved boy in Glasgow.'

In front of Melvin, Fergus made sure he was immaculately well behaved, was seen but not heard, never complained, never argued, never asked for anything, never cried, was never caught doing anything at all.

It took quick reflexes to catch even the change from the blue-eyed stare to the shifty gleam that meant a lie successfully told or something brewing that he thought he was going to get away with.

While Melvin had been in the Army the problem of Fergus had simmered down. She had tried to pay him a lot of attention, to listen patiently to his exaggerated tales about school and football and fights and his frightening gory war stories of air-raid victims or battle casualties he had heard or read about. Her own repressed, yet excitable nature, was irritated and distressed by his but she had all the time struggled with herself and tried to keep her voice floating along in pleasant normality.

'Gosh!' she'd say. 'Fancy that, son. Oh, my goodness. Yes . . . fancy . . . oh, dear . . . What a shame . . . You don't say . . . Gosh!'

She felt it must be good for him to be able to express his emotions and if he was angry she did not discourage him from showing it and she tried to explain that if he was upset there was nothing wrong in finding release in tears.

No matter what he did to upset her she never remained angry for long. She forgave quickly and always made a point of tucking him in last thing at night with a goodnight smile and kiss.

She had been rewarded every now and again by unexpected bursts of affection, bear hugs that nearly strangled her and from which she was forced to seek escape. Or if she happened to have a cold or something wrong with her he would insist with demonic deterrnination on looking after her.

'Don't get up, Mum. Don't get up. Just lie there. Lie there. I'll look after you.'

'But I must get up, Fergus,' she'd protest. 'I've a hundred and one things to do.'

He kept knocking her roughly back and holding her down.

'No. No! Don't get up, Mum. Don't get up. Just lie there. Lie there. I'll look after you.'

She always lay for as long as she could, her eyes and ears closed against chaos in an effort to ignore dishes being broken and milk and sugar being spilled in Fergus's excitement in making her a cup of tea.

She considered her efforts well worth while but effort took energy and since Melvin had returned her energies were being stretched far beyond their normal limits.

There was so much to think about and do in connection with the shop. The old man had regained some enthusiasm and pride in acquiring a business again but he was too old to be of much practical help and just shuffled about the place getting in everyone's way.

Sometimes he did not bother going into the shop at all, and Melvin told him:

'Da, you might as well give up. Go on, retire and enjoy yourself!'

The only thing for which old Duncan never lost any talent was hanging on to money. It was like squeezing a lemon to get him to lay out capital.

Melvin wanted the bakehouse at the back of the shop to be the best and most modernly equipped in Glasgow.

But the old man kept repeating in his high-pitched nasal whine, 'What was good enough for me is good enough for you. You've always had too many big ideas. That's always been your trouble!'

Melvin blustered on at his father in hearty good-natured attempts to keep things moving. He seldom allowed himself to become angry with the old man. This was a luxury he kept for Catriona. He nagged at her continuously, only stopping if someone else was there. He became a Jekyll and Hyde character with, for the most part, a surprisingly mild, amiable front to outsiders that only changed to a perverse whittling edge when he was alone with her.

It did not seem to matter what she did or how hard she worked, it was impossible to please him. He found something to criticise in everything she accomplished and yet he continued to pile on tasks big and small.

'You phone about that order, Catriona,' he would say. 'Tell them we've waited long enough for it. Tell them the war's over now. Tell them we don't need to put up with this and we're not going to!'

Then while she was phoning Melvin would keep whispering instructions, and afterwards he would grumble bitterly.

'You should have spoken up, been firmer. You sounded like a nervous schoolkid. What good do you think that's going to do? You're no use. You're weak, that's your trouble.'

She tried to be firm and capable, to acquire a more forceful voice and brisker, more efficient manner, but it never seemed to do any good. Things got worse instead of better. Blame continued to be heaped on her head. His criticism lashed her already deeply rooted sense of guilt until to do something right became a masochist challenge. Her determination became desperation. She would do something right if it killed her.

Since they had moved into the house in Botanic Crescent exhaustion seemed to be already nibbling her life away. Half the time she wandered about in a daze. The mess the children made with their dirty feet or their untidiness, and her father-in-law with his tobacco all over the chairs and carpets and his whisky and beer splashes, often reduced her to helpless weeping, not so much because she cared about these things, it was the measure of nagging she would have to suffer from Melvin if he saw the mess that tormented her.

Her mother came over to help wash the windows and scrub what seemed miles of floors and stairs, yet she only made things worse and tightened the screw of her secret anxieties.

'May the Good Lord have mercy on you, Catriona. That man's trying to kill you like he killed his first wife!'

'I'm perfectly all right,' she assured her mother, but cries echoed louder and louder inside her from a deep well of fear.

'May God forgive you, Catriona. You know perfectly well that's a downright lie. I don't know what he did to his first wife but I've seen some of the things that man has done to you. Remember how he forced you to go to the Empire Exhibition and you nearly gave birth in the middle of all these thousands of folk? It was disgusting as well as dangerous. Then there was that horrible miscarriage you had . . .'

She kept on scrubbing the floors and her mother kept on talking.

'He's trying to work you to death, that's what he's trying to do, sacrifice you to his own conceit. I told you no good would come of you marrying that man. I told you you would be punished. You should leave now before it's too late. Think of the children. Do you want them to be left alone in this big house with that man?'

Catriona wanted to leave. But it was all very well to talk blithely about leaving. It reminded her of Melvin's big talk and how she was always left to face and work out the small humdrum practicalities of the matter.

It was all very well too for a decision like this to be made and put into practice by someone happily free from the exhausting effects of the situation; someone whose health was not affected, someone who was fresh in mind and body; someone who was not debilitated by neurotic pressures from childhood. Someone with a different character.

Directly she moved out of Melvin's house her mother would leap on her like a man-eating tiger. If she escaped from Melvin how could she escape from her mother? What could she do without money? Where could she go? Accommodation of any kind was at a premium. Squatters were moving into flats, houses, even offices, shops and Nissen huts. What could she take with her? Melvin would certainly allow her nothing, not one teaspoon, not one face towel, not even a suitcase. He had always made it very clear that his money had supplied everything and everything was his.

She would have to leave without telling him and when he was out so that she could scramble a few necessities together and dart furtively away clutching the children and cases and cardboard boxes. But Melvin worked nights and was in the house most of every day. He slept badly if he slept at all and the slightest movement wakened him. How could she leave without him knowing, when at all odd unexpected times he was liable to appear at her elbow with blood-orange eyes and moustache spiking over sour mouth?

Over and over again she tried to plan how she could organise the practical details of escape and how she could overcome all the difficulties. Threads of action kept spinning across her mind, weaving this way and that in a web which strangled her with its complexity.

And all the time her mother nagged at her about Melvin and Melvin nagged at her about her mother.

'She's an absolute menace, that woman. You keep her out of my house, do you hear?'

But he no longer said anything to her mother's face and this apparent sign of weakness gave more persistence to her mother's voice. She felt like a bone between two dogs, a thing to be used or misused.

Then Da began to worry her by doing dangerous things like dropping burning paper or matches on the floor of his room. Singed, smoking, smelling patches and holes multiplied on the carpet and she began to notice burns on his sheets and blankets too. She realised his hands were getting shaky with age but the knowledge only increased her fears that one night he would set the house on fire and burn the children in their beds.

She worried constantly about the children yet her irritation with them seemed to increase with her concern. Their bickering if she asked for their help became unbearable. It was one thing Fergus ministering to her. It was quite another matter if she asked him to tidy up his room or weed the back garden. She always told Andrew to do his share but in a few minutes the bickering would start.

'You left these there!' Fergus accused.

'I did not!' Andrew protested.

'Come on, Fatso, put them away.'

'No! I hate you. Big Skinnymalink!'

'What did you say? What did you say?'

Then there would be a yelp or howl or scream of pain from Andrew and she would rush through to slap wildly at Fergus or at Fergus and Andrew and cry out near to tears.

'Oh, get out, get out of my sight, both of you. I'll do it myself.'

Yet there was an affection between the boys too. If someone

else attacked Andrew and the opponent was too big for Andrew to tackle successfully by himself, he would shout:

'I'll get my big brother to you.'

Fergus always battled to his aid.

More and more each day she seemed to split in two. One part of her knew the right thing to do, the other tormented her by doing the opposite. Her mind pointed out with painful clarity that she should not have snapped at Andrew:

'Oh, shut up and get out of my way. Why can't you just leave me alone? It's Mummy, Mummy, Mummy, all the time. I never get a minute's peace.'

He had been telling her something of importance that had happened at school.

She should not have shouted at Fergus:

'No, you cannot go out to play. You should be working, not playing. Why should a big useless article like you do nothing but play while I'm being worked into the ground!'

There was no reason for him to stay in and nothing he could do at that particular moment.

It was Melvin and the old man she really felt like shouting at. But she was afraid of Melvin because he seemed to be waiting for any excuse to start nagging at her. His voice had become like rat's teeth gnawing the very flesh from her bones. She found it safest to say as little as possible to Melvin. No use being angry with Da either. He was getting more and more fuddled.

Often she started quite sensible conversations with him and then for no apparent reason he would become 'thrawn' and contradict something about which they had previously been agreeing. Then the conversation would rapidly deteriorate into a maze of contradictions and foolishness.

She knew she was taking it out on the children and was tortured with regret yet she continued to surprise them with sudden vicious outbursts that sometimes reduced them both to tears. Sometimes she wept helplessly along with them. Then in an effort to console them and to soothe the pain of her conscience she gave them money and coupons with which to buy sweets or to pay for a visit to the local cinema.

If Melvin happened to be there, however, she did not get the chance to console the children. He immediately pounced on her in front of them and verbally tore her to shreds.

'You're weak,' he kept saying. 'You're no use.'

Every despicable fault imaginable was attributed to her. It was like stripping her naked before the children's eyes and she hated him for it. She found herself retreating in an ever-shrinking pattern of behaviour and speech in order to avoid any confrontation with Melvin. Fergus soon realised this and became completely undisciplined behind his father's back knowing that she dare not say anything to him or call on Melvin's help. A kind of blackmail situation arose. If Fergus did not get what he wanted or was not allowed to do as he liked, he would either complain to Melvin, or make Andrew suffer, and Andrew never dared tell what happened to him no matter how much she questioned him about why he was crying in bed at night, or why he was terrified to go upstairs alone. Occasionally she would find out through Madge's children that Fergus had said there were ghosts under Andrew's bed and a witch hiding behind the door in the bathroom.

Or something precious to someone in the house would disappear or be mysteriously broken.

Melvin always blamed her and displayed his anger by haranguing her with words and upsetting her in whatever way came into his mind. Once he had grabbed her best dress from the wardrobe and torn it to shreds literally under her nose. Often he turned Andrew's photograph face to the wall or he would make a fool of the child, until Andrew complained that it was obviously better to be a bad boy. He shouted at her angrily, his freckles like brown chocolate drops against a white milky skin.

'Fergus does what he likes and nobody says a word to him. But everybody gets on to me. It's not fair. I'm just getting fed up with it!'

He stamped away, desperate to hide from her his tears of rage and frustration.

She heard afterwards, again from one of Madge's children, that Andrew had made an attempt at running away from home but after a few hours he returned because he felt hungry.

Visions of Andrew wandering about lost in the dark tormented her. Catriona tried to protect him, cushion him from further upsets. She always kept alert, keyed up, listening, watching, trying to keep track of where everybody was all the time and if Andrew was alone in a room with either Fergus or Melvin she kept making excuses to be there too. Even if she were in the middle of making a meal and Andrew was in the sitting-room she would keep coming through to make casual conversation with Melvin or to pretend she was looking for something.

Sometimes she told herself that if she could just hang on long enough things would get better. Fergus was a good boy at heart and he would surely grow out of this difficult stage. Melvin was worried because he had used up all his money paying for the house and furnishing it and it was a terrible strain on him to be continuously fighting to prise money out of the old man in order to get the business properly organised. What he had suffered during the war, of course, could account for much of his irrational behaviour. Often she would look at Melvin's ravaged face and know she could not leave him. Yet she felt just as certain she could not go on the way she was doing.

Chapter 18

Catriona began to suffer from headaches, and coughs, and pains in her chest, and legs, and back, and stomach, and throat. Often she vomited. In attempts to relieve her perplexing symptoms she experimented with different tablets and powders and pills. She had become so convinced that there was no solution to her problems and that no one could help her, it even seemed hopeless to go to a doctor. She suspected that anxiety and unhappiness lay at the root of her symptoms and she could not see how a bottle of medicine would be able to cure that.

'Snap out of it!' Melvin kept saying. 'Pull yourself together!'

It was no good. She did not know how to pull herself together and eventually she decided to try going to the local doctor.

He was an elderly man with a grey woolly moustache like Melvin's, a stooping posture, a non-existent neck and a continuous little grin as if many years ago his mouth had cramped in that position. He shook hands when she shyly entered the room in his house that he used as a surgery. He shook hands most politely when he ushered her out again a few minutes later. He had not even bothered to examine her.

He had scribbled a prescription, grinned and assured her that everything was 'just nerves'.

The tablets made her feel dopey and depressed and when Melvin found out she had been to a doctor he behaved like a madman.

'You disgust me,' he spat. 'I could never feel anything for you any more.'

She felt as if she were going mad herself. Somehow she could not accustom herself to Melvin's illogical behaviour.

'I don't understand,' she said. 'What have I done now?'

'Don't act innocent with me. I know your sly filthy mind.'

'Are you talking about my visit to the doctor?'

'It didn't matter to you that you were my wife.'

'What has being your wife got to do with it?'

'That's typical! It doesn't matter that you're my wife. You'd let any Tom, Dick or Harry muck about with you.'

'I only went to the doctor because I felt ill.'

'What do you mean - ill? Don't give me that. What's wrong with you, then? Tell me! Come on. Tell me. Is there anything wrong with your lungs? Or your stomach? Or your heart? Come on! Come on! Tell me!'

The bulbous eyes staring out wildly from dark sunken rings frightened her. His voice stirred up fear too. It was a vulture's claw intent on destroying her.

He is mad, she thought. And for some reason or for no reason he is trying to make me the same; it sounds melodramatic and no one will ever believe me, but it's true. The terrible isolation of her predicament and her inability to cope with it terrified her.

She tried to push him aside and go into another room - but he followed close behind.

'What's wrong, then? Tell me! Is there something wrong with your heart?'

She wondered what anyone would say if they saw him now, the crazy red eyes, the wildly quivering cheeks.

'No.'

'He massaged it for you, did he?'

'Get away from me! Leave me alone!'

She ran into the hall and he darted after her. She hurried up the stairs sucking in little gasping, panicky breaths but all the time silently pleading with herself to keep calm. *Keep calm and you'll be all right. He's trying to break you, make you scream with hysteria. Just ignore him. Keep calm and you'll be all right!*

She fought her way from one room to another, pushing, punching, clawing at him, struggling desperately to close each door between them. But he always proved stronger and heaved it in and his voice, although he never raised it, became more and more obscene. The only way she could escape from him was to run outside. There she walked the streets worrying about the children and trying to gather enough courage to return.

Eventually she could not stand it any longer. Her nerves strained far beyond caring about money or accommodation or anything, she waited until Melvin left for work one night and then hurriedly began flinging clothes into a case.

'Why are you doing that?' Fergus's pale eyes watched her curiously.

'Don't just stand there!' she cried. 'Quick! Get a box or a message bag or something and stuff in everything you want to take. Tell Andrew to do the same. We're going back to stay at Granny's for a while.'

Out in the dark cold street, hurrying penguin-like, stiff-armed with heavy cases and parcels tucked underneath, she was palpitating, sweating, choking with terror in case Melvin should suddenly materialise out of the fog and confront her.

Now even her mother's home in Farmbank seemed a haven of peace and safety in her mind. She had staggered the length of Great Western Road with the boys hurrying and complaining behind her when a tap on her shoulder made her jump and brought a high-pitched strangled sound to her throat like the squeal of a trapped animal.

Both Fergus and Andrew giggled at her unexpected reaction and Fergus said:

'I only wanted to ask if we were going to see Dad in the bakehouse first.'

Shivering, huge-eyed with hatred, she whirled on them. She even hated Andrew for laughing at her and not understanding how terrified and ill she felt.

'No, we're not. Stop that idiotic snickering, both of you! Get in front of me so that I can see what you're doing and hurry up or we'll never get to Farmbank tonight.'

Never before had Glasgow seemed so enormous, or so teeming with strangers, prosperous, successful strangers of good character with orderly lives and respectable homes to go to. Struggling along the road with the cases bumping against and wobbling her legs and the parcels under her arms beginning to come undone she felt ashamed, a failure, an inadequate, an embarrassment, someone who did not fit in, who was no more than a piece of flotsam blown along the street by the wind.

The journey to her mother and father's house was one of the worst in her life. She had no clear recollection how she eventually got there.

There was only the relief of the door opening and the lighted lobby sucking her in. The babble of voices, her mother's, her father's, Fergus's, Andrew's. Then a hot cup of tea being forced into her hands.

'That man won't dare come here. And if he does he'll have me to reckon with,' her mother assured her. 'Don't worry, Catriona, you're safe here!'

But even on the sofa crouched behind the bars of the chairs she did not feel safe. Nor did she feel at home.

An urgent obsessive need to defend herself had become all powerful. Alerted by this into a continuous high pitch of tension, she could not, dare not, sleep.

Rootless, isolated, she listened to sounds lapping far away outside her. The boys giggling and bouncing on the bed-settee next door, her father's mock growl as he chastised them, only to make the giggles and the squeals swell louder and louder. The strong monotonous thump-thump of her mother's feet as she strode busily, happily about.

'Now, now, come on, boys, that's enough nonsense! Finish your piece on jam and say your prayers. Granny and Grandpa are going to bed. Come on, Robert, get through to the bedroom and leave them alone. You're worse than they are.'

'Our Father which art in heaven . . .'

'Fergus, don't you dare carry on like that while you're saying your prayers. Do you want God to strike you down dead for making a fool of him? Clasp your hands and close your eyes. Now both together.'

'Our Father which art in heaven . . .'

Chanting voices balancing along the edge of hysterical laughter.

Doors shutting. Giggles muffled by blankets. Long black silence.

Sleep stealing across. Then jerkily deserting her.

Dusty grey light. A mosquito net through which shabby furniture looms over her. Everything was too big and too close in the overcrowded room, including her mother now up and dressed and pinning an old felt hat on top of her thick coiled hair.

'I'm going along to see if I can get anything for you and the children's breakfast. They might have some dried egg and I could whip up a nice omelette. I looked in your bag, by the way, and found your ration books. I won't be long. You get up and set the table and put the kettle on. Your daddy's away to work but I haven't wakened the boys yet.'

She went away humming cheerfully to herself but she had only been gone five or ten minutes and Catriona was struggling, shivering into her clothes when the letter-box clanged impatiently.

Secretly cursing her mother for the headache the noise had triggered off she hurried to open the door and was caught off guard to find Melvin.

The sight of his broad-shouldered figure, his bushy moustache, his bulbous eyes, his twitching face filled her with undiluted hatred.

Pushing past her he said:

'What's the meaning of this?'

For a moment she was tempted to run from the house instead of following him back into the living-room but she had no shoes or stockings on.

'I left a note.'

'What do you mean - you left a note?' He pulled out a piece of paper and stared incredulously at it. '"Melvin, I'm leaving you"!'

'There wasn't any use saying anything else.'

'What do you mean, there wasn't any use saying anything else?'

Sheer animal self-preservation made her wish he were dead. A basic need to defend herself, to survive at all costs, took overriding possession of her. Eyes normally guileless pools of amber, narrowed to yellow slivers of malevolence and suspicion. Soft vulnerable mouth hardened and twisted and became ugly.

'Aw, shut up!' she flung at him and snatched up her stockings and turned her back on him as she tugged them on.

'What do you mean - shut up?'

'Go away! Die! Disappear!'

'Oh, charming! You're a great wife, you are! Supposed to be

534

a goody-goody Christian as well.'

'I don't want to be anything to you. Just go away, Melvin, and forget you ever saw me. That's all I ask. Just leave me in peace. I don't want to have anything more to do with you.'

'Don't talk rubbish. You're my wife. Get your coat on. We're going home right now.'

'No!'

'What do you mean - no?'

'Goodbye, Melvin.'

'What do you mean - goodbye?'

'I've a thumping headache.'

'Well, hurry up then. Get your coat on and come on home. I can't stand here all day. I've been slaving my guts out in the bakehouse while you've been here snoring and enjoying yourself.'

'You'd better go before my mother gets back.'

'Is this the case you took? I'll pack it. You get your coat on.'

'Are you deaf or stupid or something?'

Immediately he tucked clothes into the case, she swooped on them and scattered them wildly over the floor. Words tumbled recklessly from her mouth.

'I don't want to have anything to do with you. I hate you. I loathe you. I despise the very sight of you. Can I make it any clearer than that? Get out! Get out of here before I get my mother to fetch the police.'

He suspended in uncertainty for a minute. Then he began to shake like an old man. He looked like his father.

'You don't know what you're saying.'

'It's finished, that's what I'm saying.'

His face twisted, screwing out tears. His voice howled up an octave.

'You can't leave me. Not after all I've suffered for you and worked for you all these years. If you leave me I'll have suffered and worked all these years for nothing.'

The hatred for the chains of guilt he was welding came straight from hell.

'I wish you were dead!'

He was blubbering now and moaning.

'I will be dead if you leave me. I'll commit suicide. I'll kill

535

myself.' He stretched out hands, doughy brown floury hands with black treacle hardening under square nails. 'Catriona!'

'Don't touch me!'

'I'll kill myself.' He began banging his head against the wall. 'I'll kill myself. I'll kill myself!'

'You've wakened the children.'

She could hear their half-awake, half-frightened voices growing louder and keener with apprehension.

'Mummy, where are you? What's wrong? Mummy!'

Hatred built up like steam pressure in her head. She wanted to pounce on Melvin like a wild animal, strangle him, exterminate him, rid herself of him once and for all. Then, suddenly, the violence of her emotions exhausted her. Words dragged out heavily:

'I don't care what you do, Melvin, I don't care about anything.'

Right away Melvin brightened.

'It's all right, boys,' he shouted, mopping his face with a big greasy handkerchief. Then after noisily trumpeting into it he began issuing instructions to her.

'Tell them to come on later. Tell them to explain to your mother about me coming for you. Tell them . . .'

She made her way through to the sitting-room, ignoring the rest of what he was saying. Then having seen to the children she allowed Melvin to hustle her from the house.

She longed for help. For days afterwards she thought continuously of her two friends Julie and Madge. Julie had disappeared without a word. Mrs Vincent had called to enquire about her. It was from Mrs Vincent she learned that Julie had left her job at Morton's. The manageress at Morton's had told Mrs Vincent Julie had gone away to live and work in England.

Madge was no longer in Huntley Gardens. Apparently the police and the owner's men had broken into the house and moved Madge's furniture out on to the street and when she tried to stop them they had manhandled her and Alec had lost his head and set about them with his fists. He had been arrested and was serving a sentence in prison.

Madge and the children were in Barnhill. She had gone twice

to the institution to see Madge but on both occasions Madge and the children were out. Apparently they were put out every morning and had to stay out all day. It was only at night they were given a roof over their heads.

If it had not been for Melvin she would have had Madge living with her in Botanic Crescent. Despite the obvious harassment of adding the noise and problems of seven children to her own two, it would have been a comfort to have her friend beside her.

Melvin had nearly burst a blood vessel at the mere idea. Completely recovered from his weeping fit he raged on at her. She had never really had any hope of him agreeing to give shelter to Madge and the children and she had not nearly enough energy left to fight him.

She wept in secret for her friend. It was dreadful to think of a woman, any woman, losing all her possessions, her security, her home, being unable to protect her children.

She knew only too well what it was like.

Like a monster for ever crouched in some secret corner, the night of the air-raid towered up and spilled long shadows of horror across her mind. Recent glimpses of other insecurities added to her distress. She felt again the rootlessness and the shame of walking the streets with nowhere to go.

She cupped her hands across her mouth and nursed herself.

Now Melvin had made a will. He had told her quite casually, making no secret of the fact that he had left the new house to Fergus.

'You're no flesh and blood of mine, you see,' he had explained to her in front of the child. 'Fergus is my son!'

It was like the air-raid happening all over again every time she thought of it. It was as if she were already dispossessed like Madge, homeless, without any rights or place.

All her life, as far back as she could remember, she had longed for security, had played houses by herself as a child and pretended she had one. Continuously, day and night, it had been her dream.

She realised now that it was a basic need for every woman and it did not matter about the size of the place or what it looked like. It was the feeling of having it that mattered, of belonging, of having roots, of being safe.

Once again the world caved in, dust parched her throat. Things loved disintegrated, were temporary, unreal, like everything else.

And she was frightened.

Chapter 19

Julie moaned and retched violently over the kitchen sink. The brown paper blind was drawn down in case someone from outside might see and it enclosed the room in a funereal stillness.

Her skin clung like wet ice and prickled with pins and needles. She willed herself not to faint.

She kept remembering how when she was sick as a child one of her mother's hands supported her brow, the other had cuddled tightly round her shoulders. She remembered a cotton apron, a soft body and a strong voice.

You're all right, hen. Mammy's here. You're Mammy's brave wee lassie.

She had been thinking about Mammy a lot recently. She used to clamber into the kitchen bed beside her when Dad was on nightshift and Mammy would sing her to sleep, often with a proper song or rhyme but sometimes with just a few repetitive words, lilting softly.

> Mammy's bonnie wee lassie,
> Mammy's bonnie wee lass.

The sickness died down and she forced herself to wash her face at the cold water tap. Then she brushed her hair and slashed on fresh lipstick. She spent most of the time alone in the house but she was determined that she would keep herself looking decent. Her father had never been one to stay indoors and now, because he felt helpless and did not know what to do, he kept well out of her way.

Despite all her efforts, however, her hair lost its bounce, her face pinched in.

Her morning sickness was supposed to go away after the first few months but nearly nine months had passed now and she was still plagued with it; sometimes it lasted, off and on, for most of the day. It only needed her dad to hawk or give one of his phlegmy coughs to set her rushing boking to the sink.

As soon as she had discovered she was pregnant she stopped working in Morton's and told a story about going down to live in England. Her first thought was of the disgrace. Shame hardened around her, locked her into herself. She vowed that if anyone said anything she would spit in their eye and tell them to go to hell. She froze out her father, her glittering eyes warning him not to mention her pregnancy, daring him to utter one word.

A job in a small general store in one of the back streets of Gorbals helped her financially until her condition became too obvious. Then she left and shut herself up in the house and told her father he must do all the shopping. She would not put her foot outside the door except to go to the lavatory and she suffered agonies trying to avoid that because the lavatory was outside on the stair. She always listened just to make sure the stair was quiet before hurrying out.

Her father tried his best but often lost the shopping list she gave him and did not remember all the messages and sometimes, despite her angry warnings that she was not coming to the door for anyone, he forgot his key.

At first she whiled away the long hours by busying herself scrubbing and polishing and cleaning out cupboards until every inch of the place sparkled and she could have defied anyone to find a speck of dust or even the faintest smudge of a fingermark anywhere.

Then she got so fat and heavy and ungainly she could not manage the cleaning. She still kept the house as best she could but it was a difficult and breathless task to reach up or bend over or kneel down and once down it was a terrible struggle to get back up.

Food acquired an urgency, became intensely important, something to drool over and dream about and look forward to. If her father forgot to bring the sweets or biscuits she had been craving for, disappointment was so keen she sometimes shamed herself by bursting into heartbroken tears.

Proud and bitterly ashamed, hard and resilient, yet with an

aura of vulnerability about her, she wandered through the house like a bewildered child.

Her only contact with outside, apart from her father, was the papers and from them she soaked up a miscellany of news. She read copies of the Glasgow Bulletin avidly, hoarded them, re-read old ones. She fastened especially on serious items in an effort to exercise her mind and keep herself from stagnating as each long, blank hour followed another.

'It is an accepted fact that war is accompanied by a lowering of the standard of morals and conduct. Within the lifetime of a generation it has been possible to observe the effect of two wars upon delinquency and crime and if the results have been very much as one would expect they are not the less deplorable on that account . . . The culminative effect of six years of war has been to weaken the moral fibre and the powers of resistance. The stages of dissolution through which Britain has passed are familiar and need not be recapitulated but the black-out, the break-up of homes, the destruction of property by bombing, rationing and the black market have all left their marks upon the civilian population.

Since each war is more barbarous than the last and since the 1939-1945 conflict was fought with an unparalleled savagery and at closer quarters than its predecessor it follows that life has never been held so cheap as it is today.

The picture of early post-war Britain which has its counterpart in the United States is unlovely. London has its crime wave which ranges from highly organised theft to kidnapping and worse. Glasgow has been shocked by a particularly brutal murder and everywhere crime is on the increase . . .'

Now she flung the papers aside. War . . . war . . . It was enough to make anybody sick.

Mammy used to say, 'I'm glad you're not a boy, hen. They just take boys away and use them as cannon fodder.'

She took an unexpected pain in her abdomen but it eased away after a couple of minutes. She blamed it on all the retching she had been doing and a strained muscle was the last thing she wanted with her date only about a couple of weeks away. She did not know much about birth but she imagined that strong abdominal muscles would be a better help than weak ones.

Impulsively she hauled herself up from the kitchen chair and trailed through to the room to search in one of the drawers for a photo of Mammy. Then, finding one, she stood staring at it for a long time.

Mammy's health had broken eventually. Probably having a late baby and then losing the wee boy did not help.

She had been slightly taller than Dad, a fine-looking woman with a proud lift to her head, a gleam of courage in her eyes and a touch of red in the brown hair pulled severely back and plaited.

The photograph of Mammy was in her hands when the knocking at the door jerked her attention irritably away and made her slip it into the pocket of her smock.

She had a good mind to ignore the knocking and keep her father out. She had threatened him more than once to do it. Pain niggled her again and she leaned against the sideboard for a minute or two before forcing herself to go and open the door just a crack so that she could see but not be seen.

Mrs Vincent was standing on the doormat as small and slim and expensive-looking as ever. Normally her perfume was something Julie envied. Now it brought nausea to trigger off another bout of sickness.

'Julie! I knew you hadn't gone away. I just knew it! Oh, my dear, your face! You look so pale and ill!'

Julie turned away in anguish, fighting for dignity, but jerky spasms persisted in heaving her body and she had to run to the sink.

Afterwards she splashed cold water on her face and brushed her hair before looking round at Mrs Vincent who had followed her into the kitchen.

She saw the older woman's horror, saw the minister's daughter shrinking from the evil, fallen woman, saw Mrs Vincent's struggle with herself, her expressions changing like butterflies fluttering backwards and forwards across her face.

At last her loyalty to Reggie won. She took a little breath like a sigh then said:

'I'll do all I can to help you. What do you need? A new smock? A nightdress? Baby clothes?'

Before she sat down her gloved hand lightly brushed the

542

fireside chair clean.

'I don't need any help, thank you,' Julie replied. 'I've knitted one set of baby clothes. I won't need any more. I'm having it adopted.'

There was a tiny silence then Mrs Vincent said:

'Yes, of course. That's very sensible of you. And after it's all over, don't you think you would be better to come and stay with me? That's what Reggie would have wanted.'

'I have a good home here. Thanks all the same.'

'Oh, dear, I do feel guilty. Reggie did tell me to look after you. I'm sure if you had been over in Kelvinside with me this . . .' Her face creased as if she were in pain and she forced her eyes just for a terrible moment to rest on Julie's swollen belly. 'This terrible thing would never have happened.'

Julie reached for her cigarettes, lit one and tossed the match into the fire with a careless defiant gesture.

'What has happened has nothing to do with you. But if you must know, I love this man even more than I loved Reggie. He's crazy about me too. But he's married!' She shrugged. 'That's my hard luck. We love each other, that's the main thing, and I've known him for some time. He didn't pick me up off the street, you know!'

Mrs Vincent's face tightened again but she said:

'I would still like to help. Are you going into hospital?'

'Yes.' Energetically Julie puffed at her cigarette. 'Ten days from now.'

'Are you sure you have everything you need? A confinement is so expensive. Have you something really pretty to wear in bed? It makes such a difference to how one feels. I always believe in having a really pretty nightdress and négligée.'

'Yes. I can imagine. I've still got the one from my honeymoon. It'll do.'

'I'll get you something else. And some of the other little things that make such a difference. A nice talcum, a good soap.'

'You've no need. Thanks all the same.' She turned away, her breath catching with another pain. 'I'll make you a cup of tea. The kettle's on the boil.'

The thought occurred to her that she might have started

labour. Doctors could make mistakes. Or something might have gone wrong.

Mrs Vincent peeled off her gloves and smoothed them neatly across her lap.

'Thank you, my dear. That would be nice. I've been worrying about you so much and then finding you like this . . . I've developed quite a migraine. Nervous tension, do you think?'

'You should go home and lie down. But drink up your tea first.'

Mrs Vincent gave a little sighing breath.

'Think about coming to stay with me, Julie. It would be so nice to have you. I get lonely at times. After this is all over we'll talk about it again, shall we?'

'I belong here.'

'You would soon settle in and there's your friend in the crescent now - young Mrs MacNair.'

Stiff-faced, Julie watched her taking her time over her tea. Sipping it slowly, delicately, then each time replacing the cup gently, quietly.

'I thought she looked a bit peaky the last time I saw her,' Mrs Vincent murmured between sips. 'Of course, I don't think she has any domestic help and those houses are rather large. Then I believe she pops in quite often to the shop. I hear the business is going very well.'

At last she rose. 'Tomorrow I'll go into town and buy you some nice little odds and ends. No, you can't dissuade me, my dear. I can be very determined when I like.'

Just before she left she leaned forward and pecked Julie on the cheek.

Julie closed the door and returned to the kitchen. She felt unexpectedly upset. The pain was distressing enough, but now a new emotional upheaval suddenly gripped her chest and sent it lurching into big noisy breaths, like sobbing without tears, and made her plead to the empty room, 'Mammy. Mammy.'

The grinding pain intensified, became her only world demanded all her attention. Then it died away again and she became aware of the sweat trickling down her face.

Long ago she had saved up enough for a taxi. The money was

544

ready in her purse but her dad was supposed to phone for one and have it come to the close to collect her. Her case was ready packed. She had everything arranged.

Slowly she made her way through to the room and collected her case. It was an old scuffed one from Woolworth's and the cardboard it was made of showed through the brown paint. She struggled into her coat then went over to the window.

Her father was standing down at the corner and she fought to open the window and call out.

'Dad!'

He looked up in surprise. 'Eh?'

'Phone, right away.'

'My God! Aye, aw right, hen.'

The journey back to the kitchen was excruciating. Her grip tightened on her case and, still clutching it close to her, she sat down to wait for the taxi. She would arrive in style. That's how she had planned it. Then with any luck everything would be all over by morning. Life would return to normal. She would be herself again as if nothing had happened.

Chapter 20

If it had been an ex-Navy camp maybe Alec would have felt more at home but the Hughenden Playing Fields off Great Western Road, which belonged to the Hillhead High School, had been requisitioned by a Royal Air Force Balloon Squadron in 1939.

Now its Nissen huts sheltered a gypsy band of squatters, travelling people, rootless ones, displaced persons, the rubbish dirtying the skirts of respectable West End society, the flotsam washed up by war.

Most of the men were ex-servicemen. Some of them had had their wives and families in married quarters while they had been in the forces and after demob had been unable to find alternative accommodation. Others had returned to find that their homes had been destroyed by air-raids. Others like Alec had been unable to get work, could not pay their rent and been forced to quit.

He had been in several places, hanging on, trying to make the best of it until workmen came to cut off water and electricity and tear up floorboards and fling his furniture and belongings out on to the street.

He had missed death while serving in the Navy. Since the war he had died a thousand deaths.

The Nissen hut, as Madge said, was better than being in Barnhill but they had no privacy, especially from the children, and any amenities that existed were communal. Everybody in the camp went to the same place for ablutions and to wash their clothes as best they could in cold water. There were no facilities for ironing.

He did not mind the communal bit so much. He liked plenty of people around. What he did suffer from was the lack of clean, pressed clothes. He had always been a natty dresser and it was an acute humiliation to go about in a creased suit or wrinkled raincoat or grubby crumpled shirt. Embarrassment made his eyes become evasive and he acquired the habit of looking down as much as possible when he walked outside the camp with the ostrich-like hope that if he saw nothing, nobody would see him. If anyone, especially a woman, spoke to him he could still come out with some of the old patter and his eyes still twinkled at them, but with hasty sideways glances that betrayed a furtive restlessness. His walk did not lose its sailor's roll or its Glasgow swagger but the movements shrank, lost their jaunty bounce, became a gentle imitation.

Not that he walked much around the Great Western Road area. He did not like this part of Glasgow. He realised of course that his views were jaundiced by the unpleasant experiences he and his family had suffered in the West End.

He supposed it looked all right. Plenty of big houses and trees. Sometimes he went for a walk with Madge and the weans and looked at them all. Madge loved to stare at houses. She would keep crying out in admiration.

'Oh, Sadie, look at this one, hen. Look at its lovely big windows. How many rooms do you think this one'll have, eh?' Or, 'Agnes, would you just look at that. Oh, my, isn't that lovely, hen?'

In the silent avenues, terraces, gardens and lanes where no children played, Madge's voice boomed out with excruciating loudness. Not that they needed Madge's voice to draw attention to themselves. The mere fact that there were nine of them crowding along the pavement was enough. In the camp they blended in with the others. In Springburn's busy streets they would have merged into the background too. Here, however, they were vulnerable as if a spotlight was aimed at them, ruthlessly picking out every shabby detail.

He became acutely conscious of his own seedy appearance, of Madge's down-at-heel shoes and dirty ankles, of the children's motley mixture of ill-fitting clothes, of skimpy coats, with dresses drooping underneath them, and of Hector and Willie's knobbly wrists protruding from their jackets.

Charlie looked worst of all. His mouth was plugged with a dummy-teat but his nose was usually running and his nappy drooped down at his ankles. His clothes never seemed to meet. Bare skin always showed in the middle. Often Charlie was left to stagger or crawl along on his own, getting dirtier and dirtier, until Alec lifted him and tried to wipe him with a handkerchief. He was fond of Charlie. The other children had grown away from him and now resented him as a symbol of authority.

Madge kept shouting at them.

'I'll tell your daddy on you, you rotten wee midden!' Or, 'Daddy'll throttle you, I'm warning you.' Or she would command him:

'Do something with these weans! Don't just loaf about like the useless big article you are!'

Coming back to the camp after one of their walks, he felt especially diminished, as if all the grand houses all around were only there to emphasise the fact that he was no use as a provider. All he could manage for his family was a dark corrugated iron cave.

He tried to blot out his thoughts in drink as much as he could and one night after he had had a few and Madge was nagging him, he suddenly lost his head and struck her.

Looking back on it he sometimes thought she had been purposely egging him on. The way she had been acting anyone would have thought the war and everything else was his fault.

'Aye, you've always been all right, haven't you?' she sneered. 'Sailing around the world, having your way with women every chance you could get. Talk about the proverbial Smart Alec. Well, you're not so smart now are you, eh? An unemployed ex-con and a right wilted one at that!'

As soon as he struck her, he bitterly regretted it and the well of tenderness he had for her immediately overflowed.

'I'm sorry, hen. I'm sorry.' He tried to take her into his arms but she knocked him aside and sent Agnes running to phone for the police. When the police came, she had him charged with assault.

He marvelled at the long memories and the natural vindictiveness of women. Madge had never forgiven him for playing the field and it did not matter what he did or did not do now, it made no difference. She continued to punish him at every

548

opportunity and all the misfortunes that befell them were fuel for the fire of her resentment. Sometimes he felt he could not stand the camp, the Nissen hut, or Madge any longer, and he took the tram to Springburn and stood at his old street corner and watched the world go by. Often he would meet someone who had once been a customer, or a neighbour or a friend and they would buy him a drink and talk about old times, or the war, or the present.

Then one day he met Sammy Hunter. He could never fathom how Sammy of all people had been a conscientious objector. He certainly did not fit in with most people's idea of what a pacifist should look like. Sammy had the appearance of a prize fighter with his stocky aggressive build and broken nose and short red hair. He came from a military family. All his brothers had been in the Army and his father had once been a sergeant-major. He remembered how Sammy's father used to drill all the wee Hunters in Springburn Park and children from miles around came to jeer at them. It occurred to him that this could be why Sammy refused to have anything to do with the military. He would probably have been sick to death of army ways long before the war started.

Sammy shook him warmly by the hand and thumped his arm as if he were genuinely glad to see him.

'How are you doing, Alec? Where are you staying? I never see you around Springburn now. Come on up to the house. I've got some beer in.'

He accepted the invitation but once in Sammy's wee room and kitchen the memory of Sammy's wife, Ruth, hit him with depressing pain. He saw the photograph of her on the mantelpiece. Many a time he had come to collect the insurance money and admired that sexy beauty. He sighed and jerked his head towards the photo.

'She was a lovely girl. You were a lucky man.'

'I know.'

Sammy poured out the beer and pushed a glass towards Alec and Alec's hand reached out for it then suddenly drew back again.

'I was with her that night. She was fed up and lonely and I

549

took her to the pictures. We had just sat down when the air-raid started. I tried to get her out, Sam.'

The night when the Ritzy Cinema was destroyed by a direct hit came roaring at him through time to make him cringe. He felt sick.

'I was going to take her back home. We were on our way to the exit . . . Afterwards I clawed at the place with my bare hands. I tried my damndest to get her out but the fact remains if I hadn't have taken her there she would still be alive.'

A nerve twitched at Alec's face in the silence that followed. Then Sammy said:

'It was the war. Dessie Street got it as well. If she had been there . . .' He shrugged. 'Drink your beer.'

'But I was with her.'

Sammy paused before going on.

'I've had this horror of her dying alone among strangers. It's over five years ago now but it still bugged me, the thought of her being alone and frightened when it happened. She always liked you. I'm glad you were there.'

Alec sighed again.

'Such a bloody waste, isn't it? And I bet the Jerries'll be better off than us now. Look at me. No job. No home. Squatting in bloody Nissen huts. I admit I didn't give much thought to why I went away to fight, but, my God, Sammy, it wasn't for this. Sometimes I wonder what it was all about. Oh, I know what they tell us, but politicians tell so many bloody lies.'

'I'm reading this book just now. It says there's a sickness in Western civilisation and it's from that that both Fascism and the war grew. It's a wrong way of looking at human beings. It's the materialistic view. The idea that men are only valued in economic terms, and to the extent they submerge with their group or class, or nation, and make its ends their ends.'

Alec took a swig of beer.

'Sounds like Fascism. But we're supposed to have beaten that.'

'Don't you believe it. No, we've got to get an entirely new angle of approach to problems, Alec. We've got to reassert the value of the dignity and the rights of the individual. And we can't do that by holding an atomic bomb over their heads. We've got to build up an international morality and it's got to be supported by spiritual forces. Christ, Mohammed, Buddha, Confucius - they've all something worthwhile to teach us.'

'I don't think there's any danger of another war, though. Nobody would use an atomic bomb.'

'What are you talking about, man? They already have - twice. There were so many men, women, children and animals buried in Hiroshima and Nagasaki, they haven't been able to make an accurate count. And a so-called civilised Western nation did that. How about when they all have the bomb? And they will.'

'You're a right cheerful Charlie.'

'Just facing facts. I believe, you see, Alec, that now is the time to fight for the peace. Now is the time to prevent the worst war of all. This is the fight for real survival right now!'

'To hell! I think I'll leave this fight to the weans. They've a lot more energy than me now.'

'You had another one, the last I heard. How many does that make?'

'Seven.'

'Seven? Some guys have all the luck.'

'Call that luck? Och, they're a great bunch but, my God, Sammy, they've got mouths like Hoovers and they're growing out of all their clothes. If I don't get work soon I don't know what I'll do.'

'At least they'll get dinners and milk at school now and there's going to be family allowances. That should help.'

'Thank God for all of it but all the same I'm desperate for a job. It's slow death hanging about like this.'

'Well, Joe Banks where I work is due to retire soon. I could put in a good word for you. But it's not in the office, Alec. It's not your kind of job . . .'

'Listen, mate, I don't care what kind of job it is as long as it's a job.'

'Joe's the storeman. He works in the basement. As said, it's . . .'

'Do you think there's a chance?'

'I don't see why not. I'll certainly do my best.'

Alec got up, grabbed Sammy's hand and, speechless with gratitude, pumped it energetically up and down.

Sammy laughed.

'Take it easy. Where did you say you were living? I'll speak to the boss tomorrow and come out at night and tell you what he says. He'll probably let me know when you can go in and see him.'

'Hughenden Playing Fields, off Great Western Road. It's right next to the asylum. Handy if I go berserk. They can just toss me across the fence. I'm itching to tell Madge, Sammy.' He made for the door. 'See you tomorrow, then.'

He clattered down the stone stairs with almost as much vigour as he once had after seeing Ruth. Now he did not look back at the window as he used to but winged his way across to the camp as fast as the tram-car and his long legs would carry him.

'Where the hell have you been?' Madge greeted him above the racket of all the children. 'You've been drinking again. I smell the stink of you from here.'

'Och, I only had a bottle of beer, hen.'

'Only? The money for that could have bought the weans something, you rotten selfish bastard!'

'Now just a minute, Madge. Give us a chance.'

'I gave you your chance years ago. And look where it's got me.'

He groaned.

'I met Sammy Hunter. He took me up to his house.'

'What did you do there? Compare notes with him about his wife?'

'Once and for all, Madge, will you shut up about Ruth. She was a nice girl.'

'Oh, she was a nice girl, was she? I'll "nice girl" you!' She flung herself at him, her fingers digging and grabbing and shaking him, her face ugly and contorted.

He struggled with her and all the children began to scream and jump around them. Desperately he bawled at her.

'I've got the chance of a job, you maniac! In Sammy's place. He's coming here tomorrow night to fix it up.'

'Oh, so you think you'll soon be back to your f—ing cocky self, do you, in an office full of girls, do you? You think you're going to leave me here in this dump with this howling mob all day, do you?'

'Madge, for God's sake!'

'Well, I'll soon fix you. I'll tell Sammy a thing or two for a start and if you do get the job I'll go up there and barge into the place every day . . .'

All the time she was fighting him and it took all his strength to keep a grip on her arms or wrists.

'Agnes!' she shouted. 'Sadie! He's twisting my arms. He's hurting me. Run quick and phone the police!'

'Madge, what are you trying to do to me? I'm trying to get you and the weans out of here. This is the first chance I've got.'

She gave him a punch on the shoulder that made him stagger back.

'You've had your chance. Now it's my turn. You stay here. You watch your own weans. I'll find a job. I'll go out and work.'

She seemed hell-bent on destroying him. Finishing him off good and proper. Grinding him under her big strong foot as if he were no more than an insect.

'After I come out the nick again, you mean?'

She laughed then and it was the big blowzy laugh that did it. He suddenly lashed out at her with all his strength, all his pent-up frustrations. Afterwards, running through the quiet dark streets where Madge had often walked admiring the houses, he sweated with the thought that he might have killed her if it had not been for the children all hanging desperately on to him like leeches and the sound of Charlie's sobbing voice, high-pitched and pleading with fear.

'Daddy! Daddy! Daddy!'

He stopped running eventually and slipped in behind some bushes in the driveway of a house. He was shaking and gasping for breath and the nightmare scene he had left still imprisoned him like a shroud of icy cobwebs. It had been raining and the leaves of the bushes had an earthy smell and glistened and dripped with water. The dampness seeped through him and made him shudder as he peered through the leaves. The big villa was in darkness. Maybe the owners were out enjoying themselves at the theatre, or away on holiday. Staring at the place, it occurred to him how ill-divided the world was. What made these people so special that they had so much of the world's goods and comforts and he had so little?

Were the man who owned that house or any of the other men around here such paragons of virtue? Did they work harder than he had once worked? Were they more honest?

He had never stolen a thing in his life but now for the first time he was really tempted. If he took something from that house what would it mean to the owner who owned so much, compared with how valuable, how important, what a difference it could make to himself who had nothing.

Perhaps there was enough money in a safe in there to give to a house-factor as 'key money'. Money could get anything. If he had enough money he could get a house, a decent house. Not unnecessarily big like that one but adequate - a good-sized flat in Springburn with a bathroom in one of the decent red sandstone buildings - maybe up the Balgray Hill near the park.

The poky room and kitchen in Cowlairs Pend had been smaller than the Nissen hut.

He was still in the nightmare, he could still hear Charlie's voice. The dream of money and a house only spun across the surface for a minute and then was gone with the temptation, leaving him more tormented than ever.

He ached to run again. He could thumb lifts down south on the long-distance lorries. He could get to London. He could shake free of Madge and the weans and all his problems, no bother at all. He could manage fine on his own.

The prospect of absolute freedom, the chance to start life afresh, reared up with tantalising attractiveness. It immediately lightened him, seemed to lift the weight of the whole world off his shoulder.

He moved, restless to be away. The bushes rustled and sprayed his crumpled demob suit with water.

He said a mental goodbye to Madge and the weans. He saw them all in his mind's eye.

He wiped his wet face with the sleeve of his jacket as he

554

walked away. Then, still rubbing clumsily at his face and cursing himself, he turned back towards the camp.

Chapter 21

Catriona began reading psychology books. She read about things like transference and wondered if that explained Melvin's behaviour. Was he transferring everything about himself on to her? When he accused her of being weak and no use - was he secretly afraid of facing his own weaknesses and guilt feelings? And if so, what could she do about it? She was becoming more and more convinced that either Melvin and the old man were going off their heads, or she was. She felt herself slipping, losing her grasp, as if she were hanging on to the edge of a precipice and below her yawned a black pit.

At every opportunity she studied the Bible in an effort to cling on.

She read every paper or magazine that had a horoscope. Her ears were for ever attuned to anything that might apply to her problems on the radio, or in anyone's casual conversation. She read the agony columns but no one's agony seemed so complicated and hopeless as her own.

Everything was getting beyond her. The housework was a nightmare roundabout on which she whirled round and round without end. And Melvin still kept trying to involve her in all the problems and extra responsibilities that success was bringing to the business.

Her father-in-law worried her to distraction but Melvin pooh-poohed the idea that the old man needed a doctor.

'Da and I aren't like you, with your pills and potions and your carry on with doctors. I don't want you bringing any of your doctors into my house. Da's old and can't hold his liquor so well now, that's all.'

But Melvin did not see the old man as often as she did. Melvin was at the bakehouse half the night and it was then Da was at his worst and she did not know what to do. During the day for the most part he was perfectly all right. He never worked in the shop or the bakehouse now but occasionally called in to see how they were doing. Or he would ask Melvin for all the news at mealtimes. Then Catriona would wonder if she had imagined every nighttime when she lay sick with exhaustion, and ears straining up from her pillow, listening for the old man.

Was that him staggering about the house again? Might he not fall down the stairs? It was not the first time he bumped down the stairs and hurt himself. Was that the scrape of a match, the crackle of flames?

Rigid with anxiety she made desperate plans of how she would rescue the children if Da set the house on fire and they suddenly became trapped in a roaring furnace. A thousand times in her imagination she wakened them. Should she risk precious seconds waiting until they put on their dressing-gowns, or should she try to rush them out the window and down the drain-pipe and put them in danger of catching pneumonia through being outside in the cold wearing only pyjamas?

But they would never be able to climb down drain-pipes from this height and neither would she. They would fall and break a leg or an arm, or be killed.

She wept to herself, but quietly, so that she could still listen.

Sometimes the old man called her and she jumped out of bed and raced to his room, tugging on her dressing-gown as she went, tightly knotting her nerves and emotions along with her dressing-gown cord, retaining a quiet voice although her heart drummed noisily.

'Yes, Da?'

'Take Tam out of here.'

'Tam?'

'Tam MacGuffie. You remember Tam. There he is at the back of my bed.'

Tam had been one of the Dessie Street bakers and he had been killed in the air-raid.

'There's nobody there, Da,' she said. 'Cuddle down and try to go to sleep.'

His goatee beard bristled and he slavered with anger.

'It's all very well for you to talk. The wee nyaff's no taking up half your bed.' He suddenly whipped back the bedclothes to

557

reveal spindly legs dangling from a too short nightshirt. 'I'm getting up!'

She averted her eyes in embarrassment and then was sickened to hear the thud of him falling on the floor. Rushing forward, she struggled to lift him. He seemed only a bundle of jaggy bones and yet felt as if he weighed a ton. It took every last ounce of her strength to wrench him up and stagger with him to the bed and while doing so she felt her menstrual period, which had just finished, start again with a painful gush. She felt faint and saw the old man through a misty haze.

'Are you all right?' she asked.

'What are you doing in my bedroom?' he whined querulously. 'I never get a minute's peace. It's terrible.'

Sometimes she went to his room and he would be up and dressed and would immediately pounce on her.

'About time too. What's the meaning of this? I've been sitting here the whole day without a bite to eat or even a cup of tea.'

'But, Da, this is the middle of the night,' she'd wail. 'You had your tea hours ago.'

But there would be no convincing him and she would have to trail downstairs and wander about the kitchen half asleep cooking ham and eggs or sausage or whatever she could find, then carry it up on a tray to his room.

Sometimes by the time she got there he would be back in bed and asleep and if she wakened him he would peer incredulously at the ham and eggs and sausage, and yelp in high-pitched outrage.

'Have you gone off your bloody nut? It's the middle of the night!'

More often than not he would have fallen on to the floor off his chair. She was suspended in continuous terror of his falling into the fire, of opening his door and having to face the most appalling, horrific sight.

As it was, to watch his slow disintegration was bad enough. On the wall he had a picture of himself as a spruce, straight-backed young man and every time she saw it, then looked at the tottering, red-eyed, white-haired old wreck of a man, depression destroyed her a little.

Was this what we all have to come to? she wondered. Was this all there was to life? All the worry, the pain, the struggling, the trying to understand - it was all for this?

She sought to keep her eyes averted from the picture. She tried to look at, yet not see, the old man, to find some secret place within herself, if not in the house, where she could be free of distress, but there was nowhere.

The old man began to dominate her whole life, to take up all her time and energies to the exclusion even of caring for the children, and Catriona felt sad to think that the children's childhood was passing away and she had no longer the patience or the time for them. It became a regular job to heave Da off the floor in the middle of the night and half carry him back into bed, and somehow the menstrual period that had come back that first time never quite dried up. It streamed heavier each month and heavier and heavier in between months, until it seemed her life's blood was flowing fast away.

In terror that Melvin would find out, she planned another visit to the doctor. To withstand a repeat of Melvin's obscene tirade about going to see the doctor was impossible.

She began to watch him from the corner of her eye when he did not know she was looking. She furtively listened at the door of any room he was in. For self-protection she tried harder and harder to appear normal when she was with him, as if nothing at all was the matter. Often she chatted about trivial things and laughed while dishing up meals in the dining-room. Then she would come through to the kitchen to the cupboard in the corner for more plates and weep helplessly in shadows behind the door with her arms sprawled over the shelves and her head rolling.

Then eventually, waiting in the doctor's surgery, she was strung up in an anguish of suspense in case Melvin somehow found out where she was. Her turn came and she poised herself on the edge of the chair at the opposite side of the doctor's desk. He looked almost as old as her father-in-law.

The wrinkled mouth under the tufty grey moustache still strained back to reveal the same little yellow teeth. She stared at him without hope. She felt so terrible and it was all so complicated and she was so tired, she did not know where to begin.

It occurred to her that the people who most needed help might often be the least likely to get it. For one reason or another they might not be able to communicate their condition in either an adequate way or a way that would arouse enough sympathy and understanding.

She did not feel well enough to explain. Her mind had gone blank. She did not know where to begin. She heard herself murmur apologetically about having heavy periods and being tired all the time when a loud buzz at the front doorbell made her jump and burst into tears.

'It's maybe my husband!' She screwed herself up, hands to mouth, eyes enormous, terrified, waiting, listening to the sound of the receptionist plodding across the carpeted hall outside, listening to the door opening, listening to the mufffled voices.

The doctor said, 'It's only another patient.'

And he gave a jerky little giggle.

She froze inside. She hated him almost as much as she hated Melvin.

Now he was writing a prescription. He was rising. She rose too.

She thought, any minute now he's going to say - 'It's just nerves.'

He smiled. She smiled.

'It's just nerves,' he assured her, seeing her to the door and shaking her politely by the hand before ushering her out.

On the slow way home, like a little old woman bent against pain, walking carefully, she tried to take deep breaths to soothe herself.

She thought, 'Where can I go? What can I do?'

Turning into Botanic Crescent she passed her next-door neighbours, the minister's house. His name was Reverend John Reid and he was Mrs Vincent's father. Her feet faltered, halted, then returned to Reverend Reid's house. Heart pounding at the enormity of what she was doing she tugged at the doorbell.

She had never had anything to do with the Reids. Occasionally they smiled in passing and Reverend Reid lifted his hat but they had never exchanged more than half a dozen polite words of conversation about the weather. She had certainly never been in the Reids' house.

Now she gazed in consternation at the prim elderly maid who opened the door.

'I . . . I was wondering if I could see Mr Reid?'

'What?' The maid screwed up her face and strained one ear forward.

'Could I see the minister please? It's terribly important.'

'You're the woman from next door, aren't you?'

'Yes. I want to ask the minister's advice about something. Is he in?'

The older woman moved back and somewhat grudgingly allowed Catriona to enter. 'I'll see. Wait here.'

Left standing in the hall after the maid plodded slowly away into one of the rooms Catriona stared apprehensively around. The rosewood hall with its turkey-red carpet gleamed darkly and somehow made her feel out of time as well as place. Her nerves twitched and her thoughts raced but opposite the grandfather clock slowly tick-tocked, its heavy brass pendulum lazily, contentedly, swinging.

Knotting her hands together she strained her eyes and ears in an attempt to decipher words from the low murmur of voices coming from the room. She thought she heard a woman say something like, 'Not one of your flock', but could not be sure. One thing she did catch was the gentle sighing tones of long-suffering resignation.

Then the maid reappeared followed by a determinedly smiling Mrs Reid.

'Good afternoon, Mrs MacNair. Do come in. Jessie tells me you wish to speak to my husband. We were just about to go out but . . .'

'Oh, please,' Catriona interrupted. 'Don't let me detain you. I'm so sorry for intruding like this.'

The portly figure of Reverend Reid sailed towards her with outstretched hand.

'Not at all. Sit down, my dear. Duty comes first.'

His wife's smile was like a pain.

'I'll see about a cup of tea.'

561

'No, no, please, I'd rather you didn't,' Catriona pleaded.

'All right, if you insist.' The ladylike smile again and the polite little tilt to the head that reminded Catriona of Mrs Vincent. 'I'll leave you to talk in private.'

'Thank you,' Catriona murmured. Then after the older woman left she sat staring down at her hands.

'Well, my dear?' the minister prompted gently. 'What seems to be the trouble?'

Catriona wished she had never come. People in this kind of district did not do this kind of thing. The 'done thing' here was to keep up a respectable front at all costs. One did not talk about intimate things to strangers or neighbours, even if the strangers and neighbours were people of the Church.

By seeking help she was only making herself more of an outcast. It occurred to her that Melvin, by managing to keep up his front of normality for outsiders, would gain sympathy from these people without even trying.

For the first time she felt class conscious, even though, in a small way. Melvin was still a business man. Like his father before him he could make and hang on to money and this alone gained him respect and acceptance.

Catriona's background had been the working class, where people borrowed and shared everything including their most intimate troubles.

'It's nothing really.' She struggled to bring some dignity and pride into her voice. 'Actually I haven't been feeling too well and everything seems to have been getting on top of me.'

'Ah, well, yes.' Reverend Reid leaned back in his chair and began gently tapping the arm of it with his fingertips. 'It happens to all of us at some time or other. Perhaps a visit to your doctor, my dear. I'm sure he would be able to give you a tonic.'

'Yes, of course!' Catriona said brightly. 'How stupid of me. I should have gone there. Of course!' She blinked and blinked again but despite her efforts to be brave and discreet, tears were escaping and coursing down her face and her mouth was twisting and quivering out of control.

'My dear!' Reverend Reid murmured unhappily.

'It's my father-in-law. He's so much work. I'm up in the

middle of the night with him. He does all sorts of stupid and dangerous things. I can't stand it much longer.'

'Poor old soul! You must ask God to help you to be patient, Mrs MacNair. Old age is something that comes to all of us. You'll be old yourself one day, my dear, and you'll want your children to be loving and patient with you.'

'It's my husband, too.' She knew she was only making things worse but could not help blurting out the truth. 'I've come to hate him. I can't help it. He nags at me day and night. You've no idea what he's like. Nobody has. I tried to leave him but he came after me acting like a maniac, banging his head on the wall and threatening to kill himself.'

'Oh, dear, dear.' The minister tutted. 'Poor soul. He was a prisoner of war, wasn't he?'

'Yes, but . . .'

'God alone knows what the poor fellow must have suffered.'

She took deep breaths. Then she said:

'You think I'm neurotic and selfish.'

'My dear,' he soothed. 'Life cannot be easy for you. I'll pray that God will strengthen you, and help you to find enough love and patience to carry you through this little difficult patch.' He sighed. 'Try to feel thankful that you have your husband safely home beside you, my dear. My poor grandson was killed. Think how his wife must feel.'

She rose stiffly and immediately.

'How dreadful of me. I forgot about your tragedy. I'm so terribly sorry.'

'Reggie was . . .' The old man shook his head, unable to speak for a minute. 'Reggie was a fine boy.'

'Yes, he was.' Pleasure illuminated his face. 'You knew him?'

'I met him a couple of times. I thought he was a perfect gentleman and very, very handsome.'

'Yes, wasn't he? Yes, wasn't he, indeed?'

'I'd better not take up any more of your time when you're going out. Thank you for being so kind.'

'Not at all. Not at all.'

He patted her shoulder as he saw her to the door.

'Your husband's a fine brave man, too. Just give him time, my

563

dear. These have been difficult years for all of us.'

Immediately she got into the privacy of her own house she leant her head against the door and wept loudly and broken-heartedly.

Her problem was becoming more and more a physical one. She was bleeding so constantly and heavily that every day was an ordeal of exhaustion to be overcome.

She got to the stage when she knew something would have to be done. If she were to survive, the odds against her would have to be cut down.

'Melvin!' she burst out eventually. 'Something will have to be done about Da.'

'What do you mean, "Something will have to be done about Da"?'

'He'll have to go into a home.'

Melvin's eyes bulged. 'Toss my father out on to the street?' he shouted. 'I'll see you out on the street first!'

'I didn't say toss your father out on to the street. I said - a home - or a hotel.'

'He's got a home. I gave him a home.'

She tried to sound reasonable.

'I can't help it, Melvin. I'm sorry.'

'What do you mean, you're sorry? I've a big ten-roomed-house here and you expect me to turf my father out. You're rotten selfish, that's your trouble. Nobody matters but yourself.'

'I just don't feel able to look after Da any more. I can't go on like this. I just can't. He's too much for me.'

Melvin's mouth twisted.

'Aw, shut up, you're always the same. Whine, whine, whine! What have you ever done for Da?'

'I've done my best. That's what I've done. Now he'll have to go.'

'What do you mean, "He'll have to go"? I promised my father he would never have anything to worry about as long as he had me. And my word's my bond.'

'You had no right.'

'What do you mean - I had no right? He's my father.'

'And I'm your wife.'

'So? I've given you a good home here as well, haven't I? What more do you want? Buckingham Palace and a squad of maids?'

'I want your father out of here so that I can have a rest. I've the children to think of.'

'The children!' he scoffed. 'You don't care about them any more than you care about my father. You're always narking on at them. You make their life a bloody misery.'

She stared at him in heartbroken silence for a minute or two. Had it became so bad, so noticeable? Were the children actually suffering, really unhappy?

Melvin grabbed a newspaper, shoved it up between them, shut her out, ended the conversation.

Her lips trembled.

'Are you or are you not going to do something about your father?'

'Aw, shut up!'

She left the room and went for her coat. She went out, shutting the front door quietly. Her mind was in a daze.

Walking slowly, painfully down on to Queen Margaret Drive she tried to sort out what she could do. If she left again it could not be to her mother's. Her mother had never forgiven her for going back to Melvin the last time. And, as if she knew that it was the last time Catriona would stay there, she had turned the full force of her emotions on Rab. They were never apart now. Sometimes Hannah called for him at the bakehouse and they went straight from there to the pictures. They still argued and fought but it was as if they did not know how else to speak. It was a kind of passion that blotted everyone else out, including Catriona.

She would need to find someplace else to live, somewhere for the children to sleep and eat and have shelter. If she could find a job she could perhaps make enough money to pay for a place. But no, she knew that she would never be able to make enough money to pay rent and buy food and all that the children needed although if she had been able she would have tried. She was not able, that was the problem. She felt ill. Every now and again pain possessed her, then left her weak and nearly collapsing with relief after it faded away. Recently it had been getting worse.

She marvelled at how lucky men were, how much suffering they missed.

Reaching Great Western Road, she hesitated as if lost. Then, remembering that Madge was living in an old RAF camp further along the road, she forced herself to go in a slow plodding pace in that direction.

Madge was standing outside her Nissen hut with her big arms folded across her chest. Charlie was staggering about nearby and some of the other children were shouting and playing and racing back and forth, often knocking Charlie down.

'Hello, hen,' Madge greeted her. 'Come on in. It's ages since I've seen you. That marvellous house of yours - just makes me jealous.' She gave a big cheery laugh. 'You're a lucky wee midden, eh? Sit down, the chair won't bite you.'

'I don't feel very lucky,' Catriona ventured.

'Well, you should.'

'But, Madge. I'm terribly worried.' She gave a hasty glance around then lowered her voice. 'It's my periods. They're so heavy - they go on all the time. I feel terrible.'

Madge scratched herself then tucked her hair behind her ear. 'Drink plenty milk stout.'

'Milk stout?'

Madge laughed.

'What are you looking so shocked for? It makes blood, doesn't it?'

'Does it?'

'Och, anybody knows that. They give it to women in hospitals.'

'Do they?'

'You get your man to buy some bottles and take it regular.'

Catriona nibbled at her lip. She did not feel as if she were getting to the root of the problem.

'It's not just that. My father-in-law seems to be going off his head. Half the time he imagines he's still in Dessie Street. He gets all mixed up. Especially at night. That's the funny thing about it. He's mostly all right during the day when Melvin's in. But at night it's awful. I never know what he's going to be like.'

'Och, the poor old soul. It'll be his dotage. It comes to all of us, hen.' Another big laugh shook Madge's chest. 'Any more complaints eh? You're a scream, hen. There you are along in Botanic Crescent among all the toffs in a lovely big house with a good man. And here I am with damn all. And you come here trying to tell me your troubles!'

Catriona flushed.

'I suppose it does sound ridiculous. I'm sorry, Madge.'

'You look a right toff yourself. You suit your hair up like that. My God, some folk have all the luck. You're even made wee and dainty and, as Julie would say, tairably, tairably refained. Think yourself lucky, hen. That's my advice. You go back home tonight and think yourself damned lucky!'

Catriona tried to graft a look of cheerfulness across her face.

'All right, Madge. I will. Talking about Julie - I wonder how she's getting on? I don't suppose she wrote to you, did she? I wrote to Mr Gemmell and enclosed a letter for Julie and asked him to post it to her address in England. But I've never had any reply. I wrote to her father again and never got any reply from him either. He must have gone with her. I can't understand it, can you? I hope she's all right.'

'Och, she'll be all right,' Madge said. 'She looks as if she can take damned good care of herself, that one!'

Chapter 22

Mrs Vincent had come every day without fail to the hospital. Julie had written to Botanic Crescent right away and told her where to come, and she had headed the letter 'Dear Mum' and ended it - 'Your loving daughter, Julie'. She did not know why she had written like that. She always called her Mrs Vincent to her face and often went to no pains to hide the fact that she did not like her very much.

She was sure Mrs Vincent had no great love for her either, and she always felt that at any minute she would disappear from her life. She kept thinking to hell with her and good riddance. Yet every day Mrs Vincent arrived exactly on time and brought fruit and flowers and chocolates.

Julie kept saying, 'You shouldn't have. I don't need anything. I'm all right. When I want something I'll buy it for myself.'

But she looked forward to each visit because she trembled with eagerness to show off the baby.

'Isn't she a doll? An absolute doll.' She held the little bundle with great tenderness, savouring every silky flower-petal feel of it against her breast, studying every hair on its downy head, rubbing her cheek gently against the vulnerable softness, closing her eyes with love that was like a pain. 'She's so beautiful, isn't she? So good, too. Look at her. Look how she just lies there without making a sound.'

The fingers of Mrs Vincent's gloved hand eased back the shawl. Then she smiled and murmured agreement and before sitting down tickled the tiny chin with one finger.

'Coochie-coochie coo! They are sweet when they're tiny!'

Julie had bristled at the word 'they' as if it somehow detracted from her baby's uniqueness. No other baby in the universe was as exquisitely wonderful as her daughter.

She would never forget the first time she saw her. It had been as if she had gone in through one door of a torture chamber and

568

eventually struggled out another and found herself changed as a result. From the moment she looked at her baby she knew she would never be the same person again.

A new part of her had been tempered in the fire of pain, was hypersensitive, had subtle nuances, strange penetrations of feeling that had never been dreamt of before.

Looking at her new-born child she saw her own flesh, a completely vulnerable part of herself yet with none of her faults or imperfections. When the child cried she cringed inside and palpitated with the acuteness of her concern.

All the time she kept staring at her baby. With great care and wonderment her eyes studied the tender pink bulge of the cheek, the rosebud mouth, the little creased neck that seemed too thin, the dimpled fists. Any movement, a sucking twitch of the mouth, the slow enchanting opening of the eyes to stare straight at her, touched on ready ripened nerves like an orgasm.

All the time they kept telling her that it would be best if it were adopted and she had agreed before the baby was born. But now seeing it, now being different, she no longer could decide what ought to be done for the best. Just to think of giving the little girl away made her stomach immediately plummet down as if she had stepped into an empty lift shaft.

She kissed the baby and kissed it again and cuddled away underneath the bedclothes with it in her arms so that no one could see her weeping. She wished she could ask the child what it wanted. In the dark tunnel of the bed-clothes, through rainbow tears she kissed the milky mouth and longed to be able to converse with it.

They said it was not fair on the child to have only one parent. A child needs a father as well as a mother, they said.

There was this well-off couple up north just longing for a child, they told her. They had a lovely big house out in the country and if they adopted the little girl she would lack for nothing.

Think of the difference, they said. What had she to offer? An overcrowded nursery during the day or someone looking after the baby while she was out at work. A room and kitchen in the Gorbals at night. Not even a garden. Nowhere for a pram.

Then when the child grew up - what could she say about its father?

Holding and kissing and nursing it, her face soaking the pillow, she thought, 'If only she knew me now. If only she could remember. If only she could know how much I love her.'

But maybe it was better that her daughter should never, have any memory of her at all.

How could she bear the child to know that her father had been some faceless airman who had picked her drunken Gorbals mother off the street, and afterwards disappeared? She did not even know his name or what he looked like.

She tried to clean her mind of the memory of that night and the terrible shame in case just thinking about it in the presence of her baby might in some way contaminate it.

She knew she could never endure her daughter knowing about her and being ashamed of her.

The adopting parents were such *respectable* people, they said.

She could almost see them. They had a neat villa in the suburbs of Aberdeen or Inverness or Oban. Probably their parents had helped them to buy it. They had a big garden, of course, and a car and they went regularly to church on Sundays. They were known and respected members of the community. He played golf and she was a member of the Women's Guild. They had a joint account in the local bank. They fitted securely into all the accepted patterns.

Julie closed her eyes and prayed to them.

'Please, please, be good and loving and kind and patient and understanding always and always to my little girl.'

She did not allow Mrs Vincent to come for her on the day she left the hospital, but she promised to visit her at Botanic Crescent the day after.

She did not want anyone to be there when she said goodbye to her baby.

In front of Mrs Vincent she had always managed to maintain a brusque, cheerful exterior.

At visiting times they gossiped and laughed as if she had come to hospital for no more than the simple uncomplicated removal of an appendix.

If Mrs Vincent noticed the tragic eyes, and the face puffy and swollen with weeping, she never once mentioned it.

The last day came and panic swooped inside Julie like the big dipper at the fair.

She kept telling herself that this was not, could not be, the last time she would ever see her baby. She would never know her daughter. Never see her in all the stages of growing up, never know her as a woman. And her daughter would never know her! Shaking and weak and bewildered, Julie tried to console herself. Her baby would go to the adopting parents now but at the end of a few weeks she could still change her mind before signing the papers.

They told her:

'You'll be able to think more clearly once you get home and back to normal.'

She held her daughter in her arms. She gazed at her face, tracing its each and every contour with her finger, then eased her finger into the little hand.

The nurse was impatient to be away.

'I'll have to take her now. You've just got to be brave.'

'Sure, pal. Sure,' Julie said, handing over the baby. Then before she could snatch another look or touch or say the word goodbye, the nurse turned on her heel, clipped smartly down the corridor, and disappeared through swing doors.

Julie watched the doors wham backwards and forwards, then shudder, then become still. She lifted her case and wandered outside. Part of her heart and soul seemed to have been wrenched away. She felt incomplete. All her instincts were screaming out in protest. Bewilderment made her take the wrong turning. She thought she would never get home and she did not care.

Her father was standing at the corner as usual. On the outside it was as if nothing had happened. The Gorbals looked exactly the same. Yet had there been so many shops that sold prams or baby clothes or toys or baby food before? The sight of each shop tormented her. And each baby in its mother's arms and each child playing in the street were knives of anguish stabbing at her.

Her father had an old white scarf knotted at his neck and his cap pulled well down over his beaky face. He was shuffling from one foot to the other and rubbing and smacking at his hands and grinning.

'Hallo, there, hen. Ah've got the kettle on. The tea'll no' take a minute.'

Off he scampered up the close to get everything ready as if she were just coming; home as usual after work.

She took her time, her hand on the bannister pulling herself up each stair.

'Ah've got a confession tae make,' he said once she had arrived in the house, taken off her coat, and flopped helplessly into a chair. 'Ah bumpt intae that pal o' yours - whit's her name? A bonny fair-headed wee lassie.'

'Catriona?'

'Aye, that's the one. Well, ah was up the town the other day fur a message in Woolworth's and she collared me, hen. Ah couldni help it.'

'You told her!'

'She kept asking me. Ah didni know whit tae say.'

Julie sighed. 'Oh, never mind. It can't be helped now.'

'Here, drink yer tea, hen. That'll cheer you up. And you'll be glad of yer pal, tae. She'll be here in a minute. She wanted tae go and get you at the hospital but ah said you didni want anybody there. That was whit you said, wasn't it, hen?'

Julie sipped at her tea and did not answer. She was saving her energy for the bright brittle act she would have to put on while Catriona or anyone else was there.

'Och, never mind, hen.' Her father hesitated, groping for words with which to comfort her about the child. 'It's best this way. This way, y'see, you'll never know it.'

Tears spurted out of her eyes of their own accord. They splashed down her face and trickled along her jaw and down into the hollows of her neck.

She went on sipping her tea, not saying anything.

'Och, dinni greet, hen. Them yins know what's best for you, ah'm sure. You're a young lassie yet, and bonnie tae. Now you'll be able to meet some nice fella and get married again, eh? Fellas are no' so keen if there's somebody else's wean . . . There's the door, that'll be your pal, now.'

In obvious relief he scuttled off to let Catriona in.

Julie got up, clattered her cup down on the table and fumbled in her pockets for a handkerchief.

Surprise at the changed appearance of Catriona momentarily switched her attention away from her own problems. Catriona's fair hair was now plaited and circled her head like a little crown. She had always been small but she had lost weight and her delicate bone structure was more noticeable. She had acquired a fragile look with white skin drawn tight over her cheekbones casting dark shadows under her eyes.

In a way, although the colouring was completely different and they did not really look like one another at all, Catriona suddenly reminded Julie of Mrs Vincent.

They both seemed to possess the same genteel West End aura.

'There's a cup of tea in the pot if you want it,' she told Catriona brusquely and then raised an eyebrow in her father's direction. 'What the hell are you hanging about with a face like that for? Either sit down and content yourself or get away out the road.'

'Aye, aw right. I'll away, hen. Cheerio the now.'

The outside door banged shut. Then Catriona said:

'Oh, Julie!'

'Well? Do you want a cup of tea?'

Catriona sank gently into a chair and nodded as if she could not trust herself to speak.

'Before you start quizzing me,' Julie said, 'I'll confess all. He was crazy about me. I was crazy about him. But he's married and can't get a divorce so we had to call it a day and that's him out of the picture. They've advised me to have my baby adopted. They say it's best from the baby's point of view. A little girl, by the way, an absolute doll.'

She grabbed her handbag, found her cigarettes, lit one and breathed deeply at the smoke. Then she took out her powder compact and energetically powdered her face.

'You can't,' Catriona said.

'Can't what, pal?'

'Give your baby away. You'll never be able to forget her,

573

Julie. She'll always be part of you. If you do this it'll torment you for the rest of your life.'

'This has nothing to do with you or anybody else. It's my decision and my decision alone.'

'You've just told me you've been advised to have her adopted.'

'They say to think of what's best for the baby. That's exactly what I'm going to do.'

'I don't want to interfere . . .'

'Well, don't!'

'But I must say this. I believe no one can feel the same for a baby as its own mother.'

'I know what I feel.' Julie sent a stream of smoke darting across the room. 'I don't need you to tell me how I feel. It's my baby's feelings I've got to think about, not my own.'

'Julie, you could manage somehow.'

'There you go again - talking about me - always from my angle.'

'But are you sure . . .'

'Look, pal, I know you mean well, but drop it, will you? I've told you, this is something I've got to decide for myself.'

'Does Mrs Vincent know?'

'She found out and came to see me at the hospital. I promised to go and visit her tomorrow.'

'You must pop in and see me too when you're so near.'

'Sure! Sure! How are you getting on these days? Business doing well?'

'Oh, yes. It's a good locality, you see.'

'Oh, I see. Aiverybody's tairaibly, tairaibly refained and frightfully decent and all that. Not like in dirty, horrid, immoral old Gorbals!'

'I only meant that Byres Road was a busy main street so there's always plenty of passing trade as well as regular customers.'

Julie laughed.

'Sure, pal! Sure! And your grand big house?'

'As big as ever,' Catriona replied in a light, bright voice.

'And your husband?'

'Oh, very well, thank you.'

'And your family?'

'Fine. Fine.'

Suddenly Catriona got up.

'I shouldn't have come just now, Julie, I'm sorry. You're too soon out of hospital and have too much on your mind to be bothered with visitors. Please forgive me.'

Julie dragged at her cigarette.

'Don't give it a thought. I'm fine.'

'I'll see you tomorrow then? When you come to visit Mrs Vincent?'

'Sure! Sure!'

She saw Catriona to the door and waved cheerily before shutting it.

Then she returned to the kitchen and the tears immediately overflowed again and made her crumple into a chair and just sit listening to the clock ticking her life away. Then her father came back for his meal and she jumped up and flounced about on her high heels getting everything ready.

'Ah saw yer pal going away,' her father said.

'Oh?'

'She was saying you're going over there tomorrow.'

'I might. And then again-' Julie shrugged- 'I might not!'

Chapter 23

'Catriona! Catriona! Catriona!'

The faint wailing came from upstairs.

'Mum, you should have seen me play football today,' Fergus enthused. 'Every time I got the ball I . . .'

'Oh, shut up!' she pleaded. 'What do I care about football!'

'Catriona! Catriona! Catriona!'

Knocking Fergus aside she hurried upstairs sweating with weakness and nauseated by the sensation of raw liver slithering between her legs. More and more each day she had to increase the padding around herself, had to struggle with the difficulties of bathing and trying to retain some of her normal fastidiousness about personal hygiene.

'Catriona! Catriona! Catriona!'

'I'm coming, Da!'

She dare not visualise what she might find. Life was just carrying her on regardless, buffeting her about.

He was not in his room.

'Da! Where are you?'

She found him in the bathroom struggling with his braces. The stench was overpowering.

'Bloody diarrhoea!' he yelped. 'Came on me so quick I've shitted my trousers.'

It was then she noticed the mess of faeces on the bathroom floor and realised that there was a trail of it all the way from the bedroom. It was even on her shoes.

She willed herself not to retch.

'Came on so quick, y'see!' the old man whined. 'I couldn't help it.' He was shaking all over and staggering a little.

'It's all right, Da,' she said. She was used to saying that. It had become a habit. 'It's all right, Da,' she always said, when it was not all right at all.

She felt ashamed. She was terrified someone might come to

the door or even smell the house out in the street.

She must be something very loathsome in God's eyes. Now he seemed to be punishing her by rubbing her nose in dirt like an animal. If it was not stinking wet bedclothes it was this!

For a minute or two she just stood there looking at the mess, her stomach heaving.

The old man managed to pull down his braces but his blue-veined shivering hands still refused to cope with the buttons of his fly.

She thought of calling Fergus for help but checked herself. Fergus had a delicate stomach. He was easily nauseated; a hair, a chipped cup, a fly buzzing around the table could put him off his food. He would be ill if she brought him upstairs now.

She forced herself to go over and undo the buttons herself. She kept thinking:

'I'll never forgive Melvin for putting me and his father in this dreadful situation. I'll never forgive him. Never!'

The old man leaned on her and it took all her strength to hold his weight up while at the same time struggling to peel off the stinking trousers.

'I'll away to my bed now,' he said. 'This is terrible!'

'You can't go like that. You'll make the bedroom chairs and carpets and bedclothes all dirty. We'll get everything off and get you into the bath. You'll be all right.'

She ran the bath, then with painful avoidance of the old man's eyes she stripped off the rest of his clothes, helped him across and half lifted him into the water. She sponged him down then dried him and hauled him out again. After wrapping the big towel round his skinny body she supported him as he stomped and staggered towards his room.

Then, armed with a pail of water and cloths and a bottle of disinfectant, she set about cleaning up the mess on all the floors. Tiny moans of distress escaped every now and again as the faeces stuck to her hands and splashed on to her clothes.

She felt God turning away from her, like her mother, with the same hatred, the same screwing up of the nose against something filthy and foul-smelling.

She harboured no resentment against the old man. Now that

577

he too was weak and helpless and distressed it gave them something in common. But resentment was there, alternating in waves with her self-hate and misery, straining for release.

She kept thinking of Melvin. Their whole life together unrolled before her eyes. Every grievance she had ever nursed against him was remembered with bitterness. Especially the fact that when she had to get up early after a sleepless night, he lay on snoring for hours. He got enough sleep now all right. He knew how to take care of himself.

In her imagination she carried on long arguments with him and by the time she next saw him she was primed up ready at the drop of one wrong word to explode all the frustrations and hatreds of a lifetime on his head.

He was eating his breakfast when he remarked casually:

'Your pal doesn't seem to think much of you. Never even bothered to write and tell you why she didn't turn up.'

'Julie isn't well just now, that's all. I'll hear from her. But it'll be no thanks to you - you and your rudeness and downright bad manners when my friends do come. You purposely try and discourage them. You're so selfish you want me just to be here on my own all the time, just pandering to your needs and being a slave to your precious house. You'd have me die alone here, alone and friendless, just as your first wife was.'

His eyes bulged with shock.

'My Betty never wanted anyone else but me. You've gone off your nut.'

She was trembling violently but she went over to him and stuck her face close to his, her eyes glittering, her facial muscles tense. 'I'm not like your first wife!'

'I know,' he retorted bitterly. 'You couldn't be like her if you tried.'

'You gave her a really marvellous funeral, didn't you? And you wanted plenty of people at that.'

'All I did was make a passing remark about your pal not turning up and you suddenly, for no reason at all, go berserk about my Betty.'

'You're not going to have any fancy funeral here for me.'

'You're right there,' he bawled back at her. 'They can carry

578

you out in a bloody orange box for all I care!'

'Oh, I know you don't care about me. I know you don't care if I never have anybody to talk to.'

'What do you mean-' he began, but to his exasperation she suddenly burst into tears. 'For God's sake! All I said was . . .'

'I know all you say,' she sobbed. 'I'm no use. I do nothing. Nothing!' She repeated the word as if she could not believe it. 'Nothing!'

'It's no wonder I can't eat.' His mouth twisted down and he jerked his plate away. 'You're enough to put anybody off their food!'

'Your father could be dying. You don't even care about him.'

'Now it's my father! Aw, shut up!'

Catriona could not reply because a sudden overpowering urge to vomit forced her to retreat to the privacy of the bathroom. She hung over the basin then slithered down on to the floor. She lay there for a long time before the pain and sickness passed and she was able to pull herself up as if out of a nightmare and return to the kitchen.

In the afternoon she made her way determinedly to the doctor's once more. Surely at least he would be able to give her something for her stomach and the bouts of pain that were fast becoming unendurable.

She rang the bell of his house in which he used a couple of rooms for surgery and waiting accommodation. The doctor himself opened the door, his little grin at the ready. It always surprised her how old he looked. But this time he looked shabby as well, in an old cardigan and reading-glasses and brown checked slippers.

'Good afternoon, Mrs McNair.'

'Good afternoon, Doctor.' She hesitated on the doormat, longing to sit down and waiting for him to invite her in. But he waited too, so she screwed up her face in pained embarrassed apology.

'I'm sorry to bother you, but I was hoping you'd give me something for my stomach. I'm not so bad at the moment but I have been awfully sick.'

'If you come back tomorrow, certainly,' he said. 'This is my half-day.'

'Oh.' She stared helplessly at him. 'I forgot.'

'It's perfectly all right,' he assured her before gently shutting the door.

She stood for a long time on the doormat suspended in a fog of lethargy. It seemed to her that she had reached a point of no return. She could not go on any longer.

Eventually she turned away and wandered about the streets in a daze before it occurred to her to go into a telephone booth, search for the number of a solicitor, and dial for an appointment.

At home they were all waiting impatiently for her.

'Where were you, Mum?' the boys queried. 'What's for tea?'

'Did you remember my tobacco?' the old man wanted to know. 'And where's my paper?'

'Where have you been all this time?' Melvin demanded indignantly.

Questions, questions, questions. She avoided their eyes, hid deep inside herself in case anyone might suspect what she had done and where she was going next day. Silently, she moved about making their meal and then listlessly leant against the sink as she attended to the washing-up.

'It's time you snapped out of it,' Melvin said. 'Pulled yourself together. You go about here like a half-shut knife. No wonder you're full of complaints. That's bad for you for a start - bad posture. You should always stand straight and keep your shoulders well back. It's all a question of willpower and physical jerks. I haven't so much time to do mine now but there's nothing to stop you from keeping fit. I'll show you a few really good exercises.'

'It's a good sleep I need.'

'Well, there's nothing to stop you from getting that.'

'I'm up with your father every night.'

'Well, that's your fault. You worry too much, that's your trouble. The old man takes a few nightcaps and you make a tragedy of it. Anybody would think it was the end of the world.'

She turned and gazed sadly at him. Maybe it was the end of their world. She wanted to weep on his shoulder. But she knew the feeling of comfort and security in his arms would only be an illusion, a figment of her wishful thinking.

Just as she knew that although she desperately needed sleep, it would again be denied her.

This time she had to leap out of bed at the sound of the front door opening and closing. Dashing to the window she was horrified to see, by the light of the street lamps, the old man stomping along the crescent dressed in his striped pyjamas, his old black trilby and his working boots.

She stumbled about the room trying to dress rapidly and get out in time to catch him before he disappeared. Different catastrophes seesawed her mind. People in the crescent could see him and they would all be disgraced.

Or he could march straight into the river and be drowned.

She ran outside, her face twisted with the physical distress of movement.

Her father-in-law was nowhere to be seen.

Clutching her coat around her, Catriona hurried on to Queen Margaret Drive where she could see as far as Great Western Road. There was still no sign of him and she doubted that he would have been able to get any further.

Her overstretched nerves tied themselves in knots of apprehension. He must have gone down into the gardens. Running back, her eyes wide with panic, her mouth open and gasping for breath, she could see in her mind the brown bulging water of the river. In her imagination she plunged in to save the old man and drowned along with him, pulled down by his bony clinging fingers, and she sobbed out loud at the thought of the children being left without her.

The gate creaked open and she suddenly realised that it was dark and she was alone. She hesitated for a few seconds among the high bushes, wringing her hands and anxiously biting at her lip. Then she hurried down the steep steps to find the old man sprawled at the foot of them.

'Da?' She kneeled down beside him and he looked dazedly at her. 'It's all right, Da. Come on. I don't care what Melvin says. I'm going to get the doctor,' she said, although she had long ceased to believe that the doctor could do any good either for Da or herself.

They took ages struggling together to get up the slippery stone steps and back on to the crescent and into the house. Then she phoned the doctor and he promised, politely, to come as soon as he could.

It was morning before he arrived and she was still up making cups of tea and filling hot-water bottles for Da. Melvin had been told what had happened and he went to the old man's room, and stood pulling at his moustache and saying: 'Anything you want or need, Da, just let me know. Anything at all!'

The doctor wrote out a prescription and chatted to Melvin, and asked about the business, and said he hoped the medicine would help his father but there was nothing much anybody could do now, and added:

'It's really just his age.'

Afterwards Melvin said:

'He's no chicken himself. Quite a nice old guy, though. I don't mind you going to him.'

'Thanks very much,' she said bitterly. 'Thanks for nothing!'

She returned upstairs to tell Da she was going out to get the medicine. She felt she was on a treadmill.

He seemed quite perky again.

'Strong as a horse!' Melvin laughed. 'He's wee but he's wiry. He'll last for years yet.'

'My God,' she thought. 'My God!'

Chapter 24

Rain smeared all over Glasgow enfolding it in a damp grey mist. It blurred Catriona's eyes as she walked. Edwardian and Victorian buildings loomed up, ghost-like, all around. Crowds of shadowy people stirred about.

She recalled a verse she had once read from a poem called 'Glasgow' by Alexander Smith:

> 'City! I am true son of thine
> Ne'er dwelt I where great mornings shine
> Around the bleating pens
> Ne'er by the rivulets I strayed
> And ne'er upon my childhood weighed
> The silence of the glens.
> Instead of shores where ocean beats
> I hear the ebb and flow of streets.'

She liked the poem. She loved Glasgow. She could imagine nothing better in the world than living here, having a flat to go to, somewhere in which she could feel safe, somewhere legally indisputably her own. Home, recognisable, everlasting, part of the great sea of Glasgow streets.

Dreams wafted about her mind like mist. They had no substance against the realities of pain and sickness and worry with which she was attempting to cope.

Everyone in the solicitor's plush carpeted office had treated her with attentive deference but she could not help wondering how much of it was due to her best clothes and her Kelvinside address. She was fast becoming aware of the yardstick of money that so many people used. Now she began to worry about how she was going to pay the solicitor's bill. She seemed only to be adding more problems to those she already had instead of solving them.

'And what can we do for you, Mrs MacNair?' The young solicitor's voice slid out like golden honey and he leaned forward to concentrate concern on her.

Her gaze flickered worriedly, uncertainly.

'I need help and advice.'

'In a matrimonial problem, I believe.'

'Yes.'

She prayed for strength not to break down, not to sound selfish and neurotic. She prayed to be able to find the right words. And the right amount of words. Not too many. Not too few.

'I've been very unhappy for some time,' she said slowly and carefully, her eyes clutching at the blotting-paper on the desk as if she were reading from it. 'I feel my marriage is affecting my health. I feel that I have a duty to the children. I must get away and take them with me before they too are made miserable and ill.'

'Were you thinking in terms of divorce or legal separation, Mrs MacNair?'

She looked up.

'I don't know. Divorce, I suppose.'

His chair swung back and he caught himself by hitching his thumbs in his waistcoat.

'There are three main grounds for divorce - desertion, cruelty and adultery. Very briefly, the position with desertion is this. If you left your husband, he could keep offering you, in writing, a home with him. If you refused to accept his offers, then you would be in desertion and he could file divorce proceedings against you. This involves a period of three years.'

'I would be the guilty party.'

He spread out his hands. 'Technically, yes. Then there's adultery.'

'As far as I know my husband has never committed adultery, so I suppose it would have to be cruelty.'

'To make cruelty stand up in court you've got to have charged your husband on at least two occasions with assault. Then you would have police witnesses, etcetera, to back you up.'

'I see.' A bitter laugh jerked out. 'That seems to be it, then.'

The solicitor pursed his lips as if to say, 'Pity!'

Hopelessness swamped her. Everywhere she turned it was the same.

'Of course, if you could get a note from your doctor to say that your marriage was affecting your health, Mrs MacNair, then we could at least attempt to prove justification in leaving so that you would not be the guilty party.'

'If I left, what would I be entitled to take with me?'

'Your clothes. Articles given to you personally as gifts.' He shrugged. 'But, of course, you know what they say. Possession is nine-tenths of the law. If you managed to take more with you then it would be up to your husband to prove that the articles were his and that he was entitled to their return.'

'I see. Oh, well.' Smiling, Catriona gathered up her gloves and handbag. 'I'll go and see my doctor and then I'll be in touch with you again. Not a very nice day, is it? So dull and wet.'

'Indeed. Indeed.' Cheerfully he leapt to his feet and made the door in a few energetic strides. 'Going to be fog tonight, I think.'

Back outside, rain mixed with perspiration and wetly covered her face. She felt as if she were drowning. The journey home to Botanic Crescent stretched before her, all-absorbing, like the lonely ascent of the highest and most perilous mountain in Scotland.

Straining herself along slowly and painfully she thought, 'I'm going to die.' She sensed death very near. It did not frighten her, but she felt a terrible sadness at the thought of never seeing her children again. She did not want to say goodbye to Glasgow, either. If she never felt any home belonged to her, at least she knew she belonged to Glasgow.

Her mind clung desperately to the city. Despite her physical weakness a tough core of spiritual strength remained.

> 'I belong to Glasgow,
> Dear old Glasgow town,
> But there's something the matter with Glasgow
> For it's going round and round . . .'

In a daze she successfully reached Botanic Crescent, then, having reached it, remembered she had meant to go to the doctor's for the note. But the ordeal of another agonising journey and then the seemingly impossible task of convincing the doctor that she was ill proved too much for her. She suspected too, that the doctor would not act in any way against Melvin without first discussing the matter with him. That would result in another terrible scene and she could not stand any more.

Fumbling for her key with icy cold fingers while her life's blood drained away her mind became more and more fuddled. She tried to pierce the grey cotton wool to find someone else she could ask for help, or somewhere else she could go, or something else she could do. But she was unable to think of anyone, or any place, or anything.

Melvin was sitting in his favourite chair smoking his pipe. 'Where the hell have you been?'

'In town for some messages. It's an awful night. I got soaked.'

She went through to the kitchen to peel off her wet clothes and crouch gratefully over the fire.

The sight of Melvin had nevertheless aroused resentment in her. For years she had worked day and night as nanny, cook, cleaning woman, housekeeper, waitress, nurse, decorator, laundry maid and even shop assistant and book-keeper, because many a time she had helped Melvin fill in forms and do books for the bakery. On top of all this she had borne his children. And now at the end of all the years of slaving what had she to show for it?

Melvin had the house in his name and he owned the furniture and everything in it. He had the business. He had the earning capacity.

It struck her that there was a wicked inequality in law, and in marriage, and in every sphere, between the sexes.

Anger burned feebly inside her. She tried to fan its flames but had not the strength. Every ounce of energy was needed to concentrate on making a meal and then afterwards to face the long night looking after old Duncan.

There was no use going to bed any more. No use undressing only to dress again; to go to bed and have to rise again, to drag herself to the old man's room to attend to him or perhaps to search for him outside, in the garden, or the crescent, or perhaps she might not hear him leave and he would wander further away.

After Melvin left for the bakehouse, Catriona just sat in a chair as if in a trance, waiting for her father-in-law to call. Her head nodded and jerked as sleep played hide and seek with her. Sometimes when she thought she heard him, she went out to the hall and stood hunched up in an agony of listening in the silent darkness.

All the time her head echoed with the wailing sound of her name.

Catriona! Catriona! Catriona!

Yet the hall was devoid of all sound except the nervous fluttering of her breathing.

At last she could bear the suspense no longer, and she dragged herself up the stairs to make sure that he was all right.

Immediately she went into his room and saw the old face, hollow-cheeked and sagging-jawed against the pillow, she knew he was dead.

She leaned back against the wall, weak with relief. She admitted to herself she was glad he was dead. She could feel no guilt. She was beyond guilt or grief or caring.

But she said out loud:

'I'm sorry, Da.'

Then she forced herself to put on her coat and go and tell Melvin.

Before she reached the bakery, however, the rain-shimmered streets lapped slowly away from her. She felt herself without bones, a piece of seaweed undulating with the tide until it gradually engulfed her.

Melvin did not discover until next morning that his father was dead and it was much later before he found she was in hospital.

By that time Catriona had been through an emergency operation and had her uterus and her ovaries removed.

'You were lucky!' the surgeon told her. 'We got you just in time. Now with plenty of rest and care you should be all right.'

Melvin was the first person she saw after she was back in bed and coming out of the anaesthetic.

She thought at first she was still out on the street, still in pain and still seeing Glasgow through a misty grey blue. Then Melvin's bulbous eyes, staring wildly, came into focus. He was waving a bunch of flowers in front of her face. She tried to move her head to escape from them.

'You're all right,' she heard him shout excitedly. 'I knew it! I knew you couldn't do this to me!'

Afterwards she wondered what he meant. Was it some sort of confession of faith in her? Or was it that he had been afraid she might die like his first wife and he could not bear any more guilt?

But why should he feel guilt?

In the safe world of the hospital, lying tucked neatly in her white bed, drifting in and out of sleep, being conscientiously cared for by the hospital doctors and nurses, she could take a more objective view of her husband.

Poor Melvin. Surely he was no more responsible for harming his first wife than she was responsible for the death of her baby.

When he came back to visit her she managed to thank him for the flowers. He seemed pleased, and strolled around the bed jingling coins in his pockets and assuring her:

'Anything you need or want, just tell me.'

She did not answer him. She only smiled then closed her eyes and pretended to have fallen asleep.

She felt an instinct of quiet prudence taking root. Her first need was to survive. Layers of caution enfolded her. She drew them around like secrets she would never divulge or share.

But she wrote to Madge and to Julie and let them know that she was in hospital.

Madge said, 'I told you, didn't I? Some people have all the luck! Now you've had everything taken away and you'll never be able to have any more weans!'

Melvin and the boys had been by her bedside when Julie arrived bright and smart and talkative, yet with restless eyes that kept straying to Melvin and the children.

Madge envied her the family she could not have and Julie envied her the family she had. The next time they came and left

588

together, and before she went away Madge said:

'Oh, by the way, you'll never guess who's coming around our place now. Him and Alec are the best of pals.'

'Who?'

'Sammy Hunter. Ruth's man. He knows about Alec being with her that night as well.'

'Fancy!'

'It makes you think, doesn't it?' Madge said. 'Maybe the big midden was telling me the truth after all.'

'Have I met this Sammy?' Julie asked.

'No, hen,' Madge laughed. 'But you're welcome to come to my place any night he's there. That'll be a laugh, eh? Me as a matchmaker!'

Julie rolled her eyes.

'I only made a perfectly casual remark.'

Catriona smiled.

'He's nice, Julie. I like Sammy very much.'

'Hey, you! Less of it!' Madge punched her in the arm. 'Never you mind liking Sammy very much. You've got a man already.' She winked at Julie. 'Now that she can't be caught out there'll be no holding her back. Randy wee bugger!'

Catriona shook her head.

'Madge, you're terrible.'

But she felt a little more cheerful, a little more reassured and a little stronger after their visit.

'It's terribly kind of both of you to come and see me like this,' she told them earnestly. 'It means a lot to me. You've no idea how I appreciate it.'

Julie laughed and as if on an impulse came back to the bedside and dropped a quick kiss on her cheek.

'No need to look so serious, pal. It's a hard life, but if we keep working at it we'll survive!'

Madge strode back too and kissed her noisily on the brow. 'You're a right silly wee midden, always have been!'

For a long time after they left, Catriona felt warmed by their affection and friendship. She felt strangely cheered by what Madge had been saying about Sammy, too. It occurred to her how fascinating it was that in such odd little unexpected ways one person could influence another. Everybody was like a pebble dropping into a pool, making ripples that went on and on, their effect widening and widening.

By deciding to behave in a certain way Sammy had influenced Madge, although he probably did not know it, and now he was indirectly influencing her in her hospital bed as she struggled to regain strength and purpose to face the world outside.

Suddenly she felt keenly and urgently aware of the importance of ordinary day-to-day human relationships. It seemed to her that every word everybody ever said, every attitude, every action, helped to swell the influence of either good or bad in the world. The fact that the pebbles could not see the ripples did not matter. There was no doubt at all that the ripples were there.

And if every casual word or deed to strangers had vital importance in the scheme of things, how much more valuable and meaningful were those of family and friends. Couldn't she influence, even in tiny ways, her mother and people beyond her mother? Couldn't she influence Melvin, and the children and their children, and into the future in wider and wider reaches without end? And if Madge and Julie could help and influence her in the most unconscious and unexpected ways - couldn't she sometime, in some way, do the same for them?

Catriona felt the journey towards understanding, the challenge of life beginning. She felt thanks to Sammy, that she had managed to get herself on the right track.

It would be nice to see Sammy again. Friends were so important. Friends were the links in the lifeline to which she must cling.

Yet, at the same time, thinking of Sammy brought depression and memories of the air-raids and the deaths of neighbours and good friends and her own son.

Sadness spread out and encompassed all the other mothers' sons and all the other neighbours all over the world, the unknown hundreds, thousands and millions. She felt overwhelmed by the tragedy of war. And she was afraid of what tomorrow might bring. But she struggled with the fear and suddenly into her mind came the text:

'Sufficient unto the day is the evil thereof.'

It seemed a revelation. She had strength enough for one day.

She relaxed back against the pillow and a breeze from the open window made golden cobwebs of her hair.

Her steady gaze studied a bird floating free in the sky outside; small and delicate yet powerful; swooping and circling, climbing triumphantly, higher and higher.

Catriona smiled her secret smile to herself.

One day was all she needed.

Also by
Margaret Thomson Davis

The Kellys of Kelvingrove
RRP £6.99 – 978 1 84502 339 3

Nestled down, hidden behind the Glasgow Art Galleries, is a line of seven rented houses. Though quiet and out of sight alongside the River Kelvin, they accommodate seven very different families, along with their problems, schemes and secrets. Despite their efforts to retreat within separate lives, each household will soon find themselves mixed up in the problems of the others, as malicious schemes and secrets are exposed in Margaret Thomson Davis's thriller, *The Kelly's of Kelvingrove*.

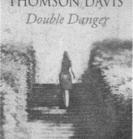

Double Danger
RRP £6.99 – 978 1 84502 325 6

Jessica McKay moves to Saudi Arabia to be with her new husband, Brian. At first it seems like paradise, but after the birth of their two children, she feels threatened by terrorist attacks on the luxurious compound where they live and decides to return home, settling in an estate that Brian has in the Campsie Hills near Glasgow. However, back in Scotland, things are not what they seem and the real danger begins. Jessica's children mistrust the attractive gardener, Patrick, believing that his charming manner conceals sinister schemes – and when a terrible accident befalls their father, they fear their worst suspicions are about to be realised.

www.blackandwhitepublishing.com